THE WAY TO
DAWN

Siege of a Nation

THE WAY TO DAWN
by
Charles Lee

Contents

Broken Wings

Chapter One

Darkness... Infinite black.

Why can't I open my eyes? My thoughts are scattered. It's so hard to think. Who am I? What am I? Do I even have eyes to open?

Low chattering. Barely hearable. It fills my space.

But who's talking...? Who's talking? Those voices... I know them. But who am I?

The voices. They're children—calling a name.

Anya...? Afearia? That name makes me frantic. But why? Who? Why? Why are they desperately calling out to her? Why won't she respond? Answer them. Why won't you answer them? They need you. Answer! Afearia!?

Afearia. Afearia. Afearia...

In a small bedroom, a red-haired woman sleeps soundly under a plaid green and brown quilt. A series of gauze is wrapped around her head with a white bandage on her cheek and jaw. Next to her twin bed are two chairs pulled close on her left, and a nightstand at the head of the bed with a lamp and clock radio. To her right is a window with parted green curtains to let the moonlight shine in.

Slowly, the young woman begins to open her eyes, just barely. She briefly closes them before opening them wider than previously. Her mismatched red and blue irises slant to the left to see the room's wooden door ajar with light coming from the hall. She slightly pushes the quilt down to reveal her white silk gown.

She prepares to sit up and immediately falls back down with a loud, pain-filled, clenched jaw grunt. She breathes heavily and tightens her eyes in pain, grunting from the pain-charged deep breaths she took. Quickly, she controls her breathing to sooth her aches. When she tries to twist, she quickly screams out in agony. Her face dampened in sweat, she brings her hand over herself and lightly touches her chest, wincing from the pain.

"Why? Why does it hurt so much?" She tries to turn her neck a little and hurts herself once more. Suddenly, she makes a face of realization, recalling the events that caused it.

Abruptly, the sounds of rushing footsteps are heard from the hall as a man with a panicked expression hastily comes through the door wearing tan slacks and a white collared button shirt.

"Afearia!?" he says in alarm.

Afearia slowly looks to him, "I lost," she says with a shaken expression.

He sighs in relief as he comes in while slightly leaving the door ajar. "Yes, but the good news is you're alive." He grabs a chair from his left by the wall and puts it near her bed before sitting. "You gave us quite a scare."

"Us? The children! Where are they!? Are they—!?" In mid-rush to sit up, she hurts herself once more.

"Calm down. Your hasty movements will aggravate your injuries even further."

She holds her chest, breathing quick, but lightly, reducing the pain. "Dr. Richards, are the kids safe?"

"Yes. They're sleeping down the hall. Fortunately for you, I still own this house placed far on the outer areas of Aster City. Though I've abandoned it, I thought keeping it as an emergency shelter would be a good idea." He looks at her bruised face and chapped lips. "Afearia, do you remember what happened at all?"

Afearia looks up at the slow spinning ceiling fan, not responding for a moment. "I remember... She... How long have I been unconscious?"

"A few days now. It was certain you were in a coma. If you were under any longer, I would've been forced to take you somewhere it posed risk in getting medical treatment." The room goes silent for a moment. "Can you tell me what happened?" She doesn't respond. "Anything." As if to be deaf, Afearia remains staring at the fan. "A name at least." He sighs and turns away.

"Minerva."

He looks surprised for a moment. "That hand-to-hand combative? She's been known to be merciless. But you had the magical edge, so how—?" Afearia quickly glares at him with eyes mixed with inner pain and anger. Dr. Richards slowly looks away, changing the subject. "I feel you should understand your situation. Your chest muscles and skin have suffered severe damage which will lead to slow healing. Your ribcage has a series of fractures, mainly through your sternum."

"You also have four broken ribs," he continues. Through stubborn will, Afearia grunts with closed eyes, forcing herself to sit up. For a moment, he calmly watches her. "You really shouldn't be moving like this. Your broken ribs, two are in the front, one on your left side, and one in your back. Through your deliberate moving, you may have noticed pain in your left thigh and right wrist. Those are just bad sprains with possible bone bruising. Your neck is in a similar state."

"Why didn't she kill me?"

"She did, Afearia."

"What?"

"Seems you don't remember that part. Assuming from your injuries, I'd guess repeated blunt blows to your chest caused your heart to stop at some point. Because of that, I've had to keep monitoring your heart rate which is still a little irregular. As your doctor, I highly recc—"

"As my doctor?" she chuckles callously. "Don't get carried away. I come from a place that prepared me for anything. I'll just perform a hyper healing spell and I'll be on my way." She raises her bruised right arm and closes her

5

eyes. Over five seconds go by with nothing happening. She opens her eyes in alarm. What the! Afearia thinks. Afearia tries again, but nothing changes.

Dr. Richards glances at her a couple times, confused. "What are you—?"

"Shut up!" She tightens her eyes before straining her focus while using her other hand to brace her right arm, but nothing happens. "Gah!" dropping her arms, breathing heavy with wide eyes of surprise and fatigue. "I can't... My link to Sovereignty and all my other swords... I can't call my blades."

"Wha-what does that mean?" he says with worry.

"I—don't know." She lowers her head and stares at her shaky hands.

Dr. Richards looks to his left. "Maybe it's because of your injuries." She looks to him with a helpless expression, then back at her hands. "Yes, I suppose not. But my real hypothesis is far more upsetting. Afearia... there's a chance you may have suffered brain damage before I rescued you."

She looks to him, looking like something broke inside her. "Before I found you," he continues, "the kids were already there. On average, it takes three minutes for the brain to start dying without oxygen. Assuming the kids found you a minute or two before my arrival—"

"How long?" she asks with gloom in her voice.

Dr. Richards pauses before responding. "It took me over three and a half minutes to resuscitate you." His words cut her once more as her eyes express distress. "I assume if you have, the section of your brain that can access that power is long gone... I'm sorry. Medical science has yet to reverse things like brain damage." When he looks to Afearia, she is shaken, staring into the bed sheets. "I'll give you your space," he says upon standing.

Dr. Richards places a bottle of pills on the nightstand. "I suggest you take these to fight the pain and prevent inflammatory issues along your sternum."

He calmly walks from the bed and heads for the door. "So…," Afearia miserably says, stopping him half out the door. "In the end, I'm nothing."

He glances at her before softly shutting the door, proceeding up the hall. As far as A.N.T.S. is concerned, yes, Dr. Richards thinks.

The next morning, Afearia's lying in bed, watching each fan blade rotate above her. The sound of the door slowly creaking open, causes Afearia to close her eyes, faking sleep. Adrian and Veronica slowly peek in on her.

"She's sleeping," Veronica whispers. "But Mr. Richards said she was okay now."

"What're you two doing?" Dr. Richards asks from behind them, startling the siblings.

"You said Anya was okay," Adrian says.

"She is, but she still needs bed rest. Come downstairs for breakfast. You two can see her later this afternoon." The kids head downstairs as he closes the door. Afearia opens her eyes and faintly sighs.

She looks over at the door, then back at the wall at the foot of the bed. She remains fixated on a single spot, focusing on nothing with a mind empty, but filled with immense self-loathing. With her eyes almost saddening, she grunts and looks up at the ceiling fan.

As each blade passes over her, Afearia plays the final moments of her fight with Minerva in her head. Like an ongoing taunt, Minerva's words echo through her mind:

You call yourself a hero. You have no conviction. You are disgusting. You're a mess.

Afearia clenches her jaw and slaps the pills to the floor. She stares at the rolling pill bottle while breathing a bit heavy. She quickly puts her hand in the air, trying to call one of her swords. She slams her fist down in frustration from another failed attempt. Bubbling anger is steadily rising inside her as she tightly holds her mouth shut. She nearly has a fit with her arm ready to swing, but she stops.

Afearia calms herself before trying to sit up. She slowly moves up with clenched pain in her eyes as she angles her back against the pillows. Once up, her forehead had dampened as she keeps her eyes closed to focus.

After a while, sitting in silence, her eyes jolt open. No chains!? Afearia thinks. No chains!? But I— Demeseus! Afearia begins to panic. "Demeseus!" she shouts.

She loses balances and falls out of the bed with an agonizing scream. "Gahh! Arrrrgh! Demeseus!"

With her mind unable to filter the words of her adversary, Afearia's breathing becomes erratic. The sound of rushing footsteps come pounding up the stairs. Emotionally broken, she stares at the floor, painfully recalling the things Minerva said to her as tears flow down her cheeks.

"I hate her! I hate her! She keeps taking things from me! I hate her!" speaking in bursts of anger. "I HATE YOU! I DIDN'T BRING SHAME—!" Afearia suddenly begins coughing and wheezing. Her eyes become wide as jolting pain begins rushing through her ribs.

The door flings open with an alarmed Dr. Richards standing in the doorway. "Afearia!?" He rushes over to the other side of the bed. He quickly turns Afearia over to try and calm her. "Afearia, you need to control your breathing! If you don't you'll damage your lungs!" Adrian and Veronica rush to the door side. "Stay back!" Afearia continues fussing. "Afearia, stop! You're making your injuries worse!"

She wasn't in full compliance as he tries to get her under control before forcefully restraining her. Afearia begins to relax herself as he coaches her down. She concentrates on her breathing until it regulates.

"Good," Dr. Richards says. "Let's get you back into bed."

As he prepares to move her, she swats his hands away. "I don't need your help," she says in exhaustion.

He stands and stares at her with no expression before walking over to grab the pill bottle and placing it back on the nightstand. He glances at her, then moves toward the door.

The kids try to look past him. "Anya!?" Adrian shouts, but Afearia does not respond before Dr. Richards shuts the door.

Afearia doesn't even try to get up off the floor. She lies there with an unhappy expression. Demeseus, why did you leave me? she thinks. I didn't mean to let you down like this... I swear. A tear rolls down her frozen face before she sorrowfully closes her eyes, drifting to sleep. I'm so sorry...

Several hours later, Afearia awakens to a darker room from the steadily setting sun. After still not moving for a few minutes, she finally decides to painfully sit herself up.

In her eye line on the bed are crutches and her tote bag. She did not use the crutches or grab her bag. Afearia just knocks all of it to the floor and gets back up on her one good leg. Moving slowly to reduce the pains in her chest and body, Afearia eases herself back into the bed.

When she brings her legs over, Afearia ends up hurting herself anyway. She grunts in frustration and punches the bed. While lying there, she looks to the pill bottle and grits her teeth before putting a pillow over her head. Why is this happening to me? she thinks. How can any of this be real? I lost. I lost to a lousy Demi of all things! Then, I lost my powers... How long? How long was I dead? How did I even lose? How!? SHE'S A DEMI!

The final set of attacks Afearia took against Minerva run through her mind. Was there really no way for me to win after that? Demeseus... what do I do? Afearia prepares to raise her hand to summon Eternity, but quickly puts her hand in her mouth, biting down not to cry.

This predicament has become a fate worse than death. I have never felt—I don't even want to think anymore! Terra! This realm only knows how to hurt! This cursed realm! I hate you! Afearia gasps at her thoughts. What am I doing? Blaming an entire realm for my shortcomings? I'm disgusting. Place blame on everything and everyone except myself. It's me... This miserable state is because of me.

Afearia recalls a memory of her battle with Yadeira. My arrogance will kill me ten times over... She knew. Her words were not an empty threat. I have accomplished so little, and yet, my journey ends here. The successor to the Eternity blade? What a joke! I really do—bring shame to Demeseus's name...

At the corner of her eye, she notices the room has darkened. She lifts the pillow a bit and vaguely sees the doctor closing the curtains before she lowers it back down. "I know you're not sleep," Dr. Richards says. He turns to her, waiting for a response before walking around the bed. "Are you going to listen to me now?" He grabs the bottle and sits by the bed. "That wheezing attack you had earlier was from you not doing deep breath exercises. If you don't follow what I'm telling you, you'll slowly die a painful death."

She continues to be unresponsive. He shakes his head while looking at the medicine, "You haven't even opened the bottle. Have you given up on living?"

He looks at her motionless body before sighing and putting the bottle back. Dr. Richards stands and leaves the room before Afearia peeks from beneath at the door.

At the hour of dinner, Dr. Richards is downstairs eating at the round wooden table with Adrian and Veronica. It's a small kitchen with little walking space and an even smaller stove. The largest appliance is the fridge which isn't much in comparison to the whole kitchen.

The three of them eat silently while Adrian mostly fork tosses his meatballs across his plate. "Is it not good?" Dr. Richards asks Adrian.

Adrian shakes his head, "It's fine. I like it." He nibbles on the meatball and takes a taste of the pasta with no change to his sour demeanor.

"Then what's wrong? If it's not the food—"

"It's Anya." Mentioning Afearia changes the air. "She hasn't even asked to see us. Why? Is she upset that we didn't listen to her? Is she really alright? We haven't got to see her since you bought us here. How is she?"

He stares at him for a moment. "She's fine," he says before taking a bite of his spaghetti.

"Then why can't we see her?" Veronica asks.

"She's not ready for visitors."

"But it's us."

"Exactly. She doesn't care all that much that it's me. She barely acknowledges me entering the room. But if it were you two... I'm concerned what her reaction may be. Most of all, I don't think it would be good for you two either. Seeing her at that building took its toll on you both. I want everyone to have their own mental recovery space. If one is not ready it can lead to a chain breakdown. When she's ready, you'll know."

"And where does that leave her?" Adrian asks.

"What do you mean?"

"Nothing. I think I'll go back to the room. Thanks for dinner." Dr. Richards nods before he leaves the table.

Adrian softly walks up the stairs. When he reaches the top, he looks toward Afearia's room. He stares at her door for a while before steadily taking a couple steps toward it.

"Don't," Dr. Richards, standing at the bottom of the stairs. Adrian looks at her room one more time before walking back to his room.

A little over an hour passes since dinner. Dr.

Richards enters Afearia's room holding a tray with spaghetti on a plate and a glass of water. He prepares to place it down on the nightstand until he notices the bottle is gone. He turns his foot and taps the medicine bottle on the floor. He makes a disappointed face before placing the tray down.

He picks up the medicine bottle, "They've been asking about you. Those kids are very worried. They want to see you." Once again, Afearia remains unresponsive to his words. "Do you want to see them?" He waits a moment before turning from her. "Then I'll go get them then."

"Do it and I'll purposely puncture my lungs."

He looks to her with a bit of irritation by her response. "What is wrong with you? I can't believe the woman I thought was so strong is choosing to handle her condition like this. Your broken bones won't last forever."

"Shut up and get out."

He grunts in annoyance and walks to the door. He sticks his head into the hall and shouts, "Adrian, Veronica, you can come see her now!"

Afearia sits up a bit too fast and hurts herself, "Gah! What are you doing!?"

"As a doctor, I can't just sit back and watch you waste your life away. So I want them to see what you've decided to become."

"No!"

"Then get up. Get up and give the appearance that you are even trying to get better." She glares at him for a moment before falling backward and pressing the pillow over her face. "You would selfishly choose to hurt yourself just because you're bedridden?"

Footsteps begin to approach the room before Afearia turns her head to him, "How would you feel if you suffered brain damage and lost the ability to help people as a doctor?"

"I would find another way and take control of my

new destiny," he calmly replies.

Afearia sees their shadows rising to the door before she glances at him a couple times. As she's about to cover her face, the doorbell rings.

Dr. Richards steps out the room and stops the kids. "One moment guys, I want us to greet her together." He rushes down the stairs to answer the door. When he opens the door, a middle aged man stands at the door wearing blue scrubs.

"Dr. Richards!" he says.

"Patrick!? What are you doing here?"

"We tried calling you, but you didn't answer."

"I'm taking a few days off to care for in-house patients."

"Yes, the chief knows, but you've been gone longer than usual and things are becoming dire dealing with this unknown virus from the south."

"What?"

"We've never seen anything like it. It kills the host in twelve to seventy-two hours. And what happens after they pass is—"

"Say no more. Wait here. We can discuss this along the way to the hospital," Dr. Richards says before rushing back up the stairs.

"What's going on?" Adrian asks him.

"I have to attend to an emergency back at the hospital. Promise me you two won't go into her room until I get back."

"We don't have to promise you that," Veronica rudely replies.

Adrian nudges her, "Although I don't like this, we won't enter her room. I guess you're doing this for her sake since you need her, right?"

"I'll be back as soon as possible," Dr. Richards says, ignoring Adrian's question.

Dr. Richards quickly walks to his room and comes

back out with a brown leather bag while putting on his white doctor coat. He runs out the door and hops into a car with his co-worker Patrick. The kids look to each other and glance at the partially open door to Afearia's room before closing it and heading back to their room.

Afearia lies staring at the ceiling, thinking about her shattered expectations. She raises her hand and attempts once again to summon one of her Empyrean Blades. She grunts with a sorrowful face. Afearia thrusts her hand up several times. But none of her swords answer her call. She flails her arms and slams them on the bed before frustratingly screaming out.

Her screams reach across to the children's room. Afearia's distressed screams rattle Veronica, who is tightly hugging Adrian as she cries. Adrian covers her ears and gently rocks her back and forth, trying not to cry himself.

"She's in pain," Veronica says in a chopped voice. "Her screams. They sound like mom's. She's in pain, Adrian. What do we do?"

"I don't know," he sadly says. "I don't know."

Long after Afearia's screams had stopped and the kids lie in bed, Afearia's door creaks open. Afearia poorly limps out the room, looking both ways before focusing quite hard to make her way toward the kids' room.

She stops partway in the dark hall, breathing a bit heavy while holding her side. Even walking is agonizing, Afearia thinks. She grits her teeth, seeming angry and exhausted. I can still feel your fists impacting my body.

Fighting through the pain, she clenches her jaw and hobbles on. Afearia reaches their room and slowly opens the door. The children are sleeping in separate beds with the covers high over their heads. She steps inside, pushing down her grunts.

"You should be in bed," Dr. Richards says from the top of the stairs. "It's four in the morning, why disturb them now?"

"I just wanted to see if they're sleeping okay."

"I wanted you to show signs of wanting to live on. This is good. You still have concern for these children."

"I promised to get them home." She turns to Dr. Richards, unable to clearly see him from the shadows of the hall. "But it is no longer possible?"

He doesn't respond to her words for a moment. "Come with me to your room."

"But—"

"They're okay." Afearia softly closes the door and limps back to her room. When she nears Dr. Richards he steps down the stairs, further into the shadows of the hall. Once she was in the room beside her bed, he stands in the blackened doorway. "You have an awful way in perceiving a promise. Because you have no powers you've decided to abandon your promise, right?" She stands still, staring into the bed with no expression. "Are you going to keep using that as an excuse for everything you can't do? Do you think parents make promises to their kids and then go back on their word just because of a slight change in plans?"

"I'm defective... I can't protect them anymore."

"You don't need powers to protect people. In this case, you still don't. All they want is for you to take them home. What does having powers have to do with that?"

She pauses for a moment. "We could be attacked if—"

"Oh, stop it, Afearia! You're just pitying yourself! Looking for every excuse under the sun to give up. Demis have been around for as long as humans; maybe longer. Humans have fought those things time and time again to protect the things they love. We powerless beings don't throw our hands up just because we can't kick through a tree. We find another way. If we can't run as fast as you, we create a vehicle that can. If we can't destroy a mass of enemies like you, we'll create a weapon that can. We accept our mortal limitations and find other ways to close the gap. A trait you may want to incorporate. Or give up and allow your defeated persona break you."

Dr. Richards walks from her room. Afearia slants her eyes at the pill bottle on the nightstand. Dr. Richards opens the door to his room and gently closes it. He turns on the lamp on his work desk and drops his bag. His once white coat is now nearly all covered in blood. Instead of removing his bloody coat, he sits at his desk in his black leather rolling chair.

He rests his arms on the desk before dropping his head. After a short while, he raises his head up to eye level. This world is doomed, Dr. Richards thinks. I'm terrified to think that my theory could be correct. Demis that can exist on a cellular level... Dr. Richards balls his fist. It's absurd!

Given little rest, Dr. Richards was only home for a few hours before he had to leave for work again. Resting in her room, Afearia has the covers completely over her head. Afearia's door slowly creaks open before Adrian steps inside with Veronica carefully following. Veronica suddenly stops and steps back.

"What's wrong?" Adrian whispers.

"We're not supposed to be in here," Veronica replies with worry.

"I want to see Anya."

"But Mr. Richards said she's not ready."

"Don't you want to see Anya?"

"Yes."

"Then stop complaining and come on."

Veronica does not come further inside. Adrian becomes upset and grabs her by the wrist, pulling her inside as she tries to resist. "No, Adrian, stop. Adrian, stop it. Stop it!"

They freeze, looking toward the bed to see if she woke. When he wasn't paying attention, Veronica yanks her hand away and runs out the room." Veronica!" he loudly whispers. He hesitates to leave as he looks to

Afearia's bed once more before leaving and closing the door.

Shortly after the kids had tried getting inside her room, Afearia lies awake, hazily staring at the pill bottle in her hand. The real question is, Afearia thinks, do I even want to get better? What good am I without my powers? What purpose do I serve if I can't do what I was born to do? The pill bottle slips from her hand and rolls across the floor.

Where do I go from here? I can't even return home—not like this. The Elders would never accept me back. No home. No purpose. No hope... I'm nothing. I'm nothing at all. Get better? There is no better. I've fallen and lost everything. This really is the worst outcome for a warrior who expected so much.

Afearia slowly closes her eyes. I could die ten times over and still feel better than this... I could even die now.

By late afternoon, Afearia wakes to find a folded paper near her face. She unfolds it and sees a poor drawing of a big smiling face with red hair and smaller smiling faces with Adrian and Veronica's names above the smaller faces.

Below is a note written in black crayon reading, 'We miss you, Anya. Get well soon.' Beneath, it's signed, Luv Adrian and Veronica'

Afearia lowers the paper to her chest with a pan-faced expression, but emotionally shaken eyes. Nothing at all, she thinks. Afearia lets her hand fall off the bed and feels a crumbled paper brush her fingers. She grabs it and brings it up to her face to read:

Anya, I don't like it when you're in pain. Don't cry anymore, ok? I still believe in you, Anya, so don't cry. Just don't cry... –Love Veronica

A tear rolls from Afearia's eye before she slaps her hand over her face. How can they—? "Stupid brats," she mutters with a shaky voice.

17

Meanwhile, Dr. Richards is sitting downstairs in his semi-dark kitchen. His head is down for a while until the mobile house phone he had placed on the table rings. "Hello?" he answers. "No, I have not heard anything about her. Yes, I hope so too. Alright, goodbye."

He hangs up rubbing his face in tire. Dr. Richards stands and walks up the stairs. He moves toward Afearia's room and looks through the partly opened door. He lightly sighs at the sight of her still in bed. You don't plan to get better, do you? Dr. Richards thinks. He turns away and approaches the stairs before suddenly stopping. He about-faces and walks inside Afearia's room.

"Afearia, are you awake?" he asks. He notices her fingers hanging slightly from the covers before sliding from view. "You know, I've tried everything to convince you not to throw the towel. A violent dramatic wakeup call is the last thing I have. But it's not in me to do something like that. Those things must have some form of sincerity that I do not possess."

"I can only pity you," he sadly says. "You once walked with an air of superiority and confidence. It amplified the amount of respect and admiration I had for you. People on Terra would see you and feel the same way. They see you and remember who they were before becoming scared mice under Derexen's rule."

Hope, Afearia thinks with a lifeless expression.

"But now that you have been gone from the public for over three weeks, those doubts are rising again. And those kids... They're the embodiment of that doubt. They haven't seen your face for just as long. Afearia... They've completely stopped smiling and talking." Afearia's eyes slightly rise to his words.

"Your wiliness to dissolve is also eroding at all the connections you've ever made," he continues. "I don't know if any of this matters to you anymore but... If you can't care enough to at least help yourself, no one else can either." Dr. Richards turns to leave, "You've always come off as a person who loves their own talents enough to overcome any obstacle. Since that seems to no longer be enough, perhaps you should put your pride into something else. Maybe those kids can be your new pride. Under their care, maybe you can move once again."

Dr. Richards leaves the room and sees Veronica coming to the top of the stairs holding a plate of cookies and a glass of water. She stares in his direction before nodding. "Did you find the cookies okay?" he asks her. She nods again before looking to Afearia's room. "I'm sorry. She's still not progressing the way I would hope. Maybe it's time you two go see her."

Veronica doesn't even crack a smile. She turns from him and goes to her room, shutting the door. Suddenly, the house phone rings from below and his room. He quickly walks to his room and sits at his desk to answer it. "Hello? Yes, I'm on my way. Try antibiotics and use a combination of—. Then just use the antibiotics."

He hangs up and grabs his coat from the back of his chair before leaving the room. He walks to the kids' room and opens the door. The children are sitting across from each other, eating their cookies with depressed faces.

"I'm going to the hospital again," Dr. Richards says. "I won't be back until late."

The kids don't even look in his direction. Dr. Richards closes the door, grabs his bag from the bottom of the stairs and leaves the house.

Upstairs in the kids' room, Adrian finishes another cookie and gently pushes the plate to his sister. "You can have the rest," he said in a saddened tone.

Suddenly, they hear a loud thud from the next room, followed by agonizing screams from Afearia. They scramble to their feet and run out the room. When they reach Afearia's room, Adrian prepares to open the door, but when the sounds of Afearia's whimpers pass through them, he freezes. Just as shaken, Veronica puts her hand over her mouth with watery eyes.

"I can't!" Veronica muffles through her hand. "I can't!" she says before running back to the room. Adrian quickly chases after his sister. "I can't, I can't, I can't!" she shouts as she crashes herself onto the bed.

Adrian stands in the doorway, watching his sister cry into the bed, "She doesn't want to hurt like this, Veronica." Veronica sniffles and wipes her face. "Maybe if we appear stronger, she will feel stronger too. We should see her."

"She sounds like mom, it's too hard!"

"Sis, she needs us. Just like mom needed us to be strong and take care of each other. It's hard for me too. I've cried many times since we've been here. But our crying is not going to help anything." He approaches his sister and puts his hand on her back. "I want to see Anya, but I can't face her alone. I need you to come with me."

Veronica looks to her brother and nods. She gets off the bed and walks behind her brother to Afearia's room. Adrian slowly opens the door as she slightly shakes with her hands on his arm. Afearia is now back in bed with the covers over herself.

Adrian steps inside until his sister tugs him. "What should we say?" Veronica asks.

He stares at his sister for a moment and looks to Afearia with uncertainty. Adrian takes a deep breath and closes his eyes, "Anya's number one!" Veronica looked at him with shocked eyes and confusion. Adrian 's focused, but obviously nervous as he stares on at Afearia in bed. "Anya's number one! We love you no matter what happens! You're our Anya and I just...! I just want to see you again," he says with a saddened voice. "I hope you'll one day feel the same."

For awhile, no one moves or says a word. "Anya?" Veronica says. "You're more than just a savior. You're our savior. Even if you feel like you've lost, I think... I think if you would open your eyes you would see we are still here. We won't see you any differently than we always have. Me and Adrian have made it through hard times because we kept pulling each other up. We want to be the ones pulling you up this time. Together, I know we can do it. Just... Just don't forget us, Anya. We're here for you..."

Afearia doesn't move. The children look to each other with meek faces before turning to leave. "Adrian... Veronica?" Afearia says, sounding out of sorts. The kids quickly turn to her as she's lying on her stomach, moving toward the bed's edge. "Oww," she says, trying to turn herself.

The kids rush over to her bedside and Veronica quickly takes Afearia's hand. "Does it hurt, Anya? What do you need?"

Adrian moves the quilt down from over her head, revealing her face. Afearia gives a tired smile with a sweaty face. "I got careless, huh?"

Adrian's eyes water before he joyfully smiles. "Yup!"

Veronica suddenly becomes quite worried as she feels on Afearia's arm. "Brother," she says in a low voice, "Something's wrong. Anya's really hot. Like really, really hot."

Adrian puts his hand to Afearia's head. "What are you doing?" Afearia sluggishly asks.

"I'll go get a cold cloth!" he hastily says before rushing out the room.

Afearia hazily watches him leave. "Why is he in such a hurry?"

Veronica fakes a smile, "He's just really happy to see you again and is in a hurry to return."

"Yeah, me too," she says with a lazy smile.

In her heavy haze, Afearia doesn't even notice how much Veronica's hand is shaking in hers. Adrian returns with a bucket of cold water and rags.

"Anya," Adrian says, "Can you to lie on your back?"

"A new game?" Afearia asks as she painfully turns herself over. Veronica places the pillows behind her head before pulling the covers down to her feet. "Veronica, I'm cold."

"I know, Anya," Veronica says. "It'll be alright."

Adrian loosely wrings out six rags and places them on her ankles, chest, wrist, and forehead. The siblings look to each other with faces of uncertainty. Seeming like she's about to pass out, Afearia suddenly begins coughing until she vomits blood, causing her to jolt forward and lie on her side.

"Anya!" the kids screamed.

Afearia's breathing becomes irregular as her eyes are nearly closed. "My chest," she says with a bloody mouth and rasp. "It hurts."

"Call the doctor!" Veronica says.

Adrian runs out the room. Veronica takes the rag from Afearia's forehead and wipes her mouth. "I'm hot," Afearia says. "My ribs, my stomach. They hurt."

"You'll be okay," Veronica says with forced optimism. "I'm here, see? I'm your light right now."

Afearia makes a faint smirk. "Light... No. Only darkness."

Adrian enters the room with the wireless house phone to his ear. "No, she just looks out of it," he says with a shaky tone. "Pills?" Adrian looks around the room and finds scattered pills at the other side of the bed on the floor. "There's some. No, not a lot. Yes, she's very hot. Okay."

"I'm dizzy," Afearia weakly says.

Adrian hangs up, grabs the empty glass from her nightstand and rushes out the room as Veronica watches, "Brother!?"

"He's coming!" Adrian shouts to his sister as he

22

rushes down the hall to the bathroom. "We have to keep her hydrated!"

While Adrian gets Afearia water, Afearia coughs up a little more blood before wide-eyed Veronica wipes it away, barely remaining calm as she tries her best to be positive. He returns without the phone and a full glass of water. Lightly pouring, Adrian gets Afearia to drink it while Veronica continues to keep her cool by reapplying the cold rags.

Afearia breathes from heavy to slow with her eyes struggling to remain open. Adrian finishes giving her the water and quickly leaves to get more. Suddenly, the front door opens with Dr. Richards running up the stairs with another doctor.

"Stay here!" Dr. Richards tells Patrick.

Dr. Richards enters the room and immediately looks Afearia over. Veronica steps back and stands by the door with her brother. He checks her pulse then pulls out a small flashlight from his coat's pocket, looking into her eyes.

He checks her heart rate with his stethoscope before pulling out a syringe. He goes into his pocket and pulls out a small glass vial. Dr. Richards turns it upside before poking the needle through the top. If I made it in time, Dr. Richards thinks, the naloxone should counteract the overdose.

After a few minutes, Afearia's breathing regulates. Now less tense, Dr. Richards turns toward the door and walks out the room to approach Patrick waiting on the stairs. "I may need some spare naloxone." The doctor hands him more vials. "I'm sorry about all this, but you'll have to cover my patients until I return. Call me if things get out of control again."

The doctor nods and is walked out the house and to his car. Dr. Richards returns inside and shuts the door before slowly walking upstairs. The kids stare into Afearia's room until Dr. Richards stands before them.

"You two did good," he says. "This could have been much worse if no one was here."

"She'll be okay?" Adrian asks.

"Yes, but I'm going to keep close watch over her. She may not be fully out the woods yet. Go back to your rooms and I'll let you two know when she wakes up."

The kids walk away while Dr. Richards goes inside Afearia's room, softly shutting the door. He approaches and pulls a chair beside her bed. When he sits down, Afearia violently coughs. He leans back with a stressful sigh while running his hands down his face. He puts his fingers in his hair and watches her rest.

Several hours past with Dr. Richards sleeping slouched in the chair while Afearia sleeps soundly. Slowly, Afearia's eyes begin to open. She turns her head to see the doctor in the chair before staring up at the ceiling. Afearia looks to the nightstand and sees a glass of water. She struggles to reach it until Dr. Richards grabs it for her.

"You're hopeless," he says. He tilts it to her mouth, but she just stares at him with heavy, annoyed eyes. "Would you rather the kids do it for you?" She continues to stare. "Afearia, drink the damn water! Or has your misplaced pride not made its point?" She turns her head to the ceiling. "Fine," he says with gruff before roughly placing the glass down and standing.

As he turns, a sandy rasp is heard. He looks to Afearia and sees she's struggling to speak. He takes the glass and tilts it over her dried lips. Once finishing the glass, she moistens her lips. Dr. Richards places the glass on the nightstand and sits back down.

"You are so selfish," he says with underlining annoyance. She looks to him with a confused expression. He places the pill bottle on the nightstand with it being over half empty. "To actually try and take your own life. How could you? How could you selfishly try and take your own life after I told you those kids need you? It doesn't get

24

much lower than that." He looks down at her with disgust. "It truly doesn't."

Dr. Richards leaves the room and returns to his study. He turns the lamp on and sits at his desk in a huff with his head lowered to the desk. He lifts his eyes from his arms and stares at the wall before looking to his phone. It's over, Dr. Richards thinks. The hope is finished.

He reaches for the phone and dials. He stares at it while hearing it ring before a man's voice is heard, repeatedly saying hello. Dr. Richards raises the phone to his ear, "I'm sorry. This is Dr. Richards, number 3-0-7-4-1. Yes—from A.N.T.S."

Diary Entry #2402

You know that feeling you get when you feel so alone? That feeling you get when you are incapable or unable to connect with anyone? How real is that? They say no matter what, there is someone in the world who feels exactly the same as you do. But they only represent one aspect of your emotional spectrum. What about my other lonely feelings? Do I need to find hundreds of people to stop my loneliness? What are the chances of finding that lonely pair? And if you are lucky over a hundred times—can anyone out there relate to being a monster? No—they can't. And that's why no matter what I do or say, I will always hurt alone... Even in a sea of pseudo pairs.

For Our Future

Chapter Two

A little over two weeks have passed since Afearia's overdose. She calmly sits with her back to the bed's headboard. Her eyes slightly lift with her gaze to the floor. After awhile, she scoots herself back underneath the covers. Once in her bed, she closes her eyes and takes in a painful deep breath, repeating this treatment several times.

"Anya?" Adrian says, peeking through the doorway before pushing his head through. Veronica wiggles her head beneath his to see Afearia. Afearia smiles softly at them before the siblings walk inside.

"How are you feeling?" Veronica asks.

Before Afearia could answer, Dr. Richards comes inside. "Good afternoon, guys," he says cheerfully. He walks to the opposite side of the bed, "How are you feeling, Afearia?" Afearia nods. "Still having trouble talking? That's really weird. Let's do a check-up," he says before turning on the clock radio. "Can you turn on your side please?" She does as requested while he readies his stethoscope. "Deep breaths."

Afearia takes several slow breaths before he removes the instrument. "You sound clear to me," Dr. Richards says. "I'm surprised you still have no infections from refusing to do the deep breath exercises."

Afearia lowers her eyes, moments before the clock radio's song begins to scramble. After the clearing of the static, a choppy voice comes on the air. "Are we on?" the voice asks. "Can you hear me citizens of Terra? Can you hear me?" she asks as the once indistinguishable voice clears up.

"What's going on?" Adrian asks.

"Must be another of Raquel's hacked broadcast," Dr. Richards calmly replies.

He leans forward to turn up the volume. "Today was a blessed day for us," Raquel says. "We were once again able to drive back the government snakes that plague or world. With effort and determination, we won this battle. But this is only the beginning. Today was proof. Proof that we can no longer wait idly by for aid from those who do not exist. We don't need divine intervention to stand up. We don't need a false jumpstart from some angel or calamity trigger. These are only excuses!" Raquel stresses. "We are the jumpstart! Mongoose will aid the rebel army and help shake this world back into place."

Dr. Richards narrows his eyes a bit after her words. That's a bold and reckless statement, Raquel, Dr. Richards thinks.

"We are ready Terra. No longer should we cower in fear. The revolution is coming, and we are the storm. We will—take back our home. This is Raquel, leader of the Mongoose rebels... and I will always protect your freedom."

The radio scrambles before returning to its regular broadcasting with a man apologizing on the air for the interruption.

"Mongoose?" Veronica says with curiously.

Dr. Richards resumes Afearia's exam, "It's a small rebel group that has been nipping at the king's ankles for six years now. I respect her passion and empowering speeches. It really moves the masses. But her declaration is a risky move to play. This will surly draw unimaginable fire her way." He stands up. "Your lungs are clear and your heart is back to a natural rhythm. All that remains is you healing the last of your injuries and you'll be good to go." Afearia remains still, looking at no one. "Well, I'm off to work," he says with an upbeat attitude.

"Hey," Dr. Richards says, walking toward the door,

"if you guys need anything, just give me a call. I shouldn't be too late tonight."

Dr. Richards shuts the door behind him while Veronica briefly ponders. "Hmm," Veronica says. "Brother, who's the rebel army?"

"Don't you think you should've asked the doctor that question?" he replies.

"This is the first time I heard there was one. Hmm, Anya—?" When she turned to Afearia, it appeared she had fallen asleep.

Veronica taps her brother's shoulder for him to look at Afearia. They both nod and silently leave the room. Once the door shut, Afearia opens her eyes, saddening her stare. Suddenly, the song My Savior by Yadee plays on the radio. She closes her eyes and sighs.

Meanwhile at Aster City's hospital, Dr. Richards walks through the ER with interns after testing their knowledge on the currently admitted patients.

"Alright, Lisa," Dr. Richards says, "since you shined so well in rounds today, Mr. Donovan will be your patient. As for the rest of you, go meet Dr. McMillan on the fourth floor for a chance to assist in his case study."

As the interns clear out with Dr. Richards looking at a chart over a patient's bed, Lisa nervously looks around. "Dr. Richards?" she says.

"Yes, Lisa?" he replies, signing the chart and hanging it at the foot of the bed.

"I may be knowledgeable about his condition and the needed treatments, but I don't think I'm ready for that kind of patient."

He sighs with a slight smile. "Lisa, you're supposed to be a doctor. If you're breaking from one patient then your future here won't last long." Lisa lowers her head. "Look, you're still new, but you need to get used to this kind of pressure fast. Hospitals have fast days and slow days. This is a slow day, so be grateful because in the future you will have a lot of patients. As a doctor, you have to be able to handle that every day. Hey," Dr. Richards says, making eye contact. "Have confidence. You're one of the brightest students I've seen here in a long time. You'll be fine."

Lisa smiles and leaves to take care of her penitent. Dr. Richards turns to leave and walk down the hall before the loudspeaker requests him to come to the third floor. He turns left to the coming stairway and walks up to the third floor.

He approaches the nurse's station and smirks, "I knew that was your voice."

"Morning, doctor," the nurse greets with a smile. "Dr. Jarvis needs you in room 326."

"Thank you."

Dr. Richards walks to the end of the hall and slowly enters the room where two armed guards stand at the foot of the patient's bed. When he walks around the curtain, he sees an unconscious man lying in the bed with black sores on his skin and a breathing mask on his face. The man's hooked to IVs and three different machines. The already attending physician, Dr. Jarvis, finishes taking notes on the man's vitals.

"He looks worse," Dr. Richards says with a gloomy expression.

"He may look worse than yesterday, but he is much better than last week," Dr. Jarvis says. "How's your in-house patient?"

"She's fine," he says indifferently. "Any headway on the infection?"

"No. Thanks to you, the best we can do is stabilize it."

"But for how long?"

Dr. Jarvis stares at the man's pulsating sore, "Maybe one or two weeks at best. Sadly, he was the only one we were able to stabilize. The rest were—"

"Yeah." Dr. Richards glances at the guards. "I'm going to the lab. Maybe I'll be able to do something there."

"You're the only one who's been able to make any progress, so go ahead." Dr. Richards nods and begins to leave. "Kerry?" He stops. "It's getting smarter. When you get to the lab, take a look at the files I've complied pertaining to this patient." Dr. Richards glances at Dr. Jarvis before leaving and taking the elevator located near the nurse's station to the basement.

Once on the elevator, he rides down to the basement and waits for the doors to part. Dr. Richards steps out and proceeds to the end of the hall where two doors await; one of which is to his right. He swipes his card on the small slot on the front door and punches in a four digit code on the keypad mounted beside the door.

As he opens the door into the four foot long hall, another door with the same safeguards was before him. Dr. Richards proceeds with the same steps as the previous door, but puts in a code twice as long as the previous door.

As he enters the dark, spacious room, he flicks one out of four light switches to dimly reveal five computers resting on long tables while the main computer's placed in the middle. All kinds of lab equipment was available to whoever had access. It's all spread across seven tables in rows of three, including the computer tables. Dr. Richards approaches the computers where doctor names are placed near each monitor.

He stops at his computer at the far end where a red flash drive with Dr. Jarvis's name on it. Dr. Richards sits down and moves his mouse to exit the generic hospital screensaver before loading up the flash drive. He opens the folder, "D-virus Mr. Monroe", sorting through the files. He selects the video files and the zoomed images of the virus.

While watching the footage, he pauses in shock when he sees late night footage of Dr. Jarvis cutting into one of the pulsating black sores on Mr. Monroe. It oozes black goo before a deformed, infantile leg pokes out and turns to ash.

Dr. Jarvis takes some of the ooze and scrapes it into a container. The footage cuts over to the recordings of the virus under scope view. Dr. Jarvis dropped a solution on it that momentarily halts the virus.

The footage cuts away to Dr. Jarvis mixing chemicals. "In conclusion," Dr. Jarvis says in the video, "the sores house stronger contagious strains of the virus from the current host. It's safe to say once freed, they immediately spread to the nearest victim. Whatever fails to kill the virus the first time will not work the second if any of its descendents survive. I've had calls made to grant me authorization to cremate the bodies two days before the virus can spread. It is unfortunately the only way to fully kill this troublesome infection."

Dr. Jarvis looks beside him before the footage stops. This isn't everything, Dr. Richards thinks. He left out something... Doesn't matter at this point. What concerns me are the host's sores. If a patient has sores, he must be near death. But its means to spread its infection isn't clear beyond the touch of the black ooze. But the creature that appeared when the sore was cut could not survive in the open. What's the purpose of such function then?

Perhaps it's a container? A sheltering sore to house it before it can mature? It's hard to study something that turns to ash immediately after death... Its sudden appearance and its functions... It's almost done with a touch of primitive engineering. Dr. Richards eyes widen in realization. Is this.... Is this a bioterrorist attack? That's a leap, isn't it? What would anyone gain from engineering a destructive pathogen like this?

Dr. Richards shakes his head. It can't be that... The virus has no solid place of origin since it spawned in three different regions from one another at the same time. It comes and goes with no sense of reason at all. Each time it appears it happens to be stronger and smarter than when it last arose. It's a troubling thing that must be stopped.

Dr. Richards begins clicking through Dr. Jarvis's files. There has to be something here that can lead to clues on how to stabilize or eradicate this monster. My work and his should have some kind of answer by now.

He suddenly stops. "The D-virus..." Dr. Richards looks over his monitor and stares at beakers. "It's worth a shot."

While Dr. Richards continues working tirelessly at the hospital, the siblings are in the kitchen at his house working on a simple dinner. "Is the rice almost done?" Adrian asks his sister while stir frying fairly burnt handmade meatballs.

Veronica coughs a few times from the smoke coming from the food, "It's done," she says while looking at the ready light on the rice cooker.

Adrian coughs a couple times. "Open a window!" Rushing to do so, Veronica struggles to open the kitchen window before it slides up. She waves her hand by her face to move the smoke. "I hope these are done," he says before reaching to grab the pan's handle. Adrian burns himself and shouts in pain.

"Brother!" Veronica rushes to her kneeling brother as he cuirasses his hand. "Let me see it!" Adrian refuses as she pries his hand out from him to see his first degree burn. "We should treat that!"

"After! We're almost done. Get me the oven mitt." Veronica hands him the mitt from the table and Adrian puts it on his other hand. He carries the sizzling pan from the stove to the large plastic bowl on the table before dumping the meatballs in. Veronica turns off the burner and turns on the cold water before Adrian rushes the sink. "Move!" He tosses the pan into the sink and shakes off the oven mitt before putting his hand under the water. "The heat was going through the oven mitt!"

"Adrian, let's treat your hand."

"Fine," he reluctantly says.

After their shoddy first aid treatments, the two of them carefully carry a loaded hot dinner plate up the stairs, sharing an oven mitt. Once upstairs, they carefully knock on Afearia's door and let themselves in. Afearia's sitting up on her bed, staring out the window.

"Anya, dinner," Veronica softly says in order not to startle Afearia. She slowly turns to them as they stand by her bedside with kind smiles while presenting the plate of rice, irregular shaped meatballs, and chopped broccoli. Afearia's eyes glaze over them, noticing Adrian's hands wrapped in gauze and many of Veronica's fingertips. Afearia looks them in the eyes. "We know," she says before Afearia can respond.

"We hope you like it," Adrian nervously says.

Afearia lightly smiles and takes the plate from them with the mitten. They calmly watch in anticipation until Veronica gasps, "Brother, we forgot a fork!"

"I got it!"

Before Adrian can even get halfway across the room, Afearia pops a hot meatball in her mouth. They silently watch her with tense eyes, hoping it will be to her liking. Afearia finishes chewing and swallows. She gives the kids a thumbs up with a closed-eyed smile. The kids are excited and rush to her bedside.

"Try the rice and broccoli!" Veronica says. Afearia scoops up some with her fingers and smiles again. "She likes it! We did good!"

"I'll be back with a fork," Adrian says as he quickly leaves the room.

"Me too! I made the rice and broccoli!" she says while running out the room backward. "Don't stop smiling before we get back!"

Afearia silently chuckles before continuing to eat with her hands and fingers. With a few rice grains around her mouth, she looks back out the window, leaving her face to sadden once again. She hears them rushing up the stairs and quickly conceals her sorrow with a somewhat forced smile.

"Here you go, Anya," Veronica says as she runs to her with fork in hand.

Afearia takes it and gestures her head as a thank you. Adrian puts down two full glasses near the clock radio. "I got you water and apple juice," he says. "Would you like the radio on?" Afearia does a soft nod. He turns on the radio at the near end of a song. "Me and Veronica are going to go eat too. We'll be back later."

As they leave the room, Afearia silently waves them off before they close the door behind them. Shortly after the start of the next song, the station begins to scramble. The transmission breaks with the rise of Raquel's voice.

"After receiving news on the imprisonment of my men and the failed liberation of Zerci town," Raquel says, "I feel I need to speak out and let all the citizens of Terra know this is not over. I have not given up and I have not lost hope. I will free my men and the people of Terra screaming for change. Change is not something Derexen is willing to give. Change can't be asked for. It must be demanded!"

"And that change is our freedom," she continues. "Our freedom should not be up for discussion. It should be a given! And if the king isn't willing to step down from his oppressive throne, we'll step up and strip him of all his power by any and all means necessary. Derexen and his dark government will turn to dust and ash like his kind deserves. Do not dishearten people of Terra. We will rise again. That's a promise, a belief, Raquel, the leader of Mongoose will always believe in," she says in a softer tone.

The station scrambles and returns to its regular broadcasting. Afearia remains motionless after the words spoken by Raquel as she stared somberly into her plate.

Hesitant, she resumes eating.

Meanwhile in the kids' room, Adrian and Veronica are nearly done eating as they're silently sitting on the floor with Veronica's back to the door and Adrian in front of her.

Veronica softly pushes her two meatballs back and forth across her plate. "Brother, when do you think we're getting out of here?" she asks.

"When Anya gets better," Adrian replies.

"Where will we go?"

Adrian bites into his meatball, "Home."

"Home. That's good," she joylessly says.

"What's wrong?"

"It's just—this may be the first time I've really thought about this…"

"About what?" sounding a bit irritated.

"That someday we will have to leave Anya," she says with a frown.

"And then she'll be alone again," he says, frowning as well.

"We used her, Adrian. We manipulated her and played dumb all the way. But… we soon began to care about her like our actual—"

"I know."

"I don't want to leave Anya alone. Not after all we've experienced with her."

Adrian looks away from her and finishes his half bitten meatball, "She's an adult, Veronica. She'll be alright. Besides, I'm sure she has prepared for the day she has to take us home and say goodbye." Veronica's frown grows. "But maybe it doesn't have to be goodbye. Maybe when she finishes her journey she could settle down in our town."

"Do you think she would?"

"I hope… I don't know if we can tie her with just that."

Veronica makes a pondering expression. "If that's the case, I'm gonna marry Anya!" she proudly says.

"You can't!" he blurts suddenly.

"Why?"

"Because..." Adrian wonders for a moment. "I don't know why, but you just can't."

"Then you marry Anya so she can live with us."

Adrian's face becomes flushed with embarrassment. "Don-don't say such crazy things!" Adrian grabs his plate and rushes out the room while Veronica watches him and giggles.

Later that night as the kids slept, Afearia remains awake with her back against the bed's headboard. After staring at the wall for a while, Afearia raises her arm with an open palm. Soon after, she drops it with a long sigh. A light knocking is heard at the door before opening partway.

Dr. Richards pokes his head halfway inside, "How's everything going?" he whispers. She nods before he lets himself in and closes the door. "The kids are already in bed after leaving my kitchen a mess. But I have to head back to the hospital." He sits at the corner of her bed. "You doing okay here?" Afearia gives him a suspicious glare before slowly nodding.

"Good, good," he says. "As long as you're comfortable here that's all that matters. Do you want me to get you something before I go?" Afearia declines. "Alright then." He stands. "Try to get some rest and don't overexert yourself. I'll see you tomorrow," he says before leaving the room.

Dr. Richards goes to his room and grabs a flash drive from his desk and a small, silver cylinder shaped device before shutting his door. He leaves his house and climbs into the passenger side of a car before driving off.

"Thanks for driving me again, Patrick."

"No problem," his co-worker says. "Did you get what you needed?"

"For now. This viral strain is causing a problem. I'm running out of ideas on how to stop it."

"Out of the three hospitals that have this problem, you and Dr. Jarvis are the closest at figuring this thing out. However big or small that may be."

Dr. Richards looks out the window. But Dr. Jarvis's methods…, he thinks. "Do any of these patients have a common place of origin?"

"Completely random. Even the symptoms take effect at different times of the day. We have yet to determine a common cause or relation."

"There has to be something. Maybe something they ate or used or—" His pager goes off. He looks to his hip before calmly looking out the windshield. "Speed up. We have a conscious infected patient."

When they make it to the ER entrance, Dr. Richards quickly runs out the car toward the hospital. He enters the building and is quickly approached by a nurse.

"He came in with a high fever," she says as they hastily walk through the ER. "He's a little delusional and is a bit coherent. He has just recently started talking about stomach pains."

"Any sores or darkening of the skin?"

"We didn't want to run any checks for that without you or Dr. Jarvis."

"Where is Dr. Jarvis?"

"Taking care of two other patients carrying the virus."

He grunts as he turns the corner. In a cornered bed lies the patient she spoke of. With shut eyes, he holds his stomach while rolling from side to side.

"Get me a needle," Dr. Jarvis says to the nurse. "Sir, can you tell me where you have been for the last twenty-four hours?" he asks while putting on some rubber gloves. The man tries to speak, but his words are jumbled. "Sir, I'm going to remove your shirt, okay?" The man nods painfully. Dr. Richards removes his shirt and sees a red lump on his chest. "Sir, do you know how you got this?" he

38

asks while closely looking at his lump.

"Tha-that-that wasn't there before," the man stutters. "I'm-I'm freezing."

"You have a fever," he says as he takes two needles from the returning nurse.

"I got two just in case," the nurse says

Dr. Richards proceeds to draw blood from the man's arm. "Check his eyes."

The moment she opens his eyes, he screams and pushes her away. "It hurts!" the man screams, rolling out the bed and onto his feet. "The light! It hurts! Turn them off!"

He flips the bed over onto Dr. Richards and swipes at the nurse's leg. She is nearly injured before running off to get help. Dr. Richards pushes the bed off himself as the eye shut man stumbles around swinging his arms.

Dr. Richards stands, trying to reason with the man, "Please, let me try to help you. We're not going to harm you. I can take you to a dark room, just calm down."

The man swings at him and misses, "Turn off the lights! It's hurting my skin! Ahhh! It burns! My God, help me!"

Security enters the room and tackles the man. A nurse follows behind them to inject the man with a syringe while Dr. Richards quickly grabs spare blankets.

The man begins to become drowsy, "The lights," he weakly says.

"Get off him," Dr. Richards says. The guards rise off him, but hold his arms and legs.

Dr. Richards calmly covers the man, "Thank—you," the man says as the blanket falls upon his face.

The nurse picks up the bed while the guards lay his covered body in the bed to restrain him. "Take him to room 334." Dr. Richards says to the nurses. He picks up all the medical supplies and recaps the syringe he drew blood with.

A few hours later, Dr. Richards is in the basement along with the feverish patient. As the man wakes, groaning a bit, Dr. Richards glances at him while standing at his medical table, "Shh. As promised, I had you moved to a room with little light." He takes a syringe and draws blood from the lump on his chest.

When he finishes, he daps his lump with a cloth and leaves the dark room. He proceeds down the hall where his computer monitor is and sits before it. He raises the syringe and shines a small light on the blood. Trace amounts of black liquid move around inside, hiding behind the blood to avoid the light. It's even worse than I thought, Dr. Richards thinks. He's gradually turning.

He sets the sample on the table and returns to the patient's room. He grabs the chart off the foot of the bed and flashes his small light on the chart for a moment. "Mr. Raymond, have you been sick anytime this month or the previous month?"

The man groans and vaguely turns his head toward him, "Last month. I had an unknown virus in my system. It gave me black sores and stomach pains."

"I don't recall seeing sores on you. How's that?"

"I don't know. I took far trips in order to get treatment."

"Where?"

"To the west to see a doctor with good ratings in their area."

"The west? How far west? What location?"

"I'm tired."

"What location?" Dr. Richards demands.

"Yolis town," he says with a series of coughs.

He turns from the man. It's all coming together now, Dr. Richards thinks. "Be patient, Mr. Raymond. I'm going to do all I can to save you."

He leaves the man's room and grabs the sample from his desk, moving to the other end of his lab. He flicks a switch on the wall to light a long table with available lab equipment. He takes a petri dish from a set of others and places it under a microscope.

Dr. Richards glances at the time and goes into his coat pocket to pull out the silver cylinder shaped recorder from home before holding the button. "10:41pm," Dr. Richards logs. "I think I may be onto something, despite my previous thought of it being bioengineered. What I do know is the two possible end results of those infected with the D-virus. You either die or become a Demi. My patient is showing possible early signs of Demi behavior and…"

He shakes the sample before squirting it into the dish. Looking through the lens, he adjusts the lens's focus several times to get the best image possible.

He holds record, "DNA." He stands and walks to a draw behind him, "Mr. Raymond claims to have had the same infections as others I have treated." He opens the draw and pulls out a small light, flashing it a couple times. "I theorized a while back that if these are exposed to UV-rays they'll die. And knowing this, Mr. Raymond went to a location with sun making it a possibility."

He looks through the scope again, "But how did they come back with different symptoms? The virus looks similar to the strain I'm treating, excluding the purple ridges on them now. And on closer inspection, they don't seem to be changing the cells or interacting with them in anyway. Could it be aware it's no longer in its host? Or maybe—"

Dr. Richards stops recording suddenly and gets another empty syringe. He enters the room Mr. Raymond sleeps and quietly puts on rubber gloves. He wipes the man's lump and takes another sample with the needle. When he finishes, he walks out into the lab and looks at the almost all black sample he extracted. He pulls out another dish and squirts the sample onto it before examining it under the lens.

His eyes widen in surprise before recording his findings, "I understand now. Theses look exactly like the D-virus but far more active. I am literally witnessing them take the remaining blood cells and rewriting them like a cancer. Which could mean the viruses with the ridges are just damaged viruses placed in a dormant-like state. Was it because of the UV exposure? I shall test this theory."

He puts down the recorder and grabs the UV light before looking through the lens as he shines it on the sample. "Incredible." He turns the light off and resumes recording. "As the active infection is exposed to UV, they cluster together as an act of unity against the attack and are unaffected. They are just now breaking apart and resuming their activities. I will now perform the same test on the dormant viruses."

He swaps the dishes and begins the same test. "Because of the ridges, the virus can't properly come together. This causes some to become a type of gray matter and dissolve. I will end the exposure to conduct more test. However, it's clear something prior must have occurred for the ridged samples to get like this. Another variant must happen before they can reach a state of vulnerability. Perhaps other elements from the sun?"

Dr. Richards looks to the other syringe. "I will now conduct another test." He takes the syringe and introduces the dormant virus with the active variant. "No..." he says in displeasure before slowly reaching to record. "The dormant cells... They've been reactivated by the unharmed strains... I'm running out of time."

"Doctor," Mr. Raymond groans from the room. Dr. Richards stands and quickly goes to check on him only to find that his hand has darkened and swelled. Even the restraints on him have begun to give way to the swelling. "I don't feel too well."

Dr. Richards stands at the doorway staring in on him with no real open expression on the development of

Mr. Raymond's condition. "Mr. Raymond... Your coming test are about to become... inhumane." Mr. Raymond, barely responded as he can only vaguely see his doctor. Dr. Richards clenches his teeth for a moment. "Just—bare it."

A week's time has passed. Dr. Richards never comes home longer than need be.

Afearia, making progress in her recovery, can now walk with difficulty. She opens the door to her room and slowly makes her way to the bathroom. Once inside, she stumbles onto the toilet seat in a huff as her concentration had broken. Catching her breath a bit, she slowly lifts her gown in order to urinate.

When she finishes and flushes the toilet, she remains seated for a moment before looking at the tub. She uses the sink and the tub's edge to help herself stand before turning on the bath water. As she watches the water run, the added sound of the bathroom's wall mounted cat clock enters her ears. The silver British cat smiles as it's yellow eyes watch from over the door while the clock hand ticks on its belly.

She tries to block it out and remain focused on the slow rise of the water in the tub. Her eyes are fixated on the flow of its movement. Steadily raising her hands, she moves them in a flowing, smooth manner, but fails to manipulate the water. As her irritation rises, her brow twitches before she attempts again to control the water.

As Afearia continues to move her hands, the sound of the clock seems to be louder in her ears, causing her to make a face of greater irritation before turning angrily toward the clock while gripping an air freshener from the top of the toilet tank.

"SHUT UP!" she screams as she hurls it into the clock, causing it to fall and break on the floor. In a huff, she stares at the clock before noticing the uncanny similarity of the cat's eyes.

In a mental flash, she sees Minerva's face appear on

the clock. In fearful alarm, she rushes to the clock and begins smashing it with her fist in panic. Though fearful as she attacks it, her fear becomes rage as she hits the clock harder, blooding her knuckles as she grunts with each strike.

When she finally stops with her hand breaking the clock to pieces, she stares at the floor for a while before looking up to see she had cracked the hanging mirror behind the door as well, showing the saddened, distorted reflection of herself.

A light knock is heard from the door. "Anya?" Adrian calls from outside. "Are you okay?"

Afearia hastily, hurting herself in the process, stands to wash her bloody hand, gathers the broken pieces into the trashcan and wraps her hand with the available gaze. She shuts off the water and puts her injured hand inside her pajama pocket. Afearia opens the door and smiles down at him.

"You okay?" he asks again.

She pats his head and walks back to her room, leaving him feeling sadly concerned. Afearia sits on her bed and slowly rocks herself while rubbing her thighs. She looks to the radio and turns it on as an added distraction. Soon after, the front door slams with slow footsteps coming up the stairs.

With a light knock on her door, Dr. Richards comes in partway, giving her a light wave in exhaustion, "I'm back." He shuts the door behind him after entering, "I've got more food for the house since I know we were low." He pulls his stethoscope from his coat pocket. "I'm glad to see you're sitting up more than you used to." She gives her back to him as he puts his scope on. He lifts her shirt and listens. "Deep breaths. Good. Another. One more."

"I know you've given up on me," Afearia says in a fairly weak rasp.

Dr. Richards is surprised for a moment, "You've

got your voice back."

"It's been back for a while."

He listens a bit more and leans from Afearia after lowering her shirt, "Is that so?" he says, walking from the bed toward the chair.

"I haven't appreciated your empty-hearted smiles. After that night, you've given up on the idea of me getting better."

He sits down and huffs, "You tried to kill yourself. That was the white flag."

She slowly shakes her. "You're wrong. That wasn't an act of suicide. It was an unintentional overdose."

"What?"

"Like I told you before, I have never taken medicine. It was only after I felt dazed that I struggled to read the label."

Dr. Richards looks surprised by what he was hearing. "And you expect me to believe that?"

"Why would I lie about this? Don't you think if I wanted to take my life I would have done it by now?" He looked away from her, seeming annoyed in his denial. "You were right about some things though. Those kids do need me. And I made a promise. As soon as I'm able, I will keep my word and get them home."

Stern and even bothered, Dr. Richards looks Afearia in the eyes, taking notice of her genuine expression. His displeasure is evident when he lightly grits his teeth. Suddenly, the song on the radio begins to scramble before a voice comes through the static.

"People of Terra," Raquel says. "My lovely brothers and sisters. We, the rebels of Mongoose have a frightful battle ahead of us. Derexen—has discovered our hideout. Even though the info is reliable, it could all be a ruse. But if it's true, Mongoose will not be fighting just for us, but for everyone. Mongoose always fights for the good of the people. Our battles are your battles. What we face is a representation of Terra's pain. This is all due to the unrelenting hand of the king."

"And although we as the people know what we want," Raquel continues, "we are marked as outlaws because of our desire to be free. Outlaws. The disease that won't go away. The ones who refuse to bend over for this world's precious king. We are slandered this way because we don't want to be governed by those who believe us too foolish to control our own lives. The place we once called home is nothing but his playground."

"Raquel, reinforcements!" a man shouts in the background.

"We are not outlaws! We are activist! And we will be victorious!"

The radio scrambles back to its station after gunfire is heard. "She's in trouble," Afearia says with genuine concern.

"It was bound to happen," Dr. Richards says almost nonchalantly. "She's hacked airways before, but the amount of times she's done it this year while threatening the king was too much."

Afearia shakes her head, "Six years. She's been doing this for six years?"

"Yes, with a small group of freedom fighters to aid her cause. They've always worked independently—until recently. I assume they received a great offer from another party."

"Or ran into a great deal of trouble."

"It's possible. She was considered one of the strongest freedom fighters until you showed up. But even now. People still look forward to her morale boosting speeches."

"Terra shouldn't jump ship yet. Raquel is very inspirational. Her speeches alone show the high characteristics of a strong leader. Hearing her... has actually been motivational to my recovery."

"Your recovery," he says with some skepticism.

Afearia looks to him with a hint of bother as he stands to leave the room. "Sounds like you disapprove," she says, stopping him at the door. "Or do you refuse to believe I haven't given up?" Without saying a word, he closes the door and leaves the house to be driven back to the hospital.

As Dr. Richards traverses the halls of the hospital and stands before a soon-to-arrive elevator, he is greeted by one of the nurse's staff.

"Hey, Dr. Richards," the nurse says. He says nothing, staring straight ahead at the doors. "How's Mr. Raymond doing? I heard he's under your care now."

When the doors part, Dr. Richards steps inside the elevator, "He's dead," Dr. Richards bluntly says before the doors close.

He rides down to the basement floor. When the doors part, he sees the front and right lab doors are wide open. He slowly walks until he hears something drop and a man groaning. He quickly moves to the darkened patients' room where two men restrained to hospital beds lie with Dr. Jarvis leaning half across one of them.

"What are you doing!?" Dr. Richards shouts.

Dr. Jarvis turns, holding a bloody scalpel from cutting into the patient's head, "Richards? Why are you back so soon?"

"What are you doing to them?"

"Finding a cure."

"It looks to me you're running evasive procedures."

"Evasive? When a medical mystery is presented to you on a table, nothing's evasive.

"Dr. Richards steps into the room with suppressed anger in his eyes, "And what could you be looking for in that man's head?"

"Not looking. Testing."

"Testing?"

Dr. Jarvis takes out a syringe and injects the man he was working on in his neck, "Nighty night." Dr. Richards watches him walk out the room and into the lab with disapproval in his eyes before following him. Dr. Jarvis stands before his microscope. "Take a look at this."

Dr. Richards gives him a distrusting glance before doing as he was asked. "Cancer cells. So what?" leaning away from the scope.

"Ah-ah. Keep looking." When Dr. Richards leans down to look at the dish, Dr. Jarvis drips a few drops of the D-virus into it. The virus attacks the cells and destroys them. "There's potential here. What if I could harness this and use it to cure all kinds of once incurable ills. I could change the world."

Dr. Richards leans from the scope, "We're trying to save these people—here! They are not your test subjects for bargaining with the devil."

"You think too small. You do not understand how much of a free pass we have here. We could be remembered forever because of what we can discover down here."

"Is that all you care about? Fame? What about being a good doctor? These people are trusting their lives to us."

"As if you ever cared about that. You don't have to work in a government protected hospital to save lives but you did it anyway for the same reason any of us did. Money and recognition. Why else would you be working so hard for a cure by yourself? It's because you can't imagine the kind of recognition you'll receive if you break this box."

Dr. Richards stares coldly at his co-worker for a moment. "Don't touch my patients, Jarvis."

"Sorry, but I ran out. They all died. So I had to find out through others you had some, two no less."

"Jarvis—"

"It's okay. I'm only injecting diseases into one of them."

"You're doing what?" he says in disgust. "Do you know how dangerous that is!? You could ignorantly create something far worse!"

"I'm not an amateur. Besides, how else can I be sure about my theories without subjects? Don't worry, most have been unable to infect the host. I guess they need a fresh body first."

"You need to stop this. You will eventual be caught and sent to prison."

"No I won't. I have government immunity."

"What?" he says in disbelief. "From who? Who would authorize such inhumane test?"

"Sorry, I'm not allowed to say."

"The hospital won't let—"

"They can't do anything. Even if they could, they don't have the skill to find impractical procedures. Even then, all I have to do is cremate the bodies and I can then fabricate any story I want."

"Have you gone mad!? Do you hear what you're saying!?"

Dr. Jarvis turns from him with a devious smile, "Don't worry. If I manage to cure three diseases, I'll put credit on your name for one of them."

Dr. Jarvis walks toward the patient's room while Dr. Richards watches him angrily. He glances at the D-virus syringe on the table and grabs it. He comes up behind Dr. Jarvis and injects the whole sample into his neck. Dr. Jarvis falls to his knees and holds his neck while Dr. Richards stands behind him, breathing erratically.

"Wha-what are you—?" Dr. Jarvis's saying, looking at him with wide eyes of disbelief. "Wh-why?"

Dr. Richards frantically kicks him in the face repeatedly until he loses consciousness. He then drags his body to the back of the lab where the bodies are cremated.

He opens the large metal door and pulls an old, discarded stretcher from the wall and straps the doctor to it before locking him inside. He stands with his back to the door, looking panicked. He turns to fasten the four bolts on the door and walks away.

Still panicked, he stands at the elevator and focuses to calm his nerves and his breathing. When he does, he calls for the elevator and rides it upstairs. Noticing his hair's a bit messed up and his expression still frantic, he quickly smoothes his hair and stands straight, breathing deep until the doors open. When he steps out, he heads to the Chief of Medicine's office.

He softly knocks on the door. "Come in," a man says from within the room. Dr. Richards comes in and closes the door behind him before standing before the man's desk. The Chief of Medicine glances at him. "What is it you need, Dr. Richards?" he says as he hangs his coat on the rack beside his chair.

"Something has happened during the D-virus research."

"Yes?"

Dr. Richards looks at him sorrowfully. "Dr. Jarvis—was infected."

"What!? How!?"

"A carless mistake. One of the patient's sores popped while Dr. Jarvis was suiting down in their patient's room. It splattered on his face and although he tried to quickly remove it, too much had already been absorbed by his skin. It's currently corroding his bloodstream. Under our expert opinion, we believe it best he doesn't leave the lab."

"I understand." The man looks to his right, shaking his head. "He's such a brilliant doctor. To make such a carless mistake."

"It could happen to anyone, sir."

The Chief of Medicine nods his head in agreement.

"Tell him I'll be down in a minute."

"Alright."

Dr. Richards leaves the office and rides down to the basement. He walks past the patients' room and enters the crematorium to find Dr. Jarvis bound and conscious. He stares at him on the gurney with a deadpan look while Dr. Jarvis thrashes about.

"I'll kill you for this," Dr. Jarvis sloppily says with spit coming from his mouth. "You hear me!? I'll kill you!"

As if he didn't hear him, Dr. Richards appears to be in thought. "I know," he says with flat realization. He leaves the room and returns with a syringe filled with a solution. "I'll just make you incoherent," he says as he approaches. He kneels down and injects him in the neck before standing. "After the chief sees you, I'll begin your treatment. Treatment you should be fine with." He grabs the stretcher and pulls Dr. Jarvis out of the room. "And because I don't care about you, I can test the possible cures I was too hesitant to try before." Dr. Jarvis drools with wide scared eyes. "Won't that be fun?" he rhetorically asks with cold intent.

Meanwhile, Afearia continues trying to strengthen her body, despite the dangers of her methods. She lies on the floor, finishing the last set of sit-ups. The pain and sweat is highly evident on her face. She attempts to stand, falling back down in exhaustion as she breathes shallowly. She crawls to her bed and leans on it.

"Even this is too much," Afearia says. She grits her teeth in annoyance. "A measly five hundred. Pathetic," she says with stronger grit.

Once she climbed onto her bed, a couple knocks are heard from the door before opening. Adrian and his sister come inside. Adrian's holding a juice box while his sister holds a box of cookies.

"Hey guys," Afearia says with a light smile.

"How are you feeling?" Veronica asks. "Ready to

take us home?"

"Veronica!?" Adrian scolds.

"Soon," Afearia replies kindly.

Both of them seem surprised by her response. "Really? Aren't you hurt?"

"Not for long. I'm getting better. I haven't forgotten my promise to you two."

"I was thinking… What if you sta—"

"Later," Veronica whispers to him. Afearia watches their odd behavior before Veronica changes the subject, "Cookie?" optimistically smiling through her offer.

Afearia lightly chuckles, "No thank you."

Adrian takes a cookie from the box, "Is there anything we can do for you right now?"

"No, I'm fine."

"Okay," he awkwardly says. "Goodnight, Anya." The siblings leave the room after Afearia waves them off.

Once in the hall, Veronica stuffs her face with cookies. "Why were you going to ask her to stay?" she asks through a crumb shower.

"I don't know. Overeager, I guess."

"Eager," shooting more crumbs.

"I just want her to stop fighting. We almost lost her, Veronica."

She stops as he turns into the bedroom. She swallows her cookies with a less cheerful expression before looking back at Afearia's room. The television is heard turning on in their room. She places the box of cookies down and walks back to Afearia's room, knocking before slowly entering. Veronica stands at the door, staring at Afearia.

"Yes?" Afearia says.

Veronica gently closes the door behind her and leans on it. "Adrian said something to me."

"Was he picking on you again?" she faintly jokes.

"It… it was sad but…" She lowers her head. "He

52

was right. We almost lost you." Afearia's light smile fades. "Since then, we can't stop wondering what we would do without you," her voice breaking a bit. Afearia stands and approaches her. "To never see you again. To laugh with you. It hurts just to think about," she says, unable to hold her tears. "Anya—" Afearia hugs Veronica's shaken body. She gently strokes her hair as she holds her tight. "Don't leave us," she says in a muffled cry into her waist.

"Shhhhh," Afearia says soothingly.

Adrian peeks out from his room, looking for his sister and notices the box of cookies on the floor. He steps out into the hall, "Veronica?"

Veronica hears his call and leans from Afearia, wiping her eyes. "Oh, don't tell Adrian, okay?" Afearia nods before she steps into the hall, heading to her room. "What what what!?" she playfully shouts a silly voice.

"What were you doing in Anya's room?" Adrian asks.

"I was just asking Anya—"

"If we could sleep together," Afearia says, having had stepped into the hall.

"Really?" he says, a bit skeptical.

"Of course." He looks to his sister who's smiling while holding her breath like she's going to burst. They both jump up with excitement and rush into Afearia's room, hopping on the bed. "I'll be right there."

She walks to the kids' room and turns off the television. Before walking out, she notices the kids' backpacks hanging on the wall by the window. She moves toward them and stops upon seeing her dried blood on Adrian's. She exhales with a joyless expression.

A few days later, Afearia's on her feet, moving around in an effort to recover. Though not fully healed, her desire to recover is gradually becoming evident by her increased mobility as she makes her way downstairs.

Afearia enters the kitchen in her pajama pants and

long sleeve shirt to open the fridge, finding wrapped deli sandwiches. She grabs two at random and sits at the table to eat them. She takes a bite and chews for a little while before suddenly stopping. She lifts the bread and tilts her head a bit. "Turkey, ham and cheese? Yum is yum." She continues eating with a bit of enthusiasm until her sleeve rolls up a bit.

Afearia stops and stares at the lacking definition in her forearm. With disappointment on her face, she stands back from the table and walks outside the house. She steps onto the cold ground and looks around the area she's been this whole time as if she's never seen the outside world before.

She takes a deep breath with closed eyes before throwing a fast straight punch, soon repeating this with a forward step into the proceeding punch. After several strikes, her last punch flows into a leaping butterfly kick. She performs it a bit poorly and barely sticks the landing, expressing a bit of pain. She grits her teeth in annoyance and does several high kicks. The high kicks turn into spin kicks which lead to leaping spin kicks that end in a backflipping kick.

She calms herself with a slow exhale as her hands slowly lower to center with her body. I can do this, Afearia thinks. I need to do this. I may have lost my powers, but I'm still here. I can still do something. It's not over unless I allow it to be. Afearia looks toward the city. I owe him an apology... Afearia sighs and continues practicing her punches, remaining outside to hone her body.

Within a week's time, Afearia was almost fully healed. And for the first time, Afearia's attempting to cook. She stands over a bowl of egg yolks and a plate of raw bacon in the kitchen. This can't be that hard, right? Afearia thinks. She tosses the clustered bacon into the frying pan before turning it on high. She stares into the pan shortly before it sizzles. The rise of the delicious aroma makes her smile. She grabs a fork from the drawer and stir fries the bacon apart. This is easy. I'm a natural, she thinks with a smile.

Suddenly the oil pops onto her face, "Owe!" She wipes it off only to get hot oil popped on her face and hands from the pan. She drops the fork and steps back wiping her face in alarm. "This can't be done safely! How do people do this!?" When she looks above the pan, smoke is dirtying the air.

Veronica comes down the stairs, rubbing her eyes, "Anya, your flame is too high."

Afearia grabs her shoulders as she neared the stove, "Hold on! It's become too dangerous to face," she says, staring at the wild beads of popping oil.

"But the house will burn down."

"Then let it burn!"

"Anya," she says as she steps from Afearia's overprotective hands and lowers the flame. She grabs a fresh plate and uses the tongs from the drawer to remove some of the burning bacon. "Some of it is ready." She puts the plate down and grabs butter from the fridge.

"Wow. You weren't afraid of the oil?"

"As long as it's not a lot on your skin, it won't leave a mark."

"Where did you learn to be a fearless cook?"

"My mom—" Veronica pauses for a moment. "Mother taught me."

"Oh..."

"Yeah... I forgot to wake up Adrian," she says, readying to go.

"No, it's fine. I'll get him." Afearia walks out the kitchen and heads to the kids' room. Entering slowly, she watches him sleep a little before nudging him awake. "Breakfast. Downstairs."

Adrian rubs his eyes and looks at her with surprised sleepy eyes. "Anya, you're dressed."

"I know. It's a bit battle torn, but still okay until I get something new."

He sits up and slides to the edge of the bed. "You're feeling better?"

"Sure. I got to keep my promise, right?"

He lightly smiles, "Yeah. Let's go eat." They head downstairs to find the table had been set for the three of them to eat. The three of them sit down with Adrian being the first to try the bacon. "It's really crispy," he says with a bit of surprise.

"I don't cook well," Afearia says with a hint of disappointment.

"You made the bacon?"

"Well, I started it, I suppose. You could technically say your sister salvaged what she could from my work."

"Ooops!" Veronica excitedly says. She takes Adrian's plate and exchanges it with hers. "Sorry, I like crispy bacon, you like soft bacon, and Anya likes a mix."

"Breakfast made in three different ways?" Afearia says with impressed brows. "Was that difficult?"

Veronica giggles, "Not at all."

"Perhaps I should take lessons from you," she says before taking a bite out of her eggs. Veronica smiles and eats her breakfast.

After breakfast, the three of them are in Afearia's room as she packs a bag while the siblings play a hand game with each other whilst the radio plays in the background.

"Is tonight our last night here?" Veronica asks.

"No," Afearia replies, "but I'd like to make this week our last."

The children stop playing. "We're—leaving?" Adrian says with some displeasure. "But, you just got better."

"Yes, but why wait?"

"Anya… it's dangerous."

Afearia stops packing for a moment. I wish I could say all will be fine like I normally do, she thinks. But now...

Afearia makes a face of discontent, until the radio begins to scramble.

Once again, Raquel, the Terraian rebel has hacked the airwaves. At first, it is silent with only the occasional sound of her breathing in the background. But this breathing... Raquel was afraid and is doing her best to control her fear. The sound of her moving steadily is heard before a another pause of silence.

"From beneath the trees that strangle our homes, we fight," Raquel says, sounding eerily tranquil. "From hiding in tunnels to burning our homes, we fight. From our blackened skies to the ends of the world... we fight."

Afearia stands straight and faces the radio. The children stop their game and look to the radio as well, feeling the disturbing calm coming from Raquel's words.

Back at the hospital's lowest level, a personal radio's playing the broadcast. Several feet from the table is Dr. Richards sitting on a stool with his body slouched while his coat's stained in fresh blood. With baggy eyes and thick facial hair, he perks his head up a bit as he listens to the odd broadcast.

Without warning, an explosion is heard over the broadcast. "As humans," Raquel continues, "it is only natural that we wish to live free. And so... we fight. And we will always fight." Gunfire is heard in the background along with the death screams of her men. "As of today, my clan, my family, Mongoose will make its final stand."

Mongoose's final stand, Dr. Richards thinks with the half lift of his head. That must be true to you. But this outcome was the likeliest of outcomes. Dr. Richards' eyes roll onto the radio. "Raquel... You messed up."

"However," Raquel exhales softly, "this is not the end. From the start of our existence, we as the human race have been through more turmoil then any of us could imagine. Time and time again, we've been pushed to the brink of extinction. Whether it's through genocide or having our sense of self taken. We have overcome. There are those of you who will turn your back on those suffering just as much as you are because of your inborn fear. Don't! Fight. Stand strong. Stand together. Stand up."

"Stand up and hold that quivering body with yours," Raquel continues. "Fear is contagious. But not nearly as much as unity. You will always feel stronger in the arms of your brothers and sisters."

With the gunfire getting louder and the screams of men getting closer, a distant shout is heard in the background, warning Raquel of the coming attacker. Shortly after, a loud scream followed by a thud arose.

All gunfire, screams of pain, and scuffling has stopped.

At the Richards residence, Afearia and the children listen with wide eyes, fearing what may be coming.

Raquel takes a slow, subtle breath, "As long as one person is willing to stand... Just one... The right to live free will never die." The slow creek of an opening door is heard. Unsettling, slow footsteps eerily move toward the microphone. Step by step. The footsteps conclude with the onset tension of a heavy shadow over every listener's shoulder. A moment of silence grips their hearts. "And someday, we shall see our shining skies once again. Because today..." The sound of a chair sliding on a hardwood floor is heard upon her calming breathes becoming faint as she stands from the microphone. "We fought for our future."

Without warning, the splattering sound of blood painting the walls is heard; followed by a near-unison thud and drop of the microphone. Veronica screams immediately, covering her mouth to silence herself as she and her brother freeze. Afearia's eyes are angry as she balls her fist. A long silence is present before the station softly scrambles back to its regular programming.

Back at the hospital, Dr. Richards somberly lights a cigarette and takes a puff. He leans back against the corner of the wall and stares up at the ceiling with his mouth barely open. I was wrong, Dr. Richards thinks. You didn't mess up. You passed with flying colors. Farewell, Raquel. Leader of Mongoose.

At the Richards residence, Afearia slowly turns off the radio and sits silently at the edge of the bed with folded hands before her mouth. The children remain shaken, staring at the radio.

"Did she just—?" Adrian asks with disbelief on his face.

"Yes," Afearia softly replies.

He looks down to his right with sadness, until noticing his sister was still stunned. "Hey," he gently says, nudging Veronica a bit. "It's okay."

"It's not okay," Veronica says, sounding as if to be at the brink of tears. "I hate that sound. That life ending blood splatter. I hate it!"

"Anya, I'm gonna take Veronica to lie down."

Afearia nods him off before they leave the room. Soon after, she lies down and stares out the window. Even with my powers, I couldn't have saved her, Afearia thinks. So why do I feel guilty? Afearia turns on her side before closing her eyes and clutching her clothes in aggravation. Because I should have. That's why.

By midnight, she slowly wakes from her tossing and turning. She opens her eyes and sees the door's ajar. When she rolls over, Dr. Richards is sitting before the window, startling her. "Geez!" she says, quickly sitting up. "What is wrong with you!?"

"Sorry," Dr. Richards says, looking elsewhere through the glass. "I didn't want to wake you."

Though bothered, Afearia relaxes her expression

with a sigh. "It's okay." She swings her legs over to dangle on the opposite side of the bed. She huffs once more. "Dr. Richards... I owe you an apology." He turns his head in her direction. "From the very beginning I didn't trust you. Even after all you've done, I still didn't. It was unfair of me to not give you a chance. I judged you preemptively. For that, I am sorry."

Dr. Richards shakes his head with his mouth trying to remain neutral and unashamed. He wipes his hand over his face and exhales with dismay, "You shouldn't be apologizing to me." She turns her head to him. "Even though your actions were instinctive, they weren't wrong."

Afearia stands to face him. "What are you talking about?" she asks sternly.

"You weren't getting better. I truly thought you had given up at that point. Or maybe." He looks away, "That's just what I keep telling myself to justify my actions."

"You better start making sense, Dr. Richards," she nearly threatens. He says nothing, just keeps his eyes out the window. She rushes over and lifts him out his seat by the collar. "Talk! What did you do!?"

"I really was on your side, Afearia," he grimly says, looking to the floor. "But once my research funding began to dwindle, and after witnessing that pitiful, yet false suicide attempt, I thought, if she's out, then maybe I can make something of her wasted life. And maybe... save those she couldn't. So I made some calls."

"Who did you call?" she asks with a weary head turn while not breaking eye contact.

"Just some government thugs who were looking for a promotion. When I told them you were alive, they couldn't believe it. As far as anyone who ever knew you, you're dead. And they want proof."

"You didn't..."

"I gave them the address today. They'll be arriving soon."

Afearia grits her teeth, looking away from him. "And what do you get out of this?"

He finally looks at her. "A shit ton of money," he says with a lackluster smile of deviance.

Her hands shake in anger before she punches him, knocking Dr. Richards to the floor. She steps away from the fallen doctor and looks down at him with a disappointed gaze, "You're scum," she scorns. She grabs her tote bag off the floor and slams the door behind her.

Dr. Richards remains on the floor, frozen-eyed. "Yeah... That's true too."

Afearia barges into the kids' room, "Adrian, Veronica, get up!"

They slowly sit up as she gathers their belongings into their bags. "Anya?" Adrian says, groggy and confused.

"Hurry up and get dress. We have to leave, now."

"But what's going on?" Veronica asks.

"Now!"

The children quickly get out the bed and change into their street clothes. Afearia hands them their bags and rushes them down the stairs. Leaving the front door wide open, the three of them leave the residence, heading further north east.

In less than an hour, two men show up at the Richards residence in a car, stepping out in casual business attire. Both in slacks, one wears a mustard colored dress shirt and the other forest green.

They briefly look over the surrounding area before entering the house and moving upstairs. They split up and check each room. The man with the mustard colored shirt enters Afearia's room and slowly raises a cell phone to his ear.

He hears ringing and sees a blue blinking light from the other side of the bed. "Hey!?" he shouts to alert his returning partner as he slowly moves around the bed. They discover Dr. Richards lying on the floor staring off into space. The man hangs up. "Where's the girl?"

"What girl?" Dr. Richards replies.

The man grabs Dr. Richards halfway onto his feet, "Don't waste our time! You called us! You said Afearia was still alive and in your house. Where is she?"

"I don't know what you're talking about," he replies lightly without breaking his stare at the empty space beside him.

"Are you fucking with us?"

"I would never."

"Then why did you call the government citizen's office?"

Dr. Richards looks up at them with a hazy smile. "Because I like making dogs bark."

He pushes the doctor to the floor and kicks him in the stomach. "Come on!" he orders his partner before they leave.

Though having trouble breathing after being kicked, a hopeful smile appears on Dr. Richards face before he looks up at the window, chuckling to himself.

The two of them move to the ground floor and spread out. "If you find anything, say something," the leading man tells him. Coming from the kitchen, the man wearing the forest green shirt hands him a drawing of three stick figures. Two with blond hair and one with long red hair and mismatched eyes. "Just doodles of a child. No telling if it's recent."

"Should we look into this?" the man in the forest green shirt asks.

"No. I'm sure that idiot upstairs meant what he said." He balls the picture and tosses it before heading out the door, "Should've known better. Derexen is very thorough about eliminating threats." Before the man in the mustard shirt can leave, his partner pats his shoulder. "What is it, Ben?"

"I saw the fridge. For someone who lives alone, he

has a lot of food. She may have been here, Duncan."

"Maybe. But it's still not enough to go on. For now, let's head back to HQ." The two men, Afearia's ex-acquaintances from Armport, leave the house and step into their car before driving off into the distance.

*What can I say about Reggie. Haha. He was amusing when
I was eleven. I used to sneak out of my room at night and
enter the palace kitchen where the servants and maids
would talk about everybody. I always hid in the ovens,
pantries, and cabinets to hear their dirty little secrets about
the elders. Most of which I was already aware of. Like
Helios' ongoing advances against female staff.
One time, I fell out of the cabinet while spying on them. At
this point, I was getting too big and it was becoming harder
to be in small places. When I hit the floor, they all gave me
a nervous look like the "beast" was on the hunt.
Every time I see that stare in people's eyes, I'm
immediately overcome with rage. And when I stood to
actually terrorize them, Reggie stepped in front of me. He,
despite being afraid, asked me kindly to go back to my
room. I declined and sat in the middle of the little circle
they make every time they dish.
Of course all chatter stopped as they awkwardly looked at
one another. An hour passed and all they did was glance at
me when they thought I wouldn't see. I became irritated
and shouted BOO, making them jump. After that, I left.
I hated how mean they were to me. I was the walking
monster of paradise. So, let me live up to that name I
thought. I caused mischief everyday for them. I stole
silverware, broke dishes, attempted to bite them like an
animal. I would even jump out the bath and run down the
halls naked. I was downright bratty. Most of the time the
blame fell on Reggie. He always did everything he could to
keep his co-workers out of trouble. And this dynamic went
on for three years.
One day, when I was coming down the hall from training,
Reggie was coming my way with a food tray for the Elders.
When we were about to past each other, I tripped him and
he dropped everything. Part of our dynamic was me less*

than genuinely saying, "whoops." And as always he would say, "that's alright." I always hated him doing that. I pulled my leg back to kick him until Xenler shouted Reggie's name from down the hall. He stormed up to Reggie yelling at him about destroying a rare item from his collection. Something I did after Reggie cleaned Xenler's room. Like a little devil, I was smiling at his submissive posture. And Reggie glanced at me and knew immediately who was to blame.

Through magical means, Xenler slammed him against the wall. My smirk fell. If Xenler ever uses magic, it is rarely something you want to be on the receiving end of. He was going to punish him—bad. I was going to come clean, but Reggie quickly took the blame before they vanished in a flash of light.

I didn't see him for two days. When I did, he had bandages all over and his eye was... taken. I felt like...

I asked him why. Why didn't he tell the truth. He said, "You're royalty. And you should remain so. And even if you are mean spirited sometimes, you deserve to be a kid once in a while."

It was then I knew he had been watching all this time. He knew of my life and my struggles and wished not to cause me more trouble... even when I deserved it. I left Reggie and his staff alone after that. And till this day, I still feel like crap.

Frail Trust

Chapter Three

After a risky escape, Afearia and the children proceed to the nearest location leading northeast. Along the way, Afearia had filled the children in on the reason for their sudden departure from the Richards residence.

"I can't believe the doctor would betray you like that," Adrian says.

"You can't trust humans," Afearia coldly responds. "All they care about is themselves. And to think I actually wasted a sincere apology on that greedy sack of crap."

"Where do we go now?" Veronica asks.

"I don't know. We'll reach the next area and I'll decide what to do from there."

"Anya?"

"Hmm?"

"Your eye patch."

"Right," Afearia says before going through her bag to put on a navy blue eye patch.

"Anya, if we're attacked by Demis, what do we do?" Adrian asks.

"We run for now."

"What if we can't get away?"

With no response, Afearia increases her speed and moves on ahead of them. Adrian looks to his sister who shrugs in confusion about the matter.

After traveling for a while, the three of them come across a black paved road. The kids stop as Afearia crosses over. "Wait," Adrian says, getting her attention. "We should follow the road."

"I'm trying to get you home," Afearia says.

"But maybe we should replenish our supplies first."

"Since when have you been concerned about supplies?"

"Can we at least look over the map?"

"I already know what's in this area. Look, we're wasting time here. Let's go," she says, fully crossing the road.

"Anya, wait."

"What?" she loudly says in annoyance.

Adrian pauses before responding to her. "It's a known fact on Terra that there are less Demis along public roads protected by government law. A black paved road like this is government owned."

Afearia crosses back over, "Why are you so eager for us to travel roadside?"

"Even we have tricks to make long journey's easier, Anya. We're just trying to help."

"Fine, we'll do it your way. But we're traveling this way," Afearia says, pointing to her left. "Since nearly all roads from this point are connected, it should still lead us in the right direction, right?" They nod, not fully sure if she's right. "Right."

"Can we still see the map?" Afearia goes into her bag and hands him the map. He unrolls it and looks it over with his sister.

"I really wish you guys would just tell me where your home is. I don't want to keep going off of your occasional directions."

"Yes, this road leads closer to home," Veronica says with a frown.

Afearia takes the map and puts it away before the three of them resume their journey along the paved road.

Along the way, the sound of a fast moving vehicle is heard from behind them. Afearia begins to move the three of them off the road. Adrian looks to his sister and winks. Veronica gives her brother a slight smiling nod before suddenly coughing and falling to the ground.

"Veronica!" Afearia worriedly says as she kneels to lift her.

The flatbed truck slows to a stop in order to avoid hitting them. The four wheeled truck isn't large, more like a jeep with a flatbed designed with four wide rails around it to secure cargo.

The pudgy driver quickly steps out of his vehicle to approach them, "Oh my God, are you guys alright?"

Before Afearia can speak, Adrian explains it himself, "My sister... she's very sick." Afearia looks to Adrian who's leaned from the man's view as he wipes Veronica's forehead. He winks at Afearia. "We're trying to get to the nearest town or city to get her a doctor, but she's having trouble breathing and walking."

"The next town is over a hundred miles from here. Please, let me help." Without facing the man, Afearia bunches her brows in awkward surprise that he's buying their act. "I'll drive you there. I wouldn't be able to deal with my conscious if I didn't help when I could."

Afearia rolls her eyes in disbelief, "Look, help us get to the nearest town and I'll pay you."

"No, no, I couldn't—"

Afearia tosses money at his neck. "Take it," she says before carrying Veronica. "We'll ride in the back."

Adrian looks to the confused driver, "I'm sorry about that. We've been through a lot lately and it's all starting to wear my mother out."

The man kneels down to pick up the money, "That was rude and uncalled for. But I will still do what I said I would."

"Thanks," he says before stepping away from him.

"Wait." The driver opens Adrian's hands. "Take this. I don't want it. Just keep it out of her sight until I get you guys there."

Adrian nods and hops in the back shortly before the driver gets back in his truck. Right away, Afearia hops out and the driver sees this in his side view mirror.

"Something wrong?" Adrian asks.

In brief, Afearia puts her hand up, gesturing for the driver to halt, "What the heck was that back there?" she asks, sounding a bit angry.

"We were just trying to make travels easier," Veronica says.

"Easier!?" She glances at the peeping driver who looks away as if to be minding his business. "Have you two learned nothing in the last few hours?" she says in a lower voice. "People can't be trusted. How is getting help from a stranger making things easier?"

"We were just trying to help," Adrian says.

"Well, don't. In fact, don't do anything without running it by me first. And don't help me unless I ask for it."

"But you never ask for help—ever."

She stares at their sad faces for a moment. "That's because I don't need it." She slams the flatbed's railed door and bolts it before approaching the passenger side door. "I'm riding up front," she says to the driver through the half open window.

The driver nods a few times and unlocks the door before she lets herself in. Afearia buckles up and the man drives off.

As they speed down the road with little to no cars passing by, the driver glances at Afearia, "So, where are ya' from?" Afearia doesn't answer, just stares outside the window. "Have you three eaten?" Unresponsive, the man glances in his rearview mirror to see the kids sleeping on each other. "Maybe they should ride up front. It's safer." He glances at her again and sighs, "Ma'am, I'm trying to—"

"Stop talking to me. I don't want to be your friend. Just drive. Or do you need another hundred to shut you up?" He turns his head from her, loudly exhaling in frustration.

For the remainder of the ride, the two of them do not speak until reaching the next town. He drives the car past the entrance and puts it in park.

"There ya' go," he says in a bothered huff.

Afearia raises fisted cash at him, "I know you gave the boy back the money. Take it. I will not owe you anything."

"I don't want it."

She opens the car door and throws the cash on the dashboard before slamming the door behind her. Afearia walks to the back of the truck and unbolts the gate to let the kids hop out. They walk beside the driver's side door and the kids thank him as he smiles and waves them off.

Afearia carefully watches the chatty town's people, "We won't be here long, so there's no reason to rent a room."

"So we're going to sleep on the street?" Adrian asks.

"We're not staying. We're going to replenish supplies and move on. But first, I need to make a call. If you spot any inns, let me know. They usually have a phone in their lobbies." As the three of them look around, Veronica points to a motel further ahead across the street. "Perfect."

When they reach the motel, the kids sit patiently on the bench inside while Afearia's across the room making a private call on a wall mounted payphone. She turns to watch the kids while holding the phone to her ear as it rings. She holds up a small note with a number on it as she waits for the ringing to stop.

"Hello?" she says. "Otto?"

Back in Vale city, Otto's face is in shock as he stands at his couch. He slowly sits, "Afearia?" still in disbelief.

Afearia smiles a little. "Hey."

"It's... It's been so long. How have you been?"

She turns from the kids, "I've been better... and I need a little aid." She waits for him to respond as silence comes between them. "Otto?"

"It's good to hear from you. We were all worried."

"It's been hard. But I'm fine."

"I know... There's been so many rumors about you and I've heard nothing but the worst. But enough of that. What can I do for you?"

Afearia hears a door slam over the phone. Roy walks in from the front door and enters the kitchen, "Who's on the phone?" he asks before turning on the faucet.

"Afearia."

"Who!?"

"Afearia!"

"Who's Atearia!?"

Afearia lightly chuckles and shakes her head. "Uhh!" Otto groans while rolling his eyes. "You were saying?"

"I'm kind of in a bind," Afearia explains. "I'm low on money and I have no one to trust for temporary payment. I was hoping you could use your contacts and see if anyone could hire me where I am."

"And where's that?"

"Loggingdale."

"Hmm, sorry, no one in that town can help. Head for Loiotes and find a man named Elliot Lockhart. When you do, tell him I sent you. And when he asks what you need, tell him 'Clear Sailing.' Everything should work out after that."

"Got it. Thanks, Otto. You really are the only one I can trust now."

Otto leans forward to take a coffee mug from Roy as he walks past him, "Sounds like you were betrayed," he says as Roy sits beside him.

"More than once already."

"I told you this could happen. I just hope you're not back to shutting out the world."

"I'm trying to survive. The world thinks I'm dead."

Otto exhales, "So I've heard. Listen, call me when you reach Loiotes."

"I will. And thank you."

"Hmph," he grunts with a smile before hanging up.

Otto sits back and sips his coffee. "So who were you talking too?" Roy asks before sipping his coffee as well.

"Afearia."

Roy spits his drink back into his mug. "And you didn't let me talk to her!?" Otto chuckles and lifts his foot to rest upon his knee as he takes another sip of his coffee.

Afearia walks back to the kids, "We're going now. Our next destination is Loiotes." As she gathers their bags, she notices a male employee staring at her a bit fearfully. "May I help you?" she coldly asks.

"No-no," he replies. "I just thought I recognized you. But I was wrong."

Afearia glares at him for a moment. "Where're your restrooms?"

"Around the corner."

She gestures for the kids to grab their things and follow her. In the ladies room, she goes through her tote bag and pulls out her white and gold scarf from the beginning of her journey. She uses it to wrap her hair up with only her bangs exposed. She tucks her hair up all around the edges before standing straight to sling her bag over her shoulder. Once done, the three of them leave the restroom and exit the motel.

As they pass through the town, Veronica looks up at Afearia, "Anya, when are we gonna eat again?"

"Right now, it's best that we just leave," Afearia replies. "We'll get food elsewhere."

Veronica's stomach growls, "Oww," she says with

a saddened look.

Afearia sighs and stops. "Earlier when we were walking I saw a small store. Maybe they have some food we can take to go." They head back a few blocks and reach the small grocery store she mentioned. She counts out a bit of money and gives them each an even amount. "Get whatever you want, but make sure it will last until Loiotes."

"Okay!" the kids say before running inside.

She remains outside, watching the passing people cautiously. After ten minutes of waiting, Afearia becomes impatient. "Where are they?" She looks around a bit more before heading inside the store.

As she enters, she sees the store's clerk reading a magazine at the register, even though the store's lights are rather dim. Afearia searches the three aisles from right to left while calmly calling the kids names. She walks to the back again and proceeds up the middle toward the register.

"Excuse me?" she says to the clerk. "Have you seen two children come in here recently?"

"Nope," he says, not even looking up at her as he flips to the next page.

"Really? Because I saw them come in but they never came back out," now standing before him.

"I think I would notice that a couple brats came into my store."

"You didn't even notice me." He ignores her as she begins to glare a bit. She slaps the magazine across the room and grabs the man by his shirt. "Let's try this again. Two kids came into your store and never came out. It's a small store, so tell me where could they have gone?"

"You better get your hands off me."

Afearia glances at the door to his left and pushes him against the wall behind him. She comes around the counter and tries to open the door, but it's locked.

"Open it," she demands.

"There's no one back there, lady!"

73

"Then open it so I'll leave."

"I'm calling the cops." As he reaches for the phone under the table, she grabs it and pulls it out the phone jack. "You're crazy!"

"Open this door!"

"Lady, stop this!"

"That's it!"

As she prepares to hurt the man, he cowardly puts his hands up, "Okay, okay! Take the keys from under the table! The one with the red key cap opens the door!"

She takes the keys and opens the door. It's dark inside as she slowly walks in. But before she can go too far, Afearia's clubbed over the head with a pipe by the clerk, knocking her out cold.

When she wakes, Afearia is unable to move and her vision's blurry. Her head and face feels tight. Her sight clears a bit more as she realizes that she's been hung and tied upside down to a ceiling pipe. Her arms are tightly bound to her sides by rope.

"Good, you're awake." Afearia looks to her right and sees the kids tied to back to back chairs while the store clerk stands next to them, "Glad we can see you're still lively."

"We," Afearia nearly slurs, still coming to.

From the shadows, the motel employee comes from her left, "That's right, we." He walks past her and stands with the grocery clerk.

"Let them go," Afearia demands.

"I really wish you wouldn't make such a fuss." He pulls out a switch blade and glides it over Veronica's unconscious cheek. "Especially since I have the upper hand."

"If you hurt them I swear—"

"You'll what? What can the powerless Calamity do?" Afearia is surprised by his claim. "I heard you can sense Demis. But you couldn't sense me when we met at the motel, could you? So, either you're a fake, or you're the real deal but seem to be having a power shortage. Either way, we're turning you in."

The store clerk walks up to Afearia and takes her eye patch off, "She's got the red eye thing." Afearia grunts loudly at him and tries to get free. "And that temper is accurate too."

"Could be contacts."

He pulls off her scarf and grabs her by the hair, bringing her close to look into her eye. "It's real," he says upon releasing her, seeming a bit surprised as she leers at him.

"Good, then we're going to get rewarded."

The clerk turns to the motel employee. "I was thinking. What if she's faking?"

"Oh, please. She wouldn't let it go this far. I never heard a tale of her letting herself get captured on purpose," he says while meeting Afearia's glare. "Boy are you mad. Did you call them?" he asked the clerk.

"Spoke to Valerie herself. Those Elites give me chills. But good news is she's sending someone right away."

"That could be anyone, probably not even an Elite." He places his blade back on Veronica's cheek. "This could be a while."

"Hey!?" Afearia shouts. "You got me, alright? Let the kids go. It's me you want."

"You're right. These kids were just a means to bait you into our trap. But now that you are here." He draws a little blood from Veronica's cheek, "I see no reason to keep them alive."

"You filthy—!" Afearia begins to wiggle and swing, trying to get free.

The clerk kicks her across the face, "Shut up!"

Afearia continues to wiggle as she groans at her captors. "Gag her!" the motel employee shouts.

The clerk takes a dirty rag from a storage bin in the corner before approaching Afearia. When he attempts to gag her, Afearia bites down on his fingers. The man screams out and tries to pull away. She increases her bite force as he bleeds into her mouth while she shakes and tugs away at his fingers like a rabid dog.

Standing straight up, he tries to pry her mouth open. Because of this, Afearia has enough lift to pull him down. When the clerk begins to fall, she lets him go and uses the swing or her momentum to headbutt him in the nose. The clerk's out cold.

"Stupid bitch," the motel employee says as he storms from Veronica's side. Right away, when he approaches Afearia he stabs her in the stomach. He holds it inside her for a moment and yanks it out. "That won't kill you, but it should calm you down a bit."

She coughs and almost gags as she loses momentum. The store clerk wakes and looks over to see she's bleeding out. "You... You killed her?" he asks.

"She won't die! And even if she does, so what? Look, she may not be worth as much dead, but at least we won't die collecting what's ours."

The store clerk shakes his head, holding his nose as he complains about how much pain he's in.

Afearia's eyes begin to flutter as her five senses begin to fade. Again? Afearia thinks. Am I really about to die again? And still... I was too weak to protect what was important to me. This isn't right... it shouldn't have...

Afearia's vision goes black. But inside the dark space of her mind, a faint voice is heard, calling her name. The dangerous, masculine tone of something inhumane called with almost unnoticeable seduction. It repeats with growing intensity, sounding human and familiar after the first few calls.

As the sound of the desperation becomes clearer, the calls are coming from Adrian. Her eyes jolt open with clarity. She looks over and see's Adrian's bloody nose and teary eyes as he's on the floor, crowded by the once human employees slowly shifting into their Demi forms.

Afearia's eyes intensify in a rage as her whole body shakes and her jaw is tight with teeth bearing. She screams out as a pulsating set of veins appear on her neck and a couple on her forehead before a violent burst of four bloody chains shoot from her back and whip wildly around the room, bursting all the lights and placing them all in darkness.

They all freeze up, until they hear the faint sound of unraveling ropes and a thud hit the floor. The two Demis revert to their human states while on full alert.

"What the hell was that?" the clerk asks. "I thought you said she lost her powers!" he loudly whispers.

"Shut up and calm down!" the motel clerk says. "The dumb broad turned out the lights. We have the advantage." The two of them cautiously spread out. The Demis eyes turn black, enhancing their night vision ability. "She's hiding," he says as he looks around.

"In this little room? Won't do her any good."

The motel clerk stops inches from tripping over a stretched chain leading under a table much further across the room. He signals for his friend to come over. They stand on opposite sides of the chain and kneel down. They glance both ways, not sure which end the chain begins from. The Demis nod at each other as they place their hands at different ends as they ready to pull.

Simultaneously, the two Demis yank on the chain in opposite directions. To their surprise, all they got is more chain. They look at each other, confused on where she may be. Suddenly, the chains wrap around their wrists and pulls them down, holding them to the floor.

The clerk begins to panic as he looks around, "Wait-wait-wait-wait—!" Immediately, with the splitting sound of steel to bone, the clerk is decapitated in the darkness.

The motel employee looks around in alarm. I didn't even see her! he thinks. "Hey-hey! Get out here! Stop hiding and—!" Suddenly, he feels the gripping of fingers at the back of his head before he's lifted onto his feet. "Spare me?" he nearly whimpers.

"Spare you?" Afearia says from behind. Piercing the dark, her mismatched eyes move from his right with the turning of her head. She looks to him with devil-like intensity. "I rather swim through hot garbage than allow you to continue violating the air I breathe." She tightens her grip to painful measures. "You're in my space," speaking with a deathly air.

With the splatter of blood, Demonweaver emerges through the front of his skull before dropping his dusting corpse. Demonweaver glows anew in a bright red aura as it slowly sinks back into her palm. When Afearia's chains retract, they return violently, painfully slapping into her back with enough force to drop Afearia to her knees.

"A-Anya!" Adrian shouts.

"I'm fine," she replies. She puts her hand to her stomach, realizing she's almost completely healed. That's strange, Afearia thinks.

"We have to get out of here!"

Afearia stands and grabs her fallen scarf and patch before untying the kids. Adrian grabs their backpacks and hands Afearia her tote bag. She carries Veronica and takes Adrian's hand as they run out the store and down the nearest alleyway. Afearia places Veronica down on a supplies crate before putting on her patch and retying her scarf.

"Anya... you're hurt," noticing the bloody tear in her suit.

She wipes away most of the blood over her stomach, revealing reddish inflamed skin, "No... I've healed."

He sighs in relief. "That's good."

Afearia expresses concern as she runs her fingers along the gash. "We should get to Loiotes," she says upon picking up Veronica.

Afearia begins to walk out the alley with Adrian soon following, "But our supplies."

"We'll get them at the nearest location from here, but for now, we must go. We've caused too much attention to ourselves already." She notices some people staring too curiously at them as they walk up the streets. She takes Adrian's hand and picks up the pace.

In the realm of light, at the holy palace, the four Elders hastily move down the halls with an armored palace guard steadily ahead of them. "While we were on watch," the guard explains, "several loud crashes and flashes of light came from within the chamber. We didn't know what to do, so—"

"Silence," Xenler rudely demands.

When they reach the doors, Grayson gestures for the remaining guards to open them. When the doors are unbolted and pulled open, the Elders push past the guards and enter the chamber. The doors are shut behind them while the four of them carefully look around the chamber.

"Everything looks accounted for," Helios, being jovial as he looks around.

"A bit early to assume that," Xenler says. "This isn't the only floor."

"We'll split up once we reach Kings Road," Grayson says, walking ahead of them with his wrinkled hands tucked in his robe sleeves.

When they reach Kings Road, they stand at the middle and carefully look around. Xenler becomes surprised and points to the north east. "Eternity's case." Grayson walks up to the empty, cracked altar with shards of the case's barrier on the floor before Xenler comes beside him. "What do you think happened here?"

"It's not just Eternity," Carnavess says, calmly gesturing his head to the east floor below. "Tenebrous is gone too."

"Hmm," Helios says, stroking his goatee before flash warping two floors below. He walks below and looks around before flash warping back up top with them, approaching the other men. "Demonweaver and Sleight are not in their cases either." He stops beside Carnavess. "Am I the only one seeing the strange pattern here?" addressing his fellow elders.

"The blades that have vanished are the blades that were assigned to Afearia," Grayson says with eyes still on Eternity's empty altar. He turns to Carnavess. "Who was presumed dead."

"It's not like I was there to confirm it," Carnavess replies.

"You will be. Go find Afearia," he says with lax eyes. Xenler and Helios look shocked. Before Xenler could say anything, Grayson interrupts, "It's alright. I don't see the harm in sending Carnavess to Terra. He is her first guardian after all."

"Then I shall be on my way." Carnavess turns from them and slowly walks down the steps, moments before a sinister grin crosses his face and the haze of his pale greenish-yellow irises gleam.

Diary Entry #1

I don't know what the expect me to put here. Umm…
Helo Dierie?

A New Beginning

Chapter Four

Within a few days, Afearia and the children were able to reach the nearest village before Loiotes. There are few buildings in the area. It's quite sparse with open and narrow pathways for navigation. If it weren't for the few people who're actually walking through the streets, one may think from a glance that this place was condemned.

Although the village has a fairly gloomy appearance with its crumbled buildings that don't rise over two stories, it seems the few villagers present are fine with their home's state. It would seem this village would be completely drowned in gray if it wasn't for the colorful flowers placed at the front of almost every store and home.

As Afearia sternly walks through the village, Adrian and Veronica become chatty about the hard to miss flower shop with basket-filled bouquets placed out front. A woman comes from inside the shop with a purchased basket of her own.

"Brother, look at the pretty flowers in that lady's basket!" Veronica says, excitedly pointing at the flower shop.

"Orange, yellow, red! She has the rainbow in a basket," Adrian adds. "I wonder who she's going to give them too."

"Maybe to someone who's sick. Or maybe to wish someone happy birthday!" As they pass by the shop, Veronica narrows her eyes on something with a faint glow in the shop display basket. "Oooh! Blue roses!"

"Blue roses?" Afearia says with a face of odd disbelief.

Adrian narrows his eyes as well, "Whoa, you're

right. I've never seen those before."

"That's because they don't exist," she sternly says, walking past them toward the shop.

The kids quickly follow and enter the flower shop. Once inside, the kids take a deep whiff of the air. Veronica loudly exhales, "Oh my God, it smells so good!"

The siblings swiftly begin sniffing flowers by the dozens as they grabbed them by the neck. "Please, don't touch the flowers!" the female florist says as she comes from the back room behind the counter to their left.

The frail, pale woman angrily stared at the children with the dark circles of her eyes making her glare scarier than it should be. She shoos the kids away with her blistered, scabby hand and bandaged fingertips. Scratching her dry neck around the collar of her eggshell colored blouse, the woman places her hands on the hips of her ankle high denim skirt before noticing Afearia's approach.

"Where did you get those blue roses?" Afearia getting straight to the point.

"Huh?" the florist says. Afearia carelessly grabs the rose and drops it on the counter, "Please—!" she blurts in an insistent cringe. She puts her hand to her forehead with a near slump in her posture. "Please don't touch the flowers."

"Answer my question."

The florist takes the rose and places it in a separate vase behind the counter and gently fluffs it, "They're a rarity that can only be found here in Ozon. It's one of the rarest flowers on Terra."

Afearia slams her fist down, startling everyone, "Found where!?" The florist turns toward her with annoyed eyes. "You're wasting my time."

"At the outskirts of Ozon lies the Life Tree growing deep within a crater. Only there can these flowers be harvested."

"I saw a couple other flower shops beyond yours. Why are you the only one selling these?"

"Because. Collecting these flowers is a risk on your life."

The kids come stand beside Afearia. "What do you mean?"

"They're not found around the tree, but inside the heart of the tree."

"Then I assume you're a part-time tree worker."

"That's not necessary in this place. Our tree is one of the earlier planted ones. It's been here long enough to maintain itself while occasionally being check on by government officials."

"Then how—?"

"I answered your question. You wanted to know where I got the roses from. Now you know. Leave my shop." Afearia glares at the woman before walking out the shop.

When they walk a fair distance from the shop, Adrian looks to Afearia, "Anya, why did you upset her like that?"

"Because she's hiding something."

"I thought we stopped here for supplies."

"We are."

"Then let's get them and go to Loiotes."

"I shouldn't have to remind you, but I do have a job to do. If I see a chance to restore Terra, you know I'm going to do it." She stares straight ahead for a while. *I don't see it,* Afearia thinks. *Those trees should be impossible to miss. Even still, I should be able to at least smell it. But I can't smell anything. I better be careful. My senses must still be gone.*

"Anya," Veronica says, staring at the flower shop. "The flower lady's watching us."

Afearia looks back and see's her suspiciously watching them with a scowl. She nudges the kids along and they continue into the village. "We'll restock, then take refuge at the local inn."

"What then?" Adrian asks.

"We'll discuss that once we secure a room."

Partway through the village, Afearia's at a local market, holding a basket of assorted supplies. "What else do you guys need?" she asks with subtle strictness.

"Umm, oh candy!" Veronica says as she readies to take off.

"I said need," she almost scolds, stopping her from running off.

"Aww. Umm. Uh. Umm—"

"You're done. What do you need, Adrian?"

"Uh, I'm fine, Anya," Adrian replies.

"Okay. I saw the local inn a few blocks back. We'll head their and prepare for Loiotes."

"Brother, you don't want anything extra?" Veronica asks with some concern.

"No. I'm fine," Adrian flatly says.

"Yay, then I get more stuff! Anya, I want—"

Afearia walks right past them and gets on line to purchase their items. Veronica looks at Adrian, who seems a bit saddened by Afearia's actions as he looks elsewhere.

"If I buy these and you two are still standing around, we're going to have a problem," Afearia tells them without turning around. The kids quickly move behind her on line.

"Adrian—?" Veronica whispers, seeming a little worried.

"Just stop it," he orders her in a loud whisper. "Just stop and do what she says. Veronica sulks while Adrian's face is just as displeased.

After purchasing their supplies, Afearia rents a room at the inn she spoke of. Once inside the room, Afearia lays out some of the items she brought across the bed. "You are allowed to only eat what I lay out for you, got it?"

"Yes, Anya," the kids reply, sounding a bit sad as they stand behind her.

Afearia walks over to the window and lifts the blinds to get a clear street view. "Umm, Anya?" Veronica mutters.

"You two should be safe while I'm gone," Afearia says. She moves toward the kids and summons an orange orb from her palm with ease. The orb of energy solidifies into a glowing sphere of a glass-like material. "This orb when shattered can only be heard by the caster. In Elysium it was used as a security measure against intruders." Afearia hands Adrian the orb and heads for the door. "Shatter it if something happens. I'll come right away."

"Anya?"

"Don't leave this room for any reason." She opens the front door, "I'll be back shortly."

"Anya!" Adrian shouts with his head down. Afearia stops, taking her time to face them. "Veronica's trying to talk to you."

"Make it quick." At first, the two of them were too nervous to respond. "Today, please! You want to get loud, so I hope you got something good to say!"

"You don't see it?" Veronica says sorrowfully.

"See what?'"

"You're changing."

"Changing?" seeming irritably annoyed. "Care to explain?"

"It's your attitude," Adrian says. "It's like. It's like you're becoming who you were when we first met you."

"I'm trying to keep you guys safe while staying sharp."

"Does being sharp mean you'll turn cold again?" Veronica asks.

Afearia stares at their hurt faces. Brushing off their concerns, she turns her head from them, "I have to go. Don't leave this room," she says before stepping out and shutting the door.

Afearia leaves the inn and pauses to look back up at

their room, seeming concerned before proceeding to the flower shop. Though Afearia's several blocks away from the shop, she spots the florist coming her way from across the street. Afearia quickly dips around the corner. When she turns the corner, Afearia waits a fair amount of time before trailing her.

Afearia would move into the shadows and wait for the florist to move far from hearing range and sometimes from sight as the florist turns corners, looking over her shoulder from time to time. Afearia prepares to follow again, but swiftly drops behind a public mailbox after almost being spotted by the overly cautious florist. She waits it out a while before popping her head up.

The florist had left the block, leaving Afearia to hastily run to the end of the street only to find no trace of her. Afearia steps into the open street, passing below an underpass, looking around in frustrated confusion to find the florist. With no citizens on the streets, she can't even ask if anyone's seen her.

As she turns to give up, Afearia notices the underpass she went under has a passageway blocked by a wooden board to her left. She approaches it and pulls it away. A cool draft comes up as she heads on through. Though dark and only faintly illuminated by the moon behind her, she begins to feel her feet stepping off stone pavement and onto a dirt slope.

The dip in the tunnel's ground becomes hard again, but not like stone, but like lumpy knots. The journey's short-lived as it leads to the outskirts of town, placing her at a high lumpy point beyond Ozon. She looks down and realizes the odd ground she traversed was a series of thick roots. Slowly looking forward, it is then Afearia finally gets a glimpse of the tree.

The tree is located in a deep crater where it is barely noticeable. Stretching for miles, its mighty roots pierce through all the land mass around the area. The roots are large enough to carve houses inside and still have space left over. Although the roots have made their way through the land, none rise above the canopy, unless it's a great distance from the tree itself.

Afearia carefully looks around and smirks into the distance, "There's our girl."

The florist is carrying a long, thick board and carefully lays it across the land gap between her and the tree. She slowly crosses the board on her hands and knees to enter the tree top, seemingly swallowed by the massive leaves. Afearia quickly races down the hilly roots and around the crater. Before she can get near, she sees the board's being pulled into the tree.

Afearia stops. She's smart, Afearia thinks. But wait, how did she get past the trees leaves without retaliation? Come to think of it. This tree is very docile compared to the one in Alester. Looking around, Afearia picks up a rock and hurls it into the branches. The tree's leaves and vines barely respond.

Afearia turns from the tree and walks several meters from it. When she stops, she brings her tensed hand before her with palm to the ground. She bunches her brows as she focuses.

Two chains creep down both her arms in a resistant way before suddenly snapping back into her. The force makes her jolt forward and tense her back and shut her eyes in pain as she tries to walk it off in a circle. She lowers herself to all fours and opens her tensed eyes. What's going on? Afearia thinks. Why are my powers like this?

She stands up and takes a couple deep breathes before trying again in the same manner. A white light appears in the palm of her hand as the tip of a red blade struggles to emerge. "Come on," she strains as it rises a bit more and sinks back down like a match of tug-of-war. "Demonweaver I am your *master*!" she says with bulging veins and spit droplets. "And I command you to show yourself!"

As the struggle continues for a few more seconds, Demonweaver shoots out of her hand like a rocket and lands far ahead to her side, piercing the dirt. She pants a bit and stands straight before approaching her sword. She pulls it out of the dirt and holds it up, staring oddly at the blade.

"Why was it so hard to summon you...? No, I'm alive," she says, responding to the blades slight onset glow that fades out a bit. "When I first called upon you you thought I was someone else...? No, it was me in that basement. I'm okay, I swear. But... this struggle to summon you shouldn't have been. Were you resisting me...? No? If that's so, I better go in prepared, she says before stabbing her blade into the dirt.

Afearia brings her hand before herself and concentrates to call another sword. At first nothing happens until a single bubble appears and pops. A few more appear and pop as well with no success.

"Come on, I know you can hear me," she says, gripping her wrist. She loudly exhales as the exhaustion becomes a bit apparent. "Come to me... Come out." More bubbles appear before popping, but soon after they appear in a flourish as her sword Nebulous is finally summoned. She stabs Nebulous beside Demonweaver. "Is it hard for you two to hear my call...? Magical interference?" She slants her eyes in thought for a moment. "I wonder why."

Afearia looks toward the tree, seeming a bit cautious. "I don't know what to expect in there. I can't even sense if there's any enemies nearby. I shouldn't take chances then."

She raises her hand and makes a shaky fist as blinking green symbols appear on her arm. Looking as if she may give into to an unseen weight, Afearia holds her own as she struggles to open her fist. Falling dust comes around her arm a bit before her hand forcefully opens and slamming rocks come together to reveal Bastion. Instead of catching it in her hand, she hops back and lets it pierce the ground while being hunched over to catch her breath.

"This is… ridiculously hard for me to handle right now," she says, panting. "Just having you all here is tiring me out. And I apologize Bastion for not catching you. I wasn't confident I could. My arm felt fatigued." She stands straight with a firm look in her eye, breathing with a better calm. "There's one more we need to bring to the party."

She removes her jacket and places it around Bastion before stepping a few feet away from her sword. "I have doubts I can actually call him here. But I'll try." She suddenly looks to Demonweaver. "Yes, Eternity. The blood pact…? Of course, that could make it easier for me."

Afearia walks up to Demonweaver and cuts deep into her palm using its edge. As she folds her hand up to let a small pool of blood formulate, she dips her index finger into it and draws four lines from the palm down her forearm in a curve.

She holds her hand up over her head as the pool drains down her arm, "Hear my call, Demeseus. Come fourth!"

A bloody chain worms its way up out of her palm as the blood lines glow red and change shape into chains. The chain wiggles out and moves around like a snake as the tip looks her in the face and turns a bit to analyze her. It moves around her slowly before suddenly wrapping itself around her arm and squeezing with dangerous force. The blood drawn chains grow a single spike on each links' side.

Afearia gasps in pain as she takes a knee at the mercy of the chains squeeze. "Wha-what are you doing!?" She tries to pry the chain off and does a long painful grunt, "You're going to break my arm!" Another chain shoots into the sky like a rocket before she's lifted off the ground and yanked from lift to right. "It's me! Recognize my blood, Demeseus!" The sky darkens and thunders. "Why don't you recognize me?" she says in a sad, hurt voice.

Dozens of chains shoot from her palm and plunge into the ground like an umbrella. They twist and bruise her arm's skin, causing blood vessels to break underneath.

"ENOUGH!" echoes a man's booming voice. All of the chains immediately freeze. "Put-her-down," he emphasized. Nothing happens for a moment. "Eternity, you heard me. Let her go."

After a few seconds, the chain lowers Afearia down to her knees and unravels itself from around her arm. The remaining chains retract into the ground as a funnel before revealing Eternity as it's pushed out from the dirt, returning to the sword. Demeseus's spirit appears soon after, but with an unfamiliar spirit as well.

Afearia stares wide-eyed at a golden blonde-haired woman standing firmly back to back with Demeseus. Her long hair flows in the wind in an unreal, slow manner as she glares at Afearia. Enveloped in a full body white glow, her golden hairs flow across her face, only revealing her eye of disgust.

With the turning of her head, she disappears, releasing Afearia from her enchanting, ethereal gaze by her golden iris.

Staring at Afearia, Demeseus glances behind him, moments after the woman's presence leaves his backside. "It's good to see you," he says with a weak smile.

"Demeseus... My powers. Who? Who was that?"

"Someone you'll meet someday. Unfortunately, she has never been fond of you, even more so now than ever," he says, looking away from her.

"But what did I do?"

"You died. And in her eyes that makes you weak. Something she hates. But the worst offence is that your death has interfered with me moving on."

She lowers her head, "I'm sorry."

"Afearia, that's not how I feel. I'm just explaining her reasoning and what has left your powers estranged."

"I didn't think I would lose. I lost my head and went in fighting with blind rage. Demeseus—"

"We should talk about that later. There's something inside that tree that needs to be addressed. Are we heading in?"

"What's inside?"

"You can't smell it?"

"No. Ever since I died, a lot of things have been happening to me. I can't sense Demis at all."

Demeseus looks back at the tree. "Then I'll be your third eye."

"Demeseus? How can you not be mad at me?"

"For dying?"

"Yes."

"Afearia, I don't want to repeat myself. We'll discuss it later."

"Fine," she says shamefully. Afearia reaches for Demonweaver with a concerned expression before facing Demeseus. "Did our blood pact break?"

"Perhaps due to your passing, yes."

"But when I was captured, I was able to use the chains of Eternity."

"Were you in full control? Or was it temporary? If the latter, it probably was remnants of the previous contract."

Afearia fidgets a bit, "Should we—?"

"No."

"W-why? You no longer—want to be one with me?"

"We have much to discuss. When you used the chains during your capture, I'm sure your adrenaline was high and your priorities were clear."

"But the effort to keep it up after bringing them out was beyond difficult."

"Good. Do it again."

Afearia sighs before looking to Demonweaver with

her arm raised toward it. Focused, Afearia barely manages to get one chain out of her back while Demeseus stares at the tree.

"Afearia, that girl's in trouble. You need to hurry."

Afearia grunts and struggles to get any length on the chain, "Tch, it's not working!" She grunts a few more times "Demese—"

Afearia sees him muttering something with his eyes closed. She makes out some of the words as help her. When he stops, he looks to her. "Try it now."

Although the chain rattles its way through the air, she successfully wraps it around Demonweaver's handle. The chain carries it back to her and holds its position behind her back like a wing. She approaches Nebulous and tucks it between her belt. Afearia takes her jacket off Bastion and slings it over her shoulder before attempting to lift it with both hands.

Struggling, she manages to pull it six inches from the dirt before the sword's weight proves too much and she drops it. "I… I must've gotten weaker," Afearia says, a bit surprised she failed to handle Bastion's weight. "I'm sorry, Bastion. You have my word, I will not drop you like that again."

She brings her arms to her sides and stands straight. With focused eyes, she stares at Bastion for a while before making a slow exhale. She grips it in both hands and her arms bulge just a bit as she successfully pulls it from the ground. She holds it before her and nods at the sword.

Demeseus has been watching her the whole time, seeming emotionally distant to her struggles. Much to discuss, Demeseus thinks.

Afearia approaches Eternity, "How bad is it inside?"

"Hard to say. This tree distorts my senses." As she raises her hand to grab Eternity, Demeseus raises his hand to stop her. "I can't give you my blade right now."

"You're kidding, right?"

"I'm not."

"Demeseus, what's going on? You're making me feel bad."

"Sorry, but that is the circumstances at the moment. You could always force command me, but you already experienced how that would go. Just trust me that you'll have to fight without it. But I can still be your eyes and ears."

"Meaning—?"

"Eternity stays outside."

His behavior," Afearia thinks. Why is he acting like this. As if he... "Then I have no time to waste." Afearia takes her jacket and puts it on Eternity. Eternity uses its chain to violently whip it to the ground. "Hey!" When she bends down to pick it up, the chain whips at her hand, nearly hitting her before pulling away in time. "Demeseus? Why?"

"Just leave it and go."

She makes a saddened expression. "This hateful air for me is justified," she mutters. "Because I shamed you like no other." Afearia runs off into the direction she last saw the florist.

Demeseus watches her as his stern brows softly relax with an unhappy expression. He briefly notices faintly glowing markings on her shoulders before she had run too far. He glances at Eternity before crossing his arms and disappearing.

Afearia reaches the area the florist entered from just before Demeseus appears next to her. "I don't know if this is a safe way to enter," Afearia says.

"Hold on," he says before fading away for a while. He reappears beside her. "There's a board leaning against the tree. If you just go straight ahead, there's a branch you can land on."

"Thanks."

Demeseus fades away again. She walks a fair distance backwards from the tree. With a deep breath, she take a running start. When she jumps, she raises her hands to her sides, having the wind aid her impressive jump in order to reach the branch. Once she nears, Afearia tries to use the wind to break her coming impact, but it didn't help much. She hits the tree fairly hard, shoulder first.

She holds her shoulder and rubs it a bit as she stands. To Afearia's left is a dim green glow leading inside. She follows the light and walks down the branch, leading to the hollowed hole into the tree. At the end of the branch is a flight of seemingly fresh cut, moist white wood stairs leading further into the tree. Afearia cautiously looks around before proceeding.

The source of the green glow had been coming from the illuminated leaves along the wall and the white glow of the stairs. Reaching the end of the first flight, she walks a few feet around the corner to find another set of stairs. Though muggy and filled with the scent of plants in wet soil, Afearia remains on alert, despite it's relaxing aromas and atmosphere.

When she moves down another flight, slithering vines are present along the walls. Halfway, the glow quickly shifts to a red hue. Afearia pauses before noticing the vines now moving along the stairs. She proceeds by carefully stepping between them until one wraps around her ankle. She stops immediately. The vine tightens and loosens its hold repeatedly.

I don't want to anger the tree at this level, Afearia thinks. If it retaliates now, I'm in for it. Suddenly, the vine trembles, as if to be conflicted before releasing her. All of the vines stop moving and the red hue slowly fades. Afearia takes the opportunity and quickly makes her way out of the stairway.

After sprinting her way through, she reaches the bottom to find a curved hollowed passage. She walks on to find two paths, one darker than the lit path straight ahead. While deciding, the voice of the florist is heard down the lit path.

"Ugh, I can't believe this," the florist says. Afearia proceeds and finds herself in a bright, rounded, hollowed area. Below is a fairly sizable hole where the florist is. "It's you," she says, looking up at Afearia with surprise. "Get me out of here!"

Afearia sees a ladder against the tree's inner bark to her right, "Why did you even go down there without your ladder?"

"It's the tree! It's acting weird! It carried my ladder away! Look, just get me out of here!"

Afearia glances at the basket of blue roses around the florist's arm. "And you go to such lengths for those roses. Why?"

The florist glances down at her roses and covers it with the basket's top. "Money's never been as good as it is now. I can buy whatever I want and use whoever I want. Wave enough dollars in someone's face and they're all yours. When you're the one paying for the favor, you have all of the power and none of the shame."

Afearia stares at her with some disgust on her face, "Ridiculous," she says while looking away with crossed arms.

"Get me out, now!"

Reluctantly, Afearia grabs the ladder to help her out. Suddenly, the tree's inner bark expands before shrinking the space for her to stand until she falls inside with the florist. The florist jumps out of the way before Afearia falls on her. Afearia turns over onto her back and sees blue roses lined all around the large, bulbous area.

The inner cavity's walls are dark like the tree's outer bark, but the area is lit softly by the pulsating blue glow emitted from the large blue rose bud in the middle of the space. There's also a faint blue fog rolling around the ground at ankle level.

Without picking up Bastion, Afearia stands, staring at the bud. Is this the heart? she thinks.

"Way to go," the florist says. "Now we're both stuck down here. How are we going to get out!? I can't believe I'm stuck here and—"

"Shut up," Afearia says as she curiously approaches the bud.

She observes the blue fog pulsating out from the bud's top where wooden vines connect it to the ceiling. The bud's petals are whitish-blue with dark blue spots at the bottom of each petal. Down the middle of each petal is a rich streak of blue.

Not noticing, as Afearia stands in near arm length of the bud, she had stepped on some vines, causing the vines throughout the area's inner bark walls and ground to slither.

"Not even I get that close," the florist says nervously. "Get away from it! This is the core!"

Seeming hypnotized, Afearia continues to approach before stopping far too close for safety. A vine tip slowly rises up to her face and moves to both sides of her cheeks before slowly slithering down and behind her. The florist nervously looks around, looking up a few times from below the hole. Afearia tilts her head a bit, carefully watching the pulsating glow from within the bud.

She slowly raises her hand, moving it slowly toward it. When her palm is placed upon it, Afearia is surprised by its warmth.

A shadowy hand suddenly touches hers from within, startling Afearia as she yanks her hand away and quickly steps back. She takes several steps back with stern, but cautious brows, moments before taking Nebulous into her hand.

The blue glow turns red and the vines also shift into a reddish state. "That's what you get!" the florist says. Afearia looks back and sees the florist climbing up the hanging vines that have come partway down the hole. "You've angered it! Good luck surviving, you dumb girl!"

Though she was almost out, a vine shoots up from the ground and stabs through the florist's back. Her shocked face is mortified as blood comes out the corner of her mouth. Her head droops along with her arms as the blue roses fall out one by one.

The pulsating bud is pumping red fog into the area as Afearia looks around at the hasty glow. A vine violently whips her on the back while the others move around the open space. Before she's whipped again, Afearia backflips over them and near the hole above. She looks up at the florist as the vine tosses her body to the wall before sealing the only way out with dozens of thicker vines.

Suddenly, the bud loosens up and begins to bloom open with its six large petals. To her surprise, a shirtless man with an athletic build is tangled by the wooden vines above with his arms spread out and his legs together. The vines from above hold together sections of his long chestnut hair like a bird spreading its tail feathers.

His skin is a creamy green complexion with sporadic dark green veins all over his body and neck. From his waist, down to his ankles are clustered leaves of different shapes, sizes, and colors. Only the left side of his skirt-like leaf coverings was parted open to reveal his muscular leg. At the back of his neck is a blue rose that is more radiant than the others. The rose is embed in his flesh with green roots moving beneath his skin and outside of it.

The vines attached to the roof begin to release his hair and body before slowly lowering him. The vines drop him and he groans on the ground. Keeping his head down, he brings himself to his hands and knees.

"Tres...," he says in a low voice. "You...," the mysterious man states with a stern tone this time. "You are... trespassing!" he threatens with the sudden rise of his head, staring down Afearia with a menacing expression in his deep sea green eyes.

Without a second thought, the man leaps at Afearia and swipes at her face. Afearia simply sidesteps before hopping a safe distance as he follows up with a kick toward her face. Landing on his hands, he cartwheels in her direction and lands crouched with his back to her before doing a hind leg kick, successfully hitting her in the face.

She slides across the ground with her head shifted back from the impact. When she stops, the man stands firmly. Afearia, bleeding from her lip, sternly looks at her opponent before straightening her neck and licking the bleed away with smirk.

"No better way to get back into the game than going straight into the fire," Afearia boldly says.

Demeseus appears beside her, "I suggest you don't rely on your chains in this fight since your pact is nearly dissolved."

"Eternity is a major part of my fighting style. I can only hope this Demi isn't too strong," speaking sarcastically.

"Since when?" She looks to him, a bit confused. "And you wonder why—. There's no time. Keep your eyes peeled and your mind on the fight."

The man's right arm grows a black scaly armor that travels up his arm and covers half of his face and part of his chest. His hand, nearly doubled in size, resembles a claw with a bluish-green crystallized sack at the back of his hand and in the palm. Along the arm are raised scales with red layered veins. The pointed scales and claw tips are orange in color.

"Uh, Demeseus," Afearia says. "I know every Demi there is, but what kind of Demi is that?"

With concern, Demeseus carefully examines the monster, "He may be artificial."

"Figures. I've got this then."

"We'll see."

Afearia seems a bit baffled by Demeseus's comment before the man thrusts his deformed stretching arm at her. She sidesteps and guards the grazing of his arm, causing sparks to fly as it races past her.

The moment she prepares to rush in, the monster closes the gap by gripping the wall behind her and pulling himself in, gripping her neck with his normal hand. Still being pulled along like a zip line, he holds onto Afearia and slams her into the wall, pinning her. Afearia slashes upward, but he releases her and jumps back to evade.

In mid jump, he extends his deformed hand and grabs her by the waist to draw Afearia in. She slashes with a wide swing, but he ducks and moves behind her, elbowing Afearia in the back, causing her to stumble forward.

"Tch," she grits before facing her foe. "Am I truly this rusty or is this thing actually decent?"

Demeseus reappears, "I'm surprised your arrogance hasn't gotten you in deeper trouble already," he says nonchalantly.

Although Afearia was offended, her mind thought back to her most distressing bout. She sternly stares down her opponent, "You're right. Sometimes you've got to know when to shut up and get it together." Demeseus looks at her with a slightly surprised expression. "I'm ready now."

The deformed man runs at Afearia and prepares to slash her. Afearia jumps up and spins over his head. He turns and quickly thrusts his extending arm at her. When Afearia lands, she keeps her head down and stays crouched before her left arm muscles flex and bulge slightly.

When his arm's about to make contact, she catches his fist in her left hand, surprising the monster as she holds it in place.

"Let me tell you something," Afearia calmly says as their hands shake. "I may have not been at my best since the day I arrived. But today—and each day following from here on. I'll bring a wrathful justice upon all who defile this world." Afearia stands straight up, removes her eye patch and stares at her opponent with a renewed confidence. "Because you're facing a new breed of hero."

She tosses his hand away like trash, following up with a near instantaneous sideways stomp, upheaving the ground in a straight path that knocks the monster off his feet.

"It's time to get rough." Afearia says.

Demeseus proudly smirks, "Take him down. I'm going to conserve my energy so I can maintain your increased strength."

She gives him a nod before Demeseus fades away.

The deformed man brings himself to his hands and knees and chuckles, sounding a bit monstrous. "That's good," he says, surprising her with his coherent speech. "Maybe you can take the blunt of my rage."

His deformed hand arcs up before the whole arm extends into the ceiling, creating tree dust. The arm quickly retracts before the man stands holding a surprising object. In the monster's hand is something he shouldn't possess. The Empyrean Blade, Braveheart is in his grasp.

That's—!? Afearia thinks with an astonished look. It's the sword of the murderer.

"Surprise, surprise, you're gonna die," he mocks.

"How—what are you?"

"The last of the great guardians. And it is my duty to protect this tree."

"You are completely misguided. This explains why so many Empyrean Blades never returned. Tell me the purpose of this tree."

The man's face becomes upset. "What happened to that vigor!? You're supposed to give me your best! Not running your mouth!"

With the thrusting clutch of his hand, vines lift from

the ground and race toward Afearia. The vines crash into the ground once she leaps over them and toward her opponent. She swings her sword to create four water spheres. With the following swing of her arm, the spheres create water spires that freeze and shoot out at the deformed man.

Using Braveheart, he smashes and bashes each spire before doing a turning swing to slash Afearia. Upon impact, she defends herself with Demonweaver arching over her shoulder along with Nebulous. Completing his mighty swing, he slams her into a wall of vines that entangle her.

As he approaches, the vines tightly bound her limbs. "I'm pissed you can't do better," he says.

"You obviously don't know me. I can always do better."

Using the chained Demonweaver, she cuts herself free and hurls Nebulous into the ground at his feet. He kicks it away from him and into the ceiling. Afearia darts to his far left before he takes his sword into his other hand. While he calmly watches her, vines race from the ground to ensnare her.

She twirls her hands a couple times with a yellow ring briefly outlining the twirl. Using wind, Afearia alters the trajectory of the vines to crash into the wall. She continues on her speeding path, bringing her hand to her side in an attempt to call a sword. She fails and bunches her brow, not changing her path toward her foe.

I want to get serious, but everything is so hard to muster now, Afearia thinks. Even brining Bastion from across the room to my hand is difficult. Running low to the ground, the man speeds toward his opponent. When he rushed to her side, he releases a barrage of blurred short jabs using only his deformed arm. Bastion! Afearia thinks, expressing desperation in her face as she twists her body away and holds her hand close to her.

In that moment, less than a second before the jabs can land, Bastion vanishes from the ground and into her hand, defending her from the continuous blows of her foe. Like a deranged one-armed boxer, Afearia's opponent repeatedly jabs her sword with sparks flying and slowly diminishing Afearia's shaky posture.

Kneeling on one knee from the assault, she puts her hand to the ground, focusing strongly with some grunting in an attempt to cast a spell. The sword slips a bit, soon to fully fail protecting her as he breaks her guard.

Green seals appear up her arm, causing the ground beneath her opponent to shift unevenly, disrupting his footing. Afearia shoots up and slaps him across the room with the flat side of Bastion. As he slides and bounces across the ground, Afearia jumps up and grabs Nebulous from the ceiling before coming down on him with blade tip pointed.

Lying on his side, Braveheart gains two eighths of a red essence in its fuller. His hazy expression becomes angry as he quickly turns over and does two sword strokes releasing a red light stream at Afearia. She successfully deflects both projectiles using Bastion. The red essence rises to three eighths before he does a wider swing to release several streams.

Afearia condenses herself behind Bastion, but the force is much greater than before and propels her back, breaking her guard as Bastion falls. When her body faces up right, the monstrous man had already moved above her, staring angrily into her eyes. Using his deformed hand, he extends his arm into her chest, slamming Afearia into the ground.

Once he lands, he violently shoves her deeper into the ground and swings her around the room along the wall. "Who are you!? Who am I!?" he shouts, swinging and slamming her everywhere. During his rampage, Braveheart gains an eerie red aura as the red essence nearly reaches four eighths. "I am the greatest, badass guardian this world has ever known! And you wanted to show me your best!?" he says, slamming her down two more times. "Pathetic!"

He calms down a bit and slams her to the ground two more times, moments before Afearia's scarf falls to the ground. "Let me see your face," he says, retracting her from the dust clouds. To his surprise, he's holding a rocky figure in her shape. "What!?" He crushes the figure and looks closely into the dust.

Dusty and bloody, Afearia silently rises from behind him. He jerks his head to react, but Afearia swiftly filleted him from his lower back up to his neck, hacking his rose with Demonweaver. Almost choking as he groans in pain, the man falls face first before she wipes the blood from her right eye.

"There has only been two great guardians to have ever walked the grounds of Terra," Afearia says. "You are neither Demeseus nor Ruto Vaz. So spare me your crap." She stares down at his lifeless body and wide eyes. "I don't know who or what you are, but it's over."

Afearia watches the rose whiter before turning away. With a loud grunt, the man's shoulders hunch up as mounds move under his flesh. She readies to cut him down until vines snare him and drag his body back into the rose. The petals close up into a bud again and vibrate. Afearia does a slow upward slash with Nebulous to create an arch of water before slashing down with both hands, launching it like a bullet.

When it hits the petal, a hole is made, surprising her from what's inside. The man's half off the ground with his wound nearly healed and black tentacles wiggling around like worms from his wound. The man who appears to be dead has one of his eye's sclera visible until it's swallowed in deep sea green. Gaining awareness, the man looks to Afearia and grits his teeth at her before the damaged petal repairs itself.

"Demeseus?" Demeseus appears beside her. "That man... I think—his humanity is still intact."

"Are you sure?" Demeseus questions.

"I thought I felt something when I first fell down here. Something... I think he may have been reaching out to me. If I can save him... I have to save him," she firmly says. "But," she looks to Demeseus with pleading eyes. "I can't do it without you." Demeseus stares at her with sympathetic eyes. "Please, complete the pact with me. He looks away from her before fading. "Demeseus!? Why is he acting like this?"

Suddenly the flower petals spread open and lie flat. The angry man heaves while staring her down with murderous intent. Afearia's eyes sadden. "I want to save you...," she says. "But I can't. The least I can do is end your life like a man... scarring us both." Afearia clenches her jaw and tightens her grip on her sword. "I'm sorry."

With a violent growl, he charges in to attack. Green seals cover her arm before she takes her foot and drags her toes ahead of her in a smooth arch motion. Four irregular shaped spheres molded with wood float up. She does one hard cock back with her radiating arm of seals and thrusts her palm forward, bursting them into a showering debris.

With a double midair front flip, he creates two tall, faintly red shockwaves emit from him upon slamming down his sword. As the waves destroy the wooden debris while blowing everything in the area from him, Afearia takes the handle of Demonweaver into her mouth, biting down while the chain wraps loosely around her neck. She takes Nebulous with both hands and slowly raises it to the right of her while pointing it at her opponent.

Afearia rushes in and rhythmically has her fingers fondle the grip. Nebulous glows before leaping with the blade pointed down. Demonweaver begins to glow as well. With a midair spin, a crescent red energy is released by Demonweaver shortly before a tidal wave of water appears to carry Afearia over the man.

The energy knocks the man on his back just as Afearia comes down and stabs him in the shoulder with ice sprouting in five wide points in his wound. Without losing momentum and while still airborne, Afearia lifts him up by swinging her weight over his shoulder and releasing him off the sword toward the far end of the room.

The ice points continue to grow and spread across his back and his front. When he hits the wall, he's unable to move as the ice freezes him to it. Afearia rushes at him once again with the same sword stance as before. As he struggles to get free, vines from the room wrap around his limbs and pull him in the direction of his opponent.

The monster-like man is freed and leaps at her to attack from the air. When the five damaged icy points begin to regrow, Afearia raises her sword Nebulous' grip near her mouth, "Strike."

When she completes her diagonal slash, a blue light appears diagonally from the man's shoulder, down his torso. The man splits in two with his innards completely frozen. When his body hits the floor, vines quickly retrieve him and begin to bring him back to the risen plant petals.

Afearia crosses her arms, "Bastion!"

Bastion returns to her hand as she sternly stares at the vibrating bud. She maintains her pose for a little longer before grunting loudly to complete a hammer throw with Bastion. Bastion soars through the air and into the ceiling above the flower bud. Afearia does a slow arching slash with Nebulous from the ground to make a water sphere. She launches it with another slash, aiming it at the bud.

When it enters the bud, Afearia does an outward slash, causing the bud to explode with thin twirling streams of water, tearing up the remaining petals. Halfway from the ground is the man with his body reattached and one of his eyes reverted while holding Braveheart tightly in his human hand.

He weakly looks at her and becomes angry with half his eye becoming deep sea green and the black worm-like tentacles moving under his skin erratically. Afearia runs toward him, dropping Demonweaver from her mouth into her hand before doing heavy swings to release red energy.

The first attack disarms the man, sliding his weapon across the ground while the second cuts him loose from the vines. He falls to his hands and knees before trying to retrieve his blade by extending his deformed arm.

Afearia snaps her fingers and the part of the ceiling Bastion was lodged in, collapses, covering Braveheart. To his surprise, Afearia was near him in mid swing, looking somber.

"Forgive me," she says. Before she could end him, chains of soft yellow light pierce the tree, the man, and the ground around him, holding him in place.

Outside the tree, Demeseus is standing next to Eternity with his hand out before him, staring at the chains from the clouds that pierced the tree. He looks to Eternity, "I guess I owe you again." A faint flicker of gold hair briefly appears over Eternity. He looks back at the tree and raises his hands, raising the chains as well. He makes a fist and focuses. "Purify."

Inside the tree, Afearia stares at the man's risen body before a light radiates through him and the tree. The chain around her neck becomes like the chains pierced in the man. *Afearia, now,* Demeseus telepathically says to her. *Save him!*

Quickly taking action, she rushes to save him. With the reverting and filing of deep sea green in the man's eyes, he growls at her and extends his deformed hand to attack. Afearia keeps moving, conjoining her swords in one hand and shifts from range, getting her cheek grazed before aggressively thrusting her hand forward, releasing her glowing chain at him. The chain, grazes across his deformed arm, chipping away at it to reveal bloody human flesh.

The chain pierces clean through his longus colli, calming him while demolishing the blue rose at the back. Afearia leaps up with one hand on each conjoined sword coming down with the swords glowing pure white.

She swiftly cuts him down, scattering his blood as the chains burst into small, twinkling lights, fading away with a soft rise. He falls back with wide eyes that slowly close with the appearance of a subtle smirk as the black tentacles, armor, and vines gray and ash before he hits the ground unconscious.

Afearia drags Nebulous' tip up from the ground, "Sorry, I can't waste any time." She takes the blade and cuts her hand open twice. She bends her hand into a filling pool of blood before bringing her hand to her face. "Sovereignty," Afearia calmly says.

The blood floats up as little droplets that break apart as smaller gold droplets. Rising from the reaming blood pool in her hand is the sword, Sovereignty. She kneels on one knee and puts her hand on the man's head. Every injury on his body begins to glow gold as she concentrates with closed eyes.

Though she is attempting to heal him, nothing has changed. His injuries remain. No, Afearia thinks. It can't be too late. It just can't be. "Fight... Fight, you." His shallow breathes become still. "I said fight! Fight, you idiot!" she demands with upset sorrow in her eyes.

Suddenly, his golden wounds begin to close with dusting gold pouring upward into nothingness as all the damage he sustained closed. When his wounds have all healed, his still breathing returns at a normal pace. Afearia removes her hand and sighs in relief, faintly smiling.

Without warning, the ground cracks open in the room near them. The entire tree begins to shake as more portions of the ground crack apart. Afearia quickly scoops the man up off the ground and hastily looks around for a way out. The crumbling room and the closed pathway above leaves Afearia in a tight situation.

Assessing the situation, Afearia knew the only way back was the way she came. But the tree was only getting worse by the second. She'd never make it in time.

"I have no choice..." She kneels to lower the man before raising one hand overhead, "Odyssey, come forth!"

A transparent blue circle appears above her hand. She punches it, causing it to crack and shatter. Dropping down from it, piercing the ground to create the same blue transparent circle beneath, is a full length katana with double the standard width. The thinner, smaller portion of the blade's base is wrapped in the same blue yarn as the grip, connecting the two.

Afearia grabs the sword's blade by the laced yarn portion. Tightening her hold with the blade collar between her ring and middle fingers, she pulls the sword up from the ground. When she does, the blue circle disappears, revealing the blue luster covering one fifth of the blade's tip.

Afearia takes the sword and slashes, creating a light blue rip in the atmosphere. Holding the weakened man, she hobbles forward and jumps through. Outside the crumbling tree, the gapped slash appears next to Demeseus, standing with crossed arms. Afearia and the unconscious man fall out before the gash disappears.

Afearia rolls further than the man and struggles to push herself off the ground as she coughs. She grabs her stomach with her shaky hand and grips herself, trying to gain control over the pain inside of her. To Demeseus's surprise, he hears cracking and looks to Eternity, fracturing.

"What?" he fearfully says, uncrossing his arms.

Blood begins to drip from Afearia's teeth, "The internal damage is far worse than ever before," she says, sounding like the wind was knocked out of her. She crawls towards the man with a red face, bloody lips and trembling limbs. She couldn't stop shaking.

"I feel like I'm dying," she says as she crawls along the ground, looking at the man's unconscious body. "The distance, may have been more than I can handle." She collapses and coughs blood into the dirt.

Though she couldn't see him as she struggles to raise her arm, Demeseus watches her with an expression of coming despair. For her suffering was a hard thing to witness up close.

Reaching out, Afearia mutters with a bloody mouth, "Sovereignty."

The sword appears in her hand, just as cracked as all of her other swords. Afearia notices a bit of blood coming from the corner of the man's mouth. She stabs her blade into the dirt and uses it as a means to bring herself closer. After several stabs and pulls, she reaches him. She places her hand over his forehead and closes her eyes, activating Sovereignty's healing magic.

With the gold light outlining them, Afearia successfully heals both of their internal injuries. Her swords also repair themselves to be as good as new.

"Is he—alright?" Demeseus ask as the gold outlining fades from Afearia and the man.

Afearia sits up and remains seated with her legs underneath herself, "He is. I'm fine too. Thanks for asking."

He doesn't respond at first, just stares at her staring back at him. "I think—"

"Aren't we going to talk? Like for real."

They stare at each other, waiting for a response until a loud crash is heard from the tree that pulls their attention. Branches are falling off as the tree begins to buckle under its own weight, tilting over.

"Do you think people like him are at the heart of every tree?" she asks, watching the tree break down.

"Don't know. I wasn't at the last one, so I couldn't tell you. You could always not call upon me and just stupidly die instead."

Surprised, Afearia looks at him with hurt and offended eyes. "Hold it. That is totally unfair. You don't even know what happened."

"I don't need to know," facing her with an angry face. "I've known you for a long time, you arrogant, selfish—!" The man groans. Demeseus glances at him before calming down as he addresses her. "There are other factors to deal with. Now is not the time. You should get him somewhere safe. I'm sure he has family worried about him."

Afearia tightens her jaw in frustration before looking away from him. "Okay…"

"Summon me when this is over. Then we'll talk."

Unexpectedly, Demeseus dismisses himself and Eternity, surprising Afearia. She composes herself and looks down at the defeated man. She picks up the man and carries him on her shoulder as she leaves the area.

Back at the motel, the siblings are on the floor playing a children's hand game before they hear the door open.

"Anya?" Veronica says upon standing.

Afearia comes into the room and drops the man on the bed. Adrian stands and walks up to them. He tugs off one of the leaves on the man's nature skirt, "Leaves?"

"Who's he?"

"A life I saved," Afearia replies. "Gather your things. We're leaving."

The kids are surprised by her sudden desire to leave. "We can't really leave him like this," Adrian says.

Afearia walks up to the dresser and touches the orb for it to disappear. "I will contact the motel manger to call for help."

"But—"

"I don't have time to deal with this. Gather your things so we can go."

As the kids gather their things, the man groans a few times before opening his hazel blue eyes. He turns his head toward Afearia who's standing with her hand on her hip whilst staring back at him with an intimidating expression.

"Killer eyes," he faintly whispers with a breath of flattery.

Diary Entry #2553

It's too hard. They expect too much from me and all I want to do is be free. That's not true... I don't know anymore. I want to save Terra, but I want to also be allowed to live my own life a little. Am I being selfish? All I do is complain about what I want in these stupid entries. This confining palace is killing me! I WANT TO RUN AWAY! I WANT TO BE NORMAL!
I just want to be happy.

Waking The Dawn

Chapter Five

The long-haired man sits at the edge of the bed in a hunched ponder. Adrian and Veronica sit before him while Afearia stares at him from across the room leaning on the dresser.

"Are you going to answer my question?" Afearia asks. "Or are you going to continue being a silent stiff?"

As the man continues to stare blankly at the floor, Adrian leans over, trying to see his face, expressing concern. "Maybe he's thirsty," Adrian says.

"Or can't talk," Veronica adds.

Adrian slaps his sister on the head, "Idiot, we just heard him speak."

She nearly pushes her brother off the chair, twice, "You're the idiot!"

They begin shoving each other until Afearia glares at them, "Stop it, both of you." Immediately, they sit straight and end their roughhousing.

"Killer eyes," the man says, getting everyone's attention as he stares at Afearia with a tired, mildly saddened look. "This isn't Tarlonka, is it?"

"It isn't. Now answer my question."

He looks off to the floor, "It feels like I've been asleep for a long time."

Afearia stomps her foot, causing a hard thud that startles everyone. "Answer me," she nearly threatens.

"You asked me about the trees. What they're for. They provide food, vegetation, and protection to smaller, weaker locations."

"I want the truth, guttersnipe."

"That is the truth. Just not the whole truth. There's a

114

dark side to their purpose. Something that isn't publicly known." He looks up at Afearia. "Have you ever heard of World Guardians?"

Afearia rolls her eyes. "You're asking the wrong one. I'm a Lightbringer. A whole world of grades above the title you're asking me. Of course I know what they are."

The man seemed surprised for a moment. "I don't know what a Lightbringer is. The name must be different in other parts of the world, but—"

"It's not. A Lightbringer is a special class of warrior sent to clean up the messes you World Guardians failed to achieve. A representative of Elysium to restore balance to the realms. That's who I am."

"Hmph," he smirks. "You sure made it clear that we are not the same."

"That's right. Now continue. It's your responsibility as an ex-guardian to tell me all I need to know in order to aid my success."

"Agreed. Then I guess the spike in disappearances during the king's fourteenth year of ruling is known to you."

"It is not."

"Then to inform you, this has all been going on since the tenth year. But there was a strange spike four years after. This was around the same time the trees became commonly established. During this time, the number of new Guardians to combat the government was diminishing."

"Yes. By the sixteenth year of his ruling, aid from the light ceased."

"Wait," he says, seeming a bit alarmed. "Sixteenth? I didn't look into this until the fifteenth." His eyes move in a confused manner as he thinks. "Through the time during my defeat and capture, that year is fairly blank. I'm under the impression we are no longer in the king's sixteenth year."

Afearia's stern expression softens a little. "No."

Sitting straight, the man sighs, "How long was I gone?" he asks with distressed eyes.

"Derexen's kingdom has been in power for twenty-two years; now moving into his twenty third."

The man exhales from his nose and brings his hand to his mouth for a moment. "My God… I've been gone for seven years? Is that what're telling me?"

"I'm sorry."

He shakes his head and leans forward covering his face. The room remains silent while the kids glance sadly at each other. Afearia, being stone face, glances at the floor, showing a bit of empathy for the man.

He lifts his head, eyes looking over the floor as his thoughts race with a lost, saddened expression. "Why…?" he says. "Why did Elysium stop supporting us?"

"Because my completion was near and it became clear that no Terraian could do the job."

"Hmph," he weakly smiles.

"What?"

"I don't think that's why."

"I'm from the realm you received your power. I know."

"Do you? Then do you know why the government was snatching up Guardians to energize their trees and amass more power?"

"Meaning?"

"The population has been lied to. Derexen said the trees only operate with photosynthesis using darkness. But a tree is a tree. And a tree needs light. And in this case, blood. Sucking dozens of bodies dry every year while using Guardians to keep them charged and sustained to do what it does."

"I don't see how this amasses power."

"Think of it like this. If the ones who oppose you are turned into batteries, can they be considered allies?

Every Guardian captured can't dismiss their Empyrean Blade. Which means it can't return to the light realm. That's power lost."

That's what I thought as well at one point, Afearia thinks.

"Your Elders didn't stop because you were ready to be deployed. They stopped because they were losing power. I can't tell you how many Guardians have been trapped and turned into batteries, but it's certainly a serious issue."

"How do you know all of this?"

"The Guardian stuff or the trees?"

"Both."

"The Guardians had started seeking each other out in order to improve our odds of turning the tables against the king. By doing so, we shared information with one another. We discovered that the Elders had become more enlightening with each new Guardian brought to the call. As for the government secrets... I hacked it," he says with a prideful smirk.

"I don't understand. How can you gain information after chopping it up?"

"Uh—?" he says with a confused head tilt.

"You're a hacker!?" Adrian asks with excited eyes.

"I was before I became a Guardian."

"What's a hacker?" Afearia asks.

"It's a person who can lift information from protected security systems. The time it takes to do so depends on the system and how experienced the hacker is. In other words... This guy is super cool!" he says admirably.

"No. However..." She looks to the man, "You were caught, weren't you?"

"At the time, I was at one of the government buildings that the king frequents. That's how I discovered all of this."

"Then I guess—"

"Wait. It gets worse. Those trees... There was a hidden file. When I was gathering data, I was breeching deeper parts of the mainframe and hit a wall. It was just one. One that was heavy duty protected."

"That's a given. The king would not have anyone finding out his deepest secrets."

"It wasn't his," he says, looking her in the face, pulling Afearia's attention further. "I couldn't really get into it beyond what the trees are and how they were made, including the research that went into it. And what they are for."

"You told me what they're for already."

"No, I told you what the king intended, not what they're really for. Whoever made the trees, labeled the protected file 'Charging'. But before I could really see what was inside, time was up. I had to flee."

"This really is a problem. I had no idea the trees could be this important. They have a hold on this world similar to the dark generators."

"No one did. I was just looking for a means to stop them from the inside. But after learning of the missing Guardians' fates, I knew I had to save them too."

"When I return the world's sun, it will."

"It won't kill the trees. Maybe in a few years it may reject the Guardian and use the sun as a means of power. But the chances of the Guardian surviving are slim."

"Why's that?" Veronica chimes in.

"The tree feeds its captives, keeping them alive because it needs them. But if it realizes there's another power source, it may stop nourishing them."

"Then how?" Afearia asks.

"I don't know."

"And that's all you can tell me?" she asks, sounding a little annoyed.

He looks away from her in somber thought, "Yes."

Afearia leans off of the dresser, "Fine. You have been semi-helpful to me. You can—"

"Wait... For the past seven years, I have been unconscious to my actions and my own awareness. I don't know what it's like out there anymore. Can you fill me in, even just a little?"

"Derexen's still king, I'm here to stop him. That's all you need to know." She walks past him, "You can go home now. Kids, let's go," she says to the siblings.

When the kids stand, the notice the man's glum expression as he stares at the floor with his lost eyes. Adrian glances at his sister before following Afearia out the door. Veronica glances at the open door before putting her hand on the man's shoulder.

He lifts his head a bit in her direction. "I'm sorry," Veronica earnestly says. "I hope you find your way," she says before walking out the door. The three of them leave the motel and proceed out the town. Veronica glances at Afearia several times before sadly shaking her head. "This isn't right," Veronica says. "He's lost and sad. Anya, why did you—?"

"So he doesn't overwhelm himself with meaningless guilt," Afearia interrupts. "Besides, he'd already told me all he could," she says as she puts on her eye patch.

"Heeey!?" a man shouts from behind them. They look back and see the rescued man running after them. "Hey," he says, breathing deeply with the rippling of his chest and six pack abdominals, all being draped by his long chestnut brown hair. "Where are you guys going?"

"That's none of your concern," Afearia coldly responds.

"Come on, killer eyes."

With swift danger, Afearia points at his throat with her joined index and middle fingers. "That's the third time you've called me that. Stop it."

He smiles nervously, "Then what's your name?"

"You need not know. Just get to where you need to be."

"I am."

Afearia lowers her hand and resumes her leave with the children. But seconds after, she rolls her eyes, "Are you lost?" she says while turning toward him.

"No."

"What town is this?"

"I don't know."

"Then you're lost."

"I'm not. I know exactly where I'm going."

"Which is?"

"With you guys."

"I don't think so. What makes you think I want to walk around with another liability?" The kids glance at each other, seeming a bit hurt from her thoughtless words.

"Not sure, but I could be of assistance."

"You have no powers."

"An informant?"

"Just get out of here," she says, walking on with the kids following.

"Come on," he says, jogging up to them. "Let me be part of the team."

"There is no team, you annoying little—"

"Anya really wants you to go, so you probably should," Adrian says joylessly. "If you haven't realized, she doesn't trust you, or anyone anymore."

"Why?"

"She's been betrayed too much."

Afearia tugs Adrian, "That's enough. What I've been through is none of his business. Stop talking to him at once."

"Yes, Anya."

Though staring at Afearia from the back, his stare was quite serious, but not threatening. "Alright... I'm gonna follow you anyway," he says, quickly dissolving his sterner expression.

Afearia suddenly stops. "Let me tell you something. From the time I finish this statement, you'll have thirty seconds to back five meters from us before I view you as a threat. If you follow me, I won't protect you, I will let you starve, and I will never trust you. Now back off—before I *bury* you," she emphasizes with a dangerous glare in her eye.

With noticeable fear on his face, the man takes several steps back before quickly walking away. Afearia turns from him and continues to walk on ahead with her party. In less than a minute, Veronica glances back with a near laugh and suppressed smile bubbling up before she swallows it back down.

"Anya," Veronica says. "He's still following us," unable to hide her slight smile.

"It means nothing. He's probably scheming something."

"Hey, I'm a little chilly!" the man shouts. "Got a spare blanket or something!?"

Veronica's about to respond as she turns, but Afearia tugs her forward. "Ignore him. Sooner or later he'll give this up."

Long after leaving the town, Afearia and the kids set up camp for the night. They sit around the fire eating and drinking while the long-haired man sits quite far from them.

"That looks good!" he shouts. "Can I have some!?"

Afearia irritably drops her fork into her fruit can, "He's so annoying."

"Come on! I haven't eaten in seven years!"

Veronica almost turns to look at the man. "Don't look at him. He's like a stupid baby seeking attention. She looks down at her can and notices the label's packaging had the location it was produced. It tugs at a lingering thought she's had about the kids before looking in their direction. "Guys, we need to talk. I've been quite nice not asking too many questions, but I think it's time for some answers. I deserve that much."

Adrian swallows a halved peach, "Okay."

"Where is your home and why won't you tell me more about it?" The kids glance at each other. "I can't get you home if I don't know where home is for you."

"We'll tell you when we get there."

"Not good enough anymore." The kids continue to eat their fruits. "Look, a lot has happened since we've been together and recently you were almost killed. I have to accept it… You two are no longer safe with me. From here on, we need to move closer toward your home." They stop eating and just stare at the ground. "Why won't you two tell me? What? Is it a lie that you're from elsewhere?" The kids look up at her. Afearia looks a bit hurt. "That's what it is, is it? You deceived me as well."

Adrian sighs, "No, Anya."

"The reason is—" Veronica tries to say.

"Veronica, don't," he quickly interrupts.

"This will only make her worse if we don't tell her something."

"What are you two talking about?" Afearia suspiciously asks.

"We—" Adrian, stifling his words for a moment. "We were going to tell you before. But when we found you… We're concerned about leaving you."

"Why?"

"Because you're changing," Veronica adds. "You're acting a lot like the Anya we first met. What will happen to you when we finally do leave?"

"Nothing. I will fulfill my mission."

"How?"

"That's none of your concern."

"See! You haven't spoken to us like that since we

first met."

"Do you want to live? I can't get soft and let you die."

"Are you saying that—your dying was our fault?" Adrian says with hurt in his voice. "We make you weak?"

Though the man is far from them, the man's ears twitch a bit as he sternly stares at the ground with his back to them.

"What do you want me to say?" Afearia responds. Looking like he may cry, Adrian clenches his jaw and shoots up to run away, until Afearia grabs him by the wrist.

"I don't want to be the one making you weak," Adrian says with his voice shaken and his back to her. He tugs from Afearia, "Let go."

Without lifting her head, Afearia holds his wrist tighter. "I'm sorry. I keep making excuses for my own mistakes. What happened in that building had nothing to do with traveling with you. Adrian...," she looks up at him, "I didn't mean it. I'm sorry I spoke like that."

Adrian turns to her with eyes on the verge of tears, "Then why are you being so mean?"

Afearia slowly releases him, "I don't know. It's like I said before. I'm still under the belief that I was at my best when I kept the world at arm's length. But I wasn't better off. I wasn't sharper. Just cold as ice. I've been raised under that reasoning. Cold and sharp like a life severing katana. I guess I figured if I go back to my basics I'll become untouchable again."

Afearia places her elbows on her knees, folding her open hands before her mouth, "I've wrestled with a twisted thought back when we were under Dr. Richards care. Before I made friends and met others I cared about, I was never close to being defeated. No one could top me. But the more lives I came in contact with, the harder it became for me to win. I... I don't know if the enemies I've faced became stronger, or I've become weaker. Or it's all a

123

coincidence and it was bound to become this way. Either way, I felt my basics will keep you two safe. Protected, like a warrior should."

"But you're more than a warrior," Adrian says. Afearia turns her head away. "I mean it. You really are—to us at least."

Afearia stands with a weak smile before putting her hand on his shoulder, "I know."

In the distance, the man's wide, gazing eyes fixed to the ground as if he's experiencing something amazing quickly ends with a couple blinks when he hears footsteps from behind him. He turns partway and sees an annoyed Afearia holding a water bottle for him.

The man playfully snatches the water bottle from her, "Hey, thanks!"

"Mhmm," Afearia says before walking away.

"No seriously." She stops and looks at the genuine expression on his face. "Thank you."

She stares at him for a moment and turns to return to camp. He smirks and bobs his head a bit before cracking open his water bottle.

Afearia sits down with a sigh, "Alright, I gave him water. Now tell me."

"Leslinbrook," Adrian calmly says with reluctance. "A town located at the foot of a mountain."

Afearia unrolls her map, "Leslinbrook, Leslinbrook. Oh! We have some ways to go before we reach it. Why were you guys so against telling me?"

"It may have been put under government rule, but it's watched closely by the scariest man we've ever met. And I'm not trying to upset you. You may hate the king, but this person is far worse."

"I doubt it. Derexen's a demon. Pure evil."

"If Derexen's a demon, then he's the devil itself." Adrian checks on his sister who has plugged her ears with a fearful face, seeming to be on the verge of a traumatic fit.

"His name's Agonda. A government pillar who lives and torments the people of that town every day. The things he will do to you is only something nightmares can fuel. No one knows if this was the king's will or not. But that man... He's... He's..."

"You don't have to force yourself. I get the picture. I can understand why you couldn't tell me."

"No. At first we couldn't tell you because it's hard to talk about. But after Aster City it became our reasons to keep you alive."

"I can handle a measly Demi Anthropoid."

"Like Minerva?" he says, catching Afearia off guard. "Dr. Richards told us who you fought. And now, we are scared out of our minds of losing you. And for a moment—we did." He looks to his sister and slowly lowers her hands. "We just want to protect you."

"And I keep telling you that's not your job. I appreciate your reasoning and I even understand your secrecy. But you're trying to stop my purpose. I can never live that happy life you want for me. If I knew that I never did everything in my power to save this world... I could never forgive myself. I wish there was a way I could make you understand."

"I get it, Anya. We get it. But we'll still keep trying."

She smiles softly at him. "Then try harder."

Confident that they're making headway, the kids continue eating and talking with Afearia. The three of them joke and laugh in merriment until the kids finally fall asleep. Before Afearia can put out the campfire, she notices the man is still awake, watching the night sky. She turns in his direction before reluctantly approaching him.

When she stands behind him to his right, Afearia says nothing as she looks down at him, still gazing up at the sky. "You know," he says, "I still can't believe I've been locked up in that tree for seven years. It doesn't feel real to me. Almost like I didn't miss a day. But being out here, seeing the discolored sky. I have. How many lives have been lost due to my absence?" he says with saddened eyes.

"That is no longer your concern," Afearia answers. "Your time as a World Guardian is over."

"Hey!" he says with some jest. "Play nice."

Afearia huffs and turns to walk away for a moment. "The tree. I've been in one like it before I found you. It was nowhere near as docile as your tree was. Why?"

"I don't know. It all felt like I was trapped in a deep dream with brief moments when I could be aware of what was happening in reality. I couldn't tell the difference, but when things felt wrong in the moment, I tried to gain control over it, even though I still couldn't tell if I was affecting anything at all. It's hazy."

"You were placed in a dream-like state. So you couldn't know."

"But I do know. People still died during those years because of the delusion I was under. When they did, an unwelcomed sensation ran through my dreams. A sad, hollow feeling," speaking with saddened brows as he looks at the stars. Afearia glances at him for a moment. But when she looks again, he's comically pointing at her with his hands like guns. "Darn. I thought I could get you to smile."

Afearia walks away, "Idiot," she mutters.

After everyone had lied down to sleep, including the stranger who's back is to them, Afearia's still awake as she sits in front of a dying campfire. Afearia sighs before getting onto her feet and walking out into the distance. Her expression is in deep ponder as she struggles coming to terms with her predicament.

Everything I do has become so difficult, Afearia thinks. My magical control is laughable. To even summon an Empyrean Blade is like my early years of training. And even worse. Afearia looks at her hand and forearm, flexing a few times. My healing abilities have increased higher than ever before. Why?

She stops and sighs through her nose with her eye looking to the ground in disappointment. She removes her eye patch and pockets it. "I feel like I'm moving backwards." She turns her head, looking closely at the loose, dry dirt. A three-legged whiptail lizard pokes its head out from the dirt and races across the ground.

As she watches it scurry away, a man's echoing voice grabs her attention, "There you are."

She quickly looks around, frantic to find where it came from. Without warning, a circle of pure darkness appears beneath Afearia's feet before swallowing her up. As quickly as she was taken, the circle reappears in midair in a seemly darker atmosphere to drop her out. Flipping out of control, Afearia falls with flailing arms until a man catches her in his hand by the neck, choking her a bit.

Clutched tightly with shut eyes, Afearia tries to pry the hand off her until she opens one of her eyes, seeing who had her in their grasp. "G-guardian Carnavess," she barely stutters, fearfully looking into his menacing greenish-yellow eyes.

Afearia gasps as blood rushes to her head. Carnavess holds her with no concern, similar to lovelessly holding a puppy by the scruff of its neck.

"So... you are alive," Carnavess says plainly. He suddenly drops her at his feet, watching her cough and catch her breath while she has her hand to her neck.

When she finally gets her breath, Afearia notices the nearly black ground. She looks up at the darker than black sky with a blood red moon. The area around them is completely desolated.

"Where am I?" she asks.

"I'm surprised you're not gagging from the darkness here," he says, looking around with near pride. He looks down at her, "This is Armagevion."

Afearia stands, looking uneasy as she walks from

him to observe the scenery. Devoid of life, nothing moves through this lightless plain. It's just an open dark land surrounded by pitch black, veiling anything to be visible in the far distance.

"Why are we here?" Afearia asks. She makes a nervous realization as she turns to him, "Why are you here?"

"Looking for you, of course."

She looks around, confused to all that's happening, "Carna—"

"Elder Carnavess," sternly correcting her.

There's a moment of silence. "Elder Carnavess," she says with reluctance.

"Does walking amongst the filth cause one to lose respect?"

"My apologies," she says with a lowered head. "It was a slip of the tongue."

"The last time you used that excuse, I pierced that tongue with a needle. Two, if I'm not mistaken." Afearia nervously swallows spit just because of the thought. "I came here under the suspicion that you were still alive. I didn't think when I found you I'd have to reeducated you. Do I?"

Afearia stands her ground until Carnavess takes a single step, causing her to back step and cower. "Please!" she blurts, trying her best to hide her fearful expression. "It was a disrespectful mistake. I'm sorry... Father Carnavess."

He smirks deviously, "All is forgiven, my child." Afearia, refusing eye contact, still glances around a few times. "Still don't know how or why we are here? Don't let it trouble you. You and I have bigger problems."

"I don't—"

"You died." She stands firm after his statement, still avoiding his stare. "You died and yet you and I are here, talking. Care to explain?"

She slants her eyes, "Several months ago, I encountered the anthropoid, Minerva. We engaged in combat and I shamefully fell to its hands."

"Ridiculous. Either you're lying to me or you didn't take her seriously. No matter your reasons, you're pathetic. All your life you trained for this. And just like that," he says with a snap of his fingers, "you bite the dust like a worm. You've gone soft. Walking with the apes have made you weak, hasn't it?"

"That's not—"

"I'm taking you home." Afearia's surprised by his sudden words. "You're no good to me like this. You need to be broken down to the bare bones and built back as new. I need you to be perfect. Not another pusing meat bag." He begins to approach her, "It's time to go."

Afearia slowly walks back, "No," she softly says.

"Yes."

"No."

Carnavess stops and raises his hand to her. "Yes," spoken with a near hiss. A faint red spiked chain appears in his palm and around Afearia's neck. She trembles to her knees before falling to the ground, shaking in agony. She twitches around with her hands on the chain and her mouth open. "You will do what I say, mutt. Dogs should not bark when their masters call."

Afearia's eyes begin to water as her body continues to rive in pain, trying to scream out with not a sound being freed from her throat.

"When I release you, I want to hear, yes, elder Carnavess. Understood, puppy?" he says, still smirking deviously.

When he shuts his palm and lowers his arm, the chain fades away, freeing her. Squealing in pain while holding her neck, Afearia catches her breath as she rolls around like she's on fire.

Afearia begins clawing closely to her neck and

chest, as if something was harming her. She turns over onto her stomach, regaining her normal vocal tone as she breathes deep and drags herself a bit, coughing into the dirt. Her heavy shivers begin to subside as she lifts herself onto her feet.

"Yes, elder Carnavess," she says, causing him to make his devilish grin grow. "Walking in the mortal realm has changed me. But I don't believe I'm weaker—just careless."

"That's how you justify your defeat?" he says with annoyance. "Carless? You really have become pathetic. Lowering yourself for the sake of playing human."

"I'm not playing human. I'm doing the task that you and all of Elysium has assigned to me. I would never do anything to compromise that," she says, looking him in the eyes.

"It's a little too late for that. The little vacation you took playing dead has set us back. Forty percent of Terra should've been restored by now. We still can't intervene here. Derexen has gone through great lengths to keep us out of the realms. Your time here is not being well spent. Have you even seen him?"

"No... I don't know where he is. And Derexen doesn't find it necessary to confront me personally either."

Carnavess paces around for a bit before moving toward her while nodding slowly. Suddenly, he quickly wraps his fingers around the back of Afearia's neck, "I'm beginning to think you're not doing what we asked of you."

"I am," she says, sounding a bit fearful as she stared into his eyes.

"You're not. If you were, a lot more would have been accomplished by now. This is a functional government that he believes he owns. What was the one thing I told you to do if you wish to flush him out immediately?" Slowly, but fearfully, Afearia looks away before shutting her eyes in pain. He shakes her once in his grip, regaining her fearful attention. "Destroy a town. Burn a city. Flush—him—out." he emphasizes.

"I was asked to protect life. Grayson and Helios said—"

He shakes her again, "Who raised you!? You listen to me! I don't have—!" He pauses for a moment to collect himself. "We don't have time to waste while that lunatic aims to control the universe. Sooner or later he'll come for Elysium again. And when all realms are bathed in hell's fire, you'll be the one to blame—forever."

Carnavess pushes her away, "This problem should have been settled in two weeks. Now, what will it be? Will you come home, or will you do as I ordered you to do?"

"But to end so many lives... I—"

"What—will—you—do?"

Afearia lowers her head with shut eyes, wishing her answer would be better. "I'll do it," she says in a low voice upon opening her eyes. "Just give me one month."

"Why not now?"

"Please?" she says, staring back at him with shaky eyes.

"Do you think I pity you?"

"No, sir. You never would."

Carnavess approaches her and roughly pokes her in the sternum, causing her to stumble a step. "One month. I'll be waiting." She nods sadly. "Get back to work, Afearia. Stop pretending you're human."

Carnavess walks pass her to leave. Afearia quickly turns around, "G-guardian Carnavess!?" she calls in a stutter, sounding a bit surprised before stopping him. "Are you—leaving me here?" Carnavess turns halfway toward her. "I—I have to get back." Carnavess' expression becomes suspicious. "My-my things that I travel with. I-I need them." Carnavess' expression remains unchanged as he watches her desperate display. "I have a-a map with details and—"

131

"Shut up." Afearia quickly closes her mouth like a scolded child as she lowers her head. She trembles a bit as she focuses to control her shakes. Carnavess slowly walks up to her before violently palming her panicked face. "Hold your breath and close your eyes."

Doing as she's told, Afearia suddenly feels weightless. With the sensation of rushing wind on her body similar to falling, her weight returns to her. Carnavess roughly pushes her away, causing Afearia to stumble. She turns as she tries to get her footing. But when she does and turns back toward Carnavess, he had left the grounds with not a trace of him to be found.

Soon after, Afearia falls to her knees. "I have to kill—so many people," she says, looking at the ground with distress. She balls her fist, closing her eyes in pain before sitting up straight with a deadpan expression. "I am a warrior. The lives lost before me are nothing more than sheep," she lifelessly says.

Back at the camp, everyone continues to sleep soundly, except for the rescued man lying on his side. He stars off into the plains before closing his eyes upon the sound of approaching footsteps. Afearia returns and sits before the sleeping children, staring emotionlessly at them before putting on her eye patch and lying down. The man opens his eyes and curiously shifts them to the ground.

Despite her efforts, Afearia could not sleep. After hours of turning, she decides to sit up with a bit of a frustrated expression. Afearia rubs her weary eyes before sighing. She glances at the peaceful siblings sleeping before standing and walking into the distance.

Once far from the campsite, Afearia takes off her eye patch and puts it inside her jacket before stretching her arm out, focusing. Her arm throbs for a moment before wild chains come from her shoulders, retracting almost as quickly. She sucks her teeth before she grips her wrist, still holding her hand out.

The chains, seeming like they're trying to resist her call, creep up her arm before rapidly appearing to shape up into a cylinder, summoning Eternity. Breathing heavily, she stabs the sword into the dirt with both hands, leaning her weight on it.

"It really shouldn't be this hard," she says, catching her breath.

"You're wrong," Demeseus says, suddenly appearing before her. "This is Eternity's true burden."

"What are you talking about?"

"Are we alone?"

"Yes."

"It's time we had our talk."

"Aren't you curious why I summoned you here?" she says with a slight playful tone.

"This isn't a battle, so I'll be frank. I'm not interested about why you brought me here."

Afearia slants her eyes from him with a joyless look, "Okay..." She steps back from the sword and fully gives her attention to Demeseus. "What's going on?" Though Demeseus doesn't respond, Afearia can see how serious he is. She rubs the back of her neck, lightly smiling, "This feels kind of like the calm before the storm."

Demeseus looks away, trying to unclench his bolted jaw. "I'm trying to find less than violent words for you," he barely manages to say. Afearia's eyes sadden in surprise... with brows faintly exposing her concern of his judgment. "But I don't think you deserve as much from me."

Demeseus shakes his head and takes a few steps from her. She stares concernedly at his back as he shakes his head a few more times before turning toward her, "How could you...? Did you think I wouldn't notice?"

"Notice what?" she says sorrowfully. "What did I do to you?"

He exhales in disbelief. "You know, the fact that you don't acknowledge it makes all of this that much worse."

"Acknowledge what!?"

"How about dying and not giving a shit about anyone else!"

"That's not fair, Demeseus! You weren't there!"

"And whose fault was that!? I told you to call me when you're in danger!"

"I—"

"You know what pisses me off the most? The fact I can bet on everything you did not take your opponent seriously."

Afearia looks to the ground, "You don't know what happened," she mutters.

"I do know. And the thought. Every time I think about it." He stomps his foot several times, "Of all things, you're foolish arrogance is surely the one thing I hate about you!"

Like being hit with lightning, Afearia's head shoots up and looks at Demeseus with wide eyes glossed with tears. "No! You can't say that to me! You can't!" she shouts, taking a few steps toward him. "I'm—! You're my—! Demeseus, you can't mean that!"

Seeming barely fazed by her dramatic words, he stares at her almost coldly, "I do. Because your arrogance tore you away from me. Another person, lost and blinded by their own faults," he says, lowering his head in regret. Afearia calms herself a bit, staring at him with her hurt eyes. "Don't you see? Don't you see how stupid that was? To die just because you wanted to stroke your ego? How do you think I felt knowing your presence had suddenly faded away. Unable to do *anything* about it. It hurt, Afearia. More than you realize."

Afearia takes time to collect herself. She looks to him with self-pity. "You're right," she says. "When we started, I didn't use everything I had to win. If I played to my strengths it could have gone differently. Something an

134

enemy heeded me about. But Demeseus. You don't know how it felt when that—**fiend** blatantly paraded about taking your life."

Demeseus is taken aback by the open revelation of his death. "I lost it!" Afearia angrily continues. "I went into a blind rage in an all out attempt to kill that devil! I wasn't thinking! All I wanted was to avenge you with all that I had! So don't tell me...!" she says sorrowfully. "Don't tell me I left you and didn't care because you were the only one I was THINKING ABOUT!" she screams in desperate sympathy.

With her voice echoing through the plains, Demeseus stands speechless and shocked by the ach in her that he's ignored all this time.

Afearia falls to her knees, sadly lowering her head, "And you say you hate me," she says in a hurt, shaky tone. "After all we've been through when I was little. After all I've done to better fit the shadow you left behind. And to see you after so long... You coldly tell me—you hate me," she cries a little. She slowly shakes her head looking in the dirt. "How...?"

"Afearia. I hate your arrogance, not you."

"That's still me! The thing you hate is still me! I'm not perfect... I'm not you."

"Nobody's perfect, Afearia, not even me. I used a strong word out of anger. I even tried to rationalize my mistake. I'm sorry I said I hate you. But my feelings still stand about your terrible approach toward every battle you engage in. Afearia, it's reckless. I don't want you to meaninglessly throw your life away over it, especially with vengeance on your mind. I've already lost one friend to that. I'm not looking forward to losing another."

"So what?" angrily wiping her eyes. "I should just let that fiend get away with what it's done? I won't! I won't allow this to go unpunished!"

"Perhaps we should revisit this subject."

135

"There's nothing to revisit! I'm ending that devil's life," she says with a stern fervor.

Demeseus stares off into the distance. "You can't hear it, can you? The hate is already taking root inside you."

She grunts in annoyance, "You just don't understand."

"I do. I've seen it many times on my journey. I've even been in that same darkness myself. It will change you, Afearia. If you don't take control now, you'll end up hurting innocent people, or worse. You'll be like Greyshio."

Surprised by his words, Afearia glares at Demeseus. "How dare you compare me to that monster? He was a blight on the World Guardian name. He killed and sacrificed thousands of people to satisfy his twisted goals. And you openly compare me to him!? To that!?"

"Listen to yourself!" he says upon quickly facing her. "Are you telling me this is Afearia!? This is the level-headed warrior who always keeps her emotions in check!?"

"That's because you don't know how I feel!"

"You're right, I don't! But I know what you'll become if you don't stop this!"

"You can't stop me, Demeseus!" She takes a moment before pointing at him with conviction, "I'm gonna string Minerva up high for all to see."

"Even if that means losing me?"

"How would I lose you?"

"Hate takes many forms. Down the line, your hate will destroy those closest to you in ways you never dreamed you would. Innocent lives will soon become hindrances on your journey of hate. Then they'll become cannon fodder for your prize. And in the end, they'll have no value at all. Just things that drift around in your world of hate. And your friends? Even your loved ones will just be meaningless casualties on your road of hate. Afearia," he says, pulling her attention further. "Take it from someone who's seen it up close. How hate morphed a gentle soul into something unrecognizable."

Afearia turns her head from him, "My hate runs deep. Your words may not be enough..." She looks to Demeseus, "But I'll closely heed them."

Demeseus stares at her for a moment, then looks off into the field, "How are your powers?"

"Screwy. Everything is unreasonably hard to access now. I can't even summon an Empyrean Blade without panting and sweating. What's wrong with me?"

"I know."

"You do?"

"Afearia, what I'm going to tell you is something I've only recently discovered. It's about the Elders and their relation to the Empyrean Blades."

"What do you mean?" she says with a confused expression.

Far across the dark plains of Terra, traversing the empty fields, Carnavess has not returned to Elysium. Instead, he calmly treads the lands before a sinister grin crosses his face.

Diary Entry #2222

Sometimes I just can't take the pressure. That internal build up of being alone and feeling torn up inside. I just want to let it out because I'm starting to feel like I'm going to explode. Holding this all down is really starting to wear me thin. My body actually feels like it's under pressure, especially in my chest. I honestly ask, is it possible to physically explode from your own suffering? Doesn't matter. Who's going to miss me? I can only hope you will...

The Guiding Currents

Chapter Six

Seemingly to be walking with no destination in mind, Carnavess' eyes express a serene focus. He suddenly stops, looking somewhat suspicious. He closes his eyes and takes a slow, deep inhale through his nose while gradually spreading his arms. Carnavess sinks into a small pool of light with creeping darkness at the edges, vanishing from the plains.

Elsewhere on Terra, Afearia waits to hear Demeseus's explanation. For a while, the two of them just stare at each other.

"Well?" Afearia impatiently says.

"I'm hesitant," Demeseus replies.

"Why?"

"Because you need an open mind for this. And let's be honest. Speaking ill about your elders has always been an icky subject between us."

"That and other things, Demeseus. Don't hold back now. It would be against your character," sounding a bit annoyed.

Demeseus takes a breath. "Alright. How far back does your knowledge of the Empyrean Blades stretch?"

"Possibly further than yours. To be specific, around the time they were first being gathered."

"As a means of balance, right?"

"Yes. The unpredictable changing of hands between the Empyrean Blades was causing too much destruction."

"Which in turn gave the Elders control over the most powerful weapons in existence."

"Well, not control, balance."

"No, Afearia. Control. The Empyrean Blades are

139

now contained and forced to choose their next owner by who is presented to them. Which means the Elders can now select candidates based on their agenda. In other words, they can select less than promising guardians in hopes they won't succeed."

"That's ridiculous! They wouldn't do that!"

"It gets worse. Realize there are Empyrean Blade ranks. If you were to save the world, you would choose the best wielders and the best blades. Wielders who possibly already have combat experience, giving you an edge for combative warriors. And yet they choose people who are too young, too inexperienced, and armed with low tier blades. Why would they do that? Why give weak swords to a world in danger?"

"I don't buy the decision on how they choose people. They must've saw something in you and others that's beyond experience and age. And as for the swords given, it shouldn't be hard to understand. High tier blades are too unstable, you know that. And the only reason Eternity was an option for you is because Derexen had Catastrophe."

"And I wonder how he got that."

"Don't you dare! They would never do that! Even if they did, they probably thought he was a good choice for—"

"For what, Afearia? The world wasn't in danger."

"As far as you knew back then."

"Look, I don't know if he was chosen or not. But you can't deny the possibility. And if he was chosen, what for? What was he meant to prevent? As far as you and I know, the world was fine until he got an Empyrean Blade."

"He wasn't chosen. No one knows how he got an Empyrean Blade, so enough with the false accusations."

"It's still something to consider."

"Are you going to tell me about my powers or not?"

"This is about your powers. Yours and every

Empyrean wielder to ever serve. I assume not only have your powers been harder to use, but there's been a significant difference in the weight of your blade. Even your spells must have become difficult due to those abilities partly being given to you from your weapons. The reason for this is because since the day you were chosen, you have been only using a fraction of your swords' powers."

"I don't believe it. I've spent years gaining mastery over my companions. And I know all the best ways to use them."

"You think so? When you first got Eternity, how long did it take for you to swing it in fluent motion?"

"I don't know. A day?"

"How long until you could manipulate chain mass and shape?"

"A day or two."

"And it never occurred to you that mastery over one of the most powerful Empyrean Blades in existence was coming to you a bit too easily?"

"By that time I had already gain much experience with magic and Empyrean Blade usage, so it only made sense it didn't take as long as it did when I was nine."

"Then allow me to be blunt. You've mastered nothing. Just a set of limiters placed on you from the start. All weapons have their weight masked because of the elders limiting how much of the sword's abilities may be used. Even I didn't know it until I went to Elysium. Well, I theorized, but couldn't confirm. Until now."

Afearia thinks to herself for a moment, looking around in disbelief. "That—that doesn't make sense. Masked weight. Limited power access. No. That can't be done. It makes no sense."

"Why not? Old magic used by experienced casters puts all things in the realm of possibility. You should know that. It's the same with Eternity's secret power. There is a transformation called Eternity's Armor. Few wielders advance that far, but if they do, they only get to use fractions of it. It's a struggle to call upon and no one has ever done a full transformation."

"Ridiculous. All of it. I mastered my weapons because I was ready. Those who've used Eternity fail to reach that level because no one has ever been strong enough to do so. They just weren't ready."

"No. There's a deeper reason for it. It not only requires a blood pact, something the Elders only teach elysian soldiers. It also requires iron will and complete access to Eternity's power. You, nor I have ever had complete access to Eternity's power, and it's not because our companions denied us. It's because of the divider placed on chosen wielders during initiation."

"You're wrong... Where did you even hear this? None of it is making any sense."

"Long ago, people were chosen at random. But once the Elders captured the swords and chose who pacifically would be next in line, they had to be smart. On the off chance their chosen wielder would turn on them, they had some fail-safes put in place. One would be limiting how much access and control the wielder has over their chosen weapon. This same magic is key to leading dismissed blades back to Elysium, even in death."

"They bind the Empyrean Blades and have an auto-recall spell to keep them," Demeseus continues. "With this intricate binding, it limits the burden of being exposed to the raw power of their blades. A foolproof way to keep their power and limit the rise of potential threats."

"You're wrong...," Afearia says with disbelief in her eyes. She shakes her head, "You have no proof, none," she says, sadly looking down to her right.

"Then look at it this way. Think about a surge protector. With it, you can reduce the electricity output from any port. All of your appliances still function. You wouldn't even notice the difference. Until you want to operate at heavy duty levels. That's when the protection kicks in. Your appliance either fails to completely perform or it just shuts down. This is no different. And what makes it so perfect is if you have operated at less than optimal levels your whole life, you'll never question there being something greater."

Afearia walks to her left, still unable to believe the words she's hearing. She chuckles, "You are ludicrous. You're just saying random things and you still haven't proved anything to me." She chuckles again, much like before, a nonbeliever's chuckle, "This is all just you making things up to make sense of what's happening."

"Afearia, your struggles are proof. Your body is currently trying to adjust to this sudden burst of energy and you're paying for it. Your control is terrible, and although you haven't said it." Demeseus suddenly looks to his right, as if someone said something to him. "Yes. I'm sure you are feeling physically out of your element. Your chest is tight, right?"

"What?" she says, surprised by his accurate question.

"Tight chest and an elevated heart rate that has yet to stop causing irregular beats. Your nerves are on edge, and your overall senses are heightened."

"How—? How do you know that?"

"It's the surge. This is a side effect of having so much energy running through your body unbound. Because your swords no longer return to Elysium, they have to return to their true master. You. They are now constantly present from within you."

"They're—in me?" she says, putting her hand to her chest.

"Your death was like a system reset. This broke the divider within you, destroyed the limiters and our pact." He notices she seems to be frozen by his last words. "I know

143

this must be overwhelming to hear all at once, but it's the truth."

"As if I would believe a word of it." She looks to him with bothered eyes. "Not a word."

"Why would I lie to you, Afearia? Me, of all people. Remember who's always been by your side. I would not deceive you—ever."

With a near glare, "You've lied to me before."

"When?" She tilts her head in annoyance, expecting him to know what she's speaking of. Demeseus nearly rolls his eyes, "The story of my death wasn't a lie. I just didn't tell you what happened."

"A lie by omission."

"A lie is when someone deliberately tells you false information. When you asked me, I told you the truth about what you asked. When you asked who, I didn't want to discuss it. I didn't lie." She doesn't stop giving him her bothered stare. "You're pissed, I know. But perhaps when you calm down you'll realize—"

"Perhaps when you stop rationalizing your reasons, you'll realize how much that hurt me!"

"You're changing the subject. You're deflecting the situation to something else."

Afearia throws her hands up in a huff and looks at the ground, shaking her head with hands on her hips, "You're right. I'm still focused on this whole hidden truth about who killed you and whatnot. Please, continue," she sarcastically says.

"You still think I'm a liar? A jerk who likes toying with you?" She shrugs angrily as she stares at him with irritation. "You're serious? For God sakes, Afearia, I would die to keep you alive!" Though angry, her expression mellows a bit into guilt. "Is that not good enough for you? Because I'm trying to help you. So even if you despise me, better that than you dying for stupid ass reasons!"

She sighs, relaxing her uptight posture. "Alright... I

believe you. I don't truly think you would steer me wrong. But all of this... Demeseus, they raised me. They watch over the realms for the sake of balance and peace. That's how it's always been."

"More like how it's always been told. But if that's what you believe, I'm fine with that. All I ask is that you hear me out, despite me painting them in a bad light."

"Fine," she says with some gloom.

"For a long time, the Elders have had a strong hold on the realms by controlling how power is divided. But this is your chance to turn things around. At this moment, you have a chance to be stronger than you've ever been. Right now, you are a radical. A free agent. You are no longer bound. You can finally place your hands on the wheel of fate."

Afearia's eyes slant. "Not quite," she says in a low voice. "I still belong to Carnavess, regardless how much I wish I wasn't shackled to his sadistic magic."

"The Chain of Obedience..."

"It's still in play. Etched into every molecule in my body... I'm his... forever more."

"I don't want to believe that. But for now, we'll tackle things one step at a time. Let's first awaken your true strength."

"I think I'm plenty strong already, thanks," she says with a smirk, looking off to the side.

"If you don't quit this cocky shit, I can ensure you that you'll die again. No second chances."

"Whoa, hey now, no need to be rude."

"You're the rude one. It's like you've learned nothing. The next time you fight an Elite, are you going to just scoff at them like they can't touch you?"

"Well, obviously I'll turn it up a bit after I toy with them for a while. But I take my fights seriously."

"No you don't."

"Yes I do!"

"You don't toy around when a life or death battle is taking place. Especially if your defeat means the ongoing suffering of billions. I shouldn't need to explain this to you. You're not a damn kid!" Knowing her tasteless comment was ill used, she turns her head in shame. "This is not a game, Afearia."

"I know."

After staring at her for a while, his eyes become a bit firmer on Afearia's distant pose of shame. "You want to emulate me? Be my successor? Then it's time to cut the shit. Take your fights seriously. I admit in the past I have stroked my ego in a fight, but I never fought my foe like they were lesser than me. If I hold back, it's not because I don't think you're strong. It means I'm searching for something in this fight. It's usually hope," he softly says.

Afearia looks up at him, realizing his sincerity was there since the beginning. "There was never a fight I didn't treat like my last," Demeseus continues. "And that's what you need to do. Treat every fight, every struggle, like it's your last." Demeseus looks into the distance with a smile, "You'll be surprised what an altered mindset can do for you. You might gain more than you expected from this caged Eden. Not every fight has to be fueled with negative emotions. Sometimes there's mutual respect." He glances at Afearia who's giving him an odd look, causing him to laugh a little. "You'll understand it, someday."

"Sure, I guess. But I hear ya'. No more arrogance. Wait," she says, realizing something. "Is that why you were so short with me when I summoned you?"

"It was. That, and I wanted to teach you a lesson in effort. To fight like it mattered. And when you did, I helped. By the way, how's the guy you fought?"

"Pfft, he's fine," she says, rolling her eyes.

"Good. But that was risky though. It could've backfired."

"A dangerous gamble, but it had to be done." She

frowns a little. "I'll try, Demeseus. I really will. But from here on out, I'll have to be careful. Much more than ever." Demeseus's expression becomes a bit serious. She closes her left eye, "The beast inside me never sleeps," she says before opening her eye. "Greater exertion means greater slipups in control."

"Has he made any returns?"

"Not since Yadeira. And he almost came out during my fight against Minerva. But since I've been back... Demeseus. I can't sense him—at all. I heal like a speed machine and I can no longer smell darkness."

"Fast healing... That is odd. But that may be an added effect of Sovereignty's innate healing abilities being infused with your body."

"Even still. I know he's still there. If he wasn't, my eye wouldn't bare his mark. Do you think it's a side effect of the Empyrean Blades?"

"Sounds reasonable. I can't be sure though." Demeseus notices the sweat coming from Afearia's temple. "Are you alright?"

"I'm fine."

"You look a bit flushed in the cheeks."

"I felt warm earlier and now it feels really hot. But I'm okay."

Demeseus turns his head a bit, looking to his side as if something was whispered to him. "We should probably do the pact now."

"What's the rush?" she jokes.

"You currently have ten nukes resting inside of you. The fact that you haven't exploded yet only further pushes my belief that you have boundless potential. But this energy flowing in you is unstable. If we wait any longer you're going to have a heart attack."

"Will I lose my heightened senses?"

"You might. Right now, I'm more concerned about your life."

Afearia sighs. "I hate this part." She sits on her knees and unzips her top down to her pelvis, revealing her gauze wrapped chest. She removes and folds her jacket before placing it down. Afearia takes her arms out the suit and presents them with open palms to Demeseus. "I'm ready."

Demeseus steps forward, "I hope so." He extends his arm toward her. Two chains slowly come from Eternity and rattle slowly in two directions, hovering over her palms. "Here we go."

The chains suddenly slash her palms open and slither into her wound and into her arms. Afearia closes her eyes and breathes in a near sensual way as the lumpy chain links gently wiggle up her arms as she lightly trembles.

Without warning, Afearia's body jolts and she screams out in pain. She quickly jerks forward with arms still up, barely holding on. Afearia is clenching her teeth, breathing madly through them with spit flying out while she shakes in pain as the chains multiply and course through her torso.

The chains work up into her neck and through Afearia's face, causing her to tremble harder in stiff shakes as she still tries to fight the pain and remain in control. As her head trembles harder than the rest of her body, Afearia suddenly falls backwards and starts to jerk uncontrollably.

"STOP!" Afearia screams. "IT HURTS TOO BA-A-AAD! PLEASE! ARGH!"

Tears roll from her eyes as her skin becomes inflamed, bruised, and a bit of tearing starts to occur. Demeseus looks down at her with concern, but doesn't stop. Afearia, Demeseus thinks. You know I can't stop now. If I do that, you'll die immediately. As she coughs and briefly gargles, Demeseus' face becomes a bit regretful as he looks away for a moment.

The chains begin to move through her whole body at the speed of a fleeing snake, causing her to scream horse as she digs her nails in the dirt and kicks her feet around. Her body begins to move around in impossible ways, causing her to look mangled from time to time. She continues to beg Demeseus to stop as he stares at her with sad, suppressed revulsion.

"I CAN'T TAKE ANYMORE!" Afearia screams with her voice being distorted by the rushing chains in her neck. "I'M GOING INSANE! STOOOOP!"

Back at the camp, the man slowly opens his eyes before shooting up to the sounds of Afearia's tormented screams. Noticing she's missing, he quickly rushes off pass the camp to find her. He suddenly stops and turns back to grab the kids in his arms as he runs off as fast as possible with them.

Demeseus, still performing the pact, stares at Afearia with a troubled expression. This isn't good, he thinks. Not at all. She's going to break in two if this doesn't end soon.

Afearia's back continues to arch harder than each previous contortion as her eyes bulge in pain and her face is red and veiny like she's choking.

Suddenly, the chains instantly halt, holding her arched body in place. With an immediate retraction of all the chains, Afearia's body drops. Only two chains remain, slowly moving down the sides of her neck. Afearia lifelessly lies on the ground with wide eyes and an open mouth, barely breathing.

As the slithering chains make their way out, Demeseus makes a relived expression, "That was close. She almost died. This was nothing like last time." Demeseus suddenly looks upset and quickly turns his head. "What!? Why didn't you tell me that a pact without restrictions usually means death!?" His eyes express that he's listening to something before calmly looking back at Afearia. "No. I suppose it wouldn't."

As the chains move further out of her body, Afearia

finally blinks with a deep inhale of air. After taking a couple surprise breathes, she cringes just as the chains slip out of her palms. She turns over and painfully strains to do so, shaking in fatigue to sit up. With the same agonizing exhaustion, Afearia manages to slip one arm into her suit.

"Are you alright?" Demeseus asks.

Afearia, still breathing like she finished a light run, is hunched over a bit, looking into the dirt with her weary eyes, unable to respond right away. "I feel like every muscle from in my body has been worked beyond their limit," Afearia says with a horse voice. "Like to the edge before you experience an inevitable tear. I'm bruised and sore everywhere. It's never felt so bad."

"I'm sorry."

"I'll live. I still have this healing factor of his."

Demeseus flickers a few times. "Your exhaustion. It's high. I'm starting to fade."

"Sorry. I don't think I can hold on much longer. Sorry."

"No, you did great. As always, Afearia outperforms everyone as the strongest warrior the world's ever seen," he says with a confident smirk. She chuckles before coughing a bit. "Call me again as soon as possible. There is still more we must do."

"Demeseus... I...," she says with a bobbing head. But before she can say her last words, Afearia passes out, causing Eternity and Demeseus to disappear in a flash of white.

Far across Terra at Derexen's palace, Valerie is calmly walking through the hall while reading through multiple files in a folder. She adjusts the collar of her robe as she turns the corner to descend down the center stairs leading to the ground floor.

Once she reaches the bottom of the first half, the double doors to the palace entrance fling open wildly, brightening the room a bit by the sun's rays. Unexpectedly,

Carnavess comes strolling in before the doors slowly close.

"Well, this is a surprise," Carnavess says with a grin.

Valerie continues reading for a moment, "If you're looking for the king." She closes the folder by clasping her hand before fully addressing him, "He's not in right now."

"When I was heading this way," walking toward the middle of the room, "I felt someone brushing against my essence. You, right?" he says condescendingly with a swift, brief point of his finger.

"Correct."

"You sensory types cause a weird kind of itch when you probe me. But when I knew, I found a way to shake you."

"Yes, but I got a beat on you about half a mile from here."

"You did. But if I wanted to, I could've shown up right at your doorstep and you would be none the wiser."

"Oh?" she says with lack of care.

"You seem disinterested."

"You can travel between realms, right?" Carnavess has slightly surprised brows by her accusation. "It was a working theory. Thank you for confirming it."

"Heh," he smirks. "I figured you'd have panicked and scrambled when you felt my presence again." Carnavess makes an expression of stern realization as his eyes dart just a little. "But from those distances..." He looks up at her, "Perhaps I should've questioned that before." Valerie stares at him with no readable emotion. "Where's the runt?" he asks, looking around. "I know this is where he likes to hang his cowl."

"Under world law, you shall be—"

"What? Banished!?" he lightheartedly blurts, finding her words outlandish.

"Executed," Valerie sternly replies.

Carnavess chuckles. "Well, well. Look at you acting

all brave. You've grown—a bit."

"Funny. Didn't think you looked my way back in Elysium," she says, dismissing the folder she held in a puff of white smoke.

"Sorry, I tend to do that. When insects get in my eye view I ignore them. Because like the Mayfly," he raises his arm beside himself and summons ten orbs of light in a ring behind him, "They'll only live for a day. Now. Where's my favorite juvenile?" She says nothing while remaining still. "Oh? So you remember this. Since you're the weakest, I'm sure this will be—"

Valerie begins calmly approaching him, activating each orb with every step. All orbs are deployed by the time she reaches the bottom step. With smooth evasion tactic, Valerie warps from right to left ten times, still moving toward him before centering herself several meters from Carnavess.

Valerie stands firm with cold eyes on him, "I didn't think so back then. But today. That was probably the most inefficient attack I have ever seen. Atrocious."

Carnavess' grin lessens, "Watch it, kid. You think you know me."

"Lord Derexen and I know more about you than you think."

He stares at her for a moment before closing his eyes. "It changes nothing," he says, raising his hand before him.

As if to be from another dimension, a sound of howls erupt from a green and black light out of the floor, pushing up Carnavess' mysterious saw-like Empyrean Blade. He opens his eyes after wrapping his upside down hand around the grip, dismissing the light below. His sword briefly steams green and black before he holds it to his back between his shoulders.

Valerie narrows her eyes at him, "It changes everything."

She makes a mildly stern, yet nervous expression before rushing in to attack, with a leaping jump kick. Carnavess leans to the side from the attack, letting her pass by. In that moment, Carnavess does a blindingly fast arching sword swing from behind himself while still standing sideways, not even looking at her.

Valerie's eyes are wide as her body splits in two before hitting the floor. Blood sprays everywhere, soiling his garments while he remains still. "Sensory types. Such a useless breed." Suddenly, the spraying sound of blood abruptly stops. Carnavess looks down and sees his robe's completely clean. What? Carnavess thinks.

Coming from behind him doing a dragon kick is Valerie wearing her casual business attire. At the last second, Carnavess avoids the kick the same as he did before. As Valerie's about to pass him, she wraps her arm around his neck and swings herself around him, drawing her dagger from behind herself.

Just as she's about to stab him in the face, Carnavess flash warps toward the stairs knelt half down with his back to her. Carnavess slowly stands, "Should've known. Illusions is a core ability for your kind," he says as he turns to face her with a small cut on his forehead. "Not a wise choice to reveal your best talents so soon."

Valerie raises her arms before herself and crosses them while having one hand partially open and her dagger tightly gripped in the other. Carnavess smirks while lifting his sword's tip off the ground, "I don't know who you're trying to fool with that thing, but don't hurt yourself."

When Valerie takes a step forward, Carnavess quickly dashes first to make the offensive. He follows with a wide sword swipe. Surprisingly, Valerie blocks it with her dagger gripped tightly with two hands. She struggles as he press on. He turns his sword downward, sliding off her dagger. In that movement, he turns his back to Valerie and kicks her up into the air before quickly doing a reversal slash across her waist, cutting Valerie in two.

Grinning proudly was a short-lived act once he looks up at Valerie's body and sees she's grinning too. Her body disappears in a puff of white smoke.

Carnavess stands straight, chuckling in annoyance, "Oh ho-ho! Again!? Really!? You sensory types are nothing without your one-trick pony." Once again, Carnavess' sword discharges black and green steam before he swings it, "Disillusion!"

A transparent purple veil steadily moves across the room in a wave. When it passes the pillars near the doors, Valerie is revealed beside it. She quickly looks around as he stares at her.

"Yeah, I can see you," Carnavess says. Valerie grunts and comes out from behind the pillar. Carnavess' sword stops steaming. "You know I've been around for a very long time. I think I can dispel an illusion or two. And if you know me as well as you imply, that should be a given." Valerie gets back into her dagger stance. He makes a mischievous grin. "Hmm. I'm so tempted," he covertly says, confusing her. "Heh, fuck it. Why not."

Carnavess raises his hand before a swarm of large skulls made of light come flying out at Valerie. They all bypass her and crash into the wall, busting into a blinding light with a disruptive high pitched ring. Valerie shields her face with one arm as the ring and brightness fade at an unnaturally slow pace. Moments after, Carnavess appears behind her in mid sword swing.

She ducks low and rolls around him with closed eyes. Leaning forward on one leg, Carnavess does a back kicking sweep for her head. Valerie leans from the kick's range, seconds before he follows up with a sword stab she narrowly avoids by twisting to the side, causing the sword to be wedged between her arm and body.

Carnavess completes the attack by slashing upward in an attempt to remove her arm. She twists around him with her arm raised straight up to avoid the attack while positioning herself at his vulnerable side. Just as she's about to stab him in the ribs with her dagger, Carnavess snaps his fingers and the dimming light and ring amplify a maddening amount.

Because of the loud pitch, Valerie begins yelling as she holds her ears, though her screams are completely drowned out. She warps behind a distant pillar, trying her best to drown out the sounds as she grunts with shut eyes. With the combination of blinding light and high pitch noise, Valerie's senses are being distorted.

Unknown to her, Carnavess' sword pierces high up through the pillar she's hiding behind and quickly begins coming down on her. As the light and distorting noise begins to fade from the room, Valerie begins to faintly hear the stone above her beginning split apart before she warps away.

Valerie appears far behind him upside down with hand tucked in the waist of her pants. She smoothly throws a black carbon knife with a silver edged tip. Carnavess swiftly pulls the blade from the pillar and holds it behind him flatways, deflecting the throwing knife. She vanishes once again before he turns with a grin, carefully looking around the room.

Carnavess slowly walks across the room before suddenly dashing to his left, piercing his sword through another pillar. On the other side, Valerie has a stunned expression with blood coming from the corner of her mouth after being stabbed.

He leans around to the left of the pillar, "As fun as that may have been, I'm no fool."

Without warning, he yanks out his sword and stabs Valerie, who happens to be behind him with her dagger raised over head. The lifeless illusion behind the pillar puffs into white smoke. Carnavess lifts Valerie as she moans in agony before dropping her dagger to try and prevent herself from sliding down his blade.

"What's wrong?" Carnavess jokes. "Not an illusion this time? I've met many of your weak ancestors in my era. You always slip up by getting carried away with your illusions, thinking someone like me can't tell the difference between the real you and a phantom." He lowers the blade a bit while still keeping her toes off the floor before steadily jerking her back and forth. "Skewered jerky!" he jokes. He pulls her in from the neck, "I told you you were weak." Valerie mutters something. "What?"

"I said...," Valerie says with a smirk. She locks her arm with his, looking him directly in the eyes with confidence, "Welcome to the now."

Without warning, blood shoots from Carnavess' side with Valerie ducked low, bearing her dagger deep into him. Impossible! Carnavess thinks. Another illusion!? He glances at the fake Valerie on his sword before it puffs into smoke. He attempts to backhand Valerie, but she warps away before he can connect. She reappears to stab him on the other side.

He quickly turns to resist with a sword swing, but Valerie stops her attack, jumps far back and throws a carbon knife into his neck. Carnavess flash warps toward the double doors, holding his neck before kneeling down. The Valerie that was attacking him, stands straight and disappears before the true Valerie comes walking from behind another pillar, standing in the middle of the room.

"You think you know me and my illusionist, Carnavess. But you know nothing of what I'm capable of." She coldly watches him bleed out as a small pool starts to form on the floor beside him. "Pride goeth before a fall."

Carnavess remains gasping for breathes, struggling to stand. "Talking out your ass," he says with rasp before spurting a bit of blood from a cough, falling to one knee again. He glares at Valerie. "That's not even how that idiom's spoken."

Valerie crosses her arms, getting back into her dagger stance. "Like I said. Welcome to the now."

She takes a few steps before darting toward him. The moment she nears, Carnavess grins and chuckles before doing a heavy upper slash to her torso. Valerie's arm goes limp as she stumbles back with blood dripping. The attack had cut across her chest and deep into her deltoid. Clutching her bloody dagger, she watches Carnavess stand straight up, breathing calmly while staring dangerously at her.

"Not possible," Valerie says. "All of my attacks were vital. You shouldn't be standing, let alone moving."

"Oh?" he sternly says. "I thought you knew me. I admit I was a tad carless. But I still think your kind is trash."

Valerie focuses her determined eyes on him, "You will never hurt the king."

"So damn brave. Tell you what, kid. I'll give you one more shot before I cut your face clean off." He raises his arms. "Come on. Impress me." Taking a glance at his dripping wounds, Valerie warps, appearing by the stairs. Seeming a bit disappointed and bothered, Carnavess lowers his arms. "Less than stupid I see."

Suddenly, black and green steam endlessly seeps from Carnavess' sword. Soon after, he rushes in doing a sideways sweep with his blade. Valerie switches hands and blocks the attack with her dagger, deflecting his sword to the floor before suddenly puffing into white smoke. Carnavess grins and does a hard back kick, knocking Valerie across the room. She repeatedly coughs and turns over holding her stomach.

Carnavess turns and approaches her with a menacing grin, "That's all you sneaky belly floppers do. Attack from behind, attack from behind. And once that's out, illusions, illusions. Take those two rabbits out the hat, you all become trash at your opponent's feet."

157

Valerie glares at him. I don't know how he dispelled me just now, Valerie thinks. But it shouldn't matter. I purposely did meaningless things to stall the fight as he bleeds out. We are well over the time. Why isn't he dead?

She notices the bags under his eyes and that his skin has paled quite a bit, but his movements and vigor is still as if the battle had just begun. Valerie slowly stands as he nears, warping once more to reappear above him with dagger raised to be plunged in his head.

With no worry, Carnavess calmly slashes the illusion from above into nothingness without even moving his body. He raises his hand to his left, blocking Valerie's kick, holding her foot. She stands there with complete shock as he turns his head in her view.

"Nice kick," he says before effortlessly stabbing the illusionary Valerie. He turns with a smirk. That's how she got me last time, Carnavess thinks. This is a combination of illusions and sensory distortion. She's good.

Swiftly, Valerie comes from behind a nearby pillar and closes in on him. She does a sliding kick Carnavess avoids by jumping up. As she readies to leap up and attack him from below with her dagger, Carnavess slashes down with his blade going through her fading hands and suddenly halting inside her face. When he lands on his feet, the illusion suddenly pops, revealing Valerie struggling with her dagger to keep his attack back with one arm.

Losing the battle to halt him by the second, she glances at the steam and is immediately surprised as she stared at it. "Good girl," Carnavess mocks. "You're finally understanding what's happening here." His grin drops as he stares at her with dark intent. With no effort at all, he pushes down on her poor stance, hurting Valerie's arm enough for her to loudly groan. "We're done here."

With one arm, Carnavess uses the flat side of his sword and slaps her dagger to the floor before knocking

Valerie across the room and onto the stairs with a swift blow from his forearm. Before she can sit back up, he smashes his foot into her chest. She struggles to lift his foot, grunting under his weight before suddenly having a surprising realization.

"How?" she grunts. "I can't warp."

Carnavess dangles his sword tip over her face, "The Miasma. There's currently too much of it inside you. Your best tactics have been sealed." Valerie's eyes become panicked as his piercing stare and haunting voice digs into her. "You should've called your king." He holds his sword properly and raises it over his head. He looks down at her with his pale green eyes, not giving a hint of a smirk at his frightened foe. "Pride goeth before destruction, and a haughty spirit before a fall."

When the sword drops down, Valerie fearfully shuts her eyes. Filling her ears is the sound of clashed steel. Waiting for the pain that never came, Valerie opens her eyes, surprised to see Derexen standing beside her holding Catastrophe over her, blocking Carnavess' sword inches from her face.

Though she's concerned about his sudden arrival, there is a slight sense of relief on her face. Derexen is staring Carnavess dead in the eyes before glancing at his steaming sword, "Miasma. Odorless. No wonder she thought this steam served a different purpose."

"Well," Carnavess grins. "Look who's out from hiding."

Derexen takes one hand off his sword and roughly palms Valerie's chest. A sphere of light appears on his hand, extracting the green and black miasma from her body. Derexen's eyes remained locked with his foe while Carnavess glances at Valerie a couple times.

"So you knew," Carnavess says. "In another two minutes had I slain her or not, she would've been dead either way."

Valerie's surprised and looks over to Derexen. "I assumed," Derexen calmly says. "The true power of your sword's Miasma is it's sudden death effect. It first seals away your powers in a painless, unexpected way. With every breath, your opponents fall closer toward their own demise."

"Interesting. Then I expect—"

Without warning, Derexen and Valerie disappear in a puff of white smoke. Carnavess' sword hits the floor, leaving him a bit confused before turning toward the double doors behind him. Derexen is standing before the doors with Valerie behind him, still extracting the miasma from her body while carefully watching Carnavess.

"If that was to gain distance from my miasma, you're wasting your time," Carnavess informs them. "The room is filled with it, even though you can't see it."

Valerie stares at Derexen's back. Although he's trying to keep me alive, Valerie thinks, I'm starting to fear for his prolonged exposure. Valerie glares at Carnavess. Even if this is his power, he has been exposed to this much longer than both of us. Why isn't he—?

Derexen lowers his hand from Valerie and quickly summons Genesis before sheathing Catastrophe to his side through his black leather belt.

Derexen holds Genesis up before him, "Repel."

A transparent bubble of light grows out from the handle and surrounds Derexen and Valerie in its protecting light. Derexen holds the blade close to his chest, extracting the miasma. With a stern expression, Carnavess begins to approach them.

"This bubble has a six foot diameter," Derexen tells Valerie. "Stay in the center and only step a maximum of five feet from this point at all times." He turns his head halfway toward her. "Don't stray too far from my side." Valerie sternly nods at him before they stare at their nearing adversary.

Carnavess' sinister grin becomes wide as he slowly approaches while twirling his giant sword, creating thicker miasma. The entire room gains a smothering dark tint. The surface of much of the room begins to gradually corrode as the miasma gains strength. Carnavess makes a fist, causing dark liquid to drip from between his fingers. Derexen's bubble begins to flicker as it wards off the fog engulfing the room.

The room soon becomes too dark to see beyond a foot from the protective bubble. Derexen's eyes narrow a bit concernedly. He's getting serious, Derexen thinks. It's safe to say a single breath of his miasma now is instant death.

"Ooooh, how long it's been," Carnavess suavely says from the deep black, filling the air with his demonic desire. He opens his pale green eyes, piercing the dark as he stares down his foes. "Since I've felt this good."

Valerie stares at him with a shocked look before nervously focusing on the battle at hand. This is it, Valerie thinks. The last piece Derexen needed to know. His darkness... Derexen stomps his foot and spreads his arms in a grunt, tripling the brightness and the strength of his nearly collapsed bubble. She looks to Derexen with worry. I can feel it. Where ever lord Derexen just came from... he is not in top form. Valerie raises her hand, inching toward him. Maybe I can warp him out of here.

"Do it and I'll kill you," Derexen says.

"But—" Valerie utters.

"Don't get soft on me, Valerie. Prepare for battle or prepare to die."

Valerie's face becomes deadly with a true no nonsense appearance... A terrifying, lightless stare. "Does this mean I can?" she asks in a chilling voice.

Derexen hesitates to respond upon glancing in her direction. "If it comes to that... Just be on your guard and don't do anything I've long forbade."

"Yes, lord Derexen," she replies, greatly calming her dangerous stare.

Carnavess closes his eyes, concealing his location. For a moment—it is quiet. The sound of him briefly walking to their right is heard before he turns his raised fist upward. With a flick of his middle finger, a laughing black skull is released, colliding with Derexen's barrier and becoming a black ooze upon impact, eroding it like acid.

Derexen points to the weakened portion with his sword and tries to strengthen it, but the substances is eroding his defenses too quickly. Derexen bunches his brows a bit.

"Having trouble?" Carnavess asks. "The black erosion cannot be stopped. Once it comes in contact with a form of matter it will continue to eat until it's no more. Now, as I showed the girl before, I can release dozens of the cursed skulls in seconds." He opens his eyes with clouds of even darker smoke seeping from around his eyes. "This is what happens when cowards play defense." Multitudes of laughing murmurs are heard. "They die."

"Valerie," Derexen says. She looks to him. "I'm about to gamble our lives. Cover me."

"Of course," she says.

Silence blankets the room.

Shattering that calm like a flock of screaming birds, the skulls come flying at them, eroding all that they touch. Derexen clasps his hands tightly around Genesis.

"Purify!" Derexen shouts.

With a mighty explosion of light, the bubble expands with rapid speed while eradicating the miasma and the skulls. As this mighty light comes for Carnavess, a noticeably large smile comes across his face. He raises his palm and all the light generated by Derexen is being absorbed by Carnavess' hand, sequentially healing his wounds.

His pale skin returns to normal and the baggy eyes

he once had fade away. When the light was gone, the room returned to its normal hue. The steam from Carnavess' sword ends before he calmly stands straight.

"Well, that was quite a fun setback," Carnavess says with a sinister smile. "Thank you. I shall be returning to Elysium now."

Carnavess raises his sword over his shoulder and lets it rest on him before moving toward his foes. Valerie watches him closely, ready to strike while Derexen lowers his arms as he approaches. When Carnavess comes close enough, he walks right pass them with no interest to fight, surprising Valerie.

"I played right into your hand, didn't I?" Derexen asks.

"Perhaps," Carnavess replies.

"You needed a surge of light to mask your darkness as you return. Healing yourself was another added benefit."

"Heh, can't go back and raise suspicion. I took it upon myself to come here. This was not Elysium's intention. But I'm no fool." He turns to face them with Valerie being the only one to face him. "I played into your hand as well. Twice, I presume."

Derexen turns his head partway to him, "Twice?"

"Oh? So this girl wasn't cannon fodder like my Afearia?" Derexen fully faces Carnavess. "Perhaps I gave you too much credit."

"If Afearia isn't your trump card, then what is she?"

"Imagine a living weapon with enough power to destroy an entire species while killing itself in the process. Or in this case, greatly weaken a foundation in its mad dash to its doom before the last wall comes tumbling down. After that, the real conquest begins."

"Conquest?"

"It's all about control with you people," Valerie says with disgust.

"Dig through a few layers, and yes," Carnavess

says. "Dig a little deeper and," he snaps his fingers, sparking green flames for a moment. "You get dead. But don't worry. Few have gotten that far." A portal of light opens on the door. As he prepares to go through, he pauses, "By the way. How's the book?" Derexen bunches his brow a bit with Valerie seeming quite surprised. "Don't worry. I think I'm the only one who knows. It just wouldn't make sense if you didn't."

Carnavess turns his head to them, "I'm a bit jealous of how much you kids have been offered this generation. You've all been given such nice toys by a generous hand. But heed my words. The greatest lesson leading to adulthood is learning toys are only distractions from the truth only *real* men," with his index and middle fingers, he points to his eyes, then Derexen's, "can see."

He lowers his hand and steps into the portal, disappearing shortly before the portal does. Derexen slants his eyes in thought.

"What do you think he meant by that?" Valerie asks.

Derexen looks toward the doors, "In another life, there may have been a lot he would have taught me." She stares strangely at him before he turns toward her. "We may have created the wrong idea about Afearia while she was with us. But no matter. He doesn't know she's dead. Luckily, we removed her before she could do the intended damage she was meant to."

"Yes, that's for sure. But I still don't understand the reasoning. Why train her?"

"The illusion of freedom. It's perfectly unseen puppetry. As long as the puppet doesn't know it's on stings, it has no reason to look above."

"I suppose so, but—" Surprising her, Derexen has put his hand on her chest again before the light encircled his hand. "Sir?" she says, staring at him with confused eyes.

"Quiet. I have to remove the last of the miasma."

"But what about you?"

"Quiet, Valerie.

With much warmth, Valerie lightly smiles at him as he single-mindedly extracts the last of the miasma within her.

Meanwhile, back in the far dark plains of Terra, Afearia remains unconscious on the ground. Over the horizon, the man she saved is surprised to see her lying on the ground. He lowers the kids down and runs toward Afearia.

"Hey!?" he shouts. "Heeey!?"

The kids begin to wake from his shouting. Adrian sits up rubbing his eyes, "Wha…" He begins to notice the man running down the hill toward Afearia. "What is he—Anya!?" Veronica shoots up. "Anya!?" he shouts again before getting on his feet and running down the hill. Veronica quickly stands up and runs behind her brother.

The concerned man reaches her first and lifts Afearia's head off the ground, shaking her a bit. "Hey!? Wake up! Killer—"

Afearia immediately wraps her hand around his mouth before calmly opening her eyes. With his thick eyebrows, he expresses a nervous, nonthreatening face as she glares up at him. "I thought I made myself clear," Afearia says.

"Anya!?" Adrian shouts as him and his sister come racing toward her. Afearia releases the man and sits up just in time for them to hug her. "You're okay."

Afearia puts her arms around them, "Of course I am," she says with a smile. They lean from her with relieved faces. "How did you two find me?"

The kids look toward the man. "I heard screams from the distance and saw that you were gone," he says. "So I decided to go look for you."

"Is he lying?"

"We were sleep," Veronica replies.

"When we woke, you were on the ground," Adrian adds.

Afearia smiles at them before sternly looking at the man, "You carried them here?"

"I didn't want to leave them alone," he replies. "It can get dangerous out here in a heartbeat."

Afearia stares at him for a moment, gauging his sincerity before fully putting her leather suit and jacket on, "Though this may be an exploitive ploy, I will thank you for not being selfish and watching over them while I was away." She zips up her suit before standing. "You have earned the right to tell me your name."

He smiles before standing, "I go by the name Azaiah. But you can call me Zaiah for short."

"Zaiah?"

"That's right. Zaiah the Strong," he says with comical pride.

Afearia just stares at him with a deadpan expression before walking pass him, "I'm not calling you that," she says while putting on her eye patch. The kids quickly follow her back the way they came.

"Oh, come on! It's catchy!" he says before doing the same as the kids. "Can I at least know your name?"

"Quiet, Idiot."

"But I'm Zaiah."

"And now you're idiot."

Zaiah sighs in a playful bother as he heads back to the campsite with Afearia and the children.

Diary Entry #5212

Though it is forbidden to dig this deep, I must've read through over a hundred Guardian files. More than that at this point. But almost all of them were classified as failures. Even Demeseus was in there. What is the Elders definition of a flawed Guardian? I thought Demeseus was great. I tried to understand their system, thinking flawed meant those who died without finishing the mission. But they had Guardians who were successful also part of the failed files. I cross-checked to see if it was based on skill, but one of least talented Guardians were filed as successful. Ruto Vaz was filed as successful too. Perhaps if I compare Ruto and Demeseus I can figure out their system.

A Tool for Destruction

Chapter Seven

After returning to the campsite and gathering their things, Afearia and company proceed to their next location. While the siblings walk close to Afearia, Zaiah is forced to walk several feet behind them.

"Why do I have to be so far away!?" Zaiah asks.

"Because I don't trust you," Afearia replies.

"I mean you no harm. And hey, I made sure your kids were safe, didn't I? Even you admitted that." He begins to walk faster to catch up, "Hey—"

"Keep your distance, Terraian. I won't warn you again." He makes a sideways smile as he falls back. Adrian glances back. "Do not give him attention. Keep your eyes forward and ignore him."

"But—" Adrian was saying.

"Adrian," Afearia firmly says.

Adrian lowers his head. Veronica glances at her brother before looking to Afearia, "Anya, where are we going?"

"I already told you. Loiotes."

"How far is that?"

"Far. It's going to take some time before we get there."

"But I'm hungry."

"I swear your hunger is insatiable. Just get something from your bag. Something small."

Veronica pulls her bag forward and pulls out a large banana. "When are we going to eat sandwiches again?" she asks with a full mouth.

"I don't know," she replies with an annoyed tone.

"I want more subs. Can we have more subs?"

"Eventually."

"Oh, and cookies too! Like the crunchy ones. And the soft ones. And—"

Afearia stops, "Would you please!" The children are startled and freeze up, looking at her. She kneels down and wipes away the mushy banana from around Veronica's mouth. "I'm sorry. I didn't mean to shout." She brushes her hair with her hand. "You okay?" Veronica nods. Afearia stands with a sigh. "Give me a second."

Moving away, Afearia walks a fair distance from the kids. She pinches between her brows and loudly exhales before putting her hands on her hips in a huff.

"Is everything alright?" Zaiah asks, having had inched quite close to her without Afearia noticing.

"I thought I told you to stay back," she says, not facing him.

"Yeah, but—" He respectfully takes several steps back. "I just want to make sure you're okay. You seem troubled."

"Stop prying. All I did was yell at Veronica. Nothing serious."

"You wouldn't have walked off if it was only about that. What's the matter?"

Afearia faces him. "What do you want?" she asks with suspicion.

"I just wanted to see if you're okay—uh. I still don't know your name. Should I call you Anya?"

"No. No one in the world is allowed to call me Anya other than Adrian and Veronica."

"Then—"

"Enough. I will not disclose my name to you. And my problems are none of your business."

"So there is a problem," he smirks. Afearia leers at him. "Look, I get it. I'll leave it alone. But my advice. If your choices conflict with your own sense of fortitude, then it's the wrong choice." He begins to walk away. "Never compromise who you are."

Afearia looks to the ground, pondering his words for a moment before returning to the children. She looks up and notices the man was walking toward the kids.

"Hey, hey, five meters away from the children!" Afearia protectively shouts.

Zaiah freezes then jogs away from them, "Sorry!"

"Anya, is everything okay?" Veronica asks as Afearia nears. "I didn't mean to get you angry before."

"It wasn't you," Afearia says before standing before her. She lightly smiles as she looks into her big eyes. "Tell you what. I'll get us some delicious cookies and eat them with you."

"You promise?"

"Promise." She pats her head. "Come on. Let's hurry and get to Loiotes."

The three of them continue on with their journey while Zaiah follows a safe distance behind them. Afearia glances back at Zaiah who smiles at her and politely waves. She turns her head forward and rolls her eyes.

Traveling long and far, the team finally take a rest for the night. They had set up camp and sleep soundly, except for Afearia. Afearia had left the area and has placed herself far in the distance.

Out alone in the dark, Afearia's firing chains into the night while wielding Bastion. She swings as if to be facing an opponent before leaping back, attacking again and sidestepping to counter with a rise of rock columns after a foot stomp. She fires chains into it, pulls herself in toward it and slashes it in half with Bastion as she glides pass it. Afearia's sweaty, huffing and puffing with her limp chains on the ground and Bastion's tip in the dirt.

"Stop resting and practice," Demeseus says, standing far behind her with crossed arms. Eternity is behind him with Afearia's jacket neatly folded beside it.

"It's not—that simple," Afearia says with fatigue.

170

"It isn't suppose to be. Effort must be given every time you wield. You must push your old ideas of exertion to new heights."

Afearia lifts her sword and struggles to hold it with one hand before green seals appear on her arm. With an upturn of her hand, massive rock columns rise up from the ground. Her chains retract before another column she had called begins to rise beneath her. She jumps back while raising Bastion above her shoulder, but loses balance upon her landing due to the unexpected weight of Bastion.

"This is ridiculous!" she says. "Since when has Bastion been this heavy?"

"Since always. I've already told you—"

"Then don't tell me again!" she irritably says before standing.

Afearia turns her palm up and summons Demonweaver with no issues. She tosses it up high into the air and does a energizing shout, summoning Nebulous without issue as well. One chain slowly comes from Afearia's shoulder and takes Nebulous from her before she leaps forward at the columns, catching Demonweaver before coming down to slash them.

She slashes one in two and hops out of the way before it falls on her. She then jumps off another column toward one adjacent to it. Using her gaia magic, she makes the column fire pieces of itself at her. The chain holding Nebulous rises over her shoulder to point the blade tip at the coming rocks. Nebulous creates large ice spires and fires them at the nearing projectiles.

Dust and ice fill the air as she goes right through it and stabs the big rock. Afearia slashes the column in half and jumps toward the next one that happens to be slanted. She turns in midair and tosses Demonweaver into the falling half of the column she just cut. Taking Nebulous in hand, she guides her hand over the blade in synch with water covering it. She swings it and wets the surface of the slanted column before waving her hand to freeze it.

Landing crouched while holding Bastion out to her side, Afearia slides up the column, facing the falling half she recently destroyed. She fires a chain to wrap around Demonweaver. Using her great strength, Afearia pulls the slashed column toward her with much speed.

Afearia grips Bastion with two hands, hurls it into the coming rock, smashing it to bits. With the rock bits flying in all directions, she raises her hand to call Bastion back as a means of defense. But as it vaguely materializes in her hand, she fails to call it back.

Afearia's hit in the stomach and the chest, knocking the air out of her and her body off the column. As she falls toward the ground, she regains control with an angry expression. Using her manipulation of the wind, she slows her fall and lands on the ground roughly, not even sticking the landing. The rocks come down on her and she yells in frustration before green seals appear on her arm and she punches the ground.

Several layers of thick rock shields protect her from the rubble by nearly covering her whole body. When the falling stopped, the shields explode the rocks all over the field with Afearia standing in an angry huffing manner.

"That went completely wrong!" Afearia complains.

"Maybe you should start slower," Demeseus says. "You're jumping straight into complex practices."

"Maybe you should—!" Afearia catches herself and runs her hands through her hair as she paces around for a moment.

"Either something is bothering you or you owe me an apology. That's twice you snapped at me, Afearia."

"Regardless, I owe you an apology." She breathes out slowly to calm herself before facing him. "I'm sorry. I know you're just trying to help. It's just... frustrating. I've never been on this side of it before."

"The side of what?"

"Mediocrity. To put forth so much of myself and still fall short of what I once was when the world was so different to me. No matter where I walked or what I faced there wasn't much doubt in my mind that I could truly be defeated. I saw myself here," she expresses with her hand at the highest point of her body. "And now I'm here," she says with her hand below her waist. "Is this what it's like to not be gifted? To be like everyone else? Me dying... It really feels like I've been reborn in another life. A less lustrous life where everything is bronze and I'm at best a dull iron."

Demeseus uncrosses his arms. "It's the curse of being gifted. Though all who are not will envy you at some point for having a natural talent at excelling at all you touch. There is a stark difference between the two. The gifted and the ninety-nine percent. From the start, people like me who didn't possess natural talent fought tooth and nail everyday to be more than we were yesterday. To stand shoulder to shoulder or even above those godly people who made light of all our struggles just by simply attempting what we found so impossible."

Afearia, now seeming less frustrated, listened carefully as Demeseus elaborated. "Whether it's a sport, a skill, a matter of IQ, there will always be that one person who just is. So you fight and climb and bleed and scream just to reach the height of this gifted being. And when you do, you only find out that they've already surpassed this level long before you even got halfway... It's a never ending need to reach that world of the one percent that you may never reach. Some give up. But others... They don't know the meaning of the word."

"Because of this," Demeseus continues, "we already knew what hard work and dedication was. We already knew what it looked like and the kind of fruit it bore. Because we weren't special. We weren't gifted. So for us, gaining our wings in the sky was a challenge from the start, while you and many others like you were already born to fly. Through adversity, we know how to fly head first into a storm and come out roughed up because that has been our whole journey. But you. Even a minor storm will knock a gifted person on their ass because they have no idea what a genuine struggle really is."

"And you're saying that's where I stand," Afearia ponders.

"Yes. To say you are not gifted anymore is stupid."

"Well, I think—"

"No, I mean what I'm saying to you here. Your gifts have been shackled up to this point. And they still are when it comes to other hindrances. What you're doing now is learning to walk. That's all. You've started your life running. Now it's time to take a step back and learn to walk."

Afearia sighs. "Even still. Demeseus, I don't have time to build myself up like that."

"What's the rush? As far as the government knows, you're dead. You have time. You don't need to force this progression."

She wipes her face with irritation, "But I do."

"You're not making sense."

"Demeseus, just understand that I do," she sternly says.

He stares at her for a moment, trying to understand her. "Alright. What's really going on?"

"Nothing."

"I think we've been together long enough for me to know when something's off with you. It becomes more apparent when I'm telling you something and you swear it doesn't work for you. What is the underlining reason for your impatience?"

With anxious brows, Afearia stares at Demeseus. "What...? What do you want me to say? It's nothing. I just don't have the time you think."

"Because?"

"Demeseus!?" She walks from him before abruptly turning toward him, "I'm getting pressured by all sides," she says, returning to where she was standing."

"By who?"

"It's… the children."

"The children?"

"They're counting on me to get them home. The people of Terra are counting on me too. And the longer I take, the faster Derexen will potentially regain the little power he's lost."

"I can understand that. I can. But haste will only—"

"I've already wasted enough time! I've been here for months, fast approaching a year and I have yet to do any real impact to this prison!"

"No impact? Was destroying that generator nothing? What about when you liberated Armport from that government official? What about saving your friends and keeping those kids safe every day."

Afearia waits for him to say more. "Is that all you've got?"

"What?" he says with an appalled expression.

"Only one of those things had a real worldwide impact. And you know what else? That sleazy doctor got more right about me than wrong. I've ruined more lives than I saved. Demeseus, I've condemned entire towns more than once. I've had people die because of my inefficiency to act fast enough or to realize the size of the danger. And the lives I saved. They're doomed for just knowing me," speaking lowly.

Demeseus shocked expression had not changed. "What the? What the hell's wrong with you? I've never…" He soon simmers to a face of pity. "Afearia… How much did you lose that day?"

She tightens her jaw in shame. "More than I wish to admit." She puts her hand to her face. "I don't know if it's all just sinking in or I really am this coming calamity that these Terraians fear."

Afearia lowers her hand and looks up at the stars, "You know, I thought—. I thought if I just do as I was told, things would turn out alright. That I already had all I needed to make a difference down here. I thought I could save people without destroying myself in the process. But I was wrong. I couldn't do either. I can't follow orders and be who I wish to be. My ideals and their expectations cannot co-exist. I'm trapped," she mutters, shaking her head.

"Afearia, what are you saying?" Demeseus asks with concern.

She looks in his direction, almost as if she wanted him to see through her coming words. "Duty over self—is the governing law of a Lightbringer. And you cannot defy it." Afearia walks over and picks Bastion from the dirt before about-facing with sword raised. "Let's continue."

"Afearia—"

"I'm ready to keep practicing." She swings her sword and takes a straight stance, holding Bastion's tip to the sky with the edge facing her while she faces the fallen rubble. "Are you going to help me or not?"

"Just tell me one thing." She turns partway to him. "Does it require sacrifice? The kind that stains the soul?"

She turns from him, "Did Alexander?" He makes a solemn displeased expression. "Sometimes... your back's against the wall. And it's not bricks pushing up against you. It's..." Her eyes slant to the ground. "Let's continue. You need not to worry about me."

"For once, it's not you I'm worried about."

"Good. At least your heart's in the right place." She slams her sword down, raising several rock columns up for her training.

Hours later, she finishes her practice session and returns to the camp. She lies down in a loud huff before closing her eyes to sleep.

The following morning, Afearia's looking through the map with the children standing beside her. "Are we close?" Veronica asks.

"I doubt it," Afearia replies. "But," she says, running her finger across the map. "If we cut through the town Hillstar instead of going around it, we'll reach Loiotes faster."

Adrian looks over at Zaiah who's patiently sitting with folded legs, harmlessly swaying to a tune he's humming. "Is he okay?" Adrian asks.

Afearia glances fairly quickly at Zaiah. "He's fine," she says with complete lack of concern. "You know what's odd about that idiot? I've been without food and water before. After two or more days without water it becomes pretty hard to do anything. But he..." The three of them look his way and Zaiah notices before politely waving at them.

They look back down at the map. "He really does seem fine," Veronica says.

"Then he's fine," Afearia says before standing and rolling the map.

"But we've been out here for over a week," Adrian says.

"I know." She glances at Zaiah again. "Have you two been giving him anything to eat or drink?"

"No."

"Yes," Veronica nervously says.

"Why!?" Afearia loudly asks. "This is like feeding a stray cat. The longer you feed it the longer it will come around."

"I'm sorry, Anya. But I didn't want him to die out here since he's been so nice to us."

"When will you learn. He's tricking you. People are not nice. They're dangerous. You don't know what he's capable of. He may actually be a government spy."

"I'm sorry," she sadly says.

Afearia shakes her head and kneels down to Veronica, "You are very kind, Veronica. Much nicer than I. But in this world, that kindness will be used against you in every way. You have to be careful who you show your heart to, okay?"

"Okay." Afearia stands and looks to Zaiah. "Excuse me," she says before approaching him.

Zaiah sees her nearing and stands with a smile, "What's up? We moving on?"

Afearia intimidates him when she pushes Zaiah with two fingers, "Stay away from my kids."

"What are you talking about?"

"You know I don't want you near us. I don't care if they approach you first. You back yourself up!"

"Alright, I got it," he says, genuinely accepting of her demand.

Afearia turns and walks away before stopping to point at him again, "And stop taking their food. I meant what I said. I will let you starve out here. It's your own doing."

"I understand." Afearia begins to walk away, "If I may. Where are we going?"

"*We* aren't going anywhere. You're just an annoying stalker."

Unfazed by her callousness, Zaiah just watches her walk away. As Afearia walks pass the kids, she gestures for them to follow in order to continue their journey.

Long after departing, Afearia is cautiously looking around.

Something's been troubling me since we've started traveling again, Afearia thinks. Although I can't sense darkness anymore, why have we yet to be attacked by wild Demis? I've theorized there being an active generator nearby but there have yet to be signs of that. No rumbles, no shots of darkness. Nothing. There may be another reason Demis are absent from this region. You would think I'd find this lack of danger good. But it's quite the opposite. With hyperactive senses I feel like I'm going to explode.

"Anya?" Adrian says, trying to get Afearia's attention. "Anya? Anya?"

She blinks a couple times, leaving her own thoughts before looking to him, "Yes, Adrian?"

"That man, Zaiah. He's trailing us further back than usual." She looks back at him. "You said if he did anything strange and we see it we should tell you."

Afearia narrows her eyes on him since he was too far to accurately identify. "What is he up to?" she suspiciously asks herself. A gentle wind blows from behind them. Afearia's face mellows with a hint of confusion. "Do you guys smell flowers? Like roses maybe?" The kids glance at each other, shaking their heads. "Never mind. It must be my imagination."

Despite her suspicion, Afearia and the children continue their travels for the better part of the day before stopping to rest. As the three of them sit around the campfire eating bread and soup, Afearia's facing in Zaiah's direction who's sitting at a greater distance than ever before.

He knows we stopped, Afearia thinks. But he insist to stay a great distance from us. From here, at least I can tell what he's doing.

"Anaya, try the chicken soup," Adrian says, handing her his can.

"Huh?" Afearia says, being taken from thought. "Oh, okay." She takes his can and eats some. "Yeah, it's really good. Want to trade?" They trade cans and resume eating. "Hey, you guys have been doing pretty well keeping up on these lengthy travels. Your bodies must be getting used to it."

Adrian weakly chuckles, "Yeah, I guess," he says,

179

glancing at his sister.

Afearia takes a bite of her bread while staring at Veronica. "You're not hungry?"

Veronica's can is unopened and her bread is untouched as she sits tightly with knees to her chest. "I am," Veronica says with a smile. "I'm gonna eat real soon."

"Veronica... You look tired."

"I do? But I feel fine though."

"Okay." She glances back at Zaiah. "I'll be back," she says upon standing. She pats Veronica's head while walking pass her, "Eat something."

"Okay!"she says positively.

Veronica looks back and sees Afearia's walked a bit from the camp. She looks to the bread and reaches for it with a trembling hand. She slowly raises it to her mouth, struggling to do so.

Adrian takes it from her and breaks off a piece to put in her mouth. He quickly pops the can open and stirs the soup inside. "I really hope Hillstar is close," Adrian says. "You're really overdoing it," he says as he raises a full spoon of soup to her mouth.

Veronica slurps the soup off the spoon before he dips into the can for more. "But we're still not telling Anya, right?" Veronica asks.

"She'll find out soon if you don't get better. Stop talking and eat so you can go to sleep," he says as he raises another spoon full.

Away from the camp, Zaiah's sitting calmly with folded legs and closed eyes before Afearia steps before him. Shortly after, he slowly opens his eyes and looks to Afearia with a light smile.

"Hey," Zaiah greets.

"Why are you—?" Afearia looks around strangely, getting a whiff of the flowery scent she smelled before. "Do you—?" she was saying before looking down at him.

Zaiah just stares up blankly at her. "Never mind. Why are you traveling so far behind us?"

"Is that a problem? I don't want to cause any more trouble for you."

"If that were true, you would leave us alone."

"I'm bothering you guys?"

"You're bothering me!"

"I'm sorry you feel that way. Would it help if I don't talk?"

"It'll help if you go away." Zaiah just stares at her for a moment before kindly smiling, irritating her further. "I'm warning you. Whatever you're planning won't work. I'm watching you."

"Thank you," he politely says.

Afearia grumbles before storming off. When she returns, the kids had finished eating and Veronica's lying down sleeping.

"That man is aggravating," Afearia says as she sits.

"What happened?" Adrian asks.

"He refuses to leave us alone."

"But isn't he doing as you asked?"

"That isn't the point. I don't want him near us at all."

"Why?"

"Because I don't trust him. I'm not interested in being fooled anymore."

"But he doesn't seem dangerous, Anya."

"I'm not doing this again. We already had this conversation." Afearia watches Veronica sleep as she adjusts herself a bit beneath the blanket. "She's already sleep."

"Yeah, she was pretty tired."

"Hmm. I guess we can set out a little later than I intended then."

"I think we should leave when you decided before. I think Veronica just needs a good bed to sleep in."

"I think you're right. If we move fast and take one break we should be able to get there later today."

"Then I better sleep," he says before standing to lie with his sister.

"Okay."

He crawls under the blanket with Veronica, "Goodnight, Anya."

"Night."

Long after the children had fallen asleep, Afearia remains awake, staring at Zaiah in the distance. Why is he still awake? Afearia thinks. I can't tell if he's facing me or not, but he hasn't moved in a while. Is he sleeping sitting up? Though I need to practice, I should keep an eye on this guy. Afearia grunts before lying down and using her jacket as a blanket.

Several hours after lying down to sleep, Afearia wakes with blurry vision. She sits up rubbing her eyes before looking into the distance. Her eyes widen as she looks around in a near panic. Zaiah was nowhere to be seen. She nudges the kids several times.

"Wake up guys," she hastily says. "Get up."

The kids begin to wake while Afearia keeps looking for Zaiah until the clouds roll pass the moon to lighten up the area. She then sees Zaiah standing in the distance looking back at them.

"Is everything alright!?" Zaiah shouts for her to hear.

Afearia's expression becomes annoyed. This guy..., Afearia thinks.

"Anya?" Veronica says. Afearia looks down at her weary eyes. "I don't mean to be a burden, but can we rest at Hillstar?"

"I don't think we can rest as long as you think." She suspiciously looks at Zaiah. "I can give you a day at best. But after that we must move on."

"Okay."

They gather their things and continue on their journey with Zaiah following far behind. Though they haven't been traveling long, Veronica had been roughly coughing for the past half mile. Adrian pats her back as she coughs again.

"Are you alright?" Afearia asks.

"I'm fine," Veronica replies before coughing again. Afearia stops and kneels before her. Veronica's face is damp and her eyes are droopy. Afearia puts her hand to Veronica's forehead. "Anya, I'm fine."

Afearia suddenly picks Veronica up and puts her on her back as they proceed. "You are not fine. You have a fever and a slight wheeze in your cough."

"That wheeze has always been there," Adrian says. "She has an unknown breathing problem that comes and goes. Mom never got it checked."

"I figured she had one from when we first met."

"Anya, put me down... I'm fine," Veronica says as she slowly drifts to sleep.

Afearia feels her weight fall on her back as she sleeps. I don't want to alarm Adrian, Afearia thinks, but depending on how bad her prior condition was, a fever tends to make many things worse. And veronica's lungs sound a bit blocked.

After traveling at a steady pace, Afearia and her team reach Hillstar. The four of them walk the less than busy streets where few pedestrians move about their day shopping and entering their houses.

The houses are small like convenience stores. The buildings throughout the small town have a unique design similar to cabins in size and design with brownish white tops while the other buildings are of modern design.

A bit after Afearia and the children enter the town, Zaiah enters and slouches his shoulders with a sigh of relief before standing straight with a smile. "We made it!" he says cheerfully.

Adrian and Afearia stop and look back at Zaiah.
"Wait here," she says to Adrian before approaching Zaiah.
She stops a couple feet from him saying nothing.

Zaiah looks around, seeming a bit uncomfortable,
"Uh—"

"I need you to stop following us now."

"Is something wrong?"

"It's time for us to part ways. You can start your life
over in this town."

"But—"

"Leave us," she says as she turns to walk away.
Taking two steps from her position, she bumps into Adrian
standing behind her. "Adrian!?" surprised he was standing
so close. "What are you doing? I told you to stay put."

"But, Anya, your hair."

"What about it?"

"You said you need to stay out of sight by hiding
your features. I went through my bag and I didn't find your
scarf."

Afearia pondered for a moment. "Yeah. I definitely
lost it along the way," she says, slightly turning her head in
Zaiah's direction. "I'll need to get another if I plan to move
through here."

"I'll get it," Zaiah says.

It's silent for a moment before she continues to
address Adrian, "I could send you in, but I'm a little
paranoid after last time."

"I'll do it," Zaiah says again.

"Perhaps we should continue traveling to Loiotes,"
she says, ignoring him.

"But Veronica needs rest," Adrian says.

"But we're out of options." Adrian glances at Zaiah
and then sadly looks at Afearia. She looks ahead of him,
"There has to be something I haven't thought of."

"I can do it, really," Zaiah continues to suggest.

"Anya…," Adrian says as Afearia's brow twitches

in annoyance.

"It's not a problem. I can—"

Afearia quickly turned to him, "Idiot, it appears you don't listen when people tell you to go away."

Zaiah looks to the seemly pale Veronica. "That child needs nutrients and rest."

"I didn't ask for your weigh in… But I may have some use for you. I'm in a bind you can assist with," she says sarcastically. "I don't need your help, but this is faster. Adrian, take some money out my bag." He does as he's asked and brings it to her. "Thank you. Idiot," addressing Zaiah. "I need you to go get me a scarf. In exchange, you can buy yourself some clothes too. That way, I owe you nothing."

"Alright."

When he stepped forward, she stepped further in front of Adrian. She holds her hand out for Adrian to give her the money. Once he does, she hands it to Zaiah. When he tries to take it, she doesn't let it go.

"If you betray us, you'll be sorry," Afearia warns him.

Zaiah looks her in the eye before she released the money. He nods and heads into the town. After much waiting around, Adrian's sitting on the ground with his sleeping sister in his arms. Afearia's impatiently looking toward the town while tapping her foot with hands on her hips.

She turns to Adrian, not talking directly to him, "This is taking too long. He's not coming back. That selfish little—"

"Anya, look!" Adrian says, pointing toward the town.

She turns around to see Zaiah slowly approach with a large bag and a smaller bag. Afearia practically stomps toward him, "Where were you!?" Afearia snatches the large bag from him before ruffling through it.

"The store was actually further in than I thought," Zaiah replies. "And getting your items were—"

Afearia snatches up an item from the bag, "What the heck is this!?" she says, holding up a long tan garment.

"Oh, I couldn't find a scarf good enough to hold your hair so I got you—"

"What's this!?" she says, holding up a small plan white brooch with pins.

"It's a brooch. It can be used to pin the shawl to create a hijab appearance." Afearia just stands frozen, staring at him with anger. "In a hijab, concealing your unique features will be much easier. Here, let me," he says, reaching for her.

She pulls away from him, "I can figure this out myself. Now move."

"Uh, okay."

Zaiah walks pass her as she glares at him for a moment. She looks down at the bag of items, specifically the ones he got her as she stares a bit confused at them.

"Hey, I got you a hero sandwich, champ," Zaiah says to Adrian.

Afearia quickly turns to them, "Hey, stay away from—" Zaiah and Adrian are far from each other as they stare oddly at her overreaction.

"He tossed it to me, Anya," Adrian says.

"Hmm... it could be poisoned. Give it back."

"But I'm—"

"Give it back!"

Adrian sadly tosses it back to Zaiah as it rolls across the ground to his feet. "Poisoned?" Zaiah says as he kneels down to grab the sandwich and pull away the wrapping. He bites into the sandwich and smiles. "Poison's never been so good!"

"You think you're funny?" Afearia sternly asks. He swallows the food and rewraps it before rolling it back to Adrian. "Hey!?"

"If it's poisoned we'll both get sick. No fool would lace a sandwich and ingest it himself in order to gain trust."

Afearia gives him a sideways look of distrust. Afearia looks to Adrian's puppy dog eyes before reluctantly waving him off a couple times to eat the sandwich. He quickly preps up and begins stuffing his face. Zaiah kindly smiles at the irritated Afearia. She scowls harder at him, causing Zaiah to look away.

By the time Adrian finishes his sandwich, Afearia finishes using the items she received to conceal herself. "Alright, Adrian, let's go," she says, standing behind him.

Adrian turns and bursts out laughing, "What are you—!?" unable to finish, he begins laughing again.

Zaiah turns in their direction, "What's–oo–who!" he hilariously blurts with hand over his mouth.

Afearia has wrapped her head down to the shoulders like a mummy. The pins and brooch are arranged without purpose to the shawl.

"What?" Afearia says with a shrug.

"I'm sorry," Zaiah says, trying to control his laughter, "but that's not how the hijab looks."

"I know. I didn't want to wear it that way," she claims.

"Really?" he says with disbelief.

"No!" Adrian blurts in his ongoing laughter.

Afearia looks in Adrian's direction, ending his laughter a little. Zaiah simmers down and puts his hand over his face as his laughing slowly stops. "Regardless, you can't go walking around like that."

"Why not?" Afearia asks.

"You'll draw attention with your odd appearance. I was drawing looks just by walking around like this. Come on, let me do it for you."

"No."

"I'm just trying to help you. You can't put together something you've never seen before. I mean you no harm."

"And I should trust you?" He remains calm and innocent as she stares at him. "No funny business. I'm not kidding."

"I swear," he says with his hands up.

After taking one step, she halts him, "Stop. You stay where you are."

She approaches Zaiah and stands a few inches from him. Zaiah smiles and raises his hands, touching the shawl, "This may be the closest we—"

A sharp poke is felt against his stomach. He looks down and sees the tip of Demonweaver coming from her palm. "No funny business," she says with a menacing glare.

He looks back up at her with a calmer expression. "I promise." She retracts the blade a couple inches. "Please, let's sit." They sit before Zaiah slowly removes the shawl from her head. She keeps her eyes closed until he removes it fully. Being up close, he begins admiring the sharp contours of her face... like he's seeing an ethereal woman. A higher being. "Wow..."

Afearia opens her left eye, "What?" she asks with annoyance in her voice.

"Nothing...," he says with a clean sincerity.

Afearia's bothered expression calmed a bit after his strange reaction. Zaiah looks back down at the shawl he's readying. He rests it unevenly on her head before bringing both sides together to be pinned with the brooch under her chin.

Afearia flinches from the light tickle under her chin, "Don't touch me so much!" she exclaimed.

"Sorry," he calmly says with a gentle focus.

Afearia stares at him with both eyes, seemingly pouting a bit, not realizing she's doing either of these actions. Shortly after, Zaiah finishes, giving her the hijab appearance while covering the top right side of her face. Underneath is her long braid loosely wrapped around her neck.

"Looks good," Zaiah enthusiastically says upon their standing.

"Whatever," she says while walking away from him. "Let's go, Adrian," picking up Veronica.

The three of them walk onward and enter Hillstar. As they move through the streets, Veronica briefly coughs and mumbles in her sleep.

She doesn't sound good, Afearia thinks. Afearia stops a passing pedestrian and asks for directions to reach the nearest motel. After getting the information she needs, Afearia hastily walks to the motel. She glances at Adrian struggling to keep up, "We need to get her inside. She's feels hotter."

"Don't worry about me," Adrian says. "I just want her to be okay."

Moving quickly, the three of them arrive at the small motel. Afearia sits Veronica on the lobby bench before Adrian sits beside her, leaning his sister into his arms. She slightly opens her puffy red eyes.

"Hey, sweetheart," Afearia says, "it's going to be okay. We're going to get you rested, alright?" She looks to Adrian, "Watch her," she says before heading toward the entrance. Just as Zaiah enters, Afearia walks him backwards through the doors with her index finger pushing his forehead. "Stop," she tells him. Afearia crosses her arms. "I won't let you sleep in the same room as us. Get lost."

"Where will I go?" Zaiah asks.

"I don't care. Go anywhere you wish, just not with us."

"Okay, but—"

"Enough from you. Do yourself a favor and just stay away."

"But—"

Afearia turns around and goes inside, leaving Zaiah staring at the closing doors. After leaving him behind,

Afearia gets herself a room key and approaches the kids.

"Anya, where's Zaiah?" Adrian asks.

"The idiot's gone," Afearia answers as she picks up Veronica into her arms. She immediately becomes alarmed. "She's burning up!" Afearia races toward the narrow stairs, "Room 215, Adrian! Hey, hey, you with me?" she says to Veronica while making her way down the hall.

"Running," Veronica slurs.

Afearia quickly opens the room door and rushes inside to lay Veronica on the bed. She rushes to the bathroom and turns on the light to fill the tub with water. She comes back in the room, turns on the room light and sits beside Veronica, sitting her up.

"Veronica, sweetie, you need to wake up now, okay?" Afearia says while removing her clothes. "Veronica, do you hear me?"

"Anya running," Veronica says, barely awake with her closed eyes.

She scoops Veronica into her arms and takes her to the bathroom. Afearia kneels down to turn off the water.

"Veronica, brace yourself. You're not going to like this." Afearia submerges half of Veronica's body in the tub of cold water. Immediately, her red eyes open up and she screams and panics as she tries to escape the tub. Afearia forces her back into the water while she cries and screams for her to stop. "You have an intense fever. I need to drop your body temperature."

As she struggles to get out, Adrian comes rushing into the bathroom. After awhile, Veronica fights Afearia less as her body begins to acclimate to the temperature. She settles down and shivers in the water. Afearia lovingly rubs Veronica's back and smiles kindly.

"Veronica, I'm going to submerge your head under for five seconds."

"No-no-no, Anya," Veronica stutters as she shivers. "I'll die."

"I would never bring harm to you. You are not going to die. Not as long as I'm here with you." Veronica hesitates, but nods. "I'm going to do it now. Hold your breath. Adrian, get your sister's towel out the bag."

When he leaves to get her towel, Afearia slowly dunks her head under. When the time was up, Veronica shoots up coughing.

"It's over," Afearia said, softly smiling at Veronica. Adrian hands her the towel, "Thank you," she says before wrapping Veronica snuggly and carrying her out the tub. "Adrian, drain the tub please."

Afearia sits Veronica's shivering body at the edge of the bed before going into her bag grabbing her PJs. She carefully dries her off and dresses her with the same soft, motherly smile she had in the bathroom.

"I see you're falling asleep already," Afearia says. She finishes putting on her shirt and grabs a water bottle, twisting off the cap. "Drink some of this before you lie down." Veronica does as she's asked and drops to the bed. Afearia shakes her head and picks her up to pull the covers back and lay her underneath. She tucks her in and kisses her forehead. Afearia turns to Adrian, "You okay?"

"Is she?" Adrian asks.

"She will be." Afearia stands and grabs some money out her bag. "I'm going out to get us some supplies. I'll bring food too. We'll stay here until she gets better," she says while moving toward the door. "Keep it down while I'm out."

She leaves the room and heads downstairs. The lobby floor was darker than when she first came into the building. She looked to the desk and saw no one present. As she's about to walk out the door, a voice seeps from the dark corner of the steps near the front desk.

"Still playing human?"

Afearia jumps up in alarm and quickly turns to face the shadowy area near the stairs. Creeping out from the dark to reveal himself is Carnavess.

"Fa-Father Carnavess?" Afearia stutters in disbelief. "You're-you're supposed to be—"

"Gone? No, I'm never truly gone. I still have business with you. You remember what we talked about?"

"You said I had a month."

Carnavess grins, "There's been a change of plans. I think we've given you more than enough time to make a crack in this feeble kingdom."

"But—"

"This isn't up for discussion. Go out there and flush him out. Or you rather I go upstairs and pay those brats a visit?" Afearia stared at him with fearful eyes of reluctance. "Then I'll be back shortly."

As he turns to go upstairs, Afearia steps forward in desperation, "Wait! Just... leave them alone. I won't defy you any longer. I will—initiate your demand," she says with a defeated posture.

His sinister grin grows. "Good. You have one night. And one night only." She looks up at him in hesitation. "I would get going if I were you." Afearia lowers her eyes and steps out the door.

Standing against the building, Afearia stares at the ground before removing her shawl and clutching it in her hand. She tries to hold on to it but releases it out of defeat. With much suppressed anguish, she moves her eyes down the avenue before narrowing her stare and proceeding through the street.

As she moves through the street and around the corner, Zaiah comes from the building's alley with a sad expression.

Though it was late, Afearia had traveled a fair distance from the motel and into the semi populated streets with her head down and nothing to conceal her unique features. Not moving aside, she was bumping into pedestrians, aggravating many as they move along.

Afearia suddenly stops, causing a man to walk right into her. He stumbled back and began to yell at her until she lifts her head to glare at him with her right eye. He freezes in fear. The man quickly turned around and began to run.

She raises her arm, grits her teeth in distain and fires a chain into the man's back. He yells upon impact and hits the ground with the chain returning to her. Everyone around Afearia stops. All the chatter ceases with only the sound of Afearia's chain dropping to the ground. She grips it tightly and immediately whips several people to the ground.

A man took a single step to run until she wraps her chain around his neck and pulls him in. She lifts him off his feet with partly bunched brows, but no readable emotions. Like trash, she takes him and hurls him into the closest building's window, sparking panic around her as everyone runs away.

Afearia wildly swings her chains around and fires a few at the people, hitting and puncturing buildings and a few cars. After a while, as people screamed and fled from her destruction and the growing fires coming from store gas mains and electrical lines, Carnavess' voice infects the air:

"You know that won't be enough."

Afearia turns to face Carnavess, "No, this should be enough. Their panic will spread and—"

"Not fast enough. I want the king. This will only alert minor authorities." Coming from down the street, Afearia sees five officers rushing her way. "See. Unless you start taking lives, he'll never come."

Surprised by his words, Afearia looks his way, but Carnavess had already fled the area. Once close enough, the officers stop and point their guns at her.

"Put your hands up," an officer says to Afearia. She turns halfway to them with her head held low. "I said hands up!"

Afearia looks to the darkest corner of the burning building and sees Carnavess staring sternly at her. He raises his hand a bit and the glimmer of his red chain appears. Fear strikes Afearia before she fires a chain at the officers, whipping it to disarm them. She whips it around again at their legs, knocking them to the ground.

She fires five chains into the ground only to have them reappear by wrapping around their necks, binding and tightening lightly. She raises her arm, readying the command to choke them to death, but the confliction on her face becomes evident.

"Now squeeze," Carnavess says with some menace. Afearia's brows twitch as she clenches her jaw, reluctant to finish the job. "Squeeze!"

Just as she seemed as if she'll do it, she's halted by a familiar voice, "Stop!"

Afearia stares further into the distance and sees Zaiah approaching the fallen men. "You," she says with annoyance.

"Release them," he demands, standing near the officers.

She smirks, "And what will you do if I don't, human?"

"Surrender?" Zaiah jokes, not cracking a smile out of her. "Look, this...," he says, looking around confused, then at her. "I don't know what this is. But you never struck me as a person who killed innocent people for no reason."

"Heh, and you know me."

"I know enough. And I know there's something not right about this." Afearia glances in Carnavess' direction, but he was not there. "Hey—"

"Hush. You are not in control here. Either get out of my way or pay with your life."

"If only Adrian and Veronica could see you now." Afearia's taken aback for a moment, briefly losing her hold on the downed men. Zaiah notices and calmly glanced at the men. "What would they say? Those kids. They look up to you. You're everything to them. If they—"

A chain suddenly rattles around his head with the chain's tip pointed at his forehead. "You've pushed your luck for the last time, human," Afearia threatens. "You'll be the first."

Zaiah, standing firm without showing the slightest hint of fear—smiles. "I surely know it will be an honor to be your first." The chain wraps fast around his head, lifting him off the ground with the tip ready to strike. "But." Afearia narrows her stare a bit. "If this conflicts with who you are then you know this is wrong."

"Idiot. Are you gambling you life with the small interactions you've had with me? I knew you were stupid."

"Then do it. And when you do, I want you to feel every bit of your actions. I want all of your senses to be on high for this. Because this moment will either make or break you." Afearia stares him down, looking as if to strike at any moment, until the chains begin to rattle. "Well? What are you waiting for? Kill me. Kill us all!" The men look at Zaiah like he's crazy. "Come on! Do it!"

In a grunt of frustration, Afearia flings all of the men into an abandoned shop before fleeing. Zaiah stands and watches her escape until one of the officers jump up and grab his shoulder, turning him around.

"Are you insane!?" he questions. "You could have gotten us killed! I have a family damn it! How could you do that!?"

"Because I was certain she wouldn't," Zaiah says with a smirk.

"Are kidding? Do you even know who that is? She's—"

"Terra's hero," he says confidently as he still stares down the street where Afearia fled. "And it's our duty to make sure she doesn't fail."

"You're fucking nuts." He turns to one of his

officers, "We don't fight monsters. Find a landline in here and get me in contact with an Elite."

"Don't do that."

"Why? She looks exactly like that dead criminal from months back. If it is, I will do my part to let the government clean this mess up."

The officer finds an old phone that's been knocked over and begins to make the call until Zaiah pushes down the hook switch.

"Don't," Zaiah says.

"You are now officially obstructing justice. You're under arrest," he says as he's about to cuff Zaiah. Suddenly, the officers smell something naturally pleasant. "What is that? It smells like—flowers?"

Soon after, all of the men collapse except for Zaiah. He makes a big smile, "Luckkkky!" He looks at one of the fallen officers and notices his cell phone and makes a pondering expressing before picking it up.

Deeper in the town, Afearia is panting heavily in a dark alley, a bit shaken from what had nearly transpired. "Why did you flee?" a voice said from the shadows. She turns and sees Carnavess step forward. "Answer me."

"I-I," Afearia stutters. "I don't know."

"You should've just killed him and moved on."

"I was, but—"

"Excuses again, Afearia? Enough. Those kids. I'm ending them."

"No, stop!" she shouts as he turned to leave.

"I warned you. And I don't like repeating myself."

"Father—"

"I'll make it quick… If I feel like it."

Suddenly, a chain rattles through the alley and hits a passing man, breaking his leg. She turns out the alley and approaches the pain stricken man with her hand up. Carnavess turns toward her, seeing the disconnect she wears as she prepares to do as he demanded. It makes him smile before following close behind her.

Afearia stands over the fallen man. "Please," he begs. "Don't."

Afearia kicks him in the ribs and wraps her chain around his neck. The townspeople watch in horror before she draws her blade Demonweaver, holding it close to his face. The chain holds him in midair as he begs once more for Afearia to spare him. Seeming hesitant, she releases him. But before he can touch the ground, Afearia slashes her blade to cut down her first human... breaking her oath.

When his bloody body hits the ground, leaving Afearia detached completely to her own actions, the crowd scatters and flees. Slapping her hand to the ground, she upheavals the ground, slamming everyone into buildings, windows, and even into car windows. Once they were grounded, she proceed through the streets. One man tried to sit up, but she cut him down, back into the ground.

With each person who tried to escape when she neared, got cut down or stabbed. Carnavess, smiling like a demon, walked slowly in her bloody wake.

"Yes," Carnavess says. "This is it. This is your purpose. Now fulfill it."

Up ahead is a man's leg crushed and trapped under debris. Afearia stands coldly before him. "Get away from me!" he shouts. "Help! Somebody help me!" Ignoring he's cries, she raises her sword overhead.

"HEY!?" Zaiah shouts from behind her, gaining her attention as she turns her head toward him. "What the hell are you doing!?" She doesn't answer, just stares at him as he approaches. "Yeah, you! I think you missed one." She glances at Carnavess, who's standing beside another fallen civilian in front of a house's door. "No, not that one, but you're getting warmer."

She turns to face him as he stands a few feet from her. "Well, now that I have your attention," Zaiah says. "I have four words for you." Zaiah gives her an ominous smile. "You're doing it wrong." Slightly shaking her emotionless demeanor, Afearia gives him a vaguely odd look. "If you really want to kill someone, you have to do it like this."

Zaiah lifts the fallen man she had slain prior, halfway by the neck while wrapping his fingers around his throat. Afearia almost rushes forward, taking a step, but she halts herself.

"What?" Zaiah says. "Can't you tell? I'm still infected by the tree's will. After you left those officers, I couldn't help but take them for myself. Must be habit now." Afearia's deadpan expression turns stern. "But to think you were a killer this whole time like me. You just wanted to cut loose, and I can get that. I'll happily join you after I twist his neck. It's a sound I'm obsessed with."

As soon as he prepares to snap the man, a crescent red energy comes between him and the man, causing him to release the civilian in order to not lose his arm. Griping her sword, the crescent projectile was fired by Afearia's Demonweaver.

"Why did you stop me?" Zaiah says with surprise. A kind smile crosses his face, "Unless you knew this man was never dead to begin with." Afearia's surprised by his deduction. "I figured as much. Which is why I checked his pulse when I grabbed his neck. Regardless, this is messed up. Why are you doing this?"

"I have to…"

"Even if it goes against everything you believe? Harming the innocent? I can only look the other way so much. I can't let this go on much longer."

Afearia looks away from him, expressing displeasure before approaching him, "You should've fled when I gave you the chance. Now I have to kill you."

"Isn't that what you wanted to do all along?" he jokes.

"I'll take your foolishness as a sign that you want to

be a sacrifice for the greater good."

"Mmm, nope. I don't believe in doing things like that. Though there are rare exceptions, I suppose."

"Yet you wish to play with me. You're about to lose your life."

"I'm aware." Afearia stands before him as he looks her in the eyes. "Do it. Nothing can stop you now. Nothing other than you." She glances at Carnavess sternly watching her. She grunts with displeasure and raises her sword. Noticing this, he glances in the same area a couple times. "Is there something over there distracting you?"

"Have some respect! That's the father of all realms you're insulting."

"Really?" looking to his left again.

"At a time like this. How can you be so stupid? He could level you and this entire town in the blink of an eye. At least this way, the casualties can remain small... even if I have to stain my hands to do it."

Zaiah looks over to the alley once more. "Perhaps... However, there's no one there."

Afearia stares wide-eyed with disbelief. She looks back to Carnavess who's still standing where he's been. "He may have hidden his presence from mortal eyes," Afearia says to Zaiah. "They can do that."

"Even so..." Zaiah walks over to where Carnavess is and stands directly before him. Carnavess stares down at Zaiah with stern eyes. "How much of a coward must you be to send someone else to do your dirty work?"

"Watch your mouth!" she angrily says. "He's not one you should disrespect! He will kill you!"

"If he's as bad tempered as you say, then why hasn't he done it already?" Afearia's expression changes to a somewhat questioning one. "And masked presence or not." Zaiah does a strong straight kick, knocking out the door behind Carnavess. "He should have a tangible form in some sense or another, right?"

"Not exactly," Afearia says as she suspiciously approaches Carnavess. As she nears, Zaiah steps aside as Afearia stops to stare up at Carnavess with stone anger.

"Why have you stopped?" Carnavess asks.

Still staring up at him, her stone anger becomes openly apparent when she grits her teeth with bunched brows. "Twenty seconds ago, you would have slapped me to the ground for looking you in the eye like this. Who are you?" He continued to stare at her, just before she began to step away. "The better question is on me. Why didn't I see it sooner? My fear of you is a truly powerful weapon. And you know that." She sits with her back to him and meditates.

"Hmph," Carnavess says with a slight grin. "You may have figured it out, but nothing's changed. You're still a frightened little girl who's only purpose is to destroy. Our war machine. Should you not fulfill your purpose you would simply rust." Afearia stands and faces him. "Fight as you must. Cling to this false lifestyle like the germ you are. But you will never be free from what binds you. And like the unholy thing inside you, you will never be loved—*beast*," Carnavess accentuates with contempt and disgust in his chin jolt.

Afearia's brow twitched as she swallowed her feelings cut by his words. She remains as stone face as possible before raising her hand to him. "Mental Universe."

Like a flicker of light, Carnavess' body becomes transparent before small spheres of light quickly float out of him, fading into the air before he cruelly smirks at her and vanishes into nothingness.

Meanwhile in Elysium, Carnavess calmly travels the palace halls before suddenly stopping and looking out the window, sensing the dispel of his magic. He makes a disgruntled sound before moving on.

On Terra, Afearia remains still, staring at where Carnavess last stood, openly burdened by what Carnavess said to her. Zaiah cautiously takes a step toward her.

"Hey," Zaiah softly says, "are you okay?" Afearia glances at him before looking at all the damage she had done to the area. "Look, I know a lot has just happened here. But we need to run. I'm sure authorities are on the way. And depending how it's reported, government elites may show up."

"There's nowhere to run at this point," Afearia says in a low voice. "Besides, it's what I wanted anyway."

"There's still Loiotes. And I've found a way to get us there unseen." Suddenly, a car comes speeding down the street, stopping several meters from them. "That's our ride."

"I just told you I'm staying."

"Are you still saying that? Is that guy still here?"

"He never was. Just a specter he placed in my mind when he was here. Now move," she says as she shoves him.

As she began to walk up the street, the car door opens, "Anya!" Adrian shouts, quickly getting Afearia to turn around.

"If we stay," Zaiah says, "no matter where we go in this town those kids will be in danger."

Afearia rushes up to Zaiah and shoves him a few times as she speaks, "You kidnap my kids and force my hand? How dare you?"

"I was trying to stop your rampage!"

"You told them?"

"No, I'm not an idiot." She looks him up and down and begins to move toward the car. "Wait. You dropped this." In his hand was the shawl Afearia discarded. She snatches it and proceeds to the car.

As she approaches, she trips over a man's arm. Afearia looks down and sees him holding his injured leg. Afearia kneels down to help him before he franticly swipes at her and tries to move away.

"Stay away from me!" he shouts.

"Wait," Afearia says, "I can help."

"Stay away! Help! Help!"

Zaiah comes from behind her, "There's nothing you can do now. Come on."

"But I can heal him."

"Look at him." She sadly stares into his shaky eyes and trembling body every time he takes a moment to stop crawling and stare at the one who harmed him. "Do you think he wishes for your aid?"

Afearia stands and turns away from the man before proceeding to the car. "I'm sorry," she mutters.

Afearia stands at the side car door as she has her hand taken by Adrian. "Anya," he says, "what's going on?"

"Get in the car," Afearia says in a low voice, not making eye contact.

"Anya?"

Seeing that she's distraught, Adrian says nothing more and gets back in the car. Afearia goes in next while Zaiah steps into the passenger's side. The car quickly makes a left and drives off.

While speeding down the street, Zaiah sighs in relief, "That was close. Thanks again, Calvin," Zaiah says to the man driving the car.

Calvin's wearing a plain short sleeve red shirt with two buttons leading to the collar. With one button undone, two large puncture scars are visible on the lower left of his neck. His black hair is gelled and combed back at the top with the sides shaven down, but not all the way to the scalp.

"Haha," Calvin laughs. "When I got that call from you, I knew that it would be something crazy."

"And yet here we are again." Calvin smiles at him before looking back at the road. Zaiah looks back and sees Afearia parting the hair from Veronica's face as she sleeps. "You may want to sit on the floor until we leave town."

Afearia sits on the car floor, moments before patrol cars come racing pass them. Afearia looks toward Calvin,

"Thank you, Calvin."

Though Calvin heard her clearly, he doesn't respond. "Hey, buddy?" Zaiah says. "Do you think we can get out of here before government response?"

"They've been really tied up lately," Calvin replies. "If they do, it won't be for another thirty or sixty minutes. They'll probably take the usual approach by sending an elite scout and a striker to settle the issue swiftly. And since Valerie's aid is hard to come by as lead scout, I suspect Kyoto to take the role. But hopefully we'll be gone long before any of that." Calvin glances at his rearview mirror, seeing Adrian. "How's your sister?"

"She's still hot," Adrian replies.

"Around this time, kids get sick a lot, especially mine."

"You have kids now?" Zaiah says with surprise.

"We have a lot to catch up on." Calvin goes into his glove compartment and hands Zaiah a couple pill packets. "Children's medicine. Helps colds and fevers. Give her some with a glass of water." When Calvin looks forward, he sees something that caused alarm. "Zaiah, get down."

"What's up?" Zaiah asks while ducking down.

"Government car."

Zaiah looks over to Afearia who happens to still be distressed as she stared at the floor. Coming down the street is a black limousine with two mini government flags pinned at the corners of the trunk. Just as the cars come beside each other, Calvin's nervousness caused him to slightly swerve, but no impact. He looks through his rearview mirror seeing the car's break lights before stopping.

Zaiah peeks up only high enough to look into the side view mirror seeing the limousine had stooped, "You think they suspect something?"

Calvin breathes out after fearfully holding his breath, "Their windows were tented. Let's just hope they think this is just another pedestrian car fleeing."

Calvin looks into his rearview mirror one more time before speeding up to escape the panicked town.

Diary Entry #5888

When I turned thirteen, every two months my Elders would subject me to a variety of torture. As heartless as they were cruel, they're reasoning was sound. I needed to learn what certain injuries mean to my body. So I know what to most look out for and what I can take. Makes sense, I suppose. I learned certain injuries don't hold me back much while others make me curl up, even though they are not that serious in terms of fatality.
The things they've done. I've been burned, had my bones broken, had pieces of my flesh cut off and even whole body parts. They've even skinned me. I really didn't like that...
I've been poked, stabbed, nailed to objects, blinded, limbs pulled to the breaking point. I've been through more than most can dream.
Sadly, I developed a slight, slight, masochist affliction to all that pain. Or maybe I was always wired that way and it kind of just came to pass when they tortured me. I'm not saying I like all kinds of pain, just certain kinds. But I didn't really like that they were doing either.
When I could dissociate that they were my tormentors, I would sometimes have to hold in giggles when my skin was pierced and tugged...
God I'm sick...

Taking Back Terra

Chapter Eight

As Afearia and company drive outside of town, Calvin glances at the empty passenger seat, "You can stop hiding now. We've made it through."

Zaiah comes up and gets in the seat to buckle himself in, "Better safe than sorry at this point."

"You should've been thinking that way years ago."

"Wha!? Then my nickname would be meaningless." The two men laugh while Afearia remains on the car floor watching over Veronica. Adrian silently listens to the two men converse and catch up. "Kids though, Cal. How many?"

"Three. Two boys, one girl."

"Wow. Man, I can't believe you settled down and started a family."

"That's less than I can say about you. You're sitting in my car nearly naked with wild and crazy hair like an animal from the jungle. Where've you been that haircuts and clothing were taboo by nature?"

"Hehe, it's a long story."

"When is it not?"

"Let's just say it was a bad ending to a long fight."

"Right. Still not going to tell me the truth, are you?"

The atmosphere becomes a bit tense by the jokeless reply given by Calvin. Zaiah's eyes glances at him before looking out the window. He turns his head to Calvin with a smile.

"So, who's the unlucky lady tied to you for life?" Zaiah asks.

Calvin chuckles, "You know her actually."

"I do?"

"She was part of the team back in the day."

Zaiah thinks to himself before quickly realizing who he's talking about. "No way!? You tied the knot with that butch, Debbie!?"

"You know she never liked you calling her butch."

"Then she shouldn't have been born a giant with super strength."

"Haha, she actually still has super strength, despite getting smaller."

"What? Did she get sick?"

"Injured. It put her out of doing physical labor for a while."

"Damn. Is she alright?"

"It happened years ago. She can't work like she used to, but she's no longer depressed about it."

"Depression... That's some serious stuff. I'm glad she had you to pull her up."

"It didn't always work. It was a battle neither of us were prepared for. But I'm happy she could muster the strength inside herself to not give up."

"Damn, that's crazy... What happened to her?"

"Long story. I'm sure you know how that is."

Zaiah makes a sad sideways smile. "Yeah..."

"Excuse me?" Afearia interrupts. "I thank you for helping, but where are you taking us?"

Calvin says nothing. Zaiah glances at the two of them a few times before addressing Calvin, "Can you estimate the time it will take you to get us from here to Loiotes?"

"Couple hours, give or take," Calvin replies.

"Good. The sooner the better."

"Yeah. Now, despite knowing you're up to no good, how did you get wrapped up in this mess?"

"No mess, just a sense of morality. Maybe that's not the right word. Obligation?"

"Can't be any of that."

Zaiah laughs, "Why not?"

"Because it isn't in your character to be those things. Me and Debbie would know."

Calvin's remark hit a sad cord inside Zaiah. Zaiah turns his body a bit to the window. Staring out into the dark with less than a cheerful expression.

Adrian, wanting to break the tension, leans forward, "So, uh, you guys used to be on the same team? Doing what?"

"Nothing big," Calvin answers with a smirk. "We were just your ordinary freedom fighters doing what we did best against a corrupt government. Hacking, breaking and entering, stealing classified documents. You know, the classics."

"Wow!" Adrian says with excitement. "What do you do now?"

"I'm a merchant. I travel around promoting and selling goods for major companies. By the by, I have a red duffle bag with some clothes in the trunk that you can wear, Zaiah."

"Thanks," Zaiah says. "I can't very well keep traveling around like this."

"Haha, most certainly not. You look like an ape."

As the two men laugh, Adrian smiles, knowing the situation had changed for the better.

"Hey, I'm really glad you're doing alright," Zaiah says. "You settled down, started a family, and even got a great business. And you even managed to get off the grid, I assume."

"Yeah. Me and Debbie had to hang low for three years before we could move around again. Doesn't mean if we were to parade in front of the king he wouldn't have us executed on the spot."

"True. But I'm still glad. Even happier to know you two are still alive." He lowers his head a bit with a softer smile, "Truly glad...," speaking under his breath.

Calvin glances at him, "Hmph," he says with a smile.

"How did you two meet?" Adrian asks.

"You're quite interested, are you kid?"

"Yes! You guys sound amazing! Zaiah told me he used to hack too."

"Well, kid, we've been good friends since high school. But it wasn't until a few years after we became rebellious. That's shortly around the time we found Debbie at a local dive bar we went to a lot. It was that very night we formed our task force."

"We?" Zaiah says. "It was more like us drunkenly speaking out how much we were against the new government and her presenting a choice we couldn't refuse." Zaiah looks through the windshield with a bit of intensity in his eyes. "A chance to strike back."

Calvin nods in agreement. "Even in high school we felt that way. It was pretty much the magnet that brought us together. We joined the debate team and argued our points in school. We became debating partners going across the country in national debate-offs. We were hoping for a chance to do that in front of real politicians. Every year we were promised an opportunity like that. But it was always canceled for numerous reasons."

"We resorted to try and legally get our points across through public protest and many other means," Calvin continues. "But the people and the government itself acted as if we were invisible. And after our last attempt, it was clear that our years of doing the right thing against the wrong people didn't mean a thing. That's when we got drunk and ranted our frustrations to a woman who gave us a ticket to change our lives."

"Debbie was a real rebel," Zaiah says proudly. "She didn't take crap from anyone. Compared to us all full of bluster, she was a woman of action. Talk was cheap and she knew it. When she made a plan, it was going to go down, right Cal?"

"Yeah," he says with a smirk. "It's truly admirable. That unshakable resolve she had. If you didn't want to listen, she'll make you see her. Don't want to see her? You'll feel her when she bombs federally owned buildings placed in neighborhoods to drive its community apart."

"In other words, you guys were terrorist," Afearia says condescendingly.

The car comes to an abrupt stop, lunging everyone forward. "Zaiah...," Calvin says with an angry air around him and in his voice. "Shut that murderous dog up or I'll be throwing you all to the dirt."

"Hey—!" Adrian was about to say.

"Kid," Zaiah interrupts. He turns his head to Adrian and sternly shakes his head for him to let it go.

Adrian sits back and Afearia looks away from them, knowing not to interject anymore than she has. The car soon resumes its course for Loiotes."

"As I was saying, Debbie was a real no nonsense kind of person back then. She was as courageous as she was cunning. Needless to say, she was the brains of our operations."

"Hey, I had some good ideas too," Zaiah says. "Some of which she thought were pretty good."

"Didn't most of them end in failure?"

"They—! Hmm. Well, she didn't do everything."

"I can't believe you're still this petty on who's most useful in operation planning."

"I'm not petty," Zaiah jokes. "I just think I have the best ideas. Hey, who came up with the idea to steal from the central laboratory?"

Calvin chuckles, "That was terrifying. We barely got out of there. Proof of your *genius* planning."

"Okay, so I tripped the alarm on our way out. But we did get out of there."

"Yeah, after Debbie had to brainstorm the idea to

incapacitate some guards and wear their uniforms out the building."

"Pfft, I could've thought of that."

"Right," he smiles with disbelief.

Zaiah pouts before suddenly becoming enthusiastic again, "What about my idea to hack into Orcelin's top tech building?"

"Mhmm. That was a good idea," he says with a tight lipped nod.

"And we did extract some serious life changing secrets about our country and much of the world. Do you remember that, smart guy?"

"I do." He tilts his head smiling while expressing masked disgruntlement, "Then you disappeared."

Zaiah sits back, disappointed by the turn of the conversation, "Look, I know a lot hasn't been explained, but—"

"I actually don't care what the reason is."

"Calvin."

"It's cool. You disappear for years, telling no one that you're alive. Then you call out of the blue looking for a favor." Calvin leers up at the rearview mirror seeing Afearia. "A dangerous favor to help transport the supposedly dead calamity." He looks forward shaking his head, "You know Zai, we were really worried sick about you. We actually felt it was our fault for not stopping you from storming deeper into that building."

"It wasn't," Zaiah mutters.

"It wasn't, was it!? You as always, lost your head after reading a few documents and marched forward without thinking!"

"I'm sorry. But after discovering that Derexen had a plan to decimate 4.5 billion people as a means of population control, what was I suppose to do?"

Learning of Derexen's disturbing plan, Adrian and Afearia glance at each other in disbelief someone would go to such extents and call it a solution.

"Control your damn temper," Calvin grits. "You could never get that damn anger of yours in check. It's disgusting! And it's for that very reason—Debbie lost her arm," Calvin struggled to say. Zaiah turned his head to Calvin with shock and soon shame. "When you tripped the sensory alarm and the gate dropped between us and you, we weren't swarmed by just building guards. An Elite was there too."

"And we ran like hell," Calvin continues. "With all the gunfire and being winged by bullets, we hear you scream out as several other men yell in agony. That was the last time we heard your voice. We didn't know what happened to you beyond that. Maybe now you can tell me. Or will you be your usual self?"

Zaiah sighs with disappointment, "I didn't know. No. I didn't think."

"No. Like the piece of shit you tend to be, you certainly only had you in mind."

For awhile, the ride was silent with much tension in the air. Zaiah glances at Calvin. "If you hate me so much, why did you come when I called?"

"When we get to Loiotes, you'll know why."

Zaiah looks out the window, crossing his arms. "I know this isn't the time. But my selfish actions did jeopardize the mission. But you two did make it out. And the data was lifted before I waltzed off. Did you two make their dark crimes public?"

Calvin readjusts his grip on the wheel, not responding for a moment. "We didn't."

Zaiah quickly turned to him, "Are you serious!? After everything they've done? After everything we risked!?"

"There weren't any real risk until you screwed us!"

"Those files were bigger than us!"

"It was an easy decision after we escaped. If we had

went through with publishing those files, Derexen would not rest until we were dead. We already lost a friend. We weren't interested in losing each other as well."

Realizing their situation, Zaiah calmed himself and faced forward with crossed arms. "That must have been hard on you two. How long were you running?"

"Never said it was over. The hunt continues. The blunt of it died down roughly a year ago. We will always be fugitives, Zaiah. At least this way, me, my wife, and my children can have some sense of normalcy by keeping our heads low and what we discovered buried."

"Maybe I'm the one who didn't see the bigger picture," Zaiah admits, looking to Calvin. Calvin doesn't respond and keeps his eyes on the road. "I'm sorry, Cal."

Calvin takes a hand off the wheel and turns on the radio for the remainder of the ride.

After a silent car ride, Afearia and the others finally reach Loiotes. Calvin parks a fair walking distance from the town with no intentions of entering himself. Afearia steps out the car holding Veronica in her arms wrapped in a blanket. Adrian steps out behind her holding their bags.

Zaiah ruffles around in the trunk and pulls out the red duffle bag. He gestures for Afearia to come over and get her tote bag. She stands beside him, glancing at him several times, unable to gauge his current emotion through his semi carefree expression.

Afearia grabs her bag and stares into the trunk. "Why didn't you tell him?"

"Tell him what?" Zaiah replies.

"He doesn't know you used to be a World Guardian, does he?"

Zaiah slams the trunk, "My being a World Guardian does not make up for me being a bad friend and ally." Zaiah proceeds around the car with Afearia soon following.

As they pass the driver's side door, Afearia and Adrian move toward the town and Zaiah looks at Calvin through the window. Calvin doesn't look his way before he makes a somewhat sad sideways smile and walks away.

Calvin rolls the window down and sticks his head out, "Azaiah," he firmly says. Though he stopped all three of them, Zaiah was taken aback by his friend's call before softening into a solemn state.

Zaiah turns to face Calvin with a painted smile, "You called me by my full first name."

"Yeah. We're even. Never contact me again. Consider that merchandise as a parting gift between old friends and rebel allies."

Zaiah stares at Calvin for a while, seeing how far from empty his words of departure were before respectfully nodding. "Understood... Goodbye—Calvin."

Calvin rolls up his window and drives away.

While driving back the way he came, Calvin's face was sad. He takes a deep breath and sighs before he glances at his rearview mirror. He sees Zaiah still watching him. He looks back at the road and shakes his head. He gently rubs the heavy puncture scars on his neck.

"We're even...," he forlornly says.

Zaiah takes a deep breath and turns for Loiotes. Afearia and Adrian let him pass, feeling that the situation had been unpleasant for him. They walk a few feet behind him in silence. Afearia looks up at his stoic sway, debating with her eyes if she should say something.

"It's unfortunate," Afearia says, "but maybe you should've told him the truth. If he knew, maybe he wouldn't have given up on you."

"It wasn't him giving up on me," Zaiah says. "It was I who gave up on him... And Debbie. I'm just lucky he didn't punch me in the face after all of these years."

"You should have told him. It was your sense of duty as a guardian that made you leave them. He may have understood."

"I couldn't. Back then, Derexen was on a

214

worldwide manhunt for all remaining World Guardians. Just being associated with one was enough for him to come for you. After that, you deal with his specialist. An extreme tormentor. Risking their lives by revealing myself wasn't worth it. And yet, that's exactly what I did. My title... wasn't the burden. It was me," he says with regret. "I was the one not worthy of them or my duty... Even now. I'm an incompetent, sorry excuse for a guardian."

Afearia felt empathy for him, for it was the first time she kind of felt like she could relate to his pain. Zaiah shrugs and smiles at her, "So, you were pretty quiet that ride. I thought you would lose it when he insisted you stop talking back there."

Afearia looks away from him, "I have more pressing matters on my mind than dealing with an unruly human."

"I'm sorry he was like that. We saw what you were doing and I had to convince him the situation wasn't what it seemed. I then had to convince him I can calm the situation. But by that point, all he saw was a vicious attacker who I happened to want taken safely elsewhere."

"He was right not to be polite to me then. I was mistaken to call him unruly."

"No he wasn't. Well either way, I knew better. I trusted you wouldn't do something like that for no reason."

"Heh, trust."

"Yeah, trust," he says positively.

"Do you really think you can trust me? Was Hillstar not a wakeup call for you? I'm a beast who will do anything their master tells them. No good can come from someone so easily swayed to slay on command."

"Easily? I don't think we were in the same town. I saw you fighting yourself every step of the way. It wasn't fun for you."

"Doesn't matter. I still—" Afearia looks down at the fairly clueless Adrian. "If the same circumstances occurred again, it would go the same way." Zaiah looks straight ahead. "Nothing to say now, right?" Zaiah looks back at her with a kind smile. She grunts in annoyance and throws her bag ahead of Zaiah. "Hold it." The two boys stop. "Don't think I forgot that you violated my rules."

"Yikes!" Zaiah says before quickly jogging away.

"Stop!" immediately halting him. "You came in contact with my children," she says while approaching Zaiah. "You came close to me, and you even dared to get in my way." Zaiah's eyes move erratically, not knowing what she'll do. "Perhaps a thank you is in order," she says, standing before him. "Even though this may all be a ploy."

"No need to thank me," he say, seeming a bit nervous.

"Then I won't." She turns and walks ahead of him. Zaiah makes a sideways smile, seeming a little disappointed. "It's Afearia," she says, peeking his interest in a serious way. She turns halfway to him. "That's my true name."

"Does this mean you're starting to trust me?"

Afearia grabs her bag and moves on, "Not in the slightest."

"Ugh," he says with a head tilt before following with Adrian.

"We're going to see a man who's bound to use my name. And since you don't seem to understand what go away means, I figured I'd get it out in the open."

As Adrian passes Zaiah, a slight smirk comes across his face. "Still something," he mutters, readying to step forward.

"And remember, five meters, idiot."

Zaiah waits the appropriate distance before following her into Loiotes. The rising sun softly warms the town, one of the few locations who happen to receive the benefits of the destroyed generators.

Though Loiotes is an outlawed region, the place is

actually clean and well taken care of by its townspeople. The tan buildings are tightly packed together, creating narrow alleyways. Some passages are so narrow, the town had to build a street light for those passing through them.

Because of their arrival being at the start of day break, the streets are completely empty. Some stores are preparing for the day while others are closing down. As Afearia and company move through the streets, she carefully observes the town. She suddenly hears a whistle for her attention. She looks back and sees Zaiah waving her over at the entrance of an alley.

What is he up to? Afearia thinks. Zaiah continues to wave her over, but more aggressively. "What!?" she aggravatingly screams.

"Shhhh!" Zaiah hushes. "People are still sleeping," he loudly whispers.

Afearia rolls her eyes and walks over with Adrian. "What?"

"You're probably looking for a place to rest up, right? Down this alley and a couple more blocks is a shortcut to a low cost motel."

"And how do you know that?"

"Calvin said when we were looking for you that he would drop us close, but not come in himself. He gave directions saying when we pass the town bank," pointing to the bank behind them, "make a right. After we reach the end, make a left and go straight down. Can't miss it. It's all right here," he says as he pulls the note from his leaf skirt.

She glances at it and looks at him. "Since this could be an ambush, you lead the way."

Zaiah puts his note away and leads with Afearia and Adrian moving along in a single file. When they reach the end, Zaiah follows the directions from the note, cautiously checking every corner while even greeting the few pedestrians on the street. He receives smiles and returned greetings along with odd looks because of his lack of clothing.

Soon after, Adrian and Afearia come out the alley. But with Afearia's scowling, the few who happily greeted Zaiah become cautious or stone face.

After a couple blocks, Zaiah stops at the corner, scratching his head with a confused look. "Is this right?" he says aloud, looking for the motel. He looks over the note again, "Maybe it's further up."

"Let me guess," Afearia says, coming from behind him. "You don't know where we are."

"Hmm, I know I'm reading this right."

"Good-for-nothing," she says while turning back.

"Wait!" Zaiah walks up to a resident. "Excuse me, I'm looking for a motel called, Sleep-inn. I was told it should be somewhere around here."

"They moved," the gentleman says. "It's not far though. Walk straight up two blocks and make a right. It should be across the street."

"Great, thank you so much." As the man takes his leave, Zaiah turns to Afearia, "See, I told you—" Afearia had already left. Zaiah throws his arms up in exasperation before proceeding to find the motel.

Because she overheard, Afearia had found the motel on her own and checked-in. She received a ground floor room and wasted no time to get settled down the hall. When they get in the room, Afearia lies Veronica down and parts the curtains to let the sun shine through.

She goes into her bag and briefly has a surprised expression before grabbing a dry rag. "Adrian," Afearia says. "Could you wet this with cold water and bring it back to me?"

Adrian puts down his belongings and does as he's requested. She takes the rag and dabs it around Veronica's hot zones like her neck and chest before folding it to rest on her forehead. Veronica coughs a little bit and turns her head.

"Sorry, girl," Afearia says softly. "I'll slow down."
Afearia looks to Adrian. "I need to meet with someone. But
until I know she's getting better I'll hold off. All of this
excessive traveling hasn't been good on her."

Adrian looks to his sister, "I'm kind of tired too. Do
you mind if I sleep?"

"Go rest. When you wake up I'll have us fresh
supplies." Adrian climbs onto the bed with his sister,
"Adrian? Have you or anyone else gone into my bag since
Aster City?"

"No, not unless you wanted us to."

"Okay, get some rest."

Adrian kicks off his shoes and lies close to
Veronica, putting his arm around her. Afearia stands and
sees an ice pick in a bucket of ice left by room service on
the nightstand. She takes the bucket and goes into the
bathroom, filling it with cold water after removing the pick.

That book, Afearia thinks. Light's Doctrine is gone.
I honestly don't know how to feel about it. I'm not even
sure what it was. I wonder when I lost it or when it was
stolen. I know that thing was really important, but I got
carless. I was afraid of using my magic to dismiss it like
my diary. I kept it close to me. But not close enough
apparently.

Afearia shuts off the water and returns to the room.
She sits at Veronica's bedside and rinses the rag before
dabbing around her face and neck, trying to keep her cool.

For several hours, Afearia watched closely over
Veronica. Knowing her temperature was now at a safer
level, Afearia decides to leave the room to replenish their
supplies.

She calmly walks the streets of Loiotes in her
shawl, thinking to herself. With every person she glances
at, she gets a hot flash of what she did in Hillstar.

Carnavess..., Afearia thinks, looking disgusted. I
didn't even think about it. He gives the command and I go

where he ask. I kill when they ask. Even after all I've learned down here, I'm still just an attack dog. And I tell myself it was right. It was the law of Elysium. Their divine will to save this world using my hands. So why do I feel so bad?

Afearia sees a sign and an arrow pointing into an alley for customers seeking groceries. She walks a couple meters in and stops in front of the small market. She wearily stares up at it, still lost in her own head between the market window and the wooden door leading inside.

Demeseus would have disobeyed…, Afearia thinks. But even still, that doesn't make him right. Afearia slaps her hand on the glass and lowers her head, clenching her teeth. I'm so sick of feeling this way. The anger, the confusion. The tug of war between me and the people yelling around me. I'm tired, and I want it to stop!

"Just make it stop!" Afearia shouts, banging her fist on the market's door. She looks to her right and sees the fearful look in a mother and her child's eyes before they turn around and leave the way they came. She looks at her reflection in the window. And you don't have to tell me I won't be loved because if they knew… Afearia narrows her stare at herself before gruffly turning away and entering the store.

After finishing her shopping and returning to the motel, Afearia makes the kids sandwiches for lunch while they sleep. By evening, the sun has nearly set. Adrian was up watching TV while Veronica remains asleep. Afearia's sitting at Veronica's bedside until she stood to grab a wrapped sandwich off the dresser. She takes half and rips it into four small pieces.

Afearia sits back down and gently tries to wake Veronica, "Hey? Hey? Veronica, can you hear me?" She softly rocks her a few times before Veronica opened her droopy red eyes. "You have to eat something in order to keep your strength up. Here," she says, putting it in her hand. Veronica weakly raises her arm and bites a piece off, chewing with closed eyes. "Doesn't that taste good?" she says with a smile.

She hands her the second piece and watches her finish it slower than the first. Veronica turns her head just before Afearia reached for another piece, "There's two more." Veronica groans. "Come on, it's yummy," Afearia says as she prepares to hand feed her. Veronica turns her head away when she feels it touch her lips. "You have to eat. I'm feeding you half a sandwich."

Veronica slightly opens her eyes, then her mouth, eating the third piece. Afearia presents her with the last one, causing Veronica to stare lazily at Afearia before taking it and eating it.

Afearia smiles, "See, you're looking better already." She waves a water bottle in front of her, "Last thing I'll have you do today, okay?" She tilts it into Veronica's mouth. She drinks a little and breathes out, coughing afterward. "You did good. Do you want half a cookie." Veronica weakly smiles and nods at her. "Yeah, you got life now, huh?" she chuckles. "I'll go to the store and get it for you right now." She stands and looks to Veronica's brother, "Watch your sister, Adrian."

After he waves her off, Afearia steps into the hall and locks the door. Without looking, she quickly turned to leave and bumps into someone.

"Oh, sorry about that," she says as she looks up at the person she ran into.

Surprised by who she's looking at, Zaiah was standing before her, cleaned-up and mildly surprised that he ran into her as well.

Wearing a new plaid, dark red and black short sleeve open button shirt with a plain white tee shirt underneath. His smoky black jeans are a loose-fit, complimenting his white sneakers with black stripes at the sides. Zaiah's once long and wild chestnut hair is now cut to a short mid length combed with volume and lustrous waves throughout.

The two of them stare at each other for a while with Afearia seeming more shocked than he was. Zaiah smiles, putting his hands in his pockets, "You know, I was hoping I would find you here—" Afearia quickly walked right pass him like nothing had happened. "Hey!? Where are you going?"

"Go away, idiot," she aggressively says. "I thought I lost you."

"Nah, you can't lose me. So where are you going?" sounding a bit confused.

"None of your business." She suddenly stops. "Crap, I forgot my money," she says to herself. When she turns to walk back, Afearia doesn't step aside but instead tries walking right through Zaiah.

"Hey!" Zaiah says as he stumbles from Afearia's path. He runs his hand through his bangs and into his thick, silky hair before shrugging with a smile and following her again. "So, back to your room, I guess?"

Afearia abruptly stops once again. "You are without a doubt the most annoying person I have ever met. Why must you persist with this ridiculous behavior? Let me make this clear. Leave. Me. Alone."

Zaiah stares blankly at her for a moment. "So I thought you might want this," Zaiah says before taking out the medicine packets he received from Calvin. "How's Veronica doing by the way?" he asks sincerely.

"Give it."

"Sure," handing it over. "I wouldn't deprive that little girl of something she clearly needs." Afearia holds the packets, staring at them for awhile. "What's wrong?"

"I don't know how to administer medicine...," she says in a low, embarrassed voice.

"The directions are on the packet."

Afearia narrows her eyes on it, "The words are

smudged."

"Really?" he says, trying to see, but she yanks it away and bunches her brows at him, giving Zaiah a look for him to take her word for it. "Okay, well we can always go and get her fresh ones. Come on. I saw a drugstore on my way here."

"I don't want to go with you."

"I can tell you how to get there then."

Afearia sighs and walks on ahead, "Like it matters. You'll just end up following me anyway."

Zaiah chuckles before following her, "You got me there."

They leave the motel and walk beside each other with Afearia walking as close to the curb as possible, getting some distance from Zaiah. He glances at her fairly apathetic expression a couple times before smirking at her.

"I clean up good, huh?" Zaiah says.

"What?" she replies, looking at him with an annoyed demeanor.

"Me. I got clean clothes, a nice haircut, and I even showered. I'm doing pretty well."

"Congratulations. You've now done what every ten year old could do," she sarcastically replies.

"Yup. I had a big day."

"God I want to hit you," she says with a slow blink and a fist.

"That's not nice."

"You think?"

He chuckles and puts his hands in his pockets, "Sure is a nice night out," he says, stopping to look up at the stars and the natural half moon.

Afearia irritably stops and looks at him before looking up at the sky. Her face softens up from her irritable state. Under a clear sky where light pollution was not too heavy, clusters of stars are spread across the sky.

"Amazing," Zaiah says softly. "Ever sat on a beach

during a warm summer night?"

"No."

"It's an experience you should have. The feelings and the sensations. The feel of the sand between your fingers and toes. The gentle brush of the winds with the crashing waves. The sweet scent of the ocean's vapor settling on your skin and into your nose. And that salty taste of ocean mist."

"Sounds lovely," Afearia softly says.

"Someday, maybe—I can take you..."

Though it was almost unnoticeable, Afearia's eyes softened and a light smile's seen at the corner of her mouth. After a few moments, Afearia blinks, regaining her sterner expression before looking irritated by Zaiah's presence.

"Stop bothering me, idiot," she says before walking ahead. Zaiah smirks and follows.

Though quiet during the duration of the walk, the two of them reach the drugstore. Zaiah steps inside before Afearia and moves toward the nearest store clerk.

"Excuse me," he says. "Where's your cold and flu medicine for children? Specifically something to handle fevers."

The man points into the aisles, "Straight down, two aisles over."

"Thank you, young man," he says with a smile. "Come on," speaking to Afearia, gesturing for her to follow him.

Afearia quickly moves beside him, "I heard what he said. I'm not deaf."

"I know."

They reach the end of the aisle and find the medicine area for children. They skim the boxes and bottles until Afearia reaches up and grabs the bottle from the top shelf.

"Fever," she says, reading the back. Zaiah quickly takes it from her and reads the back. "Hey!?"

"I'll pay for this."

"How?" she says with skepticism.

"Calvin was thorough about his goodbye gift. He packed that bag. It wasn't already in his car. Among the many things he gave me, money was also in there. Paying for this won't be a problem."

Afearia snatches it back, "It is. I won't be in debt to you."

"Four dollars? And you saved my life. I don't think I will be closing that gap anytime soon. Do you?"

Seeing the seriousness in his eyes, she sighs and hands it back to him. "No, I suppose not. As she walks up ahead, he looks over the bottle again, "But you know. Your life is not in my debt. When I saved you, that was it." She stops and turns to him. "You owe me nothing."

Zaiah hasn't looked up at her and nods at the bottle's label a few times before walking up ahead of her, making no eye contact like she never said anything.

Once purchased, they head back to the motel, not talking much. When they reach the front of the building, Afearia stops and waves him off like a dog.

"Hey," Zaiah says as she opens the front door. "You think you can give her that medicine without any problems?"

"I can read, idiot. It's not magic."

"I know. But, I can give it to her, if you want."

"Why are you constantly trying to get near my kids?"

"I'm not."

"Then why?"

Zaiah says nothing for a moment. "I'm just saying... if you want to be on the safe—"

"Five minutes. Since I rather be sure since it is medicine, you can make sure I'm giving her the proper dose. After five minutes, you get lost."

Zaiah nods and follows her inside. When they reach

Afearia's room, she opens the door to find Adrian helping himself to a sandwich. Veronica hazily opens her eyes and looks to the door.

Adrian turns with his prepared sandwich and bites into it, "He's back?" he asks with a full mouth. "And looking cool."

Afearia locks the door, removing her shawl, "No, not cool. And he's doing us a favor, maybe."

"Maybe?" Zaiah says.

"Could be a trick, can't be sure," she says before walking pass him. She sits by Veronica's bedside while Zaiah approaches from the other side.

"How you doing, kiddo?" Zaiah asks Veronica with a smile.

Veronica weakly smiles back, "Better."

"Hey," Afearia says. "Don't talk to them."

"Right, sorry," Zaiah says. Adrian shakes his head, seeming bothered as he glanced at Afearia before sitting in front of the TV.

"Give me the medicine."

He hands her the bag as she takes it out, "Three teaspoons should do it."

"How you figure?"

"That's what it says on the box."

"Hmph." She opens the bottle and pours the syrup into the measuring cap, but it comes out too fast and overflows to the floor. "Whatever, here you go."

Veronica glances several times at her dripping hand and Afearia like she's crazy. "Uh," Zaiah says, leaning forward as he points at the cap, "that's too much."

"You said three teaspoons."

"Right, but the measurements are the lines. The three teaspoons begins far below the brim."

"Ugh," she huffs, rolling her eyes. "Then why make it bigger than it needs to be?" She pours it back into the bottle and carefully finds the line. She slowly tries to pour it, but she ends up going beyond the line quite a bit. "Come on!"

"May I?"

"No! Here, drink this, now!" Afearia says, forcing the cup onto Veronica who shuts her eyes and lips tight while squirming away. "It's good for you, drink it," she roughly says, spilling some of it as she tries to make Veronica drink it.

Zaiah quickly moves to Afearia's side of the bed, "Please, let me."

"No! She's acting like a kid when she knows better!"

"Yes, but she's still a little girl," he whispers. Afearia calms down a bit, looking a little more understanding as he speaks. "Not all of us grow up in hard times and get harder. Some of us try to hold on to that innocence."

Afearia sighs, "Fine," shoving the medicine and cap at him. As he carefully pours it, she watches him like a hawk. "If you try anything—"

"You'll put me down faster than a heartbeat," he says with a smirk. "I know. There we go," he says after measuring the perfect amount. "Aaahh," Zaiah says with an open mouth.

Veronica glances at him and the cap before raising the covers over her mouth, "I don't like medicine."

"No? But don't you miss running around?"

"I miss cookies."

"Ugh," Afearia complains, slapping her hand to her head. "I forgot the cookies again."

"Anya…?" Veronica says in a crabby whine.

"What kind of cookies do you like?" Zaiah asks her.

"Chocolate chip, chewy," Veronica replies.

Zaiah puts down the cap and bottle before standing, "Then that's our deal. I'm getting your cookies right now. You can eat five if your drink everything in this cap before

I get back."

Veronica shakily reaches for the cap. When she gets close, Zaiah grabs it and gently tilts it in her mouth to help her slowly drink. When she finishes, he grabs a tissue from the tissue box on the nightstand. He wipes the corner of her mouth and smiles when she does.

"Okay, cookie time," Zaiah says. "I'll be back in fifteen minutes. If I'm not, you get six cookies."

"Okay," Veronica says.

"I'll get something good for you too, little man," he says to Adrian while walking toward the door. He stops at the door and turns to Afearia, "Oh, you want anything?" Afearia grunts and looks away from him. "Okey-dokey," he says before leaving the room.

Afearia makes a face of confused annoyance, "Okey-dokey?"

After a while, Zaiah returns with the snacks he promised the kids. When he knocks on the door, Afearia cracks it open and looks at him. "Are those the kids' snacks?" Afearia asks.

"Yeah," Zaiah replies. "I ended up being later than I expected. I guess I owe Veronica six cookies," he jokes.

"I need to examine them. Give."

"Hmm. Are you going to lock me out?"

She just stares at him as the phone in the room begins to ring. "Give."

"But—"

"Anya," Adrian says, "Otto's on the phone."

"Otto?" Zaiah says, looking vaguely bothered.

Afearia rolls her eyes at Zaiah, "Just come in. After that, go somewhere." She lets him in and rushes to the phone by the bed. "Hello? Hey," she says with a smile and immediate loss of aggression. "Thanks for calling me back... I know, I miss them too."

Zaiah inches into the room and next to Adrian, "Hey, who's this Otto guy?"

228

"One of her only three friends in the world," Adrian replies. "She likes them a lot, especially Otto."

"What's that suppose to mean!?" he says with concern and alarm.

"I don't know. I just know out of her three friends she talks about him the most."

"Hmph," he says with a shrug, crossing his arms while looking away. "Whatever." Adrian glances at him and smirks.

"Tonight?" Afearia talking on the phone. "Isn't it a bit soon to meet him...? No, you're right. The sooner the better. Alright..." Afearia giggles, "If you say so."

Zaiah stands with his mouth open, completely in shock. "She giggled!" Zaiah pointing at her while talking to Adrian. "She never giggles!"

"Okay, I'll let you know how it goes. Okay. Bye," Afearia chuckles before hanging up with a breathy exhale of released tension. She then looks to Zaiah, seeming a bit more stern. "You're still here."

"Yeah, uh. What's going on tonight?"

"Why do you ask questions like this involves you?"

"I don't know."

"I swear you're like a lost puppy."

"Perhaps," he jokes.

Afearia grabs her shawl from off the bed. "Looks like I'll be going out again."

"Are we leaving?" Adrian asks.

"No, don't worry. We won't move on until your sister's well again."

"That's good," Zaiah earnestly says. Afearia looks to him and approaches. She soon begins pushing him out the room. "Hey, wait!"

"Goodbye, idiot." She opens the door and shuts it on him. Afearia sighs and leans her back against the door, "His persistence is unbelievable. You'd think he would take a hint by now. He's wearing me out," reentering the room.

"You still don't trust him?"

She sighs, "I hate to admit it, but he may actually mean well. I just don't understand why he won't leave us alone."

"You mean you."

"Huh?"

"I like Zaiah. Veronica does too. We think he's really nice and kind."

"How would you know? I don't see you guys talking to each other."

Adrian makes a nervous sideways smile, "We may have talked to him more than we should have."

"What!?"

"Anya," he loudly whispers, gesturing at Veronica who's sound asleep.

"I told you and that idiot to stay away from each other."

"We did, but there were times we had no choice but to talk to him."

"Ugh!" She turns around, looking quite annoyed. "No wonder he won't go away. He thinks we like him around."

"But we do like him around."

"Adrian, you're missing the point. What if he's just another Dr. Richards? He acts all nice now, but when we least expect it..." For a moment, her face saddens a bit. "I don't want to risk your lives on uncertainties. Nothing's worth that."

Adrian lowers his head a bit. "Me and Veronica felt the same way before we met you. We shut the whole world out just because of one man's evil. We couldn't trust. But if we kept living that way we wouldn't be together now. We would have done our usual routine. Take advantage of you then run away."

"Then what made you trust again?"

"We just had to believe that wasn't the world. It was ours. I wish meeting you was the full reason, but it took our own willingness to fight our own instincts to believe in you or anyone else again."

Afearia turns to him, "Must have been hard."

"Easier than you think with you at our side," he says with a smile. She smiles back at him. "And something else you should know about Zaiah. When we told him about your distrust in others, he said, bonds require you to stretch your hand out into the unknown. You never know who's going to take that hand. But that's life. Living through uncertainties in hopes for a better tomorrow." Afearia stares at the door for a moment. "Living guarded will leave you isolated. Once that happens, no light can ever shine in or out."

Afearia crosses her arms, "And you remember all of that word for word?"

"Yeah, seemed like he really wanted that to be understood and shared. I even remember the important things you've told me. I remember because it's important."

"Hmph." Afearia uncrosses her arms to grab her shawl. She heads to the door, twists the knob and turns her head halfway to Adrian. "You know, I really do see a lot of greatness in you, Adrian. Do you still not know what you want to be when you grow up?"

"No," he says, seeming confused.

She chuckles before opening the door, "It'll come to you." As she steps out and closes it partway, she sticks her head back in. "My advice. Do something life affirming. You can help more people than I ever could," she says positively with a earnest look in her eyes.

Afearia shuts the door and leaves the motel, standing out front. She carefully looks around the area. A pub called Rattle Snake, Afearia thinks. Is it seven blocks down or is it eight before two lefts and a right? Afearia huffs, "I should've wrote this stuff down."

"Hey!" a man shouts.

She looks to her right and sees Zaiah coming her way. "Did you seriously stand out her waiting for me to come out this whole time?"

"Mhmm. Pretty much."

"Fantastic," Afearia irritably says while looking elsewhere.

"Where are you going tonight?"

"You have yet to answer my question."

"Which was?"

"Why are you following me? You've got your life back. Derexen won't look for you because he'll think you're dead. You can start over. Do you really think getting involved with me is the best idea?"

"Yes," he says, looking her in the eye.

"I can't protect you. You know this."

He smiles, "But you'll want to if the situation would arise."

Afearia rolls her eyes and walks away, "Get lost."

Zaiah waits a moment before following. Afearia notices him get close and sighs. "What? I'm getting lost. I just happen to be getting lost in your direction."

"Of course," Afearia says before Zaiah smiles and begins humming. After walking several blocks and making the necessary turns, Afearia has grown tired of Zaiah's ongoing hums. "Would you please—shut up," she stresses.

"Oops, sorry."

"Look, I need to meet with someone important. I don't want anything to go wrong so I ask, please wait outside."

"Not a problem."

"I've got to admit, that was easier than I expected."

"Well, I'm not here to make things harder on you."

"Yeah, all of a sudden you're not here to make things harder on me," she says sarcastically.

"That's always been true."

"Yeah, I'll believe it when I see it."

She suddenly stops as he walks pass her. "We're here," she says, noticing the graffiti in the neighborhood.

"A pub?"

"Yes, now stay here."

The front of the pub across the street from them has a fair amount of people going in and out. The pub's name is in wiggly green font. Though it has two windows on either side of the door, it's too dark to see inside.

Afearia crosses the street and enters the pub. Once inside, she's immediately eye balled by two men standing by the door on either side. Though there are people on both sides of the room, most sitting at round tables, Afearia stares straight ahead.

She sees a man sitting at the bar with a green bandanna tied around his bicep and two women dressed in tight matching dresses on his arms. The three of them are laughing and carrying on with filled and emptied glasses of booze all across the counter.

The older gentleman is light skin with a visible scar on his right forearm in his short-sleeve solid blue button shirt that's half buttoned up, exposing his white tank top. Though he's laughing, his face has a mean demeanor because of the deep wrinkles between his brows and around his mouth. He wears a light weight black jacket with white fur lining the edges of his hood and the jacket's sleeves rolled up.

Afearia narrows her stare and moves straight for him. With each table and group she bypasses, the chatter dies down as they suspiciously watch her.

Afearia stands firmly behind the man, "Are you Elliot Lockhart?"

The girls on the man's arms look toward Afearia, seeming a bit serious in their leer. "Who wants to know?" the man responds before taking a swig of his whisky.

"I was told to look for a man dressed in similar

attire as yours at this time."

"By who?"

"His name is Otto. Otto Francis."

"Heh, yeah right."

"Clear Sailing."

Reconciling the coded phrase, he lifts his head and slowly turns to face Afearia, "And who are you suppose to be?"

"You haven't answered my question."

"Lady, you're in my town. You come in here asking for help, dropping names and expect a kind hand? Not in your life." He turns back around with the two women. "When you're done playing around in that get-up while being tight lipped, try me again."

Afearia lightly exhales before removing her shawl and keeping her right eye closed. "The name's Afearia. Perhaps you've heard of me."

The bar goes quiet before he lifts his eyes off his glass. "The dead girl. Also known as Ms. Calamity," He says as he turns back to face her. "It seems even death eludes you."

"Not really."

"Heh. And what can I do for you?"

"Then you are Elliot Lockhart."

"That's correct."

"Otto told me all I needed to say was the phrase. All should be taken care of after that."

Elliot chuckles with some people in the bar doing the same. "So confident. But you clearly don't understand business. You think because you said a code word from a good friend that's gonna to cut it?"

"I don't know what you want from me."

"Let's start by having your friend join us." Afearia becomes surprised by his statement. "What? You think I didn't know you had backup?"

"He's not backup, nor a friend. Just a lost fool

234

trying to find his way."

"Regardless, not like I haven't seen you two chatting and moving out of that motel."

"How do you know that?" she asks in an appalled tone.

"I have eyes everywhere. Or did you not understand what I meant by this being my town."

Afearia's face becomes stern. "Fine. But the man outside has nothing to do with this."

"He does. Being that he's standing outside my pub."

"Wait—"

"This discussion's over until he comes inside. Or you can try me tomorrow, alone, hopefully with a better head on your shoulders. We as a people tend to evolve every day. I'm always open to a fresh start. But it's your choice."

Afearia grunts and turns to leave the pub. As she begins to walk toward the door, the two men who eyed her before block her way. "Move," she firmly says.

"Wrong, Afearia." Elliot leans his back against the bar with arms stretched out while holding his glass from the rim. He's smiling at her with a face almost hoping for confrontation. "Try again."

Afearia turns to him, "Are you really Elliot Lockhart? Because for a friend of Otto's, you're sure not treating me very kindly."

"Ditto," he taunts.

Losing patience, Afearia grits her teeth before addressing the men blocking her, "Out of the way before things get ugly," she loudly demanded.

Suddenly, everyone in the pub, except Elliot, pull out their once concealed firearms and pointed them at Afearia.

"Yes, things can get ugly," Elliot says. "It all depends how you want to play it, Calamity."

"Excuse me, gentlemen?" a man standing behind

the two blocking Afearia says. When they turn, Zaiah's standing calmly behind them. "Mind if I cut in?"

"Idiot, get out of here!" Afearia says.

"By all means," Elliot says. "Fellas, let him through."

Zaiah walks between them as they part, "Thanks," he says with a polite smile.

Afearia shakes her head in annoyance as she stares at him standing beside her, "God you're stupid."

"Welcome," Elliot says. "We were just talking about you. Would you like a drink?"

"Sure," Zaiah says before moving toward the bar, looking at all the guns held up at Afearia. He makes a long-winded whistle before sitting up at the bar, "Quite the angry crowd here."

"They can't help themselves most of the time. But as soon as a certain someone came through, things went sour, didn't it?" Elliot says, looking at Afearia.

Zaiah laughs, "She tends to have that effect."

"Idiot, you barely know me," Afearia says.

Elliot pours Zaiah a glass of whisky. "What were you guys talking about?" Zaiah asks.

"Not much," Elliot replies. "Just you being her hired gun and her body to soon be riddled with bullets."

"Hired gun?" Zaiah chuckles. "Heavens no." Elliot watches Zaiah take a swig of his drink. "As for shooting Afearia. We can't have that."

Elliot smiles as Zaiah takes another swig, "You like the strong stuff, huh?"

"That and whatever else can impress me."

Elliot laughs, "You're an interesting man."

"I am today."

They both laugh while Afearia watches them with annoyed glances. "What's your name?"

Zaiah downs his drink and inhales loudly through his teeth before shaking off the burn. "Zaiah."

Elliot refills Zaiah's glass and his own. "Elliot." He toasts his glass with Zaiah's before they both drink. "In this town, I'm usually the guy people come to when they need a favor. So tell me, Zaiah. Is there something you need?"

"I would truly be grateful if you don't harm this woman." Elliot looks at Afearia over his shoulder. "She has a habit of getting off on the wrong foot with others. Her attitude doesn't help matters either." Zaiah looks over his shoulder and stares at her for only a moment before turning back. "But she can do better if given time." Zaiah and Elliot look at each other. "I won't go as far to ask you to fulfill her request. Only she can do that. All I can ask is for you to tell these folks to lower their weapons and give her another chance."

Elliot takes a deep breath and slowly exhales, almost as if to be displeased. He swirls his drink a bit and raises the glass to his mouth, "Put your guns away, guys," he says before drinking.

After everyone does as Elliot requested, Zaiah smiles at him, "I appreciate it." Zaiah turns to Afearia and gestures with his eyes and head for her to come over and talk to Elliot.

Afearia glances at the two men standing over her. "Excuse me," she mutters. The men barely part to let her through. She walks up to the bar and stands behind Elliot. "Elliot?" He doesn't turn to face her. "I'm sorry. I do not fully understand what I did to offend you upon our meeting but I can see I did at some point. Perhaps I shouldn't have been so straight forward when we first met. My brash tone with your men while not introducing myself properly was unfair and rude."

Elliot drinks half of his whisky before lowering it, "Now that's business." Elliot turns in his seat to face the confused Afearia. "You seem to think just because me and Otto are good friends I should just give you what you want by association. But to me, you're just a stranger."

Afearia's eyes look to the floor in thought. "Word of advice," Elliot continues. "Never presume you're entitled to anything. It creates bad relationships. Because if you did hurt my men before you left from here, I would have hurt Otto. And you'd be the one to blame for it, keeping your calamity streak alive."

"I know," Afearia mutters.

"I don't know this man sitting next to me, but in the last few minutes we spoke, I'm more willing to give him traveling aid long before you. You know why? Because he didn't come in assuming I would help him. He didn't come in hiding who he was or being guarded and vague. He sat down and had a conversation with me, despite how much he wanted to help you the moment he saw the guns. So for as far as your request goes... Denied," he coldly says. "Now get out," Elliot says before turning back toward the bar.

Zaiah makes a faintly displeased smile as he stares into his glass. Afearia stares at Elliot's back for a while before turning toward the door, "Then I'll try again tomorrow."

"And what makes you think I'll care by then?" he says before readying to finish his drink.

"We as a people evolve every day. Perhaps we can come back with a better head on our shoulders." She turns her body halfway to him. "Because we all can learn to be open to a fresh start," she says before walking out the pub.

"Hmph." Elliot smirks before finishing his drink.

As she approaches the front door, being stared down by the same two men, she makes eye contact with them. "Excuse me, gentlemen," Afearia says clearly. The men part as she walks between them.

Before she can step out, Elliot halts her, "You evolve quickly. Perhaps you don't need a whole day."

"I do. I believe you deserve a better greeting than you were given."

Afearia walks out the pub. Elliot chuckles a bit before patting Zaiah's back. "Bring her back here, would you?"

"Sure thing," Zaiah says before standing and rushing out the pub.

Elliot smirks as the pub door closes. She's just as they said she would be, Elliot thinks as one of the girls refill his drink. Which is why we need to move along. Time is short. Elliot takes his glass with him and does a head gesture to one of his women in a tight yellow dress with her right oblique exposed before walking away.

After a few minutes, Zaiah returns to the pub with Afearia. But when they come in, Elliot was no longer at the bar. "Where did he go?" Zaiah asks aloud as he and Afearia approach the bar.

"Elliot is waiting for you in the pub's basement," the woman in the yellow dress answers before coming from the other end of the bar. "That's where the real dealings are done. If you wish to still seek his aid, follow me."

The woman smiles at Zaiah before putting her hand on his shoulder, sliding it off invitingly as she walks toward the back around the bar. Afearia and Zaiah follow her behind the bar and into the kitchen. When they reach the back and take a few steps around the corner, a trapdoor is propped up by a thick stick.

The woman descends down before Afearia and Zaiah file out to do the same. Once at the bottom, she leads them down the dimly lit hall with shelves of canned goods and jars to the sides of them. Up ahead lies a dented metal door. The woman turns to them to see if they were ready before knocking on the door in an odd pattern.

It opens wide with the two men who were guarding the door upstairs now guarding this one. Beyond them is Elliot facing the door, sitting before a knee high, square wooden table on a box with the second woman from upstairs in her blue dress, standing beside him. Around the table are empty milk crates to sit on.

"Come sit," Elliot invites.

Once Afearia and Zaiah come inside, the woman who lead the way locks the door behind her and moves to stand beside Elliot. They sit at the table with Zaiah carefully looking around the small, ill lit alcohol storage room they're meeting in.

"Elliot," Afearia says, "do you really need him here?" she asks, pointing her thumb at Zaiah.

"Not really," Elliot replies. "The things I need to tell you are for your ears only."

"Tell me?"

"Otto wanted me to add informative details to your Clear Sailing packet. He's assumed that since your absence, you've lost touch with what's going on in the world."

"I haven't been gone that long."

Elliot leans back, "Long enough."

Elliot gestures with his head for the two women to leave the room shortly before the men guarding the door leave as well. When the door shuts, Elliot grabs two thick manila envelopes behind him from atop of beer cases and places it on the table.

"I'll try and keep this as simple and detailed as possible," Elliot explains. "Shortly after your supposed death, Derexen gave a speech about your passing and his coming plans in the next few years. This only aggravated the growing rebellion under his nose by the masses. But here's what shut down that uprising right away. During his speech, a man stood up and began to shout rebellious words to boost moral against the government."

"But he wasn't in the right mind," Elliot continues. "He pulled out a gun and aimed it at Derexen. I don't think anyone even had time to blink before the man's hand was cut clean off. Valerie had moved from her secure location to standing in the crowd, holding his severed hand along with her bloody dagger."

Zaiah makes a face of slight disgust, "That's a bit much, but not surprising, I suppose."

"No, except it was on public television. And deliberately, nothing was censored. Valerie looked dead in the camera with a rarely seen deathly stare that I'm sure froze the soul of many viewers. Derexen used that opportunity to clearly state he would not stand idly by as those who stand against him amass power. In other words, he's aware of the coming rebellion and he's not amused. But not everyone out there heeded his words. Have you heard of the group of freedom fighters, Mongoose?"

"Yes," Afearia gloomily says.

"Then I take it you know about their demise?" Afearia nods. "That was once again Derexen's violent response to our uprising. It seems he's taken the gloves off and is telling us to shove our demands."

"Seems more to me he's grown tired of Terra's demands and he's reminding everyone why he's in the position of power," Zaiah says.

"Well put. Part of me telling you this is because Derexen will soon be holding his annual world speech. I think this will be a prime opportunity for the rebellion and you to take action."

"When?" Afearia asks.

"At the end of this week. Four days from now."

"Then I can strike. Where is it?"

Elliot shakes his head, "Slow down, Afearia. You're getting ahead of yourself. To go at him swinging will be the biggest mistake of your life. There's a better way for you to do damage to him."

"You said I could use this opportunity."

"Yes, but brain over brawn conquerors all. He doesn't know you're alive. There's a way to exploit that."

"A sneak attack."

"Enough with the offensive, Afearia. It's not happening," he nearly scolds. "If things were different, I would have faith in that idea. But you'll be put down before you can lift a finger. Word has it that you lost to an Elite. Imagine trying to fight eight, excluding the select DA agents that may be present."

"DA agents?"

"Those guys," Zaiah says, looking away with worry in his brows.

"What's a DA?" Afearia asks.

"When Derexen created his regime, he toppled all of the old ones in every country. But not all of the old leaders were killed off. He spared quite a few. Though their countries still stand, they are under his rule with few liberties of independence. This placed those leaders a few leagues below him. Because of this, things had to change."

"A treaty was made," Zaiah continues. "When sat down at the United Nations, these fallen countries reluctantly agreed to sign if they're given some reassurance against future tirades by Derexen's hands. Thus, the DA agents were formed. An elite group of super beings who are Demi Anthropoids under direct control of their specific country. Each have the letter D following after their first name as I means of identification."

"In other words, a means to fight fire with fire," Afearia says.

"Exactly. But that's what makes them frightening. They may be government officials, but they do not answer to Derexen. They're under the command of the UN and the country they reign from."

"Not that I find it to be a good idea, but why don't the UN use these guys to overthrow Derexen's guys?"

"To simplify it as much as possible, it would violate the peace agreement they signed," Elliot says. "Going against that would cause an all out war. And that would put an unreal strain on the world's economy, resources, and the populace."

Afearia thinks to herself for a moment, "The DA

agents. Are they strong?"

"The strongest, supposedly. No one truly knows who would win if DA members and Elites actually went against one another. Not that it matters since war would ensue long before we knew the outcome."

"Regardless who's side the DA agents are on, they can't be trusted," Zaiah says. "The world has their issues with Derexen and his rule, but from what I hear, the DA agents truly play by their own rules. Did you know in some countries a DA is allowed to kill a human if it's required to satisfy their primal needs?"

"What?" Afearia says with some shock.

"It's true," Elliot adds. "In many countries, Demis and Demi Anthropoids are written off as beast without understanding or morals. No better than a dog in heat. Since they are required by law to let it be known that they are Demis in human skin, their allowed a fixed amount of unjustified carnage per month."

"That's ridiculous!" Afearia says with disbelief and shock. "How can the citizens of those countries trust such a system?"

"They don't," Zaiah says. "The point is to endlessly fuel the masses with hate and fear of Demikind. Trust will never be possible between the species because of it. In turn, fuel those same negative feelings towards Derexen and his kind, despite the fact Demi Anthropoids have proven to be more human than monster for the most part."

Elliot looks to Zaiah, "Where did you hear this?"

Zaiah closes his eyes for a moment. He goes into his pocket and puts a flash drive on the table. "Apparently, Calvin really made that bag a farewell gift." He looks to Afearia, "Remember when I said me and him stole government files but he didn't release them? Turns out he didn't destroy them either."

Zaiah holds the drive, "This is it. They're not files just from Derexen's country, but from the others as well.

243

And not that I know how, but when I reviewed it last night, Calvin obtained more than we stole that time. Recent things as well." He looks to Elliot, "I know you may want this. But it's encrypted. I'll be willing to share what's on it with you if—"

"No need," Elliot interrupts. "I don't need to know what's on there. I actually know quite a bit about the government as is. This is not a bargaining chip in your favor, I suppose. Just use this time to get information because things are going to start rolling around the world very soon." He looks to Afearia. "Starting with you most likely."

"Alright," Zaiah says before putting his flash drive away. He crosses his arms and sternly looks at Elliot. "What is A.N.T.S.?"

Afearia looks at Zaiah. He's become so inquisitive and confident, Afearia thinks. Bold even. He's in complete control and is fairly competent in a situation he had no understanding of previously... But he wishes to gain knowledge on things he can't change. Is he doing this for my benefit?

"Well?" Zaiah says, noticing Elliot is still silent after the question.

Elliot just stares at him for awhile, "Was that on the flash drive?"

Zaiah smirks, "I thought you didn't need to know what was on it."

"In that case. For reasons Afearia will soon learn, it's best you two find that out on your own."

"Why?" Afearia questions.

"Because it won't be useful to you right now. It may even cause you to make poor decisions based on what I would say. All I can say is that A.N.T.S. is important and is key to putting Derexen in his place for good. That's all I can say."

"I have a question about the DA members," Afearia

says.

"Okay."

"How many?"

"No one outside the government knows for sure. I assume as many as there are nations in prominent power. So, thirteen, give or take."

"How long will they be in this country?"

"It varies every year. Days, weeks, months. There's no way to really know."

"Last question about the DA agents. Do you think they'll get in my way?"

"No, but like Zaiah said, they play by their own rules. If they can find just cause, they may, but not by Derexen's request. It'll depend on how they view you. Are you the angel or the calamity? To be safe, just stay out of their way."

"That won't be possible for what I'm here to do."

"And many of us around the world are not sure what that actually is. But Otto and I thought of not only a way for you to make that clear, but to possibly even up the score between Derexen and his Elites. Maybe even take them down a peg."

"How?"

"By taking over the world's biggest speech with you at its core. Whenever the king opens up his plans for the coming years, he makes a large speech about it that's broadcasted across the entire world. Radios, TVs, city monitors and street speakers, you name it. But to do this, there has to be one originating source. With the team I've assembled, we can at best, take over the world's broadcast for at least five minutes."

"That's incredible," Zaiah says. "Who are they?"

"Just a small team of hackers. They're the best at what they do."

"And where do I come into all of this?" Afearia asks.

"You'll be giving your own speech. Otto thinks that if you make it clear to the world your intentions while openly letting the government know you're alive, you could boost global support and shake up Derexen and his team's confidence."

"Hold on, what supporters? Everywhere I go I get betrayed or attacked. Don't lie to me about why I should be a part of this."

"They're out there, Afearia. They're just too afraid to stand up. And the ones that do, stand up with shaky knees that ends with them turning on you to save their ass. But not in this room. Hell, you have an alley sitting back in Vale who's always going on about you. One is sitting in this room." Elliot glances at Zaiah, "And something about the look in this man's eyes tells me he is too."

Afearia looks at Zaiah who's in deep thought before he looks at her and kindly smiles. "As great as that may be," she says, addressing Elliot before looking at him. "This man's an idiot." Zaiah drops his head in a comical way. "Besides, I don't have confidence in a group of people I have never met."

"Agreed." Elliot stands, "Do you want to see them? Tomorrow, me and my crew are driving to Lorzen City to meet, prep, and strategize for this. It would not only be essential to them, but an honor if you joined us for this trip. This way you'll meet the whole team and see the entire operation coming together. Sounds good?"

Afearia sits quietly, staring into the table as she pounders. "I—don't know. I need to think."

"I'll tell you now. I'm not waiting for you. We're leaving bright and early at 6 AM. We'll drive by the motel to see if you're ready by that time. If not, we'll continue on without you."

Afearia exhales a bit loudly from her nose before looking at Elliot, "I have kids. One of them are sick. I told them I wouldn't move on until she got better."

"This isn't an obligation. Just a good opportunity to strike back and probably take out one or two Elites along the way."

Zaiah and Afearia are surprised, "You guys have a plan?"

"To reveal it now isn't something I'm going to do since I don't know all of the details yet. Besides, Otto's the one coordinating this whole event anyway. I just helped a little by gathering the teams and giving some input."

"Otto!?" Afearia says, straightening her back in surprise. "But he said he's done doing things like this."

Elliot laughs. "You should know him better than that. Being an outlaw is a big part of him. Living at the mercy of another is not a future he sees for himself. And he'll always be that way for as long as he lives. Derexen should fear men like him."

"Does this mean he'll be at Lorzen?" She lowers her head from view a bit, "I miss him," she mutters, getting Zaiah's semi stern stare upon her.

"Don't know. He's already stated it's best he stays in the shadows as much as possible in order to continue the guise of being an ordinary outlawed citizen. But that isn't important. The question is, what will you do?"

"I need to think it over."

"Then we'll swing by tomorrow. If we don't see you out front, we're going on." Elliot moves toward the door, "But I hope you'll be there." When he opens the door, the men and women who left the room were patiently waiting for him. "That envelope is for you. It's the Clear Sailing package. If I don't see you again, take care on your journey." He releases the door, letting it close while him and his people leave.

Afearia looks at the envelopes while Zaiah looks at her. "What will you do?" he asks. She looks up at Zaiah before grabbing the envelopes and leaving the room. He sighs and follows behind her.

Once departed from the pub, the two of them head back to the motel. Afearia returns to her room and opens the door to find Veronica sitting up watching TV with her brother.

"Wow, you're up," Afearia says, seeming a bit surprised.

The kids turn to her, "You're back to stay?" Adrian asks.

"Yeah, I won't be going out again tonight."

As Afearia moves toward Veronica's bedside, Zaiah quietly comes inside and gently closes the door behind him.

"Hey, Zaiah's here too," Adrian says.

"Don't get carried away," Afearia says. "He can't go beyond that spot."

"Awe."

Afearia sits on the bed, "How are you feeling, Veronica?"

"Sick, but much better too," Veronica replies. "Adrian didn't want to play leap frog," she complains.

"Because you're still sick," Adrian says.

Afearia feels Veronica's forehead and neck, "She's not nearly as hot as before. She's doing a lot better."

"Psst," Zaiah whispers to Afearia.

Afearia irritably walks up to him. "What?"

"I came back to your room to see if everyone's doing alright. But I have a room upstairs I want to rest up in. I'm in 2E."

"Didn't ask you all that."

"If you still plan to go tomorrow, mind coming by my room to get me?"

"I should sneak out and leave you behind. But I am curious to know what's on that flash drive."

"Calvin gave me a laptop, but I'm still unlocking the files."

"Hmm, maybe I don't need you."

"Huh!?"

"Heh, I don't know yet. I have a lot to think about."

"Well, if you need anything, you know where to find me."

"Idiot?"

"Hmm?" he says, confused.

Afearia steadily comes closer, seeming like she would hug him or more until she turns the door knob and opens it partway, "Get out."

"Heh," he says as he opens the door further and steps out. "Goodnight."

She shuts and locks the door behind him. "Hey, Anya?" Adrian says as Afearia walks toward the bathroom. "There's a new episode of Psy Island coming on. You gonna watch?"

Afearia grabs her tote bag, "If there's an encore episode, sure, but I really need a shower." She goes into the bathroom and closes the door. It seems times for relaxation are becoming more of a rarity these days, Afearia thinks, placing her bag on a wooden stool near the sink before taking her rag and laying it on the tub's edge. Can't even get a full day to enjoy a rented room.

Afearia runs the bath water and lets her hair down to unbraid while standing in front of the low mirror over the sink showing her reflection up to the bridge of her nose. At this point, I feel like I'm just moving without direction. Afearia pauses, Can I…? Can I even handle facing one of Derexen's elites? I'm far from peak performance right now. Simply wielding my swords is now a complicated endeavor.

Afearia resumes unbraiding her hair until it's fully out. She shakes her head and repeatedly runs her fingers through it while looking a bit sad as she stares into space. How well can I fight at all? Afearia thinks. To think the one thing I've always been the most boastful about is now under question by its proudest admirer. And I hate that…

As she removes all of her clothes, she thinks back to

her encounters since she's been on Terra, until quickly silencing the images of her defeat against Minerva. She grabs the sink's edge, leaning over it in a heavy pant and even some sweat. Her eyes move up at her own reflection, seeing the burning doubts, anger, and fear physically manifest.

Even now..., Afearia thinks. I... She's... I...

Afearia's chest feels tight, as she holds her fist to it before kneeling to the floor, shaking a little. Only becoming angrier, Afearia punches the wall, denting and cracking its plywood. A knock is heard soon after.

"Anya," Adrian calls, "are you okay in there?"

"I'm fine," Afearia loudly replies. "Go watch your show."

"Okay."

Afearia stands and looks at the water rising in the tub. She twists the knob to shut it off. She climbs into the tub and slowly lowers herself into the hot water. Her angry expression softens quite a bit as she feels the burning sensation of the water kissing her skin. She sinks herself low into the water with only her face still exposed while she looks up at the ceiling.

Everything just keeps moving without me, Afearia thinks. Even this plan was made without me. Otto, what are you thinking? Should I be suspicious? No, Otto's my friend. I can trust him. And if my plan is really to shake things up, this may be the way to do it.

Afearia heavily sighs before submerging all of herself into the water. She remains below the water for over a minute before coming up out of breath. When she regains some of her air, she lowers her head and stares into the rippling water.

"Funny... I almost didn't even want to get up..."

Roughly half an hour later, Afearia had finished washing herself and is now sitting on the wooden stool dripping wet as the tub drains and her bag rests on the hamper behind her. Motionlessly, Afearia is staring into the mirror, directly into her eyes. She slowly covers her right eye.

"Angel." Removing her hand, she slowly covers her left eye. "Devil." She lowers her hand.

All names given to me without my knowledge or consent. The humans here give me praise and grief. They think highly of me and expect much from me. Afearia bunches her brows. And that frustrates me. I expected it when I first arrived. But now that I'm living it I feel sick to their blind need to place everything on one person they have never met. Is that weakness or desperation? Perhaps a mix of self-inflicted naiveté.

Afearia looks down at her thighs with a rise in her somber expression. I'm starting to feel like I'm part of a giant game I know nothing about. I'm being pushed and moved across the board by hands I cannot see.

No matter how I see it, Afearia thinks before looking up at the mirror. My perspective on all of this is bleak and worthless. Afearia looks down before smirking and looking back at the mirror. We evolve everyday with a better head on our shoulders. And for me to do that, I can't keep letting things I can't control chain me. I need—to break free, Afearia sadly thinks as Demonweaver slides out from her dangling palm. Her brows become stern and her eyes sharp. And end my misery!

With the swift flick of her other hand, slapping her hair into the air, exposing the nape of her neck, Afearia swings Demonweaver's edge at the back of her neck with hair flying all over the bathroom floor.

A loud thud is heard and Adrian and Veronica look at each other. Adrian walks up to the door and knocks, calling to see if she's alright. Adrian begins to worry and tries to open the locked door.

In the bathroom, Afearia's eyes are closed as she's standing before the mirror and her heavy tote bag on the floor along with her hair. When she opens her eyes, a small hopeful smile appears on her face as she looks at her short hair cut to the nape of her neck.

Not bad, Afearia thinks. She glances at her long bangs. I guess I have to cut you too. She stares at the longest bang on the right side of her face. Well, not all of you. She only now realizes Adrian's near panicked calls and the fiddling of the knob. "I'm coming out!" she shouts.

Once dressed, Afearia comes out the bathroom with Adrian standing right in front of it. When he looks up at Afearia, he's wide-eyed and speechless as he steps back from her. Veronica looks at the bathroom doorway and sees Afearia herself. Her jaw drops and she freezes.

Afearia stands in the doorway smiling. She had neatly combed her hair back and kept majority of her bangs except for the left one while keeping the right bang long to hang down her face and close to her collarbone. She has bundled her hair into the bang and has it tied together with her black hair ties in X formations.

"So?" Afearia says with a weird wide smile and a simultaneous rise of her shoulders and hands.

"Nooooo!" Adrian screams. "You're hair! Why!?"

"I don't know. It just felt like it was time for a change."

"Anya, you look amazing!" Veronica excitedly says while Adrian comically paces around.

"Thank you. I oddly feel lighter, but more exposed like this. But it's good. I like it."

Adrian runs into the bathroom, searching for something, "Where is it!?" He runs around the bathroom looking through everything.

Afearia huffs and rolls her eyes, "It's gone Adrian. I flushed it."

"Nooooo!" Veronica begins giggling. "But I could've kept it! Anya—" he was saying as he turned to face her back. "Anya... I didn't know you had tattoos?"

"Tattoos?" she says, with her head partly turned toward him.

Afearia goes into the bathroom while Veronica curiously leans over. She unzips, covering her front while exposing her back. She turns her head to the mirror and is surprised by the ten brown tattoo circles lined across her upper back in an arch.

Each circle is two inches in diameter with a unique symbol in them. The one in the middle is raised a bit above the others with a faint silver and gold light coming from it, bearing the infinity symbol in chains.

The tattoo to the far left closest to her shoulder has a large castle in it surrounded by four layered walls. The next one has half a blade with four brown drops dripped from the tip. The third has the silhouette of a person meditating. Her fourth tattoo has a sea with a large iceberg. Afearia's fifth tattoo has a large lightning bolt coming from a dark cloud with rain.

The next one has two irregular shaped gashes with part of a lightly colored circle passing through one and remerging from the other darker. The seventh tattoo has the silhouette of two heads facing away from each other with one darker than the other. The eighth has three circles overlapping one another with three four point stars each smaller than the last. The last tattoo has four horizontal wavy lines and five wavy vertical lines, giving the symbol a strange warped appearance.

"What are these?" Afearia says, looking puzzled and concerned.

"They're cool!" Adrian says as he gets closer. "Why is the middle one glowing?"

"Can I see!?" Veronica says. Afearia returns to the room and kneels for Veronica. Looking to be in wonder as Veronica glides her fingers across a few. She moves her fingers along the glowing one and smiles. "It's really really warm. It feels... I don't know, I just like it."

Afearia stands, "Can you tell what they are?"

"Tattoos? When did you get them?"

"I didn't get them. I don't know how or what's going on."

"Oh well, I like the storm cloud and the warm one! One of them were kinda cold."

"Storm cloud?"

"Yeah, and the sideways eight in chains. The warm one!"

Afearia thinks to herself after hearing what Veronica was saying. She then slowly summons Demonweaver, causing the tattoo with the dripping blade to briefly flash then smudge.

"Oh!" Adrian says in surprise. "The second one smudged!"

"Really?"

Using her other hand, she summons Nebulous, causing the tattoo with the iceberg to do the same.

"Whoa! The fourth one's messed up too!"

"Is that the cold one with the wave?" Veronica asks.

"Yes?" looking unsure.

It's as I thought then, Afearia thinks. Is this about what Demeseus told me? About the blades being inside me? I need to show this to him when I get the chance. Afearia dismisses her swords and zips up her outfit. "I suppose it is cool." She moves toward the front door. "Veronica, get some rest. We have to set out again soon." She opens the door and looks back at her. "I'm sorry—to break my promise again."

Veronica stares at her for a while not expressing any emotions. She suddenly smiles and brings her hands to her mouth, kissing them as she spreads them apart.

Afearia covers her mouth in a gasp with wide eyes, blushing a little, "That was so cute!" she says in an unexpectedly high cutesy pitch. "I have to leave," she says, slinking out the door.

On the second floor, Afearia moves down the hall towards room 2E with her right eye shut. She stands in front of the room for awhile before huffing. She knocks and leans on the doorframe with crossed arms. The door opens halfway with Zaiah looking quite tired.

"Hey," Afearia says, seeming irritated.

Zaiah steps back blinking a few times before wiping his eyes. "Wow...," he says, staring at Afearia like he's seeing her for the first time.

"What?"

"Nothing... You look great."

"Hmph," pressing her lips while looking elsewhere. She glances over his shoulder and sees that his room's being dimly lit by his laptop screen. "Working late?"

"Yeah, sort of. Still trying to get inside all the files Calvin's given me."

"Yeah, look I've decided I will accompany Elliot to Lorzen and—" Afearia huffs and rolls her eyes, avoiding eye contact. "You are welcomed to join us."

Zaiah raises his eyebrows in surprise before quickly answering. "Wow. Yeah, yeah, I'll be there." Afearia nods before walking away. "Wait." She stops and turns to him. "You really want me along?"

"No." Zaiah seems a bit sad with his small tight lipped smile and light head bob. "It's not because I don't trust you." Pulling his attention back on her. "I just don't trust that I can keep you safe. I need you to understand that. It's hard enough protecting my kids because they're almost always around me. And those who stay around me experience danger all the time. Death is certain if you stay with me. Consider this our last time traveling together."

As Afearia turns and walks away, Zaiah watches her with a deadpan expression before closing the door.

The next morning, Afearia and the kids are up bright and early. The three of them are standing in front of the motel waiting for Elliot to arrive. Happily humming and turning slowly in place is Veronica, gripping tight to the scarf around her neck.

"Warm enough, Veronica?" Afearia asks, adjusting her shawl.

"Mhmm," Veronica replies "Is Zaiah still coming?"

"I told him he could, but after last night he may have had a change of heart. Maybe now he understands it'd be best if he stayed behind."

"That sucks…," Adrian says.

"Better for me. That man drove me nuts and was useless as can be."

Huffing and running down the street toward them with his duffle bag and shopping bags is Zaiah. "Awesome, I made it," Zaiah says.

"Yay," Afearia says with zero enthusiasm in her head tilt.

"Hey, guys," he says to the kids. "I got you two breakfast. You guys like bacon egg and cheese sandwiches?"

"Yeah!" the siblings loudly say before rushing toward him to get their food.

"I've got apple juice cartons too."

"Thank you, Zaiah," they both say.

"Don't mention it." He walks up to Afearia, "I've got one for you too."

"No," Afearia says with a near glare.

"Okay, more for me. Hey kids, there's donuts in my bag too," he says before grabbing his sandwich.

"Stop giving them bad food. You're like, the worst."

Zaiah chuckles before two cars come around the corner and park. Elliot comes from the driver's side of the front car. The guards from the pub come from the backseat with one moving toward the second car.

"Glad you're here," Elliot says to Afearia. He looks to his guard standing by the driver's side door of the second car. "Shall we go?" he says while moving to the passenger side door of the first car while his other guard goes to the driver's side car.

Afearia nods and moves to the backseat of the second car with the kids. Zaiah tries to follow after she gets in, but she literally kicks him out and slams the door.

"No room!" Afearia's voice muffled through the car door.

Elliot laughs, almost not able to control it. "Don't sweat it, Zaiah. You can ride in the other car."

Zaiah sighs, "Alright." He knocks on the glass. Afearia rolls it down only enough for her eyes to be seen. "Give this to the kids." She rolls it down enough to take the bag before rolling it back up.

As Zaiah takes a few steps toward the second car, Elliot calls to him, "Zaiah. This is going to be a big operation. This could really be the start of change all across Terra. I'm sure we could use all the help we could get."

"I'll do my best."

"Your best in interest to the restoration of Terra?"

Zaiah looks into the backseat window and sees Afearia playing with the kids and smiles. "In the best interest of Terra's angel," he says earnestly to Elliot.

Elliot nods and gets in the car. Zaiah gets into the second car, driving off shortly after the first car drives up the street.

A King's Role (part 1)

Chapter Nine

    While Afearia and her team of outlaws have long departed for preparations, Derexen and his team have four days left to finalize their plans for the coming day. Unfortunately, some of the government elites are being haunted by an ongoing issue. One that threatens the circle's standing itself.

    Passing through a dark forest on Terra, Minerva seems to be returning from a previous venture as her face is soiled a bit with dirt. As she moves through the area, she suddenly stops. She cautiously looks around before she hears faint rustlings. She crouches low like she's about to pounce when suddenly, she darts off deeper into the woods.

    As she quickly moves through the thick leaves, the hasty sounds of pursuers are also moving through the trees. With perfect precision, Minerva leaps to her right with elbow pointed straight. Successfully, she elbows a man in the face dressed in an all black spec ops outfit, but with less overall gear for lightweight mobility.

    She cracks his three lens night vision goggles before he flies into a tree while she keeps moving at breakneck speed. Because of the moonlight, Minerva notices a trip wire and jumps over it. Unfortunately, she triggers another wire that presses against her knees in mid hop. Just as a wide net is deployed to ensnare her, Minerva disperses into black mist, allowing her essence to pass through and rematerialize for her to continue running without losing speed as she rushes through the bushes.

    As she maintains her run, she glances to both sides of her before sprinting forward with a swift side step as two rods with electrified tips come from her sides, thrust by men dressed in ops gear. She turns around running backwards for a moment before running through leafy areas that bring her to a clearing in the forest.

She turns back the way she came, ready for the danger that seems to have found her. She backs up slowly below a tree before two men in ops gear descend upon her. One is brandishing an assault rifle and the other a large knife. Minerva jumps further into the open before they land. The man opens fire on her while the other darts at her with his knife ready. When the knife wielding man nears shortly after she ducks the brief spray of bullets, he seizes the moment to slash her.

Minerva turns to her right and leans back once he thrusts his knife at her. She prepares to disarm him until another spray of bullets is fired with a few grazing her side, causing her to stumble and allowing the knifeman to slash her shoulder. The knifeman continues his attack with another thrust.

She evades and grabs his wrist, directing his attack downward before evading the next barrage of bullets. Looking to engage the gunman, another man dressed in the same attire leaps out from the bushes she emerged from, swinging his electrified rod as he comes at her. Minerva evades, but not fast enough and is clipped on her fingertip by the rod.

She shakes the pain out of her hand as she slowly walks backwards, keeping her eyes and the steadily approaching knifeman and rod fighter. She hears the sound of the gunman behind her taking his aim.

Shortly after, two more men came from the bushes with electrified rod tips. As Minerva cautiously watches them while moving away toward the trees, the first attacker she had elbowed peers out from the bushes behind her. He jumps out and throws a circular object that releases three ropes aimed to wrap around her torso. She ducks them, but is fired upon and is hit in her left shoulder, causing her to grunt and stumble into the middle of the clearing.

Like wolves, the black ops attackers surround her. She kneels with somewhat of a focused look on her face as she stares down her foes.

"Annoying," Minerva says.

Her eyes turn yellow and her pupils sharpen. "This is it!" the man holding the knife shouts to his men. "Get in formation!"

As the men begin to scramble, Minerva speeds toward the man who shocked her finger and breaks his leg with a leaping shin kick to the side of his knee. While he goes down as she remains airborne, she grabs his face and slams it to the ground before sliding on her hip like a baseball player. She quickly stands and runs toward the others, trampling the fallen man's neck in the process.

She quickly moves to face the man with the rods. Seeming to be reaching for something, Minerva's too quick and smashes her palm into his face, embedding the goggles into his skull. She smoothly moves around the falling man and slips his large knife out of his belt holder and slits his throat before moving on to the next one in a low dash similar to a snake.

The last man wielding a rod swings at Minerva. She shifts to the side from range, moments before bullets come her way. She smoothly hops from the trajectory of the bullets and in that same moment, hurls the knife into the gunman's head. The rod wielder comes at her once more. Continuing her snake-like movements, Minerva swiftly moves around the man and hops on his back.

She wraps her legs around his head and curls herself forward to grab the knife from his belt and pull the pin to one of the four grenades strapped to his chest. Minerva follows up by leaning back to balance on her hands and slam him over herself.

He grabs her ankles and tosses her legs away from his face and rolls away to gain some distance. He quickly stands and tosses the grenade at her. Jumping to her feet, Minerva runs at him and catches it in a sprinting single spin, not losing momentum.

Without fear, the man runs at her as well. Minerva releases the grenade toward him with a soft lobbing flick of her wrist. The man attempts to slap the grenade away with his rod, but Minerva increases her speed several folds and bypasses the grenade and reaches him. Taking the knife she has, she stabs him in the armpit of the arm he's chosen to swing with. She spins around to the other side of his body and breaks his arm from the elbow by smashing her elbow near the joint while simultaneously raising her knee to met his forearm.

Smoothly, she moves low, slashes the muscles at the back of the man's knees and moves on to her next opponent just as the grenade hits the ground before him and explodes. She halts in the middle of the clearing and carefully watches the knifeman.

"Heh, you're getting slower," he says. "Or maybe we're just getting better."

"Both," Minerva says before bringing her knife forward with the blade tip turned horizontally.

He adjusts his knife as well with the blade tip facing to the ground. "Then we'll have your head in no time."

Minerva's eyes revert just as he comes rushing in to attack her with a wide slash. She blocks it with her knife. He hits her arm upward with his palm and attempts to punch her in the face with a backhand. She lightly kneels while tilting her head from range, before violently slashing his ribs. He grabs his side stumbling, but not before doing a sloppy kick that Minerva dodges easily with a light backwards hop.

He rushes toward her and does a leaping knife dive with the weapon overhead. She crosses her arms above her head, bearing the weight of his attack. He pushes harder, trying to get through. He takes his other hand and pushes down with both, making little to no change in her solid stance. He quickly ends his struggle with a swift slash to her face. Minerva quickly leans from his reach and backflips, disarming him with her toe kick.

The knife flips up into the air as she lands on her feet and bolts at her enemy. She slashes his chest and knees him in the stomach. He stumbles back as she leaps up to catch his knife. Upon doing so, she tosses both of them away and rushes him down once more.

He takes a combative stance before she throws a few jabs at him with her right arm. He nimbly dodges her punches before throwing a few of his own. As if to be imitating her form, he tries hitting her with advancing blows before doing a roundhouse that she ends up dodging. Minerva follows up with an angled roundhouse herself, aiming for his face.

With a clean hit, she continues to move in motion with the sole of her boot smashed into his face and grounds him with it without breaking contact and standing on her fallen foe's face. "Good fight," she says before applying enough pressure with her foot to successfully kill him. With half his skull buried in the dirt, she lifts her boot and looks into the deep woods while still maintaining her deadpan expression.

From the darkness in the woods, dozens of three lens goggles begin to light up, surrounding her from all sides. Minerva tilts her chin down a bit with slightly sterner eyes than she's had from the start of the chase.

Out in the southern warehouse district on Terra, Valerie's running between buildings and large stacked shipping containers as she's chased by similarly dressed men like the ones who attacked Minerva. They swiftly pursue her through the light rain, splashing puddles along the way.

As Valerie continues to flee, someone's recording her movements through green lens night vision binoculars before she slips inside a half open warehouse door. The seven assailants who've been chasing her enter as well. Four go through the front, two take the roof, and one from the left window.

The man recording under a black tarp wearing black headphones zooms in on the only available window he can see from his angle while increasing the audio pick up.

Though the warehouse is dark, it becomes fairly lit when the pursuers enter through the front and the clouds part from the moon's shine. Inside are large shipping containers stacked on top of one another. It has a high ceiling made of steel and another set of large doors straight ahead.

Valerie's standing in the middle of the warehouse between two double stacked containers with her hands behind her back, head low, and a slight smile on her face. They notice her odd behavior and stop.

"I'm grateful you followed me here," she says before her smile drops. "But this is as far as this chase will go."

"You've been lucky, demon," one of the two men hanging from the ceiling above by magnetic gloves says. "But as low as your battle rank is due to your own weakness, tonight will be when Derexen loses one of his men."

"To be so misinformed. Understand one fact. There is no such thing as weakness in Derexen's circle. Or do you not understand power?"

The two men hanging from above chuckle with dark intent before Valerie glances to her upper left, then her upper right. She slowly puts her hands into her robe while the men who entered from the front watch her without worry. She pulls out a black carbon throwing knife in each hand. After twirling them a couple times, she quickly spreads her arms, releasing them at an upward angle.

They go up and ricochet off the warehouse support

beam, going higher and faster in opposite directions. The knives cross each other and pierce the heads of the hidden attackers. One of the men hang from his magnetic glove like a dead bug while the other falls beside Valerie.

Her earpiece begins to flash yellow, getting her attention. After glancing in the direction of her piece, she stares down the remaining four in front of her. "My king calls for me. I can no longer waste time here."

The four men pull out their rods. Valerie dashes toward them, slipping her hands into her robe and behind her back. She quickly pulls out her hands and crosses them over her mouth, revealing four evenly placed throwing knives in her mouth. Valerie tucks her hands through open slits on the waist of her robe and pulls out four throwing knives between her fingers before stretching her arms back.

"She's a knife thrower," the man standing furthest in front. "Just deflect her knives and take her down." Valerie jumps up and throws four knives at them. "Above!"

As the men ready themselves, Valerie throws another four, faster than the first set. The second set hits the first set, redirecting them into a downward acceleration, stabbing the men in the shins and knees. Valerie lands behind them, moments before her earpiece falls out a few feet in front of her, trigging the piece to answer the call.

The grunting and grumbling men turn to her before she effortlessly throws her last four knives she took from her mouth. The men respond properly and deflect the knives from their heads. A couple seconds later, each of them had knives in their skulls, killing them instantly. Three out of the four fall while the one in the middle falls to his knees in shock.

"But—we—blocked—it," he says.

"How easily we forget," Valerie smugly says, pulling out another throwing knife. "I am an illusionist after all."

She throws the last knife with perfect aim, hitting

the half embedded knife in the man's head, lodging the blade deep enough to kill him. He falls on his back as she approaches her communicator. Derexen is on the line, calling her name to answer. She picks up the piece and secures it to her ear.

"Be at ease, my king. I'm perfectly fine. I shall return at once..." She listens carefully to his words. "Yes, you were correct. I shall explain shortly."

Valerie hangs up while the final assailant remains unseen, fearfully spying on her by looking between the gap of the lined, stacked containers at the left of the warehouse. How is this possible? the man thinks. Soaking his cloth mask in sweat, the man looks down. An Elite with a rank C battle strength took out six Owls? We may have been disposable, but this doesn't come close to what they said. Is her rank invalid? I have to tell—

The man looks up and through the containers to find Valerie was gone, including the knives she used to kill the men. It was only then he noticed the area he was standing in had darkened. When he looks up, he sees Valerie crouched above the stacked containers he's hiding behind, staring down at him with her chilling silver eyes.

"You're not very brave, are you?" she says. He stumbles back and falls with his legs shaking. "It's disgraceful that you would let your comrades die just to protect yourself. That makes you scum," she says with a stern tone and a deadly leer. "A life that would do all it can to preserve self over others. Gross. I can smell your worthlessness from here. You're dirt."

"Shut up!" he shouts, pulling a pistol from his waist and firing at her.

She jumps over the bullets and comes down on him, kicking his gun from his hand before landing. He quickly crawls away and scurries onto his feet with hands up to fight. He goes in and throws a hook that she easily ducks before delivering a heavy kick to his ribs. He stumbles and has his legs swept out from under him before falling on his back.

He stands up, a bit wobbly before she gives him two hard straight kicks to his chest, bouncing him off the wall before grabbing him by the throat. "If you won't fight with or for your comrades, then your only existence is to consume." Valerie ruthlessly stabs the man in the neck with her custom dagger, covering his mouth as he bleeds and spits blood into her palm. "And that is not the world lord Derexen is creating."

She pushes him to the floor and watches him twitch a bit more before he stopped. She glances at the window toward the doors she passed through before looking at her bloody dagger. Valerie takes the dagger and glides it across her face, making a fake blood slash. She tears her robe sleeve by cutting it with her dagger. Using the blood of the fallen man, she makes another fake blood slash on her arm.

Valerie repeats this on her leg, waist, and stomach before wiping the dagger clean on the dead man's clothes and putting it away. She approaches the doors she entered from and begins to fake a limp while holding her arm. Valerie passes through the parted door, limping into the open of the distant recorder's view before warping out of the area.

Out on top of the farthest stack of containers, the man with the binoculars lowers them with a sigh, "I'm sure if I had gotten any closer, I'm certain she would have taken my head off. For this is the max distance a human can remain unnoticed by Valerie Quinn. But if I were a Demi, no distance would be enough."

He pulls a radio from underneath the tarp to speak into. "I got as much as I could without being seen. Our men were not enough, but she did struggle. How about your end?" he asks, adjusting his headphones.

Back in the forest where Minerva's being attacked, a man lying in the bushes using the same equipment pulls up his radio from beneath his tarp. "I'm getting a lot," he says. "We're getting there. A.N.T.S. will be pleased. Remain hidden for a little longer before moving to the pick-up point."

"Roger," he says before putting away his radio.

I only got glimpses of her before the Owls perished, the man thinks. She took the offensive and then it got quiet. Next thing I know, it was over. And that doesn't sit right with me.

The man stands up wearing a black poncho and boots before pulling up his hood. He folds up the tarp and climbs down the ladder to reach the ground. He hugs close to the container where little rain hit him. Seeming nervous, he pulls out his wallet and looks at a picture of his son and wife standing beside a Christmas tree with him. He smiles and puts the picture away with his wallet before tucking his tarp beside the container.

My data is insufficient, the man thinks. Her sudden victory. The Owls only using their guns once. It's all strange to me. She's C rank. Then again, the Owls are only humans with slight genetic modifications. The man darts off into the rain moving low, lightly splashing the puddles. If I get footage of the bodies, I might be able to turn over better data than I have.

He moves quickly and carefully before stopping a few meters from the warehouse Valerie was in. He squeezes close to the container he's hiding behind, looking around to be sure. Shortly after, he races into the warehouse.

Once inside, he suspiciously looks around, seeing the four dead Owls. He raises his binoculars and switches from recording to capture, taking pictures of the fallen men.

Doesn't look like deaths done by supernatural causes, the man thinks. The tiny holes look like multiple stab wounds. But how can she stab so many of them so fast? She would require speed like Minerva. But she's not that fast. Even a quarter of Minerva's full speed is beyond Valerie's.

He looks ahead and sees the other two dead Owls before approaching. Same sized forehead piercings, he thinks. He looks up at the one hanging from the ceiling beam and the other on the ground. Did she actually jump up to reach them? Or did she...?

He looks up searching the higher portions of the building, noticing a scuff mark on one of the support beams. He looks around more and sees another on the second beam. She threw something, the man thinks. The slit shaped holes... Throwing knives!? the man realizes. Since when could she use throwing knives, and so well?

He begins to walk back over to the other four Owls until his foot steps in blood coming from between the stacked containers to his left. He quickly moves to the other side to find the last Owl.

Such a savage neck wound, the man thinks before taking a picture. Whatever she used on him, it wasn't a throwing knife. The man kneels down. How is this possible? Seven Owls was not enough? But a hundred or more of today's modified Owls should be enough to beat or weaken a rank C anthropoid. It's been tested. Yet she came out so soon. Then again, she was wounded.

The man raised the binoculars and took pictures of anything else suspicious before pressing a few buttons for the uploading message to appear. This is the best I can do at the moment. Maybe the A.N.T.S. network can put something together I missed. He stares at the dead Owl, seeming bothered. A hundred should be enough, right? She was hurt, badly. But if I do the math of how long it took to beat seven... A hundred wouldn't be enough. But she was hurt! I saw it! This doesn't make sense! Unless...!

The man's eyes slightly look surprised as he lifts his head from the fallen Owl, "She's higher than rank C."

"You should've gone home," a rough, threatening

voice says from behind.

The startled man quickly stands and turns around to see Kyoto in a bloody white trench coat with a chipped up bloody white hockey mask. Derexen and Valerie are also standing behind Kyoto. With no hesitation, Kyoto knocks the man unconscious with one solid punch to his face.

Kyoto, Derexen, and Valerie stare down at the man who's stretched out on the floor. "Valerie," Derexen says. "Gather the others and send them to my palace for an emergency meeting. Locate and assist anyone who isn't responding."

"Yes, my lord," she says before warping.

Shortly after she leaves, Kyoto's forensics team of humans and Demis filter into the warehouse. "I'll have this place cleaned shortly," Kyoto says.

"Good."

Derexen's about to walk away, but stares down at the man Kyoto knocked out. "Shall I carve him?" Kyoto asks.

Derexen approaches the fallen man, "Watch your persona, Kyoto. Perhaps you should switch mask now."

"No thanks. The night is young."

"And business is brewing. You can let loose later." Kyoto grunts in annoyance, seeming like he would refuse. Derexen fully faces him, giving him a stare that subtly looks threatening. "Kyoto."

Kyoto grumbles before lifting his mask. Once he does, his body begins to shiver. "It's co-co-co-cold to-tonight," Kyoto stutters.

Derexen grabs the unconscious man by the neck hole of his poncho. "Have your team handle the clean up at the designated areas. I need you at the palace immediately."

"O-okay."

Starting from Kyoto's feet like a violent storm of cylinder shaped darkness, Kyoto is shielded by its rise from all sides. When it drops to the ground, he is nowhere in sight. Derexen looks down at the man in his hands before vanishing under his powers as well.

Meanwhile, at Derexen's palace, some of the Elites have already arrived under Derexen's order. Bonnie, Glenn, and Valerie sit and wait for the others to arrive. As the three of them wait in silence, Glenn, sitting with his arms crossed, appears to be anxious as he's impatiently tapping his finger on his arm.

"I don't like this," Glenn says. "It's not like I don't know what's going on. Valerie, how many did you contact?"

"Everyone," Valerie answers. "But not everyone replied. Derexen, Kyoto, and Agonda are fine. Aquarius hasn't replied, but he sent a message."

"Which is?"

"The frozen head of one of our mysterious assailants at my feet. I would say roughly eight hundred miles from my location."

"How?"

"When I was calling him, I saw a falling, glittering ball from above. When it hit the ground, it was his signature. I know his work."

"And Minerva?"

"Minerva... She's..." Valerie stands. "I think I'm going to go to her location. Her energies are confusing me. I can't tell if she's fine or struggling," she says as she begins trying to call Minerva. But she doesn't answer. She walks from the table going toward the doors. "I'm going to find Minerva. Relay that to the King when he arrives."

Glenn stands, "I'll come too."

"You stay. Derexen's orders."

Glenn slams his fist on the table. "This is not the time for protocol! One of our comrades are in trouble!"

Valerie quickly looks back at him, seeming a bit surprised before lightly smiling. "Okay." She walks toward Glenn, "I'll warp both of us there."

As she prepares to put her hand on his shoulder, she pauses with a concerned facial expression while looking to her side.

"What?" Glenn impatiently asks.

"We need to hurry... She's gone."

"What!?"

"Oh?" Bonnie says with a raised brow and a negligible curve on her lips.

"I can't sense her," Valerie says, still frozen. "Her essence became so erratic. Then it vanished."

"Take us over there now!" Glenn angrily demands.

Just as Valerie's about to warp them, a black mist enters the room, gathering behind the chair Minerva usually sits in. When the black mist disperses, Minerva's standing behind her chair with yellow eyes and elliptical pupils. She stares at them with an appearance similar to a ferocious lioness returning from the hunt.

Covered in blood from head to toe, Minerva's face is nearly bathed in all red. Her gloves are dripping, and her robe is torn all over, revealing the fresh bloody wounds she has and her bullet shot arm in worse condition.

"Are you—?" Valerie was asking with wide eyes.

"One hundred fifty-eight men have fallen to my fist," Minerva coldly says with her near monotone response. "The first groups of five and seven were test groups," she says as she walks toward Valerie and Glenn with a noticeable limp. "The final wave of attackers had over fifty men, all of which were strangely familiar with some of my combative habits."

As Minerva passes the table, they notice a bullet hole in her side. "Minerva!?" Valerie shouts in alarmed concern.

"I've been shot three times. Two of which were sniper bullets." She stands before them and looks to Glenn, "Fortunately they weren't nearly as good as you."

"I'm calling the medical staff," Valerie says in a

growing panic as she presses her earpiece. Glenn becomes angry and snatches Minerva up by her robe's collar. "Glenn, stop she's injured!" Valerie says as she rushes toward him.

Glenn pushes Valerie away. "You stupid girl," Glenn says to Minerva. "Familiar or not, a hundred little bugs should not have gotten the best of you like this. What the hell has become of you? Do you have a death wish?"

"I'm not allowed to die, Glenn," Minerva replies, sounding a bit more monotone.

"Then why have you become so weak? You were even stronger than this when you were human." Minerva's eyes revert. "Well? Why are you letting yourself fall!?" he shouts, shaking her.

"Stop it, Glenn!" Valerie says, trying to part him from her.

But Valerie stops immediately once Glenn pulls out his revolver and points it at Minerva's head. "Long ago. The soldier I once knew would never let a man get this close and put a gun to her head, regardless if they're allies. Don't you understand the vital position we have at upholding the world's order?"

"I know," Minerva says wearily.

"Then why are you lacking?"

When Minerva passes out, Glenn holds her tighter by gripping her with both hands as she nearly hits the floor and Valerie grabs her from behind. "I'm taking her to receive treatment, Glenn," Valerie says with nervous, yet stern eyes. "Or would you rather we let her bleed to death?"

Glenn releases Minerva, "Take her. I'm sick of her shit." Glenn walks back to his seat as Valerie warps herself and Minerva from the room. He sits in a frustrated pose and props his arm to hold up his head before looking to Bonnie shortly after. "You're pretty quiet, Bonnie."

"I'm just concerned about all of these assaults," Bonnie says with a worried expression.

"Did they get you too?"

"I was in Orcelin at the time. Those Neanderthals wouldn't dare enter such a high security city."

Kyoto warps into the room wearing his hockey mask, walking toward his seat until he sees the blood on the floor. "Who's dying?" he gruffly asks.

"Minerva's injured," Glenn answers. "She'll live."

Kyoto proceeds to his chair and sits with the others. Soon after, Agonda arrives seconds before Derexen.

Derexen and Agonda take their seats. "Where's Valerie and Minerva?" Derexen asks.

"Valerie's taking Minerva to get treatment," Glenn replies. "We don't need to wait for her since she quickly gave her piece before passing out."

"She passed out?" he asks with an undertone of surprise.

"She says she was shot three times. She's becoming a liability, Derexen."

Valerie warps into the room. "Funny how quick you turn on your comrades, Glenn," Valerie irritability says as she somewhat aggressively moves toward her seat. "I was wrong about you," she says upon seating.

"Our number one priority should, and always be, upholding order throughout the realms. Part of that is making sure your team is always performing at their best. Minerva's not at her best, and you know it."

Valerie's expression becomes angrier before she could reply. "When did you notice this decline?" Derexen asks.

"A few years ago. I saw it, but I just thought she was off her game. Me and her rarely cross paths during working hours, so I didn't think much of it at the time. But today has made it clear. She's slipping."

"Enough!" Valerie shouts. "Her injuries are reasonable. She said her enemies were familiar with her habits like they've fought her before. Someone must be serving as a relay when they encounter us."

"Don't make excuses for her!"

"Glenn!" she shouts, slamming down her hands upon standing. The room's silent for awhile. "Glenn, please. This isn't helping. We're at each other's throats for no reason when we're gathered here to discuss and prevent these attacks, not point out our flaws. I know tensions are high after tonight. But we can't take progressive measures if we don't believe in our team's abilities." She looks around the table, seeing she has their attention. "Can we not speak of Minerva like she's a problem and focus on the matter at hand? Please?"

Glenn sits back and loudly exhales through his nose, "Maybe she's right. If these assailants are collecting data on our battle habits, that could be a problem."

Relieved, Valerie takes her seat. Kyoto, sitting with elbows on the table, leans forward while folding his hands. "I've noticed," he says. "Tonight, I fought fifty-seven men and had minor trouble until I used my ability. I've never had to do that before against these attackers. The moment I did, they were quickly defeated. Does this mean next time they'll be better prepared for me?"

Derexen thinks for a moment. "How many attacked Minerva?" he asked.

"She said it began as small groups of five and seven before the final set being a large mass of attackers," Valerie says. "Not sure how big the last group was, but she said in total, one hundred fifty-eight."

"That's three times in a row she's been hit with the largest assault parties. I believe our attackers think they're closer to defeating her than anyone else in our circle."

"That may be true," Agonda says. "I was only targeted by seven. But I didn't pick up on any change in their offensive."

"I was hit with twenty-two," Glenn says. "That's double from last month's. I had to reload."

"So?" Bonnie says.

"I've fought them many times before in larger groups." Glenn looks to Bonnie. "I never have to reload. I actually missed shots. For humans, their reflexes are a bit abnormal. They move much better than they did when we first started dealing with this. The attacks are becoming more frequent too. It's been five months straight, sometimes more than once in the same month." He looks to Derexen. "It's been four years and we still can't pin down who's behind all of this?"

"I can take an educated guess," Agonda says. "Only the toppled governments around the world would have anything to gain by killing us off."

"I don't think they're that stupid to break the UN's peace treaty over an old grudge," Bonnie says.

"Without proof," Kyoto adds, "this is pointless speculation."

"Indeed," Derexen says. "There are many countries that could be involved. We cannot assume they're all behind this."

"Why not?" Glenn says. "It's reasonable enough, isn't it?"

"Refer to Kyoto's statement for my response."

Glenn grunts in annoyance. "Lord Derexen's right," Valerie says. "Besides, we have allies who wouldn't turn on us."

"Correction," Glenn responds. "Compelled allies. They didn't want to be with us. They wanted to fight, but decided living was better. As Derexen made clear many times over. Die or walk with us. Those are the only choices he gives to most."

"And a smart leader would know to choose peace over war. That's why we have the treaty in the first place."

"Hmm," Kyoto ponders. "Then it could be a civil assault. An attack on home soil. It's not like we don't have a lot of those kinds of enemies here already."

"Which is why we should stop guessing and start digging," Bonnie says.

"Are you suggesting we violate our treaty with the UN and spy on other nations?" Valerie asks.

"As if those foreigners ever follow the treaties themselves. How many times have we caught spies and terrorist from other countries? Like it or not, if we're not doing it to them, they're doing it to us."

"And if we're caught, it could be the catalyst to a fourth world war. In less than two decades, mind you."

"We could always start right here," Agonda says. "If we just increase monitoring around our boarders and security in our country, the pressure could be enough to get the real culprits out in the open."

"We'll have to do it without alarming the public to anything strange on our part," Derexen says. "I don't want to draw attention. But for now, I won't do anything to jeopardize our public and overseas allies' trust in us."

"Do you think they'll strike during the world speech?" Kyoto asks.

"The ongoing pattern is that we are the targets and only when we're alone and away from society. They clearly realize that to attack when we're together would not end well for their units. Even if they do, we'll be ready."

"Then what in the meantime?" Bonnie asks.

"Everyone shall proceed as planned. I have leads on our attackers that I'm going to look into. Kyoto, check in with your team. Glenn, continue getting security up to code for the coming speech. Bonnie, make sure preparations for our arriving guest are up and ready to go within the next two days. Valerie, in several hours our monthly requisition program will begin. You and Glenn work out the security within and around the palace. Be sure the requisition list is complete before then. Agonda and I will continue looking into the assaults and the potential source."

"Should I relay anything to Minerva?" Valerie asks.

"She was suppose to assist in today's requisition. If she's not well by then, tell her she has to be ready for our guests' arrival. If there's nothing else, that shall be all."

Everyone warps out of the room except for Valerie, who remains staring into the table with a saddened expression.

Down at the basement, Minerva lies conscious on an operating table in nothing but her black floral bra and panties. She emotionlessly stares up at the ceiling of the white room with most of the lights off. The room's size and some of the décor is similar to a dentist office with two twin Demis dressed in white scrubs presently operating on Minerva's wounds.

Though both Demis have a voluptuous female figure, their skin is bright red and their ears are pointy. Dangling down the back of their scrub pants is a long, thick tail like a lizard's, but without the scales. The bottom half of their faces are covered by surgical masks, leaving their elliptical pupils and yellowish-brown eyes exposed.

Using surgical tools, the Demi working on Minerva's thigh, successfully removes the large bullet. The Demi drops it into the metal dish and dabs her wound with sterilized cotton balls. The Demi moves up to work on Minerva's abdomen while the other remains working on Minerva's left arm. Minerva makes a face of displeasure as they dig into her.

Valerie had quietly entered the room, "Are you using anesthesia?"

"She refused anesthesia," the Demi working Minerva's arm answers.

Valerie looks at Minerva who almost appears to be looking at Valerie like it's the first time she's seen someone like her.

Valerie looks to the Demi surgeons, "How bad is it?"

"The bone in her arm is split and chipped. The

bullet is embedded quite deep. I assume because of continued use after the injury. But since she has such a strong body, the other bullets failed to reach her vital organs."

"I guess you were fortunate this time," Valerie says to Minerva. Minerva turns her head back to the ceiling. "The discussion upstairs got fairly heated. You were the main topic for a little while. Glenn was adamant on accusing your decline of skill being the cause for your injuries."

Minerva remains unfazed before flinching a bit in pain as the bullet in her abdomen is removed. "But I explained the situation," Valerie continues. "They all agreed it was just the odd familiarity these people have of us."

The final bullet is removed from her arm, making Minerva groan a bit in pain. The Demis slowly remove their mask, revealing their faces to be similar to a human female, but with a slight mound over the mouth like an iguana. They lean forward to Minerva's wounds and smile at each other before slithering out their five inch pink tongues. Their tongues are nearly three times thicker than a snake's.

Valerie glances at her wristwatch. They repeatedly wiggle their tongues quite deep into Minerva's abdomen and thigh. Minerva makes a vaguely apparent face of pain. The Demis lightly suckle and kiss the bullet wounds while keeping their tongues embedded as they sloppily drool their blue saliva into her.

Though Minerva was breathing a bit faster from the pain, her hurt expression fades as she calms. Valerie looks at her watch again before an incredibly faint moan is heard from Minerva.

"Enough," Valerie says. "Fix her arm."

The Demis lean up and remove their tongues as tiny white spores continuously float out of her wounds and disappear. The Demi who was working on her arm begins to apply the same tongue treatment to Minerva's arm. The other leans forward, propping up their head to watch their partner with a sweet smile whilst making flirty eye contact.

Valerie keeps her eyes on her wristwatch until Minerva makes another sensual moan with a light flush in her cheeks. "Enough," Valerie says. The Demi's attention is fully on their actions as it continues to move its tongue in a near vibrating fashion with its eyes closed. Minerva moans a little louder while lightly squirming. "Hey!" Valerie says, shooing the Demi away. "Stop it."

The startled Demi slurps its tongue back into its mouth. "She'll heal faster if we do the full process," the other Demi says.

"The full process is unsightly," Valerie says with a sassy annoyed smile. "Get going. As always, your services are appreciated."

The Demis smile at Minerva and walk from the table. "Later, Roughshod," the Demi last licking her says, seductively walking out the room with their partner.

The door closes and Valerie shakes her head, "Though they may be the best healers we have, it's disturbing that their saliva has a strong aphrodisiacal effect that can cause climax. That's why we rarely call them."

"I do," Minerva says as her wounds slowly regenerate.

"Why?"

"Faster. Full process."

Valerie gets a chill and shivers. "You mean you let them—" Minerva turns her head to Valerie and gets another chill before looking away. "Anyway. It's been theorized that the enemy is collecting data on our repeated encounters. Lord Derexen and Agonda are working on some leads that may shine some light on this before the coming requisition begins. And judging by your current recovery rate," she says, looking at Minerva's bullet wounds, "You'll have to be excused. But our country's biggest allies are set to arrive in two days. You have to be sharp for that."

"Yes," she says, looking back at the ceiling.

"And normally, I wouldn't have to say that," she says, turning toward the door and leaning against the operating table. Minerva turns her head to Valerie's back. "But he's right. I hate to admit it, but he is. What's happened to you, Minerva? A hundred men shouldn't be able to hold a candle to you. But here you are—hurt." Valerie turns her head to Minerva. "It pains me to see you like this," speaking with grief in her voice.

"Why?"

"Why? Because I care about you!"

"You—care?"

"Yes!" She stands, shaking her head in annoyed disbelief as she walks a few steps from the table. "If it wasn't clear before, maybe it is now." She turns to see Minerva's blank expression. "But you can't understand a word I'm saying, can you? Because for some reason, your heart shattered into a million pieces and no one knows why." She rushes to the table and kneels, taking her hand. "What happened to you?"

Minerva looks her up and down, regaining her usual deadpan expression before looking up to the ceiling and leaving her hand limp in Valerie's. Valerie, releases her hand and walks from the table seeming a bit irritated by the way she was shut out.

"I just wish the old you would return," Valerie says with a saddened voice. She turns her head partway to Minerva. "I just don't want to lose anymore comrades, you know?" Minerva's eyes remain locked to the ceiling. Valerie sighs as she looks straight ahead. "Get some rest, Minerva. Hard times are ahead of us."

Valerie opens the door and leaves the room. Lying silently, the hand Valerie touched twitches a bit before she

softly curls her fingers. Valerie, Minerva thinks. She's—
warm.

Several hours later, the morning sun has marked the
day for the annual requisition at Derexen's palace. In the
crowded streets of Derexen's town, thousands of people are
lined up, filling the streets all the way up to the palace's
doors which are now open to the public. A magic
translucent staircase was erected specifically for this event
with palace guards positioned on the staircase, front doors,
and further into the town beside the massive line of people.

Inside the lobby are Demi and human guards
blocking all passages that are off limits for this event.
Going all the way up the center stairway and several floors
above are the people of Terra single filed waiting for their
turn to enter the throne room. The doors leading to the
room are guarded by hollow armored knights possessed by
Demi spirits.

The doors part as two joyful men are escorted out
by a human guard in knight's armor. "Next!" Valerie
loudly calls from inside the throne room. The throne
room's table and chairs had been cleared out for this event.
Just Derexen in his throne chair and Valerie calmly seated
at a desk to his right at the foot of his steps leading to his
throne.

Valerie sits at a finely crafted wooden desk next to
Derexen's throne. The desk has several high stacks of
documents all sorted and ready for the requisition event.

Another man comes in holding a briefcase while
being half escorted to the throne before the doors shut
behind him by the two hollow armored guards inside the
room. Once they stand at the middle of the room, the guard
proceeds closer, stopping at the steps of Derexen's throne,
facing the gentleman. Derexen stares at the man with the
briefcase before looking to Valerie.

"Edmond Law," Valerie says, looking through her
documents. "A government hired sonar specialist. His

request is in relation to his field. What do you wish, Edmond?"

"I wish for lord Derexen to reconsider the discontinued use of sonar," Edmond says. "This halt has made the use of submarines subpar at best. I've piled my reasons," he says, pulling documents from his briefcase. "With a great deal of pros if we reestablish sonar."

As the guard prepares to take Edmond's files, Derexen raises his hand to halt him. "In that well-documented list of reason, does it include the reason I ended the use of sonar?" Derexen asks.

"Yes, but I wanted to stress how advantageous it would be if submarines were back in service along with the sonar equipment."

"Edmond, did you include my reason or not?"

"I... No. But, sire—"

"Dismissed."

"Please, my lord, be reasonable," he loudly pleas. "Our submarines have no purpose now. They just sit at the base because travel's too risky. Sonar is the best means for communication, location, and anti-war efforts."

"At the cost of great amounts of marine life. Sonar kills and harms much of the living creatures in those waters. Whales and dolphins being one of the many who will be at risk. Unless you and your team can come up with safer valuable means to locate and communicate, I will not allow submarines to be used as long as I rule."

Edmond angrily grits his teeth, "It's not possible! You're just making things harder for us!"

"But easier for the world we wrongfully hold in our fist."

"We're part of the world too. You make work for government employees harder than anyone else. Why? For what?"

"Because we are the government, Edmond. We're suppose to have it harder than everyone else and be held accountable for every danger that befalls this world. If you can't understand that, perhaps you don't belong in my order."

"N-no. I understand, my lord."

"Good. Now be gone with you. And don't approach me about this again until you have a real solution."

Edmond grumbles as he's escorted out the room. As the doors part, a woman in her mid twenties, dressed in a casual business blouse and pants enters as Edmond leaves. She's a bit chubby, but not overweight. She has large moles on her face and neck and warts between her nostril and cheek, including one on her eyebrow. Though she is young, her nose seems to have been broken in the past and now looks crooked and wrinkled.

Once at the center of the room, she awaits to be addressed. Valerie, not looking to the woman, flips through her files.

"Kelly Rice," Valerie says. "She returns again, but this time seeks government lawmakers to help combat ongoing sexism." Valerie glances at her for less than a second before reading over her file, "Make your case."

Kelly clears her throat, running her hand through her half shaven head of green and black roots, "Good morning," she says with a smile. "As you know, we live in a world run and dominated by men. As a well-known and prominent activist in the feminist movement," she says with prideful snootiness, "I can truly say we've made great strides. But there remains a large amount of inequality in the world."

"Indeed," Derexen says.

"There are countries where woman cannot dress the way they wish. And at times, even here."

Valerie lifts her head, "Women can dress however they please in this country."

"Not when a woman wants to dress in something tight and revealing or go topless."

"You seem to be confusing freedom to dress and societal reaction. For centuries, people in this country and many others have been groomed to be uncomfortable with the human body. When a sudden change to the norm occurs like a woman being topless in a public place, it becomes awkward and sometimes offensive. But laws restricting how woman can dress have been removed whilst keeping with the limitations that are also placed on men. So what's the issue you're presenting here?"

"I want laws that protect women from men degrading and catcalling them when waking around in public."

"In other words, take away their freedom of speech and expression."

"No, just for this so they know it's wrong."

"Your reasoning is flawed. To do as you ask would violate an already existent amendment in this country. People are free to say as they wish, but once you start creating exception, where does it end? Your next mistake is the bias of stating only men take offence to the sight of topless or tightly dressed women while saying rude remarks or giving disgraceful stares. Even women take offence to women, why are they exempt from your proposal?"

"That's because of institutionalized sexism."

"There could be some truth to that. But how is punishing one side of the genders going to help that? You'll just continue cycling the hate in a different direction, not diminishing it."

"We are not equal right now. So even if we push it back to them this way, it will only even the tides."

"Then why did you come in here talking about making things equal between the sexes?"

"I—"

"No, you meant it literally. And I knew that the moment you came in. Screw ending the inequality and making the institutionalized discrimination and inferiority end by pointing out the flaws and seeking to make both parties happy. No, you want revenge. You want to make them hurt the way they made you hurt. Even if the ones you wish to hurt had nothing to do with your pain. But they will pay nonetheless."

She giggles, "A real woman. It's a feminist's job to tilt the selfish power from men to women. You get it!"

"I sure do," she says with a painted sideways smile. "So let's conclude. The government is not your attack dog. When you wish to use the power in this government to further a selfish cause destined to breed hate instead of end it, you immediately lose the right to ask for assistance from our hand." She stands Kelly's files up and lightly taps them on the desk to even the papers out. "I can't speak for the king, but I don't think you will be getting assistance from us this year."

"You found a true injustice I overlooked three years," Derexen says. "But every other time it seems you wish to find problems where there are none. Your request will be ignored."

"I have more request," Kelly says with a disrespectful tone.

"You're wasted enough of my time with your sexist mentality, or am I being hasty, Valerie?"

"No, sir," Valerie replies, reading through the rest of Kelly's files. "You don't want to know the other things she's requesting. Just more false victimization and male oppression."

"Wrong," Kelly says. "It's because our king is a man who wouldn't understand the wrongs placed here since he isn't a woman." She looks to Derexen, "You've even brainwashed this young lady into thinking this is okay."

"Um," Valerie says with bunched brows of annoyance and full attention on Kelly, "I can make my own decisions and I happen to agree with the king on this one. Your nasty requests are not sugarcanes and plum drops.

Their masked to look that way to hide your bitterness, anger, and jealously. Some of which is against women as well." She leans forward. "The world doesn't cater to you. Sorry you were born a woman and look like you do, but that isn't the world's fault. Make do with what you've got and clean yourself up as a person."

"You are so—!" Kelly calms herself. "You know what? You are a woman who's been neck deep in this patriarchy to fully see how bad things really are for women in this country."

Valerie looks to Derexen with eyes of annoyance by the woman's closed mind proposal while he stares at Valerie as well. "In this country, no," Valerie says to Kelly. "But others, yes. And we'll fix that. Other than this." She looks to Derexen, "Are we done with her, my lord?"

"Yes," Derexen responds. "She seems to have lost sight of her own cause. Dismissed."

The guard comes to escort Kelly by the arm until she snatches herself from him. "Hands off, pig!" she says. She walks ahead while the guard follows. The doors part as she storms out.

The next person to attend is an older gentlemen carrying a briefcase as he's let inside. He kindly greets the guard that escorts him to the middle of the room. "Good morning," the man says to Derexen and Valerie.

Valerie glances at him as she reviews his files. "Drew Stanford. "He seeks government funding for an anti-war ad." She lowers his files to the desk while looking at Drew, "Not sure why since the world has been promised no more war."

"I know, lady Valerie. But there are some who are still suffering from the repercussions of the third world war."

Valerie looks to Derexen. "Continue," Derexen says as he watches Drew make his plea.

"Thank you, sire. Though the third world war

waged against you and your Demi army has happened over ten years ago, it is not really a thing of the past for many. Some still fear another will happen while others suffer mentally from living through it."

"How so?"

"There's survivor's guilt, anxiety, PTSD—"

"PTSD?"

"Post-traumatic stress disorder. I have it all here," he says, going into his briefcase to pull out documents. Derexen waves his guard over to take Drew's files and hand them to him. "In there are the symptoms and what kind of disorders can and have happened from the war."

Derexen's carefully looking through the files, "And what exactly is your aim?"

"I want to make ads to show these people where to get help and to express further with other ads why they have no need to fear another war. On the last page I have narrations written out for help hotlines and facilities to heal those who are suffering."

Derexen flips to the last page and reads through most of the written out narrations. He then flips back to the page he was on. "You've put together some good work here."

"Thank you, your majesty."

"However, unless you fix the narration in the second ad or just disregard it altogether, I will not fund this."

"My apologies, your majesty, but if you would be willing to state what you fine displeasing about it—"

"It misrepresents your aim."

"But I wrote them myself. I don't see how."

Derexen looks at Drew, "You don't? Perhaps you should read it out loud," he says, holding the documents in front of him so his guard can deliver it back to Drew.

Drew takes the documents and flips to the last page to proudly read the second ad. "Are you afraid? Are you and your loved ones still paranoid of a coming war? Maybe even having trouble sleeping or focusing on anything else? There are others like you. Come to the MED center so you can regain your peace of mind. You no longer have to suffer in silence if you are a woman or a child. Call now—"

"Stop there. When you are appealing to the public you need to be direct and precise. That last line creates exclusion. You didn't have to state gender or age. By doing so, those men who may happen to be going through the same things will now be hesitant and maybe completely against the thought of seeking help."

"Oh, I was just thinking the common idea that woman and children come first. They do tend to get the short end of the stick," he jokes.

"Yes, because men don't suffer in silence. War only affects women and children."

"That's-that's not what I meant, your majesty."

"No? Because that's what I got from your ad. Let's say there was a man at home depressed and unwanted, feeling like no one will help. Then they see your ad. They may feel hope until they hear the narrator state only women and children. The only thing your ad will do is continue the ignorant notion that men are just accidents with no feelings and are perfect meat shields in times of terror. All people, no matter their walks of life have pains and aches. To target and exclude makes your reach limited and in my opinion, an utter failure."

The man thinks to himself for a while. He looks at his written narration again and nods. "My king, you are absolutely right. This approach was not complete. But I am going to fix this right away. Next year, I'm sure my ad will be up to your standards."

"Don't bother."

"What? But-but I swear it'll be better. I'll change it."

"Valerie."

"Yes, my lord," Valerie replies.

"Don't put him on the list next year for this ad." Drew lowers his head in shame. "Set up a meeting for Mr. Stanford to meet with the government advertising team next month. We will fund it if he follows through with the needed changes and adjustments."

Drew quickly looks up in surprise, immediately expressing gratitude, "Oh, thank you, lord Derexen! Thank you so much! You'll be pleased on how many lives we save and improve!"

"I'm sure. You can go. We'll contact you." Drew bows and is happily escorted out the room.

The next attendee is a young man holding a manila envelope. He stands in the middle of the room and adjusts his glasses. "Good morning, your majesty," he says.

Valerie turns a few pages, "Clark Clementine. An independent researcher of natural resources. He seeks funding to find a solution to Terra's impending clean water crisis. He also wants a research team and equipment provisions."

Derexen gestures for Clark to make his case. "As Ms. Quinn stated," Clark says, "Terra is, and has been for a while in a clean water crisis. We constantly overuse a vital resource in our everyday lives. Over a gallon alone is used to flush human waste. A gallon. That's terrible! We need not only find better ways to live, but we need to find an answer to our water crisis. But now we do."

"Which is?" Valerie says.

Clark begins taking documents out from his envelope, "Deep inside the planet are large rocks if cracked open hold clean fresh water that is safe to use. I've tested it myself," he says, holding out his papers to be passed to Derexen.

Derexen raises his hand to stop the guard from taking the files. "Though you are asking for a lot, I'm declining your proposal," Derexen says.

"But—sire, all creatures need water, even your kind. This is not something we can ignore. It has to be done, and fast."

"You're being denied because my government team already know about this and are working on it as we speak. They're even in the beta phase to find a way to convert salt water into fresh water. The best I can do for you is make you an addition to the team as co-supervisor of the projects. Perhaps you can be a permanent member of the team with potential of advancement."

Clark sucks his teeth and turns away, "No thanks," he says in a grumble as he walks away.

Valerie watches him with underlining annoyance, "Ungrateful little—" she was saying under her breath.

"Valerie," Derexen interrupts, still watching Clark as he leaves. "We are not allowed to verbalize our opinions during these hours. We are only evaluating whether to give direct aid or not. Being ungrateful or appreciative is solely their right. We do not judge or condemn their reactions here, understood?"

"Yes, my lord."

Once Clark leaves, a nervous woman wearing conservative clothing is escorted to the middle of the room. "Thank you," she says to the guard. She reaches the middle of the room and musters up her courage before looking to Derexen. "Hello, fair king of Terra."

"Leahnora Rodriguez," Valerie says. "She seeks...," looking down the list with confusion on her face before lowering the file and looking at the woman. "Medical treatment for her son. This must be a mistake," she says, looking the files over again. "There's no way this should've made it through processing. Personal request of this nature are not allowed."

"I know, Ms. Quinn. But the officer happens to be a good friend of mine and she told me the same thing. But I wouldn't let up until she did me this favor. See, my sick son has cancer and I can't afford—"

"Who's the officer?" Derexen sternly interrupts.

"I. I don't want to get her in trouble."

"Good. Then you'll be imprisoned for manipulating the system, ensuring your child does not receive help." Derexen waves the guard to take her.

The guard grabs Leahnora's arm, but she frantically spins out of it, distancing herself. "Wait!" she screams. "It was Carrie Grossman. Now please, my son," seeming close to tears.

"Remove her," Derexen coldly says.

The guard approaches. "Wait, stop!" she says, halting the guard. "Please, your majesty! I don't want him to die! He's only six!" she screams tearfully. Derexen glances at the guard, causing him to resume his duties. "Please don't do this!" The guard grabs her as she struggles to get free as she cries.

The guard hesitates.

"Remove her or I'll remove you," Derexen threatens.

The guard grunts. "I'm sorry," the guard says before gripping her tightly and dragging her out.

"Please, lord Derexen!" Leahnora screams. "This can be just between us! I'll do anything, just please save my boy! I beg of you!" The guard yanks her as they near the doors. "No! MY SON!"

The doors part before she's thrown out and apprehended by guards on standby. She screams through the halls as she's taken away. Valerie silently watches with sad eyes.

"We don't judge," Derexen repeats, staring emotionlessly into the hall.

Valerie looks down with a saddened expression. With our hearts..., Valerie thinks. No—we do not.

"Valerie."

"Yes, my lord."

"Make note to have Carrie Grossman fired and permanently unable to get a government job again. And if Leahnora lied, have her imprisoned for five years with rights to know about her son's condition."

Valerie's momentarily surprised before bitterly taking notes. "Yes, lord Derexen." With our hearts... We do not, Valerie thinks. "Next!"

The requisition event went on long into the day and only reached its end the following day at 4:30 in the morning. As the last person is seen and sent on their way, the exhausted guard turns to Derexen.

"You may go," Derexen says. "For working the full shift you may have the day off."

"Thank you, my lord," the guard says. "Goodnight."

As he leaves the room, the armored guards prepare to close the doors until Agonda strolls inside, almost knocking them over as if they weren't there.

Valerie looks up from her papers, "Agonda? What are you doing here so late?"

Agonda stands in the middle of the room with his hands behind his back. "Though the event is meant for the residents of Terra," Agonda says, "there are some request that need to be made on my part. I figured this would be the best time to openly discuss them."

"Agonda, that's not how this works."

Derexen gives him a long stare before exhaling through his nose. "Valerie, organize and file all of the accepted and denied request for this year. When you leave, take the palace guards with you."

"What?" she says, seeming confused as she stares up at him. Derexen does not look her way, he just continues to stare at Agonda. "Understood." She stands and walks from the desk toward the doors. Valerie glances at Agonda, but he does not look her way. When she nears the parting doors, she snaps her fingers, "Follow," she commands the hollow suits as the doors close behind them.

Though the room was fairly dark, the air Agonda brought in with him made everything seem ominous.

"As you know," Agonda begins, "it's fair to say after yesterday's assaults it must have been a wake-up call. Not only for you, for all of us. We need better means to deal with these transgressors. For far too long you've been lenient and it's starting to cost us. You want to protect these realms? You need to remind them why you're king."

"And what is it you request?" Derexen asks.

"Less ethical, yet more effective ways to get information from our enemies."

"I wouldn't think that would be a problem for you."

"It's not. But sometimes we need answers faster than I can get them. If enemies know all they have to do is wait me out until backup arrives or their objective is completed by others from their team, then the mental fortitude to do so will be harder to break. And truth be told, I believe some of them already got the memo."

"State your request, Agonda."

"I want you to allow a previous request I made to be passed. Project Babble. Bonnie was making headway with that. A truth serum through forced drug test on captured spies."

"Denied. That's what I have you for."

"I want permission to start Project Deconstruction. This gives way to shock treatment, drug dosing, sensory deprivation, and repeated reformatting in hopes of building a new person from the ground up. A doll for a soldier."

"Denied."

"I want to activate Project Shadow. Through countess physiological testing through stress and mental tearing, I want to create a sleeper agent."

"Denied."

He pauses for a moment out of irritation as he slightly readjusts his jaw. "Reinitiate the Child to Army program."

"Denied."

Agonda, seeming annoyed, practically glares at Derexen. "Do you want to protect this country or not?"

"Your pet projects are all for you to toy with people's lives in very harmful ways in an attempt to achieve effects that may or may not be favorable."

"That's why they're called projects. Experimental research is needed to see if it can be done or not."

"I'm not giving you consent."

Expressing a cold anger, he stands a bit straighter. "Alright. You want a sure thing? Release the restrictions you've placed upon me to extract the needed information from our enemies. Allow me to use my personal tools. And before you say no, remember. You've seen my work. I always get what I want. You won't need to find some crazy experiment to get what you need. Just my skills. And for as long as I am in your service," Agonda does a bow, not rising back up before looking Derexen in the eyes, "You'll always be two steps ahead."

Derexen stares at Agonda for a moment. He looks away, slanting his eyes, leaving silence in the room. "Granted."

Agonda widely smirks, "Excellent. You'll have immediate progress before the day is out." He turns and takes a few steps toward the door before stopping. "Please give the boys at the vault the okay for me to retrieve my tools." Eerily, he turns his head to Derexen. "I'll be in my office. I'll see you in nineteen hours," he says with a sick smile.

With the coming of scattered screams, Agonda uses his powers to warp out the room.

The next day, Derexen, along with Valerie, approach a satellite and communications government owned building in the famed city Orcelin. They pass through the large blue carpeted lobby and are greeted by passing employees before getting on the elevator.

"Which floor, lord Derexen?" the elevator operator asks, standing by the button panel.

"Seventy-four," Valerie answers.

The operator presses the button out of the one hundred thirty-two floors. They reach the floor they needed to reach uninterrupted before stepping out walking to their left. At the end of the hall is the broadcasting department. They enter the room where a small group of employees monitor and control various forms of nation-wide media.

They take a couple steps before a hasty man jumps in front of them wearing tan slacks, a headset, and black shoes matching his shirt with the initials CSC at the left of his chest. "Good afternoon, lord Derexen and lady Valerie," the man says. "I am the new broadcasting manager, Steven. What can I do for you during your humble visit?"

"What happened to the original manager?" Valerie asks.

"He made me his replacement. He wanted to pursue his career in a different light. Now, how can I be of assistance to you two? Is this about the world speech?"

"Yes."

"Ah. The previous manager put me up to speed on that while giving specific instructions in order to maintain smooth broadcasting. I promise you, all is in order for the coming day. There isn't a government owned location that is not hooked up to our network to receive our broadcast. We even have several radio stations under or network ready to go."

"Have you run any test to ensure that?"

"Yes, ma'am. Sound and video are optimal. And if anything would need to be primed for this event, our control room down the hall is at top form."

Derexen turns and leaves. Valerie glances at him as he departs. "Thank you for your hard work. We'll be in touch."

She follows Derexen into the hall, noticing he had taken a call and is now hanging up. "After we visit the staging area, I need to further our arrangements," Derexen says. "While I'm away, be sure to finalize our guests' schedules and resting reservations."

"Understood," Valerie says. "Before I forget, Bonnie has requested an audience with you, but hasn't been able to make contact. She's currently in the main technology building. Should I tell her to reschedule?"

"No, we'll see her after. She needs to be informed about tomorrow and her involvement."

When they reach the end of the hall, the two of them enter a fairly dark room with a series of large control tables and wall mounted monitors showing satellites, space, and Terra. At the metal table that's connected with the floor are men and women adjusting functions through their mounted controls with their team.

Derexen and Valerie approach the largest monitor that has a view of Terra and small computer windows being toggled. In front of the monitor are two men working a table that's slightly elevated above the rest. They stand behind the men for a little while before Valerie clears her throat, causing them to jump a little as they look back.

"Gentlemen," Derexen greets.

"Good day, lord Derexen," they greet simultaneously.

"Give me an update for this month."

"As you wished, the last of your satellites have been launched," the man in the right chair says. "You now have fifty-seven operational satellites separated in three requested categories."

"That's good."

"But there was a minor problem recently. Sometime last night, the team and I lost control over one of the satellites."

"For how long?" Valerie asks with expressed

concern.

"A terrifying five minutes. During that time, it ran a self-maintenance program, changed rotation for a few seconds and even aimed itself in random directions."

"Which type was out of control?" Derexen asks.

"The anti-war satellite. What may or may not come as alarm is that this isn't the first time. This has been happening for the last few months. It happens most frequently with the anti-war ones and some of the communication satellites."

"And why is this the first time we're hearing about this?" Valerie asks.

"We didn't want to raise alarm over something that tends to happen to new satellites put into orbit. It occurs most with satellites with complex functions like the anti-war types. But since last night was the longest we were not in control, we felt concerned."

A printer at the end of the table begins printing while Valerie thinks to herself for a moment, "By any chance, do you know what time this occurred?"

When the printer finishes its few pages, the man in the right chair takes them and does a quick glance before handing them to Valerie.

"Around 3:30 in the morning," the man in the left chair says.

Valerie carefully looks over the satellite abnormalities from the last few months. Seeming bothered, she walks away from the men. "Keep up the good work, gentlemen," Derexen says. "If anything else comes up, alert a government pillar immediately."

"Yes, sir," the men say.

"My lord," Valerie says low enough for Derexen to hear as he approaches her reading through the documents.

"What is it?"

"I'm not sure about the rest, but last night and last month's times the anti-war satellites were out of our control sync up with the times we were assaulted."

"Are you sure?"

"I'm certain." Valerie's earpiece glows for an incoming call. "Excuse me," she says while handing Derexen the reports to look over. Valerie steps away from him to answer the call while Derexen reviews the reports. Valerie rolls her eyes. "I heard you the first time. Stop being irritating," she says with a raised voice. Valerie hangs up and walks back to Derexen, "She's so annoying sometimes."

"Bonnie again?" Derexen guesses, still looking over the reports.

"She knows we're in the city, so she continues to call telling me to have you come by."

"Then we'll go to her."

"We don't work on her time table. She needs to wait."

"We're already here." He lowers the papers and looks elsewhere as he walks out the room. "No need for extra trips." Valerie sighs and follows him.

At the heart of the city are three tall buildings surrounded by two other buildings. The two shortest buildings, standing at ten stories, surrounding the three diamond positioned ones are gray in color with the tallest white building in the middle, standing at sixty-five stories. The other two buildings squeezed beside the white one are blue, standing at forty stories.

Down below at the front of the technology buildings is a fountain with a statue risen higher than the water can splash. The metal statue of a young man in a lab coat and fist on his hips has an engraved plate below that reads, 'Orcelin's Technology and Science Departments'. Beneath that is a quote from its founder:

"Through the punishing flames of knowledge, lies the embers of humanity's future." –Technology and Science founder, Dr. Raizoral Yesian

At the mid floor of the tallest white building, Bonnie stands in her large office. She's staring down from her window wall with hand at the corner of her mouth and one arm crossed over her diaphragm, supporting her other arm.

Bonnie's wearing a sleeveless royal blue dress with shiny floral patterns and a white lab coat over it. Her heels are black with a strap going over the foot and locking with the gold buckle at the side.

To the left and right sides of the room are bookshelves stretching across the whole wall. The whole room is carpeted in different shades of gray, mostly dark grays with the initials B.V. at the center of the carpet in yellow script and a yellow circle to enclose the letters. On her large black desk is scattered notes and sheets with equations and scribbles.

A light knock is heard from her black office door. "Yes?" Bonnie says.

A Demi slightly opens the door and comes in wearing all white patent leather with only one bulging yellow eye exposed and a slit across its mouth. It has a child's physique with the exception of its gumdrop-like head and its low placed arms beside its ribs.

"My lady," the Demi innocently says with the voice of a little boy. "The king and the department head have arrived."

"Show them in." The Demi shuts the door before she lowers her arms and turns toward her desk behind her to face the door. Shortly after, Derexen and Valerie walk in, the phone on her desk rings. She picks it up and holds up a finger for her guest to wait. "Answer faster when I call. Tell my chief I want fresh sushi made in front of me in thirty minutes. And don't skimp on the roe." She hangs up before sitting in her tall, black leather swivel chair. Bonnie smiles, "Pardon the delay, lord Derexen." She looks to Valerie. "And you."

"What was so urgent for you to rush lord Derexen's systems check?" Valerie asks.

Bonnie leans back, "I thought he'd be happy to know that Windnull was completed today," she proudly says before stretching her arms up and behind her head.

"That's it?"

"With the completion of Windnull, we can counteract a very troublesome being and one of the long plaguing disasters that terrorizes Armagevion. We can now move onto the most difficult project. Quakenull. I already have my team working on theories to cancel or weaken a quake. I also thought you may want to see a live demonstration of Windnull."

"Bonnie," Valerie says, pointing her thumb behind her, "we're supposed to be preparing for the world speech. Something you should be doing as well. So unless you have something else to tell us, or in relation to the coming day, we need to get going."

Bonnie stares at her, still smiling, but with a smile of suppressed irritability before she opens her draw, revealing three manila envelopes and her RK pocket watch from long ago. She hands one to Valerie and two to Derexen. The envelops are in bold black ink reading, 'Bionull Projects'.

"Don't be foolish," Bonnie says with a straight face. "The Bionull projects are important. And as for the coming speech, I haven't forgotten. But first..." She looks to Derexen. "Lord Derexen, there's something dire we must discuss. Afterward, I'll relay to you about the request you asked of me for our coming guests."

"And what might that be?" Valerie asks.

Smirking, Bonnie keeps her eyes on him while he continues to briefly look through the envelope. Derexen locks eyes with Bonnie and lowers his envelopes, "Valerie."

"Y-yes?"

300

"Head over to the staging area and make sure all matters are in order. If I don't arrive before you finish, it just means I've undergone other task."

Valerie glances at Bonnie with suspicion. "Understood." She looks at Bonnie once again before taking her leave.

As the door shuts behind her, Bonnie takes a small black remote from her draw with three white buttons on it. "I have something to show you," she says. Bonnie pushes the center button to activate the black shades for the window. Before the room fully darkens, Derexen turns to the door.

A projector comes down from above her head and produces an HD image on loop of a swirling black mass spinning violently like a whirlpool in the ground.

Derexen walks to the other side of the room so the image can fully show. "It's not like Valerie doesn't know about this," he says.

"I know, but this update may cross the lines of why I'm here."

Bonnie takes two one inch plastic clamps off her desk and clamps them on her index finger and thumb. A small green light comes from the clamps. She joins her index and thumb tips together before spreading them in order to zoom in on the image. She points to a shadowy figure inside the dark mass.

"You see that?" she asks. "I've come to discover that something lives at the heart of that storm. And after much surveillance, the only time that pressure producing mass weakens is when that figure surfaces."

"Last time we spoke about this, you told me the darkness in that mass is equivalent to seven hundred tons. How much is it when that thing appears?"

"Six hundred-fifty. Still too strong for any living being to enter, no matter their methods."

"What about firing projectiles."

"In theory, yes. But due to the rotation and the gravitational pull those walls create, it'll be torn apart before reaching its target. You may even spook what's in there. However, even if you could hit your mark by using the anti-war satellites, the destruction from such a powerful attack may cause the mass to explode and kill everything. And I do mean everything."

Derexen stares at the image for a while. "How much time do we have?"

"Through distant research I've gathered and the current rate of the realm's destruction, Terra and Armagevion have less than eighty years before all life in both realms end." Derexen does a noticeable exhale in a calm, but openly bothered manner. "But you should know," she says as she presses the remote to end the image and part the curtains to a dusk sky. "That estimation is inaccurate."

Bonnie removes the clamps and stands to look out her window, "The rate of realm destruction and the power of that mass permanently increases at random intervals. We could have eighty years. We could have fifty. Just recently the mass reached over one million eight hundred thousand. But Adam Markeith's research was thorough enough to give us a head start."

Bonnie turns partially to briefly glance at Derexen who remains with his back to her. "Unless we can get some kind of visuals from inside or even obtain a valuable sample, progression to stop this will remain at a snail's pace. Maybe if—" she says as she's turning to him.

Without warning as she turns, Derexen thrusts his hand over her throat and chokes Bonnie as he lifts her off her feet. Derexen stares at her with deathly intent, slamming her back to the glass. "We've reached it, Bonnie. I have no further use for you."

"Wait," she strains as she kicks and squirms, struggling to breath as she tries to pry his hand free from her. "Lord—wait."

"How long I've waited to do this to you. You have no clue," he says before squeezing harder, causing Bonnie's face to redden further and her eyes to tear up.

Air flow for Bonnie was almost completely blocked. She slaps his hand several times trying to get free, even attempting to grab his face before he immediately pulled her hand down, squeezing it as well. "Fuck!" she spat, barely staying conscious as her legs knock things off her desk. "Please—I can—fix this."

"You're progress is at a snail's pace. Translation. You can't do anything."

"It's offspring." Derexen becomes a bit curious to her words as his brows untense a little. "When it emerges it sends out offspring. If we capture one and run test we may have answers." Derexen looks away for a moment before viciously shaking her one time as he looked up at her. "It's—it's not now. And you know it," she says as her eyes flicker a little. "You... need—"

Derexen drops her to the floor as she coughs and desperately gasps for air. He stares down at her as she holds her neck with saliva all over her mouth. He kicks her fallen glasses toward her and turns to walk out the office, "You have one week to provide me some kind of progress on this. I'll fax you your duties for tomorrow and the day after."

Derexen leaves the room and shuts the door.

With her mouth open, Bonnie remains staring into the carpet with wide teary eyes as she takes in every breath. After awhile, she shakily puts her glasses back on and climbs into her chair. She puts her hands to her face as she rests her elbows on the desk.

When Bonnie closes her mouth to swallow spit, it hurts her bruised throat, causing her to loudly groan in unexpected pain as she holds her throat, stomping her feet like she's on fire. She calms herself and stares into her desk for a moment, looking a bit hopeless before a sudden burst of anger takes her.

In a fit of rage, Bonnie sweeps all of her things off the desk and quickly stands to hurl her chair into the window. The glass receives numerous cracks on impact, but doesn't shatter. She angrily huffs and puffs as she stares at her reflection in the glass. She controls her breathing and tightens her jaw.

How dare you continue to put your hands on me—a genius, Bonnie thinks. Walking all over me like I'm some kind of disgusting insect! I'm not the insect here! Bonnie punches the damaged glass, distorting her reflection while also cutting herself. "You're the insect," she says with her glasses below her eyes and the blood from her fist filling the groves of the glass. "I'm one in a billion. And you're..."

Back in Derexen's palace, Valerie's sitting in the meeting room alone, organizing files, signing documents, and making notes on her clipboard. The double doors open and she remains writing until the shadow of the person who entered was upon her.

"I covered your duties again today," Valerie says before she continues to write. "Tomorrow, you have to do your own assignments. I won't cover for you." She flips to another page and seems to be signing it with a bit of increased aggression before huffing and ending her signature to look up at the visitor, "Are you even list—"

When Valerie looked up, Minerva had presented to her a dozen yellow iris flowers tied together in a pink bow. With soft eyes, Valerie looks at them in frozen surprise. Minerva hands her a folded index card. Valerie takes it and reads it aloud.

"The yellow iris flower has many meanings. But it's most prominent characteristic is its symbolic ties to friendship." She looks to Minerva with wide eyes. "You— mean it?"

Minerva gently plays with Valerie's hair, making

her blush a little. "It matches you," Minerva says. Valerie nervously swallows spit as she had become a little flustered. Minerva shows her the flowers again. "Accept?"

"Y-yes," she says, slowly taking them. Valerie raises them up to her nose and takes a soft whiff before smiling into them. "The smell. It's so warm. Like—summer. Thank you, Minerva."

Minerva does a light nod before walking out the room. Valerie watches her leave with fondness before pressing her face into her flowers and taking another whiff.

Elsewhere, in a gray crumbling building of a small village located on a high mountain, the man who spied on Valerie sits in a chair inside a dark room where a dim dangling ceiling bulb sways overhead. The stone floor is wet with stains of blood all around him. Only the square space he sits is made of old wooden planks. The rest of the room is too dark to make out since the light only spreads out around the man and not much further.

The man has on no shoes or socks. His shirt is torn open as he sits covered in his own blood and sweat. The skin on his right arm has been peeled up to his elbow with most of it hanging off him like a banana peel. Most of his fingernails have been pulled off and replaced with thumbtacks. His arms are tied together at the back of the chair and his legs tied and bound to the chair legs.

The man lifts his head revealing cuts, bruises, and burns on his face. He bounces his head before lowering it and shaking his head in a whimper as the sound of damp footsteps approach. He fearfully looks straight ahead as the steps come closer.

Stepping into view is Agonda wearing a dirty white tee shirt and blue jeans with old blood stains. Draped over his body is a bloody black leather apron and a belt filled with assorted tools and deep pockets. The belt has assorted cutting tools, hooks, pliers, and ice picks, all of which are rusted. He pulls on his long latex gloves before stepping his

305

rubber fisherman boots into the blood puddle at the man's feet.

"Stop this," the man whimpers. But Agonda looked at him with pitiless eyes. He goes into his pocket in his apron and pulls out a sandwich bag with a white powdered substance inside. "What is that?"

Agonda tilts his head. He takes an eye speculum out from his pocket before opening the bag. He then kicks the chair from underneath the front legs, dropping the man onto his back, crushing his hands in the process. Agonda slowly kneels down and uses the eye speculum to open the man's eye and lock it's position. He grabs a fair amount of the substance with his two fingers and leans over for the man to hear him speak.

"When you're done screaming," Agonda says, "let me know what it's like to have poorly grounded glass in your eye." Agonda sprinkles the grainy glass into the man's eye before removing the speculum. As the man screams loudly, Agonda tugs on the man's eyelid and rubs the man's glass-filled eye. He smiles and exhales in satisfaction as blood drips from the man's eye. Agonda sits on the man's knees and props his head up with his bloody latex glove. "You really make my skin all tingly."

Agonda wipes the blood from the man's cheek and smears it on his chest. "It's that good, huh?" Agonda says. "I thought I might have lost my touch. But you squeal like a beautiful sow ready to mate." He happily exhales again, "Alright." He stands and lifts the chair back on its legs. "Play time is over, sadly." The man is still screaming with closed eyes. "Hey," Agonda says, but the man keeps screaming in agony. "Hey?" Agonda thinks for a moment. "Okay, okay, I know what you need."

Agonda kneels down and takes needle-nose pliers from his belt and clamps it on the man's middle toe. He slowly squeezes it, increases the pressure until the bone collapses between the pliers. He twists it and begins to gradually pull it from his foot.

"STOP, STOP!" the man begs.

"Quiet. I'm waiting for the skin to tear so I can see the muscle fibers." He continues until he can see beyond his bloody skin. Wiggling his tied ankles, the man couldn't stop squirming from the pain. Agonda stops and sighs when he loses sight of the man's torn toe skin. "You need to stop moving," he says as he goes into one of his pocket.

He pulls out many long, thick nails before taking a hammer from the waist of his belt behind him. As if he was just doing a mundane task, Agonda hammers a single nail into each of the man's foot joints. He then takes two large rail spikes from his belt and nails them though the man's ankles.

Agonda smirks, "Very good. Less moving, more screaming. You're getting it." He stands and lifts the man's head, staring at his bloody, swollen eye. He puts away his other tools and pulls scissors from his belt. He roughly grabs the man's eyelid. "If you don't let that breath, it could get infected." As if he was styling a doll, Agonda slowly scissors off the man's eyelid and drops the skin on his lap.

He steps back and leans forward as if he's about to speak to a child. "Can you see me through that eye?" Agonda loudly speaks. "Mr. Otis, I want you to tell me more. Who hired the Owls? Who's their leader?"

"I told you all I know! Just KILL ME!"

Agonda stands straight with a stern expression. "Taking one's life isn't an admirable skill. Preserving one's pain is," he says with a hint of optimism.

He walks into the dark before wheeling a two shelf silver cart into the light. The cart has small bottles of various liquids, hooks, pins, knives, small but dense hammers, bags of live worms, maggots and parasitic creatures.

Agonda walks up to the man and leans forward with

his hands on the man's shoulders, "We've got all night, Mr. Otis. And I've got two more carts right outside this room."

"You're… You're mad," the man barely says, exhausted from all the pain he's endured.

Agonda smirks. "Not mad. I just take pride in my work as the Connoisseur of Pain." Suddenly, the metal door behind him opens just a bit. He turns his head to it. "You're early."

"Are you done?" a man with a raspy voice asks from the door.

"More or less."

"Come." Agonda leans from the man and heads toward the door while undoing his apron. He hangs it up on the nail by the door before shutting it. He slowly walks down the hall with Derexen beside him. "What have you learned?" Derexen asks in his usual voice.

"They're called Owls. They're genetically enhanced humans who's primary function is to collect battle data by combating and usually dying for the purpose of creating counter measures for the central battalion."

"Who sent them?"

"He claims he doesn't know. His orders are given through delivered messages that are left somewhere for him to find. Apparently, these people are nothing more than fodder before the rise of some massive resistance."

"I see."

"One other thing. These guys don't leave a trace. I had his blood delivered to Kyoto. He's not in the world database."

"Neither were the ones killed. I had all of their bodies checked."

"Someone's working us from the inside out. But your guess of what organization they're from was correct." Derexen looks to Agonda before they stop. "It's A.N.T.S., Derexen. Their operations are spreading and it's starting to crack this kingdom's foundation."

"Then we only need to control how and when they can operate. If we do it long enough, they'll be forced to reveal themselves."

Otis incoherently screams from the torture chamber. Agonda glances behind him. "And what would you like me to do with our spy?"

Derexen briefly thinks. "Does he have a family?"

"Does it matter?"

"No… Kill him."

Agonda bows, "As you wish."

Agonda walks back to the chamber while Derexen continues to take his leave. As soon as Derexen turns the corner, he hears the tortured man scream out once more.

A King's Role (part 2)

Chapter Ten

Two days before the coming speech, the world's allied countries also prepare for the major global event.

Far out overseas, beyond where Derexen and his pillars reside, in a cold snowy country, a woman stands between two men on a small fountain before a crowd of underprivileged citizens. In the semi sunny, cobblestone paved town, the two men are dressed in long black coats and ushankas branding the country's insignia of a hammer crossing a sickle with a star above them. These armed men are soldiers for their country, brandishing loaded AK-12s.

The woman standing with a height of five seven, wears a custom-made white velvet parka with large gray raccoon fur around the edges of her hood and collar. Her half skirt parka extends to her knees with the same fur lining the bottom. Much of the fur bulks the inner portion of the skirt. The coat has a black St. Peter's cross on the lower front and back half of her parka, including smaller crosses on each of her sleeves at the wrist. The crosses are also on the sides of her parka skirt half.

Around her waist is an all white leather belt with a silver buckle of a grieving angel. Keeping her feet warm are tall white boots extending up to her knees with white laces. The woman's also wearing an all white furry ushankas with the ear flaps tucked.

She lightly touches up her black hair with the ends curled up a bit outward as it bounces at her shoulder blades. She smiles warmly with her light copper toned complexion. Her yellow irises have a fine pure clarity of a topaz gem. From cheek bone to cheek bone, going across the bridge of her nose is a fine sprinkled pattern of freckles. Around her smooth neck is a black choker with a gold St. Peter's cross hanging from a single gold loop.

As the crowd mumbles to themselves about her odd decision to stand on the fountain with a bright smile and hands on her hips, she nods softly at the turnout. A man who apparently was selected to hold flyers for her appears to be becoming frustrated from the wait as she looks into the crowd that has gathered.

"Hey, monster," the man holding the flyers says to the woman. "Can you begin before they leave?"

"Hand me the flyers please," she politely asks.

She kneels down when the man comes and hands her the flyers. She holds onto the flyers as he slightly steps back with annoyed brows as she remains looking at him, still smiling kindly. Without warning, an unseen force slams into him and sends the man flying through the crowd and into the wall of a building with a large red banner of the country's insignia, splattering his blood all over it.

The man's out cold as flyers are scattered through the air, coming down to the ground. "I am a child of God," the woman proclaims. She stands straight. "To speak with such disrespect for something he made is blasphemy. But I forgive you and your sinful ways." As the fearful crowd stare at the unconscious man, she extends her arm up to regain their attention, "Yoo-hoo?" she says cheerfully. "Gentlemen. I'm glad your curious minds have brought you here, but now's not the time to be distracted. For I have the opportunity of a life time to offer you."

She slowly walks along the fountain's edge, "Our country's gone through many changes since the king has come. Even our great military has fallen in power due to him striping away our might. It's deplorable. So, we rebuild. Whether you wish to strengthen our nation or give us a political edge to become more valued than we currently are—join us," she says, extending the flyer for the crowd to see.

311

The men at the front of the crowd look at one another, unsure of her proposal. "Don't you love this glorious land?" she says. "Don't you love what this country stands for? Don't you love our culture? Don't you want to protect all of it? This is your chance to serve your motherland like never before."

One of the men pick up a fallen flyer, looking it over, "To protect our land... A life altering experience. What does that mean?"

"Do you not trust our president?"

"Well, I—"

"Then how about this. Do you trust the word of God?"

"I'm-I'm not religious," he stutters.

The woman gasps with hand over her mouth, genuinely shocked. "A dirty sinner. How could you be so foolish. Do you not care about your eternal soul?"

The man nervously looks around, feeling the judgment of those around him who are believers. "Y-yes. I just never had the opportunity to learn about God."

"Oh," she says with a relived exhale. "You're just lost. But today you're about to witness something great." She puts a hand on his shoulder, "My brother, an act of God has already been performed here. You've always wished to learn about God, and God has brought you to me. Listen, brother, if you sign up for this program, they have bible classes for beginners and beyond. You see? If you ask, you shall receive."

"Is this true?" he asks, looking over the flyer. "Can I trust this?"

The woman smiles into his eyes, "Yes, you can. Just give us all your trust. Your soul shall be saved."

"Al-alright!" he excitedly says. "I'll do it!" He rushes to grab a pen from the table set up in front of the fountain below her.

"Anyone who joins will receive training, benefits,

salary, paid vacations, shelter, food, everything you could ever need to survive in this cold challenging world. Do you want to make something of your life and the world we share? The answer's here. Join us," she smiles with her hand out to the crowd.

Most of the people in the crowd take flyers from the ground and approach the table to sign up. The woman enthusiastically hops down and walks through the crowd until she's confronted by another soldier dressed in black.

"Chloe D., yes?" the soldier asks.

"Yes?"

"The president said to find you and have you escorted back to base in order to join him for his departure to see the world king."

"Splendid!" she says with a big smile and a clasp of her hands near her face. "Lead the way."

He walks toward an active parked black car and opens the rear door for her. Once she enters the car, he shuts the door and sits at the passenger side before being driven off.

Elsewhere, under gray skies in a neighboring country, a man slowly treads through a drizzling, foggy forest with hands in the pockets of his wool trench coat. It has eight dark gray buttons, four alongside one another. Because of his above average solid build, his coat is a perfect snug-fit, almost like his dark gray trousers.

To offset his outfit is a long red scarf that goes around his neck and lower half of his face, complimenting his butter cream complexion. The rest of the scarf hangs over the back of his shoulder. The man's mid length black hair is styled wildly, unlike his calm burgundy irises.

At the end of the dirt road, surrounded by trees is a town and a man in a blue rain poncho and hat.

"Hmm?" The man in the trench coat calmly says, stopping after noticing the person up ahead.

"Welcome back, Kalju D.," the man in the rain

poncho greets. "Was your two month journey into the wilds worth your time?"

"It was needed, but nothing life changing." He proceeds toward the man. "It's always so peaceful and quiet out here. Even the Demis in the forest have found a way to live in harmony with our country's habitat."

"They're still primitive beast that need to be expunged," the man crudely remarks as Kalju stops near him. "Hopefully your kind will go with them."

Unfazed, Kalju shrugs, "Probably."

"Anyway, the president ordered me to retrieve you and get you packed and ready to see the world's king and his demons. Like every year, I'm sure you'll fit right in," he cheaply remarks.

Kalju remains unfazed by his lowbrow taunts. The man pulls out a cigarette and puts it in his mouth. He takes his last match and lights it, but before he can light his cigarette, a drop of water falls from the trees above and puts it out.

"Ah-damn it! Hey, do you—?"

Like striking a match, Kalju's fist in his black leather glove becomes red hot as he executes an uppercut at the man's face. Knocking him off his feet, Kalju's punch leaves a brief fiery streak in the air, followed by smoke. The man fearfully stares at the tip of his lit cigarette, taking no injury of his own since Kalju was only inches from hitting him.

Kalju relaxes his striking pose and proceeds toward the town, "You're welcome."

Still afraid, the man stands after awhile as he watches Kalju casually leave him behind. He becomes angry and grits his teeth. "You damn monsters." He looks at his lit cigarette and throws it down into a muddy puddle out of frustration.

Further along the continent, an abnormally large man sits on two stools in a poorly lit bar with few customers. His upper body is as broad and wide as if you were to line up two hefty men side by side. Even his head was equivalent to a large watermelon. Although large, his arm and leg length is oddly small for his body, but thick like tree trunks. A muscle-bound giant he was, but despite that, this mammoth sized man's height only reaches five eleven.

He wears a black jumpsuit with two large breast pockets and a zipper down the middle halfway zipped, revealing his white tank top. He also wears partially torn navy blue overalls with one of the straps undone. The man lightly coughs, rumbling the bar and rattling the shackles around his ankles and wrist. The bartender comes down the bar, looking frightened, but trying to remain composed.

"That's your eighth pitcher of cherry ale," the bartender nervously says. "I know you're a DA, but can you please pay for your drinks?"

The hulking man looks to the bartender with his big brown irises. The man fearful steps back. But despite his menacing appearance, the man smiles big and wide, revealing his straight white teeth, offsetting his tannish-gray skin.

"Sure," the large man replies with an inhuman base to his voice. "I was going to wait until the end, but here you go."

As he takes his colossal sized hand off the pitcher to get his money out his pocket, the bartender freaks out and moves up the bar in a near sprint. "You can leave the money on the counter!"

The man scratches his short dark brown hair in confusion. He sighs and raises his pitcher to his mouth and drinks, loudly breathing through his broad nose. He happily chugs his drink until his smartphone rings on the counter, playing the nursery rhyme 'Hush Little Baby' with the image of a little brown-haired boy being hugged by his mother. He struggles to answer the call because of his big hands.

He slides it off the counter and into his hand before
sliding the screen to answer the call. "Hello, this is
Ludwig," he answers. "Yes, yes, I'm on my way."

He smiles and hangs up, placing his phone in his
large breast pocket. He finishes his pitcher before standing
and placing crumpled euros on the counter before leaving
the bar, shaking the room with each step. He stops and
stares at the big Ludwig-shaped hole where the entrance
once was.

The bartender's gossiping with his co-workers as he
and everyone else in the bar watch the giant's sudden stop
with bother in their eyes because of Ludwig.

Ludwig suddenly faces them with a big smile,
scaring them, "Sorry about this. There's a number with the
euros on a sticky note. Please call them to pay for the
repairs. Once again, I'm really sorry."

He bows and leaves the bar with everyone loudly
swearing and cursing his name and species.

Far out in the deep east end of the world is a
beautiful woman with the youthful appearance of little girl.
She sits on her knees in a spacious room of wooden floor
boards. The room is a wide square space with one open
doorway leading into a dark hallway. The walls are thin
and white with red wooden support pillars in the corners of
the room.

The young woman sits on an elevated portion of the
floor by four steps leading up to her. To the far left and
right of her are tall burning iron tiki torches. To both sides
of her are two women, one standing close and the other
kneeling behind her, both wearing red hanfus. But unlike
them, the black-haired young woman wears a far superior
hanfu.

Her hanfu is white with pinkish-purple cuffs and
hem. Her sash is a purple near white color. In purple
stitching on the sleeves and sash are cranes standing in a

316

pond, some with a fish in their mouth.

Complimenting her fair, milky white skin is her silky straight black hair being combed by the woman kneeling behind her. Her lips have a natural reddish-orange hue, and her eyebrows and eyelashes have both been trimmed and styled to accentuate her beauty. However, the woman's eyes are closed with a noticeable scar going across the bridge of her nose and along her eyes.

As the young woman smiles calmly to her grooming, another woman wearing a blue hanfu comes from the black halls holding a bowl of green grapes. Once near the young woman, she gets on her knees and presents the bowl to her. The youthful woman takes a few and puts them in her mouth, softly chewing them. Shortly after, another woman in a green hanfu comes into the room and kneels before her.

"Lady Niang," the green hanfu wearing woman says. "A call came in for you from a man who works for the emperor. Your audience has been requested."

Niang's smile grows, "It must be my favorite time of the year again."

She raises her hand for the woman behind her to stop combing. Niang stands, coming up much shorter than the other women at a height of four eleven. As she prepares to move toward the stairs, the woman in the green hanfu attempts to help her down, but her colleague holding the grapes fearful shakes her head for the woman to back off. The woman quickly gets back on her knees as Niang effortless walks down the steps before the women in red hanfus follow.

"Message girl," Niang says. "That's the second time you moved without my permission." She stops and turns to her with prominent angry brows. "I am not an infant," she scolds.

"Y-yes, lady Niang," the woman says, bowing repeatedly with her head touching the floor. "I'm terribly sorry."

Niang looks to the women following her, "Take her hands."

"What!?" she says, quickly sitting up. The women in red hanfus approach her before one of them pull out a concealed machete. The woman in green stands and slowly backs away from them. "Wait, please. Lady Niang!" she fearfully pleas while looking at her, "Please, I'm sorry! I didn't mean it, I swear!" The woman looks to her colleague holding the grapes, "Help me," she whimpers.

The woman holding the bowl fearfully looks away and lowers her head to the floor, trembling. Before the woman in green knew it, her colleagues grab her hands.

"Let's see how you like it when people pity you for your disability," Niang says before turning and walking slowly into the dark halls.

As the woman in green begged and fought to be spared, the woman on the floor began to cry and tremble, unable to control her breathing. It was then the agonizing scream of her colleague runs through her body, moments before the thud of the woman's hand being chopped off from the wrist hits the floor.

In the deep sea to the east islands, a light skinned man stands on the roof edge of a city building, looking into the distant night sky. With one hand in his skinny dark gray jean pocket, his black, hard fabric belt with silver buckles slant to the right. His shirt is a light smoky gray with the silhouette of a large cherry blossom tree on the left in black.

His snug autumn jacket is the same color as his jeans with collar fixed to rise pass his neck along with the hood. Near the bicep on both arms are zipper pockets, including near the chest. Around his neck is a short silver chain with a ring on it. The man has a slender build with neat, yet wildly styled black hair, draping over his ears, most of his forehead, his temples, and the back of his neck.

Despite the fact it's night time, he wears stylish black shades with dark lenses.

Landing on his light buttermilk cheek is a suzumebachi. As it walks to the faint dimple in his chin and raises it's lower half to sting him, he suddenly punches himself in the face, killing the suzumebachi.

Shortly after, a black helicopter comes hovering ten feet overhead, blowing the dead bug off his face. When the side door opens, the man bends his knees and hops into the chopper before it flies off. He calmly sits down before an army soldier tosses a cloth his way. It lands in his lap before he uses it to clean his face of bug juice.

"Something tells me we're not going back to base," the man in the shades says.

"As if you didn't know," the soldier replies. "Every year you do the same thing. Disappear from contact, stand on a tall building within the city and wait to be found. You DA agents swear you can do whatever you want. But as long as that chip's inside your people's head, we can always find you."

"If I really wanted to get away, you people wouldn't find me. So, where to?"

"I'm taking you to the Prime Minister's private plane so you can meet with the others by tomorrow morning."

"Are the rumors true about the western conflicts between the citizens and the king's elites? I hear the warrior from the stars caused quite a stir."

"You know I'm not ranked high enough to inform you about any of that. But I'm sure you'll be completely informed once you meet with our Prime Minister tonight. You're our nation's *ideal* DA for a reason, Takashi D."

Takashi lowers his shades a little, staring at the soldier from his right eye, revealing his purple iris and elliptical pupil. "That's true," Takashi confidently says before raising his shades back up.

The soldier makes an uneasy expression. You and Chloe may be the ideal DA agents, but you're all still freaks, the soldier thinks.

"Better a freak than a coward who will never be remembered for his talentless efforts," Takashi says, shocking the soldier. He smirks afterwards and looks outside the chopper, watching the city go by below.

Only one day remains before Terra's largest global event occurs. Currently, Derexen and his elites are in route to pick up their coming guest in three black limousines; driving through a sunny, desert-like plain.

In the leading car is Derexen sitting with Valerie, and Bonnie sitting across from him. Derexen's wearing a black suit with matching shoes and a white button shirt. His black tie has diagonal gray stripes. In his breast pocket is a camellia flower with a mix of mostly white and soft blends of red and pink. His black belt has a cursive large silver D as the buckle.

Valerie's wearing her usual business attire with a one button suit jacket, exposing the top of her blouse. The jacket's hem is white, including the pockets, but not the bottom edges or the three button cuffs. Her black peep toe block heels also have additional height because of the thick sole.

Bonnie wears an unbuttoned wine blue suit jacket with a large collar folded and pressed to the jacket. Her white blouse is buttoned all the way to the neck with the collar folded over the jacket's collar. Matching her jacket is her business skirt extending down to the top of her knee. Her black closed-toe heels have shinny diamonds around the sole. Her fingernails are painted a rich red to complete her attire.

Rarely seen, Bonnie's long silky hair is not tied up. Her hair's hanging low with the lower half done in rich curls extending down to the middle of her back and a clean part down the middle of her head.

Bonnie looks down at the tablet on her lap when the screen turns on with a silent notification. She begins scrolling through times and dates on her calendar, "Although we are a little behind schedule, we should be able to arrive at the country boarder before they arrive with a few minutes to spare."

"Good," Valerie says before looking to Derexen, noticing his unique accessory. "Nice flower."

Derexen glances at the flower. "It's a gift from Minerva. It was cultivated and modified by her. She says it represents how a select few in the elite circle feel about me."

"Wow. Until recently, I forgot she had a side hobby of understanding the meaningful language of flowers. What does yours mean?"

"It's a camellia. She says it means admiration, perfection, power, and love."

"Love!?" Bonnie and Valerie simultaneously say in shock before glancing at each other and looking away in bother.

"But because she made an unnatural flower, she gave it another meaning..." Valerie looks at him as he stares at his camellia. "Endless devotion."

"Whoa... I wonder why she went through so much trouble."

"How are today's arrangements?" Derexen asks Valerie.

"We're all in the green," Valerie replies. "Everything is set and finalized. I foresee no problems for the next few days."

"Good. We'll return to the palace first before taking them to the selected destinations we arranged in advance."

Behind Derexen's vehicle are the other two limousines steadily spacing apart fairly wide from each other before the trailing third limo reaches equal speed to the second car. They both trail evenly from the leading car as they cruise along. In the left limousine, Minerva and Agonda are sitting across from each other.

Agonda's wearing a light gray suit with a black shirt and red tie. At the corner of the shirt's collar is a gold pin of the government's flag. His black dress shoes are polished nice and shiny for today's meeting.

Minerva's suit is made for men. Because of this, her navy blue suit with black pinstripes is a little loose. Underneath is a white blouse with the cuffs exposed. Tied beneath her neatly folded collar is her baby blue tie. Even though her suit is mannish, her footwear is not. On her feet are black high heel sandals with risen soles.

Resting her chin in her hand, Minerva calmly stares out the window, seeming to be mentally elsewhere.

"Derexen said you and I have to give the tour of our defense department," Agonda says. "But we are not to show them anything vital, just the statistics and the procedures." He looks to Minerva. "I suppose I'll handle all the talking as usual," he says with noticeable irritation to her solemn demeanor. "I'm talking to you, potato," Agonda sneers upon leaning forward in a threatening manner.

However, his remark and his body language changed quickly when Minerva swiftly kicks her leg toward him, causing him to immediately lean back as she holds her heel less than an inch from his eye.

"Respect me," Minerva says, staring at him with her upper body unchanged.

He swallows spit and slightly moves to the side while her eyes follow him, "Excuse the insult. I'm just asking for you to acknowledge what I'm saying to you."

She lowers her leg and looks back out the window. "You're rude. Do all the talking. Manage the tour. Train the new hires."

"But you said you would train them!"

"Obey."

Agonda grunts. "It'll be taken care of." The soulless

witch is being vindictive, Agonda thinks. I brought that upon myself, I guess. "Will you at least overlook the tour?"

"Obligated."

"Perhaps we can—"

"Stop talking."

He crosses his arms and looks away from her. Good idea, Agonda thinks with a disgruntled expression.

In the last car, Glenn and Kyoto sit across from each other. Kyoto wears a half white half black suit jacket with the two colors on a slant much like his tie. From his right shoulder down to the middle of his abdomen is white while the rest is black.

In his right breast pocket is a white daisy. His trousers are white on the front and black at the back. Even his shoes are half white and half black. Pushed up on the top left side of his head is a white mask molded like a male human face. From the top right, spreading across most of the mask is a black design similar to cracks.

Glenn's suit is a grayish-blue with a matching tie that has thin diagonal white stripes. His suit is fully buttoned, only exposing a little of his powder blue dress shirt. Like Kyoto, Glenn has a fully bloomed flower in his breast pocket known as the holly flower. Glenn lifts his foot to rest on his knee, revealing his dark brown leather shoes with the heel of the shoe lined with shiny silver.

"Wh-why isn't A-A-Aquarius with us?" Kyoto stutters.

"When does he ever show up for these yearly get-togethers?" Glenn replies. "I question myself if he's actually a government elite or not. I honestly don't know what he does other than join the occasional battle or sit in on one to two monthly meetings. But lately he's been absent far more than usual."

"I ca-can't understand that-that man. He's too mis-misleading."

"I know. He takes a strange sense of enjoyment

323

leading people through his narrative before he locks you in a room of false truths. He's the king's joker, but he's got to be here for a reason."

"Wh-wh-why don't-don't we know? That's odd."

"It is. But I don't pick fights with the king over things like this. He picks his players very methodically. So I'm never worried about that. My concern always lies on what his final decisions may do to the worlds he rules. That's all."

Kyoto smiles slightly at Glenn, expressing a subtle admiration. He turns his head out the window. "Truly heroic," he mutters.

"What?"

"N-n-nothing," Kyoto says, leaving Glenn to just passively shrug and stare out the window.

Nearing the end of the hour, Derexen and his team arrive at the country boarder. As far as the eye can see, stretching from left to right is a towering stone wall with exposed gears in the wall and skyscraping doors extending far above the wall itself. The doors are wider than necessarily required. Wide enough to have a small army pass through.

Derexen, Valerie, and Bonnie exit their car before the others do the same. The others walk toward the leading car while Agonda walks up to Bonnie who's still fiddling with her tablet.

"So how long do we have to wait?" Agonda asks.

Bonnie closes a few apps while keeping a counting timer down in the corner with five seconds to spare, "Should be any moment now."

When the clock hit zero, a horn is sounded from above the wall. Gears and motors begin to turn as the barricades unlock and slowly part. Once opened, the metal doors behind it begin to part, revealing five white limousines as a group of people approach.

Minerva's eyes narrow on them. Glenn puts his

hand to his belt, near his tucked blue revolver, partially pulling it up with finger on the trigger. Kyoto fearfully puts on his mask before calmly, but menacingly watching the coming group. Valerie and Derexen calmly look ahead, watching their coming guests.

Passing through the doors are the five DA agents side by side wearing matching black suits and white button shirts underneath. Each of them also have black leather gloves, black ties, and black shoes and heeled loafers for the women. Takashi and Kalju are the only ones wearing sunglasses, Kalju's being only lightly tinted gray lenses. With them is each DA's corresponding country leader dressed similar to each other for the most part.

Derexen walks toward them to greet his guests. "At ease," he tells his pillars.

Though he told them to settle down, the elites barely do so. Minerva's eyes untense a bit. Glenn removes his finger from the trigger while Kyoto half lifts his mask. As Bonnie begins to follow Derexen a fair distance, Chloe lowers her head down and smirks.

Without warning, Chloe, Takashi, and Kalju bolt toward Derexen with remarkable speed, coming to attack Derexen from three different directions. But Derexen doesn't lift a finger, nor does he show signs of fear or alarm.

With flawless timing, Glenn is behind Chloe with his gun to her head as she was about to strike quite low from the ground. Valerie has her dagger pressed to Takashi's neck, deathly staring deeply into his eyes with their faces only inches apart. Minerva holds Kalju's arm up from the wrist whilst having her other arm wrapped around his neck, pointing his body close to the ground while she's knelt down.

Ridiculous! Kalju thinks, with a fearful appearance.

Fast little bugs, Chloe thinks, appearing annoyed.

Not bad, Takashi thinks with a smirk.

The chubby Prime Minister from Takashi's country slow claps while speaking enthusiastically in his native language wearing a dark brown suit and checkered white and gray tie.

Takashi smirks again, "Splendid, splendid," he translates. "As swift and thorough as ever."

"Must we always do this when we meet?" Derexen asks.

Bonnie slowly walks up from behind Derexen and his attackers, relaying Derexen's message with a smile. The Prime Minister chuckles while replying. "Well of course," Takashi translates. "I can only feel relived knowing the king's walking around with the best and not a bunch of jokes for guards." Takashi ends his translation and looks to Bonnie. "Long time no see, Bonnie."

"Likewise, Takashi," Bonnie politely says.

"Can we cut the chit chat?" Kalju says with a hint of bother in his voice. "I feel like Minerva's about to crush my wrist. And I'm sure Chloe's tired of having her head low to the ground with a gun pressed to it."

Chloe remains motionless with a comical expression of puffed cheeks as she holds her breath. "At ease my elites," Derexen commands.

As soon as his three elites released them and relaxed, the DA agents did the same. As the eight of them give one another space, the rest of the country leaders and their DA agents approach with the remaining elites. As the two groups near, Niang suddenly stops, looking as if she's come to realize something.

Niang's hair is neatly combed with two evenly spaced buns on the top left and right sides of her head. The buns have white silk covers on them with pink flowers. The remaining length of her hair comes from the buns like tassels. Over her forehead is a heavy set of bangs, mostly to the left near her eyebrow.

Niang turns her head in Minerva's direction. She

bunches her brows in irritation before Minerva takes notice of her. Minerva's stare intensifies for a moment. Like the lioness she tends to be, her irises turn yellow and her pupils sharpen. Niang's face is completely angered by Minerva's reaction.

"You dare bare your fangs at me, woman!?" Niang angrily shouts, getting everyone's attention. "With such nefarious air around you, you boldly aggress my presence?" Niang emphasized with her hand to her chest. She gets into an angry pounce stance with one hand toward the dirt and the other beside her. "Worthless criminal who forever runs, I will deny your false prominence!" she threatens with terrible intent in her voice, showing her clenched teeth and her always present sharp canines.

Niang's hands become veiny as she tenses her dangerous hands before one digs into the dirt. As her anger mounts, little wrinkles on the bridge of her nose appear like an enraged wolf until Ludwig puts his giant hand on Niang's head with his fingers hanging half down her face. This immediately calms her before he briefly lifts Niang like a doll and turns her around to face him.

"Come on, Yao," Ludwig optimistically says. "You know what you're about to do is forbidden by law and the UN treaty." He smiles down at her. "It's always better if we just get along, right?"

Niang looks away from him, seeming almost pouty. "You're such a softie, Ludwig," she mutters.

Derexen looks to Minerva. She glances at him and quickly reverts her eyes before looking off into the distance. Glenn leans over to Minerva, "No matter where you go, the ghost of your past refuse to let you live." Minerva's eyes slant a little in thought.

The leader of Niang's country speaks to Derexen in his native language. "I apologize on behalf of my monster, lord Derexen," Niang translates. As he finishes his statement before laughing, Niang makes an annoyed sideways smile, "Yao D may be on its period. I'm sure a box of bloody chocolates will sooth my monster."

The Emperor of Niang's country wears a dark brownish-yellow suit with a matching tie and brown shoes. He happens to be the most robust of the leaders.

"That's quite alright," Derexen replies.

Bonnie translates to the Emperor in a cutesy, cat-like manner. The Emperor is in awe before blowing a kiss at her. Derexen turns his head to Bonnie, pawing at the Emperor before nervously noticing Derexen staring coldly at her. She immediately stops and stands professionally.

Niang is rudely scolded by her leader, even slapped on the arm before he tells her to follow. Though scolded, Niang didn't seem to show any ill resentment for her leader's response. Once all of the leaders are standing before Derexen with their respective DA agents, Bonnie stands beside Derexen and smiles at them.

"As our nation's foreign ambassador, I welcome you," Bonnie says five times in each respective language.

"We don't have much time before my world speech," Derexen says as Bonnie translates. "I suggest we head to my palace now."

As Bonnie happily translates, Valerie stares at her with jealous eyes. Every year at this time, I feel utterly useless compared to her, Valerie thinks. No matter how I feel about her, Bonnie is the only one well-versed enough to be lord Derexen's mouthpiece. Who can openly say they fluently speak thirty-eight languages other than her?

"To keep things as civil as possible," Derexen continues as Bonnie clearly translates what's necessary. "I would like for President Duskin and Emperor Zhao to ride with me, along with their DA agents. Chancellor Heibel will be with Agonda and Minerva. Glenn and Kyoto will accompany Prime Minister Minami and President Härma."

Once Bonnie translated what each leader needed to know in shorter detail, everyone moved to their assigned cars before driving off. With Derexen's car leading the way, the foreign leaders and their agents sit across from the king and his elites.

"Ms. Niang," Derexen says. "I have yet to congratulate you for reclaiming your family's estate."

Emperor Zhao chuckles and says something to Derexen. "No need for formalities with my pet," Niang translates. "Just call it Yao D."

"He understood me?"

"No, he just heard you use my family name. But yes, I thank you for the congratulations, but reclaiming my family's estate wasn't a victory. Just a delayed birth right."

"I see."

President Duskin speaks to Derexen in his black suit, red tie in a full Windsor knot and black loafers. "What happened to the little girl?" Chloe translates in her strong, native accent, coming off with a deep voiced femininity when she speaks. "She always rides with you."

"When we reach my palace I shall explain, but in short, two of my elites have passed," he says while Bonnie translates.

"Perhaps she didn't accept God in her heart like all should," Chloe tells him. "God protects. God loves. His guiding light would have saved the girl."

"Now is not the time to talk about this," Valerie says, seeming a bit bothered by her words.

"There's never a bad time to talk about God. Why would you say such a thing?"

"Enough, Chloe," furthering her irritation.

"I mean no disrespect," she says somewhat earnestly.

"I'm sure," Valerie crossing her legs with a hint of disbelief.

President Duskin looks to Bonnie and makes a small comment that makes her giggle. She responds giving thanks with a classy hand pose to her chest and a charming sideways smile.

Chloe nods in agreement as she listens to what they're talking about, "Yes, she does look quite beautiful."

"Derexen," Niang says. "I'm sorry for your loss."

Derexen stares at her for a moment before looking out the window, "It is always unfortunate to lose a percentage of your power. But if history has taught me anything, there's always more power for the taking."

"I expect nothing less from the king of Terra. Nothing less."

In the car behind Derexen's, Agonda and Minerva are sitting across from Ludwig and his country leader. "I'm glad you were able to join us again this year, Chancellor Heibel," Agonda says. Ludwig translates while the somewhat chubby Chancellor straightens her sandy, baggy brown slacks and her lose-fit eggshell button shirt. She nods after the translation. "I hope you will join the tour we—"

Before he can finish, she says something to Ludwig. "Agonda," Ludwig says. "The Chancellor wishes to discuss business later. She just wants to enjoy the ride."

"My apologies, Chancellor."

Ludwig relays the message before looking to Minerva as she's resting her chin in her propped hand while staring out the window. Her eyes suddenly move in Ludwig's direction. He lightly smiles at her.

"Yes?" Minerva says.

"This is such a surreal moment for me. I finally get to meet and talk to you face to face without the need to discuss business." As if to lose immediate interest, Minerva's eyes move back out the window. "Your position in the government is indeed strong, but not as strong as your sense of morals. The journey that got you here today and the many lives you had protected is certainly a wonderful thing."

She looks back at Ludwig. "Sincere?"

"Of course. Only a fool would turn their nose up at all you've accomplished. You're like a modern day knight with the most noblest endeavors on your resume."

"Charming," she says with a near raise of her eyebrow.

In the last car, Glenn and Kyoto sit across from their foreign visitors. Glenn stares sternly at Takashi as he seems to be doing the same. "We're in a car," Glenn says. "Must you always wear your shades, even indoors?"

"My shades are my concern," Takashi answers with a smirk. "You don't see me getting bothered by Kyoto's masks. You didn't even say anything to Kaiju about his shades."

"I can see his eyes. You on the other hand—"

"Do you not trust me? We've been government employees for years."

"Not our government."

Takashi shakes his head with a lighter smirk, "But aren't they one and the same?"

"It's a big world. It's hard to run with so many people with individual beliefs of their own."

"That's true. An old regime dog like yourself should know that better than anyone. But I can assure you that these distrustful shades of mine are purely for medical purposes. I'm quite sensitive to light and bright colors entering my retinas."

"Then assure me."

Takashi leans forward and lowers his shades to only reveal his right eye before sitting back and fixing his sunglasses.

"My eyes are in a constant elliptical state for the same reasons a cat's eyes would adjust to the light. This isn't to flaunt a Demi trait, just a bodily response to protect my eyes. Unlike the brawling maidens in our governments, my eyes do not change in response to releasing my demonic might. Now if you don't mind, I'd like to enjoy the rest of this ride in silence. I'm a bit jetlagged."

Glenn turns his head out the window while Takashi folds his hands and leans his head back. He doesn't turn his head, he just moves his hidden eyes toward Kyoto, seeing him stare at him with firm eyes. He has good instincts too, Takashi thinks. Such well chosen soldiers you have under your wings, Derexen. I wonder how you do it.

After picking up his guests, Derexen and the others arrive at his palace. For this special time of the year, Derexen has a room just for them.

Inside the largest conference room, a round, black mahogany table has the same elite chairs in the same order as the usual meeting room. At the head of the table where Derexen's chair lies, Derexen's metallic chair is larger and taller than everyone else's. It has armrest and a red cushion on the seat and backrest.

On the table is a red table cloth with yellow edges and dinning plates with silverware set before each seat. Bread baskets, juice pitchers, and water pitchers are the only present food and beverages. The room itself is rounded with grayish-white pillars with glittering black fragments in it. The pillars line the walls with windows in between them, covered with black blinds. Above the table is a large chandelier with a light passing through the violet crystals.

The double doors open with Valerie coming through before the other elites come in behind her with the DAs and world leaders. The elites stand behind their chairs while the world leaders and their agents sit at their respective seats where their country's insignias are placed on their plates using place cards.

Takashi and his leader sit at the end of the table with their backs to the doors. Kalju and his President sit beside Kyoto. Chloe and her country leader sit beside Agonda, moments before Ludwig and his leader sit beside them. The only ones who've yet to arrive are Derexen,

Bonnie, Niang and her country leader.

Everyone takes their seat except Valerie who remains standing to speak to the table. "I'm glad you all could come. We will begin as soon as lord Derexen and the Emperor arrive. In the meantime, let's patiently wait for brunch." She opens her hand to the table, "Help yourself to croissants, bagels, juice, and water."

"Oh!" Chloe excitedly says, pouring water into her glass. "Will we be given any delicacies?"

Valerie grabs a croissant using tongs before sitting, "What do you mean?"

"Come on. Anything to make any egg sandwich worthwhile when wrapped in Terraian bacon."

"All bacon is Terraian. You'll have some when the palace cooks finish."

"Oh goodie!" she says with little rapid claps. "Derexen has finally ridded his country of the ridiculous rule of no human cuisine," she says before barehanded grabbing a croissant.

All of the elites look at her with shock in their eyes. Valerie turns her head in disbelief while not blinking and staring at Chloe like she's mad. "Eating humans is a major violation in all countries."

"If it's such an unnatural thing, then why is it so vitalizing? It is proven to provide better body nourishment than anything else we can eat."

"You dirty—!" Glenn angrily says upon standing. "We can arrest you here and now with passable execution. By world law, it is only acceptable as a last resort, and such circumstances should never arrive. You've committed a crime, and you will be punished."

"You've made a huge mistake," Valerie says before standing. "To openly admit your crimes here. As far as Terraians know, we Demi Anthropoids are not capable of such things. But because of your evil, we—"

Suddenly, Chloe bursts out laughing, innocently

waving her hands about while the DA members either chuckle or smirk at the elites. "I kid, I kid, you uptight stiffs!" Chloe says. "Yes, I've had human before, but not since I've been under Derexen's rule." Valerie and Glenn sternly stare at her, not buying her words. "Really, I swear," still laughing a little. "But I do want bacon," she says with a smile and her eyes devilishly looking up right.

Valerie and Glenn glance at each other, briefly trading a mutual thought about Chloe.

At the far end of the palace halls, turning up the stairs is Derexen and Niang with Bonnie and Emperor Zhao walking and talking several feet behind them.

"Your palace is wonderfully crafted," Niang says as she glides her hand along the banister and walls as they stroll along. "Not nearly as gritty as I imagined," she jokes.

"I have to maintain appearances after all," Derexen retorts, making her giggle.

Niang becomes a bit solemn. "I really am sorry Yadeira is no longer with us. Her plans of global education to less fortunate countries via conference link was a good idea. It would have brought a diverse, fair share of education, preventing bias teaching and giving everyone a chance to learn and grow."

"Agreed. It was still in testing before her passing. Hopefully, others in her department can realize her vision."

"I have no doubt they can." Niang turns her head a bit toward the chatty Emperor. "He's enjoying this little tour you've granted him. Especially his company with Bonnie." She faces forward. "Though I enjoy the pleasantries and the kind regards of me reclaiming my estate, something tells me you have more serious topics in mind." Derexen glanced at her. "This is about Minerva, right?"

"It doesn't have to be. But that little spat could have ended badly for all of us. If you or she even laid a finger on each other, that could have been a war between us and your country. As this world's ruler, I would have no choice but to engage in something so devastating over someone's petty vendettas."

"Petty?" she angrily and loudly says, stopping to face him while Derexen sternly does the same. Emperor Zhao and Bonnie stop before getting near, watching them with concerned expressions from the mounting tension. "You and this country can dress her in all the titles, medals, and honorifics you want, but she is not worthy. There is nothing she has done that deserves admiration. And because you've set up these laws to protect her from the past, doesn't make her misdeeds clean. Murder, vandalism, abduction. This is not someone you protect. And for you of all people to do such a thing is a sure sign of corruption."

"It's a law to exempt her of past crimes, not of any under my rule."

"And yet," turning her head to Bonnie, "others are not so fortunate to receive your blessed hand." She turns back to Derexen. "You can't choose whose past deserves eternal punishment and whose deserves exemption. That's nepotism."

"No. That's kingship."

"Kingship. Of course. I wonder how pretty that crown will look when the world's blood runs from it."

The atmosphere becomes palpable, even dense by an unseen pressure. "Was that a threat, Ms. Niang?" Derexen asks with dangerously calm eyes.

"Not a threat. A prophecy." She slowly moves closer toward him, "You can guard her with your laws. Hide her behind your walls." She stands less than an inch from Derexen, seemingly looking right up at him. "But a criminal's a criminal. And that doesn't change because you switched out your blood soaked garments for a clean wardrobe. Your hands... are still dirty."

Emperor Zhao questionably says Niang's first name. "I feel you're trying to say the same about me,"

Derexen says.

Niang pompously raises her eyebrow, "Isn't that a thought."

Niang walks on ahead. Derexen looks to Bonnie and gestures for her to lead with Emperor Zhao. Bonnie causally plays down the situation to the world leader as the two of them move pass Derexen before he follows.

Once Bonnie, Emperor Zhao, and Niang enter the conference room, moving to their respective seats, Derexen walks in shortly after. Everyone stands as he walks to his seat. They remain standing until he sits down. Valerie and Bonnie move their seats a little closer to him before sitting down.

"Once our meals arrive," Derexen says, "we can open discussion." Bonnie translates to the nation leaders.

"Thank you for having us, lord Derexen," Ludwig respectfully says. "Your home is lovely, and the townspeople are very welcoming. They weren't scared of us at all."

"Terraians are understanding that the Demi race isn't anything to fear unless they have harmful intent."

"I wish my home was like that. The treatment overseas is quite different."

"If it's uncomfortable, you should take it up with your nation leader."

Ludwig glances at the stone faced Chancellor Heibel. "That won't be happening," he says with a smile to Derexen.

"Not that it's necessary," Takashi adds. "They have every right to fear us. We are monsters after all."

"A protector should not be feared," Glenn says.

"Of course they should. If no one fears your power, then it's fair to say you never really had any power."

"Only an enemy should fear you, not the people under your protection."

"Now that makes no sense," Chloe chimes in while

shaking her head in disagreement. "At any given moment, anyone could become your enemy, even a long time ally." Glenn and Valerie glance at each other. "You all think it's fun and games now, but under the right circumstances, that ally of yours may be worth betraying. Whether it's for self-preservation or to protect another. No, my neighbors. All who walk can be enemies," she says with an unpleasant smile.

Derexen's elites become a bit tense. "Then they weren't your allies to begin with," Ludwig says, getting the room's attention. "Must we agents always speak with such cynicism? A true comrade would never dream of hurting their team."

Minerva tilts her head a little as she stares oddly at him. She puts her hand to her chest, seeming taken by something he said. "You are admirable," she says, surprising few of her teammates. "But foolishly naïve." She looks to Ludwig before expressing a hint of displeasure upon looking away. "I'm sorry."

Derexen's elites are in a bit of disbelief in Minerva's behavior. When's the last time I've ever heard her be sorry about anything? Glenn thinks.

Ludwig stares at her for awhile, "Is that so?" he says, sounding a bit disappointed.

"Tch," Niang gripes. "Of course. Who better to confirm such things than the master."

"Yao, please. For the sake of order."

"But—"

Ludwig turns to her, "Yao... please."

After awhile, she turns her head away from him. "You're such a softie," she mutters.

He kindly smiles. "Thank you."

"She's right though, Ludwig," Kalju says. "Minerva that is. It's not like teammates are sitting around hoping to harm one another. But if the right pressures are applied, they may find it to be necessary. Every civil war could tell that tale."

"I refuse to believe it. When someone's truly a valued partner to you you would never raise a weapon to them."

Sounding as if she choked, Minerva hunches over coughing before biting hard enough into her hand to draw blood. "Minerva, what's wrong?" Valerie worriedly asks. Minerva just muffles into her hand, coughing a little, not responding. Why is she acting so strange? Valerie thinks. "Minerva, if you need to talk we can for five minutes. I've cast an illusion through the room. As far as everyone else is aware, you've only sneezed. But if I use anymore power, Derexen will notice."

Minerva continues to bite deeper into herself, still not looking Valerie's way. "Minerva stop biting!" Valerie says, almost freaking out. "You're really hurting yourself!" Valerie gets up and walks around the table to stand beside her. She tries to pry her mouth open, "Why won't you listen? Stop this!"

Loosening her bite, Minerva's teeth nick Valerie's finger and cut her. For less than a fourth of a second, the illusion broke with only Derexen noticing the sudden disappearance of Valerie in his peripheral vision before he turned his head to her.

"Hm?" Valerie innocently says as she looks at him.

Derexen looks back at the table of all his conversating guests, "Nothing."

Behind the illusion, Valerie's crouched to the floor holding her blood dripping finger while Minerva stands behind her, looking as concerned as she can with her usual dead demeanor.

"Are you alright?" Minerva asks. "I didn't mean to be so emotional."

"You call that emotional?" Valerie looks to Minerva with mildly upset worry. "What is wrong with you? This isn't okay. You acting like this. If lord Derexen saw you just now he would do away with you."

Minerva slants her eyes, looking vaguely disappointed in herself. "I know... Give me a moment."

Minerva warps out of the room. Valerie quickly stands, "Minerva!?"

Valerie turns around several times looking really worried and unsure what to do. She holds her finger, wincing a little before Minerva suddenly returns with a bandage and her usual lifeless expression.

Minerva takes Valerie's hand and cleans her finger using a disinfectant packet. "You'll be alright," she calmly says. Valerie stares at her with calm surprise. "I'm okay now. It won't happen again. Ludwig's words blindsided me. He..." Valerie waited, feeling she wanted to tell her something sacred to her. "Ludwig's spirit reminds me of someone I once knew..."

"Someone bad?"

"No..." Barely noticeable, it almost seemed like Minerva was smiling, but not nearly close enough to be considered a true smile. "A good man..."

"Minerva..."

"Are you alright now?"

"Yes."

Minerva puts the bandage on Valerie's cut. "Take your seat."

The two of them calmly sit back in their seat. Minerva seats back straight and nods at Valerie to end her illusion. Shortly after the unseen shining glamour falls, Demi servants enter the room with the brunch dishes they've been waiting for on carts. The rat-faced Demi servants bring all kinds of breakfast dishes to the table, including freshly cut fruits. Gleeful Chloe becomes when the bacon piled dish hits the table.

Once the table's set, the servants file out the room. The world leaders don't serve themselves, but instead make their DAs serve them. Derexen's elites and the DA agents

339

begin to make their own plates while passing around the large dishes.

President Minami speaks to Derexen, "I know this is the time of year for you to tour us around in order to maintain good faith," Takashi translates, "but I would like to begin discussion on our pressing matters."

"Start us off," Derexen says before Bonnie translates.

As President Minami talks, Takashi continues translating. "Have you given any thoughts on my request? The situation has become troubling."

"I assume you're talking about the issue with the Flux of Demis in your country."

Niang and Chloe are asked to translate what's being said by their leaders.

President Duskin addresses Derexen, "We are also having a similar issue as well," Chloe translates.

Once Takashi relays what was said, he translates his leader's words, "Might I have the floor first, President Duskin?"

"Pardon me," Chloe translates while loading her plate with more bacon. "Forgive my rudeness." She sips her water before suddenly spitting it out, getting the table's attention. "Вы называетеето водка!?"

As everyone stares, Glenn comically does a lost double blink, "What?"

Bonnie clears her throat, "She said, you call this vodka?"

"Why would we serve vodka at this hour? It's not even two o'clock."

"She said there was vodka," Chloe says, irritably pointing at Valerie.

"I said water," Valerie replies.

"Vodka!"

"Дорогой, вода," Bonnie says to Chloe.

"Well, we're not drinking this," she says while

pushing her glass, the president's glass, and the pitcher away from them. She even pushed other DA agents' glasses away. "I-wanted-vodka!" she rapidly demands, slapping the table upon the emphasis of each word.

"I don't even understand how she misunderstood that?" Glenn says, looking at his fellow elites.

"Well!?" Chloe loudly says. "Vodka! Vodka! Bring Vodka!" she says three times, hitting the table each time.

President Duskin scolds her upon angrily shouting her name. Like a bratty child, she stares into the table, perfectly still as he lectures her.

When he finishes, Chloe addresses the room, "I'm sorry for my outburst. It won't happen again, for I shamed my country and the king."

Derexen nods before looking to President Minami to continue.

"My soldiers are doing their best," Takashi translates for President Minami, "but I'm losing more men than I wish to. Unlike you, we don't have a large Demi army or a group of elites to assist us."

"A choice you made," Derexen replies.

"You know how I and my countrymen feel about Demis, it's no secret. But fire against fire is the best course sometimes."

"And what is it you want? Some of my Demi soldiers?"

"Of course not. I will always believe man is superior to monsters. Perhaps you'll be willing to loan me six hundred of your human soldiers."

"So you'd rather my men die than yours?"

"Don't misunderstand. Your armies have more Demi experience than mine. With their aid, I'm sure we can drive them back and learn how to deal with the problem next time."

"I suppose it would be fair," Valerie says, getting Derexen's attention. She looks to him, "For the past few years their country has provided us with hard to gain materials for our projects, including our bionull research."

Derexen looks to Minami, "Indeed. You will have your soldiers."

"Thank you," Takashi translates. "That'll be all."

Chloe is speaking with President Duskin about what had transpired. "You granted his request?" Chloe translates to Derexen. "I would also like a generous hand with my monster problem. But I don't want your soldiers. My army is strong enough to fight without you. But I would like some extra hands in completing the barricades due to the rise of Demis entering."

"Summit to me the type and the amount of workers you need and I will fulfill it."

"Thank you."

"Is there anything else?" he asks the table.

President Härma bites into her croissant and brushes the crumbs off her long burgundy dress before addressing Derexen, "Not so much as help, but rather a curious question that itches me," Kalju calmly translates. "As my intelligence agency reported, that sudden meteor shower destroyed the generator you had placed in my country."

"Yes, Bonnie informed me before I got your call."

"Under Bonnie's orders and aid by coming to my country, we managed to clean up and quarantine the area. How long before you send over a replacement?"

"Not for several years."

"Really? Then can you perhaps not replace it? My people have come to enjoy the sun's return and—"

"Part of our agreement of sparing your pseudo country was that you would hold things for me, including one of the ten generators. It will be replaced. This is not negotiable."

President Härma leans back like she was just slapped in the face as she glances at Kalju and Derexen before taking her hands off the table and looking away from the group.

Niang is softly eating the diced fruits on her plate until Emperor Zhao leans in speaking to her. "Lord Derexen," Niang says with a full mouth of kiwi before chewing and swallowing the fruit. "Emperor Zhao would like some clarification on why you did not seek our aid on eliminating the world's troublemaker, Afearia." The table goes quiet and the elites look at one another until Emperor Zhao speaks to the table. "Is this not supposed to be talked about?" she translates. "It should be no surprise that the angel's deeds would reach overseas."

Derexen stares at Emperor Zhao, not answering his words. "I don't say this to insult your honor," Niang continues to translate. "You're a close ally of my country and it's only natural for us to want to help a friend."

"Though I appreciate the concern," Derexen responds, "that minor nuisance has been handled. She's dead."

Some eye contact is made between the DA agents and the leaders as talk in their native languages transpires. "How efficient," Chloe translates for her leader.

Derexen looks at Chancellor Heibel, who's whispered to Ludwig several times since the beginning while Ludwig translates only loud enough for her to hear. "Chancellor," Derexen says, getting their attention. "You've been very quiet most of the morning. Do you not have anything you wish to discuss?"

"Nothing you haven't already heard," Ludwig translates.

"I see. Then you must still be displeased with my decision."

"I think you should reconsider. Perhaps you and I can speak more privately before my trip here is over."

"It won't make a difference."

"A trial then. I'm sure you can find use of him within the time we're here. If suspicions are what I expect is your reasoning, keep his jobs superficial."

"Why do you insist to push this idea?"

"He will never be truly one in your circle. But the idea to be able to lend our best for one of yours in certain times of need is just smart business. It makes it easier to assign jobs to those who are more suited for the task at hand. In the end, this could help us both, even strengthen our alliance."

Derexen thinks for a while before glancing at Valerie who's sitting with a fairly stern expression as she watches their guests. "We'll see. I think I'll open the idea to my team through a vote. For now, just enjoy your brief stay here."

Heibel accepts his words and resumes eating and talking to Ludwig. Derexen calmly watches over his conversing guests with an empty plate before him. He glances at Valerie once again, noticing her less serious facial expression had turned subtly worrisome.

Once brunch was over, everyone remained seated while still speaking to one another. "DA agents," Derexen addressing the table. "Translate this to your leaders since Bonnie will be with me for a while. I have a guard outside these doors who will take you to the limousines. We'll be taking you to our government's crowning locations very soon. Wait outside and we'll be right with you."

The DA members translate and filter out the room with their leaders. The elites silently wait until they can no longer hear their guests outside the doors.

"Before we tour them," Derexen says, "I'd like to know how you all feel about Chancellor Heibel's proposition."

"Which is?" Glenn says. "She was as vague as she could possibly be."

"Her idea is to trade government elites for a set amount of time to complete missions best suited for their skills. Thirty-six hours is the discussed longest time I have to give one of my own. I can have hers for longer."

"I don't like it," Kyoto quickly says. "After everything that's happened, it's important to know who our real allies are. For all we know this could be a trick."

"Chancellor Heibel has always been a trusted ally," Bonnie says. "She's the only one who willingly complied with our demands during the early stages of controlling this realm."

"Yet she still signed the UN treaty to have her own super solider," Glenn says.

"It's only natural to protect yourself and your own, especially when an unknown ruler emerges."

"It's true," Agonda adds. "No alliance is truly formed under the belief they can trust their partners. It just so happens cooperation can yield benefits. And this is no different."

"This—could burn us," Minerva says.

"I agree," Glenn adds. "This is hard to even consider at the moment."

"It will always be that way," Agonda says. "There will never be a time this feels comfortable. But what do we have to fear? We hold more power than anyone else on the planet."

"That's true, but…"

Deep in thought, Valerie lifts her head to speak, "I object. This couldn't be a more terrible idea. Each of us hold positions too important to leave unfilled."

"Yes, but there is some leniency that can be applied to some of us," Agonda says. "People completely unable would be you and lord Derexen. Minerva on the other hand could be useful in both countries."

"Why Minerva?" she asks in an irritable tone.

"Why does it matter?" he responds in kind.

"I'm curious."

"Fine," he says with bother, "Glenn. They could both fill the role, myself included."

Glenn ponders for a moment, "I'm actually starting to lean in favor of this."

"Glenn?" Valerie says with some confusion. "Why?"

"Think about it. If they really are the enemy, this could be an opportune time to learn from them. For example, we still don't know what abilities the DA agents possess. And under treaty, we're not supposed to. But if we're working with them, sooner or later we'll see their cards."

"And you think they're not thinking the same way? We have more to lose than they do. If this is the game they're playing then it's a game too dangerous for us to play," Valerie says to the table.

"If so...," Derexen responds, "Then it's a game we shall play."

"Sire?" she says with some disbelief.

"Though this is all speculation, we shall put it to the test. Whether this is a trick or not, it is still a double-edged sword. If they're looking to gain insight on us then we'll do the same. Heibel has offered me a trial period to lend me Ludwig for no one in exchange. It'll only be for a week before she makes her own request. I'm looking to entertain it."

"There's no vote, is there?"

"Everyone's vote was made when I heard the circle's opinions on the matter. That should be enough." Valerie slants her eyes to the floor, appearing troubled. "Are you losing faith in me, Valerie?"

"N-no! Never! How could you even think that!?"

"Your body language."

She lowers her head a bit. "I just don't want to take this risk."

"Everything we do here is a risk. Just a calculated risk with the right strategy."

"Right," agreeing, yet feeling concerned.

Derexen stands, "Let's proceed to our patient guests."

By nightfall, the long day touring his guests around his country's government buildings has ended. The political leaders and their DA agents have all checked into a fancy hotel set up and paid for by Derexen. Each leader and their DA agents are all checked into their own rooms. The leaders are at the highest floor while the DA agents are one floor below. Though the leaders have resided in their respective rooms for the night, the DA agents are all gathered in Niang's room enjoying themselves.

This five star hotel room has a separate space with red sofa chairs and a two seat sofa. The chairs are arranged in a circle for them to face one another. A dining table is set beside the kitchen and the TV over the fireplace a few feet from the kitchen. The room's carpeted in burgundy with a blue stripe leading to the bedroom.

Sitting in the main room, the five of them are gathered around a table, drinking champagne from their glasses with an ice bucket holding two more chilled bottles.

Chloe's tie is completely undone, her shoes are off and so are her socks. Her pants are rolled up to her knees as she lazily drinks. Kalju and Takashi only undo their ties and open their jackets. Niang has removed her jacket and tie, unbuttoning the top buttons of her blouse.

"It has been so long since we've gotten together like this," Takashi says.

"Coming to this country is the closest we get to having a real vacation," Kalju replies.

Chloe pours herself another glass, "This is not vodka," she says with some disappointment.

"Ugh, again, Chloe," Niang irritably says while reaching for the bottle for a refill. "Don't start shouting in here, damn it. I won't deal with it," she hiccups before taking a graceless swig.

"Yao, you're drunk...? That's fucking cute."

"For a woman of the cross, you sure swear and partake in things that others would consider a sin," she says, hiccupping again.

"Others would, but not my Father. I admit, I swear too much, but that's why religion is a practice and why I wear my sacred crosses inverted. Since am not good enough in this life to decorate myself in God's divine relics, I let it be known I only strive to be what he wishes me to be."

"Chloe..." Niang lazily says as her head lightly rotates like a disc on a pin. "All I heard was, blaaaaaaaaaaaaaaaaaaaaaaaaaaaaaaaaaaaaaaaah vhat he vishes me to be," she mocks with exaggerated facial movement not far from Chloe's usual expressions.

Chloe shoots up, spilling some of her drink, "Да ладнух!? Маленькая девочка, ты плохо говоришь о Боге. Я тебя убью, сука."

"Hey, hey, quit it!" Kalju says.

A knock is heard at the door. "Мы не закончили," Chloe says, pointing at Niang like she's a child.

Chloe opens the double doors to Ludwig holding a couple bottles of high proof vodka and one bag of food.

"Hope I didn't take long," Ludwig says, turning sideways as he pushes himself into the room.

Chloe excitedly takes a bottle and uncaps it to drink immediately. She exhales loudly after drinking half. Whooooo! It burns so good!" She turns to Niang in a sassy manner, "Vodka," she says, running her finger under the word printed on the label.

"At least you can say something right," Niang sneers before taking a far more graceful sip of her drink.

Chloe grunts at her before handing her glass to Ludwig and taking the other bottle. "Hey!" Ludwig says before taking the bottle back.

Chloe playfully laughs, running away after Ludwig gave a brief chase. She jumps over the back of the two seated sofa and plops down next to Takashi, almost spilling his drink and smiling at him after he nearly freaked out.

"This trip has been great so far," Ludwig says as he comes in and sits on the floor in the circle. "I've never been here before. Nothing's as I expected."

"Really?" Takashi says. "So hearing that Derexen walks around with a jagged stick up his ass doesn't ring true?"

"He wasn't so bad, none of them were, really."

"No shock, I suppose," Kalju says. "He said the same thing when he first met us."

"What? It was a new experience, much like meeting you guys. It was interesting seeing them work together up close."

"Really?" Takashi says before he's nudged by Chloe leaning forward to grab one of the chilled bottles and pop the cork.

Chloe takes a glass and let's them both go. They float in midair and begin to come toward her as the bottle pours itself into her glass and she drinks more vodka from the other bottle. With another loud exhale and wide smile, she leans back with arms stretched along the back of the sofa and head tilted back while the bottle floats into the bucket and the glass into her hand.

"Then how do you feel knowing you may be working side by side with them?" Chloe asks Ludwig.

"You know, I'm pretty excited about it," Ludwig answers.

"You shouldn't be," Niang says, seeming a bit more serious. "Despite whatever you've been told, we're suppose to view them as the opposition. It is why we are here and it is why we will remain here. Excited shouldn't be the word you're looking for. It's cautious. They may off you."

"No way. They have honor and morals."

"Not all of them," she says with a sterner expression.

"Maybe so, but I'm sure I won't be paired with anyone like that."

Takashi smirks and shakes his head, "Forever the child."

"I don't wish to assume the worst in people."

"Then see where that gets you."

"Leave him be," Chloe says. "If he likes the opportunity, good for him. Tell us, big monster. What has you so excited about this?"

"I've heard many things about them over the years and I thought about what it would be like if I was in their circle."

The four of them seemed a bit surprised. "Are you a Judas?"

"N-no, Chloe! I have respect for them and I admire many of the things they have achieved, but I am happy with my current position as a DA."

"Is that so? Who's on your list?"

"I like Glenn, but I don't think he would ever trust me. Valerie seems kind, but I doubt we would work well together. But if I could choose, it would be Derexen and Minerva."

Suddenly, Niang abruptly stands, grabbing the last bottle before walking toward her bedroom. "Lock my door when you guys are done drinking my champagne," she says before slamming the door behind her.

The four of them stare at the door until Takashi leaps up out his seat, "Nah, I'm good. I'm going back to my room." He walks out the room, "Night guys," and shuts the door.

Chloe glances three times at the concerned Ludwig's hand holding the vodka bottle while he stares at the bedroom door. She swiftly snatches the bottle and runs out the room laughing like a giddy child. Ludwig was in mid attempt to stop her, but doesn't as he looks back at the door.

Kalju stands up slowly and pats Ludwig's shoulder, "Get some rest. We still have a lot of week to get through."

Kalju leaves the room and shuts the door while Ludwig remains behind, debating on what he should do.

In her bedroom, sitting on the edge of the bed, Niang is slowly brushing her hair. As she preciously smoothes her black hair over her shoulder with every stroke, Niang moves her head around to a personal hummed tune in her white knee high nightgown. Though the nightgown reaches to her knees, Niang has surprisingly thick, muscular legs for her size.

A knock is suddenly heard on the bedroom door, causing her to pause. "Who is it?" she asks. The door opens with hard footsteps of someone approaching the bed from behind her. Seeming like she's trying to figure out who, she softly smiles and continues brushing. "Even if you don't say it's you, I can always figure it out by your monstrous heartbeat. Gives you away every time. What's on your mind, Ludwig?"

Ludwig walks around the bed and stands beside her with his pelvic meeting her face and an evident elephant-like bulge in his pants steadily growing. "I can sense you standing next to me. Ludwig—" She looks surprised upon turning herself and feeing her head hit against it. She uses her palm to pat his bulge and rub it up and down a few times, still seeming surprised before a sultry smile showed. "So that's what's on your mind."

He gets on the bed and moves behind her, gently kissing her porcelain neck. Niang tilts her head back and to the side, making an open mouth smile to reveal her ever-present sharp canine teeth before exhaling loudly in a moment of bliss. He strokes her hair back as she remains still to each of his advances.

Soon after, she turns around and pushes him to the bed. Using his elbows, he repositions himself to have his head at the headboard while she remained on top of him.

Niang swings her legs over his bulge and slowly grinds herself on top of him. She takes two fistfuls of his shirt into her hands as she maintains her balance by holding on to his chest.

Niang undoes a few of his buttons and leans forward to untie his loose tie with her teeth. When pulled off, his open shirt reveals some of his scarred chest where some places are held together by a strange black, gooey stitching. She unbuttons more of his shirt as she grinds a bit more desperately. She leans forward and bites his nipple and licks across his chest slow and sloppy, gliding through the groves of his muscles.

She leans up and beings to ride him, breathing heavy with moans in between. "Did I upset you earlier?" Ludwig asks.

"When?" she moans, losing herself in his unreal girth that bulges her stomach a bit.

"When I mentioned Minerva."

Niang stops, tilting her head down at him, "Seriously, Ludwig?" she says a bit out of breath. She stands up and climbs off him as he turns over toward her. "You really know how to kill a girl's drive. Bravo, dumbass."

Ludwig sits up while she sits at the edge of the bed not facing him as she brushes her hair. "Why do you hate her so much?" Niang doesn't answer, as if he wasn't in the room. "Would you be upset if I work with her?"

"Stop being ridiculous. You're an adult. You can work with whoever you want. Not that you have much choice in the matter."

"I just want to further understand what makes her so noble."

"She's not noble."

"Even if you say so, I still want to understand what makes her so strong. What is her drive, her thoughts, her process."

"I'm stronger," she mutters with annoyance.

"I know that."

She huffs and throws her wooden rose brush into her open travel bag in her closet, "Whatever, just get out, Ludwig."

"You don't want that," he says with a semi smirk, but still concerned eyebrows.

"Go, asshole. You ruined my mood."

"Did I?" he says before moving to the edge of the bed. He runs a couple of his fingers across her leg, but she slaps his hand away. He tries two more times before she just turns her head to him, still looking upset while not stopping him. "Then why are your legs wet?"

"It's the remains a good time. Now get out."

"Yao, are you serious?"

"I'll finish myself off. Get the fuck out."

"Yao, I'm sorry. I wasn't—" he says as he reaches to touch her cheek.

Yao reactively grabs his hand and swings him off the bed and into the wall near the door. She gets on her feet with veins bulging from her hands and bunched brows.

"I said go," she threatens, pointing to door.

Ludwig stands and moves with his back to the door while she slowly follows him. "But—"

With a hefty kick, she sends Ludwig through the door and over halfway to the front door of the hotel room. "GO!" she demands, pointing the way out. Ludwig gets on his feet and turns to leave until she runs up and grabs him by the hand and swings him over her shoulder and onto his back. Ludwig's confused as some of the air was painfully knocked out of him. "On second thought," she says, looking and still sounding angry. "I need to finish." She mounts him and begins to choke Ludwig. "Don't say mama doesn't love you," she says with an evil smile revealing her teeth.

The big morning has finally arrived with the last

preparations for the coming speech underway. At Derexen's palace, Valerie, wearing her business attire, makes her way down the hall while holding documents as she reviews them. She reaches black double doors, looking up at it with some concern before knocking. Her knocks sound hollow and delayed as a reflective translucent purple barrier ripples with each knock she did.

Deciding to let herself in, Valerie looks around like she's up to something secretive before her joined index and middle fingers gain a white aura. She cuts down the middle of the door. Once she reaches the bottom, the barrier glows completely white before the light pop sound similar to a distant balloon is heard. The barrier falls to the floor like the sudden end of a rushing stream.

When she enters, the room's pitch black with no light entering beyond a few feet from the doorway. "Lord Derexen...? Sir? Lord—"

Suddenly, the sound of loud hoofs hitting the floor come her way. She stares forward before the thing from the dark steps close enough to feel its hot breath on her. Vaguely making out its monstrous features, the creature's large ivory tusk and its stubby thick legs were dangerously hard. She could tell as it violently jerks its head, scarring the floor with its tusk and stomping around spreading cracks through the floor.

Valerie steps back, nervously looking at it before the sound of beating wings are heard. The monster is abruptly slammed against the wall inside the dark. A scuffle is heard with the demonic grunt of a man, moments before the monster squeals in pain with the added sound of its blood being splattered. Some of it hit the floor in the light of the doorway, nearly getting on Valerie.

"Lor—Derexen?" she fearfully says with uncertainty.

"Valerie," Derexen replies, sounding fairly demonic with the echo in his voice piercing her. The flap of wings is heard again with a faint breeze coming from the dark. A devil-like black tail creeps from the dark, scaring her a bit before it rises up and gently runs its furry tip under her chin and back into the dark. For some reason... its touch put her at ease. The slow sound of bare footsteps come her way.

"You know coming here is dangerous," he says in his usual monotone. "And undoing my seal is also not something you should be doing unless it's an emergency."

"Was that—?"

"Why are you here?" She doesn't answer, just stares into the dark with a near sad yearning in her eyes. "Are you going to answer?"

"Do you trust me?" Derexen's silent. "Do you trust me, my lord?"

"Beyond my better judgment."

"Step into the light."

"No."

"Please. I do not fear the man in the shadows. No matter what demons he may hide," she softly adds.

At first there is only silence with the eerie sounds of shifting flesh. But soon after, Derexen steps forward wearing black sweat pants and no shirt. He's sweating all over his lean, rippled body. His muscular physique was that of what men strive to reach without becoming bulky or skinny. Just lean and strong with every muscle exposed like a fine cut diamond.

However, his body wasn't perfect. The scar he received many years ago against the deceased World Guardian, Greyshio remains deeply etched across his torso. Along his right oblique is a rarely seen sight. Like Afearia, he has two tattoos symbolizing his Empyrean Blades in a vertical lineup. The first is the golden glow of a galaxy inside a circle. Below it is a purple glowing circle with the image of a black hole.

Derexen stares down at her with glowing red pentagrams in his eyes. The pentagrams spin a couple times, making her focus on the illegible text and the red and black veins on his sclera. His expression seemed normal, but his eyes looked like they were in pain, including the fact they look as if he was on the verge of tears.

"How far this time?" Valerie asks softly.

"Too far," he replies just as softly.

"Shut your eyes."

"Why—"

"Shhhh," she gently hushes him. "Shut your eyes. Regain control." Derexen slowly shuts his eyes while she remains looking over his face. She tilts her head a little, almost raising her hands up to his face before resting them back at her sides. He opens his eyes, having them completely reverted to their original, soft cyan color. "You're back," tenderly smiling.

"Yes."

Valerie's face becomes less relieved. "Why do you keep going inside that angry place? Those things can just rot away inside that space you created for them."

"Not all of them," he says before walking pass her. He stands with his back to her, but she doesn't turn to face him. "Some will live on unless something takes their life for them. Worse of all, the longer I leave them in that space, the weaker the seals grow. Sooner or later they will break free and bring havoc to the realms all over again. So it is my obligation to become stronger and pull them out one by one for a personal execution."

"And what if you pull one you can't handle? We all stopped them together for a reason."

"Each bout is magically timed. If I can't erase them in two minutes, then they'll be sucked back inside."

"My question remains, Derexen." He turns to her. "You speak so casually as if you dying isn't a problem."

"It isn't."

She balls her fist in irritation, "I wish you not to speak like that before me," Valerie nearly exclaims, barely hiding her anger. "I know I have no right to ask such a thing, but you are wrong to say it. This world could not function like it is without you. That was—insulting to hear you say. Disgusting... Did you not think before you said that?"

Derexen momentarily stares at her back before approaching. The sound of his footsteps coming behind her takes her out of her anger a little. She turns to him, looking upset, but calmer than when she spoke.

"We weren't looking at my response in the same light," Derexen explains. "But in a larger sense, you are not wrong. But at the same time, you are. My true goals remain out of reach. And if my death becomes the final push, so be it."

"I'm sorry, but I can't accept that."

"I know..." The two of them just stare at each other before she turns to walk away. "Why are you here? You broke my seal knowing you may have released something onto this world that should remain locked away."

"A mistake. But I came to collect you. We need to oversee the final arrangements for the speech."

"I see. I'll be ready in an hour."

"Good."

As Valerie walks away with evident anger in her departure, Derexen watches her until she turns the corner. He glances into the dark room before shutting the doors. Derexen recasts his dark seal by drawing a circle in midair. It creates a purple glow before he touches the door with his index and middle finger. Derexen turns his fingers like a key which sparks a brief puff of darkness at his fingertips and the echoing sound of a locking door before he walks away.

At the staging area where the speech is set to take place, most of Derexen's elites and all of the DAs and their leaders stand behind the podium. A row of black chairs are set against the staging wall with Derexen's elites to the left and the world leaders and their DA agents to the right. The world leaders are sitting patiently waiting for Derexen's arrival.

A large crowd is gathered throughout the city filling every place humanly possible to stand and sit. From the sidewalks to the streets, people have come far and wide for this moment. Although it is morning, the skies only look like the near dawning of the sun's rise.

Back at the broadcasting station, the building's staff is assessing the network in preparation of Derexen's speech. "Are we ready to go?" a man at the front control panel asks Steven. Steven, sitting at the central control station is staring at the main monitor as he alters a few settings before smirking at an upload he's started on a separate monitor through his flash drive.

"Oh, yes," Steven says. "We're quite ready."

Back at the staging area, Derexen, Valerie, and Bonnie warp outside the staging area dressed in their business attire. Bonnie looks up at the few steps leading to the stage and sees the others waiting.

Bonnie proceeds ahead of Derexen and Valerie, "We should begin. The others have already arrived."

Derexen takes a few steps toward the stage before Valerie jumps ahead of him. Thinking she was going to nag him as he tilts his head in a near sense of asking her not too. She changes her stern expression to a softer one with a light smile before readjusting his jacket.

Valerie straightens his tie and runs her hands down the collar of his jacket to crease it better. "Are you ready?" she kindly asks.

Not responding, he stares at her, looking as close to puzzled as he could before she smiles a little more and walks on ahead. Derexen soon follows her onto the stage. Bonnie steps out onto the stage and stands between Agonda and Glenn. The world leaders stand as Valerie comes to the stage. Seeing her approach the podium causes the crowd to settle down. The cameramen do a five second countdown using their hand as they focus on Valerie.

The monitors in the area stabilize with Valerie's image in each and every one. "Good morning," she says into the mic. "Today we gather to be blessed by the words of the world's finest leader to have ever ruled. He has not only driven this world into a better direction, but he has also given many of us hope for a brighter future under his wisdom. Ladies and gentlemen, it is my honor to introduce the world's mighty king, lord Derexen!"

Valerie humbly gestures Derexen's entrance while the citizens applaud. She steps back as he approaches and then stands firmly at his side. Derexen apathetically waits for everyone to settle down while he calmly watches them applaud his appearance. When everyone begins to calm themselves, Derexen tilts the mic slightly.

"Every year," Derexen speaks, "Terra's renewable power reserves deplete at a level unfit to be useable in the years to come. And sad to say, despite human wishes, it continues to be that mankind's greatest power is to destroy. As a species, humans consume more than they produce. It's disheartening. We produce waste that most of the time is either hard or not possible to be biodegraded back into our planet. But that ends now. We have to treat this world as if it's one of our own kin. Because in many ways, it is."

"Starting late this year," Derexen continues, "I will be implementing a new irrigation system, one that will not waste our fresh water. This project will cause wide spread inconveniences for several years. But its end result will have your future generations thanking you for your selfless cooperation for as long as time allows."

The crowd's already becoming disgruntled by Derexen's plans for the coming years. "There will also be a change on how we dispose of our food in this world," Derexen says. "Starting this winter, the food you wish to dispose of must be either donated to the shelters or any organization struggling to keep food, fed to the local wildlife, or biodegraded."

Boos begin to fill the air. "This is not a choice I'm giving. I'm making this for you. Furthermore, Terra must remain vigilant in these pressing times. I know the destroyed generators are affecting the surrounding areas. This will not be the responsibility of Terraians to pull up their boot straps and deal. It's mine. Me and my team take full responsibility and we will be visiting each location to provide direct aid and financial support to get you all back on your feet. And I know everyone is putting up a fight against these changes, but there are many more to come. If you'd like, I'm open to questions, but only a few."

Many hands go up, but Valerie is the one selecting who gets to speak. Men and women holding microphones come from the back of the stage, entering the crowd in order to give everyone a fair chance to speak. Valerie points to a woman at front and a stage worker holding a microphone approaches the woman so she can speak into it.

"What kind of problems does Terra face when you begin the irrigation program?" the woman asks.

"One issue you'll face is the time of day you can use fresh water and for how much you will have access to per day. My advice is when the time comes, practice time water management. Store some inside jugs and put it to the side so you'll never have to wait for the given hours of water use or worry that you won't have enough."

Hands go up and Valerie points to a woman much further back before another stage worker holds a mic to her. "Who will be forced to comply to the food laws you plan to create?"

"Many food chains. At the end of the day, they throw away more food than you can possibly know. Good food that is fresh, but won't be sellable due to FDA policies. Private residents will not be forced to follow these laws. Are there anymore—?"

Interrupting Derexen's speech, is a scrambling image on the jumbo monitors and white noise to follow. When the image stabilizes and the noise stops, a shock hits the crowd when everyone sees Afearia on the screen. She's sitting in a well-lit room with nothing particular inside but a framed picture of a bird on the stone gray wall behind her.

"Surprised to see me?" Afearia says through the monitor.

Derexen taps his microphone, realizing his connection was completely cut. Kyoto's eyes widen in anger at the sight of her on the screen.

"I know I would be. It took a lot for me to even consider revealing my return like this. But after all that has happened, I needed a new tactic. First off, this isn't a trick. I am alive. Second. Many of you don't know who I am, while others out there do. Perhaps you all know me better as the calamity trigger and the angel." People in the crowd look at one another after hearing those phrases. "By now you've all heard those words spoken without placing a name to the face."

Afearia looks dead into the camera with a stern expression, "I'm that face. The one you've all so wrongly placed so much faith and blame on. In the time I've been here, I've been called many names. But there's two that are a constant reoccurrence. Angel and calamity. Despite the common use of those terms, neither of which is how I see myself, nor is it how I wish to be seen. Because after all is said and done. Today is the day what I do and say will get inside your head. And you can't do anything about it. Because I *will* get inside your head and make you listen."

"Don't look away from me!" Afearia shouts, almost as if she knew they would. "I mean it! I'm not backing down! And neither should you! Citizens of Terra. No more sitting idly by for a sign. This is your world! Why are you letting this—*thing* run it like it's his own!? He lost that right when he became what he is today! Band together and

361

over throw this monster! Do that, with me! Stop wasting your wishes for a better tomorrow. Our time has run out! Our future is now! Fight!"

The citizens mutter to one another while Derexen calmly watches the opinions of the masses sway against him. Derexen leans to Valerie, "Find out how this is being broadcasted and stop it." Valerie warps from the area in a puff of white smoke.

"This sick Eden he's created is coming to an end. This whole conflict is bigger than me. And from here on out, I'm going to treat it like it is. And it begins by destroying everything this monster has ever built. From the people he colludes with, to the things he cherishes. You hear me, Derexen?" she loudly says, getting him to focus on the monitor with him and her seemly to be staring directly at each other. "Enough is enough."

Afearia slams her hands down on the table upon standing, "Don't ignore me! Because I'm tearing it down. I'm tearing down the walls around this system. For I'm the only one strong enough to pick a fight with the lawless! And with me at the helm I'm going to shine a light in this darkness! I'm Terra's angel? I'm it's calamity? Good! I'll be whatever you want me to be if it means you'll fight back! Look! I'm the moon, I'm the sky, I'm the sun!" she sarcastically says. "I can be it all!"

She calms herself and looks down at the table with a pondering solemn expression as her head lowers a bit. "And from the ends of the world…," Afearia, slowly lifting a remote to the camera, getting everyone's attention in a cautious manner as her thumb lies on a red button. She looks directly into the camera and pushes it. An explosion is vaguely heard and felt through the ground. The partially dark skies suddenly clear with the darkness fleeing from the bright blue sky itself, revealing a glorious sunny day. "I've come," she announces with a vengeful stare.

Elsewhere, back at the broadcasting station before

Afearia's detonation, all of the employees are unconscious by a gas that has spread through the room. A man is standing in the gassy room wearing a gas mask with his back to the door in his lumpy nylon jacket. Facing the control panel, he types in a few commands, locking the system. Once done, he leaves the room, only partially closing the door behind him.

As he looks back several times while moving down the hall, he removes his gas mask, revealing himself to be Steven. He raises his wristwatch to his mouth, "Mission complete. A.N.T.S. has locked the broadcast. Returning to base."

When Steven lowered his arm, a throwing knife is lodged into the back of his left elbow. He holds his arm and fearfully looks back to see Valerie running at him with determined eyes. Steven runs down the hall to escape her. He turns right, taking the stairway further up. Rushing like mad, he manages to lap three flights up until Valerie appears at the top of the next flight in a puff of smoke.

Standing before Steven, Valerie kicks him in the chest, sending him to the bottom of the flight without hitting the steps. Slamming against the wall deepens the knife in his elbow before he hits the floor breaking his left hand from the height of his fall. He painfully gets on his feet and passes through the door next to him.

Steven hobbles through the hall, jiggling the door to any room in order to escape. The heavy panic in his breathing gets worse once the building alarm sounds and he moves as fast as possible. Valerie slowly comes from the stairway. He looks back as his heart races with the desire to reach the end of the hall. Unfortunately for him, armed building guards come around the corner and block the path he was working toward.

Steven looks to his right and tries opening the door beside him, but it was locked.

Valerie points at Steven, "Apprehend that man."

The guards raise their weapons and fire rubber bullets at Steven. He's grounded immediately, groaning in pain. But he doesn't submit. Steven uses one arm to drag himself upward and rest his back against the door. He goes into his jacket and pulls out a grenade.

"Grenade!" a guard shouts to alert his team. Steven throws it at them, but one of the guards with a plastic shield, deflects the grenade back. "Oh no! Valerie, get down!"

With the flick of her finger, small bundled rings that are barely visible, speed over the grenade, making it disappear. Everyone's confused until Steven becomes fearfully wide-eyed when he hears the sound of his grenade drop behind the door he's resting against. It goes off and blows him into the closed office room across from him. Valerie walks on toward the room while the guards soon do the same.

Steven is half leaned up against a smashed desk with his arm resting tight across his jacket. His body's fairly mangled after the explosion as he poorly breathes, waiting for his enemies. Steven's eyes are barely open as he hazily tries to make out who's standing before him.

Valerie mercilessly looks down at him with the guards lined horizontally behind her with guns pointed at Steven. "How do we stop the broadcast?" Valerie asks.

Steven's chuckle sounds like a wheeze, "You can't stop change, demon. The tides of progression will always be. No Kingdom can reign forever. Especially not one as fucked up as this!" he says before coughing up blood.

Valerie snatches up his beaten body by the collar, "You will stop the broadcast."

Valerie's eyes express realization when she looks down at his jacket after only now noticing a faint beeping. "You hear that?" he says with blood coming from the corner of his mouth, giving her a sly raise of his eyebrow. "Like the universe, change comes in a bang."

Suddenly, getting everyone's attention, a slight tremor is felt before Valerie and the guards see a massive expanding dome of darkness, light, and fire from the window in the deep distance beyond the city. Seizing the moment, Steven quickly opens his jacket to reveal his bomb wrapped body. He yanks out several wires, triggering the bomb.

The explosion blows the room apart, blasting glass and debris out from the upper floor's window.

Back at the stage of the world speech, the confused audience look around in caution after the blast. An alarming sound is heard from Bonnie's clothes. She pulls out her tablet and slides the screen to see the alert.

"What!?" Bonnie says. "Lord Derexen!? Another generator has been destroyed!"

Though most of the men and women on the stage are surprised, Derexen turns back to the jumbo monitor to stare at Afearia. "If you're ready to face me for all that I am," Afearia says. "You better come full force, because I'm not holding back," she says with a deadly glare and head tilt.

The broadcast goes into a loop of her last words before freezing.

Kyoto stands with an angry realization, "I know that place!" he says in his gravelly voice. "She's broadcasting from that rebel Raquel's hideout!"

In less than two seconds, Kyoto's encased in a dark matter that widely wraps around him in a shell-like casing before fading off stage.

"Kyoto, wait!" Glenn shouts too late.

Kyoto reappears in a stone hallway with wooden floors in front of a metal door. The dark matter unwraps him as he cautiously looks around the hall before proceeding. Hearing faint creeks and voices from the other side, he slowly opens the door to find no one inside.

When he enters, and the door softly closes behind

him with a light clicking once shut, Kyoto briefly observes the empty room. While looking for the source of the noises, he notices the three window blinds to his left are down. Bloodstains remain from Raquel's murder, stained deep across the table and wooden chair.

He steps forward to the table where a laptop plays a looped track of floor creeks and incoherent talking. He stares suspiciously until the clicking he barely noticed before becomes rapid and loud for a second. Suddenly, the sound of the door locking itself is heard.

Kyoto's about to rush toward the door until the loop ends when a video plays with a group of armed men in fatigues standing behind Afearia, Zaiah, and Elliot.

"Surprise," Afearia calmly says. Kyoto sternly turns to the laptop and approaches with angry eyes. "That broadcast was two days old."

"Clever," he says in his aggressive voice.

"You remember these guys? They're the remaining members of Mongoose with one last mission to fulfill. With the help of A.N.T.S. they wanted one last shot at you and whoever else was involved in the death of their leader. They believed using this place would cause the ones responsible for Mongoose's end would return to the scene of the crime. They were right."

The blinds in the room automatically rise, revealing flashing C4s taped along the window frames. Kyoto rushes to the door and hastily grabs the jagged knob that has been disfigured to have a sharp surface. He cuts his hand and quickly pulls away.

"That door won't open," Afearia says, upsetting Kyoto further. "You're in check," she says with a near leer.

With quick thinking, Kyoto uses his powers to warp out the room. He appears at the lowest floor where there's open doorways leading out the building. But the ones in his view are lined with bombs along the frame, excluding the emergency backdoor.

He speed walks down the hall where he hears a looped track of Afearia repeating what she said before he warped below. The beeping becomes faster before he runs straight ahead, passing many doorways with a laptop in each repeating her words as the bombs flash.

With this much C4, I can assume they left and planed to crash the whole building on us, Kyoto thinks. Best I retreat for now and kill her later. As his dark shell begins to appear, initiating his warp as he runs, Kyoto quickly stops it, seeming a bit surprised. That murky energy... It's her! Beyond that door!

Kyoto bursts through it with a shoulder rush. Immediately halting him is Elliot, standing before him holding a pistol equipped with a silencer at his chest.

"Checkmate," Elliot says before firing.

With quick hands, Kyoto had already redirected his hand, causing Elliot to shoot the ground, still holding onto his wrist.

"Weak," Kyoto says before kicking him across the alley and into the wall of the next building.

Elliot falls to his rump before Kyoto stands over him. Before anything else could happen, Kyoto lifts his head and looks calmly to his right, seeing Afearia standing further into the alley.

"And here you stand," Kyoto states. "You'll pay for what you did," he says as he faced her. He begins to approach, "I only came here for you. Because I put down monsters. No one with a conscious would kill someone the way you did. Was it that easy? To hurt her like that?" he asks in a less gravely tone. "Just because she was of a different species? And you call us the lowly ones? I will never—!"

Without warning, a dart is shot into Kyoto's neck. Kyoto looks back to see Elliot holding up his gun at him before raising his hand to remove the dart, "Whatever you got in there won't do you any good. The government elites are—"

Before he could finish, Kyoto falls stiffly to the ground with wide eyes. Afearia and Elliot stand over his paralyzed body. "Now, what were you saying about elites?" Elliot taunts. Men who're members of A.N.T.S. come from the edges of the alley and from the building doors holding firearms.

"I guess we're all gonna die," Kyoto strains in his rough voice, sounding like he was suffocating a little.

"What, because of the bombs?" He pulls out a remote and hits a button to shut the noise and lights from the bombs off. "Remote controlled duds. But you couldn't have known that."

"I'm go- gonna ki—"

"It's getting harder to talk, huh? After a double dose of those drugs, I would think so."

"Dru—drugs?"

"You were being watched by hidden cameras. When you hurt your hand, you were introduced to a drug that turns whatever you guys got that keeps you immune from things like this inert. The dart was the finisher once the defenses your head scientist Bonnie placed were erased. For the next six hours, you will be paralyzed and fatigued. Best of all, your powers will be sealed for just as long. Not bad for a human bug, huh?"

"H... How?"

"You have your science, we have ours. But a little outside assistance never hurt anybody. A few months later and presto! We had our hands on some super drugs to take down monsters like you."

"Bite me—scum."

"Heh, tough guy over here," he says, looking to his men. "We have never gotten this far before. The tables are turning. And this bag of shit will be feeding us all the information we need to know. Their secrets, their weaknesses, all of it. Right, bag of shit?" addressing Kyoto.

"Kill me," Kyoto calmly says in a submissive tone while looking at the ground.

Elliot puts his foot on his head, "In due time. After some friendly torture so you cough up all that you know."

"Kill me."

"Are you even listening? You will be telling me what I need to know."

"Kill me."

"You little—" Elliot does a swift kick to Kyoto's ribs before a few of his men join in stomping on him as they laugh together like common thugs. Afearia watches from behind them with a deadpan expression. Elliot steps back, wiping his mouth of spit after getting carried away kicking Kyoto with his men. "That's enough boys. We need to hurry and get him transported."

The men lift Kyoto by the arms just as his earpiece flashes. Elliot removes it before he proceeds out the alley dragging Kyoto's tiptoes along the ground. Afearia watches as the men dressed in Mongoose fatigues don't follow as one larger man roughly Afearia's height comes from behind her, putting his hand on her shoulder.

"This was a victory thanks to you," he says. "This may be all the remaining members of Mongoose can do, but it's more than we would have been able to do alone."

She turns her head to him, a tanned skinned man with a full head of black hair and a scar on his cheek being partially covered by his beard. He's dressed in old torn green and brown fatigues like the men standing behind him. Around his neck is a greenish-brown scarf as he smiles at her with his broad jaw.

Afearia makes a somewhat dissatisfied face, "I'm sorry you lost Raquel. She was very inspirational, even to me when I was in my lowest moments."

"She will be missed. I wished to continue her goals, but I can't lead and raise morale like she could. All I can do is find her peace and carry her ideals with me." He looks to watch Kyoto be dragged off. "And it feels good to know her death was not in vain." He looks back to Afearia. "Afearia. I may not be a part of a big group like A.N.T.S. but if you ever need anything in the future, I will gladly help you anyway I can," he says, handing her a piece of paper with his number.

She faces him and takes it with a handshake, "Thank you, Cyrus. Please be safe. You and your men are still wanted."

"We will. Mongoose may be gone publicly, but not internally. And we have built our own connections and hidden safe havens away from prying eyes. We'll be fine." A vehicle rolls up and honks for Afearia to hurry. "You should go. Derexen and the others won't be long since one of his best has yet to return."

Afearia nods and lightly smiles at him before running off to the van. Cyrus looks to his men and waves them with his arm as they all rush down the other end of the alley.

Back at the stage where the crowd has become loud and rowdy, Derexen curls his finger for Glenn to come toward him. Glenn leans close. "End this event and get the chatter of the masses under control," Derexen orders him.

Glenn gets on his piece to call for backup while approaching the podium in order to get everyone to settle down as they fight, rejoice, and yell. Derexen exits from the side of the stage while Bonnie follows along with the other elites and the DA agents escorting their leaders through the same path.

"What happens now?" Bonnie asks Derexen as they travel through the back of the stage.

"Get the world leaders to safety and head to the palace afterward."

Emperor Zhao not far behind says something aloud. "If you plan to exclude us from this then you are mistaken," Niang translates. Derexen looks over his shoulder to see

Emperor Zhao. "My monster explained the situation and I think we could be of assistance."

Derexen stops, "I'm in a hurry. Bonnie, bring the world leaders and their agents to the palace. Minerva and Agonda, Kyoto has been gone for too long. Go to the location where Raquel was executed. We will discuss measures as soon as I return. Go," he orders his team.

As his elites begin to warp, he turns from them and warps to the control room at the broadcasting building. As the building has alarms going off and alerting lights flashing, he looks down at all the dead workers of the building lying on the floor under and above debris. He walks up to the main computer and sees a flash drive in it.

Derexen turns to walk away while summoning Catastrophe. Without looking back, he swings his sword behind himself, creating a black hole to swallow all the bodies and the equipment in the room into oblivion before stepping into the hall.

As he moves through the hall filled with smoke and running workers trying to flee or save others, Afearia's hacked speech finally stops. As he proceeds, he notices the blood on the floor and kneels to touch it. With the dab of his finger, he tastes the blood before sternly spitting it back to the floor.

"Not hers," he says upon standing.

Derexen continues to follow the blood drops. After turning the corner and taking the staircase, he reaches the floor where Steven blew himself up. Fire was spreading and debris was falling every so often. Derexen can hear the fire trucks on the streets coming to the building and law enforcement arriving as well. But he was focused on one task, despite the fact he shouldn't be so close to the location of the blast.

Derexen stops before the gaping area of the building where Steven killed himself. There were mangled pieces of limbs everywhere. Derexen looked around, as if he was trying to sense something, but couldn't…

"Valerie…," he says in a minuscule, near impossibly noticeable sense of mourning.

In a puff of white smoke, Valerie appears behind him, seconds before Derexen reacts by quickly swinging his blade toward her neck. He halts his swing mere centimeters from her neck as she remained calm, standing before him with torn clothes and blood coming down from her brow, dripping along her bruised face.

His brows untense a little as he lowers his sword, "Valerie." She points to her ears and shakes her head. "You can't hear me, can you?" Valerie nods after reading his lips. "But you can read my lips. Are you alright?" She nods again.

Derexen stands closer to her. He raises his hand and hesitantly, but gently wipes blood from going into her eye. He focuses on her brow before having a double take at her marvelously bright silver eyes. Upon his second look, he lingered, staring into them much longer than he necessarily would. His face—softened. His lips parted, as if he were about to say something, but his earpiece begins to flash.

"Yes…?" Derexen answers. "Understood." He sternly looks to Valerie after hanging up. "Code Red."

Valerie looks surprised before collecting herself with a more serious expression. She nods, moments before they both warp out of the building.

Diary Entry #6177

There is something I have been thinking about lately. I don't know if dying is what caused it but... I feel like some of my hostility is misplaced. It makes no sense though. Derexen is the bad news in all realms. His existence spills blood wherever he is. He must be stopped. But when we met... I... No... I will kill him. He's evil, that's it! There is no in between!
Sigh...
How can this world and its inhabitants be black and white when the universe is draped in gray? I... I hate this feeling. The pressuring inner struggle of confliction.

Running Under the Gun

Chapter Eleven

At Derexen's palace, the king and his elites, except for Aquarius, discuss immediate action on their missing member.

"It's been six hours, no word," Glenn says. "Minerva and Agonda discovered vehicle tracks, but he wasn't found."

"Unfortunately, Valerie's confirmed she cannot trace him," Derexen says.

"Does that mean—?"

"I don't want to assume," Valerie halting his troubling words. "But the second I can pick up on his essence, I will create a telepathic link between him and the chosen team."

"Team?" Glenn says with a mildly confused expression.

"My elites," Derexen says. "We are tied up at the moment. This all happened at a very busy time. But rest assured, I will not allow them to torture one of our own for information. In doing so, I have already dispatched a small searching party."

"Wouldn't we be more suited for that?"

"This could be a trick to lure out more members. But with the plan I've put together, I promise success. For the next twelve hours, I want each of you to be stationed at the assigned locations to monitor the skies," he says as Valerie hands out envelopes. "Kyoto may be out there. And if he is, we'll know. This operation is only the first part. Read your packets and head to the given locations immediately. You're dismissed."

Derexen and all of his worthy elites warp out the

room to begin their task.

Out on the open road, three vehicles drive close together. One car is leading the others. The second car trailing has Zaiah and the children sitting in the back seat. The last trailing vehicle is a van with Elliot and Afearia sitting in the back to keep an eye on their captive, Kyoto.

Kyoto lies on the floor with his hands tied behind his back and his ankles bound together.

Sitting on the bench screwed to the back seat of the driver and passenger side with a plastic divider above the headrest is Elliot smirking while staring at Kyoto.

"This still feels like a dream," Elliot says. "Once we get this punk to our destination, we can extract as much information as we want. This is a true victory for us. We're ahead of these bastards."

"Hmph," Kyoto scoffs.

"Something to say, monster?" Kyoto keeps his face to the floor. Elliot stands. "You don't have to talk right now. Because sooner or later you'll be crying."

"Heh, maniac."

Elliot rushes over to Kyoto and kneels beside him with an intimidating expression, "What did you say?"

"You and your extremist are so eager to restore a flawed system of greed," Kyoto fearlessly says. "Like spoiled children, you miss being a fat-cat with stuffed pockets while the poor spend the better part of their day licking the dirt off your boots for nourishment." Kyoto looks up at Elliot. "You realize that's the world you'll be restoring."

Elliot punches Kyoto, knocking off his mask. Kyoto turns his face to the floor to hide himself, "No-no matter wha-what," he stutters. "You-you can usurp as many of us as-as you wish. But-but even if you cast this wor-world back to black. We'll-we'll just take it back." Kyoto looks up at Elliot with a confident smirk. "By one maniac at a time. We will take it back."

Elliot punches his face to the floor before standing. "You know what pisses me off most about you guys? It's that you all wholeheartedly believe that you're the heroes of this world. You're not!" he shouts before repeatedly kicking Kyoto in the stomach.

Afearia watches Elliot in stoic judgment. Elliot stops, leaving Kyoto to painfully cough and spit, trying to breath freely. He backs away huffing before lightly sniggering. He looks to Afearia, "You want to get some?" he asks, pointing his thumb at Kyoto.

"I'm waiting for the interrogation," Afearia replies stone face.

"Good, good. We don't want to soften him up too much before that." He sits next to her on the bench. "We should be there shortly. We have expert torture methods to make this guy talk."

"I will never—betray my comrades," Kyoto says somewhat angrily.

Elliot grunts, looking like he may hit him until Afearia tilts her head a little. "Why?" she asks. Kyoto glares at her before slowly turning his face to the floor.

"Ha! Chump," Elliot taunts.

Afearia glances at Elliot before leaning back and crossing her arms as she patiently waits for them to arrive.

After a considerable amount of time on the road, Afearia and the members of A.N.T.S. arrive at their destination. Out in the midst of nowhere they park at an abandoned building with no top half, just the first floor with little of the second floor. Mostly crumbled stone stairs lead up to the building's doorway. Nothing remained inside the concrete building but half smashed and damaged pillars.

Afearia and Elliot sit quietly until the van doors open with three men standing outside. The men grab Kyoto and roughly take him to the building.

Elliot hops out with Afearia following. "This used

to be an extension of our ex-government's intelligence team," Elliot says as they walk to the middle car. "Until Derexen crushed them during his rise to power." They stop beside the car, "It's taken a long time, but we'll win in the end."

Zaiah, the driver, and another man comes out from the car before Afearia approaches Zaiah.

"How are they?" Afearia asks.

"Sleep," Zaiah replies. "They're concerned and nervous, but they're okay." Afearia nods before looking into the dark plains. "Are you okay?"

Afearia gives him a near glare for a moment, ready to give him a cold retort. But the sincere concern for her wellbeing was written all over his face. It made her drop her guard a little bit, a truly rare thing for Afearia. Just as she was about to reply, screams are heard from the building.

Everyone quickly run toward the stairs, but Afearia quickly stops Zaiah. "Stay," she says.

"But I—"

"Please. I need you to look after them." She glances at the kids before he nods and let's her go with uncertainty in his expression.

After Afearia races up the long stairs and enters the building, she discovers the three men who had carried Kyoto up to the building had been slaughtered. The bloody corpses had been tossed around. The men who came in after have minor injuries, including Elliot, holding his bloody shoulder.

Standing before them is a young man dressed in black jeans and sneakers, wearing a white long-sleeved turtleneck. Lying beside him at his feet is Kyoto who's still tied up.

The man is smirking at them with his hands behind his back. Slender and fit, he tilts his head for his black mid length spiky hair to slant a bit. Afearia notices the small silver hoop earring in his left earlobe.

"Well," he says, raising one of his bold brows as he stares at Afearia with his blue irises. "It's the dead girl."

"Who are you?" Afearia asks sternly.

"Heh, I—"

"Don't play around with her!" Kyoto interrupts, now wearing his mask. "I don't know who you are, but—"

"You're not supposed to. Lord Derexen sent me. I'm part of a special guard unit only he can mobilize. So to answer your concerns, no I am not weak, nor am I naïve to who stands before me."

Without warning, Kyoto is pulled away, surprising the mysterious man. A chain had wrapped around Kyoto's restraints and brought him to Afearia's hand.

"Not naïve. Bah," Kyoto says in irritable sarcasm.

The man makes a meek smile from his blunder. "Elliot," Afearia says. "Take Kyoto back to the van. You and your men get out of here."

Elliot and his remaining men grab Kyoto. "Okay, but we're not leaving you," Elliot tells her before they rush out the building.

"Phew," the man exhales in relief. "For a second I thought I would have to chase you guys down. That would've sucked."

"Your name, puppet," she says while summoning Demonweaver and Bastion.

Her shoulder glance was less than a second, but the brief dip in her shoulder came from the great weight of Bastion.

"Puppet?" he says. "The name's Tristan, Afearia."

"Good. A name to the face. Ready?"

"Straight to business, huh?"

"The talking was done the moment you killed those men."

"That's true. I only have one objective. Find Kyoto and retrieve if possible."

"Is it possible?" she asks with eyes of focus

Bending his knees as if to combat with hands raised, "Absolutely," Tristan replies with a confident smile.

While holding Demonweaver, Afearia turns her fisted hand upward and flicks her middle finger at Tristan, firing a wind bullet. Barely evading, his cheek is grazed by the bullet before his whole body's moved to the right by the bullet's pressure impacting the wall. He whistles because of the close call.

In rapid succession, going along each digit, Afearia continues to fire bullets in this fashion. But Tristan's now light on his feet, dodging each bullet with ease as dust in the room builds. Moving around sporadically, he is surprised to see Bastion flying straight for him. He leaps out the way before Afearia's chain cuts across the room horizontally.

Tristan ducks before she whips it back at him from overhead, but he evades it. Within that moment, Afearia calls three chains from her shoulder, having them whip at him like wild snakes before rushing in herself.

As she nears, Tristan manages to evade multiple chains. He ducks one of the returning chains aimed for the back of his neck, and still side leans out of range of Afearia's dashing pierce attack. While dodging, he spins with his arm stretched out and fist tight to backhand Afearia at the back of her head. On impact, Afearia's eyes are wide, seemingly taking more damage than expected.

Afearia flips over herself and lands on her back before her chains automatically retracted. Not down for long, Afearia swiftly kips-up back onto her feet. Tristan wipes the blood from his grazed cheek using his thumb.

"I think that's enough," Tristan says to Afearia. When she turns to him, her head bobs a little, a bit dazed from the hit she took previously. "Hurts, right? It was more than a fist that clipped your noggin."

Tristan points his index finger upward before dust

forms at the tip and creates a stone coin with Derexen's government flag on it. "I can manipulate particles in the air to form anything I wish," he explains. "The more particles present, the faster and more proficient my formations can be. There was more than enough already here, but I figured what's a little more?" Chains inch from Afearia's shoulder blade. "Derexen says my power has ancient lineage." He chuckles. "Apparently it falls under the category of creationism."

"Hmph," Afearia arrogantly scoffs. "Particle formations through trickery. Shouldn't be too hard to counter."

The token dissolves back into dust. "Never underestimate the small things we carry everyday with us."

Without warning, Afearia fires three joined chains at Tristan. To her surprise, they're stopped by a rapidly forming five foot stone golem holding her chains in its giant hand. It has no legs, just a pile of dirt and rocks as a base. It's upper body is lumpy with a humanoid shape connected through rounded pieces of stone. It's head has hollowed out eyes, but no mouth.

Afearia yanks back one time, but fails to retrieve her chains. Tristan raises his hand and creates two more golems to appear around Afearia. Green seals briefly appear on the side of her neck as the two golems throw a punch at her head. The fists of the golems collide immediately after she ducks.

She slides her hand along one of the golems. By doing so, Afearia manipulates its body to produce stone columns that launch from its body to destroy the others. Afterward, she jumps up high into the air only to find Tristan had vanished. Looking around the room, the sound of sand and dust is heard from behind her.

Afearia crosses her arms over herself and thrusts her palm forward to fire a gust of wind to disrupt the dusty formation. The dust swirls around her, gaining in size until it looks like a sandstorm.

As Afearia descends, shielding her face from the particles, the rocks below from the destroyed golems become dust particles and form upward as she nears the ground. The dust solidifies around Afearia's body and forms into a stone column, immobilizing her from the neck down.

After she briefly struggles to escape, Tristan steps from behind a crumbled pillar, "Dust is as present as the air we breathe. I hope you didn't think you could evade all that I can do. Heh, I'm not even trying yet." Tristan begins to approach. "Word around HQ is that you killed Yadeira. I struggle to believe that. Derexen trained her himself, specifically to fight Empyrean Blade wielders. There's just no way," he says, standing before her.

Strangely, Afearia starts making noises as it appears she's trying to kiss Tristan from afar. Tristan smirks with a less serious demeanor, "Coming on to me now?" As he stares at her mouth, a small spark appears. He makes a sudden face of realization before leaping back.

Afearia sighs, "Ops Augenda." She breaks free, looking disappointed. "Even now I can't cast flames from my mouth without the lip to hand seals," she says before approaching him.

Though he expected her to attack, he was not ready for the width of the flames she blows after doing the lip to hand seal. Tristan is burned a little, hopping further back to avoid most of the fire.

"Ops Augenda," he says while patting out the flames on his shoulder while keeping his focused eyes on her. "That's a pretty old spell. Strength enhancement. Where did you learn it?"

Afearia stops and extends her arm to latch a chain around Bastions handle. She yanks it and swings it toward her foe. Tristan raises his folded arm in a defensive manner before a thick stone wall formed to defend him.

Tristan immediately darts forward before his defensive wall crumbles. With each quick and fluent motion of his hand, a rock would form from the dust and shoot toward Afearia. She dodges two aimed for her face and horizontally flips over one large rock aimed for her legs. As her body stiffly spins over, green seals edge up along her neck before she lands down slamming her palm to the ground.

A large wall rises to separate them. Almost as soon as it rose, Tristan turns it to dust before rushing through it. "All of creation," he says. "Gaia based material are—"

Before he could finish speaking, Afearia smashes the sole of her foot into his jaw from her low position. She quickly gets on her feet and attempts to slash him with Demonweaver.

Without warning, a giant hand forms and grabs her whole body. Afearia screams and drops her sword and releases her chain on Bastion. Following the formation of the hand is an arm, leading to the formation of a massive, towering golem with a crown.

Tristan lands on his shoulder before calmly standing. He turns to her with a stern look, "Crush her."

The moment the golem began to squeeze, chains burst through its hand, whipping around until it's hand crumbled. Afearia falls backward before bringing her hand forward.

"Tenebrous," she whispers.

A silver pronged sword with a faint shadow mirroring itself appears before both vanishing. Expressing unexpected surprise by their disappearance, Afearia turns herself and shoots chains into the walls to halt her fall. The sudden stop puts a strain on her shoulders, causing her to painfully wince and groan.

She hears the rocky giant ready itself to attack. Afearia retracts her chains for a softer landing before jumping to the side to avoid the golem's fist. She quickly raises her hand, but nothing happens.

"I said come!" she shouts before Demonweaver returns to her hand. She leaps forward to slash the fist, but because of her delay, she misses her chance as it rises up. Tristan comes walking across the golem's shoulders and sits.

"Something's off," Tristan says. "Are your abilities hiccupping on you in battle? Is that possible?"

"Why don't you shut up and fight," Afearia says angrily.

"Are you embarrassed?"

Frustrated, she swings her sword at him, releasing an abnormally small crescent energy that he simply dodges with the tilt of his head.

"You know, there was word that Minerva killed you. That was what was reported. It was a finalized report. How did you do it? How did you trick her?"

"Shut it!"

"Maybe you didn't. Maybe you're just a broken doll fighting to die. That's why your abilities have been lacking punch."

"I am not broken!" she yells before leaping up to him.

Extending her arm across her body, bubbles begin to flourish. Unfortunately, they suddenly burst in her failed attempt to summon Nebulous. Tristan seizes the moment and creates a box of stone, trapping her inside.

Like a rocket, Afearia burst through the top and close to Tristan as her captive box crumbles to dust. Wasting no time, Tristan creates another box thicker than last. As it falls with her inside, Afearia slashes her way out the box and continues her ascent toward her foe.

Bringing his whole arm over his chest, Tristan makes a fist, exploding the golem's entire left arm to dust. Pointing his palm at Afearia, she brings her arm over her chest, manipulating the wind to scatter the dust. Though surprised she made it to him, he evades promptly as she sings her sword.

Swinging at her opponent a second time, Tristan protects his neck by forming an unusually large knight's sword with the lift of his finger.

"I'm getting closer," Afearia grunts.

"Not close enough," Tristan responds before fending her off.

As she falls back down, Tristan suddenly hears a chain rattle. He looks at his golem and notices she has pierced it's chest. Before she lands, Afearia uses the Lost Arts strength spell and lands on her feet. Immediately, she pulls the giant with her great strength, bringing it crashing down to the ground.

Before him or his creation could hit the ground, Tristan turns his golem back to dust. As he comes falling toward Afearia head first, he forms a cone shaped rock spire over his arm, pointing it at his opponent. She leaps up toward him, moving to his right, slashing the cone in two as she bypasses him.

Upon the cone's split, Tristan turns his back to the ground with a shallow gash in his arm. Using the dust around him, a multitude of stone daggers are made, flying up at his ascending foe. The first half of the volley is blown off course after meeting a mighty wind barrier formed by a swing of Afearia's arm. Following soon after was the second half of the volley.

Afearia tucks her blade under her arm and concentrates harder than her previous attempt, successfully summoning Nebulous this time. With the strike of her fiery lips and the release of hollow spheres of water from her sword swing, the combination makes a steam rain fall on the rising daggers. The attack disrupts the steam enough to reveal to Tristan that Afearia had vanished.

Swiftly, she slides behind him on the ground in alignment with her foe. She leaps up after with blades tucked in order to draw them both to cut him down. As soon as she attempts to slash, stone forms around her forearms, connecting down to the ground.

Tristan turns over and comes upon her with another, yet smaller cone shaped weapon on his arm. A chain comes from her back and wraps around her stone bindings, crushing them.

Once freed, she bolts toward Tristan who is quite close to hitting the ground. She leaps up with both swords raised and ready to end the fight. Without warning, a man with a large physique twice the size of Tristan and covered in a rocky armor, comes from above and smashes his fists into Afearia's lower back. She slams into the ground with this man landing on her with his dark energy covered fists firmly pressed into her.

Upon impact, the dark energy lights the area, alerting Elliot and the others of the growing danger from within. Afearia lies on the ground wide-eyed, twitching with Nebulous in her hand while the large man holds his striking pose before standing.

"Any longer and I would've been finished, jumbo," Tristan says, approaching the man as his cone weapon crumbles.

The man smirks with an identical face to Tristan, excluding his long black ponytail. "Sorry, bro," he says to Tristan. "I had to be sure I could get her clean."

They both look down at Afearia. "Well done then." Afearia tries to stand, but fails to even sit up as her legs barely twitch. "Don't bother. Hassel got you good. You probably won't be walking for a few hours or weeks. But a second measure can't hurt." He gestures for Hassel to strike Afearia once more.

Hassel raises his foot over her back. Afearia tries to recall Demonweaver as she raises her hand, but Tristan pins her wrist down with his hand. But just as Hassel was ready to stomp—

"Gentlemennn," Zaiah oddly emphasizes upon walking inside. "I think you've made your point."

"Excuse me?" Tristan says in an annoyed, confused tone.

"Your point. You're big and bad trying to lick the king's toes. We get it. So, would you two mind stepping away from the lady?"

"Zaiah..." Afearia says, sounding to still be in a bit of pain.

"I'm going to pretend you weren't talking to us and tell you to wait your turn," Tristan says. "We'll be getting to your band of merry-men soon enough."

"Jesus, that wasn't a request," Zaiah somewhat chuckles while giving an unexpected air of seriousness.

"Tough guy," he says upon standing. "You're starting to piss me off."

"And you've long since done that to me," he smiles, seeming to not be taking the situation serious enough. He loudly exhales, almost playfully while running his hand through his hair for a moment. Zaiah sternly looks into Hassel's eyes. "Did I stutter? Step away from Afearia."

Though Hassel does not heed Zaiah's words, only smirks, Tristan and Afearia sense a strange danger coming from Zaiah. Ignoring him, Hassel raises his foot to stomp down. Tristan was in mid reach to stop Hassel from attacking, but before either of them can finish moving, a streak of white light brushes pass Hassel with a strong rush of wind following shortly after.

The brothers are wide-eyed and Zaiah is knelt behind them with Afearia in his arm and a glowing white right hand brought across his chest. Zaiah turns his head toward the brothers, moments before Hassel's served leg comes falling from behind Zaiah. Hassel screams while staring at his missing leg. Getting his pain and shock under control, he hobbles himself to turn and face Zaiah.

"You bastard!" Hassel yells. "How did you do

that!? I won't let you get away with this!"

"Hassel!?" Tristan warns.

"I'll kill you! You and that broken whore!"

Zaiah's brow twitches before he vanishes in a bolting white light passing unseen between the brothers again. Zaiah now stands where he once was with Afearia held close so she can stand as he holds her. Though they didn't see him move pass them, Hassel felt it. He slowly turns his head toward Zaiah with wide eyes.

"Brother," Hassel says with a rasp. "Be careful with this one."

The stone armor on Hassel splits open with blood gushing out before he collapses to the ground dead. Tristan stares at his fallen brother in disbelief. Zaiah's right hand stops glowing while Afearia stares at him with astonishment.

"Zaiah...?" Afearia faintly says.

"Yeah?" Zaiah responds with a light smile.

Without warning, she punches him in the stomach and as she's falling, attempts to slash him. Zaiah, despite flinching from the pain of her punch, still had enough reflexes to jump away from her sword swing. Afearia hits the ground and turns over with angry eyes on Zaiah.

"I can't believe this whole time we've been traveling with a Demi!" she says with disgust.

Zaiah, struggling to get back on his feet, stands with his hands moving around submissively. "Whoa, hold it! I am not a Demi!"

"As if I would buy that! You took advantage of my inability to smell Demis! I can't believe I was fooled again!"

Zaiah sighs. "I really wanted to stay out of your way. But in your current state, and the fact you think I'm an enemy is leaving me with little choice here. I mean, can you still win?" he says with a strange smile, but mildly uneasy brows.

Afearia, still struggles to stand, but manages to get her legs to move somewhat, but not fully under her control. "You double crossing—! I'll cut your freaking heart out, demon. You won't get away with this!"

Zaiah sighs once more in a more relaxed pose of bother. "Damn it... I'm really going to have to do this," he mutters. Afearia, seeming like she's about to cast a spell to attack Zaiah, is suddenly halted when a bright light shines from Zaiah's chest and begins to move down his left arm. "I would never deceive you, Afearia," he says as the sound of the charging light moves into his forearm and hand.

Zaiah closes his eyes and holds his hand to his chest, "Hear my voice. I call upon your power once more as the Guardian you once knew. As a man—not a monster. Hear my call. BRAVEHEART!"

With a burning flash of light pouring out of him filling the room before slowly fading back to the source, Zaiah's now holding Braveheart with a slight change in its appearance. The sword is the same as it's always been seen in the past with only a slimmer blade and gold armor decoration in three rows going around the base of the blade. At the base on both sides of the blade is a small gold lid.

"I didn't mean to play powerless," Zaiah says, staring at his sword's fuller which has the red essence filled two eighths of the way up. He raises the blade up to his chest as he looks at Afearia. "I really just wanted to stay out of the way."

Though Afearia remains in shock, staring at Zaiah with such wide eyes, she eventually calms herself back down to a more serious expression. "Out of my way, huh?" Afearia balances herself on her hands, shakily lines her feet up and stands, nearly falling over as her legs shake a little. "Then what do you call this?"

"I—"

"Save it. I think we've kept this freak waiting long enough," Afearia says, looking at Tristan.

"Oh, right. Heh," he smirks, "shouldn't be too tough since he's alone now."

Staring at his brother's body, Tristan smiles before looking at them, "I'm not alone. After all—what's a creationist if he can't recycle used goods?"

Forming before Tristan is a rocky figure of Hassel nearly perfect in form. He walks over to his fallen brother while forming a dagger in his hand. Tristan cuts off Hassel's finger and stands before his rocky look alike. The rocky clone opens its mouth before Tristan drops the finger inside. It chews the finger before Tristan points to Hassel's body. The rocky clone breaks into many large rocks before mashing Hassel's corpse repeatedly until he's mush. It lies on top of him and absorbs his body into it, reforming into a perfect, complete copy.

"What the hell?" Zaiah says with surprised grotesque.

Afearia bunches her brows, "This is a new low for your kind. Truly the value of life means nothing to you."

"Oh, please," Tristan says before turning to face them. His eye is completely gone with the open cavity of his eye socket pulling the blood back into his head. Much of his inner tissue is exposed, including some of his brain from some of the bone dissolved inside. "This is nothing, believe me."

"There's a cost for using such magic," Zaiah analyzes with focused eyes.

"But it's two again."

"Still in our favor."

"Is it?" Tristan says before creating another Hassel copy.

Afearia sighs, "In my current state, I may have to call on another."

With the brief appearance of pronged swords, one with gold prongs and the other with silver prongs, they create a shadowy gap between each other. The sword's copper base is rectangular and it's hilt a smooth metallic white. The sword never touches her hand, just floats close before drifting forward. It suddenly fades away with a shadow figure of Afearia crouched before her, standing shortly after.

The shadow fills out as a perfect replica of Afearia in every sense. The two Afearias stare at each other with stern expressions until the doppelganger squeaks out a laugh it tries to control before silently sniggering with an eerie Cheshire-like smile. It covers it's mouth like a little girl who's being devilish while sniggering.

The doppelganger walks to Afearia, still sniggering in the same manner before touching Afearia's messy hair ends. Afearia smacks its hand away, "Enough!" Her doppelganger pouts with big lips before plopping down to the floor. "Get up!" Like a cute hurt creature, the doppelganger looks at Afearia with big sad eyes, bouncing it's bottom lip.

"Awww!" Zaiah says with ecstatic cuteness.

"Shut up!"

"What, she's cute," he mutters.

Afearia shakes her head with hand to her face as she sighs, "Tenebrous, I would really appreciate your service right now." Her copy becomes excited and quickly gets on their feet. "I'm not at my best right now so," she says while holding her hand out to her copy. Afearia's doppelganger glances at her hand before looking devious and wagging its finger at Afearia. "Oh, come on! Not here!"

The doppelganger crosses its arms and huffs with a swift look away. "Fine," Afearia says with strong aggravation. "Zaiah."

"Hm?" Zaiah responds.

"If you make a single sound, I will kill you."

"Uh, okay?" he replies, oddly confused.

Afearia stares at her doppelganger who still isn't looking at her. "Come on already. You win. We'll swap

DNA your way."

The doppelganger turns its head a little and peeks at Afearia with one eye before fully looking at her when she lowers her arms. The doppelganger smiles and gently runs its hands up and down Afearia's arms as it gets closer, somewhat intimate. Unexpected to those watching, the doppelganger tongue kisses Afearia.

Afearia roughly pulls away with hand over her moist lips, "Enough! Are you ready now?" she asks with bunched brows of annoyance. Tenebrous, her doppelganger, turns to face Tristan and his brothers. She looks back at Afearia and double taps its lips with a smile. "Yes. We'll start with that."

"Alright, let's do this," Zaiah says as he raises his sword on his shoulder.

"No."

"What?"

"You'll just slow me down from here."

"Hey, hold on, I could—"

"You could what? Lie to me some more? Stay out of this."

"Fine," he regrettably says before lowering his sword and stepping back.

Afearia nods at her doppelganger to commence. Tenebrous takes a comically deep breath. With puffed cheeks, Tenebrous blows out a mighty wide range of flames at Tristan and his brothers. All but one leap high enough to evade the flames with Tristan while the other is blown away.

To Tristan and the Hassel clones' surprise, Afearia has leaped behind them with fingers pressed to her lips and she blows fireballs by rhythmically moving her rapid fingers on her lips to change the balls' sizes, speed, and trajectory. They lean from the path of the fireballs before Tristan creates a stone wall between them and the attack. From his blind side, Afearia's doppelganger appears with a vaguely visible saber of wind enveloping half her arm.

The Hassel clone pulls Tristan from the attack's range, but the completed slash releases a shiny circular wind disc that slashes Tristan's shoulder. Tristan is painfully surprised until he's hit by a raining fireball by Afearia above, crashing him down to the ground.

While Hassel looks down where his brother crashed, Afearia shoots a fireball at her doppelganger who repeats their previous attack to recreate the circular wind saw. The combined attacks create a blazing wheel aimed at Hassel. Hassel crosses his arms to defend, but like a saw, it quickly begins cutting through his armored forearms as it carries him across the room.

Hassel's back slams against the wall as he's failing to deflect the attack, "Brother! Brother, help me, ahhh!"

Tristan stands bruised and burned. He looks to Hassel and uses his powers to make the fallen duplicate fly over to Hassel, colliding it into the blazing saw in order to destroy it.

Hassel falls to the ground on his knees once the attack was destroyed by Tristan. His bloody arms drip before one completely falls off. Tristan grits his teeth before thrusting his palm forward, recreating Hassel's lost arm with rock and full functionality. He raises his arms, creating a stone lion with a curly mane for him and his brother to mount.

Hassel jumps on the lion after Tristan before they ride toward Afearia. Afearia glances at Tenebrous before brining Nebulous close to her face. "Drip," she whispers before the blade endlessly drips beads of water. Tenebrous moves her arms in unison as the green seals appear for her coming gaia spell. The ground becomes uneven and the large stone lion falls forward, causing the brothers to become airborne.

Tristan destroys his creation and reuses the material to create cobras for him and Hassel to ride on. With two swift slashes, Afearia releases two crescent water projectiles that sever the heads of the snakes. The bodies of the snakes crumble and reform with renewed heads of greater size as they come down upon Afearia and her doppelganger.

The cobra mouths open wide to swallow Afearia and Tenebrous. With the appearance of blue seals on their foreheads, Afearia stabs Nebulous into the ground, "Deluge!"

A massive wave rises up high above the looming attackers. As soon as half of the cobras enter the wave, Afearia and her doppelganger turn halfway from each other with their hand pointed in their opponents' direction. The rising wave instantly freezes, halting the stone cobras and causing the brothers to launch toward them from the sudden halt in movement.

Afearia and her doppelganger nearly hunch their bodies in unison as they watch the brothers come their way while holding their arm pointed at Hassel and Tristan. Using the ice around them, they liquefy a large amount of it and create a wall before them that spikes out and freezes. Seeing the coming danger, Tristan creates a layer of rock between him and Hassel.

Afearia and Tenebrous join their legs and raise their arms up like the letter Y. All of the ice becomes water and the cobras fall to the ground, leaving the brothers to continue on their path toward Afearia and Tenebrous.

When Tenebrous creates a wind saber with pockets of water in the blade, Afearia flicks her hand, holding it upward as green seals move around her wrist. The rocky defense Tristan made suddenly receives numerous cracks, moments before Tenebrous steps forward and slashes the wall and the brothers in two from the waistline, causing their upper halves to flip over the Afearias.

Before they could hit the ground, Tristan creates prosthetic legs of stone for him and Hassel. They land on their feet and turn to their opponents. After they take a couple steps toward them, the brothers could no longer move.

"What?" Tristan says, confused as he looks at his legs and now his stiff arms.

"Another pathetic performance from beings lower than myself," Afearia coldly says as Nebulous begins swallowing up the room's water.

"How-how are you doing this!? Is it telekinesis!?"

"You're so stupid," she lightly chuckles. "I just showed you that I could manipulate rocks much like yourself. How do you think my partner cut through your defenses so easily? Now that you're even less of a man, I can simply manipulate you," she says while pointing at him with green seals along her index finger.

Tristan turns sideways on command, trying to resist, but can't. He grits through his teeth before looking at her. "You can't stop us. I have power even Derexen acknowledged! You can't—!"

"Actually, I already did. At least Hassel." Tristan looks to Hassel and is shocked to see Hassel's head held low and drooling.

"Hassel?"

"He's gone, Tristan. His brain has been oxidized above all limits thanks to Tenebrous." Tenebrous winks at Tristan with a huge smirk on their face. "When Tenebrous cut through, Hassel, the water pockets that were gathered from Deluge entered his opened wound and—"

"I know what you did!"

Afearia's brows bunch a bit in annoyance, "Must be hard. Exhausting even to lose at your own game."

Tristan angrily grunts and growls as his face reddens before bursting off his own stone torso toward Afearia. He comes zooming at her with fist raised before he encases himself in a large stone replica of his angry action pose to defeat Afearia. Though he was almost half the size of the side of the room he was coming from, Afearia stands fearless.

"Apparently," she says as her eyes close and blue seals appear. She looks straight ahead at her coming foe, "You've learned nothing."

Inside the stone structure, Tristan's eyes suddenly roll to the back of his head, moments before drooling as he had succumbed to the same fate as Hassel. The stone replica of Tristan hits the ground and breaks into pieces. With her seals faded, Afearia turns and walks away shortly before Tenebrous follows with a carefree step in her walk and a worry-free smile.

"That was... intense," Zaiah says as Afearia and Tenebrous approach him. "I knew you were amazing, but Tristan should've known better than to fight two Afearias."

"The genderless being Tenebrous is only a reflection of what I can potentially be," Afearia says. "Together, we didn't have to try very hard. Either way, I'm still better."

Tenebrous silently snickers with hand over its mouth before continuing its ongoing silent chuckles while wagging a finger behind Afearia in disagreement.

"I never said you weren't," Zaiah replies, a bit confused. Zaiah looks over her shoulder, "Uh...?"

Afearia turns just in time to catch Tenebrous making silly faces at her before poorly acting nonchalant. "You can go, Tenebrous. Thank you for your assistance." Tenebrous bows and kindly waves goodbye at them before fading back into its sword form and splitting in two like previously before fading from sight.

"I guess you really didn't need me," Zaiah jokes upon dismissing Braveheart. Afearia leers at him. "What's the—?"

"I knew I couldn't trust you."

"What? I told you why I couldn't say anything."

"You lied to me."

"When?"

"You still had your powers."

"I never said I didn't."

"A lie by omission."

"That doesn't even make sense. A lie is when someone deliberately feeds someone false information. If information isn't exchanged, how can a lie form?"

"You're not helping your case."

"That's because there is none. Look, Afearia. All I want to do is be there when you need me most."

Though Afearia wanted to remain angry, her brows showed her mixed feelings about his desire. Suddenly, Tristan's corpse punches up through the rubble. He slowly drags his upper body with one arm like a broken doll. Zaiah's about to take action until Afearia stops him as she sternly watches Tristan come closer.

Tristan stops and snaps his body upright and tilts his head while his eyes make no contact with theirs. "Derexen has a message for you," he says in a dual gravelly voice.

"What's going on?" Zaiah asks.

"It's a spell," Afearia cautiously replies. "One that only activates under certain conditions. They're rare and hard to use." Afearia grits her teeth, "And if I'm right, this one turns your pawn into a vengeful corpse."

"Meaning?"

Tristan's lopsided shoulders shift, "You made a mistake coming out of hiding. But nothing bigger than challenging me and abducting one of my men. Ready yourself, elysian. You will not know rest until you return to the grave you once came."

Suddenly, Tristan gags before darkness begins seeping out of his body and reentering through his cavities. His body begins to shake like he's having a seizure.

"Let's go," Afearia says, slowly backing him and herself away.

"But—"

"Run!"

They flee the area moments before Tristan's body begins to swell.

"Start the cars!" Zaiah shouts as they race down the stairs.

All of the men jump into their vehicles. Before Zaiah can get into one, Afearia grips his arm, "This isn't over. I'll be watching you the whole way."

She releases him and they both get into separate cars. An explosive dark light shoots into the sky from the ruins, coloring the surrounding area in a purple bright hue as they drive off into the open plains.

Elsewhere, Valerie's walking an empty street in a city until she notices the purple hue in the sky off in the distance.

"What is that?" Her earpiece flashes. "Hello?" Valerie answers. "Yes, I see it. Understood. I'll inform the others." Valerie ends her call and walks faster while calling another. "Afearia's been found. Lord Derexen has confirmed it. Yes. The hunt begins."

Diary Entry #6109

I was told—Eden cannot be achieved by any measure. The concept of Eden was invented to grant peace in one's self. Ease of mind in the midst of a chaotic world. Acquiring Eden is a devil's task. You see, if Eden's a garden in one's mind, a concept to help them coop, then it's wrong to force your Eden on others. Your peace, your ideals are yours and yours alone. To try and reshape a world to fit your Eden only means you are a selfish child who can't stand being told no.

No Rest for the Angel

Chapter Twelve

At Derexen's palace, the elites, the DA agents, and their leaders gather once again in the dining room. "We don't have much time, so I'll be brief," Derexen says. "Nation leaders, I apologize for this bothersome time. I ask for your patience." He looks to his team. "Kyoto's location as you know has been discovered. As I speak, he's being tailed by hunter-type Demis. It's time to retrieve him. Unfortunately, since this is at a bad time, I can only send two of our best."

"Two?" Glenn says with dumfounded displeasure."

"It's not what I want. It's what I can spare."

"Derexen, this is—"

"Pardon me," Takashi interrupts with a translation from his leader. "Maybe we could be of use."

Derexen looks to Prime Minister Minami, "I appreciate your concern, Prime Minister," Derexen says while Bonnie translates. "This is a western issue that should be handled by western control."

Ludwig leans from Chancellor Heibel, "The dangers of the calamity isn't just at your doors. It's at all of ours. She threatens order beyond just your country. Which is why I again lay my offer on the table. Allow Ludwig to assist you."

The elites look to Derexen as he carefully thinks. He faintly sighs with closed eyes. "I accept your offer."

"Derexen," Valerie whispered with a turn of her body toward him.

"It's fine. I'll accept Ludwig for this operation."

"Then the party is of three," Glenn says. "Who are the other two?"

"You'll be a part of the team, but Minerva will be your party captain."

"Good call."

"Would you like another?" Niang translates.

"No," Derexen says. "I know anything beyond the current offer will only lead to you and others wanting more."

"You are not mistaken."

"In the meantime, I ask the DA agents and their leaders to wait back at the hotel until we continue our foreign duties to you later tonight."

Derexen nods at Valerie before she stands to speak, "Before I escort you all back to the hotel, there are some things we need to discuss. As I hope you already know, I can't stress enough how this is a western affair. You are not allowed to interfere in any shape or form. Doing so will result in a major punishment that will affect your entire nation. And Ludwig," facing Ludwig. "Even though you were allowed special permissions to assist us, you will abide by our laws and commands. Are we understood?" after all is translated by their DAs, the leaders nod in agreement to her words. "Good. Please follow me."

"Minerva, Glenn, Ludwig, you may begin now. Bonnie, you will be Heibel's main translator until Ludwig's return."

Valerie walks out of the room with the world leaders and their agents following her. The remaining elites, including Derexen, warp from the palace. Chancellor Heibel, Bonnie, and Prime Minister Minami casually talk amongst one another. Trailing behind them, Niang calmly walks with her arms behind her back. She hears a pair of footsteps coming from behind her until its one set of footsteps.

"Chloe," Niang smirks. "Did President Duskin send you?"

"He wants to talk to Bonnie. And I want to talk to

you."

"About?"

"The angel as we know—lives. But I have my doubts about her strength. She can't really be all she claims."

"I agree. To lose to Minerva screams weak."

"Right. And as God's apostle, it is my job to ensure all is in the benefit of my good Father. If she's one of the many keys to salvation, we need to be sure she's ready."

"Minus the religious overtones, I see your point. What do you suggest?"

"A test."

"Test?"

"Yes. We find the angel first and raise her up right. She's probably soaked in sin after being in the West for so long."

"That's all well and good, but if Derexen's team finds out—"

"They won't. We go before night and return with results."

"Our leaders won't like this."

"Our secret."

"Still."

"Maybe Minerva will show up too."

Niang's eyebrows twitch. "Three hours. If we can't find her or prove her strength in three hours, we flee and return to the hotel." Chloe smiles while Niang smirks from her view.

Far from the scheming DA agents, Afearia and the A.N.T.S. members are waiting at an outdoor station to board the recently completed bullet train. The silver and blue train is being boarded at the ends of each car, which happens to be numerically marked for passengers to find their car. Each passenger has their ticket checked before boarding the train.

At the last car, Elliot is speaking with two bullet

train crew members who monitor passengers boarding. Afearia stands between Adrian and Veronica, waiting near the vehicle they arrived in.

"This is taking too long," Afearia says, impatiently tapping her fingers on her crossed arms.

"This is still better than being out in the open," Zaiah says, standing beside Adrian.

"I didn't ask you."

"Are you still mad at me?"

"You lied."

"I didn't!"

"What's going on?" Adrian asks them.

"We're waiting for Elliot to secure a spot for all of us," Afearia replies sorely.

"That's not what he meant," Zaiah says.

"Yes it was," playing dumb.

"But it wasn't," Adrian adds.

"Oh? Then what did you mean, dear?"

Zaiah rolls his eyes to Afearia's phony oblivious attitude, "Oh my God... You know why she's mad?" directing his question to the kids. "Because I revealed myself to still be a World Guardian."

"Really!?" Veronica excitedly says, bouncing up and down on her toes with Adrian. "That's cool!"

Zaiah wildly flails his arms before presenting the kids like a major reveal. "That's how you should've reacted!"

"They're kids," Afearia responds. "They don't see the point."

"You sure about that?"

Afearia stone stares at Zaiah until she notices Elliot approaching. "That was harder than I thought," Elliot says. "It's risky using transit systems owned by the government, but I'm betting Derexen wouldn't expect us to."

"So the man agreed?" Zaiah asks.

"It wasn't easy. He almost called the government

office on us. But wave enough dollars in someone's face and you're good."

"That solves one problem. How are we going to get the cargo on board?"

"In a trunk. No one will question it as long as we act natural."

"Do we even have one?"

"Already being taken care of," he says just as two of his men come carrying a locked black trunk. The kids give each other displeased looks. "Come on. We have to board." Elliot walks toward the train.

Just as Zaiah's about to do the same, Adrian tugs his shirt, "Zaiah?" sounding a bit hesitant. Afearia raises an eyebrow at them. "This... This doesn't feel right."

"Why are you saying that to him?" Afearia irritably interrupts. "Shouldn't that have been said to me?"

"But, Anya you wouldn't understand. You hate the people in the world government. To you this is fitting." Afearia seems a little taken aback before calmly looking away.

Zaiah kneels to Adrian's height, "I think I know what you mean. The inhumane way these guys are treating him rubs me the wrong way too."

"Newsflash," Afearia says. "That thing in the trunk isn't a person. Just a monster."

"But still," Zaiah says upon standing. "Don't you think their means are excessive? Maybe even less humane than the man you wish to kill?"

"Enough!" snapping at him. "You two, on the train," rushing the kids along.

Zaiah sighs and follows behind them. The four of them board the train where Elliot had waited for them before getting on himself. Once on, the train car was cleared of passengers as they walked down the wide, gray carpeted walkway with dozens of cushioned leather seats. On one side of the train, the seats are all facing one another in sets of two and sets of three at both ends of the car. The other side of the train has the same seating arrangement.

The kids run up front and sit between two of Elliot's men. Afearia notices the trunk the men are resting their feet on. "No," she says to the kids. "You two go sit in the middle of the train."

Without question, the kids do as they're told, running pass the rest of Elliot's men. Afearia sits at the opposite window where the men are and Zaiah comes sitting in front of her. Elliot soon takes his seat between his men.

"So," Elliot says, carelessly dropping his feet on the trunk. "We should be arriving at the safe zone in a few hours. We've got to leave the East. Too much government influence. At least where we're going there's a fairer chance for us to remain safe."

"Elliot?"

"Yeah?"

"Is he in there?"

"Of course it's in there."

"I haven't heard a thing."

"Oh?" He takes his feet down with his men doing the same as he unlocks the trunk. "That's because it's drugged out of its mind," he says upon opening the trunk.

Inside, Kyoto had been squeezed tightly into the trunk with his head turned, pushing his neck to its limits since he didn't fully fit. With large dark circles under his eyes from fatigue and bruising, he lays motionless in puddles of his own sweat as he drools.

"He's barely breathing." Afearia says. "Don't we need him alive?"

"Of course we do," Elliot says before roughly propping his feet up on Kyoto's face, causing him to groan. "But there's no need to give it basic rights. It's just a Demi."

Elliot and his men begin chuckling while Zaiah just

judgingly looks at their faces, seemingly with mild disgust. Afearia suddenly stands, interrupting their laughter.

"Excuse me," she says before walking down the aisle.

Afearia sees the children sharing a window seat and sits in front of them beside the window. The children are giggling and commenting on everything the train zooms pass, including the leafy forest.

Adrian does a double take looking at Afearia, losing his smile before tapping Veronica's shoulder. As they look at her with concern, she lightly smiles and gestures for them to continue what they were doing. The two of them do as such, playing and pushing each other to look out the window. With fist to her mouth, Afearia props her head up as she leans on the armrest watching the trees pass by.

Afearia sees Zaiah coming down the aisle and looks forward before he comes and sits on the armrest across from her. "Hey," he says. "You left kind of abruptly. You okay?" Without out her usual threatening leer, Afearia just stares at him. "Talk to me."

She rolls her eyes and looks out the window. Afearia remains silent before lightly sighing. "You know, there was a time I would be just as excited to be riding this train like they are. But now... It seems like the time to marvel and enjoy things has become a lost pastime. Like the childhood I never—" Noticing she's divulging too much, she glances up at his concerned face. "It just seems like I'm worse off than when I began this journey. Like I'm moving further away from the right path."

"Really...? Afearia, you remember what I said about not fighting yourself? You're doing the opposite—still. Follow the call in your heart."

"But what if I'm wrong? What if I have an emotional reason that doesn't belong here?"

"If you're in a situation where morality isn't a factor, I think you've already found your answer." She looks up at Zaiah. "Do the right thing, Afearia. Not just by what's expected of you, but by yourself. You won't find peace by defying your own morals—believe me."

Afearia stares almost softly at him before he smiles at her. Drawing their attention, the door leading between cars gently slides opens. Two white cloaked individuals with purple flower stitching at the edges of their clothes, enter the train car. Their cloaks have large hoods closed pretty tight by their long drawstrings. The shortest one walks ahead as the other follows. They both sit across the aisle from Elliot with the taller person's back to Afearia's group further down.

"I thought you paid to have this car closed off to us," one of the men whispers to Elliot. Elliot suspiciously watches them before gesturing one of his men to stand and talk to them.

Zaiah slowly stands, looking just as suspicious as Elliot. "What's wrong?" Afearia asks.

"I don't know," Zaiah says. "Something's—off."

Another of Elliot's men walk over as the two cloaked passengers and the two men laugh with one another. The tallest cloaked person suddenly lets out a feminine giggle. Zaiah narrows his stare and begins to approach.

"Before you come any closer," the shortest individual says, stopping Zaiah and revealing herself to be female. "Where did you learn to charm my friend so well? I swear she's never like this." The other woman giggles and gives her hand for the man to kiss. "She's quite smitten."

Though the four of them have continued to carry on, Zaiah remains still, almost frozen even. I am more than certain she was talking to me, Zaiah thinks. She spoke loud enough for me to hear and now I can't hear her at all.

Afearia stands behind him, "What's going on with you?"

"Those women..." Zaiah takes one step forward.

"To move so bold," the shortest one loudly says for Zaiah to hear. "Marriage? So soon?" The men continue to flirt before the four of them laugh amongst one another.

Zaiah turns to Afearia, "Every time I try to approach, that woman says something I am certain is for my ears."

"Stop it, you're being ridiculous."

Zaiah glances at them as they continue to talk and laugh. "No, I'm not."

Just as he's about to step forward, she grabs his shoulder, "Leave it alone, you're just going to cause a stir."

"They shouldn't even be in here," he loudly says. "This car was paid off."

"What's is you're problem," she loudly asks, looking him up and down like he's losing it. "You're acting nuts."

"They—I feel like—"

"Enough. You want to bring an end to this, watch."

She walks pass Zaiah, "Afearia, wait!"

The shortest cloaked woman's head lifts a bit in alertness before the taller one slowly leans over to barely peer at Afearia from her seat. Afearia makes eye contact, moments before a yellow rod of light, slightly thinner than a pen, but equal in length is shot through several chairs and pierces clean through Afearia's bicep.

Kneeling down in a painful groan as she holds her arm, everyone looks to Afearia, puzzled by her sudden injury.

The woman who was being flirty a moment ago, now has her smoking index finger to the back of the hole in her seat. What a displeasure," she says. "I didn't expect your reaction speed to be slower than one one-hundredth of the speed of light."

The women stand up and push the stunned man into the seats across from them as they step into the aisle toward Zaiah and Afearia.

"She's already failed the speed test," the shortest woman says.

"Oh!?" the taller woman exclaims with realization. "I caught her off guard. That doesn't count." She points her glowing index finger at Afearia.

Elliot's men pull out their guns, "Stop, fools!" he orders. "Don't use your guns on this train!"

One of them pull out a knife and run up to stab the taller woman. Not even looking his way, the shortest woman effortlessly deflects his attack with her hand while also disarming him all in one motion. He follows up by throwing a punch and has his fist deflected downward, causing his weight to bring him too close to his enemy. When his face nears, the woman elbows him hard in the bridge of his nose, neutralizing the target.

Two others readied to approach for close combat until rods of light pierce their foreheads and kill them. When they dropped, Elliot stumbles back in fear while his other man grabs the one with a broken nose off the floor.

"Damn it," Zaiah says, seeming to be moving into an offence pose.

In that moment, the shortest woman moves low to the ground, much faster than he expected. She comes up below him with her hand stiffened like a claw. The taller woman crosses two of her glowing fingers to turn the tips of the shorter woman's claw-like hand bright.

Aiming to remove his heart, Afearia comes between them with Nebulous and has her sword held up high by the woman's fingertips. The woman turns to her right and sees Afearia swinging Demonweaver toward her face. She drops her body backward and kicks off of Afearia, gaining distance while pushing her and Zaiah back.

Zaiah and Afearia maintain their footing despite the stumble. Afearia's eyes remain on her slowly standing foe as she carefully glances at both of these mysterious attackers.

Afearia does a double glance at Zaiah, "What?" she roughly asks.

"You defended me," Zaiah says with a light smile.

"Idiot, shut up and protect Adrian and Veronica. I'll handle this." The taller woman watches Zaiah usher the kids to the other end of the train. Afearia steps into her eye view. "Over here."

The taller woman smirks, "Awe, worry not. We've come here for you, Ms. Angel."

"She's right," the shorter woman says.

"If that's true," Afearia says before quickly cutting a large irregular shaped hole in the train's ceiling. "I'll make this quick." With the upward flick of her middle finger, she commands a small gust of wind to blow off the damaged portion of the roof, letting in a lot of air pressure. "Zaiah!?" she calls out, pointing her sword at him. "I'm trusting you beyond my better judgment! You protect my kids with your life!"

"Anya!" Adrian shouts.

Afearia smiles at him. "I promise with my heart and soul. I will come back to you this time."

"Like hell!" the taller woman says before running at Afearia.

Afearia kneels low and thrusts her leg forward to ruin the woman's run. Afearia strikes her foot, causing the woman's fall. Afearia brutally seizes the moment and does a strong upward slash into her jaw, sending her opponent soaring out the train car to be carried away. Afearia leaps up to pursue, leaving the shorter woman to do the same.

Despite the circumstance, the taller woman was seemingly unharmed as she had been running up the train against the wind. Afearia tries to do the same, but the sheer wind pressure is making it hard for her to run let alone walk. The shorter woman comes completing her leap directly over Afearia. When she lands, she's slowed by the wind and almost falls over before regaining her footing and darting up the train as well. Almost mockingly, the shorter woman catches up and looks Afearia's way while moving at equal pace before darting off ahead.

Afearia crouches low to reduce the wind's impact. In a yellow glow, she air writes a sideways P and slashes her finger through it before overlapping the symbol with an infinity sign. The symbol glows bright before fading away only to reappear on her temple. Slowly standing, she raises her arm and majority of the wind parts to her sides. She immediately races up the train to catch up to her attackers.

After hopping several cars, she notices the women had stopped and are standing beside each other, waiting for her to get closer. She reaches the train they're on and slows down as she carefully watches them.

"Well?" Afearia asks as she stops. "Get to it."

As the shorter woman's about to step up, her partner comes in front of her. "Ah-ah," the taller woman says. "He who is without sin shall cast the first stone. John 8:7."

"That's not what it means," says the shorter woman, seeming a bit confused.

"Ms. Angel," ignoring her partner, "will you come with us?"

"I'm already here," Afearia replies. "Let's not get carried away."

The taller woman raises a finger, "Suit yourself."

Afearia runs in to attack first. Upon completing her diagonal slash, a burst of sparks appear, but her sword's edge is stopped three feet from the woman's body. In that moment of confusion, a rod of light is fired into her bicep once again, causing her to roll backwards and drop Demonweaver. Afearia sits up clutching her wound.

"Why you heal so fast?" The taller woman asks almost playfully. She looks to her partner, "Why she heal so fast?"

"I read about this in the files," the shorter woman replies. "It wasn't this fast and it depends on the extent of

410

the damage."

"Oh?" she says with a devious smile. "So more **damage**!"

Without warning, an invisible force slams down upon Afearia. She screams in pain as the force continues to push her body flat into the train. The force gradually increases as it begins to dent the trains roof and put Afearia's bones at their limits. Even her breathing became near impossible.

When the train dents further, the shorter woman pulls the taller woman's shoulder, "Stop! You'll break the train!"

While distracted, the hold on Afearia weakens. She struggles to bring her arm before her. The symbol on her temple glows brighter before the radius of the parting wind around Afearia spreads forward and between the women. The sudden rushing sound of the air crashing back between them once the spell is cancelled, causes the women to lose balance. They struggle to not fall off the train.

Afearia swings her sword Nebulous to create a crescent water wave wider than the train and at the shortest woman's neck level.

"Help us, Father!" the taller woman panics.

Before the lacerating water could reach, Afearia is released and the attack is smashed by an unseen force. Afearia stares wide-eyed and dumbfounded, but quickly regains her senses.

Doing a series of upward one-armed slashes, Afearia deploys vertical crescent water waves that slice the roof they're traveling along. Splashing into puddles against an unseen force, the taller woman calmly watches each attack be destroyed while her partner simply dodges three with two hops and a slow one-handed cartwheel.

"Why is she not fighting?" The taller one asks her partner.

"This might be her best," the other woman says.

"We must push harder. She's unacceptable right now."

"Heh, I was thinking the same thing," Afearia adds.

The trails left by the water waves evenly spreads water across their half of the roof before turning into an icy sheet. The taller woman falls immediately while the shorter one struggles greatly to remain standing.

The taller woman tries to get back on her feet but continuously slips, leaving her on all fours. In two spins, Afearia releases two roof cutting vertical water waves at the women. She then follows up with a wind bullet fired at the shorter one. The short woman evades the bullet, but slips and falls doing so.

The water waves curve toward the women and melt down into the ice sheet. The icy sheet rises half a foot over the taller woman's legs and arms, freezing to hold her in place. The shorter one sees this and tries to prevent it, only to get half of her limbs frozen to the train and the remaining water freezing high to bound her elevated arm.

Afearia does a running slide and quickly lines herself with the taller woman before doing a blinding V-shaped slash on the train's roof around her opponent. She plunges her sword into the train and a bursting pressure of water sprays up from the lacerations she made around her and explodes the top off, leaving the taller woman to fly into the forest.

Without hesitation, Afearia swings her blade toward the fallen short woman, but is suddenly halted and squeezed by the unseen force and quickly whisked off into the woods just as quickly as the other woman.

"No!" the cloaked woman says. With brute strength, she manages to break her limbs out of the ice. She stands and sternly looks back to the forest. I've traveled too far to find her on my own, the cloaked woman thinks. I can't jump off safely, nor do I know this area to be capable of teleportation. "Chloe... Don't do anything stupid."

Pinkish-white plumes of energy bubble around her feet before bursting upward as pinkish beams of light equivalent to her height. The light silently crashes into the train's roof with her being nowhere in sight.

Though hard to see as she crashes through the branches, Afearia faintly sees Chloe crashing through the forest before the train roof finally becomes wedged and sends her flying off somewhere while Afearia continues soaring along. The unseen force that has been squeezing her finally releases Afearia.

To protect herself, she encases her whole body in chains before finally hitting a tree and landing on the forest floor. After remaining still for awhile, the chains retract to reveal Afearia with a cut on her forehead and a few scratches on her arms as she suspiciously looks around.

Afearia sits up and shakily summons Bastion. She stands, still being carefully for any danger as the sound of forest crickets fill her ears. With a slow exhale, she begins walking back the way she came. Afearia doesn't get far before the sound of abrupt rustling is heard. She looks around, unable to pinpoint where she heard the noise. Looking up at the sky, the moon's light is being greatly blocked by the leaves above.

Suddenly, the sound of something loud and fast is coming her way from the treetops. In a brief gleam of light being reflected off the object, Afearia instantly hops back with much fear in her panicked expression. Barely escaping, Afearia had dodged the thrown train top which had pierced mostly through the tree behind her.

Afearia quickly turns when a quick rustle is heard and she sees Chloe in midair aiming to kick her in the face. Afearia ducks and stumbles forward before facing her enemy. Crouched down, Chloe slowly stands to dust herself off with her back to Afearia.

"Now this is a problem," Chloe says. She turns to her with a joyless expression. "This wasn't part of the plan.

But I'll clean up my mess."

"Who are you?" Afearia demands, sounding on edge due to her predicament. "You're not one of Derexen's men."

"No. I'm from overseas. Taking care of something his majesty can't. Chloe D. Dorcas. DA agent of the human government."

"I've heard of you DA agents. A means for the human ruled governments to fight fire with fire. But why are you here with me if Derexen can't order you around?"

"The ex-regime has its own plans for you. I'm just here to see if they're backing the right horse."

"I'm not you're government's plaything," Afearia says irritably.

"Oooh," she lightly chuckles. "Sweetie. Open your eyes. Since the day you arrived you've been everyone's plaything," she smiles, furthering Afearia's irritation. Chloe begins to remove her cloak, "One thing I—" A large piece of ground was hurled at her by Afearia, but it is smashed into something Afearia cannot see. Even the dusty dirt in the air dissipates from Chloe. "Impatient," still removing the cloak while not looking her way or showing any concern. "Once I capture you, you'll see why we want you."

"I'm not going anywhere with you."

"No?" Chloe tosses her cloak aside to reveal her parka attire. She unties the flaps from her ushankas as it hangs back in her hood. She flips it onto her head and secures it snuggly. "Better. Let me ask, Ms. Angel. Who better to clean up this world. A know-nothing foreigner or its natives?" Afearia remains cold face. "Neither. The natives are too scared of change so they grasp at anything familiar to them. The foreigner is too distant from the issues to understand the needs of the people."

"Can I kill you now? I don't care about your politics."

"But you should. You're currently at the heart of all these issues, including some that are beyond a political aspect. Why can't you see that?"

With the thrust of her arm, Afearia quickly fires a chain that is stopped midway from hitting Chloe in the face. Afearia's eyes are wide in shocked confusion. Chloe slowly closes her eyes, shaking her head before almost glaring at her.

"You still don't get it," Chloe says. "You're a pawn in a game of kings." Pulled and lifted by her chain, Afearia is swung into a tree. Upon hitting it, an invisible force smashes into her torso, pinning her as Chloe approaches. "I don't think you're strong. How many times have I knocked you down?"

Struggling, Afearia coughs a couple times, leering at Chloe. "It's not about how many times you knock me down," Afearia strains to say. "It's about how many minutes shall pass before I smash you to piece."

The pressure lifts from Afearia, allowing Afearia to breathe normally. Chloe just watches her catch her breath, completely unmoved by her threat. "I still don't get it." Chloe puts a finger to her lip as she ponders. "Why do they need you?"

Suddenly, Afearia throws her weapon Bastion into the dirt in front of her opponent before clutching her fist to her chest. In a heavy wave of soil, Chloe's covered in a high piled dome. On to her feet, Afearia readies to swing Nebulous at the mound, but she hesitates.

"Go ahead," Chloe says in a muffle under the dirt. "I wasn't going to stop you."

Afearia grits her teeth with irritation before snatching Bastion out the ground with her chain and leaping far back. She does two slashes with Nebulous to release two crescent water strikes, crashing into the mound. Hollow sounding in its strikes, much of the muddy dirt is smacked away, revealing Chloe's smiling face beneath the sliding mud.

"God is truly good," Chloe states with positive flare. Afearia tensely watches the mud wiped away by an unseen force. "I've never been afraid of a fight. Do you want to know why?"

"I don't care."

"Faith," she says, pointing up. "In Him. As long as you love Him unconditionally, all fears, pains, and worries pale in comparison to his divine light. God—is love," talking without pause.

There must be a way, Afearia thinks. Her defense is clearly not all around or she wouldn't need to shift herself. There are blinds spots. I just need to confirm where.

"And his love flows through me," Chloe had rambled on. "It protects me every second of the day. It's a power meant to protect and smite heathens who do not serve the Lord."

"Could you shut up and fight? I'm in a hurry."

"When one is being shown the light of God, one should listen." She slowly raises her hand, oddly moving her digits as they glow yellow. "It might save your life."

Chloe runs at her opponent with tense glowing hands. She slashes at her like a tiger, leaving a quickly fading yellow strike of her fingers in the air, something Afearia dodges just in time. Using a flurry of strikes, Afearia blocks each swipe with her swords before jumping back from Chloe's widening strikes. Seizing the small opening given to her, Afearia does a spread arm sword slash at Chloe.

Chloe instinctively leaps back from range. However, Afearia's slash with Nebulous releases a crescent water wave. The crescent wave meets the unseen force, once again protecting Chloe. Not relenting, Afearia follows up with a strong upper slash, calling forth a towering water wave. The wave burst up in the air on impact of the unseen force and pours back down. With the blue glowing symbols

416

on Afearia's forehead, she blows out freezing winds from her mouth.

The water freezes around Chloe in uneven segments, briefly distracting her. Taking advantage of Chloe's broken focus, Afearia had swiftly moved behind her in midswing.

"You're open!"

Chloe smiled with joyous cheeks, "God's Love." In an instant, all the ice shatters, Afearia's attack is deflected and her body slammed up against a tree. Chloe hugs herself with lightly flustered cheeks. "Mmmm. So warm," she intimately mutters. "Can you feel it, Ms. Angel? The endless blessings God casts on his chosen few? Wait a minute," turning to face Afearia struggling to her feet. "Can you feel it?" asking with genuine concern.

"Feel what, lunatic."

Chloe's eyes are wide with surprise. "But I thought this was a test. I thought you were a test."

"What are you talking about!?"

"You. You came from the sky. You're an angel from Father, right?"

"Geez, you really are insane. I never said I'm an angel."

"Oh," slanting her saddened eyes while turning away, lightly touching her worried cheek. "Will you now give your heart, body and soul to the Lord? Only hell awaits if you refuse to worship our Father."

"I am so tired of hearing this," she mutters with hand to her forehead, "Shut up and fight!"

"I see," lowering her arms. "You've repeatedly rejected the love of our Lord and savior. It's true… You are no angel," sounding quasi-aggressive. "You are not only a threat to the world, but an affront to God's will." Chloe turns toward her with cold eyes. "Taste despair, Calamity Afearia," she says as the ground lightly rumbles and the air around her faintly wavers.

Afearia's eyes dart around for a moment, assessing the situation. Chloe aggressively brings her hands together, creating a great blowback that breaks branches and blasts Afearia deeper into the forest. Afearia stabs the ground with Nebulous to prevent herself from being sent too far into the woods.

Stiffly floating forward, Chloe raises one glowing hand before herself. Using the last of the blowback, Afearia swings her body up and over Chloe to avoid her grab. She comes down overhead with the flat side of Bastion and bashes Chloe into the dirt. Following up in the same fluent motion, Afearia rips Nebulous up out the ground in a spin to create a crescent water wave strong enough to carry Chloe away in the dirt, breaking up the ground.

Though difficult, Chloe turns her body and grabs the crescent wave, bursting it in her grip, flipping herself back onto her knees. Suddenly the ground breaks up around her and is sent flying toward Afearia. With quick thinking, Afearia air writes in a yellow light an R with an arching shape through it before bringing her sword Bastion down like a hand fan. The power of her spell and swing was enough to send the rocks back at her foe. Before they could reach, all the rocks stop in midair.

Afearia leers at her foe. Only counter strikes seem to work, Afearia thinks as a chain comes from her back to hold Bastion behind her. Afearia's hand moves to her hip, bending her knees like a samurai. I'll be sure to make the next one count.

Chloe stands as the rocks move behind her while dusting herself off. Just as she's about to send the rocks back, Chloe's eyes bulge as she grunts in pain. Puncturing her stomach is an abnormally long silver blade. Holding the hilt is Afearia with her body in a completed drawing slash pose for Sleight to pierce.

"That was Sleight's Quick Draw ability. Less than one hundredth thousand the speed of light. And you mocked me? Such weakness."

"Weakness?" Surprising Afearia with how clearly she spoke despite her injury. She calmly looks at Afearia. "You cockroach."

The rocks resume and come speeding at Afearia. She's hit several times before using Bastion to shield herself. But the pain and muscle damage causes her to collapse to the ground.

"Weakness is not in my country's vocabulary," Chloe says while approaching Afearia as she unbuttons her parka. She untucks her thin, long-sleeve black wool shirt to reveal her stomach. The shallow stab wound was small with no blood. "Even if you can hit me," she says as her wound closes in seconds. "You will never break my skin. For I—am God's chosen."

Diary Entry #6214

*I've been through so much. But nothing like this. Never a
loss like this. This pain... It's beyond all I can bare. I
think... I think it's killing me. I'm... I'm so sorry.*

Chosen by God

Chapter Thirteen

Afearia sits up hunched over holding her side. "He's always been there," Chloe says, tucking in her shirt and rebuttoning her parka. "Watching and protecting me, then and now. God is—"

"There is no God," struggling to her feet. "You're just delusional." Afearia is suddenly slapped across the face by the unseen force, breaking the little balance she had.

"Blasphemy. How dare you speak such filth, heretic?"

"You're the filth," getting back on her feet. "You speak of following the laws of a divine ruler, yet you kill who you want when you want. You destroy lives. You strip away people's rights."

"I destroy sin!"

"You destroy! Nothing more! You destroy those who don't believe what you believe. How loving of you," she sneers.

"I'm trying to save your soul, just like everyone else's. I love God's children! But I hate sinners," spoken with loathing grit. "Last chance, Afearia. Let me save your filthy soul with God's touch," speaking in earnest.

Afearia stares tensely as her breathing has begun to regulate from her injuries. "How about you save yourself. There's no one here further down the sinner's road than you—sharing the cursed blood of bottom-feeding Demis—demon!"

Chloe was taken aback for a moment. "My rebirth was also of God's wish, unlike you. There's a rumor you harbor a deadly monster that may be the embodiment of evil itself. God had no say in your unholy union and you dare shame me?" speaking with hurt in her voice. "God gave me a new life that allowed me to be stronger."

"You're nuts."

The moment Afearia spoke, something unseen grabs her whole head, lifting her high. "You speak when I say, heretic! I am not like you! I am chosen!" slamming Afearia into the ground.

Afearia tries to stand but winds up being slammed into the ground again by the unseen force. "God saved my spirit when it was waning under the sins of this world— begging to pass on. He knew more work by his devoted follower must be done."

"More delusions from a demon," she strained in her voice, barely able to push up.

"And you continue with the insults. You know demons can't use light magic. But I can. Do you recall? You see I'm special in more ways than most. My endless devotion to the Lord is why."

"You really love hearing yourself talk," pushing up off the ground. "If you believe you're such a savior, why don't you go and defeat Derexen now?" Chloe's brows twitch. "It's because you're on a leash. If you were to act on your own, the human government wouldn't have it. Heh, God's chosen but can't do God's work. Your God must be puny."

With the rise of her angry fist, Chloe brings it down with the unseen force widening the hole. "You will not speak like that in our presence." She raises her hand and repeats the strike, burying Afearia deeper into Terra. "To insult my Father like this is unforgivable. You're garbage!" Once again she strikes, deepening the crater. "Garbage! To spit on the Lord! GARBAGE!" ending her outburst with another drop of the fist shaking the forest. "It's been decided. You are not the answer. God doesn't save garbage."

"Artes Celeri!" Afearia says in an echo, surprising

her foe.

Instantly destroying the ground from beneath Chloe, Afearia's slashing her sword at insanely high speeds, appearing invisible to the naked eye. Chloe's defending herself with crossed arms as she's rapidly slashed into the air. Her clothes are being slashed to bits with her hat being obliterated. Her thick skin looks like slashed car tires, but she has yet to bleed.

"God, help me!" Chloe called out.

From nowhere, a giant palm appears, blocking the attack and quickly descending to crush Afearia.

"Demeseus!" Afearia calls.

Numerous chains burst from the ground below them, including from Afearia's back. The ten dozen chains collide into the palm and hold it in place—for a moment. It has slowed, but it continued its push. Chloe lands below on solid ground breathing a bit heavy as her wounds heal.

Chloe frustrated, tears away her tattered parka, "She thought she could stop the hand of God," giving off a deranged chuckle. "Impossible! Show her that you're with me Father! Reveal yourself and crush this heathen!"

Appearing behind Chloe is a man roughly half the height of the trees with his entire head obscured with light and a flowing white ceremonial robe. At the soles of his bare feet is light emitting with a white fog slowly falling endlessly around him.

"Again!" Chloe says with a wide open mouth smile as she raises her finger over head in unison with her god's hand.

As it comes down upon her once more, Afearia retracts all her chains shouting, "Odyssey!"

Afearia swings her unarmed hands, summoning here blade. She grabs it and swings it behind her, creating a blue gash before leaping back to vanish just as the giant hand came down.

Chloe, holding her pose, does not notice the gash's

sudden appearance behind her. Afearia leaps out holding her while wielding Eternity in the other hand.

Swiftly, Afearia does a cross slash in Chloe's neck, only to have her swords unable to cut deep enough to be fatal.

"You sneaky whore," Chloe says crassly, surprising Afearia. She turns her neck into the blade, finally bleeding as she leerily looks at her. "How did you do that?"

"You monster. Do you not fear death?"

"I have God and his angels protecting me." Ray's of light begin to fall around her. "Why would I fear what God forbids of my fate?"

Using her strength, Afearia completes the attack, beheading Chloe. Her head rolls across the ground and her body falls to its knees. Chloe's God takes a knee and becomes transparent.

Breathing heavily, Afearia lowers her arms. She falls to her knees holding her chest as her heart painfully races.

"You're overdoing it," Demeseus says before appearing beside her.

"I still," struggling to speak, "can't handle your presence with so many other Empyrean Blades in my command. Currently—five are present."

"Are you insane!? Dismiss us, now!"

Before she could, the faint rays of light brighten around Chloe. Her blood returns to her neck before her head rolls up her body and reattaches. "It's good to know my thick skin has resistance against Empyrean Blades," Chloe says as her raspy voice clears up and she slowly straightens her neck. "I'll have to remember that when the time comes."

"How are you—?"

"Alive? The angels, I told you. They keep me alive instead whisking me off to heaven. My healing factor is a government secret." She stands and points to her head. "In my skull is a brain chip. When I'm hurt, my brain sends signals activating the chip to assemble the billions of nano machines that were injected into my body."

"You really do talk too much," readying herself for battle. "Now that I understand your revival and I can see what's been attacking me this whole time, this will go in my favor."

"You still don't get it. It is *you* who's at a disadvantage. I have an entire nation's technology inside me. Their backing, plus divine protection is more than one sinner can handle."

"Shut her up," Demeseus says irritably.

Wasting no time, Afearia calls Nebulous in her hand and swings down to send fast forming icicles toward Chloe. "God's Love," Chloe says with a calm haughtiness.

Chloe's god vanishes and reappears behind her, kneeling down to do an embracing hug like a parent hugging a small child. Afearia's attack hits the embracing arms of Chloe's god doing no damage. She repeats the attack with the same result.

Chloe smirks and turns to her protector, "I love you, heavenly Father."

"What are you doing!?" Demeseus asks Afearia. "You have many spells stronger than that. Why are you still holding back?"

"I'm not the best battle strategist," Afearia replies, "but I'm certain nothing I do can get through her defense. The only time I've been able to hit her is with counter attacks and even then I've done nothing beyond the beheading."

"Yoo-hoo!" Chloe alerts them. "Who're you whispering too?" Her god makes a rippling sound as she happily looks up at him. "A spirit, you say?" seeming intrigued while frightening Afearia and Demeseus in cold surprise. "A man... A man who is lost and needs to move on," looking slowly back at them with dark intent.

Chloe leaps toward Afearia with her god moving in unison. With a glowing claw swipe from her foe, Afearia leaps to the side and doubles her distance to place herself behind Chloe. Chloe's God smashes its fist into the ground, crumbling it beneath Afearia. Chloe follows up with a low leg sweep with her god doing the same.

Afearia leaps up high above both of them and brings fourth her hand to call Sleight. "Extend!" Afearia commands, pointing the tip at Chloe.

A column of light erupts from Chloe's feet up to Afearia's elevation. In nearly that same moment, Chloe and her god vanish, reappearing before Afearia within the light. The blade of Sleight didn't even reach the ground yet, nor has Afearia's brain processed Chloe's movements. Using her frightening speed, Chloe moved behind her and delivered a glowing swipe of her hand across her opponent's back.

Afearia's blood splatters, leaving her in a gasping pain. Her blade reaches the ground moments before she begins to fall. Quickly, Chloe's god does the impossible. It uses its giant hand to grab Demeseus' entire body. As he struggles, Afearia hits the ground with Sleight while Eternity is frozen flat in midair below Demeseus.

"Calamity!?" Chloe shouts, floating effortlessly in the air. "Did you know God can destroy unholy spirits and cast them into the great beyond?" Afearia's eyes widen in fear. "Want to see?" she says devilishly.

"No...," barely able to push up off the ground. "Don't you do it. Don't you do it!" she panics.

"Heh, purify the sinner, Father."

With the might of Chloe's protector's squeeze, Demeseus began to scream out in pain. Afearia was helplessly watching, unable to stand after such a damaging blow to her back.

"Stop it. Stop it, PLEASE!" Afearia pleas. Demeseus' body was beginning to become compacted by the hand's pressure, worsening his cries. "You're killing him! Enough, stop! I said STOP!"

Afearia angrily slaps the ground, causing a rise of many rock spires to attack Chloe.

"Barrier," Chloe says in a cutesy, playful tone as she loops her finger in a ring of light.

A barrier made of light erects, crumbling the spires on impact. Afearia quickly air writes a U shaped symbol with three angled vertical streaks through it before being propelled at great speeds toward Chloe.

Afearia angrily grabs Eternity upon her rise with unexpected, yet barely visible silver armor appearing on her forearm. Before even getting close, Chloe fires a series of needle thin light rods into Afearia's body, sending her back to the ground. Eternity is yanked from her as it rubber bands itself back where it was in the air.

Bleeding from her head, Afearia hears the strain of Demeseus' dreadful screams grow as they now become audible to even Chloe.

"Wooooo, boy! Those are some mighty powerful lungs," Chloe cruelly jokes. White cracks spread across his cheek as Afearia's eyes tremble to the sight of him. "I think he's about to see the light," seeing the white cracks in the night.

"DEMESEUS!" reaching out with a call. Eternity vanishes.

Unexpectedly from below, a crescent wave of white energy sparkling black electricity severs Chloe's arm. Afearia is now on her feet with Eternity in hand standing in a completed swing heavily panting. Demeseus gently falls to the ground like a feather while Chloe screams holding her nub.

"You've sealed your fate," Afearia threatens. "You want the calamity? I'll show you all I have to offer."

"Afearia, don't," Demeseus weakly says, getting on one knee.

"You're okay," lightly smiling in his direction with relief. She sternly looks at her foe. "Don't worry about me. Even now I can't feel him, so this may be a rare opportunity for me to cut loose."

"Afearia—"

"I won't lose myself. I promise," she says before lightly smiling at him. "It's time for me to send you back so you can heal."

"Okay...," he says with reluctance.

Once dismissed, Chloe leered down at Afearia as she had collected herself from the surprise attack. "And you send away the one weapon you had that could hurt me. You fool."

"The only fool I see is you since you're stupid enough to hurt someone close to me." Afearia's eyes narrow a cold glare that reached even Chloe's icy heart. "Chloe. I'll break you."

Air slowly rises around Afearia, gently blowing her hair up as she slowly lifts her hand. Shortly after, faintly seen electrical waves appear around infrequently. Quickly looking up at the dark clouds gathered from above, her hand's raised to receive a massive bolt of lightning to engulf Afearia's body. As it swirls around her in blinding light, it slowly shrinks into itself while she calmly walks through the funnel of lightning holding a new blade.

Afearia's new sword is all silver with an endless migrating aura of blue electricity. The blade's thin with a slightly curved tip. Near the tip on the blade's sides are black cracks by design. Its round guard is transparent with a silver hue and silent clashes of white lightning bolts within. It's grip is woven black with a basic gold katana pommel. Dangling at the pommel is a silver chain accessory with an active lightning orb.

Since the arrival of her new sword, faintly visible bolts of lightning hit the ground around Afearia in a small radius, lightly popping pockets of dirt. This sudden addition

428

to Afearia's came with an appearance change. Her hair has become bushy with spiked ends, along with a white glow outlining her body.

Chloe, sternly intrigued, lowers her hand from her once gushing nub, "What's that you carry?"

"Monsoon," placing it behind herself as it generates an electrical charge, allowing it to hover over Afearia's back. "And the beginning of your end."

"No," firing a light rod from her finger.

Bursting from the ground to successfully defend Afearia is Bastion, twirling before her to deflect the attack elsewhere. Taking Bastion from the grip, she raises the weapon to her face as green seals appear along her neck. With a heavy howl, she strikes the ground to explode large rocks into the sky.

"God's Love!" Chloe shout's with her god wrapping his arms around her as they float to the ground.

With a downward thrust of her arm, Afearia commands all the airborne rocks to come down on her foe in a funnel. Chloe's immediately buried—for only a moment. With arms spread, including her now freshly regenerating arm, Chloe breaks out the ground and takes one mighty leap toward Afearia.

"Nebulous!" Afearia shouts upon leaping back to keep distance. Dozens of ice spires emerge from the ground piercing Chloe everywhere, holding her in place. Recalling Sleight, Afearia quickly hurls it in the air. "Extend!"

"Guardian Angels!"

Sleight's blade shoots down only cutting into Chloe's neck because her god had grabbed the blade, greatly reducing the blade's propulsion power. Chloe grits her teeth as blood drips around her teeth from the trembling blade. The blade slowly enters her as she briefly screams before her eyes widen in pain.

"Judgment," Afearia says, calling a bolt from the sky to strike Sleight.

"Tear me," Chloe says in a gargling voice.

Her god rips her out the spires and the sword, cutting her neck open. Avoiding the shock still left Chloe in a vulnerable position as she is tossed across the ground with a fatal neck wound. Looking to seize the opportunity, Afearia sprints toward her until her god kneels down and wraps its arms around Chloe.

With a clenched jaw of annoyance, Afearia hunches over a bit as she rotates her shoulders. Chains come from both shoulder blades.

"Return," Afearia commands in a near grunt.

Held by the chains are Odyssey, Nebulous and Sleight in her hand. Before she could retrieve them all, her loudly thudding heart aches her as she quickly clutched her chest. Refocusing on her opponent, Afearia slashes the ground with Odyssey, creating the black gash. She points Sleight's blade at it and extends the sword into the black. The blade soon emerges from beneath Chloe, piercing her off the ground. The lights from Chloe's previous skill fade moments after.

"Let's see if she can revive herself in such a critical state."

"I can," Chloe says, sounding as if she's being choked.

Chloe lifts her head and grips the blade with one hand—then both as she strains to push her body up off the sword.

"No," Afearia says coldly, further extending her blade into her.

Chloe struggles in small breathes, weakening by the second, only mildly slowing the blades ongoing puncture.

With face gone red and veins bulging along Chloe's forehead, she utters, "God—please."

With a mighty swing, Afearia's backhanded into a tree, disarming her of all her swords except Monsoon and Odyssey. Afearia now on all fours, spits blood into the soil as she struggles to hold herself up. I should've dodged that, Afearia thinks. It's the Empyrean Blades... they dull my reactions under this strain. In this case, Afearia thinks, watching Chloe get on to her feet. Less is more. But not yet. Not until—

Chloe's Guardian Angel lights begin to fade, "I've decided. I won't hold out on you anymore. I'll bring this fight to an equal level as if you were Derexen. I'll show you," crossing her arms over her chest before levitating. "Why I was chosen."

Knowing something worse was on the way, Afearia grabs Bastion and Nebulous. "Chloe. Not only will I break your spirit. I'll break your faith," staring down Chloe's god.

Simultaneously, Afearia's advanced gaia and water seals appear. Chloe quickly hovers toward her opponent with arms still crossed. The god swings at Afearia, but with a tight grip on her swords, she deflects with a risen wall of rock, aiding in the nullification of the punch and redirecting it with her swords. The god did not relent. He continued to barrage her while Afearia defended continuously with the same tactic while crashing water pillars assist in nullifying his punches.

With every opening Afearia could find, she would swing her swords at Chloe who effortlessly leans, ducks and uses side twist to avoid being slashed. After several seconds of this, Afearia cross slashes at Chloe to cut her cleanly in two, but Chloe backflips from range and leaps back into action like a bullet for Afearia's heart.

In unison, Chloe swings down her hands with her god to push Afearia's swung blades down to the ground. Using this opening, Chloe comes in delivering a hard punch to Afearia's chest, creating distance from each other.

Chloe had floated upward before thrusting her palms like talons toward Afearia, "Sinner's Blight."

The long rods of light have pierced Afearia all over but have caused no puncture wounds anywhere to be seen.

However, she was now completely immobilized. Creating a hard light trident, Chloe comes down and perfectly pierces through Afearia's chest. To her surprise, her opponent was transparent. As Chloe frantically looks around, the person she thought was Afearia turns into blue lightning and shocks Chloe's body.

"Argggh!" stumbling back from the shock. Her rods fade as she looks more collectively for her opponent. "How did she...? Did she escape?" Chloe stands straight as she searches the silent forest with tense eyes. "Father. Help me find the sinner. She cannot be far."

He floats up high above the treetops looking over the area. Chloe looks from both sides of her several times before a faint bluish-white blur rushes pass her, moments before she's struck across the face, reddening her cheek. Nearly falling over, a weak sonic boom fills the area, scattering some leaves. Standing up straight, she is struck across the cheek again from the other side as the blur returned.

"GOD!? What's happening!?" she screamed in aggravation.

With the short-lived return of the blur, something trips Chloe from the heels. The moment her back touches ground, she's impaled by Odyssey. With a deep gasp and wide eyes, she sees Afearia over her pushing Odyssey into her with both hands as her hair crackles with lightning. Unfortunately, Afearia's blade did not fully breach Chloe's chest cavity. Barehanded, Chloe grips the blade, slowing the weapons tip sinking into her heart.

Chloe drags her other hand across the dirt and clutches it. Suddenly, Afearia loses breath as the indentation of fingers appear around her neck. She falls to her knees as Chloe slowly sits up.

"I share my power with God. I can extend my will to him and create phantom limbs." Chloe smugly gets onto her feet and tightens her grip. "You could never hope to defeat a child of God with the power of evil."

Failing to free herself, Afearia slaps her palm to the dirt. From the forest, an arched rock column comes speeding toward Chloe. Afearia holds her sword straight as Chloe's hit from the back, deepening the puncture. They both drop down and the grip vanishes from around Afearia's neck. As Chloe hung limp over Afearia, she gets on her feet to only feel the return of the grip.

Lifting her head, Chloe's tense glare sets onto Afearia's while she bleeds from her mouth and around her chin. With the stomp of Afearia's foot, the column resumes its push momentarily into Chloe's back. Twisting her foot in the dirt, the column pushes Chloe beyond Afearia's hands and across the area, pressing Chloe into a tree. Chloe releases Afearia from her grip as she is too occupied holding herself from the tree with her legs while trying to remove the sword pressing into her chest.

Afearia faces Chloe and raises her fist to do a motion similar to banging on a door. Doing so, the column pulled back enough for Chloe to flip over only to have the rocky column smash into her chest. Her eyes bulge as she gives Afearia a resentful glare with bloody teeth afterward. Afearia repeats her command on the column two more times. As the column holds its position, Chloe amazingly manages to not have the sword pierce her heart as she continues to hold it tight.

"Where's your God now?" Afearia mocks. "Stupidly hanging in the sky like you told him to? That's not God if he can't act independently from you. Look up, fool!" Chloe looks up to her god. "He's not even looking at you. He's like a doll put on a shelf. Motionless and dull. That's not God. He's just an extension of your psyche."

"Shut your blasphemous mouth you shit eating maggot! You're filthy! FLITHY! You disrespect the Lord—"

Afearia smashes the column into her again. "I was

433

hoping to catch you off guard. But I'm sure another hit will send that sword into your heart."

As Afearia readies to attack again, Chloe looks up as if to be seeing a dream. The column comes speeding toward her until Chloe's god swoops down and backhands the column into pieces. Looking half dead, Chloe's god hugs her from behind. She weakly smiles and nuzzles her head into him.

"Dear heavenly Father," Chloe says, "do not fret. I do not fear this monster. As we know, I have faced death many times back home. Even more when my country subjected me to awful test of mortality. From knives to guns, from tanks to city crushing bombs. They tried them all. But, Father, I never forgotten. Though I walk through the valley of the shadow of death, I will fear no evil; for thou art with me; thy rod and thy staff they comfort me."

Suddenly, Chloe's god slowly spreads its arms as a light shines down upon her. Odyssey is gradual pushed out from her wound on its own until it hits the ground. Her wound closes with all the blood on her body evaporating.

Closing her eyes, Chloe spreads her arms, "Thou preparest a table before me in the presence of mine enemies: thou anointest my head with oil; my cup runneth over." She raises her head higher under brilliant light. "Surely goodness and mercy shall follow me all the days of my life: and I will dwell in the house of the Lord forever." Chloe warmly smiles. "Ahhh. A new power has been bestowed upon me by the heavenly Father."

She inhales deeply through her nose before slowly exhaling out the mouth. A long crescent blade of hard light grows out the back of Chloe's forearms up to her elbows. Suddenly, tiny, gradually becoming visible light particles appear around Afearia's surprised face as she slowly turns her head toward a cluster. The particles burst with the effects of a flash bang. Afearia kneels down rubbing her teary eyes.

"Blinded by your envy towards God's love for me has riddled you sightless," Chloe says with nigh stoicism. "Sins cripple your senses, as you are now experiencing." The pain of her eyes was unbearable. Afearia screamed out as she lowered herself further in a squirm. "Under my Father's guidance, I will not fall to you, Calamity. Guardian Angels," she calmly calls while raising a hand. Chloe gets into a near spread arm pounce pose. "This is for my Father and the motherland. You shall fail!" darting at her dazed foe.

When Chloe neared, she slashed with the hard light blade that Afearia miraculously ducks. Afearia quickly stands and does a ducking dodge roll to evade the second attack and counter slash Chloe's back upon positioning behind her.

Chloe stumbles forward. "Faker!" she shouts, realizing Afearia faked her eye injuries upon facing her.

"I evaded long before the flash. You just missed it."

Can she really be that fast. Chloe thinks in disbelief. There has to be a drawback. How long can she maintain this form?

"Mystified?" Chloe shakes herself from thought before irritability looking ready to fight. "Don't bother. The longer Monsoon's with me, the faster I'll become."

"Try me, wench. We DAs know of your speed and Derexen's team's speed. We have measures."

"Then why can't you stop sweating?"

Chloe looks surprised, even offended by her remark and haughty demeanor. "Perhaps I've pulled my punches for too long."

"Then get serious!" tossing Monsoon up into the sky. The sword fades away into the clouds. Afearia's aura fades, her hair relaxes, and the lightning surges end. Afearia gives Chloe a cocky smirk, "I'm starting to feel like my old self again."

She effortlessly calls Nebulous to her hand. She

435

takes the blade's tip and draws a circle around her before enclosed walls of water shoot up into the air. It quickly ceases with Afearia's stance held and the blade still to the ground. But something was different. The hilt of her sword was steaming. It fires off two loud expulsions of steam before Afearia looks up at her opponent.

"I'm starting to acclimate to these powers raging inside me," Afearia speaks with absolute confidence. Her smirk fades. "Let's go."

Though deadpan, Chloe's eyes expressed death. She bends her knees before suddenly leaping forward with enough force to crumble the ground behind her. Chloe thrusts her arm and her god's arm toward her foe. Afearia side turns with a strong backward lean from their speedy grasp. She follows up with an upward slash that Chloe guards against with her light blades.

After guarding and deflecting the attack upward, Chloe reaches in and grabs Afearia by the neck. She swings her around to slam her body to the ground. In mid toss, Afearia slashes the ground beneath her with Odyssey, creating the blue gash for her body to go through. Once it closed, she reappears above Chloe and bashes the pommel's of her swords into her cheeks.

Chloe hits the ground like a rock and slides a little. Almost not noticing, a crescent wave of water splitting the ground speeds her way. Her god defends her with his body before she flips off the ground to position over Afearia and come down like a hawk with light blades ready. Afearia sidesteps and kicks her opponent away. With swift recovery, Chloe comes charging again.

Afearia was ready to combat her until she detected a sudden shift in the air. Looking up, Chloe's god had its massive hand coming down on her. With pursed, slightly open lips, Afearia commands the wind and moves swiftly to her right. With a shot of light from her finger, Chloe manages to finally disarm Afearia of Odyssey.

Quickly trying to reclaim Odyssey before it went out of reach only played into Chloe's strategy. Little particles of light cluster around Afearia's hand before bursting and causing mild burns. Chloe rushes in close and low, rising up at an angle to split her in two with the light blade.

Barely capable, Afearia dodges her strike and counters with a stab to Chloe's ribs. She violently yanks her sword out of Chloe as she stumbles sideways holding her wound.

"You're too reckless after Guardian Angels," Afearia says.

Afearia leaps in to take her head. Chloe poorly, but successfully guards against her using the light blade. She stumbles from the force and regains footing with a leaping one-eighty turn, striking back to pierce her face. Though Afearia evades by spinning from range, she still wasn't fast enough, taking a bloody graze to her cheek. Afearia slashes at her midriff but winds up getting her sword snagged by Chloe's god holding her sword.

When Chloe attempts to kick her hand, Afearia releases her sword and spins in close with a heavy downward punch to Chloe's face. Though her recovery was quick, Chloe got her faced punched in two more times before her god grabs Afearia by the wrist and lifts her up high. Chloe jumps up to cut her in half, but Afearia quickly kicked her hands to ruin her aim and immediately wrapped her legs around Chloe's neck, choking her mercilessly with her iron thighs.

In less than five seconds, Afearia had easily broken Chloe's neck before dropping her to the ground. Chloe's death causes her god to freeze up and become transparent, releasing Afearia. She lands down and quickly grabs Nebulous.

She looks up at the light around Chloe and glances at her hand that faintly surged electricity with a glow. Two shots, Afearia thinks, seeing the lights fading around Chloe. I've only got two shots. Afearia looks down at the hilt of her sword as she tilts it to release streams of water to envelop Chloe's head in a sphere.

"Drown," Afearia coldly says.

Upon her wounds healing and her neck repairing itself, Chloe's consciousness returns in a panic as she inhales pint after pint of water. She struggles, screams and inhales reflexively before dying again. Afearia clutches her hand and freezes the sphere on her head before walking under the steadily fading lights. She glances at the immobilized god and calls Odyssey back to her hand.

If my timing's right, she has twenty more seconds before her spell ends and five before she revives. Afearia crosses her swords before her and continues on toward Chloe's body with focused eyes. I'll finish her in seventeen seconds.

Chloe suddenly sits up in the time Afearia estimated. She beings to panic and choke as she holds her neck since not only was the sphere frozen, but the remaining water in her throat and nostrils was as well. Afearia runs at her, noticing Chloe's god had awakened with a sweeping palm aimed at her.

Afearia jumps to her left, hurling Nebulous into the dirt, "Ice Wall!" When the wall erected as protection, it did not stop his hand from breaking through. However, it did slow the attack, giving Afearia enough time to toss Odyssey up and wrap a chain around the hilt. She clasps her electrified hands together as she uses the chained Odyssey to open a pathway in the ground to escape. She jumps toward it upside down and disappears into it.

The gash reappears on the ground a meter in front of Chloe with Afearia emerging from it upside down with her lightning charged appearance restored. Afearia's pointing her finger at Chloe like a gun with her other hand tightly grasping her wrist while appearing crouched down in midair. The dirt, leaves, air, and even the ice around Chloe's head are being torn apart by the radiating orb of sparkling whitish-blue electricity at the tip of Afearia's finger as she rises to Chloe's chest level.

When the condensed energy tore all the ice away from Chloe's head, the lights from her spell fade as she's finally able to see the orb's burning light. "It's so powerful," she says in fearful suspense as the last of the ice breaks away from the crevices of her eyes.

In that moment, Afearia fires the energy dead on into Chloe's gut. The orb instantly expands five times its size, carrying her off into the woods as she agonizingly screams like a gutted siren. Afearia's shot off in the opposite direction, almost into the nearest tree. As her slide across the dirt comes to an end, a large electrical explosion goes off in the distant direction Chloe was shot in. Afearia sits up holding her arm, noticing Chloe's god is gone as well. Her opponents are vanquished with nothing but a burnt path were Chloe was launched.

Looking almost in disbelief, Afearia couldn't stop staring down the smoldering path of scattered embers. She cautiously gets on her feet, waiting a bit, catching her breath. Only taking a foot forward, she nearly falls over in a stumble. She continues to stammer as she holds her head, feeling quite dizzy.

"Overkill", Afearia weakly smiles. I put too much into that shot, but it was now or never, Afearia thinks. She looks up into the night sky. I fear how much I've lost. But this was a fight not like others.

She stares back down the cooling path with some relief on her face. With speed greater than she could detect, an abnormally long spear of hard light comes speeding down the path, piercing Afearia's shoulder and bending into the dirt to anchor her. Leaned back, she's screams out in pain, dropping Odyssey as she stares at the bloody wound she's received. Afearia trembles from the ache as she angrily stares down the dark path.

"To crush evil, one mustn't see evil," Chloe says with closed eyes, arms raised, and clothes torn asunder from the blast as she daunts the charred path with her god following behind her. Chloe's nearly naked with little to cover her lower half and upper body other than the rags she tied together herself. "To crush evil, one mustn't *speak* it," clutching her fist to make the spear sprout a flexible appendage to bind Afearia's mouth.

"To crush evil, one mustn't hear its cries… Your attacks will no longer reach me, for my Father has bestowed upon me another gift. As for all gifts, beliefs, and truths originate from our Father in heaven. For the Lord is my rock," she says loudly with arms up higher, head held high, and light falling upon her, "and my fortress, and my deliverer; my God, my strength, in whom I trust; my buckler, and the horn of my salvation, and my high tower!"

Afearia's brows bunch in frustration watching Chloe lower her head in the fading light. "There was a burning in my skull," Chloe continues. "My brain chip was frying until I remembered my faith. You said you'd break me from it, but you can't. Do you know why? Because you're facing a true child of God. You can never beat me, as long as I believe it so." Afearia begins to look a little overwhelmed. "Is it sinking in now? No matter how hard you try, or how much potential power lies in your spark, it'll only take me higher," floating off the ground in a burst of wind. "To infinity," Chloe says with her eyes flashing a yellow glow.

Diary Entry #4289

*There are hidden records about past wielders the elders wish to keep secret. I've been able to unlawfully uncover some. I normally don't reveal much I secretly uncover because I know Xenler steals my book and reads it. The records I found they know about because I got caught and punished. However... There is one whose name was even stricken from the records. All I know is that they filed 'Her' as **impurity**. Who is 'She', and what happened eleven years after Demeseus's time?*

Divinity's Nature

Chapter Fourteen

Still glaring, Afearia readies to cast a spell until Chloe commands the light spear to tighten, bending her further back from the blood wound while wrapping and binding her other arm with another light appendage.

"My light cannot be shatt—" With the sound of broken glass, Chloe expresses closed-eyed surprise as Afearia is hunched over holding Eternity with six chains coming out her back. That sword is problematic, Chloe thinks.

Huffing, Afearia looks over to Demeseus, "You ready yet?"

"Been ready," he sternly replies, staring down their foe.

"Good. I've been waiting for this." He looks her way. "I'm pushing it. My chest feels tight and my heart is really racing, almost aching. But this woman is really strong."

"Do you know how to win?"

"I do, but I need more time... I'm still... The strain is heavy, but do you think I can at least call Eternity's shield?"

Demeseus sighs before closing his eyes. "I can hear your heart and the unstable energy flowing within you. You'll be lucky to hold it for five minutes—assuming she allows it."

"More than enough," she smirks. "I can't have you summoned for long. I'm getting dizzy."

"Do what you must. I've got your back."

She smiles warmly at him. "I know you do."

As Chloe patiently waits for Afearia to make a

move, Afearia focuses on the threat before her. With quick hands, Afearia strikes her lips to release a ball of flame at Chloe. Chloe doesn't move, but instead allows herself to be hit. The flames oddly enough go out almost as soon as she's hit.

"Is that one of her abilities?" Demeseus asks in surprise.

"I guess she was serious about the invincibility thing," Afearia says as she fires four chains at her.

The four paired chains part on impact in separate directions. Chloe grabs them in a chuckle and pulls Afearia through the air.

"Don't let her take you!" Demeseus says in near panic.

"I know!"

As one of Afearia's chains drag on the ground, she uses it as an extension of herself in order to manipulate the dirt as green seals run through the chain links. The dirt breaks up as muddy chunks traveling up her chain to gather together around her wrist and hand. When she nears Chloe, she quickly creates a spiked gauntlet. Delivering a solid punch to Chloe's face with the gauntlet, it had no effect as it crumbles on impact.

Chloe grabs Afearia's face with both hands, slamming her to the ground and savagely jumping on her stomach. With a short-lived scream, Afearia retches. Chloe strikes her across the face—pausing before doing it again with heightened excitement. Preparing to strike her cheek again, Chains wrap around her arm, but they had only slowed her before suddenly falling limp, giving Chloe the opportunity to strike Afearia again. Chloe straddles her and begins viciously choking Afearia with both hands.

"And with the closing of the eyes," she says with sick glee, "may you find eternal rest under the hand of the Lord."

Afearia's face has reddened and her forehead and

neck veins bulge as she does all she can to fend her off. Punching Chloe's forearms and grabbing violently at her face did nothing. Desperately fingering around, she digs her fingers under her eyelids, surprised to see Chloe's eye pointed off elsewhere like she had checked-out mentally. She tries turning her head but she was solid and unrelenting like a bull. Afearia's arms drop and her eyes flutter.

"What're you doing!?" Demeseus shouts. "Stop her!" Gaining a second wind, Afearia grips Eternity and stabs Chloe. But like a pin to a rounded glass surface, Chloe receives no damage as it slides off her. "No effect…? Use a spell to gain distance from her!"

Afearia slaps the dirt and has the ground uplift to carry her away at an angle. However, Chloe had not released her. She mindlessly hangs onto the ground carrying Afearia with one hand. Demeseus sees Afearia had seconds before losing this fight, feeling helpless and frantic before having an idea.

"Use the ground to form rock casing around your neck, DO IT NOW!" Demeseus desperately screams.

Rock quickly forms around her neck, separating Chloe's grip. Slapping the ground again, she explodes the ground carrying them, leaving Chloe to fall smoothly on her feet while Afearia bounces around a little, gaining distance before flipping up right crouched on one knee. She slowly stands taking sloppy deep breaths over the ordeal. With a deep grunt, Afearia winces as she swallows.

"Focus," Demeseus says. "Use long-ranged attacks until we know how to hurt her."

"Won't last with her like that."

"She didn't start like this, you said you hurt her before."

"I know, but she just keeps getting stronger. It all started when—" Afearia realizes something. "I have an idea," she calmly says.

"You do?"

444

"I've been struggling to deduce what her powers were since we met. But if her abilities work the way I think they do, it should turn the tables."

"Are you sure it'll be enough?"

"No, but I feel confident on what I've gathered."

"What's the plan of attack?"

"No attack, a method," she smirks. "A little something I learned from a friend."

Demeseus proudly smiles at her. She's growing, Demeseus thinks before looking forward. "Her creature's been docile for a while now."

"Something I plan to use against her. It's time to push it. I'm calling Eternity's shield."

Chloe crosses her arms and smirks, "When are you going to let me save you? My Father's patience may be infinite, but mine's isn't."

"Your father can bite me."

Chloe tightly bunches her brows. "What did you say?" speaking with a calm anger.

"What? Are you hard of hearing? Heh," she chuckled callously. "God. What a petty being to worship. No better than pig sweat."

Angered in seconds, Chloe stomps her foot, faintly shaking the ground, "DON'T YOU DARE—speak of my Father like that!"

"He acts like a child if he doesn't get his way. A big child with big powers and an even bigger ego. If you don't give him attention, you burn forever. Sounds just."

"You don't have the ability to understand God! God is LOVE, you stupid girl! Only sinners with hate in their heart speak like you! You don't understand anything!"

"I think I do. Your sad pathetic god is insecure, so he made man to fill his insecurities with praise and expected obedience. Such weak character. That of a fly."

"Shut it," she gritted through her teeth.

"And you still worship such a petty thing? I guess

445

faith is just a matter of weakness. You reach out because you are lost."

"Shut—UP!" stomping her foot again, shaking the ground.

A branch falls and scuffs her cheek, but she doesn't notice in her burst of rage. Afearia's eyes cut to the graze on her cheek before leaning slightly forward and vanishing. Quicker than Chloe can react, Afearia appears behind Chloe and backhands her into the dirt, breaking up the ground a bit. She hops away before Chloe's god could counter.

Chloe shoots up on all fours with open angry eyes, "How!?" Afearia fires a chain to wrap around Chloe's ankle before landing. Though she pulls her in successfully, Chloe extends the length of her light blade and slashes Afearia's torso. "Don't you dare, wench!"

Afearia releases her while holding her wound, but she quickly rebounds to whip Chloe with her chain. Before she's struck, Chloe closes her eyes and is belted across the face, taking no damage. Quickly after being struck, she does a spinning turn to place herself behind Afearia and slashes her back, causing a stumbling fall on all fours. Chloe leaps forward and attempts to cut Afearia in two until she raises her arm to call a few chains to wrap around the deathly blade.

Having her blade held in a standstill, Chloe struggles to push through, but her facial expression remains calm. "You're quiet," Afearia grunts. "Are you emulating the actions of your god? Silence in times of turmoil?"

Chloe smiles, "I am not in turmoil. You are."

"You—mentioned living a hard life, right?" she strains as her arms shake more.

"Yes," she optimistically says.

"What did God do for you back then? Was your prayers ever answered?"

"Father does not always speak to us in words but

446

through the world around us."

"Then his response to you last time was more pain?"

Chloe's brow twitches for a moment, then she smiles a bit wider. "What did I tell you? You cannot break me. My faith in my Father is too strong."

Chloe bares down further, coming that much closer to cutting Afearia down. Afearia's knees shake as her arms come close to buckling, "Faith is a delusion. And your god can eat the excrement from a rat's crap hole!"

Chloe grits her teeth in immediate anger. "Such filth! How dare—!?"

Without hesitation, Afearia stabs Chloe in the stomach with Eternity. Because of Eternity's great mass, this wound was fatal. Afearia prepares to pull it out only to find it won't budge. Chloe had firmly wrapped her hands around the sword.

"How?" Chloe painfully utters with blood dripping from her mouth.

"If I told you, it wouldn't be effective, now would it?"

With full force, Afearia yanks out her sword with a trail of blood and entrails. As Chloe's falling backwards, she softly mutters, "Father... My life... will you save it?" Chloe hits the ground cold.

Afearia stands straight, staring down at her fallen foe.

"Is it over?" Demeseus asks.

"You never know with her."

Afearia leaps up to cut her opponent to pieces when suddenly, Chloe's god began moving on its own, catching Afearia's blade. "If you ask," Chloe's voice echoes from her cold lips, "you shall receive." A light falls upon her body. "Guardian Angels." She slowly begins to magically rise with arms wide open and her wound rapidly closed. She sweetly smiles at her opponent. "You just can't keep a good girl down, can you Father?"

"It's time," Afearia says, panting in fatigue.

Demeseus sternly notices the exhaustion on her face before looking over her injuries, "You've lost a lot of blood. Maybe you should—"

"Don't you dare, Demeseus. You're the last person in the world I want to ever doubt me. I can beat her. It's all in motion. You trust in me, don't you?" she asks, looking to him with eyes of near plea.

"Hmph," looking forward with a smirk. "Don't misunderstand my protective nature over you as doubt. This fight would be a cakewalk for you if you'd stop messing around."

Afearia lightly chuckles to herself. "Alright. I'll get right to it then."

Using Eternity's chains, Afearia places Eternity behind herself as the chains firmly wrap around her torso. She makes a tight fist and focuses greatly with eyes locked on her forearm. Suddenly, a bloody tear shoots up to the top of her forearm. She shakes for a moment from the jolt of pain, regaining her focus. With increased breathing, a bloody chain faintly surfaces from the slit in her arm before submerging. With her face reddening and breathing now irregularly heavier, Afearia's focus rises.

Chains violently burst from her tear to circle her body in a layer of chains. The chains form a dome, tightening as they rattle along one another. The dome briefly loses form as the painful grunting reaches pitch. Afearia accepts the pain and screams out, causing the chains to stop for a couple seconds before rapidly retracting into Afearia's forearm.

On her arm is a large round shield with a red outer edge etched with rotating glowing white Archaic Latin text repeating the words, *defense in endless reflection*. The face of the shield is a cleanly reflective chrome surface that glows a soft white.

"Before," Afearia begins to explain. "Before I choose to use this, I needed to be sure of your powers. Despite the fact you kept your eyes closed, your senses were sharper than ever. I thought senses sharpened by losing your sight. But you adapted too quickly. Your god became your eyes and ears. But that wasn't the biggest discovery of your powers I put together. It's how you believe."

"You talk too much."

"It's so strange, and yet so interesting. Your power is belief, but it goes beyond the idea. It's actually how your powers work. If you believe it to be true, then your ability is true. If you believe you can't be harmed, then you won't be. Just like you believe you can use the power of light and God's at your side."

Chloe laughs a little, shaking her head like Afearia's silly. "How stupid. Looks like you don't understand my powers at all."

"NO! It is YOU who doesn't understand their own powers. Think it's a coincidence that when I rattled your faith your invulnerability stopped? But I'll show you," bending her knees. "Why even given the opportunity, you would have never defeated Derexen."

"And you called me ignorant," she scoffs. Chloe closes her eyes. "I won't let you trigger me again."

"I won't need to anymore."

"Father," she innocently says for her god to raise its fist over Afearia's head.

His fist comes down full force, but Afearia remains calm till the last second, defending with her shield. On impact, a loud resonating tone fills the air and enters the being's body, immobilizing it with vibrations.

"Father?" Chloe says in confusion looking left and right. "Father? Father, what's wrong?" Seizing the opportunity, Afearia rushes at her, alerting Chloe's senses. "I hear you, wench!" sounding like a vicious animal. "You can't touch me! I'm blessed by—"

With a successful backhanded bash to the back of her head using her shield, Chloe's slammed head first, breaking up the ground with her face. Afearia rips her up from the dirt by the neck. Bleeding from her crumpled mouth, Chloe quickly slaps Afearia's hand away and jumps back for distance. To Chloe's surprise, her god did not follow her movement. He was still trapped in place, only slightly responding to Chloe's shift in position.

"What have you done to my Father!?" Chloe yelled as her folded jaw and teeth regenerate. "And what have you done to me!? I don't believe in your power!"

"Quartz Charm. Creates a frequency under certain conditions and matches it to lock those similar in place. As for you, I rather you see for yourself."

When Afearia rushed forward, Chloe panics and fires a shot of light from her finger. Afearia raises her shield and reflects it back as darkness. Chloe startled by what she's witnessing, still manages to tilt from range, leaving the energy to pierce through several trees behind her. Seeming aggravated, she takes the initiative and attacks Afearia with her light blades.

Though relentless in her offense, Afearia still finds an opening and does a wide swing with her shield. The attack is blocked when Chloe joins her forearms together using the light blades to guard her.

Chloe soon follows up by tripping Afearia with her ankles wrapping around hers as she drops herself to the ground and shifts her opponent to the right. Chloe was about to slash her, but Afearia quickly locked hands with her, leaving them in a power struggle on the ground. Chloe glances at her god before light particles appear around them. They swell and grow brighter with size, ready to burst.

Chloe chuckles within in her struggling grunts, "I'll survive, but I don't know about you." Releasing Eternity,

chains come from Afearia's back, each wrapping around
the orbs and crushing them into a dying light. "Grrr, damn
you—Father, help me!" she says in a desperate panic.

As if to be invigorated by her call, Chloe's god
breaks from its hold and looms over to smash Afearia.
Afearia deliberately bites the inside of her mouth before
turning to spit blood on Eternity's guard. It drips down to
the blade and is absorbed by the sword. Without warning, a
chain emerges from the atmosphere and smashes through
Chloe's eye.

She yells out and rolls away from Afearia, covering
her eye while screaming and crying. Afearia had rolled in
the opposite direction, evading Chloe's god.

In a pant, Afearia's back on her feet while Chloe
continues to roll around with her god knelt beside her. With
jaws tight, she growls in anger before a sudden bright
yellow aura pours from her. Looking vicious, Chloe glares
at Afearia with her good eye before leaping high into the
sky.

Removing her bloody hand from the goo that was
her eye, Chloe raises it above her head with the surgence of
a large yellow ball.

"Heavenly Rain!" Chloe ragingly yelled.

A heavy down pour of piercing light streaks down
on Afearia and the forest. Everything was being pierced
cleanly with smoking holes, but Afearia defends herself
with her shield, reflecting everything back as upward rising
streaks of darkness.

Chloe drops the sphere upon Afearia before softly
descending herself, but Afearia's defense holds as she
deflects the sphere of light as a sphere of darkness with a
purplish light. Chloe's god cups its large hands over her,
letting the returned attack disperse upon impact while
Chloe's eyes are stunned from what she's witnessing. She
finally lands with her god opening his hands for her to step
down.

451

Chloe's expression remains the same as she stares at Afearia, "How much evil rests inside you? I've never seen someone convert light into darkness like you do. How?"

Afearia stands straight and lowers her shield, "Now ask yourself that same question as if you were me. Because it's been my thought for a while." Chloe bunches her stern brows in confusion. "I've told you. Beings of darkness can't do what you do."

"They are not chosen, that's why."

"Chloe... Your powers are based purely on what you believe. Think about it."

There's a long silence between them before Chloe smirks. "There is nothing to think about when it comes to your twisted tongue. When I died after my father beat me to death—something he swore would one day be my fate if I did not *please* him as God intended, the first thing I saw was darkness with a fuzzy image trying to get through, shrouded in night. All went black until a great light came for me," looking to her god as he looks to her. "My Father came for me. To love me."

Afearia shakes her head in pity. "God...," she mutters unironically. "I almost feel bad to be doing this. But to win, I need to end your delusions. Because I can't die here with you." She smiles softly. "I have people waiting for me. And that's not a delusion."

"How unfortunate for those waiting for you. You're a demon. Converting light into darkness is not the marks of an angel."

"True. But it's not me. All I've been doing is sending back your powers without the delusions."

"You lying snake!" she nearly snarls.

"Chloe Dorcas. Look closely into my shield," slowly raising it before her. "Tell me what you see being reflected back at you. Is it God?"

Chloe's eyes widen with intense fear as she sees heavy waves of foggy darkness behind her. "Wha... What

452

is that...?" trembling before slowly turning to face something foreign to her eyes.

When she looks back, she sees her god, but when she looks in the mirror, she sees a monster. She does several frantic twist, looking at the mirror and her god until the image she's been seeing reflects reality... Because she always had a monster behind her. She fearfully crouches in a ball with hands over her face and yells as if she's seeing something nightmarish.

"Don't look away from it, Chloe! What do you see!? What do you see!?"

"Stop it! This can't be! I'm a devout believer in our Lord and savior! I pray! I pray! I pray EVERY DAY! I endlessly seek for God's forgiveness and divine guidance! I HONOR my Father!" sounding as if to be heading for a mental breakdown. "I do not partake in promiscuity, dark desires, sinful acts against his word! I believe in God!" voice cracking. "I BREATH IN GOD! I LOVE GOD! I SPREAD THE WORD OF GOD! I FEEL GOD! HE'S WITH ME! HE'S—" looking back to get a full view of what's really been protecting her.

The creature behind Chloe is legless and shrouded in a dark haze. From the waist up, its body's shriveled. The paper thin skin covering its stomach is sunken, similar to a mummy. The lower half of its ribcage is exposed with its gray bones broken outward. Its long boney arms are nothing to the abnormal size of its hands easily capable of grasping an entire truck.

Its face is covered heavily in the same dark blue, purple, and black haze surrounding its presence. Upon looking down at its master, the haze fades enough to make out its eerie, lipless smile of human-like teeth. It's eyes, though gazing upon Chloe, are completely white, dripping an endless black ooze from its eyes and down its shriveled cheeks, turning into haze soon after.

Chloe screams in disturbed horror and crawls

backward from it. Instinctively linked to her, the creature follows behind with a deep, howling sound as it moves, much like the deathly cries of a mourning whale. Something of the undead...

"Nooooo, get away from me!" Chloe cries as she continues crawling in a panic. Her back hits a tree as it slowly loomed upon her with a creepy, yet oddly innocent wide arm embrace. "Nooooo! Get away from me! Stop! Stop getting closer!" now nearly on top of her. "I said STOP!" her voice sounding distorted in her desperation.

Chloe's hands are over her head as her eyes are shut tight. The only noise filling the forest now is the faint, frightened breaths of Chloe as her muffled, soft cries edge up from her exhales. But the creature had stopped. Frozen by her command.

Chloe looks up slowly at it, trembling softly with wide eyes filled with tears of painful loss. "You... My... Where has my Father gone? His love..." she weeps. The creature begins to float toward her again. "Don't come near me!" halting its movement. "Why—have I? All this time... I... I was beginning watched over—protected... by a *demon*," she says with a stern voice and angry eyes at the creature.

Chloe dry heaves a few times before getting a hold of her angry disgust. "Disgusting! Vile!" spiting in a rage. "I banish thee!" The odd demon slightly tilts its head. "Go to hell! Leave me, you vile ABOMINATION! I purge you from my being! Go! Burn in hell, you demon!" As if it could feel—the demon begins to tremble, releasing an airy sound of sorrow. "Fuck off! I want you to die! I hate you! I hate you! I hate all deceiving agents of the devil! Go back to hell and die! LEAVE ME!" Chloe angrily cries, echoing her voice throughout the forest.

Suddenly, the demon's shakes become worse as it looked like it could ball into itself. With a deep bellow of agony, a dark vortex appears from within its ribcage and begins to break it apart bit by bit with its destructive suction. Fighting its own demise, the demon desperately reaches out to Chloe as it's body rips off into the void. It loses the ability to float, it crawls toward her with much of itself now bending inward.

Only inches away from touching her face, its face begins to tear, "L—love... Chloe," it says in an emotionally wounded, deep, hollow voice.

But there was nothing left in Chloe's eyes but hate for what's been her protector for years. She smacks its hand away, leaving it to be completely swallowed by the unknown. The anger melts away as she emptily stares into the dirt, muttering.

"It's true," she says with a sad uplift of her brows. "The devil's greatest trick was proving he didn't exist. And yet, for all these years, I've had the devil cozily at my back—guiding me along the primrose path. How could I not tell the difference between God's love and the evil digging its claws in my heart?" Afearia narrows her stern glare before approaching. "Father... I was fooled. I never meant to stray so far from your hand."

As she continues to mutter, Afearia stops and suddenly clutches her chest. "It hurts," Afearia says, suddenly out of breath. "I'm fading out..."

Demeseus turns to her with concern, "You've done too much. Afearia—"

"I'll make it. She slowly looks up at the sky with fatigue written all over her face, just before a roll of thunder is heard. "It's already over for her... Demeseus... I have to dismiss you for now."

Demeseus looks at her with a firm, yet compassionate expression before looking forward. "Don't lose."

Afearia smirks. "Who do you think I am?"

Chuckling to himself, "Sometimes I tend to forget—how strong you really are," looking to Afearia with a confident smile.

Afearia rolls her eyes in bashful flatter. "Don't butter me up so close to the end. I'm going to make it."

With a nod, he looks onward to see Chloe still muttering under her breakdown. "I will never doubt you for as long as you give it your all."

"I won't falter."

"Then go get 'em—my successor," he says proudly before fading away under the dismissive light of Eternity.

Chloe, muttering, rocks herself back and forth until Afearia's shadow engulfs her space. Seeming wide-eyed and afraid, Chloe has stopped moving before looking up at the opposing woman standing over her.

With clenched teeth, Chloe shoots up, "I will fear no evil. "Do you understand!? I've been freed from the devil's hold! I can still purify myself! I can!"

She attempts to slash Afearia with her dark forearm blade. Seeing her once light blades reflect darkness, catches her by surprise, leaving her to have a slow offence. Afearia effortlessly backhands the blade into pieces, grabbing Chloe up by the neck.

"Your faith's been broken. Knowing you got all those abilities from that monster makes your will to use any of them as fragile as—" Chloe tries to slash her with the second blade, only to have her blade shattered with a simple punch. "Glass." Afearia grips Chloe up by her wrist, pinning her arm to the tree. She then proceeds to choke her. "You can't keep fighting knowing that thing gave you these powers." Chloe's panicked eyes begin to roll up toward the tree tops as she gasps for air. "It's over."

But unexpectedly, Chloe began to gradually push Afearia's arm down just before grabbing her hand from around her neck and managing to steadily pull her off.

"Not all my powers," pulling Afearia's arms down to her sides. "My faith was shaken, but I told you before. You cannot break me," looking deep in her eyes with a scary resolve. "This was a test. To see if I would have the fortitude to banish evil blessings or selfishly hold on to them to save my life. And as always." Chloe squeezes hard enough to greatly hurt Afearia's wrist. "I choose God," she says with absolute confidence. "Guardian Angels." Dark light shines down upon her. "I believe he's with me in this fight and I aim to prove it by killing you."

Afearia headbutts Chloe in the nose, freeing herself and jumping back for distance, "Still using your dark gifts?" she says, summoning Demonweaver.

Chloe, hunched over a bit, looks up at Afearia with her bloody nose and licks it away with a smile. "Maybe the evil you see is just a reflection of your own dark heart. All I see is light and the brave singing angels willing to protect me."

"You delusional—"

Before she could finish her sentence, Chloe had zipped over toward her and slammed her to the ground by placing a leg behind Afearia while pushing her down. The moment her back touched dirt, Chloe stomped her hand holding her sword, breaking her fingers and causing Demonweaver to be dismissed. She kicks her hard enough in the ribs to cause Afearia to be airborne, recreating the distance Afearia tried to gain. Instead of hitting the ground, Afearia lands on her feet, nearly buckling from the pain.

"You're getting tired, Calamity," Chloe taunts as she approaches. "You can't hope to compete with a chosen like me. I'm meant for so much more. For my Father. For my country. This world—" She stops and gives a smug look of pity. "I wanted you to be chosen too. Maybe when you die you—"

Not waiting, Afearia punches her across the face twice before kicking her in the chest, knocking her on the ground. Mounting her foe, Afearia proceeds to clobbering her face several times before having her fist caught in Chloe's hand. Though her eye was swelled half shut, Chloe is still able to express surprise when Afearia begins to push her hand back.

"What?" Chloe says. "Does the laws of good and evil even apply to you, Calamity? Don't you see!? You should be losing! You should—!"

Afearia pulls back with arms high, coming down with the edge of her shield into Chloe's throat. "If I'm losing anything," she says with head down, breathing hard. "It's my patience. But not this fight!" She raises her shield and comes down once more, nearly decapitating her. Chloe's fingers and feet twitch a few times. "Stay down!"

"As long as I believe," Chloe's voice echoes. Chloe slaps her shield bearing arm upward to dislodge it from her neck. Her head regenerates quite fast as her eyes roll on to Afearia. "I will triumph!"

With enough force, she punches Afearia off of her. "Child of darkness," rising to her feet, generating a black aura that somewhat worries Afearia. "YOU ARE NOT STRONGER THAN GOD'S CHOSEN!" Chloe roars with the darkness thickened into an upward rushing mass. "EVIL CAN NEVER BE GREATER THAN A CHILD OF LIGHT!"

Chloe leaps with fist cocked for Afearia. Waiting till the last second, Afearia leaps back from the punch's range, but Chloe put so much of herself into the punch that when she curved it, the ground crumbles up with just the force alone. The crumbling expansion races toward Afearia as she hops back several times to avoid being caught within it. Chloe quickly zeros in on her with a downward, sideways hook punch.

Barely fast enough, Afearia defends herself with Eternity's shield, blowing off nearly all of Chloe's flesh, down to the bone from its magical recoil. The collision sounded as if a bomb went off underwater. Afearia rolls forward with shield first and breaks Chloe's balance from behind with an advancing thrust.

Afearia shield chops her by swinging outward across Chloe's skull, wedging it partway into the bones. Violently dislodging the shield, she spins in the opposite direction, using the built up momentum to increase the might of her bare shield backhand, grounding her opponent deep into the dirt.

Panting like she's just run a marathon, Afearia's shield suddenly receives a shocking array of glowing white cracks. After a couple seconds of golden white blooming feathers, the shield shatters into light fragments to reveal chains layered over her forearm. The chains quickly retracts, hard enough to rock her balance.

Displeased, Afearia glances at her shield-less arm before low, angry groans are heard from Chloe's face rising from the dirt. Afearia grunts in frustration seeing that Chloe can still fight after all this time.

"You—cannot beat God's plan," Chloe says. "My awful life will not be in vain. It was every beating, every labor, every assault, every **gut** turning service I provided for my seniors that led me to this," regenerating from all her injuries. Like a rising smoke, her dark aura returns. "The abuse. The neglect. Even... my death. It was all for a reason." She turns her head to Afearia with deranged murderous intent as she creepily smiles at her with one heavily bloodshot eye. "And I'll be dammed if I let a sinner like you walk out of this forest alive."

Chloe slowly looks back down into the dirt, almost lifelessly. She balls her fist into the soil before her aura explodes into the sky. "I WILL SUCCEED!" she boldly exclaims with an echo in her voice. She stands with her mangled arm regenerated enough to hold before her. "I will triumph! I have an entire country at my back, and... ! My Father's still watching me!" she yells with a burst of more darkness. "I hear him, I hear him!"

The power of Guardian Angels has begun to fade, but Chloe has failed to notice this herself. With her arm fully recovered, she bends her knees and balls her fist at her waist before leaping forward at her opponent like a bullet.

"EVIL WILL NOT PREVAIL!"

Afearia swiftly, but barely, manages to sidestep her wild attack. In mid motion, Afearia ducks to dodge Chloe's followed through back kick delivered before passing by. Chloe strikes back with a powerful punch for her head. While crouched, Afearia swings her body over her arm, using her shin to direct Chloe's destructive punch toward the ground.

The ground crumbles into a small crater, blowing Afearia away somewhat. Landing on her feet, there was no time for rest. Chloe had already closed the distance with a kick aimed for her face, taking the skin off her cheek as she arched her back from the kick's range. Afearia uses this moment to complete a series of backflips to regain distance.

Chloe digs her foot in the ground and up kicks the ground, flinging large rocks at her foe. With the flash of her green seals, Afearia twists her hand on the ground to create a semi rock wall behind her just as Chloe races toward her. Like a revolving door, the rock wall defends against the rocks, obscuring Chloe's view long enough for Afearia to be in mid motion to release a stream of fire once the wall opened up.

Chloe covers her face with her arms and successively runs through to close the distance between them. With hand still to the ground, Afearia digs her fingers into the dirt, creating rising rock spires just as Chloe jumps in to attack. Though a spire pierced between her jaw bones, this only slowed her down.

Ripping the spire out, Chloe throws it at Afearia. The rock wall revolves around to defend Afearia while she simultaneously raises a wall of water to freeze against the wall, doubling her defense. The spire shatters on impact along with Afearia's guard. Chloe jumps up the moment the wall shatters and grabs two chunks of it, hurling it down at Afearia's face.

Afearia slaps them away with the synchronization of her chains following her movements. As Chloe comes at her, Afearia swiftly moves from harm's way and positions herself to place Chloe in a chokehold. Struggling only briefly, Afearia's flipped onto her back.

Chloe cocks her arm back to bash her skull to bits, but the moment she struck, Afearia throws her hand up to grab her fist while simultaneously summoning four chains to wrap around Chloe's wrist. Immediately, Chloe goes for a kick for her head as well. Using her seals, rows of rock line up to stop the kick, but it couldn't be stopped. She breaks through and lands a weakened, poorly aimed kick, hitting her collarbone.

Though it was weaker, the force was great enough to lift her off the ground and several feet from Chloe. She bounces off the ground a few times before getting on her feet and falling to her knees. Afearia, huffing in pain and fatigue, holds her collarbone, but Chloe won't relent and rushes in to assault her.

In a barrage of fast fist, Afearia hastily straightens up and begins to evade at the best of her ability. However, the punches are a few leagues above her reflexes, many grazing her body, bruising or striping the skin right off of her. With each failed punch the intensity of her attacks grow and Afearia's evasive maneuvers become dull.

Like divine judgment, the dark skies part and a bolt of lightning comes down and strikes Afearia, blowing everything and everyone away from her in an expanding dome of lighting. Chloe's back slams up against a distant tree while Afearia's agonizing screams rattle Chloe's skull and the ground shakes. Once the electrifying power from the sky ceases, Afearia's glowing aura returns twice as bright with her hair spiky and charge.

Afearia turns her head at her enemy, looking like a beast with teeth bear just before getting low to lunge.

Roughly jerking her hand behind herself, lightning pulses around her with a light surge running along her teeth as she growls at Chloe. Chloe gets on her feet and points a finger to fire a rod of darkness. Though too fast for Chloe's eyes to follow, Afearia had shifted from its range. Chloe bunched her brows and tilted her head in confusion before firing another.

Seeming visually instant, Afearia has evaded with a sidestep, holding her pose as she had moved much closer. Firing rapidly, Afearia has evaded every shot while getting closer every time until Afearia's eyes are staring deep into Chloe's, being as she was a breath away from Chloe's face. Startled, Chloe fires a final shot at pointblank range.

With no worry, Afearia had menacingly placed herself behind Chloe. Afearia lightly puts her hand on Chloe's shoulder, making her jump up forward. She turns and frantically throws a flurry of punches. It was short-lived. Afearia dodges every punch and delivers an electrifying one of her own, knocking Chloe back several feet in the woods. She struggles onto her feet only to discover Afearia had vanished.

"This again," Chloe sounding fed up. "If you think for a second—"

Before she could finish her sentence, Afearia close lined her across the face. Chloe flips around and lands on her neck. She quickly sits up in anger, but Afearia was gone again. Wasting no time to get back up only lead to her taking a second close line. Chloe then attempts to get up faster, but doing so ensured her getting hit even harder. With her nose and mouth quite bloody, her frustrated expression had become worried and nervous as she looked around in an antsy manner before crawling along the ground.

Suddenly appearing before her, Chloe looks up at this supped up enemy glaring down on her. Afearia stomps her foot, breaking up the ground with bright lights and heat coming through every crack before torrents of lightning rises up sending Chloe soaring above. Being battered by rocks and bolts, she breaches the tree tops as her mighty adversary prepares for one more strike.

Afearia bends her knees, charging up as she glows brighter and she bites into her lip as the pain of the lightning coursing through her body begins to run wild, even burning away her hair ties to give her hair full on spiked frizz. With her body shaking for control, she lets out a mighty warrior's cry and moves at breakneck speed toward the nearest tree and runs up it, leaving a flaming path with the lightning preceding it. She leaps up higher from the top, placing herself in alignment with Chloe.

Chloe's eyes are wide by the rise of the woman who's closed the power distance between them for this one final moment. "GOD'S LOVE!" Chloe panics, not thinking as her eyes go wider in realization that the creature she banished was a fatal mistake born from her blind faith.

In that moment—all sound had left Chloe's ears. Sight and the very sensations of the wind in the air had become null. Darkness was all she could see as the thoughts of salvation became less of a reality in her mind... My God..., Chloe thinks. My gracious Father... Why have you forsaken me...?

Tightly griping her wrist while pointing her finger like a gun, Afearia's veins bulge on her blood red face before firing a condensed lightning blast aimed directly at Chloe's heart. When that yellow and blue swirl of energy hits, Chloe's screaming in violent agony as she's carried across the sky like a shooting star while wildly flailing her arms around. The lightning running through her blood fries Chloe's brain chip, ending all possible recovery.

The shot, increasing in velocity, brutally tears through her skin, shatters her ribcage and engulfs her heart, bursting it out Chloe's back to carry it on without her. Chloe falls in a deafly silence as the light leaves her eyes while her rapidly beating heart travels further and further before bursting into a bloody splatter.

Afearia descends slowly before riding a bolt of lightning down to the ground. Standing half hunched over, breathing slow and heavy as her glow fades and her hair relaxes. A loud thunder is heard from above before Monsoon descends from the clouds. Afearia falls to her knees just before Monsoon floats in front of her.

Her heavy eyes look up at the sword, "How many?" An electrified five appears from the sword, fading and expanding as it nears Afearia. "Five years, huh? Could be worse."

Monsoon lightly floats up and down almost like a nod. A bolt hits Monsoon and it rides up into the clouds with its disappearance. Once the clouds clear, Afearia fruitlessly tries to stand with her head slumped. Still on her knees, taking in air but failing to regain regularity, Afearia raises her hand before her. Her arm can barely stay still for a second as chains try to come forth nearly retracting. Though barely, Afearia summons Eternity but falls forward due to the sword's weight.

She pierces the ground with it, leaning on it like a fallen knight. Demeseus' spirit soon appears before her. "I won...," Afearia weakly says. "I won and I didn't fool around." Demeseus calmly, but with concern watches her weary arms shake. "All I knew—was I could not let anyone down. Not again." With nearly shut eyes, she leans her head on Eternity's hilt. Unknowingly to her, the sword was absorbing her blood. "Did I... do good?"

Demeseus' corporeal hand comes down and gently pats her head. "Well done," he says with a remorseful pride. "I couldn't be more proud of you."
Afearia's baggy eyes widen before looking like she was on the verge of crying. She shuts her wet eyes before moving closer to practically embrace the sword. "Thank you...," she weeps. "Thank you... Thank you..."

Diary Entry #4024

Though I'm nearing the end of my childhood, I don't feel like I missed much. I never went to school. I never made friends beyond these walls. I've never held someone's hand to express affection. I've never been hugged. I've never been kissed... These are all meaningless in the build of a strong warrior. I see why my Elders deemed it unnecessary. I don't need it. I don't need any of it... Today.

Fair Dealings

Chapter Fifteen

Being forced to stop at the nearest city due to Chloe's assault, Zaiah, Adrian, Veronica and Elliot's team depart from the train so it may undergo a lawful investigation. As Elliot and his men step out the train and walk toward its rear cars, Zaiah and the kids closely follow. The children sadly keep their heads low in silence.

"Don't worry guys," Elliot says to them. "I know this was unexpected, but there's a place nearby we can hide out until the police conclude their investigation."

"Is it safe?" Zaiah asks.

"Very. After that attack, I think I better arrange for a chopper. We are traveling with precious cargo after all," glancing at Zaiah, then the kids.

As they proceed to retrieve the trunk holding Kyoto, Zaiah sees the kids sullen faces unchanged since Afearia departed. He slows his walking pace to match theirs, "Worried about your Anya? Don't be. She'll definitely be alright. She's—"

"You don't know," Adrian sadly says. "The last time she got separated from us she... She..." Adrian almost lost himself in the thought of Afearia's passing.

"We got lucky," Veronica says. "But Anya. She didn't come back to us the same. It took her a long time to even get out of bed with a smile. Zaiah." She looks up at him with sad eyes of worry. "She might die again."

Zaiah stared at both of them. Before sternly looking forward, grasping the seriousness of their concerns, "No. She won't."

"But—"

"Trust one thing. You don't fall in this world like

466

she did and not rise up again without great purpose. She came back for you two. She won't let herself be beaten like that ever again."

"How—can you be so sure?" Adrian genuinely asks.

Zaiah shines a big smile on him, "I saw it in her eyes when she slayed me. That woman has returned to this world as an unstoppable force."

"Hey, let's pick it up," Elliot calls.

Zaiah walks closer to Elliot. "Elliot. I've been meaning to ask you. Afearia's still out there. What are we going to do?"

"When we reach our pit stop I'll have someone go look for her and bring her to us. There's no point for us to look for her."

"She could be hurt, Elliot," he says in a lower voice to not alert the kids.

"She's fine. Besides, even if we don't find her I'm sure she'll find us."

Zaiah makes a slight face of suspicion. "You sure?"

"Positive."

Zaiah glances back at the saddened children, seeming a bit saddened by their displeasure as well.

Deep in the forest where Afearia recently claimed victory over Chloe, Afearia remains flat on the ground in a slumber. Softly, her eyes slightly open as she looks around in a hazy blur that clears every time she blinks. She pushes herself up from the dirt and slouches her head, seeming woozy.

"Ugh. I feel so drained." She raises her hand to her head to ease the dizziness. "I'm still far from Adrian and Veronica. I have to find them," struggling to stand, only to collapse back to the ground. "That last attack really taxed me. I won't be any good for at least another two hours." Her heavy eyes begin to shut involuntarily. All I can do is wait for my strength to return, Afearia thinks. Until then...

Wait for me.

Out on the open road, a government limousine speeds down the streets with bold trees lining the edges of the road. Within the limo is Derexen's hand selected raiding party fresh from the meeting hall. Minerva sits with her back to the driver while the rest of her team sit before her. She soberly stares out the window resting her head back watching each tree whiz by.

Glenn, seeming nearly impatient, ends his near erratic glances when he focuses on Minerva. "I've waited long enough," Glenn says. "We've been driving for hours and you've yet to say anything about our objective or how you plan to achieve it." Minerva remains silent, not even looking his way. "Obviously you must know their location. Why are you choosing to drive when we could just teleport?" Still, she remains unresponsive to his onset aggravation. "Captain, tell me something, anything to give me insurance that your head is in the game."

Minerva's eyes roll onto Glenn before she leans off the headrest. "His location has yet to be finalized. We're following a remnant of a trail left by a personal guard of Derexen's. Upon his defeat," pulling out a PDA-like device with red dots on a digital map surrounding the area, "he leaves an odorless scent on you that won't last for too long."

"Really?"

"It's part of his altered genes by our science team for such missions."

"How much longer do we have?"

"Thrifty-six hours."

"And the dots?"

"Each dot represents what his odor came in contact with. To warp to each spot would be a needless waste of energy."

"Then what makes you so sure we're on the right path?"

"It's either here," pointing to dots near the station. "Or here," pointing to one in the forest."

"That's not enough," stifling his aggression.

"It is. These dots were once one. They're the only dots to have fled after the guard's defeat. However, the one in the forest has stopped moving for a while in an area unfamiliar to us. Logically, the one heading to the nearest city makes sense."

"I was told that an accident occurred on the train. Assuming Kyoto was trying to get away, the destruction would be credible. This initial dot here," pointing to it, "may just be a lone casualty. Perhaps the ones at the station as well. If they still have him they'll need new transport. Which means the dot will move independently from the station. And if they don't have him but were involved, punishment must still be dealt."

"Are we to kill the ones responsible?" Ludwig asks Minerva.

"I rather capture. We may learn a bit about our enemy."

Glenn glances at Minerva's bouncing leg. "Are you tired?" Glenn sincerely asks Minerva, getting her attention. "You've dug your nails deep into your leg, enough to break skin. You're even shaking a little, captain."

"You deserved a response. No more questions."

"Understood," leaning back calmly.

Minerva releases her leg and returns to her reclusive state watching the trees. Ludwig glances at them twice before looking toward Glenn. I was told Glenn isn't prone to taking orders, Ludwig thinks. But when it comes to Minerva, there seems to be a sense of respect. "Uh, Glenn, I wanted to—"

"Don't. "

"But—"

"Whatever it is you wanted to know, I would never share with anyone outside of our government circle. I'm not thrilled about this arrangement, but I'd like that we keep things strictly business."

"Sorry." Ludwig sits back looking out the window, and instead of taking offense to Glenn's words, he lightly smirks. Loyalty, Ludwig thinks, even pondering about his teammates. This is already an improvement, even for a makeshift operation team.

Not far ahead of their pursuers, Elliot and the others have successfully made transportation by car to the city building in wait for their next ride. Elliot is the first to step out of the passenger side door before Zaiah and the kids come from the back seat.

"This is it," Elliot says as the second car arrives with the rest of his men. "We'll be hiding out here until we can secure air transport. This high building is one of the few that actually have a helicopter pad."

"Hold on, Elliot," Zaiah interjects. "You sound like you're willing to leave without Afearia."

Elliot turns to the second car, watching his men retrieve Kyoto from the car's trunk. "If things get rocky, we may have to." The men pull the trunk out and march toward the building. "If we wait too long we'll draw a lot of heat. I'm sure by now we already have. If anything, we can arrange for a team to bring her to our final destination."

Adrian tugs on Zaiah's shirt, "I don't want to go without Anya."

"We won't," Zaiah responds. "Right?" sternly addressing Elliot in a passive aggressive way for him to agree.

Elliot turns his head to them a little, "Right. Come inside. I've got to make some calls," walking on ahead.

Zaiah places his hands on the kids' shoulders to guide them through the many glass doors to the building's entrance. They enter the dark office-like lobby with four elevators straight ahead and a security guard standing beside the check-in desk. Zaiah looks around, noticing the dim lights by the check-in desk and the shut door leading to the staircase as he followed Elliot who lightly nods for the security guard to place a call. Elliot's men had long since gone upstairs. He calls for the elevator and it arrives rather quickly, allowing them to gather onto it for a lift.

Pressing fifteen, Elliot stands in front of the closing doors. As they silently ride up, he turns his head halfway toward Zaiah, "You do understand how critically important it is for us to defeat Derexen, right?"

"Of course," Zaiah replies.

"This causes us to use unsavory methods sometimes." He stares at his own reflection in the golden chrome doors. "The assault on the train was evident enough for us to take this matter in full. We're leaving the minute our chopper arrives."

"What!?"

"Zaiah," Veronica looking to Zaiah with worry.

"I just told you we are not leaving without Afearia."

The elevator slows to the fifteenth floor. "Zaiah," Elliot says. "I wasn't giving you a choice."

The doors open with thirty plus men aiming assault rifles directly at them. Kyoto is on his knees with two men pointing their rifles at his head while he's tied and gagged.

Zaiah slowly pulls the kids behind him while sternly looking at the armed men, "So by precious cargo. "

Elliot slowly steps out the elevator and stands behind the armed men, "Don't do anything stupid. Obey or lose everything for nothing."

Zaiah becomes surprised when he feels the kids start to tremble as they hold onto him. For less than a second, his face became extremely threatening before he pulls it back, breathing a bit harder with a clenched jaw.

"Alright," Zaiah says reluctantly. "What do you want us to do?"

"Follow me," Elliot says, walking to his right.

Zaiah and the kids follow with two armed men

proceeding directly behind them. Walking through the dark cubical office space and black tiled floors, lies a clear space leading to a vault. At the end of the path is a split leading to a closet at Elliot's left and another leading to a stairway to the right. He nods for the two armed men before him to open the vault.

"To maintain a sure thing, we need to put them somewhere reliably secure. Kyoto will be in here soon." He turns to Zaiah. "Step inside." When they proceed, the two men behind them grab the kids by the shoulder. Zaiah quickly turns to their panicked yelps, but stops himself once he sees the rifles turned on them. "Only you, Zaiah."

Zaiah lightly moved his head where Elliot stands, "You are really crossing a line here."

"Yes, the finish line. You can't flee without these kids. And don't get cute in this vault. We'll know if you try anything through the hidden cameras. Now, get in."

Zaiah looks back at the kids who desperately watch his predicament worsen, but he confidently smiles before proceeding toward the vault. Just as he's about to step in the vault, Elliot places his hand on his shoulder.

"For the record," Elliot says, "this is nothing personal. But we must do everything we can to reclaim Terra by any means. We promise to keep you three safe."

Zaiah gives him a deadpan expression before entering the concrete walls of the safe. The two men guarding the vault shut him inside as Elliot turns to his captives. "Take them to the closet and lock them inside." The kids struggle as the armed men easily drags them along. Elliot huffs and walks back to his team of men. "I need four of you to guard the lobby. The rest of you must keep watch over all potential entry points. We've come this far. We can't let A.N.T.S. down now."

Elliot looks to the battered Kyoto, "Bring him over here." Elliot turns away as the men go to secure the building while the two holding Kyoto follow Elliot into a cubical. Elliot sits at the desk while his men roughly drop Kyoto in the chair across the desk. One of the men sloppily put Kyoto's mask over one fourth of the upper corner of his face. Elliot just stares at Kyoto, poorly suppressing his underlining anger for his kind. "You can speak now, right? Enough time has passed for the drugs to have weakened grip over your motor skills."

Kyoto doesn't respond. One of the men hit him across the cheek with the butt of their gun, leaving him to twitch for a moment and grunt, looking angrily at Elliot.

"I'll take that as a yes," Elliot continues. Elliot sneakily looks around as he stands to look over the cubical before sitting back down. "Although I was given orders not to interrogate you unless told, I think I'm gonna take first crack at you." He leans forward with dangerous intentions, "Because I know I can break you. You're weak. Your whole damn species is weak. Just a bunch of immoral cowards the lot of you."

Kyoto smirks, "I thought I told you I would never expose my comrades to the enemy—ever."

Kyoto gets struck across the face again. "Question one. How large is Derexen's demon army?"

"About the same size of go fuck yourself."

The gunman strikes Kyoto, knocking blood from his mouth and tearing the bruise on his cheek. "Does Derexen know who's leading the rebellion?"

Kyoto does a bloody snigger. "Do you?"

The armed man was about to strike him again until Elliot raises his hand to reframe. "Then answer this. You're loyal. You're still scum, but nonetheless you're loyal. So tell me, how can you be sure Derexen is a pure sinless hero without darkness?"

Kyoto chuckles to himself while almost laughing too loudly as his laugh simmers out with the slow shaking of his head. "This is exactly why he's above everyone else. Clean of sin? Are you fucking retarded? No man who walks this planet can be. And he knows that. He doesn't deny who he is. He doesn't pretend he's some kind of prophet of the light." Kyoto proudly smiles with his head held high. "Derexen's a hero because he not only embraces his own sins but he embraces the sins of humanity as a whole. And he fights everyday to right the wrongs of yesterday. Heh, you putz. Long live the demon king."

Elliot's face becomes a bit frustrated. "This isn't his world. It's *ours*. We didn't ask for his help."

"Nor did the starving children and the helplessly abused people in this country. And now they praise his efforts every day. Be grateful someone got off their ass and actually did something for this world."

Elliot stands. "You half breeds really have forgotten what it means to be human and what significance there is in being self-governed." He walks over and stands under the light, taking a large knife from his belt. "If I were to kill you now, would Derexen's government even skip a beat by your absence?" holding it close to Kyoto's face.

Kyoto lowers his head and closes his eyes. He tilts his head and smirks before looking up at Elliot. "The only beats that will be ceasing in the next few seconds are yours."

"What?"

"Eleven o'clock!" Without warning, a bullet whizzes through the window, piercing several cubicles and into Elliot's knife holding hand. Kyoto joins his feet together and kicks Elliot over the desk as he falls back losing his mask, "One o'clock!"

With two shots, the armed men receive bullet holes in their skulls before dropping dead. The men in the office scramble in disarray until the center elevator dings upon reaching their floor. The men point their guns at the doors. When the doors part, Minerva calmly strolls out with Ludwig. She carefully analyzes every man in the room and every corner with her blood chilling yellow irises.

Coming cautiously from around both sides of the elevator edges are two men attempting a sneak attack. However, both Minerva and Ludwig glance at each other, for they've already sensed their advance. The moment they jumped into view, Ludwig had extended his arm with an open palm. Detaching his wrist, wiggly black flesh fibers increase his range and allows him to grip the attacker's face. The other man points his pistol when Minerva slides in toward him with her back unbelievably low to the ground. He misses both shots before she leans up with a leaping upper cut to knock him out cold.

Hearing the commotion, Kyoto gets on his feet to escape until Elliot pulls him down in a chokehold and puts a gun to his neck.

"Don't make a sound," Elliot tells him. "We're going to the roof."

As they both slowly proceed low to the ground, Minerva spots the back door to the stairwell open.

"Ludwig," Minerva says, pointing to the stairwell.

Elliot stands up and drags Kyoto, "Open fire!"

The men do as commanded, leaving Ludwig and Minerva to take cover behind one of the many large pillars on the floor.

The sounds of screaming children is heard up ahead, "Hostages?" Minerva says. "I shouldn't, but Ludwig, your priority is to save the hostages without casualties."

"Understood, captain," Ludwig nods.

Glenn, Minerva telepathically thinks. *I've lost my link with Kyoto.*

Across from the building, Glenn is crouched in a dark room by the window facing out to their floor while perfectly maintaining aim with his sniper rifle. *So did I,* Glenn responds to Minerva. *And although this window may have the best vantage point, I can't cover the whole floor. Kyoto was my eyes for the blind spots in my vision.*

*Alright. Cover me and Ludwig. I'm going after
Kyoto. Do not kill any of these men.*

Roger.

Minerva looks to Ludwig. "On my signal." Ludwig
gives her a nod.

Minerva does a silent count down from three using
her fingers. At zero, the two of them spring into action,
racing from behind the pillar. Ludwig detaches his joints
from the shoulder, wrist, neck, hip, and torso, scurrying
into multiple cubicles like rats. As Minerva uses quick
martial art takedown moves like Aikido and Jujitsu, Glenn
was sniping guns out of their attackers' hands and taking
perfectly aimed shots at their legs to bring them down.
Despite all the gunfire, Minerva had successfully made it to
the back door Kyoto was taken through.

She races up the stairs with many pursuers while a
set few stay behind to find Ludwig. Moving like a speedy
spider, Ludwig's hand races across the floor and walks up
the storage closet to twist the knob with enough force to
break the locking mechanism within the knob. Once
opened, the rest of his body parts filed into the closet.

From the feet up, Ludwig rapidly pieces himself
back together before twisting his neck to loosen the tension.
When he opened his eyes, no one was inside. Taking only a
step forward, he knocks over cleaning supplies and two
brooms.

"It's so cramped in here," Ludwig says. "Hello? My
name's Ludwig. Me and my colleges have come to help.
Anyone here?"

Hiding behind a stack of boxes are Adrian and
Veronica crouched low as they fearfully stare at the open
gap to see his shadow sway. Not moving, not blinking, not
even swallowing spit in fear of being discovered. Ludwig's
hand crawls over the boxes and freaks the kids out, causing
them to scream and run into Ludwig's view. They were
about to run back until the hand jumps down and runs

between Adrian's legs to reattach itself to Ludwig.

"Please," Ludwig says to the kids, hoping to keep them calm. "I'm only here to help get you guys out of here."

"W-who are you?" Adrian asks.

"Ludwig D. A proud member of the DAs human run government."

Veronica looks to her brother, "What do we do? We're trapped."

"Trapped?"

Adrian looks to Ludwig, "Everyone here is a danger to Anya. I don't know what to do!" putting his hand to his head, stepping back.

"Anya...? You two must be the kids the Angel travels with. Where is she?"

"We won't tell you anything!"

"Is she safe?" he earnestly asks, surprising the children. "Is she in the building? My orders were to help hostages."

"She's... She's not here."

Ludwig exhales with relief. "Good. It would be a shame if she couldn't handle criminals of this caliber. Is there anyone else here who needs help?"

The kids stare at Ludwig with distrusting eyes before looking helplessly at each other. "There's... I..."

"You know, when I was a child, my mother always told me to be mindful of users, but be open to kind hands. When people distrust you, you must prove to them you can be trusted in a world of liars and users."

Ludwig looks around before grabbing a black garbage bag. He covers his torso and opens the bag with the sound of his waist opening up before something heavy falls out of him and into the bag. He places it on the floor and slowly steps back from it with his black flesh tissues hanging out of it from him. A strong beating pulses in a fine rhythm within the black bag.

477

"Inside the bag is a means to hurt and kill me," Ludwig says, seeming to be lightly sweating and faintly trembling in stifled pain. "Even the clutching grip of a child can easily immobilize me. The bag is yours until I get you kids out of here safely." The siblings look at each other for reassurance. "Give it a squeeze if you wish. B-but be gentle!" he blurts.

They slowly approach the bag with Adrian attempting to lift it, "It's heavy."

Veronica helps him, "It's beating, like a—"

"Heart," Ludwig says. "You've got it, but don't look inside. I don't want you guys to feel sick." They place it down and Adrian presses his fist into it, making Ludwig tremble and grunt. Adrian pushes harder and nearly brings him to his knees. "O-okay. I'm aching pretty bad here," sounding as if he may pass out.

"Sorry," Adrian says under his breath as he removed his fist.

"Over here!" a man shouts from outside the door. "Stay close!"

"Guys, we got to go," Ludwig says as he peaked outside the ajar door. "My captain ordered me to save all hostages. I can't fail."

"Wait, what about Zaiah?" Veronica asks.

"Zaiah?"

"He's in the vault."

"Hmmm… Hold that bag tight. I'm going to carry you guys out." The kids grab the bag before he scoops them up in his giant hand and holds them close like kittens. "Alright. Keep your heads low."

Outside the closet, two men inch closer toward the door with one of them moving directly in front of it before Ludwig busts the door down rushing out. Before they could react, Ludwig leaps up through the ceiling tiles. When the men try to crowd the hole, Glenn pins their movements by shooting at their feet.

Inside the vault, Zaiah stares at the door with an irritated, contemplative look on his face when suddenly, the stone ceiling several feet before him cuts into a large square and comes down with Ludwig falling through with the kids. Zaiah quickly jumps back, looking aggressively at the potential threat that has entered the vault.

"Is that him?" Ludwig asks the kids.

Zaiah approaches in a confused distrusting manner, "What is the meaning of this?"

"He's saving us—I think," Veronica, looking up at Ludwig.

"It's true," Ludwig replies. "I'm—"

"Ludwig Bierman," Zaiah says with stern, cautious eyes. "I know who you are."

"Oh?" genuinely surprised his name has traveled overseas. "Strange, but I don't know who you are."

"What are you doing with those children?"

"I'm sorry, but we don't have a lot of time. You have my word I'm only here to save hostages and one government elite." Zaiah's eyes remained fixed on him. "Uhh..."

"Zaiah, it's true—I think," Veronica says, seeming just as complacent as before.

Zaiah did not change his belief of this man as he stared him down. "Okaaay..." placing the kids down and backing away. "If you want, you can take them and I'll just lead the way out."

"I think we'll manage," Zaiah says as he waves the kids over to him.

"Maybe, but one false move and these kids will be put under gunfire. But I know a way through where guards aren't stationed."

Zaiah looks down at the black trash bag by Ludwig's feet. "What's in the bag?"

"My heart," speaking almost casually.

"What?"

"I needed to gain their trust. If I lied or deceived them they could kill me at anytime."

"Interesting," he smirks.

The kids grab the bag and return it to Ludwig. "Please help us, Ludwig," Veronica innocently asks.

Ludwig couldn't believe this little girl would put such blind trust in him. He smiles warmly at her before taking the bag and allowing the black fiber tissues pull his heart back inside.

"Is this okay with you, Zaiah?" Ludwig asks him. "Once I get you guys out, I promise to walk away, no matter the outcome."

Zaiah stares on before slowly approaching, looking dead in his eyes as he stands before the kids, "Led the way. But the kids will stay with me."

Ludwig respectfully nods before leaping back up into the ceiling. He dangles a bundle of his black tissue fibers, grossing out the children.

"Suck it up," Zaiah tells them. "Follow me." He grabs on before they soon follow.

Though he's wounded, Elliot is pulling Kyoto up the stairs as he continues to tell him to hurry up in a panic. Like a mountain lion, Minerva had arrived by jumping from wall to wall and banister to banister until she was able to jump over Elliot and snatch away his gun in the process. Elliot rushes himself and Kyoto down the stairs. Minerva tosses away the gun and leaps down the stairs, kicking Elliot in the leg. Though Kyoto falls down with him, Elliot continues to tumble down another flight without his hostage.

Minerva quickly helps Kyoto to his feet while Elliot's aided by four of his men. The men quickly open fire upon the elites. Minerva grabs Kyoto and hustles up the stairs with the men pursuing until Elliot halts them.

Elliot grabs the radio from the waist of one of his men, "All available units, Kyoto is escaping. Head to the top floor immediately. Kill all intruders who are not our captives." Elliot throws the radio. "Let's go. We'll cut them off."

As Minerva rushes up the stairs with her comrade, Kyoto's stamina was beyond poor. "Minerva, wait," he requests. They both stop with her seeing him hunched over. "The-these cuffs... They're meant to-to suppress the-the power of our kind. Take them off, please." Using brute strength, she grabs the cuffs and pulls them apart. "Thanks," rubbing his wrist.

A dark liquid comes from his left hand and moves beneath his clothes and up his neck to create a replica of his mask before hardening over half his face.

"Can you warp yet?" she asks.

"No."

"Come on. We'll leave once we regroup."

When she runs up ahead, Kyoto oddly lowers his head in thought before following. As they near the top floor, Glenn telepathically speaks to them. *Minerva, we've got trouble. Elliot's men. They've vanished.*

Vanished how? Minerva replies.

I don't know how, but it may be safe to say they're using our stolen tech. I don't know where they are. Be careful. I'm going to cover all my vantage points.

Don't . Just head to the lobby floor and remain hidden with rifle ready. We'll be out soon.

Understood.

Minerva looks to Kyoto, "Did you hear that?"

"Yeah."

Upon reaching the last flight, Kyoto suddenly stops. "What's wrong?"

"The mission. What was it?"

"Search and rescue."

"But not to kill or apprehend the criminals."

"You are top priority. Derexen's orders." Kyoto looks away in thought. "If it makes you feel better, I'm

481

anticipating for them to follow us up top. We'll capture the leader in addition. Derexen won't like it, but I feel it's a call I should make."

Kyoto remains in thought before lifting his head a little, "And Afearia... any word?"

"Still at large."

Kyoto punches the wall, denting the concrete with his left hand covered in the hardened shell from his body. "Not good enough," speaking with a gravelly voice as he angrily looks to Minerva as his mask gradually covers more of his face.

He approaches his deadpan comrade as a darkness similar to mercury seeps from the pores of his left arm. It covers his hand becoming claws. Only the top left corner of his face remains exposed as he stands dangerously close to Minerva.

"We can leave right now, Kyoto," Minerva calmly says, standing before his intense rage. "Don't do something I can't fix."

"I will not return until she dies."

"Kyoto," speaking as calmly as she could. "We need to get you back."

"NOOO!" shoving her aside and punching the door open.

The moment the door opens, Kyoto is shot in the face and hits the ground. Minerva stops all movement as dozens of armed men are aiming at her while Elliot's in the back by the windows.

"You idiot!" Elliot scolds the man standing before him with the smoking barrel. "You killed him, damn it!" He paces for a moment in frustration before setting eyes on Minerva. "The Nymph. Take the Roughshod Nymph! We can't come back empty handed!"

The moment they began to advance, Kyoto's legs slowly rise straight to the ceiling before he does a kip up into a crouched posture with his back to the men. A wrinkled bullet falls from his face before jerking his head toward them with a light snarl.

"You're gonna wish you killed me one bullet ago."

The now shiny and tinted shell covering his face has become a full helmet gaining finer details. Eye slots appear in a rectangular shape with similar vertical slits over his mouth. The black liquid trickles down his right arm to give him a second pair of black claws.

Swiftly, Kyoto turns and bolts forward yelling angrily under muffled echoes. Minerva called for him to stop in one final plea, but her words were just background noise in his all consuming rage. Kyoto runs up to one man and double slashes him; first slashing his gun, then his face. His gun parts into pieces, moments before his shredded face splatters. Keeping low, Kyoto was already closing on his next target.

The men fire, missing many of their shots while the rest are swatted away. Kyoto trusts his claws into one man, lifting him up while growling menacingly in his face with wide demented eyes before tossing him into two others. Kyoto takes several shots to the head, knocking his head upward, but no damage was taken. He aggressively faces his shooters and rushes between them with blinding speed. He's crouched several feet behind them with crossed arms extended down his waist. Though it appears his attack failed, the men's heads suddenly part similarly to his spread claws.

The others shoot at him but he jumps over them with his body condensed like a ball. Breaking from his condensed flip, Kyoto slashes his arms outward, creating red claw marks in the air over several men. Though he did not reach physically, the men below suffer fatal claw damage. Elliot, struck with fear as he watches each of his men fall one by one, unable to understand how Kyoto can kill without touching most of them.

Kyoto's holding up two men with his claws buried

in their bowels before jerking them twice and slashing them to the ground, disemboweling them in the process. The last man fearfully shoots his hand gun with the bullets being easily swatted by Kyoto. The man stumbles back, missing the rest of his shots as Kyoto approaches. So afraid, the man trips over his own feet only to have his throat slashed out of his neck from an unseen range. Kyoto watches him fall before making deathly eye contact with Elliot, the last of the rebels.

"I've known men like you," Kyoto making his way toward Elliot with a dangerous leisure. "You come off as sane, thoughtful, and even just. But when you get your prize..." The slits over his eyes and mouth melt away with the mask creating beastly fangs over his mouth. "You begin to look just like me."

Elliot slowly backs away, trembling, "This just confirms it. You-you're all monsters! At the drop of the hat you all turn into your true selves and kill without remorse." Elliot's back presses up against the large glass window as Kyoto's practically breathing down his neck as his eyes sink into his soul. "I wasn't wrong to call you a monster. I was wrong to believe you could know the difference between man and beast—especially since...," looking down at a severely wounded man aiming his gun at Kyoto, moments before Minerva notices. "Man is suppose to have dominion over beast."

Just as the wounded man was going to fire, Minerva misdirects his shot when she kicks his firing arm. The gun shot makes Kyoto look back, only to be immediately stabbed in the stomach by Elliot. Kyoto slowly faces Elliot as his blood drops down the base of the knife.

"You think you can tame me?" smugly sizing the frightened Elliot up. "Something this boy couldn't do his whole life?" gesturing his hands toward himself. Kyoto grabs Elliot by the neck and lifts him. "Think again."

"Kyoto, put him down," Minerva says. Turning his

head halfway toward her, the dark shell over his head begins to change shape again. "Kyoto?" He looks Elliot over. "Kyoto, no more. Don't descend any further into madness." Elliot, choking on Kyoto's grip, stares him in the eyes with a dying light filled with hate. With an angry snarl, Kyoto jumps out the window holding Elliot out before him. "Kyoto!" rushing toward the shattered window watching them fall.

As they fall to the ground below, Elliot is screaming until he looks up at Kyoto's face, leaving him in a frozen silence. His eyes and brows express an intense malice while the dark shell has completely reformed over his lower face. It has shaped into the mouth of a lion with its canine teeth edging out the sides of its mouth while a dark smog seeps from between its teeth.

At the building's quiet lobby, a portion of the ceiling is suddenly cut and collapses with Ludwig coming out. He carefully checks the area before waving Zaiah down from the hole. Zaiah jumps down with the kids in his arms. He slowly places them down while seeming suspicious as he watched Ludwig's back.

"Through the double doors behind me lies a series of easy to navigate hallways," Ludwig says. "They will take you to the other side of the building. Exit there and escape."

"You lied to us, didn't you?" Zaiah asks with suspicion. "You may not know who I am, but these kids? Afearia's the most wanted woman in the world. Clearly you know she doesn't travel alone. Am I to believe we are not just bait to lead you back to her?"

Ludwig doesn't face them, faintly tilting his head before doing so, "Yes, I know who those kids are. And this is a prime opportunity. But if I do that. If I lie and take you as hostage I will not only bring shame to my kind but I'll be no better than the men above us. Worse of all—I would bring shame to my mother. She told me to never use my gifts to bully the weak." His eyes shut, sorrowfully reminiscing. "Help those in need—my son," he mutters. Veronica comes beside him smiling.

"The giant with a heart," Zaiah says. "I guess the rumors were true."

Ludwig looks to Zaiah with a friendly smile on his face, "I still have to capture your friend. But I promise not to harm her. If anything, I rather we talked first."

"That's stupid."

"It is," he chuckles. "But she's saved a lot of people. That doesn't sound like a bad person to me."

"She isn't!" Veronica blurts, getting everyone's eyes on her. "Anya is... an amazing person. She cares about this world. Please, Mr. Ludwig. Stop hunting her."

Ludwig stares sadly at Veronica, "I'm sorry. But Afearia is still a terrorist. I have to bring her in." Veronica frowns. "Maybe... Maybe I can convince the others to—"

"To do what?" Glenn says, surprising everyone as he comes through the lobby's glass doors. "Let her go because she saved a few people? Quit the bullshit and capture those kids." Ludwig doesn't move, irritating Glenn further as he marches up to him. "I don't know how they do things in your country, but here we get things done. That includes the apprehension of suspects."

Ludwig turns to Glenn, "I promised I wouldn't."

"Then that's your mistake. Take those kids and—" Zaiah steps from behind Ludwig and gives Glenn a sideways glare, stopping him in his tracks. "You're...?" appearing quite surprised before looking annoyed. "The ghosts just keep coming out the woodwork, huh?"

"I won't let you touch these kids," Zaiah warns.

Glenn slings his rifle behind himself before summoning one of his mystical guns, aiming it at Zaiah. "We'll see about that." Without warning, Elliot's body comes crashing down on the roof of a parked car outside the building, setting off the alarm upon impact, distracting

Glenn. "What the—"

Ludwig quickly looks to Zaiah, "Go!" Glenn quickly faces forward and fires at Zaiah. Ludwig jumps in front of the bullet's path and opens his mouth wide to create a vibrating, boorish roar that's rapidly reaching higher heights in volume. The power of this scream slows the bullet until it's flung back. Glenn is covering his ears while slowly being pushed back with feet still firmly on the floor. The glass doors vibrate rapidly until shattering and sending Glenn flying out the building. "Hurry!" facing Zaiah and company. "Now's your chance!"

"You're serious?" Zaiah says. Ludwig just stares at him before Zaiah respectful nods and turns to escape with the kids.

Zaiah hurries them along until Veronica breaks away, "Wait!" She rushes to Ludwig's side and takes his hand. "Thank you, Mr. Ludwig."

Ludwig seemed fairly suppressed before smiling down at this tiny, tiny girl who didn't see a monster—but a man. "No, Veronica…. Thank you."

Veronica hugs him and runs back to Adrian and Zaiah. Zaiah gives a final stoic nod at his enemy and runs off with the kids through the hall leading to the other side of the building. Glenn, now regaining his senses from the impact, peels himself off the car he slammed into. Upon his wobbly stand, he looks over and sees Elliot had fallen to his death. Looking to the pavement after, he notices a large black stain splattered before balling his fist.

"Kyoto…" Glenn mutters in grit. Glenn looks toward Ludwig before stomping toward him. "This. This is an obstruction of justice. I won't tolerate this any longer."

"No disrespect, Glenn, but I am certain Derexen said our top priority was to rescue Kyoto. To pursue them any further would be out of personal reasoning. That would surely be an obstruction of justice." Glenn's face only becomes more irritable. "I was only following orders.

Captain Minerva told me to rescue the hostages and that's what they were."

"It's true," Minerva says, approaching the building's entrance as she steps on broken glass shards. "I didn't know the hostages were in connection to Afearia, but it would not have made a difference."

"Where's Kyoto?" Glenn asks.

Minerva moves right pass Glenn, not answering his question as she kept her gaze on Ludwig till she's standing before him. She continues to stare lifelessly into his eyes, almost as if to be looking for something before finally answering Glenn, "He fled. But not before taking our tracking device and murdering every man in this building. He must've taken it when he shoved me," pondering aloud. "He's even managed to sever the mental link Valerie set up for us."

"Are you serious?"

"It's a casualty report that the king must receive."

"Wait," Ludwig interrupts. "What's going to happen to Kyoto? Where is he?"

"I have a guess. Glenn, lock this place down and compile a report for the king to review.

"Understood," Glenn says, seeming bothered before looking resolved and taking his leave in a mutter, "Justice for all."

Ludwig watches him leave to take the stairs before looking to Minerva, somewhat nervously by her unflinching gaze, "Captain—"

"We're on a hunt. Our destination is the forest where the incident occurred. You *will* follow my orders."

"Y-yes... But, Captain, did my judgment seem misguided to you?"

Minerva turns away and proceeds out the building. "Whoever's traveling with those kids stole a vehicle. They may be looking for Afearia. They may be looking for no one. You saved them. They are now no longer your concern." She stops and turns her head toward him, "Now—we hunt."

"For Afearia?"

Her eyes slant to the ground before she proceeds. Ludwig watches her for a moment before following her lead.

Out in the dark forest where Afearia sleeps, she finally comes too and sits up feeling the onset pains of sore muscles. She looks up at the night sky, covered in cuts, dirt, and bruises, almost taking a mental break from herself. She regains her sterner expression before standing to look around with the aim to leave. Taking only a few short steps, a beeping hits her ears. She stops as it gets louder and the footsteps have come close before ceasing along with the beeps.

"They couldn't find you because they don't know the area," the gravelly voice of Kyoto speaks. She turns and sees him holding the tracking device Minerva used to find him. "But I do. After all," he crushes the device in his grip." No forest, no mountain, no sea in this world could ever keep you away from ME!"

Hiding her displeasure of the current events, Afearia focuses her sharp glare upon her sudden foe, balling her fist in anticipation.

Diary Entry #1881

Fear of failure. Could you imagine being the worlds' last hope and not being good enough? I'm sure many others before me felt the same. But they succeeded. Where does that leave me? How do I know I've got what it takes? I need to talk with Demeseus.

Agent of Hate

Chapter Sixteen

Driving out on the road is the government owned limo transporting Minerva and Ludwig. Ludwig's face expresses uncertainty and nervousness. He frequently glances at his captain's crossed arm and leg demeanor as she stared out the window.

"Captain?" he speaks with near hesitance. "Do we—have to hunt Afearia now? I thought our main priority was saving Kyoto." Minerva does not acknowledge his concerns." I suppose it makes sense. Kyoto is not in immediate danger and she's a wanted criminal. But don't you think we should consult Derexen on what to do?" Minerva turns her head toward him with no readable change in demeanor. "I'm-I'm not trying to undermine your authority. I just want to be sure this is what he wants."

"What he wants... You can't understand," she mutters. "From here on out, you must follow my orders completely. Do you understand?"

"Yes," sounding regretful.

Minerva turns her gaze back out the window. "Or you could follow your heart without regrets." Ludwig didn't expect such a response from her. "Just beware. No free act comes without consequence."

Ludwig becomes a bit sullen. "For a long time... I've wondered if my mother would be proud of me. I always want to do what she used to teach me. But in this line of work, such things cannot be done. Do you think— she hates me?" asking Minerva as he looked toward her.

Minerva's eyes were closed, leaving him to sigh in disappointment as he looked out the window. She opens her eyes, briefly looking at Ludwig before looking down with a saddened slant. She shuts her eyes as she sinks in her own thoughts.

Out in the distant woods, Kyoto was finally standing before the object of his hate. "You," Afearia says. "You're one of Derexen's elites. And you were Elliot's prisoner. How did you get here, monster?"

"Me? Are you seriously calling me a monster? After all you've done. You are certainly the true monster between the two of us."

"Again, you speak as if I should know what you're implying."

"No implication, Afearia. I know it was you. And for that, I will not rest until you're dead."

"Great," summoning Bastion. "That makes two of us."

"This is a game to you?" With a quick curl of his index and middle fingers, two red claw streaks appear in the air at shoulder level of his enemy when a sudden out pour of blood escapes from a double gash wound in Afearia's neck. She stumbles sideways several times with wide eyes of painful surprise. "Oh ho-ho, careful," he chuckles. He approaches with his head tilted and mocking brows. "Tip toe," imitating her wobbles before she falls over holding her juicing neck. "Try to keep your blood from going cold." He stands over Afearia with a dark glee. "I'm not done with you yet."

"You—" Afearia's bleeding becomes quite excessive after speaking.

"Uh-oh, there it goes," he mocks before walking around her quivering body. "You said too much now it overflows." He kicks her in the face. "Looks like this could be it." He walks from her body, pass her feet. "But I promise to make this hurt along the way. I will desecrate your—" A gold flash lights the area. Kyoto turns to see Afearia holding Sovereignty as the claw wounds are glowing gold as they rapidly close "A hard one to put down. Like a termite," he grits.

"That is richly insulting. Even more so coming from something as foul as you. The worlds' abominations. The Demi race."

"You hateful puke!"

The moment he runs at her, Afearia quickly does the same. Once in range, she swings her swords outward, only to have him evade by jumping over her in a near cartwheel fashion. While passing over her, Kyoto slashes his claws outward like an arcing rainbow of red claw marks. The moment he lands, Afearia's back is gashed open by his unseen claws. She was surprised, unable to understand how he's able to wound her so badly from his distance.

As she falls to her knees, Kyoto leans his head back halfway, "Tch, you're trash." He arrogantly runs his hand through his hair until he hears chains rattle. "What?" looking down at his chain wrapped wrist.

Afearia shoots up and yanks him toward her through the air. She slashes him across the chest, but her attack was blocked by his shell covered forearms. As he whizzed by, Afearia yanks him back and smashes her fist in his face, bouncing his head off the ground to stun him. When his body rose up from the blow, she came down with her sword in hopes of decapitating him. However, acting independently from Kyoto's will, his left arm moves erratically before punching Afearia in the mouth, effectively ruining her attack.

She stumbles, moments before Kyoto's eyes roll onto her. He flips onto his feet with arms ready to slash outward. Not sure if she's in range or not, Afearia swiftly takes two major backward jumps.

Kyoto stands straight with relaxed arms and carefully watches her. Strange, Kyoto thinks. How did she get those chains around my wrist? I should've heard or felt them long before she got me. I didn't even see them. Looks like both of us are at a disadvantage when it comes to understanding our opponent's abilities. Kyoto makes a cheeky smile as he watches Afearia become sternly alert to his expression. Too bad for her, I'm the best analysis fighter in the government.

Afearia calmly raises her arm and waits a moment before firing a chain into the forest. It nearly hits Kyoto in the face as he fearlessly waits for her attack to complete. The chain returns on the other side of his head and goes around Afearia, shooting into the ground between them. When Afearia's green seals appear, the chain bursts up into the air, coming down on him with three elephant heads made of rock. Kyoto smirks, shaking his head while looking away as if her attempts are futile. With little effort, he slashes with one claw, creating the bloody streaks, bursting the heads into rubble.

"Be better," he says with mocking disappointment.

With debris and dust filling the space between them, Afearia seizes the moment and zips pass him, confusing Kyoto. The chain that nearly hit him before, wraps and yanks him by the neck in the direction she fled. Pass the dusty clearing as he's carried through the air, Afearia parts the dust with the tip of her sword Sovereignty being thrust into his face. Though caught by surprise, Kyoto's mask begins to transform in response to this deadly blade less than an inch from his iris.

In the blink of an eye, the shell covers his whole skull, protecting him from Afearia's thrust. Sliding off the blade and pass her, Kyoto's released from the retracting chain as he slides in the dirt feet first before coming to a stop.

The shell opens four vertical slits over Kyoto's mouth. Honeycomb shaped holes appear over the ears, "You make it angry," he says as his left arm twitches. "I hate that you killed her... She was the only light... The only pure soul to ever walk in our midst. A true angel amongst sinners. But it..." He grabs his left arm as its twitches were becoming violent. He holds on to it until it stops. "Every time I think of her—my heart aches," he says as circular holes reveal his sad eyes resting upon Afearia. She remained on guard, just as a thin tinted red shell glows and covers his eyes. "Because you took her away from me!" he roars with a claw slash.

Afearia leaps back as the ground she was standing on takes deep gashes while she receives minor scratches on her leg. Kyoto flips up behind her and slashes down with both claws. When the slashes disappear, Afearia is cut up into multiple bloody slivers. He figured this was his victory, but a sudden realization hit him as he frantically looked around, no longer believing he had won.

He landed, looking confused and panicked before taking his claws and cutting into his own arm—breaking the illusion. With a quick down turn of his head, followed by a backflip, Kyoto was evading the rising blade from beneath him in the nick of time. Afearia was crouched low, swinging her extended blade, Sleight. In mid flip, Kyoto slashes at her, but with fast thinking, Afearia grabs the grip of Bastion who's tip's buried in the ground, and twisted it to encase her body in a thick rocky dome. The claw gashes tear into the ground and through some of the dome's top.

He readies to slash again, but Afearia comes bursting from the dome's side, firing a chain from each shoulder blade. Kyoto deflects one with his left arm, but fails to do so with his right, having it ensnared by her chain. He's turned around and pulled down toward her. With the swift upward thrust of her hand, a rock column rises up slamming into Kyoto. As he tries to roll off it, she quickly races three full laps around the column to bind Kyoto to it with her chain. He struggles until he sees her calmly walk before him, standing below with Bastion to her back and Sleight tucked away.

"What are you waiting for?" Kyoto says. "If you

think you have me I suggest you go for it."

Looking like she was about to run up the column as she bends her knees, Afearia stands straight, meeting his gaze. "Kyoto. Why are you angry with me?"

"HA-HA! Like you give a shit!"

"I shouldn't. I really shouldn't... But your attitude towards me is... I guess after being down here for so long I'm starting to lose my way. You Denis are suppose to be monsters destined for extinction. Balls of dust once slain— as if to never have existed at all. It has always been a simple concept for me. Smite evil. Move on. Perhaps," taking a moment, redirecting her concerned gaze elsewhere. "Perhaps it was naïve to expect that way of thought as truth. Something I refused to believe—despite how Yadeira tried to explain it to me," she mutters.

Kyoto's eyes widen before a dangerous anger over comes them. "Don't you dare..." Afearia looks his way. "Don't you dare—speak her name, MURDERER!"

Spreading his arms as far as possible, Kyoto down flicks his wrist, creating the claw marks in the air to destroy the base of the column in order to free himself. With an angry slash, Kyoto aims his attack at Afearia as she leaps back from the falling rocks. She raises her sword Bastion before her as well. Despite her efforts, she still received four deep gashes along her torso, arms, and face. She drops Bastion and falls to her knees holding herself.

"It can't be done. You can't defend against my Phantom Claws!" he shouts before charging at his wounded foe. He slashes at her again, but this time at the flaps of her jacket to separate her from Sleight and Sovereignty. Though wounded, she struggles to get on her feet as she walks backward from him. "No more healing! No more mind tricks!"

When he slashes, Afearia jumps as far as she's capable to her side, but her hindered ability leaves her to take a shallow slash to her leg. Before touching down, she fires a chain into the woods and allows it to carry her deeper into the forest. Shockingly, Kyoto grabs her ankle and is carried along with her, "I want you to despair!" he says as his mask had become skin tight and melted fangs form over the mouth instead of slits. "I want you to despair just like she did! Then—I'll feed you your own guts!" he threatens with dark malice edging from his eyes as he squeezes her ankle. "Just like you did to her."

Diary Entry #5328

I've come to learn that most people wield knowledge as a weapon, not as a means to provide aid. Why would they? Doing so can be a danger to the world you swear to govern. As Elder Helios once told me: Too much knowledge with little wisdom, can be just as volatile as ignorance.
Sometimes I think he sees something his equals do not.

The Man and the Monster

Chapter Seventeen

With Demonweaver edging out her palm, Afearia swings her sword to cut him off from her, but he releases her before that can happen. Afearia is about to cast a fire spell, but a sudden onset of fatigue takes over. She lands and almost falls over as she stumbles. Kyoto continues to pursue and uses his Phantom Claw ability again. To avoid damage, she jumps to the side, moments before his attack can scar trees. With the swing of her arm as she flees, green seals appear to create sharp rock spires from the ground to pierce him. Kyoto sidesteps from the spires but doesn't lose his pursuing speed.

She repeats this twice with not a single hit being made. When he closes the distance and Afearia tries to guard with Bastion, he brings his claws together and slashes down on Bastion. "You blocked again," he says as she stumbled and hopped back. "Heh, old habits must die hard, even though you should've realized by now no shield can keep you from my claws." Another set of bloody claw marks appear on Afearia, straight down her left shoulder to her hip. Panting heavy and almost falling over, she drops all her swords and dismisses them to only bring forth Nebulous. "You seem sluggish, Afearia. Is it the blood loss or something else?" he smirks.

Still breathing heavy, looking as if carrying her own weight was too much, she raises her sword at Kyoto. "Why...," Afearia pants, "do you hate me?"

"Are you seriously still asking that question in your current condition?" She did not break her focus as she waited for a response, thus angering him further. "Grr, why do you even care!? We're enemies no matter what! Stand tall and fight!"

"Tell me why first."

Kyoto was truly vexed. His mask melts away some of its nightmarish features, including half his teeth and one of its eye lenses. "Because..." Looking saddened, he balls his shaky hand into a fist. "Why'd you do that—to her?" looking into her eyes with his hurt ones. "Was it because she was a Demi? She—! She was innocent! She had never taken a human life—ever!" Afearia sternly, but with a steady calm, observed his emotions while slowly letting down her guard. "She was as pure as they come. Loving... Even to me," he says sadly. "Worst of all," unballing his fist as his nightmare features return with swirling lines moving through the mask's design. "Why did you have to kill her like that!?" he shouted in his demonic voice, stirring the winds around them. "It was the act of a demon!"

"You—! I don't—"

"Of course! You wanted to hear it so it can get you off! Sadist! I will make you pay for—!"

"For what!?

"For the death of Yadeira," he said in a calm, hurt anger. Afearia becomes wide-eyed to the dark memory awakened in her. She shamefully looks to the ground. "You can play dumb, but it won't help you, it'll just piss me off more and make your death that much more gruesome."

She looks to him with regretful brows, but stern eyes. "It wasn't me."

With a dead serious face, the conversation had ended for him as he initiated the first attack by running at her. He swipes his claw at her from close range, leaving a purplish black scar in the air after Afearia evaded. Kyoto's attack left him open to her backhanded blow to his head, grounding him. Afearia's breathing has not improved, instead it's become phlegmy before a series of coughs lead to bloody ones. She falls to her knees, shaking.

Kyoto gets on all fours, "Though you evaded it, that swipe was for your heart," looking pleased with a deranged joy.

Getting on her feet, Kyoto rushes down to attack her once again, but not before Afearia swings her blade to create countless water droplets that condense to create a thick fog. He rushes right through it only to find she had fled. He screams out in anger, flexing his monstrous vocal cords.

Deeper within the forest, Afearia's sitting behind a tree, holding her wounded self in a pant. Shortly after, she coughs up more blood, covering her mouth to stifle her sounds. Afearia looks down at her wounds, noticing she was healing quite slowly compared to when she was fighting Chloe. Kyoto screams her name in the distance after a loud thud is heard. I need to conserve energy, Afearia thinks as she summons Sovereignty. I'll channel water from the ground instead of producing it myself.

As her wounds heal with the aid of Sovereignty, her weapons dismiss themselves without command. Looking confused, she notices how shaky her nerves have gotten as she's summoning Sovereignty once again. With a sudden ache in her brain, she jolts in pain holding her head with Sovereignty vanishing. She holds herself for several seconds before slowly opening her exhausted eyes. Afearia was at her limit. A second fight against such an opponent was not something she could handle at the moment.

She lowers one of her hands with a faint light enveloping her palm. If I want to stand a chance, Afearia thinks. I need to rely purely on the fundamentals. She slowly looks forward, almost as if she's come to a realization. "The basics…" She looks both ways. Let's see if all these years of training have paid off, eh Helios?

Suddenly, the upper half of the tree she's sitting behind is slashed apart. She rolls forward and turns to see Kyoto with his arm across his chest. "Follow the golden light and you'll find your illicit killer."

Afearia stands with her shallow wounds no longer bleeding in excess. Kyoto jumps the stump, looking to be ready to tear her apart until he's hit with a small gust of wind and light. It halts his advance, leaving him confused. Afearia's hands are up much like a semi-professional boxer. He shakes it off and was only able to take a step forward before she does a hook swing to produce the same attack but as a whirling mini twister. Though he blocks it, the force turns him around. He aggressively swings himself back forward, "You annoying little—" Afearia had vanished from the area once again.

From a high tree branch, Afearia's crouched down with her arm extending, forming chains from her shoulder blades to create a bow. An arrow of wind and light begins to form as she pulls back the bow and fires. With accuracy, the arrow hits Kyoto in the head, bursting into a harmless ring of fading light. He slowly looks up at Afearia.

"Not even a scratch," tapping his helmet. "You'll never shatter this. It's my manifested hate-filled resolve to kill you."

Afearia jumps down with her chains retracting. "Then I'll break it. Because your hate is misplaced. When captive, you spoke as if to hold the ideals of a hero. But that's not who I see before me. If it was a perfect world, I rather be fighting him."

"Tch, too bad. I'm running the show now," he says, confusing her a bit. "After all, I'm still imaging how you'll look dead."

"That won't happen since I'll be killing you first. You just won't be dying a hero."

"Who cares!" racing toward her. "I'm anything but!"

Fading into view, a staff made of hard light as Afearia's body moves in accordance, up smashes into his lower jaw, launching him backward. His feet touch ground and he stumbles a few feet before stopping and angrily looking at Afearia.

"It wasn't me," she tells him.

"Liar!" he says with a dramatic swing of his arm.

"It's true! I... I was indirectly responsible. But I still feel responsible."

"Because you are."

"No. It was something else."

Looking like he's about to lose his temper, he manages to simmer down. "At this point it matters very little. All I want now is to rip you in two, sounds good?"

Afearia's eyes finally gain their signature icy stare as she bends her knees to do combat. "So be it."

After a brief standoff, Kyoto makes the first move. The second his arm begins to move, Afearia reacts with twice the speed and does a half upper cut to bust him in the jaw with a wind gust, knocking his balance. Kyoto refocuses on her to see she has closed the distance from midair, spinning toward him with tucked legs.

She smacks him across the face with the pole. He recovers quickly and tries to swipe at her. But Afearia was nimble, ducking the attack and following up with a double swatting with the pole across his head. Kyoto uses his claw to slash in an upper cut motion. With an aggressive side lean, she evades and counters with a solid blow to each side of his ribs.

He tries to grab her until she flips over him in a tight ball with staff extended before herself, bashing him at the back of his head. He stumbles forward as she lands down low with spread legs and staff held to her side. Seeming unfazed, Kyoto quickly turns and slashes in her direction, creating the red claw marks. She rolls and hops to her feet, still failing to avoid the damage of his attack. The shallow scratches leave Afearia kneeling.

Kyoto slashes outward with both hands, scaring the air and making the trees around her fall on top of Afearia.

Before she's crushed, she turns and leaps backward. The moment the trees hit the ground, Kyoto had leaped in the air above the trees and double slashes over them to scar the atmosphere. Seizing the small window, Afearia uses the wind to propel her toward Kyoto, ramming the end of the staff into his forehead.

"If I can't predict your range, I'll just move toward the source!" Afearia says as she continues to push until the staff slides off his helmet and she moves pass him. Though she thought she had stunned him momentarily, she looks down to see his sinful smile upon her.

Kyoto grabs her ankle. "Dodge this."

Using his claws, Kyoto savagely separates Afearia's leg from its shin. Her weapon vanishes as she hits the ground screaming while she holds what remains of her shin. Kyoto lands down with his back to her. As he stands, he brings Afearia's limb half above his stomach.

"I can hear the pain in your screams," he calmly says. "Tell me. Did she scream like this?" He faces her with a far less menacing air. "I don't know how people like you can do it. I actually feel bad for you right now. But... When I think about what you did to Yadeira." His left hand twitches a few times before clutching hard onto what remains of her leg. "It makes your pain all the more just!" he says with his aggressive voice. He tosses the leg aside and jumps onto Afearia, choking the life out of her. "I want to see it! I want to see the light leave your eyes!"

She struggles to pry his hands open, even hitting his arms until the shell rose from his hands to protect them. Her legs are kicking up dirt as her mouth is covered in spit with the blood rushing to her head.

Seemingly by accident, Sleight was summoned from nothing in her hand, rapidly growing in length and growing through Kyoto's left shoulder, severing his arm. Releasing Afearia as he falls back in pain, he nearly chokes on his own air from the sudden arrival of this pain in his

504

arm. Sounding almost monstrous as he nearly squeals and snarls rolling wildly from Afearia until he managed to get on his knees, hunched into his lap.

Afearia happened to be in agony on her own as she turned over holding the back of her head. Sleight hits the ground and cracks before vanishing. Afearia's nose bleeds as the tight, swelling pain in her skull subsides. She opens her eyes seeing everything in a blurry, heavy light before it calms to its usual hue. She slowly sits up and finches to the throb in her chopped leg.

Kyoto is partially whimpering, holding his bloody wound as his dark shell melts off his body to the ground. He sits up breathing heavy with teary eyes, looking around as if he doesn't completely understand where he is.

He looks down at his leaky nub. "My-my-my-my-my ar-ar-arm," Kyoto stutters. "You-you're—you're scary A-A-Afearia."

Afearia, quite out of breath, stares at him for a moment, almost falling over for a second. "I didn't mean to."

"S-stop lying to me!"

"It's true! My powers are unstable. And at that time… I don't recall fully what happened, but I'm sure I know what took place…" Kyoto was actually listening to her." Inside me—lies a monster I can't control. When I fought her, I had no intention of killing her. But my anger shifted my intent and I wanted to end her life. Then I blacked out… I'm sure she wasn't the only casualty, but she was the most regrettable. That's what I wanted you to understand. Because I was hoping you weren't like them."

"Like who?"

"The humans. Not all, but some of them are quite vile. Derexen as well."

Kyoto faintly laughs. "Derexen you say?" chuckling sadly, lightly shaking his head before looking at her with pity. "You don't even know the man. Not that you care to try. You're at an opposition to not believe me." He narrows his eyes at her. "Just like I won't believe you." The black liquid comes from his wound and covers it upon extending. Kyoto looks down at it with surprise. "S-stop. I'm-I'm not done tal-talk-talking to her."

The liquid extends to reach for his fallen arm, returning it to his body. "S-s-stop!" Kyoto stutters. As his arm reattached, his demeanor changed to something sinister. "We'll stop when this murderous woman's dead," sounding nearly like a different, darker man with cold eyes locked on hers. "She killed Yadeira." He blinks, returning to his nervous self. "But-but maybe she—" His attitude changes back to his alter ego. "She lies. Let's kill her."

As his arm is nearly attached, his hands begin to be recoated in the hard shell to create his dangerous claws again. His head's covered in his protective dark shell as he slowly stands, fully ready for battle. As he marched toward her, Afearia crawls away on her elbows before he snatches her up by the ankle and tosses her behind himself next to her bloody leg.

She grabs it before hobbling away. "You're messing with my head," he mutters. "To even try and appeal to me." Kyoto swipes in her direction, breaking up the ground beside her using Phantom Claw, "What for!? We, the Demi race are still your enemies! So why bother!?" swiping to break more of the ground ahead of her.

Afearia stops and aggressively turns to him, "I don't know! I shouldn't care about any of your reasons or personalities. After all this time, I seem to be losing sight of who my enemies are. Because things are not clean cut down here." Kyoto seemed to have a sudden understanding for her at that moment, lessening his rage. "But don't get the wrong idea. I will fight every last one of you and end your lives when you face my blade."

"Heh. I wouldn't have it any other way."

Afearia fires a chain into a distant treetop and is

pulled far away. Kyoto grits his teeth and immediately chases after her.

Hidden far from her original location, Afearia sits behind a large tree breathing poorly with head bobbing. I've lost so much blood, Afearia thinks. My head is spinning and I can barely see straight. I... I have to end this. Afearia looks at her trembling hand. Twice in one night... I will shave away my life. Afearia faintly smiles. But to see their smiling faces. I will do anything.

Afearia closes her eyes, just before a gold light emits from her skin. It condenses to her hands and begins to spread through her veins. She begins to shiver as the gold light moves throughout her circulatory system. As it travels through her chest and up her neck, the shivers worsen as it seemed she was on the verge of a panic attack. When the gold filled her face, her eyes shoot open with her chest jolting forward. The gold fades with her body slowly hunching over.

"Immensus," she deeply mutters in a faint echo.

Almost mechanical, Afearia immediately sits up straight with alert eye. Every seal engraved in her body glows bright, energizing her as they shine. With just her finger, she used a combination of water and light to reattach her severed leg. She slaps the tree's trunk and slowly pulls away with a smoothly crafted wooden combat staff. Commanding the wind, it brings Afearia gently onto her feet. The winds softly turn her toward the tree, releasing her the way you would a dove. With a long, but light exhale, Afearia stares straight ahead like she can see the entire forest without trees.

With a vertical leap and a sprint, Afearia races up the tree with the winds aiding her movements and balance. She reaches the tree top and leaps over the forest. Though her vision is blocked by the leaves, it seemed to hold no issue. Afearia locked onto a leafy area and dives down at an angle.

When she plunges through the treetops, Kyoto looks up to see Afearia coming down in her luminous glory with staff pointed. He hops back before she can skewer him. Using her momentum of the staff being embedded in the dirt, she swings around her weapon and thrusts her body in his direction, smashing her joined feet in his face. As he stumbles, she advances. Kyoto attempted to swipe, but she had already come close enough to grab his wrist, halting his Phantom Claw.

She guides his hand downward and strikes his face with her knee. She follows through upon his second stumble by spinning in close and back handing him in the same part of his mask and doing and open palm strike to his ribs. Kyoto slams against a tree, but Afearia doesn't wait and attempts to kick his face in. He ducks and double jumps back while doing two breaststroke motions to release his Phantom Claw attacks. With an overhead down swing, a pillar of water shoots Afearia up into the air from her feet.

His attack destroys the trees behind her as she comes down on her foe below. Kyoto slashes the air, but Afearia was ready and uses the wind around her to aid her sharp evasion to the left. Though she was ready, trying to read the range of what you can't see still proved difficult. The attack nearly rips her right arm in two. She grabs the meaty flesh of her arm and focuses using light and water to restore her arm like she did for her leg.

When her arm is healed enough not to flap in the wind, she extends her left hand and fires a chain into the ground near Kyoto. Every chain link gains small green seals identical to the ones Afearia has on her body.

Suddenly, three fast snapping Venus fly traps made of rock come up swallowing Kyoto one by one with each larger than the last. Once she lands crouched, Afearia retracts her chain from the ground. Kyoto explodes through the top of the trap and into the air. He comes down on her with claws out. Once in range, she moves low in a half turn, bashing her back knuckles into his face, hitting the same mark as all the previous times before. He attempts to scratch her, but Afearia hops a small distance and taps the ground between them with her staff to cause a watery pillar to rise.

Kyoto quickly rolls around it to maintain his pursuit of her. However, the moment he got near, the staff's tip is rammed in his face. As he stumbles back a bit hunched, shaking off the daze, the first crack along the forehead of his mask has finally emerged.

With a roar, he rushes her down with a piercing claw thrust. Afearia swiftly ducks it and taps the ground with her staff again to bring forth a water pillar between them. Though she hopped back at an angle, his arm is hit, almost carrying him up to the sky before yanking his arm back. He chases and swipes at Afearia twice as she nimbly dodges before taping the ground repeating the same tactic. As he leaps at an angle, she drags her staff in the dirt to leave a line across the ground as the chase continues.

In equal length of the line she drew, a wall of water rises up in her defense. Kyoto rips through the water wall with his claws and jumps through. Afearia guards, but quickly steps back after her staff is split in two. She catches the halves and spreads her arms apart to release a watery crescent attack which stumbles him up against the water wall. To his surprise, he could not remove himself from the water's hold.

With a series of rhythmic taps of her broken staff to the ground and back hops to an unseen beat, pillars of water shoot up around Kyoto one by one. Looking panicked, Kyoto notices that the previous water pillars never stopped, only intensified with the new ones. Afearia tosses her staff prices up in the air and snaps her fingers, bursting the watery pillars into a dense white fog. She was gone.

The moment he begins to struggle, Afearia's staff pieces break through the fog and hit him in his face from the jagged end. The attack becomes rapid jabs that are chipping away at his mask with his cheeks, right eye, and some of his mouth being revealed as glimpses of her thrusting hand is seen from the fog. The wall collapses as Kyoto stumbles back in a daze, holding his face as he falls to his knee.

Coming from below his knees in mid swing, Afearia cracks her staff across his jaw, breaking off a large piece. He momentarily falls on all fours before bouncing back up. He makes a second back hop and slashes downward, but before he can complete his slash, his opponent jams her staff into his armpit and swings him wildly to release his body high up above. He screams as he is unable to break the might of the momentum carrying him away.

Though barely able to see, Kyoto vaguely sees her zip through the air above him, then coming down like a bullet as she melds a knight's sword using hard light. As he tries to retaliate with his claws to defend, he was at her mercy. Afearia slashes down through his mask, shattering it and his claws to reveal his shocked face. Kyoto hits the ground and lies still, looking up at the night sky, almost with peaceful eyes. He groans a couple times before turning over on his hands and knees. Before he can lift his head all the way, Afearia's sword rises beside his face from behind.

Kyoto slowly looks up , "You-you-you," he stutters. "Yadeira did-did-didn't deserve this," lowering his head for his impending judgment.

Afearia holds her saddening gaze for moment, lowering her sword only a bit, "She didn't."

Kyoto's eyes widen in surprise to her response. He is quickly angered afterwards. "You dare mock me!" he says with dark liquid edging from his neck a little. "You piece of—" jerking his head back to see she was expressing genuine shame and sadness. He didn't expect it, softening his eyes and stopping the return of his dark liquid.

"This—isn't fun for me. You and I have something in common. Vengeance. That burning desire feeds a darkness in us. It gives birth to something that is no longer us. Every day we struggle to control what that is. You believe you're a hero. But what are you if you fall prey to your own hate? You have every right to hate me. I'm the reason she's dead, despite my wishes. But don't become the very thing you live your life to fight against. Don't let the beast define your existence," she advised in a near personal sentiment.

Kyoto looks forward with sad eyes. "It's too late…" he mutters. His eyes rise toward the forest. "Your friends are here."

"What?" In the distance, Afearia can hear Adrian, Veronica, and Zaiah calling out to her.

"Go to them."

"But… I don't know what to do about you yet."

"If you kill me now, that's a fine step. If you don't, I'll still have a job to do. It just won't be driven by hate. Either way, the outcome is not favorable for you." Afearia looks toward the direction she hears the kids' voices calling. "Go." Hesitant, she takes a few steps before he halts her, "One more thing. Yadeira… Did she get to play the piano one last time before she passed? Heh…," vaguely smirking. "She loved that thing."

Afearia weakly smiles, "She did. And it was the best piece I've ever heard."

Kyoto lowers his head with a sorrowful smile and closed eyes as he silently cried. "Marvelous," he mutters.

Afearia lightly nods before racing off into the woods. Kyoto lowered his body further to the ground, crying a little harder as his breathes puff into the dirt.

"Kyoto," a woman says from the trees beside him. He lifts himself up a bit and looks into the trees as Minerva steps forward with her yellow eyes piercing the dark. She emotionlessly stands beside him, looking down coldly.

511

"Under governmental jurisdiction, you are currently under apprehension."

Out in the woods, Zaiah and the kids continue calling out for Afearia. They press on until the rushing sound of a fast approaching person comes their way. Zaiah swiftly pushes the kids behind him and faces the rustling. It stops, moments before an unhappy Ludwig emerges.

"Ludwig!" Veronica says with glee. "How did you get here so fast!?"

Ludwig turns his head from them, "Forgive me..."

"Huh?"

Ludwig slowly raises his hands and launches them at the children. The hands snare them and brings the kids to him. "No!" Zaiah says, late to stop him. "I knew this was a set up."

"Captain Minerva ordered the apprehension of the kids. But you're expendable."

"Ludwig...?" Veronica says with sad eyes. "I thought we were friends."

Ludwig's eyes fill with grief. "I... I have no choice."

"There's always a choice," looking him in the eyes. "Anya taught me that. No one makes that for you. I would've thought your mom would feel the same."

Ludwig is torn as his eyes downcast. "I... I..."

With the raise of Zaiah's greenish-white glowing finger, wood spires come from above and pierce Ludwig's biceps. He drops the kids as the wood spires grow and enter the ground and take root as young, leafless trees. Afearia soon lands down before Zaiah holding her staff. She stands with her back to him as she watches the pinned Ludwig with caution.

"Anya!" the kids happily say as they run up to her.

Zaiah smiles and attempts to greet her. "I asked you to keep them safe," Afearia says, stopping his advance and ending his relief to see her. "Could you be anymore useless?" She turns her head halfway toward him with a glare.

"I-I had it under control," Zaiah responds.

"Yeah right." She turns to face Ludwig while guiding the kids behind her without breaking eye contact.

"It's you," Ludwig says, looking quite surprised. He notices despite her appearance, Afearia's hands were lightly trembling. "Fear? No. You're tired. Exhausted even. Are you sure you can handle a fight with me?" Because of his keen observation, Adrian takes notice as well, seeing how much she's sweating and the irregular breathing she's trying to hide. Before he could speak, Ludwig detaches his arms from his stitched elbows and creepily has them independently pull the saplings out by the root, causing them to wither and die, releasing him. "Afearia," he calmly says as his arms' stringed flesh wiggle about to partially reattach. "Will you come peacefully?"

Afearia twirls her staff and gets into a battle stance with her weapon pointed at him. He sighs, taking steps toward her until Veronica stands between them.

"Veronica!?" Afearia shouts.

"Please," Veronica pleas to Ludwig with hands joined together and teary eyes. "You're supposed to be my friend. Don't do this, Mr. Ludwig." He stares at her with an emotionless face. Despite that, Veronica runs at him with determined belief.

"Veronica, don't!"

The moment Afearia stepped forward to stop her, a strong sensory disrupting migraine hits her. She falls to her knees holding her head in glaring pain as all her usually unseen seals begin blinking in a slow, pulsing rhythm. Adrian and Zaiah run up behind her in concern while Veronica kindly, but bravely, takes Ludwig's hand while looking in his eyes with the same innocence.

"Mr. Ludwig," Veronica says to him. "You are a good person—a hero! I... I can't be wrong. You're so nice.

You—"

Ludwig pulls away, taking a few steps back and turning his back on them. "I'm only doing what I was told. Capturing Afearia is my duty. Individual ideals and wants are not allowed for a united body to function. That's how cancers are formed. And when you're a cancer." He turns partway to stare at Afearia glaring in pain at him. "The body seeks to remove it." He looks down at the sad, hopeful Veronica. "Never thank your enemies. For it falls on deaf ears."

Like a speeding snake, his detached arm grabs Veronica inside his hand and carries her over the group. Zaiah turns back to Ludwig and screams in anger, but was suddenly snared by numerous black flesh threads from head to toe. The threads had also captured Adrian and Afearia as they squirm to get free. Suddenly, they all feel a light-headed free falling sensation for a moment. When it stops and their feet touch ground, the black threads unbind them.

They look around to find themselves beside the car Zaiah stole in search of Afearia. "What just happened?" Zaiah asks.

Veronica walks ahead toward the bushes, looking around just as confused as them. Barely catching it, a glimpse of Ludwig's detached limbs scurry away under a bush. She lightly smiles and looks up into the forest.

"Thank you," Veronica mutters.

"Come on," Zaiah says. "Let's get out of here before he realizes his mistake.

Adrian helps the weakened Afearia into the backseat of the car. When Zaiah tries to help, she slaps his hand away. "Don't touch me," Afearia snaps. "Just drive."

He huffs in disappointment and rushes to the driver side door while gesturing for Veronica to hurry along. They hop inside and immediately flee the area.

Back in the forest, Ludwig stands alone staring up at the moon with peace in his heart before smiling. Kids..., he thinks. Only when they shed their tears can it rekindle the lost innocence in our hearts.

When Ludwig's arms return from the woods and reattach to his body, he puts his hands up and gets on his knees as Minerva steps out into the clearing from behind him. Dragged beside her is Kyoto cuffed and bound limb from limb with a black rubber-like material. The same material even binds his mouth and eyes as she effortlessly carries him from the connecting chain on his wrist and ankles.

"Your treason will not be overlooked," Minerva speaking to Ludwig.

Ludwig lowers his head. "No. I would think not."

"Punishment is imminent."

"Yes."

"Then why?"

"Hmph," he smirks. "Sometimes we as individuals have to forge our own paths. And we can't very well do that under the iron hand of a ruler, can we? Sometimes... we need to find our own inner hero in order to sleep at night." Kyoto's head perks up a little. "If we don't, we lose ourselves and only become an extension of someone else's will. And that—is a sad life to live. Empty—and without heart.

Minerva's face can barely pass as astonished, though rarely present and hard to see, she was expressing something through her deadpan demeanor. Empathic understanding. With speedy composure to match, Minerva rushes over and double chops Ludwig in the back of his neck and his major neck arteries. He drops cold to the dirt. She calmly stares into the dark of the forest, seeming to reminisce. Minerva tosses Kyoto atop of Ludwig and presses her dominating foot on Ludwig's head before warping the three of them elsewhere.

Hours after their capture, Kyoto remains bound as he calmly awaits his judgment while kneeling in the middle of Derexen's meeting room floor. Derexen stands several feet before Kyoto with Valerie at his side holding documents. Standing beside Kyoto as insurance to keep him subdued are Minerva and Glenn.

"On the accounts of this investigation," Valerie continuing to read out his crimes, "we've discovered unlawful actions with witness testimony. Manslaughter. Murder. Disobedience. Murder through manipulation. Vol—"

"Murder through manipulation?" Minerva asks, looking to Valerie with her yellow irises.

"Yes."

"Back at the building," Glenn explains, "Kyoto calibrated for my shots. The first set killed two men, both head shots. A deception I did not appreciate," down cutting his eyes at Kyoto. He leans into Kyoto's view as he remained solemn with shameful eyes fixed beyond Glenn's presence. "Just because you're a monster, doesn't mean the rest of us want to take a ride to hell with you."

No one spoke after Glenn stood back in position. Valerie, seeming reluctant to continue the report as she glances at Derexen who has not broken eye contact with the somber Kyoto since they began. She takes a moment before regrettably continuing.

"On the account of your actions, how do you plead?" Valerie asks Kyoto.

"Guilty," Kyoto sadly replies.

"You're aware your actions… will result in execution… if not proven false."

"Yes."

"Any defense?"

"None."

Valerie lowers her documents in sorrowful frustration. "We were coming for you, Kyoto. Why couldn't you just—?"

"Lady Valerie. Do not burden yourself with rhyme

or reason. Carry out your sentence. Lord knows I deserve it."

Valerie sadly shakes her head before looking down for a moment. She looks up at Kyoto and steps toward him with a heart of pity until Derexen raises his arm before her.

"Stand away from him," Derexen orders them. Minerva slowly backs away while Glenn turns his back on Kyoto, sucking his teeth in disgust and walking away.

"And you wanted to be a hero," Glenn grumbles.

Kyoto's eyes slightly lift from his lifeless stare as he seemed to almost be waking inside, "Yes. To create a better world. A better world," slightly raising his voice, getting Glenn to stop and face him. "What dreams I've had of it. Being a hero. Having others look into these eyes and upon my face, filling with joy on sight. But how can that happen? When the one they believed in is covered in bloody bodily tissue and the tears of the fallen. What will they say then?" looking up at his comrades with tears in his eyes. "Will they hug me? Hold my hand? Will they thank me?" he strongly says as his bottom lip quivers. "No. They will condemn me. But no worse than I condemn myself. A slave to his dark desires," weeping with a defeated dropping of his head.

Derexen, ever so slowly, begins to approach Kyoto. "I once thought if I could be a hero like other men, I could be happy," Kyoto continues. "And loved. But I wished for the impossible. Because my heart is filled with dark desires. Dark lustful want and burning hate—consuming me from the inside out." Kyoto looks down at his twitchy left arm. "And the outside in."

Derexen brushes back his coat, revealing Catastrophe pressed firmly to the right side of his waist as he neared. He raises his hand over the pommel, ready to cut him down. Everyone waited with tense eyes for what was soon to transpire.

"For tonight, all has been made clear," Kyoto

talking indirectly. "The monster… the thing I'm always fighting to hold back was never real. It was never trapped in my heart. It was trapped in my soul." Derexen halts with the most miniscule twitch from his hand hovering over his sword's pommel. Derexen—had hesitated. "For all these years I've pointed the blame on everything outside of myself. This thing. I've created this image." The black mercury-like liquid rises up his neck, causing everyone to take cautious measure, except for Derexen, despite being the closest to this possible danger.

"For this savage image merely reflects," Kyoto says in a gruff voice as his mask nearly completes. When the liquid encases his head and hardens, it is reminiscent to an oni mask, "The unholy travesty that is my heart!" he cries, looking up at Derexen through the wide sleek eyeholes."

Staring into each other's eyes, the raw anguish in Kyoto is undeniable. Valerie stood with bated breath as her eyes are on the verge of bursting with tears as she watches his heartbreaking reveal unfold. Even Glenn's anger toward him has vanished as he could barely believe what he's seeing.

In a sad low huff, Kyoto's head bobs down, staring into the marble floor in disgrace, "Lord Derexen. Why was I reborn with this deformity and no opportunity for repentance? Tell me." Derexen, staring down at him, still holds his hand over his sword, knowing what he had to do soon. "I would rather have stayed the corpse I was than come back as the man I am." Glenn and Minerva's eyes meet with a common thought for their broken comrade. "Stop hesitating… You've let this fool meander long enough. Come take me. End this beast that grovels at your feet." He looks at Derexen as his mask melts away to reveal his tear soaked face covered in a serene acceptance of what's to come. "I've already lost to my demons. Don't let me walk out of this room and do it again."

The moment Derexen grips his handle, Kyoto

slowly closes his eyes, lightly exhaling from his partially parted lips. Yadeira… Kyoto thinks in the peaceful sunny meadow on the hill of floors where Yadeira waits with her back to him at the top of the grassy fields. I'm coming…

With masterful precision, Derexen cleanly decapitates Kyoto with his bloody head flying across the room. Valerie had jumped and greatly stifled her unintentional scream into her hand. Though everyone knew this was going to be the outcome, everyone was taken aback in one way or another, including Glenn, as he watches his ex-comrade's blood wet the floor.

Nobody moves, including Derexen. He holds his pose for a few seconds before slowly lowering his sword and dismissing it into the darkness. He turns, taking two steps toward the door. "How easy was that for you?" Glenn asks with stern eyes. Derexen pauses for a moment, but doesn't acknowledge Glenn or his question before proceeding out the room. "Easy enough, I suppose."

Derexen takes his time to descend to the lower levels of his palace to reach his dining room. Parting his double doors, he enters leaving it ajar before taking his seat at the head of the table. Derexen leans back and stares through the dark crack in the door, not blinking for a moment as his mind dwells. Soon after arriving, Valerie almost comes in view, hesitating as she stands at the edge. She takes a silent breath and enters the dining room.

"Yes, Valerie," sounding vaguely exasperated.

"I-I don't mean to disturb you, but we do have another problem that needs your attention. It's Ludwig."

"He refused orders from a higher-up in my council. That is not a problem, Valerie. Let his country's leader handle it. Have Minerva see to his deportation since he has openly obstructed justice in my land."

"Yes. Understood."

"Is there anything else?"

Valerie lightly lowers her head. "Before collecting

Kyoto from the palace dungeon, he had written down a message for you to read. He said it was a parting gift by you allowing him to be a knight in your court."

"A message?"

"Detailed information about Afearia's abilities and skills to be mindful of when facing her."

Derexen slowly nods to himself. "Even in death, you emerged a better man...," he mutters about Kyoto while looking away from her. "Will that be all?" seeming more sullen than before.

"Yes, sir. I'll get to work."

Valerie turns away and glances at Derexen, noticing he had already drifted off in thought as he stared at the wall. She lightly sighs and walks away.

Down in Derexen's dungeon, Ludwig sits in a dark, concrete cell with power suppressing cuffs. He sits in thought, staring at the stone floor until he hears his metal cell door unlocking. Minerva stands before him with judging eyes.

"Let's go," Minerva says. He stands and approaches her. She grabs him and pushes him forward to walk ahead of her as they move through the aisle of cells. As they proceed, Minerva is repeatedly glancing at his back before balling a fist so tight that it hurts, briefly causing her eyes to flash her deadly irises. "Though I respect your resolve to a degree, some decisions are selfish and irrelevant to a grander cause like ours. You may have a clear conscious, but you've wasted your life."

Ludwig stops, causing Minerva to almost run into his large body. "In terms of human achievement, what cause is grander than self-fulfillment?" She does not answer, just cautiously watches for any settle movement from him. "You're wrong on this one, captain. No life is more wasted than living purely under the wishful whimsy of another." Minerva's eyes slightly widen in understanding to his moral compass. He turns his head halfway to her. "I admire—everything you've ever done for this world and your country. But every time I see people who brazenly walk the selfless road to a promised land, I have to ask myself. Is this the embodiment of a being with unrivaled strength to bare the sins of man, or is this the soul of a person who's got nothing else to live for?"

Minerva stared into his eye, as he did not turn away. Ludwig wanted an answer from the solider he holds the most admiration for. "I can no longer feel happiness in my heart. But loyalty and duty does not require self-satisfaction. To expect such a thing can only mean you were never fit for the cause. Your heart was never fit to harm."

He turns away from her and softly smiles. "You're right." He moves along with Minerva soon following.

The two of them reach Derexen's lobby where Kalju and Takahashi wait to pick up their traitor. "We apologize for his insubordination," Takahashi says as the four of them approach one another. "It came to a surprise for us all."

Coming in the middle together, Minerva pushes Ludwig toward them, "Just get him out of here." They take him by the arms and turn to leave, but Ludwig doesn't budge. He turns his head to Minerva and smiles at her, nodding farewell. Kalju pulls out a warping device to transport the three of them out the palace. Minerva stares where Ludwig once stood before turning and taking the center stairs up the palace.

Diary Entry #6200

Love. I've come to learn there is a difference in loving someone and being in love with someone... I now have both.

When the Levee Breaks

Chapter Eighteen

Derexen's palace is silent. Teleporting into his lobby is Valerie. She slowly looks around, then proceeds in a cautious manner. Valerie climbs her way up to Derexen's bedroom floor with her anxiety starting to rise. She nears his double doors with one of them ajar. Valerie inches to enter before suddenly pressing her back to the shut door, breathing a little heavy. Calming herself with a saddened face, she turns her body to the door and presses herself to it, feeling the door almost tenderly with her palm.

Valerie slowly slides her hand down the door, looking sadder as her eyes move about in a searching manner. Her hand moves toward the knob, but she suddenly halts with a slight gasp. Valerie warps down to the lobby looking a little panicked as she walks to the middle of the room. Her shoulders lower as an onset sigh leaves her.

"I knew you'd leave the moment you felt me." She turns her head to the palace doors. "Derexen," she says with a heavy heart, warping from the palace soon after.

After driving non-stop from the frost, Afearia and her party arrive at the nearest town. The car's parked a safe distance from the town to prevent being spotted. Zaiah steps out the car, checking if they were safe. When Afearia and the children step out, Zaiah halfheartedly smiles because of her stern expression.

"I've been here before," Zaiah tells them. "We should be able to get rest and all the supplies we need in no time." Afearia takes the kids and walks toward the town. "Hey, hold up!" Rushing behind them. "I know the area. From this side of town the motel is only two blocks straight down. We should go there first and—"

Without warning, Afearia turns around and punches Zaiah in the face. He hits the ground as the kids watch him lie still in astonishment. "You had one job," Afearia irritably says. "I trusted you. And you let them fall into enemy hands."

"Anya!?" Adrian shouts as he pulls on her to stop.

Zaiah sits up wiping his mouth, "I didn't expect him to be there. It caught me by surprise. But I swear to you that I wasn't going to let them get hurt. I had a plan."

"It shouldn't have gotten that far to begin with."

"You're right," getting onto his feet. "I was overwhelmed by the dangers around us."

"I should knock you back on your—" readying her fist.

"Anya, stop it!" Adrian still trying to hold her back. "It wasn't his fault! Elliot betrayed you and took us hostage. If he went against him, Elliot would have killed us all. Ludwig was unexpected."

"Hmph, sounds like excuses for his incompetence."

"I swear I had more control over the situation than not," Zaiah adds. "I swore I would protect them and I mean it." Afearia's vision suddenly blurs for a moment while he's still talking, almost losing all ability to hear. "If I—"

"Enough," Afearia waving off his reasoning. "Be useful and take them to that motel you were mentioning and wait for me. Or is that still too much to ask?"

Zaiah huffs at her doubts about him and walks beside the children. "Come on, guys. Let's get you two somewhere safe."

The three of them walk into town while Afearia limps behind the car panting as she slides down to the ground holding her leg. She looks at the mess of her severed leg which is being held together by magic alone. A magic that was failing due to her injury beginning to leak blood. Afearia nervously holds her leg, sweating in a dizzy pain.

"Please. Don't fail me now."

Taking several deep breaths, she calmly raises her hand to summon her Empyrean Blade, Sovereignty. Afearia carefully focused as the light and water poured away with the rapid stitching of her leg tissues. When she's fully patched up, she dismisses her sword and leans her head back, exhaling loudly in relief. The moment she stood up and took a single step, her eyes are instantly swallowed in black for less than a second.

Afearia screams and falls on her back holding her eyes as the painful feeling of strained dried eyes becomes abundantly overwhelming. Suddenly, all the pain stops. She slowly removes her hands, looking around in confusion. She sits up, cautiously looking around before scurrying on all fours to the car's side view mirror. She looked her eyes over in every way, even pulling her eyelids, but there were no signs of blackness in them. Though there was no evidence of trouble, she slowly stood with highly concerned brows before heading into town.

Afearia easily finds the motel and enters with her right eye shut. She sees Zaiah standing and talking with the kids while they somewhat frown sitting on the lobby's bench. She comes up behind him and irritably glances at him before cutting his story short.

"I'll get us a room for the night," Afearia addressing the kids.

"I hope it doesn't bother you, but I already took care of that," Zaiah says. "I got my room on the lower floor. You guys are on the third. Is that okay?"

She just stares coldly at him before presenting her hand, "Keys." Zaiah hands her the room keys, still aware she wasn't pleased with him. "Kids, let's go." She turns to walk, but the kids remained seated. "Hellooo?" emphasized with annoyance.

Reluctant, the siblings stand and begin to follow

her. "Gu-guys?" Zaiah halting them. "I'm—really sorry I
didn't do better. I—messed things up and put you two in a
lot of danger. I wish I did a better job. I just thought you
guys should know that."

"Thank you for looking after us the way that you
did," Adrian says. "We wouldn't have survived without
you."

"Thank you, Zaiah," Veronica says before forcing a
smile through her bitter feelings of the situation. "You did
great," giving him an optimistic thumbs up.

The children walk on up the stairs while Afearia
maintained her cold stare at Zaiah until she catches an
unexpected glimpse of someone standing behind him. But
only for a moment.

"You alright?" Zaiah asks, almost touching her
shoulder.

Afearia brushes his hand away aggressively, "Mind
your business." She storms off toward the stairwell to
follow the children. Afearia and the kids reach their third
floor room and enter with heads hung low. Afearia turns
the light on and locks the door while the kids stand lost in
the middle of the room with eyes to the floor. "How much
of our stuff did you guys manage to keep?" turning to see
their frowning faces. "Alright, what's wrong now? I came
back, didn't I? No need to—"

"I don't care about that," Adrian says under his
breath. "Why…? Why? Why do you always have to treat
people like that!?"

"You need to lower your voice," holding her finger
at him with rough eyes. "Be mature and speak your mind
without the attitude."

He grits his teeth, but quickly calms his temper.
"You hit him. A man who only wants to help and be close
to you—to us. What for? Ever since you've been back
you've been cruel to everyone. No better than the Demis
you kill. Pushing around the weaker. You're no better. No

better than," readying to angrily say something he doesn't mean. "No better than the king himself! You're just like Derex—"

With crazed rage, Afearia fires a chain to wrap around Adrian and yank him into her balled fist, lifting him off the ground as the chain rattles and she stared deep into his eyes with vicious intent. She drops him to the floor as her chain retracts, but she glares down at the teary-eyed boy who quickly wipes his tears and runs out the room.

"Brother!" Veronica shouts as she chases after him.

"But Afearia doesn't follow like a good parent would," the intrusive narration of a man says. "As she stares into the floorboards, the nagging thought grows greater. Is she incapable of having this makeshift family love her back as much as she loves them?"

Stepping from a darkened corner of the room is a fair-skinned man dressed in a white tux and a blood red tie. Appearing to be in his mid thirties as he leans on his white cane with a rounded jade gemstone as a handle, centering the cane between his outpointed white snake skin shoes. The man smirks with the brim of his white fedora hiding half of his face while leaving his well-groomed black beard in view. His curly black hair is near shoulder length along his strong jaw.

"She knows," the man continues. "She knows this is just another step. Another step into the gray. Afearia... You're losing them," he says with a charming glee as he lifts his head to stare at her with his dark brown eyes, sharp pupils and a part shaved into his left eyebrow. Afearia doesn't acknowledge his presence, she just turns her head away from him. "You were going to hit him, right? Maybe beat him red like a common brat. The nose would have been the first punch. Then his...," looking as if to be sensing something in the air. "Nose again?" looking devilishly proud and surprised. "Merciless to even those you care about."

She storms off toward the bathroom. He watches her with a smile, and as soon as she enters the next room, he's standing in the bathroom corner as she stands before the sink, staring at her own reflection.

"Afearia's breathing has become a bit irregular as her fears have begun to manifest," the man in white narrates. "She stares at her reflection, wanting to be calm in the face of the likely danger that's blooming inside her." Afearia closes her eyes and starts muttering, causing the man in white to make a quizzical head tilt. "Wishing to block me out, she recites an old mantra taught to her in order to fight her demon. But it won't do much good. Because deep down, she misses it. Don't you?" addressing Afearia directly.

Afearia's muttering becomes auditable as he walks up behind her with a judging, sly expression. "In my darkest hour, this is my space. Free of negatively, I will be safe." Afearia repeats these words in an effort to ward off the intrusive thoughts in her mind.

The man in white lightly smirks, "Even now you're thinking how can this be? Is Adrian okay? What do I do? I wanna taste." Afearia stops with wide eyes of shock by his words. She shakes it off and closes her eyes to resume her mantra. He brushes the hair from her face as he stares at her like a pretty doll. "Which do you miss most? Is it the taste? My touch," grazing his hand over the top left of her breast.

Like an eerie chill when touched by a creeping spider, Afearia quickly moved away and sat on the toilet with knees up and head tucked as she covers her ears with tightly shut eyes. "In my darkest hour, this is my space!" repeating it loudly and with heightened panic. "Free of negativity, I will be safe! In my darkest hour, this is my space! Free of negativity, I will be safe!"

She repeats this three more times, becoming louder to drown out the endless murmurs the man had constructed.

It had become silent. She slowly opens her eyes to

see he was gone.

"Anya?" Veronica calling her attention toward the doorway. "You okay?"

Afearia, seeming confused, lowers her hands and feet to the floor. "I'm fine. Where's your brother?"

"He ran to Zaiah's room."

"Oh," seeming a little saddened as she looked toward the floor.

"He's… really mad at you."

"And you?"

"Huh?"

"Are you mad at me?"

"Anya, you've become so scary. Brother was only worried about you. We love you, Anya. We've never seen you act like this toward nice people. Why?"

Afearia remains silent for a moment, not feeling any need to address her question. "What room does Zaiah stay in?" Veronica didn't want to tell, but she knew she didn't have a choice.

A knock is heard at Zaiah's door. He hops up off the floor where Adrian sadly laid while they talked. He opens the door and sees Afearia sternly standing before him and Veronica nervously standing beside her.

"Afearia, let me explain," Zaiah says with the sense of a tongue lashing coming his way. "He came banging on neighbors' doors looking for me. I let him in for just a moment. He was really upset and I didn't want to turn him away, but I was just about to come and tell you about it."

Afearia was staring down at the saddened Adrian the whole time Zaiah was rambling. Her eyes roll onto him after he stopped talking. "Well? Move."

The moment Afearia takes a step inside, Adrian shoots up in near panic, "Zaiah!?"

"Hey, come on," Zaiah says to Adrian. "You guys just had a little spat. There's no need to be afraid."

"What?" Afearia says in an offended manner. "He

is not afraid of me, idiot. Adrian, let's go." Adrian lowers his head to the floor. "Adrian!?"

When Adrian fearfully flinches, Zaiah blocks her path, "Maybe you should lighten up a little. What's going on with you? Why are you so angry?"

Afearia gives him a nasty glare. "I'm about to remove you from this plane," causing Zaiah to fearfully swallow spit.

"I won't go," Adrian says. "I... I don't feel safe with you."

Afearia stares at Adrian with astonished hurt in her eyes. Zaiah sees this and turns himself to half face Adrian, "Hey, buddy, don't say that. I'm sure whatever happened, you—"

"I don't feel safe! I won't go!"

"Brother...," Veronica says with concern on her face.

Zaiah stands aside to invite Afearia inside, "Maybe you two should talk in a neutral space."

Afearia stares at Adrian for a long moment of uncomfortable silence before looking away to hide her pain. "No. He's right to feel that way. I am an unholy, veil monster after all." Adrian looks to the floor, gritting his teeth with regret. "Veronica, go with your brother."

"But, Anya—!"

"He's your brother, Veronica. You need to stay together at all cost. I shouldn't have to tell you that. Go."

Veronica sighs with a low head as she reluctantly enters the room. Zaiah watches her slow walk before looking to Afearia, "I don't think this is—"

"It's okay," sounding a bit defeated. "Better with you than alone," walking away and returning to her room.

Upon her return, she shuts the door and slides down to the floor. She bumps her head out of frustration at herself, exhaling in bother. "It's ironic how you lost the boy." She slowly opens her eyes and sees the man in white standing across the room, "You tried so hard to make it work. Doing all a false mother could to hold on to her makeshift family. But did you really think you could?" As she stares at him, he tilts his head at her, "I'm worried. What do I do? How can I show them I love—"

"GET OUT OF MY MIND!" angrily flailing her feet and hands before they silently stare at each other. She quickly stands and storms off into the bathroom.

"Hello to you too, dear," he says with his irises turning blood red and his sclerae turning pitch black.

Roughly splashing her face with water and washing it, her troubled feelings mount and she slams her frustrated hands on the sink, "Why are you here? Why like this?"

"Admittedly, it has much to do with how you died. I was on the rise and then—lights out. I was lost in your mind. Even I thought I died. All ways back to you were scattered into billions of false doors and intertwining roads made of yours and my memories. It was a labyrinth. It was hopeless... Until you started pushing yourself. You were opening doors, lighting roads that were once shadowed from me. Reconnecting fragmented spiritual pathways to your soul every time you pushed to your limits. You were guiding me home. And now, after passing through the last door, here I am, standing in wait for the final bough to break."

Afearia shuts the water off and walks back into the room in a frantic manner while keeping up appearances of bravery. "That won't happen."

"She tries to convince herself she can overcome, but her mind is swimming with doubts and fear."

"Shut up," looking out the window as if being stalked.

"This was new for her. Dealing with this monster dwelling in her heart has never been a simple matter. But something was not right. He's—"

"I said stop!" yelling at him.

The man suddenly ages down to his mid twenties, gaining a confident air about him as he smiles at her with devious intent. "I've paid too much attention to him. He's getting in. How the hell do I fight this?" he smoothly mocks.

"Sasano!"

He stares at her with little indication that he was concerned by her rising fear and panic. Afearia closes her eyes and begins reciting her mantra. "That won't do you any good at this stage. You're already too far along. Are you listening?" She recites the words louder and faster. "Is that what we're doing now? Drowning out my voice?"

While she tries to use her mantra, Sasano cheerfully begins to hum a song while looking off to the ceiling like he's staring up at a beautiful sky. Afearia stops and slowly looks at him with disgust.

"Stop it," she mutters. "That was a special song. Don't taint it with your evil schemes!" She turns from him and begins anxiously pacing. "Don't engage with him. Just don't."

Afearia stops pacing after awhile and takes a slow breath raising her arm summoning Eternity as the chains cone up. It was struggling to come forth until she calls the sword's name. The blade reveals itself, leaving her hunched over and out of breath with the spirit of Demeseus appearing.

"How did it—?" Demeseus was asking until he notices the frightened look in her eyes." Is everything alright?"

"He's here."

"Who's here?"

"The one who sows death wherever he walks."

Demeseus sternly looks around the room. "I don't understand. There's no one here."

"He's here and he's messing with me. Taunting me. He's—he's."

"What are you talking about?"

"Nothing works!" she freaks. "Sleep's impossible. Mental Universe will be ineffective. And mediation will get me no where since he interacts with my senses."

"Like a hallucination?"

"It's more than that. He talks to me. He... He touches me," she says with shame and a lower voice with arms crossed.

"What's he doing now?"

"Humming my favorite song. He's drowning me out for trying to drown him out." She shakes her head," I don't get it. How could this happen?"

"Well, we knew he wasn't gone. He must have been lost inside you and the stress of using your powers raw and going through such intense battles must have been a beacon for him."

"Well, damn," Sasano smirking as he sits on the hotel dresser. "He's good. Much better than you. He put all that together so quickly. How will you ever measure up to him?"

"Shut up!" Afearia screams at Sasano.

"Hey! Hey!" Demeseus refocusing Afearia's attention. "Do not acknowledge him! You're talking to me now. Let's strategize. What do we do to stop this? We talked about this, remember?"

Afearia thinks before having a realization. "You're right! The plan we—" She stops herself, looking over at Sasano seeming curious about what they're planning. She leans to Demeseus. "He's trying to eavesdropping," she whispers.

"But I already know what you're planning," Sasano says, causing her to look back at him with concern. He points to his eyes, then points at her with a wink.

"Don't care," Demeseus says. "He can't do anything to stop it. But our plan is only a last resort. You can still repress him."

She turns from him and walks over to a wall mounted shelf and stares over it in deep thought with saddened eyes. "I can't." With the wave of her arm, twelve corked vials with black felt tied tightly around the neck of each vial magically appear. Afearia sadly lines each vial in a row near the edge.

"As long as you're mentally intact, the battle for control isn't over. You can't let past failures to suppress him be a reason to just throw the towel. You have to stop... letting him have his way."

Frustrated, Afearia looks up in a huff as she leans forward. "Demeseus, I'm tired. I'm tired of this endless fight from within. The time without him pulling and scratching at me. To be allowed to freely fight, act out and feel however I wished without consequence was a long running dream of mine. It was the best gift..." She turns to him. "This isn't living, Demeseus. Constantly checking my vitals. Looking at the corners of my eyes for signs of his arrival. Adopting countless methods to slow the ravaging disease growing inside of me. And like many incurable diseases... I will break. And I will die."

"Not on my watch."

"Demeseus—"

"What? You have more reasons why you don't want to fight? Because that's not what I want to hear. You are so much stronger than you could possibly know. You can reach the end of this tale, never letting him roam again. You've made it this far. No reason to stop now. So you have to live in a cautious manner from time to time. But he can't take your loved ones unless you let him."

"But don't you see how tiring that is!?" she says as she walks toward the window beside Sasano.

"I do... Which is why we've taken precautions. And no. Those you've been forced to kill are not your fault. As long as you give it your all to resist, how can it be? But if you give in now because it seems hopeless, it will be."

With crossed arms, Afearia thinks to herself while tapping her finger to her elbow. Sasano had lowered himself to her tapping finger, watching it with a smile before looking up at her. "You're right. I shouldn't break stride, regardless of the situation."

"That's my girl," Demeseus smiles.

She walks up beside him, wiping her mouth, looking almost pale. "Is it alright to be scared?"

"Of course," he says optimistically. "It's all part of the human experience."

She chuckles and smiles. "Demeseus, I—" A knock is heard from the door. They look at the door, then each other. Afearia leans Eternity beside the shelf where she lined the vials before going to open the door. When she does, Zaiah's leaning his palms on the doorframe with a serious look on his face

"Can we talk?" Zaiah asks.

Afearia glances back at Demeseus. "Yeah, I suppose. One minute." She walks up to Eternity and air writes with a white glow at her fingertip. She pokes the sword and it glows white for a second. "Wait here for me," speaking only loud enough for Demeseus to hear. "This way I won't need to call you again for a few hours."

"Smart," Demeseus says. "Freeing up your mind to focus on you and not maintaining me as an expenditure."

She nods and walks out the door. "I'll be back soon."

"Afearia—" Zaiah was saying.

"Let's take a walk," she says as they leave the room. The two of them leave the motel walking side by side down the street. They silently move with eyes low into the distance, wishing to be the first to speak. Afearia lightly rolls her eyes. "Are you going to speak sometime before sunup?"

"I was trying to figure out a way to say this without having it end with you punching me."

She stops them by gently pulling his shoulder. "I… That shouldn't have happened. You didn't deserve it. You—didn't do anything wrong."

"I know," he says nonchalantly before proceeding.

Afearia narrows her eyes in irritation before following. "If you knew that then why were you looking for an apology?"

"An apology? I never said I needed one. I'm actually not here on my behalf. There's a little man I know who's losing sight of his beloved Anya."

Afearia's eyes downcast, "What did he say?"

"Without betraying his trust, you got rough with him. He spoke his mind and you punished him for it. Sounds—"

"Yes, I know. He's right to feel the way he does. I don't know what came over me then, but when compared me to that—that tyrant. I lost it."

"I think you should talk to him."

"I want to, but he sees me as a danger to him."

"Talk to him. You're the adult here. He knows it, even if he can't say it. He needs you, even when you're wrong. You approach him and make him listen. Don't let him create messed up thoughts about you that aren't true." As she stares at the ground in thought, he takes her hand, stopping her. "Talk to him, Afearia," looking firm, yet gently into her eyes.

She stares up at him with wide eyes before snatching her hand away. "Don't get familiar with me, dimwit."

"Uh, right," putting his hand down. "Well, I guess that's all I've got to say. I know you like it when I'm far away from you, so I'm heading back."

As they go opposite ways, Afearia stopped and turns to him. "Wait." Zaiah faces her. "You could walk with me, if you want. I need to pick up some things."

He smirks and nods. "Sure."

He walks up to her and suddenly seems somber. "What's wrong?" she cutely chuckles. "I thought you would be thrilled."

"I am... just. I don't know. A thought I had made me feel bad."

"Well, suck it up. I need to get back to Adrian as soon as possible." She notices his semi-troubled, pondering stare. "Why do you keep looking at me?"

"I was just wondering... Who's Demeseus?"

Afearia scoffs, "Pfft, another fool who doesn't know the legend."

"A man who fought all across this country saving locations lost to the rogues." She looks to Zaiah with much surprise. "He once went toe-to-toe with an unidentified Demi Anthropoid with insane powers in order to protect a small town. But his adventures—"

"Wait!" quickly stepping before him. "I didn't even know about that! What unknown Demi Anthropoid?"

"Don't know. They were there one minute and then gone the next. There were no eyewitnesses, but the devastation the battle caused was seen and felt from afar."

"Oh, wow, tell me more," Afearia says with big fangirl eyes.

"Uhhh—"

"How did he use his chains? Did he change the landscape with his power?" rambling questions Zaiah can't answer while excitedly speculating. "God, he's so strong."

"Anyway... If he's the Demeseus you're talking about, why did you say his name? Was he important to you?"

Afearia slowly calms down and looks toward Zaiah. "He still is. He's the most brilliant man I've ever known. He's made a lasting impression in me that can never be destroyed. He's kind, funny, and a *true* battle genius once engaged. It has always been a dream of mine to see this amazing man fight... maybe even stand side by side with him on the battlefield."

"I'm amazing," Zaiah jokes. "You could watch me." Afearia gives him a stone-cold stare. "Uh, I guess not. I get that you admire the guy, but—"

"I don't just admire him. It's far more than that."

"Love—him?" almost choking on his words.

Afearia's cheeks turn a little red. "Where are you going with this, idiot?"

"Well… word on the streets is he's dead. He's been dead for a long time. You're infatuated with a dead man."

Afearia turns toward the next block and proceeds, "Not exactly."

Confused and surprised, Zaiah quickly catches up with her. "Wait. Are you telling me it's not true? That he didn't lose his life at the rogues' stronghold?"

She slows with a light huff. "I'm going to tell you something you must swear to never reveal upon your inevitable capture."

Zaiah shamefully tucks his lips with a pressed smile. She has such a low opinion of me it hurts. "Alright. I swear."

"When Demeseus passed all those years ago, his soul did not lay to rest like it should've. It migrated. To Eternity. Every time I summon that sword, it's him I see. I don't know if that's the fate of wielders who die using Eternity, but I am selfishly grateful to have him with me. I aspire to be everything he was when he was alive by becoming a worthy successor of his sword."

"Wow… he really is important to you," speaking glumly.

"Of course he is. I wouldn't be here without him. He's my rock. The key to how I stay strong and survive. If destiny didn't bring him to me like it has I would have died long ago." When they reach the end of the block, Afearia has a double take, seeing Sasano sitting on a car hood with a smoldering look of confidence in his eyes. She quickly breaks eye contact and stops Zaiah from turning the corner. "Wait. There's something else. I rather not tell you anything, but you clearly won't go away, so I need you to do something else for me."

"Sure, anything."

"Protect my kids."

"From what?"

"Me…," she says regrettably.

"Come on, you made a mistake. You would never hurt your kids."

She turns halfway from him. "Don't be so sure. There are things you don't know about me. Neither do they. I've been good keeping it a secret, but there was an incident caused by my weakness since I've been down here. I never want it to happen again. But with things moving along as they are now… it may," looking toward the car Sasano sits on.

"What are you talking about?"

Taking a moment as she doesn't respond, Afearia moves closer to him. "Look into my eyes. This blood red eye staring back at you houses a deep secret. An abnormality of life. A darkness I usually can control. But when I can't… someone else is in control. Someone not me."

Zaiah bunches his brows with stern concern. "What do we do?"

"There's nothing you can do. As we speak, I'm still fighting for control. And if I fail, I want you to take the kids and run. Don't look back. Don't think even for a **second** that you can reason with me. Just run. And keep running. Don't let my hands be the ones to harm those children."

"Hold on. What happens to you? Are you saying there's no way to save you?"

"Every time I lose control I run the risk of never coming back. When I do return, it's due to outside circumstances I'm not aware of. My returns are always by chance... Demeseus and I have come up with a plan that can potentially bring me back from the brink."

"Afearia, not to sound pessimistic, but he can't help you. He's dead."

"We're going to perform an experiment tonight that took months to get together. If it works, we'll all have nothing to worry about."

Zaiah slants his eye for a moment in thought. "I want to help. I want to be there for you."

"Calm down, idiot. Don't get carried away because I said you could join me. There's nothing you can do for me other than keep my kids safe. Got it?"

He sighs, lightly shaking his head. "Got it."

"See? All will be okay," she says optimistically before walking ahead.

"I'm going to save you," he says sternly after she took a couple steps from him. She suddenly stops, feeling his determined eyes digging into her back. "I don't know how, but one day I'm going to be there for you when you need me the most. I place my life on that."

A long silence comes between them while Afearia somberly stares at the ground. The wind faintly blows before she lowers her head a little and turns to him. "Stop with the melodramatics and false sense of heroism. Let's go," weakly smirking at him. Afearia proceeds on ahead with Zaiah soon following.

After walking a few blocks, they reach the town's general store. There were few shoppers and even less employees. The two of them move down the nearest aisle with Zaiah nonchalantly bobbing his head to the store's music.

"So what are we getting?" Zaiah asks.

"I'm getting stuff for me and my kids," Afearia replies.

"Canned goods, right?" suddenly moving faster

than her.

"Uh, yeah, but—"

"Got it! I know exactly what they want!" shouting from down the aisle and turning the corner.

Afearia shakes her head and shops on her own. She finds herself in the clothing section picking out tee shirts and one long tee shirt for men from the clearance rack. As she turns, she's surprised to see two men dressed in casual street attire at the end of the aisle strongly staring at her. She ignores it and continues to shop until she notices their coming approach. It was then Afearia recognizes them.

"Oh!?" Afearia positively surprised. "Duncan, Ben! What are you two doing here?"

"Wow," Duncan says, looking just as surprised as Ben. "It really is you. You're alive. The rumors have been true all along."

Afearia chuckles. "I guess they were. How's Armport?"

"Doing great actually. I wish I could say the same about Woodhaven. Weren't you there a while back?" Afearia's smile diminishes a bit. "Well, Salavania should be alright. Oh, wait. Weren't they trampled because of what you did to their generator?"

"Hold it," she sternly says. "I've returned to Salavania and they're doing just fine."

"Well, yeah, no thanks to you," he chuckles somewhat callously. "But it must be a set of unfortunate coincidences. You're only here to help after all. I'm sure Basswell understood that when you ran through their streets like a psycho."

"I've never been to Basswell," she gritted.

"You sure? Because so many people died that day when you came through. If I recall the reports correctly, it said a red-haired bestial woman came through eating and shredding its townspeople."

Afearia slants her eyes in shame. "It's not true—not

entirely," she mutters.

Duncan steps up to Afearia, meeting her stern gaze. "You remember what you told us last time we met? In short, you said we were playing commando and could never be taken seriously by anyone, including Derexen. Tell you what. Let's see how serious you take us once we remove Terra's calamity."

Duncan rudely puckers his lips, making kissing noises close to Afearia's face while lightly slapping her. Instinctively, Afearia punches him in the face, several feet into a tall bin of canned food. The bin and Duncan hit the floor, causing a scene as cans rolled along the floor. As Duncan sits up rubbing his cheek, Afearia's staring down at him with a deadly anger.

Ben crouches to his side before Duncan spits blood looking up at her. "You don't know just how wrong you are. You've killed dozens of people. Condemned thousands and indirectly killed hundreds more." He stands walking up to her just before Zaiah comes from the top of the aisle slowly approaching with suspicion on his face. "I confront you and the first thing you do is punch me in the face?"

Duncan suddenly slaps Afearia hard across the face. "Hey, hey, hey!" Zaiah yells running down the aisle.

Ben jumps back to back with Duncan to defend him. Afearia stands straight and raises her hand to halt Zaiah, not breaking eye contact with Duncan. "You're a piece of shit," Duncan insults. "You ruin lives. You've solved nothing!"

Afearia stares at him for a while before straightening her posture, "Are we done here?"

Duncan seems surprised until his eyes twitch with anger. "Not by a long shot. If lord Derexen's not done with you, we're not done with you."

Duncan turns and leaves with Ben following. Zaiah walks toward Afearia, deliberately bumping shoulders with Ben, glaring them out the aisle. "You alright," Zaiah looking at Afearia's reddened cheek with concern. "Does it hurt?"

Afearia avoids eye contact and turns back down the aisle she was shopping in. "I found some shirts I'm sure they'll wear."

"I was—" he was saying, seeing Afearia had already begun to depart from the aisle.

"I see the food in your basket. You're not bad at shopping for them." When she turns the corner, he looks back at the gawking customers and awkwardly smiles before removing himself from the aisle. Turning the corner, Afearia is staring at a frozen dinner. "How good do you think these are?"

Zaiah makes a sideways smiles. "Not great."

She sighs and walks away. "I really miss meat."

Thinking to himself, Zaiah has an exciting idea. "Ever had lobster?"

"No."

"When we get out of this town, I'm going to cook you and the kids a real home cooked meal."

She stops, turning partially toward him with an intrigued raise of her brow. "You cook?"

"I'm a man of many talents."

"Not since I've known you," she says while moving further through the store. "Other than being the best at running your mouth."

"Damn, Afearia, you never give me a break. You kill my feelings."

"Then stop being so soft."

As Zaiah grumbles behind her, Afearia grabs a roll of sealed salami and tosses it behind her into his basket, startling him momentarily. "I'm serious though! I'm going to cook for you guys one day."

"Idiot, I really don't care."

"Awww, but why?" She ignores him and turns up another aisle. "I'm really good and—" He halts his words once he turns up the aisle to see Afearia motionless and staring up ahead at no one. "Afearia?" Though he can't see him, Sasano's at the end of the aisle beside the bread rack, smugly smiling at Afearia. "Afearia?" coming up beside her, gently snapping Afearia back from her trance.

"Can you—get the bread?" sounding somewhat afraid before looking Zaiah's way.

"Uh, sure," looking oddly at her.

As he walks toward Sasano to grab the loaf, Afearia nervously watches them both while he maintains his gaze on her. When Zaiah grabs the bread, bouncing it a couple times while happily returning to her, Sasano's arm suddenly emerges from his chest, causing him to groan and drop the bread as his blood splatters.

"NOO!" Afearia reaching out.

As if to have walked through a smoky mirage, Zaiah's standing right in front of her with the bread and a concerned look as he sees the fright in her eyes. "Afearia? What's going on?"

She shakes her head in fearful disbelief. "No-nothing. Let's just get what we need," turning to go back the way she came. Terrifying her into a jump scare, Sasano's standing directly behind her with demonic blood eyes. She drops her groceries with closed eyes of frustration before picking up her items while he watches. Zaiah tries to help her, "Don't!" snapping at him with her index finger up to scold his kindness.

Afearia grabs her belongings from the floor and storms off to the registers. With the tongue of a serpent, Sasano playfully flaps it like a snake while hissing upon her departure.

Back at the motel, Veronica's watching TV while Adrian lies on the bed staring at the front door. "You think he can get Anya to come back here?" he suddenly asks.

"You're not mad anymore?" turning to her brother.

Adrian huffs and turns on his back. "I overreacted.

But I'm right, right? Anya hasn't been herself for a long time. She's distant. Angrier... She's becoming scary. I feel like she's leaving us in way without leaving. I can't explain."

Veronica frowns. "What do we do?"

"I don't know. Zaiah said he'd help me figure out what's going on, but... I don't think he can. Maybe she's broken. Maybe after everything that's happened she isn't fully together. She's just—different."

"I think we all are now. After everything," she somberly says.

After staring up at the ceiling for awhile, Adrian has a sudden realization and quickly sits up. "You're right. It's not just her, it's us too. When's the last time we tried to make her laugh? When's the last time we thanked her for being here for us? When's the last time—" immediately saddening himself to his resolutions. "When's the last time we even hugged her? We said she's acting like her old self and we aren't helping that. We're all too busy walking on eggshells around one another." Adrian jumps out the bed, looking determined. "I'm going to Anya's room. I have to talk to her."

"Yeah!" jumping up as well.

"I'll be back, sis," leaving the room with a big smile.

Adrian shuts the door behind himself and runs down the hall to the stairwell, excitedly making his way up the floor. He enters the third floor running toward Afearia's room full of hope. Adrian reaches her door in panting glee as he twists her knob to find her room wrecked. Furniture was broken and overturned with shinning lamps toppled over, creating an eerie glow in the room. Eternity lies on the floor with the shelved vials knocked over and one open.

Adrian slowly walks in confused and scared. "What are you doing? Run, kid!" Demeseus warns.

Unfortunately, his voice went unheard as the door

shuts behind Adrian with Duncan standing behind it as a looming presence over Adrian. He quickly turns, backing away until he sees three men, including Ben step out the bathroom.

"We couldn't find anything to make her understand how much she's been a damaging force on our world," Duncan says. "She didn't even have the decency to apologize for all the pain and tears she's made Terra's people shed," speaking with resentment before slyly looking into Adrian's scared eyes. "But I think *one* sacrifice will get my point across."

Several blocks away, Afearia and Zaiah are silently returning to the motel together. Zaiah awkwardly glances at Afearia a few times before attempting to speak.

"You're being awfully quiet all of the sudden," he says, failing to gain Afearia's attention. "Is everything alright? Is it something I said?"

Afearia lightly shakes her head, struggling to crack even a weak smile for his sake. "No, I'm fine. I just have a really bad headache."

"The amount of lies you tell to those close to you is staggering," Sasano says as he calmly walks beside her. "Tell the truth," speaking gruffly with eyes firmly upon her. Slowing his walk, he manages to smoothly move close behind her ear between her and Zaiah. "I'm making you itch."

Afearia shivers from his tingling whisper and does a wide backhand bursting the bag carrying her purchased items. Zaiah jumps back in alarm to avoid being hit by her scattered items.

"Whoa! Time out! What the hell are you doing!?"

"I'm-I'm sorry! I wasn't trying to hit you."

"Yeah, I can see that. What's wrong with you?"

Afearia dwells deep in her mind, almost completely drowning out Zaiah as she dangerously stares at Sasano staring snidely at her up the road. "What do you know?"

546

speaking to Sasano, confusing Zaiah in the process. "Why are you waiting?" Zaiah calls to her, trying to snap her out of it.

"Because I want you to see the truth," Sasano tells her. "When your nerves are rubbed raw. Your code of justice runs dry. You have and will turn to the one thing that has always brought you comfort and release... Me. It has never been so much of me taking over you. It's you letting me in."

"NOO!" fearfully staggering in denial.

"I can see what's coming in your final hours. And since I can, I'm going to paint your final scene so that there's no doubt in your mind that you call for my possession. That I'm your two ton excuse for you to be true to your urges in every sense of the word," Sasano taunts almost provocatively. "To be a beast," giving a lingering pulse of his eyes.

Afearia charges at Sasano until Zaiah jumps in front of her and shakes her out of her hallucination, "Get a hold of yourself!" As she's being shaken, Zaiah slowly blurs into view. Her eyes widen as she rapidly blinks in confusion as her mind settles into reality. "Hey, you in there?"

Afearia suddenly saddens, lightly shaking her head, worrying him further. "Get the kids, Zaiah," she helplessly says.

"But—"

"Just do it. I need a moment. When I return to the motel, you better be gone with them."

"How... How will you find us?"

"Just trust that I will. Now go."

Zaiah hesitates before racing off toward the motel with panic and grief across his face. She called me Zaiah, he thinks. She's... She's in so much trouble. Something really, really bad is going on with her.

Afearia remains still, not even blinking as all

547

around her falls deathly silent. "Behind you," Sasano cheekily whispers from her ear before falling quickly on his back and from her shadow.

She quickly turns and sees him standing a few meters back. Afearia swallows her fear with the rise of her hardened stare. "You don't scare me."

"I never did. It's not me you fear. It's yourself. Trusting yourself to be more human than monster. But some days it can be hard to tell the difference."

"I won't give in to you!"

"But you will," holding her attention as black slowly encloses on them from every corner. "I've already seen it. I could just force you, but the lesson won't be learned. How else will you understand that you and I are one in the same."

"You're full of it!"

"Am I?" He tilts his head and points the top of his cane at her. Afearia begins to wobble. Her eyes are covered in a smoky gray hue before she begins to move toward him without moving her feet. Once she's near, he releases his hold over her, causing Afearia's eyes to revert. "See?" lowering his cane. "I've amassed the power over a month ago to do it. I just couldn't find the source. The part of you that connects us."

"Then why wait?"

"Because you must accept it. Accept that you and I are kismet. You are my vessel. The door I must pass through for a full resurrection. I don't want you thinking anymore that you're above the influence," walking around her. "Above me. I want you to choose me. To see the difference when you've let me in and I didn't force myself upon you. For when that moment all light leaves your heart. It'll be clear."

Sasano stands behind her, placing his hands on Afearia's shoulders before running them down over her body ever so slowly and intimately, giving rise to lustful

548

yearning within Afearia as she closes her eyes and gently grinds her hips into her malevolent seducer. "You are my dark queen. And this ongoing war between us has been nothing but a difference of views."

Suddenly, he violently grabs her breast, further igniting her fires as they breath heavy while she practically whines in his arms grinding her hips harder with desperation. Sasano smoothly turns his head from her, almost as if he can hear and see something no one else can. "The final scene—is now playing," slowly releasing her as his voice echoes and his fading body floats backward into the shadows.

As if time had returned, all sound, light and passing pedestrians flooded her senses all at once as she feels herself drop out from the feelings that were building inside her a moment ago. She looks around as the night air and the street lights brush her body, noticing she hasn't moved since Zaiah left. She puts her hand sadly over her abdomen and lowers it near her pelvis, feeling the lingering sensations of being under him.

Looking as if she was craving more, Afearia quickly shakes off her urges and becomes focused. "I won't succumb to your darkness. I am my own person. A strong person. I'm in control—**not** you." She takes a deep breath and resumes her venture toward the motel.

Afearia returns and takes the stairwell, but halfway up to the third floor, she faintly hears Zaiah talking to someone.

"You're kidding." Zaiah says. "How long has he been gone?"

"I don't know," Veronica says, looking concerned.

Afearia, immediately frustrated, opens the door to the second floor, "Seriously!?" addressing Zaiah as she marches toward him.

"Afearia?"

"We had an arrangement. I thought I was clear

about what I asked."

"Afearia—"

"Adrian's missing!" Veronica blurts with teary
eyes.

"What? How!?"

Zaiah shakes his head, crossing his arms, "I don't
know. I asked the front desk. No one saw him leave the
motel. He has to be—" Afearia turns and races to the
stairwell. "Where are you going!?"

"He must be in my room!"

"I was there! Your room is trashed with no sign of
him!"

Afearia stops, darting eyes in thought before facing
them. "Then we'll split up. It's not like him to wander off.
Keep Veronica close to you at all times. I'm going to check
the lower floors, you check the upper levels," running off.

"Anya!" Veronica stopping Afearia once more. "He
wanted to say sorry! He wanted to make things right! He...
He—"

"It's okay," lightly smiling. "We'll find him. I
swear it."

Afearia bolts into the stairwell. Zaiah takes
Veronica's hand and runs to the opposite end of the hall to
use the second stairwell. As Afearia moves down to the
first floor, Sasano's happily waiting beside the door. He
opens it for her like a gentlemen. She stares firmly at him
before passing through.

"This is it, you know," Sasano says before walking
close behind her side. "The final scene." Afearia looks over
all the doors lining the walls. "Knocking on each was her
initial thought, but how much time would she lose?" he
narrates.

"Knock it off," proceeding onward.

"But then it occurred to her, if he's in trouble, she
should first seek obvious locations in her search."

"Enough!"

"Check the basement," causing Afearia to worriedly stop due to his helpful, yet likely apt suggestion. "Go on." Afearia suspiciously stares at him. "The more time you waste staring at me, the worse the situation could potentially become."

She peels from his stare, returning to the stairwell to reach the basement. She pulls the door open to reach a long hall that breaks right. Two doors could be seen from her distance. One only a few feet to her left while the other's at the end of the hall.

"Afearia cautiously proceeds down the hall feeling ill at ease," Sasano narrates as he suddenly appeared leaning beside the first door.

"Stop with the narration," looking around for any danger.

"I suppose all to know is already here."

"What are you going on about?"

He smirks wide as a faint surge of red and black energy pulsed one time through the briefly bulged veins in his face, "You let me in," sounding semi-demonic. Afearia slowly twists the knob to find the well-lit maintenance closet. She closes it and continues. "What I narrate about your life has already been written or is being done."

"Stop talking to me. I'm ignoring you."

"Good. Because I want you to see this. What awaits us—you, at the end of this road. This will be another moment to forever paint your history. My return to these realms is inevitable. I will return to my divinity and sit where I've long since belonged," he says as she anxiously nears the door. "You are only a temporary placeholder. A thin membrane between me—and everything else."

Afearia reaches the second door and opens it with near hesitation to only find the electrical room. She sighs with relief before the fuzzy peripheral image of a mahogany door enters her sight. She slowly turns her head to it while Sasano playfully stares at her, twirling his cane whilst lazily leaning against the electrical room's door. She looks at him and he silently points his cane toward the final door.

When she decides to move onward, the faint sounds of scared whimpers are heard while grunted thuds and yelps of pain arose. "Adrian?" Afearia fearfully utters before running down the hall reaching the door. Sasano continues to watch while she trembles with her hand rising for the knob and her erratic breaths echoing in her mind.

"As she moves toward the door… All the lines have been written for this moment. But the painting needs one last coating from its god's brush." Afearia slowly opens the door to a disturbing sight beyond her wishes. "Ahhh… Here comes the hardest part," he says with settle, yet evident delight.

Inside the large beverage closet, Duncan, Ben, and his men have beaten Adrian bloody and blue. Lying face down and shirtless, a repulsive smell other than blood enters her nose. The men had and were urinating on him. Adrian was sniveling with tears pouring from his bruised eyes as the hall's light did nothing but highlight his pain.

Duncan, standing over Adrian, looks at Afearia with remorseless hate in his eyes. "Glad you could make it," zipping up his pants. "Ben, look at this! Never have I thought I'd live to see that arrogant look wiped off her face. She really looks like she's experiencing untold horrors. Good," he says with a heartless glare. "This is only a fraction of the pain you caused the people of this country— BITCH!"

Sasano grimly lowers his head, "Unable to truly cope. You're feeling different. Feeling strange. For this pain could never be erased." Afearia's expression remained shocked, but her hair began to slowly stand and increase in length. He partly lifts his head to watch her from under his fedora as his eyes turn to the monster he is. "Like the blackest clouds parting for the moon. Night has fallen—

where light and dark are merely one and the same."

Dropping his cane, Sasano slowly, without breaking his obsessive stare over Afearia, leans off the wall and crouches down like an animal on the hunt. His canines grow sharp and a deep growl grows from within his chest. Steady, he dangerously moves his upper body like a leopard ready to pounce.

"As the light fades from your dreams...," speaking with a demonic gravel in his voice while lightly drooling. "May my darkness reign *supreme*."
The white of Afearia's eyes are instantly swallowed in black, and the blood red hold of the devil within breathes anew.

Diary Entry #6142
They say in our darkest hours we should huddle close with the ones who love us and will protect us. But in my darkest hours... Who will protect the ones I love from me?

Come Hell or High Water

Chapter Nineteen

Racing down the first floor's halls, Zaiah pulls
Veronica along as she struggles to keep up. He knocks on
the coming door asking for Adrian and if he's been seen,
getting the same answers he's been getting all night. Before
he could move on to the next, the floor suddenly shakes.
People come out their rooms looking just as curious and
worried as Zaiah. The motel guest begin to gossip amongst
themselves, some even mentioning the boiler room.

Zaiah scoops up Veronica and press her head into
his chest. "Sorry, but we need to find your Anya and
brother." He bolts toward the stairwell. Because I've got a
real bad feeling in my stomach, Zaiah thinks. And
something feels—dark.

He enters the stairwell sprinting and hopping
toward the basement and opens the door to the lowest floor.
He runs down the hall, following the disturbing feeling
growing inside him the further he runs. Once he turns the
corner, he immediately halts himself, nearly falling over by
stopping so suddenly.

"What's wrong?" Veronica asks. Zaiah looked pale.
Frightened as the dark, empty, soulless energy seeping
through the door was making his skin crawl and feel peeled
to the nerve. "Zaiah?"

Pulling himself together, he looks down to
Veronica. "Sorry, I just had a bad feeling." He puts her
down and tightly takes her hand. "Stay close to me."

The further he moved down the hall, the worse the
knot in his stomach began to feel. Once standing before the
door, he slowly reaches for it until a puddle of blood oozes
beneath his feet from under the door. Veronica instinctively

presses herself against Zaiah's leg.

Zaiah opens the door slowly, cautiously looking into the dimly lit room where most of its dangling ceiling bulbs had burst. The only sound faintly disrupting the eerie silence was droplets within the dark hitting the blood puddle Zaiah and Veronica currently tread. Before he could walk too deep inside, Zaiah's foot taps a man's savagely torn off arm. Catching his ear, a soft whimpering is heard from the left of them.

They both look into the dark corner. "A-Adrian?" Veronica mutters as bravely as she could.

It suddenly stops. "Veronica?" Adrian tearfully replies. Spooking them, he runs out from the darkness and tightly hugs his sister for dear life. "Veronica!" he cries into her. "Help... Help—her," Veronica's eyes widen to his shaken words. "Someone please... save Anya!"

Searching this blood wet darkness, Zaiah sees the swaying illumination upon each swing of a bare leg up ahead. "Get behind me," Zaiah sternly tells the kids.

Zaiah slowly twirls his index finger in front of his lips before softly blowing to force the winds in the room to sway the bulbs harder. Clenching his jaw in revulsion while preventing the kids from seeing, all of the men who had captured Adrian were skewered on wooden pikes, lifelessly dripping blood upon the red sea below. Many had their flesh torn straight off their bones and their faces slashed apart.

Sitting at the center of this blood sea is Afearia with legs tucked and hair down over her body like a cherry red curtain. Barefoot, pants torn up to the thighs, covered in the warm blood of men deemed too wicked to live.

"I found him," Afearia whimpers while pressing her soaked hands into the decapitated head of Duncan's mortified face. "He was suffering... And I didn't want to let him down. But... This... Look at this... Look at me," she sorrowfully cries, trembling quite hard several times.

"I'm hell bound."

Afearia looks up at Zaiah with over ninety percent of her sclerae swallowed in black. The kids almost see her face, but Zaiah stops them as she struggled to push her head down. "Zaiah... run... Save them—from," her voice straining to speak. Her body begins to shake beyond her control as she sinks her fingers into Duncan's head. "I beg you. With all that I am." Tears fall onto her hands, purifying the deep red with clear steams. "Don't let him... him take... take..."

Her shaking reaches near seizure levels until she violently flings her head back hard enough to crack bones. An echoing exhale similar to that of ecstasy slowly escapes as her eyes gradually shut. As if to have fallen asleep, Afearia remains completely motionless. Zaiah, cautious and afraid, slowly walks backward with the children while whispering reassuring words to them.

Suddenly, Afearia's demonic eyes jolt open. She slowly lifts her hand with the upturn of her wrist and explodes all of the slain bodies in the room. As blood rains down upon her, Afearia seductively runs her hands down her hair like one would while taking a shower. Zaiah's eyes tremble as he and the kids had walked halfway down the hall back to back while he watches the room.

A smile twisted with glee arose across her lips before a brief, soft chuckle breaths through. She drops her head, "Hehehe. It feels so good to be back," Sasano softly, but disturbingly speaks in his dual voice. "There's no way I'm turning back." Zaiah, watching the bulb swinging over Sasano, becomes frightened when he suddenly vanished during the bulb's fourth retuning swing.

Zaiah immediately turns and hurries the kids down the hall, "Go-go-go-go-go," hastily speaking. The three of them race up the stairwell and reach the first floor. Before Zaiah can get through the door with them, Sasano's hanging above the entrance from the ceiling. He comes down and pins Zaiah to the floor. The kids stop and turn to help. "GO!"

The kids turn back and run up the hall. Sasano makes a cheeky smile, jumping off Zaiah and using his speed step skill just as the door closes. He moves along the walls, coming down near Veronica and appears several feet ahead of the children to slowly approach them in a low snigger. Veronica lightly touches her cut cheek and fearfully looks at Sasano pointing his finger at her.

"Wh-why, Anya?" backing away carefully with her brother.

Sasano sucks Veronica's blood off his finger with delight, "Mmm. Why? Because blood and pain is my pleasure. And nothing can measure." Veronica feels light headed with a sharp pain in her side. She looks down and notices Sasano had punctured her. He smiles and raises his other hand with his index and middle fingers coated in her blood. "Like a juice box," he winks while sucking his fingers clean as she passes out.

Adrian catches her, trying to keep her conscious. Sasano attempts to charge them down, but a mighty blast of wind slams him into the farthest wall. Zaiah's holding his fist out from casting the wind spell. He uses his hand to motion the kids to come his way as the wind carries them. Zaiah bits a piece of his fingertip off, dripping the blood into Veronica's puncture wound. A green glow comes from the hole just as her wound rapidly repairs itself.

Veronica opens her eyes, "Adrian."

They hug each other before Zaiah stands them up, "We're getting out of here."

With a charging fist of swirling light, Zaiah delivers a punch to the ceiling, creating a large hole leading outside. He takes the kids into his arms and jumps up and out the motel. The moment he lands outside the motel's entrance, Sasano lands behind him, scaring Zaiah. Zaiah does a back kick, but Sasano leaps over him and delivers the very same back kick, successfully launching him into the motel lobby.

Though grounded, Zaiah's quick thinking protected all three of them by miraculously bracing all the damage with his right hand through the destroyed desk and crater in the wall. His arm's muscles are greatly flexing as he trembled a little from the internal damage. The desk clerk, barely surviving Zaiah's sudden crash, stares at him in shock.

Zaiah's hardly able to stand after such a blow. Adrian looks over Zaiah's shoulder and jumps instinctively, "Zaiah!?" alerting him of Sasano's calm arrival.

"Good reflexes," Sasano commends. "Before impact, you swapped those kids into one arm and took the blunt of my kick to the right side of your body. Pity. Should've kicked you harder so the force would break all of your necks."

Zaiah pulls himself from the indentation made from the crash and wobbles a little. The clerk runs out the motel through an emergency exit near the stairwell. Shortly after, motel guest come through the stairwell trying to flee the commotion, only to be stopped by Sasano's demonic presence blocking the destroyed entrance.

"Now I'm torn," Sasano says. "On one hand I could kill all these creatures coming late to my revival party. But I have a great urge to trample my early guest," smiling at Zaiah and company. "Hmmm. Who will it be?" Looking between the crowd and Zaiah before sprinting at the innocent bystanders. "Crowd!"

As the people run, Zaiah puts the kids down and tries to intercept Sasano. But it was a bluff. Halfway there, Sasano slyly looks at Zaiah before using his speed step skill to reach the kids. Too fast for the kids to notice, Sasano's merely inches away from snagging Adrian. Suddenly, a tree root rises up between them and slaps Sasano back toward the entrance. As he stood, another root grows up through the floor and binds him from the neck.

"There's a lot of old roots slumbering in this town," Zaiah says with his arm up at him. "That's fortunate." Sasano stares at him with no readable emotion. "Afearia. I know you're in there. I... I don't want to hurt you. Stop this and come back to us."

"You really think you're talking to Afearia, don't you? Foolish child you are." With a strong grunt, hard cracks within the wooden root are heard as he tries to stand straight. He squeezes his hands into the widening, stressing the root until the cracks are visible and the root breaks with the upward yank of her head. "Shall I convince you?" grabbing up a large wooden shard.

Just as Sasano's about to throw it, the wood rapidly grows and binds his arm behind his back as it takes root into the floor. "That's enough," Zaiah says, controlling the wood binding him. Using his raw strength, the wooden fibers begin to pop as he tries to resume his throw. Zaiah uses his powers to repair the wood, but the rate of breakage was greater than he could counteract. "Kids, duck!" he shouts to them.

The kids duck just before he hurls and embeds the shard over Adrian's head. He charges at Zaiah, but Zaiah brings up an arching root to defend him. Sasano smoothly slides between the risen root and shoves his palm into his chest, launching him across the room. With no slow in his step, Sasano resumes his pursuit of the children. The kids run toward the stairwell and up the stairs with him just about to enter the stairwell until his foot's snagged by a root.

He looks back to see Zaiah crawling on his stomach with his arm up controlling the root. He nears, grabbing the root to accelerate its growth. Frustrated, Sasano kicks forward, breaking down the stairwell door well simultaneously yanking up the root and bringing the airborne Zaiah into his hand by the neck. Choking him, Sasano tilts his head, listening for upstairs movement before jumping straight up through the ceiling to the second floor, starling the children by landing before them.

The children turn back to run, but Sasano raises his hand and alters the literal structure of the hall by making it close together by clutching his fist. "Don't be rude," Sasano tells the kids. "And as for you," lifting Zaiah before him. "Quit the act. You're weak."

"Afearia," Zaiah barely says under his grasp. "Fight this. He's going to kill Adrian and Veronica."

Sasano makes a humorous face of confusion with his brow raised. "How do you think this works? This isn't a spiritual possession. Me and her are one. You're basically telling her to stop and fight who she really is."

"Liar!"

"Do you want to talk to her?" Zaiah and the kids couldn't believe it, but hoped it was true. "I could arrange that." His eyes roll to the back of his skull and his head drops before quickly shooting back up with Afearia panicking and screaming for help, even crying about being surrounded in darkness and pain. Immediately, she stops with her eyes rolling back and head dropping. Sasano begins sniggering with a slow rise of his head, then laughing aloud before wiping away Afearia's tears. "Man, it's dark in there."

"You bastard!" struggling to break free.

"That was just a reflection of what she's doing. Crying. Begging. Screaming in the dark."

He concededly tilts his head to Adrian, "She's not so tough now, is she?"

Adrian's trembling at the sight of him until he suddenly wasn't. He slowly began to approach Sasano in a dream-like daze, confusing his worried sister.

"What are you doing!?" Veronica shouts at Adrian.

Sasano does a teeth sucking noise, getting Veronica's attention. "Hey," speaking calm and friendly. Veronica freezes up and suddenly becomes just as dazed as her brother before approaching as well.

"NO!" Zaiah screams in a struggle. "Stop! Go back! Kids!? Stop!"

"They can't," Sasano says. "It is only natural for me to possess dominion over lesser beings with a feeble conscious." Zaiah struggles harder. "Still?" Looking up at him with an unimpressed smile. "You could save them if you fought me for real." Zaiah looks to the nearing kids, then angrily at Sasano. "You still won't hurt this girl, even at the expense of those kids?"

"I can find another way."

"Oh?"

Suddenly, a root comes up and wraps around Sasano's arm, pulling it down gradually. Sasano bites the root, causing red veins of energy to spread out from the bite. When he releases it, the root heats up and turns red with visible black bubbling underneath its waxy exterior. Using Zaiah as a shield, Sasano protects himself when the root explodes with wooden splitters entering him and hitting the kids. Though the kids took minor injuries, they continued to walk forward. Sasano smirks at Zaiah, looking at him with a snarky expression.

Back in Afearia's room, the continuous tremors of Sasano's violence has caused the shelf holding the blood filled vials to slant. Another tremor hits the room, causing the shelf to fall over onto the sword. Many of the glass vials break on the blade's flat side while the rest roll away. The sword gains a strong white aura that wavers upward while lightly humming feminine vocals. One vial had rolled in front of the door before a chain gently scoops it up.

On the floor above, Adrian and Veronica stands before Sasano, staring into nothing with their mouth's half open. "Anything else you'd like to try?" Sasano asks Zaiah.

Zaiah grits his teeth, "Afeariaaaa!"

"Silence!" hurling him, slamming Zaiah up against the distorted hall.

562

He immediately stands up and charges at Sasano. With the stomp of his foot, Sasano shakes the building and upheavals the floorboards to block Zaiah. Zaiah attempts to climb over, but Sasano fires a wind bullet from his finger tip, collapsing the ceiling above him.

Successfully blocking his way to them, Zaiah can only peer through. "Afearia! Afearia!"

"Now. Where were we?" looking down at the kids. "Hey, poking Adrian in the chest, bringing him from his trance. He immediately looks up in terror. "Hey there." He tilts his head a little, "Your eyes are so full and bright. I just wanna steal that light." He snatches him up by the neck, holding him close to his mouth. "And from your light, I make it my own."

Just as he parts his mouth, Zaiah explodes from the barricade running at Sasano with rage and Braveheart tightly grasped in his hand. With a glance from Sasano, a cylinder shaped piece of the building extends from the wall coming at Zaiah's side. He slashes it to pieces while still moving forward. The floorboards spike up, but he jumps over them just in time to be shot down with a quick puff of fire from Sasano. Standing halfway up, the floorboards rise and twist around his body up to his neck.

"Persistent, but still weak," Sasano mocks. He turns to sniff Adrian's body with a smile. "So pure. The fear. The hopelessness. Infantile beings are the best to taste. What a fine way to start," speaking for himself.

He parts his mouth to bite through Adrian. "Demon!" a man's voice gruffly echoes through the hall, stopping him.

In a flash, a crescent light shots up through the floor directly up the middle of Sasano. His face was frozen in shock with the rest of his body. Beads of blood well up at the middle of his face. Adrian breaks free of Sasano's weakened hold and grabs his entranced sister to hide behind Zaiah. Sasano's body begins to slide in two until he grabs his face for his tissues realign his body and heal him.

"Heh," Sasano smirks while recovering. "You'll have to do better than that."

Destroying the floor beneath Sasano, a chain is being spun like a propeller, turning him into chunks as a man is carried through with a bed of chains aiding his ascent. Catching their eyes is the man's shiny black and white swirl patterned gauntlet. Not facing Zaiah and the kids, they see Eternity hugging the back of his black jacket with a silver stripe running along the sleeves. He stands tall in his lose-fit cotton wool black pants, matching his boots.

The chains let him down, retracting into his sword. A small splatter of blood was on his black tee shirt beside his silver cross necklace. The man runs his fingers back through his dirty blond hair, seeming bothered by the bloody mess he made.

"Damn it," he mutters. "It's going to be hard to predict like this."

"Oh no...," Adrian says with sorrow on his face. He kneels before the blood on the floor. "Anya..."

"Don't move. Your Anya is—"

"Who are you!?" Zaiah yells in a coarse anger. The man turns his head partly toward Zaiah. A faint, transparent aura lightly emits from Zaiah. "I asked you a question!" breaking free of the floorboards binding him. Braveheart's fuller has its red energy move beyond the half point.

The man glances at Zaiah's sword and faces them. "My name—is Demeseus."

"Demeseus?" Zaiah says, calming down a bit. He soon after bunches his brows, looking to do harm. "She spoke so highly of you. Yet you kill her without second thought." He readies his weapon. "She may forgive you in death, but I won't."

Demeseus turns from him. "You should take the kids and get as far as you can from here. I would say—" Before he could finish speaking, Zaiah thrusts his blade at his face. Demeseus leans his head from the blade and leaps far back from Zaiah's heavy overhead down swing. "Hey, quit it! She's not—!"

Zaiah swings up from the ground, releasing a red wave of energy Demeseus' way. Demeseus almost pulled his sword on him, but instead grits his teeth and musters a white aura over his hand before backhanding the energy into the wall.

"Why did you stop?" Zaiah asks while Demeseus just stares with no answer. "Your sword! Why did you stop!?"

"Because. I only draw my sword on my enemies. And you are not my enemy. I gave Afearia my sworn word to protect those kids. Even you." Zaiah calms with the aura fading away and the red fuller in his sword sinking. Demeseus smirks. "It was hard for her to admit, but she wouldn't want you to die either."

"Then why—kill her?" sadly falling to his knees.

Demeseus sees the sadness within him and lightly smiles with an eye roll. "Zaiah, right?" Zaiah doesn't answer, he remains with his eyes locked on the blood splattered floor. "I see you care a great deal for her. But when this rare event occurs from inside, you have to fight Afearia like she's someone else. Because she is. Zaiah. She's not dead. I have to whittle down the life of the thing inside her so she can take back control."

"By hurting her?"

"Honestly, I don't know if she can feel it. I rather not know either. It'll just make things harder on me." Demeseus' face becomes suspicious as he starts rapidly looking around.

"What?"

"Something's not right. Sasano's taking a long time to regenerate..."

Zaiah stands with a tightened grip on his sword. "Is it because you screwed up and killed her?"

He slowly walks the bloody hall. "No. I'm sure it was fully him in control." He walks over to the hole and sees a blood puddle on the lower floor. He sternly looks at it, knowing it was odd. "We'll talk later. Get those kids to safety. I need to finish what I promised."

Demeseus jumps down the hole and sees a blood trail leading into the nearest room. As he cautiously walks toward the ajar door, Sasano's back is pressed to the ceiling with his glowing red eyes beating down over his head. Quietly following Demeseus after turning himself over, Demeseus stops with hand raised over the knob and smirks.

Sasano silently leaps down behind him. Briefly appearing behind Sasano, a faint image of a golden-haired woman with a white gown glares at him from behind her flowing hairs with great detest in her ethereal eyes. Chains sprout from the sword and holds Sasano up in the air.

Demeseus turns calmly, "You can't leave Afearia alone, can you?"

"She called for me," smiling at him with a little tilt of his head.

"And she called for me. One of which is not the same."

"So you've come to protect her again?" he asked with an annoyed up tilt of his head.

"Always," smirking confidently.

"Except there are a few difference." Demeseus narrows his eyes at his smiling foe. "You're corporeal." Sasano's chastising while sucking his teeth and wagging his finger at him, "Not nice, naughty, naughty, boy. As for myself. I'm much stronger than you've known me to be."

"Is that so?"

"Mmhmm."

Using his strength, Sasano attempts to break from his chains. Surprisingly, Demeseus doesn't challenge him and instead releases Sasano. During his descend from the chains, Demeseus kicks him in the face and down the hall.

With the upswing of his sword, a chain comes speeding from his sword near the floor toward Sasano. When he sat up he immediately lies down to avoid the chain from snaring his neck.

Sasano rolls to his right and kips-up to quickly charge Demeseus as he rests Eternity to his back. Demeseus swings his other arm to release another chain aimed for his head. When it nears, Sasano does a ducking spin, rotating clockwise while ripping chunks of the wall in his hands, hurling them at Demeseus while still running at him.

Like a protective whip, a chain swats away each piece thrown while Demeseus stands unwaveringly as his foe nears. Sasano leaps forward and comes down on him with joined hands. Demeseus jumps back just in time for Sasano's attack to fail and leave a hole in the floor. Wasting no time, he darts back at Demeseus with fist raised. He cocks back his gauntlet hand and runs at Sasano as well.

As their fist are about to collide, chains burst from his gauntlet and wrap his arm like a giant vibrating drill. With ease, Demeseus obliterates Sasano's entire arm and some of his body while passing through him. In that brief moment of passing behind him, Demeseus unsheathes his sword and decapitates Sasano with a single backward swing. His head hits the far wall before his body slowly drops down.

Retracting his chains, Demeseus looks to his fallen head, "Let's limit your choices."

Holding back his middle finger with his thumb, a wave of light travels through the gauntlet to his middle finger. With the flick of his glowing finger, a small orb comes from it and falls onto Sasano's head, blazing it into crumbling ash. Demeseus coldly turns to the body and impales it in the heart before lifting it into the air.

"Now then. Where were—?"

Suddenly, Zaiah jumps down the hole to the lower floor, seeing the graphic scene. "That's enough. How can you coldly do that to someone you care about? That's Afearia in there!"

Demeseus barely looks his way. "Seriously, what are you still doing here? Get out of here before—" Demeseus feels his sword shake a little, turning his attention to Sasano's regenerating body. "Are you done playing around?" he asks as he sees Sasano's head half regenerated. "Good." With an outward slash to free his sword, he immediately decapitates him again. Sasano's body drops and is deeply stabbed in the heart twice. Struggling to watch, Zaiah steps forward to intervene, "It's necessary," halting Zaiah's interference. "Do us both a favor. Afearia told you to flee for a reason. It wasn't just to protect the kids. She knew she couldn't ask you to do this. To kill her repeatedly and brutally. But I can. It's what she entrusted us to do. Zaiah's eyes downcast in hurt. "Go. I can never truly predict how these fights can turnout."

"But I can," Sasano says, surprising Zaiah by being fully regenerated while still impaled.

"Hush," Demeseus commanding chains to wrap around Sasano's smiling mouth.

At that very moment, Demeseus' face entered frozen shock of unfortunate realization. Sasano's face said it all. He had made a mistake. Conducting electricity from his body, Sasano electrocutes Demeseus, causing him to kneel. The chains loosen, allowing Sasano to free himself. He leaps away and sticks to the wall like a bug as he fully regenerates. With roach-like speed, he crawls up the ceiling and onto the upper floor.

The moment he sees the children, Sasano jumps at them with claws out. Chains burst from the floor and snare his wrists, ankles, and neck before pinning him down. Like a snarling beast, Sasano wiggles around before calming himself.

Below, the five chains were deployed from Demeseus' fisted gauntlet pointed at the ceiling. "Bastard," he says as his chains begin to rattle. Demeseus and his chains are steadily beginning pulled through the ceiling. "No way," he says with fear as he tries to resist. Almost yanked off the floor, Demeseus pulls back down with all his strength. "No way!"

Up above, Sasano was slowly getting back on his feet. Grunting as his face reddens and veins bulge all over, Sasano's evil red aura begins to appear as his malevolent eyes never break contact with the kids he wishes to murder. His grunts grow into a moral boosting yell as he begins stepping toward them.

"God!" Demeseus blurts as he tries his best to win this losing battle of strength. Looking like he may collapse as his straining, spit-filled grunts become evident. Demeseus could no longer hold this monster down. "You idiot—PROTECT THEM!"

Without second thought, Zaiah leaps up to the upper floor and over Sasano. He snatches up the kids and hops away with them in his arms. Less than a second afterward, Sasano raises his arms in an explosive flex, yanking Demeseus up through the floor. Floating up into his eye view, Sasano grabs his neck to dangle his helpless body before him. The chains retract as Demeseus pulls at his wrist.

Sasano smirks, "One piece of Eternity's armor is all you thought you'd need? Arrogant child."

"I've weeded as much of that out of my nature as possible. Look down."

With his bare hand, Demeseus gives him the finger, commanding chains to rain down upon Sasano and burst forth from below piercing his body. Demeseus easily slips from his weakened grip and takes a calm backward hop. With a clasp of his hands, the chains turn into a twisting funnel.

Before it can fully twist close, Sasano bites off his own tongue and spits it out from Demeseus' view. His tongue lands down on the floor below, faintly glowing red while regenerating. The chains spin hard enough to grind his body to bits before the chains returned. Sasano's body was mince meat. The moment Demeseus straightened his posture, Sasano burst up through the floor behind Zaiah with a stone cold look on his face.

Zaiah instinctively tries to protect the kids, but in that moment, Sasano servers his arms from the shoulders with a smooth chop of his hands. Through unseen means, Sasano snatches Veronica into the air with just a menacing glance. Before Demeseus could help, Zaiah rolls over to one of his arms and reconnects it with his feet. He blows out a string of light and it acts like self-applying stitches. He reaches up and pulls Veronica down just as Demeseus arcs a cluster of chains from below Sasano, smashing him down the hall.

Zaiah leans over and reattaches his other arm the same way. Veronica watches him with concern and he smiles at her. "Just another trick in my sleeves. My arms will be good as new in no time." Veronica looked like she wanted to cry. "I'm alright, kiddo. Trust me."

"You really don't listen well," Demeseus says as he approaches them. "You're hesitance is putting those kids in danger. I need you three to get out of here." Before they could, Sasano lifts the chains off himself and pushes himself out from underneath. "Tch, stubborn little—" He looks to the kids and Zaiah. "This fight has just reached catastrophic levels." He grabs Zaiah by his collar. "Stop dicking around and leave—now!" releasing him to approach Sasano as he stood.

The chains retract as he sternly moves toward his smirking foe. "Heh, must you always play before you get serious?" Sasano remarks.

"Hmph," Demeseus smiles.

Sasano points his loose hand at Demeseus with index finger raised at his foe. At the moment of activation, the winds he's gathering with his finger are so great, it tears the walls pulling everyone gradually toward him.

"Is this still the wind bullet?" Demeseus fearfully asks himself as he resists the pull.

With a smooth side tilt of Sasano's head, his grin growls, "Bang-bang."

With a thunderous shot, his whirling wind bullet is tearing apart the hall in a disastrous fashion. Demeseus pulls up his sword and turns it flat ways, bracing at both ends before impact. He holds the shot in place until it dislocates his elbow, knocking him off balance as it zips pass his face while tearing the flesh right off his cheek, temple and eyelid. Lying on his back, Demeseus quickly reaches back with his arm pointed at the kids and Zaiah.

"Metal Tendrils!" Demeseus shouts, tossing his gauntlet.

With his command, chains come from below to form an expansive wall growing outward from Zaiah and company. When the bullet hits, it bursts with enough force to push Demeseus onto his feet and closer to Sasano while protecting the others. When the chains retract, the gauntlet falls down the great chasm created by the rising chains splitting the motel in two.

Demeseus takes a knee, holding his head. Sasano stares at Demeseus for a moment, then points two fingers at him. "Do you want to know what she's screaming right now?" Demeseus looks at him with an intense glare. His facial expression becomes lifeless, "Please..." sounding exactly like Afearia with dead eyes. "Someone shine a light in this darkness. I'm lost and I... Can someone hear me? Can someone save me? Please. I'm sorry." Sasano's smug expression had returned. "Such a pathetic girl," he scoffed with a devious smile.

Demeseus begins to stand. "I know." He nearly falls

over, but stands tall and firm. "She's talking to me. The last thing she told me when we formed this plan was that in her darkest hour, someone needs to shine a light. To free her from the darkness deeply rooted in her heart. She looked me straight in the eye and asked me... will you be my light?"

Zaiah lowers his head and clenches his teeth as the growing inadequacy in his chest mounts up. Smirking, Sasano tilts his head a little, looking truly interested in Demeseus' words, "What did you say?"

"I told her that in her darkest hour she'll have to be her own light. But until that day...," lowering his hand and revealing the blood on his face and the skin that had been pulled together by Sasano's wind bullet.

Suddenly, his gauntlet returns in a glimmer of light, along with a metal plate on his forehead, quickly spreading over the sides of his face and jaw before completely covering the back of his skull. As if it were nothing, Demeseus does a jolting twist to pop his elbow back in its place before raising his half clutched fist toward his face. Light gathers into his hand while a fluctuating grayish aura emits from his body. The floor begins to rumble under this sudden rise in power.

"I will be the light to shine in her nightmare," Demeseus says with stern focus. "The closest thing that can free her from you. Because I do more than shine. I become light personified!"

With a clutch of his bare hand, simultaneously summoning his second gauntlet, the metal on his head triggers, enclosing his whole skull with only a hollowed out Y shape over his face. His good eye glows blue from inside the shadowy opening of his helm. Metal wings grow out from the forehead of his helm before he yanks his hand beside him, revealing a glowing gold scarf of light from around his neck. Demeseus' version of Eternity's boots appear on his feet with wings sprouting up from the calf.

Such power, Sasano thinks before smirking. "Tell me, Demeseus. Could you always reach such heights?"

As Demeseus stares him down with his flowing scarf of fringed edges, Demeseus raises his arm ninety degrees as dozens of daggers made of light fade into existence beneath his arm. Sasano's smug grin fades into a more serious expression. Demeseus bends his knees as a gentle whirling wind encircles him.

"Try and keep up with me, monster," Demeseus says in a deep, hollow voice.

With a slight shift of his body, Demeseus vanishes. Sasano's confusion only lasts for a moment as he is soon kneed in the face by Demeseus, then stabbed in the neck by a deployed light dagger to follow. The force of Demeseus' knee sends Sasano crashing through the wall. Shortly after, Sasano returns bursting through the wall with a wind bullet ready to blast Demeseus. Demeseus zips forward and palms his bullet into nothing, breaking his opponent's finger in the process. Demeseus is pushing Sasano's arm up until it suddenly stops. He notices Sasano doesn't seem even the slightest bit concerned over the situation he's in.

"Question," Sasano says with stern eyes. "How long does this last?" glancing at the light dagger. "I can't get it out."

Demeseus sheaths his sword behind himself and pulls up another light dagger, stabbing him in the shoulder. To Sasano's surprise, this gave his opponent the edge to overpower his risen arm. Pushing his arm straight up, Demeseus headbutts him in the face and follows up with a dagger stab into his ribs as he stumbled back.

Sasano swings with enough force in hopes of splitting his arm from his foe. Demeseus with his newfound speed, dodges the strike, landing on his hands and pushing up off the floor doing a spinning overhead assault by stabbing Sasano on the other side of his neck with a light dagger. The moment he lands, Sasano does a strong back kick, launching him down the hall despite bracing for the hit.

About to crash into Zaiah and the kids, Eternity sprouts a web of chains to halt Demeseus' velocity. Soon after stopping, Sasano comes stomping his feet on Demeseus with puffs of ink-like darkness per hit while laughing through his teeth as Demeseus bares every blow with his gauntlets. The chains collapse and retract, but Sasano continues as Demeseus lies on his back trapped under his rapidly striking stomps. The stomps are becoming faster and faster as Sasano's stomps emit flames while tinting the room in darkness just before the floor collapses underneath them.

Zaiah runs over watching from above, balling his fist wishing he could step in. As they go down, Demeseus times his counter punches to match Sasano's stomps to rapidly punch the soles of his feet in accordance. When they reach the floor, the powerful exchange of blows becomes a contest of speed, power, and endurance as they match each other beat for beat.

So much light, flames, and darkness are splashing through the hall as they see who'll break first. Sasano, unable to contain his excitement through his toothy grin as he crosses his arms reaching critical assault, Demeseus lets out a mighty roar as he struggles to match the demon in this contest of power.

Ending the clash with one mighty punch, the light Demeseus was generating collects into his fist and shoots up through Sasano's knee. Sasano notices the area is bright and looks up to see the light energy made from their clashing never faded but instead hovered over them the whole time.

Seizing the moment, Demeseus zips from Sasano's view and stands behind him as the light energy rains down on him. Utilizing his light infused chains, Demeseus barrages him. The hall becomes dangerously bright as

Sasano's engulfed in a bubbly ball of light. Through the light, Demeseus expresses a sudden realization. He ends his assault with the raining lights doing the same.

The light dies out immediately, revealing Sasano with his head held low with a smile, holding all the fired chains wrapped around his forearms. Sasano evidently didn't even bother to dodge the raining lights, for he is covered in numerous searing injuries that are rapidly healing.

"After all these years of seeing your heroics, you still don't cease to amuse me," Sasano says. "Kid. She's not worth it," looking up at Demeseus, still smirking but coming off somewhat earnest. "And these ridiculous mad dashes to save her aren't working. And yet you still fight so hard, even though you're the reason she bares my mark," winking with his right.

Seeming unfazed, Demeseus slightly raises his hand with the vague turn of his wrist to recall his chains with so much force it rips Sasano's arms right off. He grabs the tip of one of his light daggers before gently tossing it up. With a flashy roundhouse kick as it comes back down, Demeseus kicks it into Sasano's face.

Sasano stumbles back with his head dropped, "It's not worth it," Sasano grumbles, sounding like something heavy was on his lips. "It's not working!" looking up at Demeseus with the dagger caught between his teeth. "No wonder she loves you..." speaking almost to himself. "Your endless heroics make you look picture perfect!"

Biting down, the dagger lasted a little more than a second before shattering. His arms quickly grow back before he flexes his renewed hands, ready to attack. With a momentary standoff, Demeseus reaches for his sword, but Sasano was much faster. Before he could wrap his fingers around the grip, Sasano grabs him by the neck and leaps up through the ceiling with him.

Sasano has pinned Demeseus to the corner of the

ceiling while Zaiah and the kids helplessly watch. It wasn't Sasano's' wish. He wanted to drag him higher, but Demeseus stopped his assent using the chains he wields like a spider web. Demeseus strains and struggles to fight Sasano's pressuring force to take him higher.

"You were a fool to sheath your greatest weapon," Sasano tells Demeseus. "Then again." He squeezes his neck and pushes him a bit further to the ceiling, detaching some of the chains.

"You must've noticed by now," Demeseus says, vaguely irritating his opponent.

With one upward thrust of his arm, Demeseus is thrown up and out the building. Slowly looking toward the frightened trio, Sasano floats toward the astonished Zaiah and pokes him with a wink. "Worthless boy. These are her thoughts too," he says optimistically. He glances above. "Be right back."

Like a missile, Sasano touches down and leaps up through the hole he tossed Demeseus through. He lands on the empty streets that have long since cleared because of the motel panic. He notices a destroyed storefront and smirks as he approaches it. Swiftly, Demeseus comes from behind thrusting his blade at his back. Sasano sidesteps from range and smoothly grabs his forearm and swings him around before lowering his arm toward the ground.

Holding onto him, Sasano punches him in the face several times before Eternity vanishes and reappears in his other hand for him to do a reversal slash for Sasano's face. Grabbing his wrist before he could cut him, Sasano stops his attack and palm smashes his face three times. Upon the last strike, Demeseus shoves another dagger into his opponent's shoulder as he stumbles back.

"Seriously?" Sasano says, glancing at the dagger before seeing Demeseus hunched over, bleeding out his helmet. "What are these anyway? I can't even dispel them after they've been embedded," tugging briefly before flicking at the dagger. Demeseus stumbles a little more before swinging his arm to release a torrent of light daggers. "Still fighting for her." Effortlessly, he sidesteps from the attack and approaches. "A girl who has some of the darkest, most lustful desires I've seen in a long while."

Showing signs of fatigue, Demeseus swings his arm to release more daggers. "It's not worth it," Sasano swinging his arm covered in a dark smog that deflects the daggers away. "Her soul's accursed," deflecting the daggers downward as the smog rotates faster around his forearm. Demeseus grits his teeth and runs in with sword raised beside him. "Now you rush in to attack me? Like this ever works."

In mid swing, a strange disturbance in the atmosphere occurs in front of Demeseus in a small, twisted swirl before swallowing him. Sasano's confused until he emerges from that same reality bending swirl above, slashing his neck as he comes down pass him. Blood splatters from the attack, but Demeseus looks back upon feeling a tight tug on his ankle hanging him upside down. Sasano's head is still attached. His head was turned from the initial attack as he holds on to Demeseus.

"Demeseus," Sasano, sounding exactly like Afearia. "Why are you hurting me like this? I love you."

Demeseus angrily balls his fist, "Sasano! Don't play these games!"

"But, Demeseus—!" In that moment as he innocently shouts at him, Demeseus hurls a dagger in his face. Sasano's head jerks back with him covering his face. He slowly turns his head to Demeseus with a smoking palm and the dagger embedded in his forehead. "You're annoying me now." He then notices he also had one in his hand. "Another one?"

"Not just one," pointing at his manubrium and sternum.

"When!?" dropping Demeseus in shock he took so

many hits and didn't realize it.

"My deception led to a triple strike when you had me." Sasano grunts with a clenched jaw looking at him. "What are you so worried about?" he smirks upon pushing himself back on his feet. "You don't even know what they do."

Irritated, Sasano swiftly kicks Demeseus' feet from under him with enough force to turn him upside down and snatch him by his ankle. Like an animal, Sasano bites into his greave, causing them to shatter into a glittering dust, greatly surprising Demeseus.

"You're right , I don't," Sasano says with much bother. "But I do know how to debuff an arrogant mortal who knows nothing of my might."

Sasano prepares to bite his other greave, but Demeseus unties his light scarf and tosses it behind his foe. Demeseus becomes pure light before bursting into white sparkles and reappearing where he tossed his scarf. It neatly wraps around his neck as he comes down on his opponent with sword pointed. Demeseus pierces the ground after Sasano sidesteps from range. Sasano follows with a backhand which Demeseus dodges with a backflip, landing on his hands and doing a straight kick for Sasano's ankle.

Sasano cartwheels around Eternity, avoiding the attack and gets into an opened leg handstand to attempt kicking Demeseus in the head. He blocks it in time, being knocked several meters across the ground before bouncing up right using his hand and firing a chain to wrap around Eternity's guard. Sasano flips onto his feet and rushes Demeseus.

Demeseus yanks out Eternity, moments after sliding from Sasano's attack and kneeling. The blade's edge cuts along Sasano's back, failing to break skin upon retrieval. Nonetheless, the strike did cause him to stumble forward a little. However, Sasano fails to notice chains had not only wrapped around the sword, but along some building pipes.

In that moment, Demeseus uses the retracting power of his chain to propel himself toward his enemy and smashes his gauntlet into Sasano's face. Before fully passing by, he brings his arm around Sasano's neck, using his momentum to slam Sasano into the dirt while also chaining him. Demeseus pulls tight and Sasano kips-up holding the chain choking him. Demeseus yanks it a few times, irritating Sasano further.

With one pull, Sasano yanks Demeseus through the air toward him. Using his swift reflexes and his second gauntlet, Demeseus fires another chain near his opponent's neck to pierce the ground behind him. When the chain rattles with a flash of green, a thick wall of rock with a small slit for his chain comes between him and his attacker. He lands feet first and jumps off to his right, dodging Sasano's devastating right hook that destroys the upper half of a building and part of the risen wall.

With a yank of the chain, Demeseus pulls him against the wall and runs around Sasano to ensnare him in chains as the wall presses against his back. Several more chains pierce through the wall and wrap around his demonic foe. Demeseus comes leaping over the wall and grabs a dagger in each hand to successfully stab Sasano in his shoulder and elbow upon landing. Sasano roars like a wild beast with a wide mouth before snapping his teeth at Demeseus with an angry glare.

Watching from within a nearby store, peeking from the bottom of the window is Zaiah and the children. Zaiah's eyes are wide as he watches in thought. I hate to admit it, he thinks before bunching his brows in irritation. But she was right. Demeseus is amazing.

Demeseus stands and turns to Sasano, grabbing another of his daggers. When he nears his growling foe, Sasano snaps his teeth again to try and bite him. He calmly raises the dagger up. "It's almost over, Afearia," Demeseus softly tells her. "It's time to wake up."

He stabs his dagger into Sasano's other elbow, but something went wrong. His attack stops inches from penetration. He tries to push, but it won't budge. He glances at the now smiling Sasano before attempting to smash another dagger into his forehead. But again, inches from his target, Demeseus' attack is halted.

Sasano stares up at the dagger and smiles wider, "You asked if I noticed something earlier. I did. But I think you've noticed. These lights. The daggers. They weaken me. It explains why my powers are growing so slowly. But that's the facts. You wanted to keep me down so I was beatable. Silly Demeseus." Sasano gives him an evil leer. "The extents of my power. My boy, you cannot even fathom what I'm truly capable of."

Fearfully swallowing spit, Demeseus holds to his brave facade. "And yet you continue to live on as a parasite."

"A story for another time." With a simple outward stretch of his arms, the wall pinning him breaks apart. He immediately tries grabbing Demeseus, but he jumps far back while retracting his chains. "I saw your Gaia spell earlier," approaching him. "Sad. Allow me to show you what Gaia spell users were like back in my day."

Sasano slowly raises his arm, causing the ground to shake. Demeseus hurls his dagger at him along with his scarf. When it nearly reaches him, Demeseus teleports. From the dagger's momentum, Demeseus' reappearance is propelled with great speed while holding his thrown dagger. He moves over Sasano and stabs him at the back of his neck, sliding on his wobbly feet upon landing. The shaking of the ground ceases, even though Sasano's arm remained up.

Demeseus calls Eternity back to his hand, "I rather not."

"You continue to hinder me," Sasano says before turning to him. "But it means nothing."

Demeseus rushes in while Sasano calmly approaches. Wasting no time, Demeseus slashes low, but Sasano jumps over it and comes down punching him in the face. Demeseus follows with three more slashes, each dodged with ease.

Coming down with an overhead straight hand, Sasano chops Demeseus' wrist, disarming him and wrapping his fingers around his neck. Demeseus tries to escape using his scarf, but when he pulls it off, Sasano grabs his wrist and slurps the scarf into his mouth. With a hard swallow, it was gone.

"Mmm, tasty," Sasano smirks. Demeseus attempts to punch him but has his fist caught in his opponent's hand. Sasano sensually sniffs his arm, then glances at Eternity still half risen from the dirt with a lustful provocation. Violently, he kicks Eternity far and high up into the sky beyond the clouds. "The events that got you here today were worthwhile," giving Demeseus a sideways smile. "A second chance. Though brief it may be. All because you wanted to be her hero. Live up to this legend she's created out of you. *Foolish*," dragging his words with bother and stern brows.

"Funny. As fate would have it, jumping straight into battle without letting my body acclimate may have been more than I could handle. But there is nothing foolish about trying to live up to the hero people expect you to be. Especially if it makes you a better man."

"Hmph. Ridiculous."

"Sasano," squirming a little to get free, yet failing to do so. "Your bite dispels magic, right?" Sasano raises a brow. "Did you chew before your last meal?"

Suddenly, a burst of light daggers protrude from his stomach. Demeseus smiles, until he sees Sasano's deathly stare had not shifted from him, despite blood pouring from the corners of his mouth.

"You can do this all day, I bet," Sasano sternly says,

coughing a massive splatter of blood. "But it won't work. She's fading."

Demeseus grunts, trying to breathe easy as he is held higher. "She won't fade. You know that. You just can't admit that she's strong. Because of that, you can't accept that one day you'll have to let her go."

"Hehehe," Sasano chuckles. "Sounds like deflection. If not, I would tell you to take your own advice, but that day has already come for you." His grip tightens hard enough to silence Demeseus. "Because one day you won't be here to watch over her life and protect her fragile heart. Without you around, who's going to protect Afearia then?"

As it looked like he may snap Demeseus' neck, Zaiah turns outward from Sasano's backside with dangerous eyes upon him, "Me."

Surprising Sasano, he attempts to backhand Zaiah. He ducks the attack and spins to his side crouched down before elbowing him in the ribs. He stumbles to his side, releasing Demeseus before being shoulder rushed several feet from Zaiah.

He remains standing and swings his arm, calling a large mud snake to mow down Zaiah. Zaiah charges at Sasano using a reversal of his hands to deform the snake back to mud. He leaps forward and lands with one foot extended, sliding in front of him.

"Mud Wall!" Zaiah's voice echoes.

Four mud walls rise around Sasano. With a sweeping three-sixty kick with powerful wind edging it, Sasano blows away the lower portions of the wall, revealing to him Zaiah had vanished, but his sword was coming for him. He leans from its trajectory, but is surprised when he hears it being caught behind him by Zaiah. Zaiah does a dual-handed swing, a swing Sasano barely avoids in time by ducking. The swing draws the mud upward to form a ceiling. Zaiah jumps up, focusing to harden all the mud into rock.

Sasano follows and attempts to punch him. By evading, the punch breaks a large hole in the ceiling while a light flowing from Zaiah's hand in liquid form appears. He gently touches his opponent's fist and kicks him down in the closing rock box while he continues to rise. Zaiah seals the box, but it only took a few seconds before the deadpan Sasano emerges from the top free of daggers. With the flick of his pommel, the slime-like light hanging from Sasano's fist extends to the ground and yanks him down before Zaiah lands. It hardens and shrinks, locking him down while Zaiah walks toward Demeseus.

"That should hold her for a while," Zaiah tells him. "Whatever it is you're trying to do to save her, do it already."

Demeseus struggles onto his feet, "You really don't know what you're dealing with here. Look." Zaiah turns and sees the murderous intent in Sasano's eyes as he was slowly cracking the binding light.

"Impossible."

"Damage and exhausting his power are the best methods. Doing so weakens his hold over her and gives Afearia the chance she needs to fight back," standing as firmly as he can. Demeseus makes an odd expression looking at Sasano, then at the rocky enclosure. "No daggers...? MOVE!" stepping forward and shoving Zaiah to the ground beside him.

Breaking through the enclosure with a dragon kick and sliding toward them quickly is Sasano. He reaches Demeseus and does two angled kicks at his shins, following with a hard kick to his diaphragm, launching him several meters. Though he didn't fall, Demeseus was not able to move and was struggling to take a breath. The daggers impaling Sasano dim and waver for a moment.

"So that's the answer," Sasano says. "If I kill you, this annoyance will end." With the snap of his fingers, the

Sasano who Zaiah trapped turns into a pitch black cloud floating toward the real Sasano. "Imagine how strong I'll be once I dispel these annoying daggers. Return to me," commanding the cloud.

Before it could return, the light Zaiah had hold the fake Sasano, liquefies and encases the darkness, getting Sasano's attention. Zaiah points his sword at it, making the light try and condense, but it couldn't.

"This is…," Zaiah says with wide eyes. "Braveheart says this is pure darkness. How can you—?"

"Boy, you have annoyed me for the last time," Sasano says as he approaches him.

Focused, Zaiah tries several times to use his powers to rid the darkness from the area. "I! I can't banish it!"

"Of course not. You're weak." The oblong encasing begins cracking until a small hole appears for the darkness to speedily pour out. Sasano opens his mouth and allows it to pass through his throat. He smiles before suddenly catching a thrown light dagger from Demeseus. "Heh," he chuckles with a wider smirk. Suddenly, the dagger bursts into a multitude of smaller daggers, piercing his throat. As if stung, Sasano jerks back, rubbing his neck wounds. "DEMESEUS!" he yells with an uptick of demonic overtones.

From the corner of his eye, he sees Zaiah had swiftly neared with sword raised. Sasano blocks it with his forearm and palm strikes him in the chest and off his feet. Looking angrily toward Demeseus, he leaps up high toward him.

Gripping the front of his helmet tightly, a surge of light similar to the aura he made at the motel pours upward from his body. "This is it!"

Raining down upon Sasano, tangling him like a puppet are countless chains piercing the ground. Floating high above it all is Eternity, casting the chains itself. Sasano growls at Eternity before looking down at

Demeseus as he hangs seventy feet in the air.

"You know, I'm really starting to hate you," Sasano says. "What can't you get!? My revival is inevitable! Do you really think you can tame me!? A child!? Afearia has long given up the fight!" Demeseus balls his fist to his words. "Don't you think she would have done something by now? Nothing in this world can hold me down. Nothing!" Pulling his limbs inward, Sasano attempts to pull Eternity from the sky and the chains from the ground. Using his liquefied light on his arms, Zaiah helps to restrain him. "Futile boy is at it again."

With a breath of the corroding darkness from his mouth, Sasano dissolves the hardened light Zaiah created. As he was turning his head back to Demeseus, a thrown light dagger cleanly pierces his forehead. Sasano's stunned eyes are wide, he even appears to be unable to move nothing but his eyes.

"You know nothing about Afearia," Demeseus firmly states, even getting Zaiah's attention. "You've spent most of her life hiding and attacking her vulnerabilities like a playground bully; not knowing all you were doing was building her up instead of tearing her down. Every time you took advantage of Afearia, all you were doing was forcing her to stand up and be stronger. Such a petty little parasite," he says with savage disgust. "If you knew her at all, you'd know that there is nothing in her measure."

After a long while, Sasano's shock subsides and he blinks to look down at the man's solid conviction indifferently, "Fuck you, Demeseus."

Without warning, a crack of glowing light appears along Sasano's sclera, reawakening his shocked expression. "Hmph," Demeseus smirks, flicking a floating dagger before him with his thumb. It quickly forms into a new light scarf wrapping around his neck, "Told ya."

Immediately, Demeseus gets into a spread leg pose with one hand to the ground and another over his head toward the sky as he gives a warrior's roar to empower himself for the final blow. The light around him grows tall and dances wildly as the ground shakes. The light in the sky becomes the brightest point until the daggers protruding from Sasano gain an equally bright glow. The clouds above Eternity begin to swell open with rays of light coming through. Maintaining his charge, Demeseus' armor begins to flake off into the light, revealing his bloodshot eyes from the stressful preparation of this attack.

Suddenly, all sound ceases with all around them becoming still and gray. But Demeseus and Eternity were not affected, as he now stood at the center of a large golden array with magic symbols throughout and Archaic Latin text edging the brim repeating the words purity, cleanse, and Eternity. The array rotates slowly as Demeseus is breathing heavily in a near pant as the hand he holds to the sky glows bright for him to ball into a fist which he brings down over his chest before standing up straight.

"With this... It is my earnest wish that I can bring you back. Because I made a promise. To protect you with all that I've got. Never believe you're alone in this. Never. " He raises his mighty fist in slow motion and begins to bring it down to punch the ground, gaining speed in his slow movement as the surrounding area's color comes back. "Because I've got your back! Eternity's Seal!" his shout echoes upon punching the ground and shattering the array.

Like the hand of God parting the sky, a large cylinder of divine light comes down upon Sasano as he screams and shakes under the power of Eternity. He remains bound to the rattling chains as the daggers appear to be digging deeper into him with light spreading out from each wound like a jet engine's flames.

The daggers enter him fully, leaving no holes as the darkness in Sasano's eyes crack apart and break away like a dusting shell while even his pupils are in a constant state of reversion by the cleansing light. After several seconds, the beam shrinks inward until it is no more. The clouds close and Afearia's unconscious. Eternity slowly floats down with Afearia and lays her to the ground before retracting its chains from her.

Beyond out of breath, Demeseus nearly collapses by just trying to stay on his feet. He holds the bloody arm he used to activate the attack which caused him a lot of recoil damage. He limps over to Afearia and falls to his knees once he was beside her.

Demeseus smiles as he looks over her body. "Are you back with us, pretty girl?" he asks with such tire in his voice.

Afearia's eyes open slowly, completely reverted to normal. "Demeseus?"

"Hey, kiddo. I kept my word. It worked, and I'm here. Not sure for how much longer though."

"Demeseus?"

"Yeah?"

Afearia's eyes become wide and deranged with the return of her red irises, sharp pupils and some of her sclerae covered in fragments of black. Sasano quickly sits up and grabs Demeseus by the neck with gleeful menace.

"You gotta do better than that!" Sasano yells into Demeseus' reddening face as he's choked.

Zaiah takes two subtle steps in an attempt to attack. "Don't!" Demeseus struggles to warn. "If you attack now you may kill her."

Sasano fully sits up to mount Demeseus and choke him with two hands. Eternity uses its chains to pull on his arms, slightly loosening his hold. Demeseus is punching Sasano's forearms as it seemed he was fighting with everything to stay conscious. Eternity without hesitation raises up a white glowing chain and fires it at the back of Sasano's skull. Demeseus quickly raises his hand for Eternity to stop, looking desperately at it before slowly shaking his head.

The chain is less than an inch away from piercing Sasano, but Eternity obeys and withdraws its chain. Sasano chuckles, "That's right, don't kill Afearia. We wouldn't want to break another promise, would we?"

Darkness slowly creeps from the corners of Sasano's eyes as he gradually resists the chains binding him. Demeseus at his mercy, ended his struggle as Sasano's grip tightened and his eyes began to flutter.

Zaiah lowers his head and balls his fist tight. "Afearia...," Zaiah mutters. "Forgive me," with voice breaking a little.

Sky blue light forms around his fist and begins to become spherical in his opening palm. He bolts forward holding this energy to his side and thrusts it toward Sasano when he neared. With lightning reflexes, Sasano turns his upper body and catches him by the wrist while keeping his other hand on Demeseus.

Sasano gives his struggling foe's attack a quizzical stare. "What is this?"

Surprising Sasano, Zaiah hacks off his own forearm, causing Sasano to overexert his hold with his arm spreading out from himself by the sudden halt in resistance. Quickly, Zaiah drops his sword and grabs Sasano's arm to violently pull behind his back. Releasing the bloody arm, Zaiah catches it and aims the energy it holds into Sasano's back with one thrust.

"Eradicate," Zaiah says in a murderous tone.

A strong discharge of light rays shoot through his skin as Sasano's launched through the air, carried by the orb of light as he screams in pain. It was a short burst through the air as he rolls in the dirt onto his back. A few fragments of dark shells over his eyes flake away as he catches his breath. Sasano was barely able to sit up before Zaiah appears above him, coming down with arm cocked and another orb striking his chest.

"Eradicate!"

Pressing the powerful light into him, more of the dark fragments flake off as his nose bleeds from the violent torrent of energy running through him.

"Stop it, you're killing her!" Demeseus shouts, falling to stand up.

Zaiah raises his hand once more, "Better this than what she'll become! Eradicate!"

The energy forms, but just when he was coming down to strike, Sasano catches his wrist, bleeding from the eyes now. "I'm... not... going—back," Sasano's barely able to say. Somehow, Sasano manages to get back on his feet with purple energy covering his other hand, creating a sharp, spear-like point. "This realm will suffer. And YOU will join the many who died trying to defend it!" thrusting the energy spear at Zaiah's surprised face. With the tip searing his forehead, Sasano's frozen—unable to push his energy further as he stood wide-eyed. "No... Damn you—Afearia," he strains, shocking Zaiah and Demeseus with his words.

Afearia's pupils slowly shift to normal, but struggle to remain as such. Her head, almost as if to be stiff, is barely able to turn and look down at Zaiah. Her nose bleeds more as she sadly smiles at him, trembling to maintain control. "Do it," she painfully asks. "End it—please." Zaiah, looking up at her, receives a light nod from her as Afearia's trembling worsens.

With a determined look in his eyes, Zaiah snatches his hand away and strikes, "Eradicate!" Sasano screams as he's lifted off his feet and knocked back as the energy runs through him again. He stumbles, but doesn't fall as he holds his aching body. Zaiah charges in, "Eradicate!" Sasano screams in agony as the energy carries him until he's slammed up against a building.

With a desperate war cry of underling anger, Zaiah runs up to him and delivers a mighty hook shot to his face, then reversing it with a backhand before landing three solid cocked back punches into Sasano's nose.

Sasano, delirious from the blows, tries his best to remain on his feet. Shaking it off after leaning back against the wall, Sasano yells to reinvigorate himself. "Eradicate!" Zaiah shouts with a blow to his abdomen. "Eradicate!" delivering a mighty uppercut. Sasano's head is moving like a noodle. With such a bloody face, he looks his rage-filled foe in the eyes and faintly smirks as his eyes begin to weigh. "ERADICATE!" aiming his final killing blow for his face, using the spherical energy brimming at three times its original size.

It was then all the darkness left Afearia's eyes and her left eye returns to blue as her pupils round out. Unable to stop himself, he notices her reversion last minute and redirects his attack into the wall, blowing away not only the building she stood against but through the building behind it and half of the third.

His eyes are wide in disbelief as she hazily stared at the ground by his feet. "A... Afearia?" sounding almost sorry.

With an ever faint smile, her lips barely part, "Zaiah... the strong." As soon as she weakly utters those words, Afearia collapses into the dirt.

Diary Entry #6138

Sometimes it's so peaceful down here. Even in its darkened state, there are still moments of peace. More so when you spend it with the right people. I don't get that kind of time with them anymore. It just feels like our bonds are... I'm losing them... aren't I?

The Martyr of Our Story

Chapter Twenty

After a vigorous battle, the beast Sasano had finally been quelled. Afearia and the others have taken temporary shelter in a two-story house that had been abandoned during the commotion. Everyone except Zaiah are gathered at the second floor bedroom where Afearia's currently resting. Demeseus is leaning over her with his hand on her forehead and his other hand holding hers as he gently watches her sleep.

"She seems fine now," Demeseus says, leaning from her as the chains holding Eternity to his back rattle a little. He looks to the kids who sit concerned on the house chairs pulled beside the bed. "She just needs to rest now."

Though Veronica seems mildly relieved, Adrian appears to be in his own world. Demeseus stands in an attempt to comfort him. "Hey—" Adrian yanks his shoulder away when Demeseus reached for him. "Okay... I get it. You don't trust me. But I assure you I'm a friend of hers. She'll clear up this confusion as soon as she wakes up. Unable to get a response, he sighs and walks toward the doorway. "I'm gonna go check on Zaiah. Be right back."

Demeseus steps out the room, leaving the door ajar. He turns down the stairs leading to the ground floor with a glum expression. Before he reaches the darkened floor below, a soft, greenish-white glow comes from the room to his right. It catches his eye, causing him to stop before cautiously proceeding. When he peeks around the corner, he sees Zaiah on his knees as he holds his served limb to his nub.

When the glow faded, his arm was whole with a barely noticeable scar. He flexes his hand a few times before Demeseus startles him, "Neat trick." Zaiah shoots up and turns to see Demeseus looking deadpan standing in the pass way several feet from the front door. Only the moon's light from the kitchen window behind Zaiah lights the room. "I thought I would thank you for healing my injuries as well. How's your arm?"

"Better."

"I've never seen a spell fix severed limbs like that before. Could come in handy for Afearia in the future. Her spells only hold and mend parts if not much time has passed."

"I can't teach it."

"No?"

"It's an ability for Braveheart wielders."

"That's unfortunate."

"Yeah...," looking elsewhere with a somber expression. "How... how is she?"

"I think she'll be okay. You should go see her. She's sleep, but I'm sure she'll wake soon." With a nod, Zaiah leaves the kitchen and heads upstairs. Until he hears the door upstairs close, Demeseus stares out the window to his right. His ear twitches. "I figured as much. It didn't seem like a Braveheart skill." Demeseus pauses for a moment. "He's hiding something. Whatever it is, I don't think he means her any harm. More importantly."

Demeseus walks further into the middle of the room. "We have a problem," continuing his talk with Eternity. He turns his head to the right. "I'm still here. How is that possible?" His eyes move a bit as he listens. "So without our knowledge, we've performed a forbidden ritual. Does this mean I'm actually back...? Oh," expressing disappointment in his eyes. "How long do I have...? A catch? For who?"

Demeseus turns to his right, listening until the door upstairs quickly opens and little footsteps are heard coming down. Veronica fills a cup of water from the kitchen and rushes back upstairs spilling most of it. Demeseus glances at the unseen before slowly heading upstairs as well.

In the bedroom, Afearia's awake with Zaiah sitting in a chair by her bedside while Veronica stands near.

"How do you feel?" Zaiah asks.

"Sore, achy, and a bit battered," Afearia replies. "Is everyone okay?"

"Yeah, everyone pulled through, even Adrian." Everyone looks to him sitting on a chair in the corner of the room as he watches Afearia with nervous eyes. Though difficult, Afearia sits up, alarming Zaiah. "You shouldn't be moving around so soon!"

"I'm sore, not dead. Now move."

She stands and only takes two steps before Adrian panics, "Waa-ahh, Zaiah stop her!" Everyone was confused by his sudden fear. Afearia glances at the others, taking one more step. "Ahh!" He hops out his chair and tosses it between them.

"Adri—"

Adrian bumps up into the corner looking around for a place to run. Afearia steps back several times with sorrowful eyes on the verge of tears and hand over her mouth. She plops on the bed, staring at the floor, faintly sniffling. Adrian then runs out the room. Veronica gently places the water on the nightstand by the bed and chases after her brother into the next room. Neither sibling notices Demeseus standing crossed-armed with his back to the wall near Afearia's room.

Zaiah is torn about either following the kids or addressing Afearia's distress. He glances at the door a few times before stepping toward Afearia. "Look, I'm sure he just needs a moment. He's been through a lot." Afearia remains silent with trembling fingers over her mouth. "Hey—" reaching out to place his hand on her shoulder.

Afearia violently slaps his hand away, "Did I say you could touch me!?" she yells upon standing.

"No, I. Afearia, I was—"

"Get out!" He glances at the doorway. "Get out!" she shouts louder.

Zaiah hesitates, but turns slowly and walks out the room. When closing the door partway, he pauses and turns to see Demeseus staring at him. Seeming irritated by his stare, Zaiah proceeds down the stairs and out the house.

Afearia stands at the window with hands on her hips and damp cheeks. She lightly sniffles and wipes under her eyes and exhales with the shaking of her head before looking upward with self-pity.

"He meant well, you know," Demeseus says, standing in the doorway. Afearia turns in complete shock, seeing his lightly smiling face. "Hey there, gorgeous," smiling a little warmer.

Afearia slowly moved toward him in disbelief before running up and hugging him tight, refusing to let go. His eyes expressed a protective calm as she held him in his arms while they're swaying happily with eyes nearly closed. Afearia cries a little and embraces him tighter with shut eyes.

"You have no idea how long I've wanted to do this," Afearia practically whimpers.

Almost as if she was trying to pull him inside of her, Afearia's hold strengthens. "Hey, easy, darling," he jokes.

"I feel like if I let you go you'll disappear," her voice breaking as she cries a little more.

"I'm here, Afearia... I'm here."

They sway for a bit longer before Afearia slowly, almost reluctantly pulls herself off him, taking a step back. She sniffles and smiles at him like seeing a long lost love. "Wait? Why—how are you here in physical form?" looking confused but still happy.

"Now you ask that?" he chuckles.

"I'm sorry, I was so excited! But really, what's

going on?" asking sincerely, but with her giddy smile creeping through.

Demeseus raises his brow. "You're still smiling from ear to ear when you should be concerned."

"I-I can't help it! And you're smiling too!" Demeseus playfully rolls his eyes. "I just can't believe it. You're here. You're finally here in front of me! It's freaking crazy! You're alive!" His smile fades a little as he downcast his eyes. "Aren't you?" she asks with concern.

"It's complicated."

"Then what—?"

"Don't worry about that right now. How are you feeling?"

"I'm still in a state of happy and disbelief, Demeseus." She steps closer and puts her hand on his face. "Are you really here?" staring up at his eyes in wonder.

He softly lowers her hand. "I'm here, Afearia. This isn't a dream or a trick."

"How? Help me ease my disbelief."

"The blood. You left it unattended and during the commotion it spilled on Eternity—all of it."

"All? We've never used that much before. That was practically my entire blood volume. It was meant to be done in doses while you had me wrapped in chains for several hours as I come down from his control. But this is—"

"Taboo. At least as far as Eternity has explained to me."

"Why?"

"She hasn't told me everything yet."

Afearia glances at Eternity hugging Demeseus' back and raises her hand in an attempt to summon it. "No response. I figured as much. She doesn't recognize me as her master."

"Neither of us are. I'm just her partner. Besides, like I told you before. Your pact was with me, not her." He glances to his right. "Doesn't help she won't speak anytime you're around."

"She can't stand me…, huh?"

"No," he sternly says before walking pass her to stare out the window. He stares down below, leaning on the windowsill before Afearia turns with a concerned look by his sudden silence. Demeseus does a slow exhale in brewing thought. "We were close, Afearia. It got out of hand. We put a stop to it. But now I'm worried."

"Whoa! You-you-you and Eternity were a thing!?"

Demeseus almost jumps ten feet by her absurd accusation. "Wha-what! No, you idiot!" Eternity chain whips his face, but not too hard. "What the hell are you hitting me for!? She said it, not me!"

Afearia puts her hand over her mouth to hide her giggle. "Oh, sorry," she apologizes with a mischievous grin and offset stare.

"This is no laughing matter. I want you safe, but…" Her face soon becomes quite somber by his words." Twice in less than a year." He turns to her. "It took you several years just to have one. Now it's becoming a usual occurrence. Don't you find that worrisome?"

"What are you saying?"

"Either something's wrong here or you don't care about losing control anymore."

"You think I want these terrors to occur?"

Demeseus leans on the windowsill with his hands. "Sasano is many things, but there is always underlining truth to what he says. You were at the edge, but he can only taunt you, not push. Something triggered you."

Afearia sadly looks to the door. "Adrian…" She turns to leave. "I've got to see how he's doing."

"Again you run from one problem to the next."

"I'm not running."

"Right. The kid can wait."

"Hey, you weren't there!" stomping to the middle

of the room to address Demeseus. "He went through something traumatic!"

"Because of them or because of you?" Afearia settles down, seeming quite displeased with herself. "That's what you're really worried about, is it not? You fear he sees the monster inside you and not your face."

"I—"

"Did you kill those men?"

She turns from him, crossing her arms as she shuts her eyes and lowers her head. "I... I should be killed," she mutters. "I am no better than Derexen at this point. No. Even worse. At least he hides behind near justifiable means. I on the other hand. There is nothing just about what I've done."

"I suppose not..."

"But Demeseus, you have to believe me. I did not just let him in. I snapped. I was overcome with rage and I barely remember what happened after I charged at the first man. I hit Duncan, but that's it. Everything after that is in pieces."

"Perhaps he is partially to blame."

"No. It was me. Even in a black rage, there is still time to pull back. I didn't mean to, but when I saw what they were doing to my child... All I could see was evil." Suppressing how angry the memory makes her, she looks up at him. "I gave into my hate and washed in my morals. A moral to erase evil when in sight."

"Even if you become evil itself?" Her stare does not waver before he lightly smirks in displeasure as he looks away. "I don't mean to come off high and mighty. Truth be told, if I saw you in a distressed state beyond measure by some fuck, I don't think I would have kept my hero mindset either. I suppose it's wrong of me to place so much blame on you. He had already reached the edge of your limits without your knowledge. But at the same time—"

"Enough. You want to blame me, but you don't.

598

Either place your blame on me or Sasano. Either way, we both know it makes no difference. We're one and the same," speaking in a low voice of shame.

"If you believe that then he's already won. To think I went busting my ass to keep you grounded," he grumbles.

"Don't be like that. You know I appreciate how hard you fight for me. I just. I can't put it in words how hard it is to be psychologically in check at all times and the minute you're not, the consequences are dire." She shakes her head in a troubled manner. "Can you try and imagine what it would feel like living like this forever? Unable to let a single doubt or dark thought enter your mind or thousands may die? I... I have to accept that one day someone is going to have to put me down." Afearia looks him firmly in his eyes. "I can't do this forever. No one could do this forever, let alone as long as I have. You know it's true."

Demeseus looks away shortly after trying to meet her resolve. "No. I won't do as you ask. We'll find another way."

"There is no other way. This curse is life long."

"There's always another way. And we'll find it."

"Demeseus—"

"We'll find it!" turning from her toward the window.

Afearia's eyes fill with pity from the painful thoughts she may have pushed on him before falsely putting on her smile of faux optimism. "Maybe you're right. Perhaps something is ticking up my episodes. But what element could have caused the sudden change in my control?"

Demeseus ponders for a moment. She waits for him to respond, almost calling his name before he has a realization. "I don't think it's just one thing. It's a number of things. The continuous battles with little time to mentally recollect yourself. That's a definite factor, let alone the dark thoughts that come along with those battles. Stress. Sorrow. Damage taken. Guilt. It's a perfect cocktail for psychological chaos," turning to her.

Demeseus notices the timid entry of Veronica standing half inside the room. He gestures with his head for Afearia to turn around. Afearia turns and takes a cautious step toward her. "Veronica, I—" Trying to be positive, she felt her mind overthinking and the need to keep her distance. "Sweetie… Um, how's—?" Veronica runs over and embraces Afearia with pure love in her heart. Surprised, she stops resisting and kneels down to accept her love and give it back just as strongly.

Veronica smiles into her face. "You okay now?" she asks.

Afearia nods. "I'm okay now. How's Adrian?" Veronica frowns a little. "That bad, huh? And he won't even talk to me."

"Go to him," Demeseus says.

Afearia stands, looking toward him. "He's probably going through PTSD. Possibly because of me. I'm sure I'm the last thing he wants to see right now."

"If it's because of what he saw, there is no one more qualified to help him sort out his thoughts than you. Show him the opposite of how you feel. The truth that I know. You and that monster are not the same." With a deep breath and reluctant step, Afearia heads out the room to see Adrian. Veronica looks to Demeseus smiling quite oddly. "What?" She smiles bigger, giggling through her chuckles, making him feel awkward.

Afearia walks a few feet down and across the hall. She peaks through the ajar door and sees his legs as he's sitting behind the door. She was going to open it, but lowers her hand and takes a deep breath.

"Let's take it back," talking to him from outside. "One step at a time. Before you saw… the thing I hide. We were unhappy as of late. Perhaps I'm to blame for that.

I've… become less friendly with you two, haven't I? More in the mindset of protect them instead of love them. But it really does look more like protect and don't love them. We haven't taken time for one another in so long. How else did I expect you to react?"

Afearia listens to see if her words were reaching him, but Adrian was still and silent, so she pressed on. "I don't know. I just wanted this mission to be over already. I was even trying to rush it along. Adrian… I'm sorry for neglecting you and Veronica like I have. Aster City… was a wakeup call for me—for all of us. But I promise to do better and make things like they were." Afearia lowers her head, feeling she was not getting him to listen to her. "Assuming you can overlook a part of me that I've tried very hard to keep hidden."

Adrian raises his knees to his chest as fear begins to fill his thoughts. "I once told you my red eye was like a label for something dangerous. What you saw—was what happens when the label's torn off. A monster with no remorse. It's the reason why I take time away from you guys to meditate these negative thoughts and emotions away. It's the reason I have a sudden mood shift mid fight. They trigger the beast within. But when I saw what they were doing to you… Adrian. I snapped," she whimpers.

Zaiah, unknown to the rest of the house, had long since returned with a clothing bag on the counter while he leans with his back to the kitchen doorway, listening to the sorrowful conversation.

Afearia exhales, then breathes slowly to calm herself as she felt her eyes water. "I lost all control. But what you saw. That I wanted to harm you. It wasn't me. I would never—!" She suddenly has a realization before lowering her head a bit in shame. "But I almost did. Even when I wasn't that monster. I did try to harm you. Maybe I am a monster… Adrian," wanting to say more, but knew it was enough. "I'm… I'm sorry I've been a bad parent to you… I'll arrange a deal with Zaiah to get you two home. You shouldn't travel with something you fear. I see you two have taken a liking to him. I'm glad."

She places her trembling hand on the wall. "I'll be gone before sunrise. Her dog tags rattle as she cries quietly. She grabs them in her hand. "Is it okay that I keep the tags?" she asks with voice shaking. "Adrian?" He doesn't respond to her request. She sorrowfully nods a few times. "Okay. I understand." She removes the necklace and places it down on the floor gently. "Farewell, my little man."

Though they didn't come out the room, Veronica and Demeseus heard everything. Veronica was crying near the bed while Demeseus stood beside the door with empathetic eyes for Afearia.

Afearia walks pass her room and down the stairs. Hearing this, Zaiah tries to remain unseen by crouching and pressing himself to the kitchen walls. Afearia only goes halfway down before sitting on the steps. She covers her face with her hands, bouncing her leg as tears come forth. She runs her hands down to her mouth as she stares into the dark. Light little footsteps are heard coming down the steps.

She lowers her hands in a loud sniffle. "I tried, Veronica. Adrian hates me and fears me as he should." She shamefully shakes her head, "I am so sor—"

To her surprise, her necklace is rattled before her as tiny arms come from behind and wrap lovingly around her body in a warm embrace. Her eyes are wide in disbelief. Adrian rests his cheek behind her head.

"Don't ever leave me again, Anya. I love you," Adrian speaking soft and calm.

Happy tears could not be held. Her heart was touched like the first time the kids opened her world with nothing but a simple hug of affection. She lowers her head in a smile, placing her hands over his while they clutch the tags that symbolizes their bond. He held onto her for a long time. Afearia did want to ask him more questions, but his embrace was more than enough to clear her thoughts.

Afearia looks up with a cheeky grin. "Zaiah, if you don't come out of hiding I'm going to beat your face in," semi-joking.

Zaiah rushes before the stairs. "I-I wasn't hiding or nothing!" he blurts. "And I didn't hear anything!"

Afearia gives a playful, but an obvious face of disbelief. Veronica happily screams before running out the bedroom and hopping on her brother's back to hug them both.

"Ugh, don't scream, stupid," Adrian says as he struggles from underneath her.

"You're stupid, stupid," Veronica says as happy as she can be.

Afearia laughs before standing for the kids to slide down and hang from her arms like a jungle gym. She curls the kids in her arms a few times, getting playful giggles out of them.

"I thought I would never see the day," Demeseus says from atop the stairs. Afearia lowers the kids down and smirks up at him. "The stone cold warrior actually showing a softer side. Though you told me you'd changed since meeting them, witnessing your heart open to people other than me brings comfort. I'm proud of how much you've grown."

Like a shy schoolgirl, she blushes a little and looks away while beaming with joy. Zaiah notices her glee and bunches his brows a bit in jealousy. "Anyway," Zaiah mutters. "Hey, Afearia, I got you some sleep-ware and some new traveling clothes. I figured you'd want something other than those torn rags."

Afearia turns sternly toward him. "What are you trying to say? That I look filthy and unkempt?"

"No-no, I just thought—"

"Idiot," quickly looking away from him.

603

Zaiah slouches with a sigh. I've been demoted back to idiot, Zaiah thinks.

Demeseus clears his throat. "Forgive my unplanned intrusion by being here, but I would like to be brought up to speed on—" Demeseus notices Afearia's pure smile as she teases the kids with pokes while mussing their hair as they play.

She realizes he stopped talking and looks toward him. "Hmm?" looking bright-eyed.

Demeseus smiles warmly at her. "I was just wondering if any of you were hungry? I'll happily go get something for us."

"Oh—thanks."

"I want a sandwich," Zaiah says with attitude and blunt aggression.

"You'll get nothing," Afearia quips.

"Uhhh, what is this guy to you again?" Demeseus asks.

"Just an idiot I can't seem to shake from my tail. Seriously, it's become quite annoying."

"Is that so? Well in any case, let's go to the room so I can write down everyone's stuff," he says as the kids stand atop of the stairs as well.

"No need. The idiot will get it for us."

"What!?" Zaiah says. "Come on, the guy offered. He needs to earn his keep somehow."

"Why? You don't."

"Ouch," Demeseus sniggers.

"Hey, shut up, DeMeSeUs," mocking his name. Though they were all laughing, except for Zaiah, Afearia suddenly keels over in pain. "Hey? You alright?"

The kids run to Afearia's side as she holds her stomach with shut eyes. She looks up at them with a smile but a moistened forehead from the ache that hit her. "I'm fine," she tells them. "Must be a lingering injury from the battle."

As she stands walking up the stairs with the kids at her side, a barrage of murmurs hit her ears and loudly bounce around in her head for a moment. She gasps and falls to her side while holding the banister.

Zaiah rushes to the bottom of the stairs, "Hey, what's going on!?"

Afearia shakes her head for them not to worry, but her face was getting sweaty and her breathing was becoming erratic. "I'm fine, I swear," she says. Struggling back onto her feet, when she's finally standing, a bloody trail runs down her right eye like a tear. She slowly touches it and begins to quiver in fear. "What? What's happening to me?"

The moment she finished her sentence, Afearia's eyes roll to the back of her head and she violently slams herself against the wall several times before banging her head against it in a dead doll-like manner, then flinging herself down the stairs.

Zaiah quickly moves up and catches her body as she furiously shakes in his arm, "She's having a seizure!"

"Get her up here, now!" Demeseus shouts.

Zaiah rushes up the stairs and runs to the bedroom with Demeseus. He places her in the bed holding down her arms while Demeseus holds her legs. The children stand a safe distance as they nervously watch Afearia shake uncontrollably while muttering incoherent babble. Her seizure soon comes under control as she appears to be experiencing painful jolting spasms as she groans in agony. Blood has rushed to her upturned head with prominent veins bulging on her neck. Afearia's eyes are barely open as they remain rolled back as she foams from the mouth.

"I need some assistance here!" Zaiah says as he tries his best to hold her down by the shoulders. Demeseus helps as she continues to spasm. She arches her back up a few more times before easing back down for the last time. The two men look at each other, missing Afearia's eyes suddenly opening wide with her pupils sharpened and her right eye completely changed to its demonic state.

She instantly sits up and chokes both of them. "Afearia," Zaiah struggles to say.

Adrian, terrified, begins to run out the room until he stops himself. He trembles in the doorway with balled fist as he muster all the inner strength he held within. He turns to Afearia who appears to be mindlessly choking her friends. Looking like his knees would buckle, Adrian manages to step forward.

"Anya, stop it!" Adrian cries.

Immediately, Afearia's face becomes alert and scared. Realizing what's she's doing, Afearia struggles to remove her hand from them. As she lowers her hands gradually in a tremble as if they're fighting against her, she stares at the men as if she didn't recognize them. Focusing as her body seems to be working against her, she barely manages to bring in her arms and cross them as they try to pull out from her. She then begins to struggle as she lowered her head from everyone's view.

Suddenly with a hard drop of her arms and a swift up turn of her head as she looks at the ceiling wide-eyed, Afearia inhales fast and deep as if to be breathing after a dive. Her eyes are now completely reverted as she breathes loudly, catching her breath. She falls back with unblinking eyes and her mouth barely open. As she lies motionless, the men are rubbing their necks, cautiously watching her.

Zaiah moves close and looks into her vacant eyes. "Afearia?"

Afearia's eyes roll onto him and a sad, scared expression begins to form on her face, "What's happening to me?"

"I. I…" unsure of what to say.

Demeseus steps forward and puts his hand on her shoulder. "We'll figure this out. I promise."

Afearia looks up at Demeseus before her right hand

begins to tremble a little. She pulls it under the sheets before sitting up and bending her legs inward while putting her hand to her forehead in a stressed out manner. She looks toward the wide-eyed scared children and puts on a false face of optimism.

"I'm fine, guys," Afearia tells the kids. "Stop looking so worried. It's not healthy." Seeing they were still worried, she sighs and nods. "I know. I'm sorry I'm making you two worry. I hate when I'm the reason for your concern. But I do have a favor to ask." The kids nod to comply before she steps out the bed and approaches them. She kneels to them with a genuine smile. "Ignore the reason. I want you two to hug me again." They do as they were requested as all three of them hold one another. "Tighter." They squeeze closer. "I love you two very much," greatly surprising the children by her words. "I truly do. You both taught me so much; even saving me from myself many times. Unseen rescues that I will never forget." She leans back and kisses both their cheeks." Thank you, my loves."

"Why-why does this make me sad?" Veronica whimpers with her brother whimpering as well.

"Because she's saying goodbye," Adrian replies.

"My little man, don't say that. I'm a fighter to the bitter end. Now," Afearia says upon standing. "I need to have a private conversation with Demeseus. Please wait downstairs." Though hesitant, the kids do as she asks while she walks them into the hall and watches them go before returning and gently closing the door.

"Okay, what the hell was that?" Demeseus says. "Why are you scaring those kids with your gloom talk?"

"We need to talk," she says joylessly. "And I think you know about what."

"No," he quickly and firmly says.

"It may have come to this."

"I'm not."

"Who else? No better time than now while all is still in my command." She suddenly notices Zaiah is silently, but sternly watching the conversation between them. "You don't have to be here for this. Demeseus has been through this enough times to understand. You can go."

"I'm staying," Zaiah firmly says.

"It's not worth wrecking your head over." Zaiah just watches her with his stern eyes upon her, not moving a muscle." I'm not trying to be mean to you, I'm trying to—"

"I'm staying," he says louder and harder.

Afearia sighs through her nose and gives him a mildly irritated stare. "Whatever. Do what you want." She looks to Demeseus who seemed a bit on edge. "Demeseus—"

"No," Demeseus says once again.

"Oh my God, just listen! This isn't like all the other times! Something. Something's wrong."

"What happened on the stairs."

Afearia casts her eyes down. "Ever since I woke, my body's been heavy. Felt like I was under pressure."

"Nothing new."

"But not right away. Anytime I lose control and return to normal, it's like a giant reset. But not this time. And worse of all." She takes her shaky hand from behind her back and makes a fist. "This isn't me. The trembling is me fighting my hardest not to kill you both. He's here. And my control is fading."

Demeseus paces for a moment. "But what's changed beyond what we discussed? Why can't you hold him down anymore?"

"I'm too weak," she sadly says.

"Or it's too strong," Zaiah interjects.

"No, it's me."

"You're wicked strong, physically and mentally. I find it hard to believe something you've dealt with for so long is suddenly too strong for you."

Afearia scoffs, "Look at you, talking like you know what's going on here."

Demeseus stares at Zaiah without judgment, just his attention. "You mock me, but I don't know what triggers him for you."

"Then let me clue you in. Anger. Rage. Lust. Pain. Hate, stress, fighting, doubts, and so much more!" getting fired up over just explaining herself. "It never stops!"

"And yet, I'll say you are fairly good at keeping all those things in check."

"Did my disgusting display of control not ring any alarms in your head hours ago about the falsehoods of my control?"

"All I'm saying is there must be something giving that thing an external boost. An edge you are clearly not aware of."

Afearia shakes her head in disagreement. "You're such an idiot."

"No," Demeseus chimes in. "What he's saying sounds reasonable. It would explain everything. We're missing something."

Looking like she may vomit as she hunched over a little, getting everyone's eyes on her, she stands straight in a light tremble, composing herself to the best of her ability. "Nevertheless. I am running out of time... And Demeseus... The way this feels. I don't feel like I'm going to sleep like how some of the changes are, nor do I feel like I'm suddenly being taking into an illusion from inside my own mind." She looks up at him. "I feel like I'm fading away..."

"Shit," Zaiah pacing in growing worry as he runs his hands through his hair. "What the hell do we do?"

Afearia shakes her head like she's pushing through a sneeze before looking to Zaiah. "What was in the bag?"

"Huh?"

"You had a bag when we were downstairs. What

was in it?"

"Is that really important right now?" She stares at him until he sighs and gives in. "It's just clothes like I said before."

Demeseus raises his brow at Afearia for asking a question she should have known the answer to already. "I guess you know my taste now?"

"I—"

"Get it. I want to see." Seeming distrustful, Zaiah doesn't move. "Please. Just come right back." He continues to stare at her, glancing at the door a few times before walking out the room. He looks back at her once more before she nods him off as he closes the door. Afearia turns to Demeseus. "My chest is tight with the want to kill—you specifically," rubbing her chest, seeming to be in pain. "But it's truly not my wish. This slow consumption within. It moves with no resistance no matter what mental defenses I mount. If worse comes to worse, we need to do what we discussed. I need you to kill me."

"I can't do that." Demeseus glances to his side a few times before focusing back on her.

"What did she say?"

"… Nothing," avoiding eye contact.

"I can tell you what she said." Demeseus gives her a peculiar look. "Don't worry," gaining an unwelcomed dual voice. "I won't tell her your dirty little secret." When Zaiah returns, Afearia jerks her head in his direction to telekinetically slam the door and hold it shut.

"Sasano," Demeseus says with stern eyes.

Though both her irises are red, her sclerae is only tinted black, not pitch black. The room slowly darkens as he suddenly smiles. "Hero of the past or not, we all have desires. I can't take the risk that you'll act on yours."

"And what's that?"

"You haven't been back long, but you have to admit it." He slowly approaches Demeseus while Zaiah continues to bang on the door calling for Afearia. "You'll love to live again," standing inches from his face.

Demeseus smirks. "What a surprise. You and I have finally found common ground."

"Heh," giving a creepy, wide, sideways smile with eyes nearly closed.

Eternity's chain suddenly latches on Sasano's wrist, ending his smile as his face sours. "But. Unlike you, I won't stop at nothing to get it. Especially if it means harming Afearia."

Looking dead face, Sasano suddenly smiles, but looking more human while doing so. "I'm touched." Without warning, he punches Demeseus in the face in a downward strike nearly knocking him down. "But you're no better than me."

Demeseus suddenly retaliates with the same manner of punch, but barely budges him. "As they say, misery loves company. But you're not pulling me down with you."

Sasano delivers the same punch but harder, bringing Demeseus to his knees with a bloody lip. "Release me," looking deadpan. Demeseus shot up to return the punch, but Sasano easily catches his fist. He squeezes his fingers into his knuckle joints, causing him to wince in pain. "You really think we can dance on the same stage, don't you?" He twists his wrist and Demeseus kneels and screams with clenched teeth. "Infuriating." He looks down at him and smirks. "Although, seeing you like this is a pleasing example of what the world will be doing when I return. Kneeling. As it was suppose to be written," speaking with underlining resentment.

Demeseus manages to get off his knee. "You won't be—returning," he grunts. "We'll see to that," he says before thrusting the tip of his materialized light dagger in his face.

Unfortunately, the dagger's stopped by an unseen force. Sasano glances at it. "To me, your ongoing existence is only a temporary hindrance. But you'll never be the cure she so desperately needs. Enjoy the girl for a little while longer." He releases Demeseus and turns to approach the mounted mirror near the window. He stares at his reflection with no emotion before fixing Afearia's hair after being previously punched. Sasano also looks to see if there is any bruising before flashing his sharp canines with a smile. "I'll allow it," smugly straightening her shirt.

With the closing of his eyes, Afearia's body drops to the floor and the room lightens to its natural hue. Zaiah busts through the door looking around in a near panic.

"Is she—?" Zaiah asks with worry.

"No. She was swallowed and didn't even realize it…," he says, staring at her resting face. "This is becoming a terrifying ordeal. I don't know how to fix it."

Zaiah grunts in irritation and marches up to Demeseus. He tosses away the bag and yanks him up by the collar. "Then think of something!" he threatens with a clenched jaw.

"There's nothing. This is completely different than all of our encounters with him. It's almost as if his soul is taking dominant capital. As if to be—pushing her out."

Zaiah narrows his angry eyes on him. "You'd like that, wouldn't you?"

Demeseus aggressively slaps his hand away. "What the hell are you talking about?"

"I heard what that thing said. Something about you bringing harm to Afearia for a second chance. What does that mean?"

"Who knows."

"You're lying!"

"Do you really think this is the time to discuss this?"

"It is if you're holding out on us. What are you hiding? Can the progression be stopped? Are you really here to help? Or have you been waiting for this chance to return to this realm by betraying her trust?"

Demeseus, seeming unfazed, stares at him for a while. "It'll cost more than her trust. Treating me like the enemy will not remedy this situation. You have a problem with me, and we'll get to that. For now, let's focus on just saving her life."

"That's your job, you idiot," he shouts in a rising anger. "She put all of her trust in you, for YOU to figure out!"

Demeseus turns from him and stares out the window for a moment. He looks down at Afearia before carrying her off to gently place back in bed. He kneels at her bedside in deep thought while lovingly holding her hand to his mouth.

Demeseus closes his eyes for a moment, subtly expressing his internal desperation before looking to Zaiah, "No one's allowed in this room unless I'm in it. I'll figure this out."

"You—"

"Get out!"

Zaiah grits his teeth and turns to leave. He opens the door and steps halfway out the room, "I don't care who you are to her. If you betray her like that thing believes you will—I'll kill you."

He shuts the door and stomps down the stairs, alerting the kids. "Can we see her?" Adrian asks.

"No," he aggressively responds before slamming the front door behind him.

Wearing his anger on his face, Zaiah treads far from the house. His cautious eyes move about as a deeper crinkle forms in his brow the further from the house he gets. Not soon after, Zaiah had left the town and reaches the widespread forest they once fled from the pursuit of Minerva's hunting squad. In an ongoing mutter of bother, he enters the forest kicking branches and small rocks.

Where the trees were a little more spacious, his

613

muttering becomes coherent. "Damn stupid Demeseus. Like he's her only hero. Meanwhile, I sit on my ass crossing my fingers for good luck. Damn it! I can't do anything for her!" kicking a rock into a distant tree within his eye view. After staring at the ground for a while, looking a bit out of breath, he looks up toward the tree, noticing the edges of a white robe fluttering in the wind. "You're a lousy hider. Show yourself—now!"

"I wasn't hiding," the man behind the tree lightly replies. Stepping from behind the tree is Aquarius, moving forward from the trees' shadows and gradually into the moonlight.

"Then what were you doing?"

"Watching..."

Zaiah narrows his eyes, clearly looking for any reason to take offensive action. "Why don't you—"

"She's in trouble, isn't she?" sounding and looking remotely concerned, something that surprises Zaiah for a moment.

"Who?"

"Little Afe, of course," moving closure for Zaiah to clearly see him as he smiles.

Surprised to have been approached by an elite, Zaiah's eyes quickly expresses anger. "You! You're—!"

"One of the jerks who trapped you in that tree," he says with rolled eyes and hard sarcasm. "Anger, revenge, hate," dramatically posing with each given word before slouching, "so bored. Look, you know better than most that I play to the beat of my own drum. Not often does what the realms' haughtiness has to say ever makes me eager to assist. But that day was kinda needed."

"How!? I should rip your throat out!"

"Trust me, we all have roles to play. Besides, I thought a few dozen years would be long enough for you to simmer that temper down. It gets you in more trouble than not. Or have you forgotten?"

Zaiah, knowing he wasn't wrong, swallows his anger the best he's able. "What do you want?"

"Wrong question. You kids always ask the wrong questions. What do you want?"

"I'm—!" He balls his fist and breaths slowly before replying. "I'm trying to be calm, but you want to mess around and play games."

"My dear tree child, time is quintessential here and you're wasting it by being overly cautious. She's dying, kid. Can't you understand that?" seeming to seriously be trying to reason with him.

"I… I know," he sadly admits. "I just want to save her."

"Then you shall."

"I can't. I know nothing about this beast and Demeseus says it's different this time. Says he isn't sure how to stop it."

"Demeseus is back!?" Not knowing why he was so surprised, Zaiah silently glares at him. "Interesting," scheming as he turned from him for a moment. "Almost wonderful even. Hehe. He is right though. Things are different. That thing is as old as—well it's hard to explain. I assume she can no longer control it."

"I don't know. I guess so."

"Darkness is all around us," looking and sounding ominous. "It is old and vast. That old magic powers his being. Though he is not one with the "source" anymore, he has other means. He relies on her instability to feed the endless abyss that is his essence."

"She mentioned something about that."

"Her time in Elysium is the farthest she's been from the darkness. So keeping him at bay wasn't such an immense task. But being here in a place smack dab in the middle while also having the realm of darkness pouring itself into this one; Afearia's never been closer. Because of the odd circumstances of two realms partly merged, she's receiving a larger dose of darkness than she should."

"Then the problem is her location?"

"That's a large factor. But the trick he's pulling now is something he can only do once per host and under strict conditions. He probably thinks fate is smiling on him since all is in line for this to happen," he thinks aloud. "She can't win this. He is literally in the process of devouring her soul."

Zaiah runs up and grabs him by the collar, "Then what are we talking for!? You lied to me!"

Still smiling without an ounce of worry, pries a finger off his robe. "I wouldn't dare. All I'm trying to say is only old things can defeat old things." Aquarius glances at his hand several times before Zaiah releases him. He brushes off his robe and straightens it. "She can't win alone, but with a little help," digging into his robe pocket to dangle a silver talisman between them. "She might stand a chance."

The small, white gold talisman is constructed in a wire fashion with a small red gemstone decorated by two green ones above it. Though it clearly is held together by finely woven white gold wiring, it can not be seen through from the gaps, apparently darkened by an odd magic.

"What is this?" Zaiah asks.

"Repellendum malum hoc, et in hoc vivat inaeternum scream de tenebris lucem. That's how you begin the chant."

"That's. That's old magic… That's lost art magic! How do you know—!?"

"Retro invocabunt in lucem. Exspellam eum in tenebras. That part must be chanted with all you have. You don't stop until he's back where he belongs. At the heel of man," Aquarius explains, looking quite serious as he stares Zaiah in the eyes.

"This—spell. It should save her?"

"The chant. It should, if done right, will save

Afearia from her current fate. Yes. After all, you're the only one who can," he says with an ominous sincerity.

"And you expect me to trust you on this?"

Aquarius smirks and holds it closer to him. "Nope. But you could always take it and not use it." Zaiah watches the talisman sway for a while, almost hearing a faint blowing wind from within before snatching it from him. As he pockets it, Aquarius puts his happy fist on his hips. "See? Was that so hard? Just make sure—" Without warning, Zaiah violently grabs Aquarius and cocks his fist back to punch him out. "Oh!" falsely surprised before collapsing into a puddle of water.

In that moment, Aquarius slithers into the forest as Zaiah had punched the air. He reforms several feet from him running into the woods laughing obnoxiously while wishing Zaiah all the best as he escapes. Zaiah watches him with much distrust before heading back to the house.

Quiet, Demeseus is on the ground floor where the kids sleep soundly on the living room couch across from the kitchen. Looking frustrated, he stands beside the kitchen window staring into the streets. The only solution I can think of is what I refuse to do, Demeseus thinks. Upstairs, Afearia screams in a brief, pain-filled moan load enough for him to hear. He looks up and sighs at his inability to help before a loud thud is heard above. Just as he turns to possibly investigate, Zaiah returns from his walk. "You're back."

"Yeah," Zaiah replies, softly shutting the door with his back to Demeseus. "How is she?"

"She's…" Afearia screams in pain up above, pounding the floors. "Barely hanging on."

"Should I see her?"

"She wouldn't want you to. But I insist you do."

"Why?" turning to face him, seeing the vague sadness in his eyes.

"Because… Just go." Zaiah slants his eyes for a

moment then nods at Demeseus before slowly walking up the stairs.

Crawling around on the floor in the kiwi gown Zaiah bought for her, Afearia's shaking as she moves toward the window. She manages to make it and sits up with her back pressed against the wall. Shaking so bad as if she'll seize any moment, Afearia pounds the floor three times in frustration, bringing her shakes to a minimum while breathing strongly.

She stares into her shaky hand and slams her head back, looking into the hanging moon with a hard face. Like a sudden itch in her throat, she coughs a few times through tight lips. "I—" only saying one word, she begins coughing again. "I really want to believe in miracles right now, but—" Her face contorts for a moment as the pain rises up inside her. "I don't want to go like this."

Afearia balls her fist, fighting back tears as well. "To leave them like this… Why!?" She looks around, feeling hopeless as tears flow and she slowly shakes her head in defeat. "Please," looking up at the moon. "I ask for a miracle… for a second time in my life. The unlikely chance you're out there and have heard me for all these years… All I asked. ALL I ASKED WAS FOR YOU TO WATCH OVER ME! WHERE ARE YOU!? PLEASE—!" She falls over, struggling in tears to sit back up, soon giving up with face turned into the floor. "Please… Help."

A light knocking is heard from the door. Afearia musters all the strength she has, only able to sit up halfway. "Afearia?" Zaiah says before cracking open the door but respectfully doesn't enter.

Afearia rolls her eyes with a faint smirk. "Come in, idiot," she jokes with noticeable strain in her voice as if she's carrying a heavy object.

He comes in with an uneasy smile before closing the door. "I just wanted to see if you're—" giving her a suspicious brow raise. "Why are you on the floor?"

618

"I thought it'd be a fine place to rest," she softly smiles.

"Can I—?" he was asking with kind arms stretched. He lowers them shyly. "May I assist you, Afearia?"

She softly nods with consent. He walks over and takes her arm behind his neck before lifting her off the floor. With loving confidence, he slowly walks her back to the bed. When Afearia stares up at the strong man carrying her close to his chest like one of his own, he catches her stare and smiles.

Afearia quickly looks away, partially covering her face. "God, this is so embarrassing for me," she mutters loud enough for him to hear. "I regret this already!" giving false aggression that anyone could see through.

"I know. A super woman like you would only see this as a fate worse than death."

She giggles. "This is true." Afearia relaxes and turns her head from him, looking to be on the verge of sleep. "But it ain't all bad," this time speaking too low for him to understand.

Zaiah sits her on the edge of the bed and steps back a little. He watches her as she tiredly stares down at the floor. She remains inside herself for quite some time before he boyishly puts his hands in his pockets while looking elsewhere.

"So, I see you like the gown I picked out."

"I don't," she rashly responds.

"Oh…" seeming disappointed in himself before looking at her warm smile.

"Green's not my color. But the thought means more than the color. Thank you…, Zaiah."

He shyly smiles and happily rolls his eyes to avoid eye contact. "You called me Zaiah."

"I did," Afearia nods.

Zaiah's smile fades into gloom. "And that troubles me all the more. Why?"

Afearia stops smiling and looks off to the floor farthest behind him. "I asked the hardest thing from Demeseus. A burden he never wished to bear."

"What did you ask him?"

"I requested he take my life."

Zaiah's eyes are wide and shaken by her outlandish request. "Are you nuts!? Don't do that!"

"It was only as a last resort. However, I fear he will not be able to go through with it. He proved that when he fought my possessed body as Sasano," looking to him. "You—remember?"

"I can always hazily recall bits and pieces."

He brushes off her reply and steps toward her. "Look, I don't know him like you do, but you weren't there. That man was brutal as hell. He exploded you at one point! I think if you give him the word he'd do it without second thought."

"You're wrong. He was ruthless when he knew my life wasn't in danger. He's sweet. If he knew I could sometimes feel the damage dealt, he would surely hold back, which is the last thing you should do when the monster in my body arises."

"Then I need to talk to him. I won't let him kill you. We'll find another way."

"Don't worry, he won't. Not like you would," staring fairly seriously at him.

"Wha—what do you mean?"

"I saw you out there when I regained partial control of my body. There was a deadly look in your eyes. The way you kept striking me. You were truly prepared to take my life. So I figured, the rightful person to ask is you. Zaiah? Will you be ready to take my life once again?"

Zaiah had not responded. He harmlessly gives Afearia a deep, yet stern stare as she awaits for him to agree. "No," somewhat surprising her. "There's another way."

"I wouldn't be asking this if there was."

"I can't," turning his head from her.

"You're the only one who can."

He shakes his head and takes several steps from her while stressfully rubbing his face. "Yeah—people keep saying that," he mutters with hands on his hips. She continues to stare at him, hoping he'll come around to her way of thinking. "What do you want me to do!? Cut you down and shrug, I don't give a damn!?"

"Absolutely not. You will strike me down, Zaiah. You'll do it. But you'll do it with a heart of kindness. Show me that before I pass. It's all I ask."

"That's not a simple request, Afearia!"

"I know… I'm sorry."

Not looking her way anymore, Zaiah repeatedly shakes his head in a manner of denial. "No. No, I won't do it," walking toward the door.

"Zaiah."

"No, we'll find another way."

"Zaiah!?"

"I'll find another way!" Swinging the door open and stopping half out the room. He turns to her with sorrowful eyes, causing Afearia to empathetically watch him try to keep it together for her sake. "I'll find another way. I will. I promise."

He slowly shuts the door behind him. Afearia shifts her body toward the window, staring at the full moon. "A miracle," she softly says with underlining desperation.

Walking frustrated down the stairs, Zaiah immediately turns into the kitchen. "What if we infuse her with light?" speaking to Demeseus who half turns to him from the window.

Demeseus turns back with arms tightly crossed as he leans against the frame. "Tried it."

"Then I'll erase it like before."

"If that was the answer we wouldn't be here now.

This isn't a simple task like removing oil from water like it tends to be. What's happening now is like trying to separate ink from tar. Telling the difference from where one ends and the other begins has become impossible."

Zaiah paces a little before impulsively punching the wall, startling the kids awake. "Damn it! There has to be something!"

"I... need to talk to her."

As Demeseus turns and heads for the stairs, Zaiah stands in front of him. "No way. She may think you can't, but I beg to differ. You're going up there to kill her, aren't you?"

"If only you could understand the vast consequences that will befall the billions of people living in this world if we let him run free."

Zaiah shakes his head with an annoyed smile. "You know, she loves you. A lot, yet it really isn't hard for you to off her at all."

"Trust me. This is harder than you'll ever know. I've been with her since she was a little girl. The idea of this rivals a choice I refused to make in my past life. But now I know better. Feelings are the last things that should stand between us and what needs to be done."

"She isn't your redemption story," sounding quite threatening. "She's Afearia. And I'm not letting you up those stairs."

"I'm sorry. But you don't have a choice." His gauntlets appear and he raises his fist to do combat. "I'll make this quick."

Zaiah calls Braveheart to his hands. "So much for the hero of the people. I guess I'll be sending you back to the land of the forgotten where you belong."

Demeseus glances over his shoulder, doing a double take. "Wait, where are the kids?" he asks in alarm. Zaiah looks back to see they truly had left. The men glance at each other then race up the stairs.

They open the door to the bedroom in a hurry to find Afearia sitting under the window with the children soundly sleep with their heads in her lap. She softly strokes Adrian's cheek and Veronica's hair while smiling down at them.

The two men cautiously come further into the room. "Afearia?" Demeseus asks oddly.

"They're adorable, aren't they?" Afearia calmly speaks. "I could eat them up," looking up at them with a shift in dual voice and eyes tinting dark.

With quick thinking, Demeseus swiftly presents his gauntlets to release chains. They wrap around the kids and are yanked from Sasano and into his arms. Sasano shoots up and bares his hand to telekinetically blast Demeseus and the children out the room. Zaiah had stabbed the floor with his sword to prevent himself from being blasted away as well. Demeseus had taken the blunt of the blow by holding the kids to his chest and having his back slammed up against the wall.

The force of the attack knocks Demeseus out cold. Zaiah turns toward him in alarm to his predicament. The moment he attempts to see if he was alright, the door slams shut and becomes magically sealed with a dim purple light edging the door. Zaiah quickly turns and draws his sword on the growling beast. Sasano slowly moves toward him, smiling sinisterly.

"What are you?" Zaiah asks, backing away a little as Sasano comes in a near swaying motion of evil intent.

"Something far greater than you could ever know," Sasano responds.

"And what do you want with Afearia?"

"That name is nearly a faint memory to me. And in memory of that, I'll have this body devour all of her—"

"Afearia?" Sasano tilts his head like a confused dog. "Are you really gonna let this thing have you? You're better than this."

"She's checked out. Ask Demeseus."

"Come on, Afearia. If you go, who's gonna call me on all my crap? It's been a long time since anyone has. I can't let that go now. I can't let you go."

Sasano smirks. "Stupid boy."

Sasano rushes to attack, nearly ripping a piece of Zaiah with him after evading his clutch. He follows up with a kick that slams Zaiah up against the wall. Sasano appears before him almost immediately as he pins him. He brings out his fangs, moving to bite his neck.

"If you do this, you'll truly be lost, Afearia," Zaiah calmly tells her. Just as Sasano's about to bite into him, Zaiah does a surprising reversal and slams his back against the wall, holding Sasano by the neck. "Afearia, PLEASE!"

His strong plea and emotionally shaken eyes spark something fragile inside Afearia's core, reawakening her. She manages to suppress close to three fourths of the darkness flowing in her eyes. Her pupils revert a couple times before normalizing. Her breathing begins to calm. Her erratic eyes gain focus upon the man who's heart bleeds for her.

Shocking him like a child seeing the first snowfall, Afearia begins to cry before him in such a sorrowful manner; almost as if to be begging for his help without saying a word. She shuts her eyes, looking more defeated than he's ever seen her. He never wanted her to hurt like this. Afearia's arms tremble as she slowly nods at him.

"Please," Afearia whimpers so softly. "I can't. No more. Please, Zaiah. I beg of you. Right now… Zaiah. Do it—**please**," sounding as if she almost became Sasano again when her head jerked for a moment.

Watching her beg for death under such circumstances was more than he could bear. Reluctant, but ready, Zaiah raises the edge of Braveheart to her throat. He tightens his grip, soon shaking at just the thought. She closes her eyes in acceptance, still twitching and shaking.

624

Zaiah balls his wavering hand. Lowering his fist down, he bumps his pocket, lightly hearing the talisman he's hidden. He reaches in his pocket and holds it in his palm before glancing up at Afearia.

Zaiah lowers his sword slowly before gradually raising the talisman up between them. He wraps the chain around his fingers with the centerpiece resting in his palm. He keeps his arm stretched and backs away to be roughly at arm's length from her.

"Repellendum malum hoc, et in hoc vivat inaeternum scream de tenebris lucem. Repellendum malum hoc, et in hoc vivat inaeternum scream de tenebris lucem." Now repeating the first portion for the third time, Afearia lightly opens her sad eyes. "Retro invocabunt in lucem." She turns her head a bit sideways, looking vaguely confused by his actions. "Expellam eum in tenebras!" his voice echoes with the room being basked in a splendid luminous light from the talisman.

At that moment, Afearia's head sharply turns with her eyes wide and alert. Her body shakes rapidly as vibrations are emitting from within. Slowly, a darkness so deep that not even the talisman's light could penetrate, crawls up the walls like tentacles from behind her. With her body mysteriously pinned to the wall, Afearia's speaking incoherent babble with much vile. Voices of howling spirits begin to fill the room, speaking many languages while screams creep up behind them. Zaiah witnessing this knew something was working and pressed on harder than when he began.

"Repellendum malum hoc, et in hoc vivat inaeternum scream de tenebris lucem!" he vigorously chanted two more times.

The screams of pain and loss grow louder as Afearia's body seems to be fighting with itself as she keeps making sudden sharp movements in a manic way. The shadowy tentacles moving up seem to be ready to engulf the other half of the room as they're coming down on Zaiah. Suddenly, the talisman's light intensifies greatly, halting the wiggling appendages at the edges of its light.

Grasping herself wildly while jerking around and slamming her head against the wall, Afearia screams with the voice of a man screaming in sync with her, but not as a dual voice. Her right eye turns full demonic while her left remains untouched by the demon's curse.

"Retro invocabunt in lucem et expellam eum in tenebras!" he's been shouting, doing his best to override every other voice in the room.

In his ongoing desperate chanting, Zaiah's spitting with a reddening madness as he puts all his heart in this chant to rid Afearia of this monstrous aliment.

The shadows on the wall and ceiling begin to soften and fade away like crumbling pillars of sand. A dark humanoid shadow rises up behind her with a white shadow equal in size, except the white shadow is virtually a silhouette of Afearia. The two shadows split apart violently, creating a sonic boom that cracks the walls. Like puppets, they join close back to back and sink into Afearia.

In a final attempt to resist, Afearia viciously rushes at Zaiah with hands spread like claws to slash his eyes. Without pause in his chat, Zaiah palms her face and slams her to the floor, chanting even louder as he holds the talisman closer. Continuing to claw at his face like a wild animal, she manages to scratch into his cheek, but he doesn't even flinch.

After finishing the final line of the chant, Afearia's body stiffened with arms up, eyes wide, and mouth open as the lingering darkness spills out into the talisman. As she releases a long, wispy exhale, her body falls limp and her eyes finally shut.

Zaiah breathes heavy as he cautiously stands over her. The light of the shimmering talisman fades and holds a dim vibrancy. Suddenly, it begins yanking itself from his hand like a scared kitten. Despite now using two hands to keep it, he nearly falls over before it yanks free from him and shoots through the window, flying over the town in a slow descent.

Out on the edge of the forest of an overlooking hill, a man's hand goes up, moments before catching the talisman. He slowly brings his hand down and looks into the dim lit item. Removing the hood of his white robe, Aquarius smiles staring at his returned talisman.

"Heh. And yet so much more has yet to come." He irritability grunts as he comically digs in his ear with his pinky. "Grr, that's going to be annoying for the next few days. The damn ringing!" he grits.

"Aquarius," a woman says from behind. Aquarius is genuinely startled as he quickly turns to find Minerva calmly, but lifelessly watching him. "What are you doing out here? You've been missing for weeks."

"Getting quite good at hiding your presence there, Roughshod. But as you know, there's nothing strange about me being M.I.A. every once in a while. Besides, what brings you all this way?"

"Evidence. Much has happened since you've been away."

"I bet."

"Afearia couldn't have gone far," causing Aquarius' ear to twitch up.

"That ol' gal? How long ago did you see here?"

"Roughly fifteen hours ago."

"Then you're wasting your time." Like a sudden itch, Aquarius begins digging in the same ear again. "Grrah!"

"Why do you keep picking your ear?"

"Because someone yelled at me for being negligent and now I'm half deaf."

"Amusing."

"Not half as much as this search you're

627

orchestrating. I was already here and never saw her in the town. Just a rough, beaten up car driving off in the distance."

Minerva makes a dull pondering expression. "It may have been her." Aquarius smirks from her view and turns to enter the forest. "Perhaps I should get Valerie's expertise."

He stops a couple meters behind her. "That bloodhound?" turning his head toward her, looking quite unamused.

"Don't call her that. It's an insulting name the people of Terra have slandered her with and she finds it quite unflattering."

"Regardless," turning to face her back. "Why bother her? Derexen and Valerie have high priority task to handle at nearly all times. This wild goose chase is not worth their efforts."

"Maybe because you have a habit of lying and obstructing information."

He smiles a little. "You're quite talkative today. Still though, you lack any and all emotions. Something must be swirling in your head to be saying so much. Something's triggering you. Something's trying to claw you out of that husk you've sadly become." Surprisingly, Aquarius' smile becomes far less mischievous and quite genuine. "It's a good thing, hatchling."

Silence passes between them. Minerva just stares at him before turning sideways to reach for her ear, "I'll call her now."

"Are you sure about that?" halting her call. "This is your hunt. If you call now, this will come off as incompetence; and coming from a pillar no less. Unless of course," stopping himself as he playfully shrugs. "Never mind. Call her. It's been a long time since I've seen her."

Though in thought, she tilts her head at him, seeming to not be swayed by his prose. "You must think of me as I was. Still with the slickest silver tongue in all the realms," shaking her head.

"Haha, that may be, my old friend, but my words ring true about this nonetheless."

She looks off in the distance and turns from him. "True. I'll be letting lord Derexen know that I've found you. He'd likely—"

Not even waiting to hear her out, Aquarius warps from the area, only getting her to halfheartedly look where he once stood. Minerva looks back into the town about to turn away when suddenly noticing the silence from below and the damaged buildings off in the distance. Her eyes narrow a bit, vaguely expressing her suspicion.

Meanwhile, several hours after Afearia and those close to her survived the storm, the worst was over. It was clear by how playful she was as she wrestled with the kids in bed. She batters them with pillows as they try to jump her and fail while laughing nonstop.

By the time Demeseus walks in, Afearia has both of them pinned under blankets. "Afearia?" Demeseus says almost awkwardly. Afearia looks at him like a kid caught sticking their hand in the cookie jar. The siblings pop their heads up looking at Demeseus just as blankly. "Didn't mean to interrupt, but I thought we should get going. It would be best we rest up somewhere further than here."

"Agreed," Afearia says. "Alright you two. It's time to go," patting both their rears. They both complain as they lazily get out the bed. Afearia playfully throws a pillow at them. "Pack you two." They run out the room, yelling and racing each other over who can come back the fastest after packing. Afearia watches them with a smile before noticing Demeseus doing the same to her. "What?" hiding her blissful expression.

"Nothing. Just seeing such a pure emotion worn on you is so good. I've know you for so long as the super solider that I forget you could smile like that."

"Oh, please," looking sort of shy as she looks away.

A shopping bag is tossed beside her bed. She looks down and sees folded clothes inside. "It's a gift from him. You should see him." Afearia pouts. Demeseus smirks and turns leaving the room. "Give credit where credit's due, Afearia. It builds character," shutting the door behind him.

Down in the living room, Zaiah is calmly sitting in deep thought with his red duffle bag beside him. Staring at the wall, he has a cotton bandage on his face where he was previously cut. With the back of the couch facing the stairs, soft footsteps come up behind him.

"I was wrong," Afearia says from behind him. Zaiah's startled as he quickly stands up and faces her. "You do have good taste," she shyly says with hands behind her back while twisting her foot in her new black block booties.

Afearia's wearing a black leather jacket a bit off her shoulders with gold lined chest zipper pockets and side pockets. Her top is a thin, sleeveless black sweater and her matching black pants are tight but made with a strong flexible material.

"Well, I did have to make an exchange first," Zaiah jokes.

"Mmm. Much black," she says in a walking exhale.

"Too much?" he asks as she moves pass him.

"A bit," standing in front of the window.

"Next time it'll be better."

It is silent for a few moments. Zaiah was going to speak, but he hesitated. "I don't fully recall what happened or what you had to do. Honestly, I don't want to know. But you are what I remember... You." She turns to face him with a beautiful smile worth a thousand laughs. "Thank you, Azaiah. Thank from the bottom of my heart. For saving my life." Zaiah is astonished to the fullest at how sincere she was with him. He couldn't even blink. She looks to her side. "I guess this makes us ev—"

"We should get going," Zaiah interrupts as he turns

from her.

"What? Azaiah, I'm trying to—"

"Yeah, we better move before they catch wind of us."

"Zaiah—"

"Okay, I'll get the kids," about to run upstairs.

"Idiot!" stopping him in his tracks. "God, the level of stupid in you," she snips as she angrily walks up the stairs.

Zaiah watches her storm off before briefly smiling a little. "Why did you do that?" Demeseus asks, standing with his back to the wall in the kitchen.

"Is this what you're going to do all the time? Standing in the corner of every room like you're deep and edgy?"

"What she was trying to do is hard for her. She was trying to thank you."

"No," he says as he grabs his bag off the couch. He walks up to the front door and opens it before stopping. "She was trying to get rid of me." Zaiah softly shuts the door behind him.

Shortly after Zaiah had left, a car horn is honked from outside. "Time to go, Afearia!" Demeseus shouts.

"Coming!" Afearia shouts back. Folding the last of her belongings into the brown backpack Zaiah got for her. The kids restlessly wait with Adrian walking in circles and Veronica rolling on the floor. "You two can wait for me in the car. I'll be right there."

"Kay!" the children say.

Adrian playfully pushes his sister back as they race toward the door and he makes it out first. Veronica chases him and they both race out the house. The door downstairs is faintly heard shutting. Afearia shakes her head with a smile at their silly antics until a tingling sensation runs down her back, similar to but faintly like the feeling of knowing you'll fall. She stands straight, looking around herself carefully before all of her surroundings are suddenly swallowed in black.

Turning rapidly in panic, all the blackness surrounding her clears. Afearia finds herself standing in the middle of the neighboring forest. "Where? What the? What?" looking around in confusion.

"How long have you waited for this moment?" a deep voice asks from behind her. Afearia stiffens up as her eyes move slowly to her right and her body soon follows. To her great disbelief, standing only a few yards from her is the sole reason Afearia, the 72nd Lightbringer has been deployed to Terra. Derexen had finally made contact with another fragment of his destiny. "Today," drawing his sword Catastrophe on her. "You will answer to all you've done."

With the point of his blade and the cold stare of determination, Afearia comes face to face with an opponent she shouldn't have met... yet.

Eyes of the Future...

Though it is believed nothing's written in stone when speaking of the future, much can be said that unless you're the one writing the book, you can never know. However, even as a tome scholar, there are some futures that are fated to be no matter how many times they've occurred.

Armagevion has been mostly a barren world of nothingness for centuries. Dark cliffs, mountains, and dry land as black or gray as burnt ashes. Finding life out here is difficult, but if you happen to find yourself here by some foolish chance, it is wise to always flee and hide. There are old things still living here that are far too dangerous to be in contact with.

But a new, young danger walks these lands. Something that has never been recorded in these realms before. Something not Demi. Something not human. Wearing a black raggedy cloth with terribly frayed edges from head to toe is a humanoid, barefoot being aimlessly walking the northern dry lands in search of something. The empty winds lightly blow the bare bush branches and the loose grains of dry soil as this creature repeatedly mutters few words.

"Hate... Vengeance... Hate... Vengeance... Rage... Rage..."

It seemed weak and lost, dragging a large shadowy veiled thing behind it as it loudly rakes the land in the endlessly rising darkness covering its features up to its arm. It speaks to itself as if it's trying to hold on to its purpose. Holding on to what remains of its existence. When the winds blow south, the creature stops. It stands a little straighter, lightly bouncing its upper body, still muttering.

"Hate... Vengeance... Hate... Vengeance..." When the winds blow once more from the north, the bouncing becomes greater and its words grow louder and faster. "Hate. Vengeance. Hate. Vengeance. Hate. Rage. Rage." Darkness begins to seep upward slowly from its body. Thick and strong, something is awakening within this being. "Hate... HaTe!" it grits in a growing anger as the darkness comes up faster with red energy mixing in.

The lower half of the creature's humanoid male face is seen from its hood as it lifts its head. "De... De... Der... Der—rex... Der. Derex!" shaking as it seems like it's fighting for consciousness. Its darkness was beginning to bubble, rising up faster with red energy trapped in the bubbles while red steam overlays the creature. "DEREXEN!"

With a bloody roar, it spreads its arms screaming Derexen's name as this chaotic energy explodes from its body blowing away the dead plants and loose dirt from his surroundings. It bends its knees and runs north at an outrages speed before gliding over the soil at near mach three speeds, howling like a mad demon in distress.

The world burns under the might of its rage as all in a two mile radius can hear the whaling screams of the creature who's believed to be hate incarnate. Born twenty-five years ago with a body that can't be destroyed and a power that can't be stopped. This creature has made itself know to all who enter this realm as it hunts and kills everything that moves with the aims of destroying one man.

This remnant has been dubbed the D-Reaper.

*Your past can and **will** shape your future. The problems of yesterday will always become the problems of today. Placing a tourniquet on it or holding off to address it only raises the likelihood of that issue remerging as a greater force or worse... In greater form.*

Much further than the location of the D-Reaper is a fallen civilization where three mighty catastrophes harmlessly spend time together. Though they've never heard or meet the D-Reaper, they wouldn't care regardless, for the three of them have a belief. All that isn't about them isn't relevant or worth a thought. But that belief has been challenged. There's actually a world outside themselves and interestingly enough, HE showed them that.

The ruins of this once great Demi civilization has broken stone monuments, pillars, homes and the city temple scattered throughout. A large, muscular man lies upon the temple ruins with his relaxed limbs spread and the rest of him half dipped in between the stones. His head's leaned back with shut eyes as he bathes in the moon's glow.

Up several fallen stones above him is a finely dressed man in a black suit who's leaned back on his hands. He watches the clouds pass by from under the brim of his fedora, faintly content with his thoughts. He frowns a little with eyes expressing inner disappointment.

"I'm about to lose our game, am I Trisha? It's been almost ten years and I still can't find my happiness." He sighs and watches a distant flock of avian Demis fly across the moon. "You should've gave me pointers. A little help." He smirks. "I bet you're enjoying this. But I won't lose. I will put on a splendid show for you. If I fail... I guess we both die," speaking grimly.

"Cecil, is it time?" the man below asks.

Suddenly, two dusting birds come falling before them. Soon after, a girl dressed like a punk rocker with a pink mohawk comes swooping down, bouncing on a massive bubble made of gum. Her headphones play loud metal music as she keeps rocking on her air guitar. When the song ends, she drops her headphones to her neck, loudly chewing her pink gum.

"Is it time?" she says excitedly with a full mocha dimple smile. "The revival of the games by the return of the exiled villains?"

"Yes," Cecil says calmly. "It is time we make our comeback and remind his highness we're still here." He stands as the clouds part down upon him as he adjusts his thin black tie, "And we're done waiting." A devious sideways smile comes on his face before he shoots his gaze forward in the distance. "Let's go catch our hero." Wind loudly swirls around him, blowing the smaller rocks away and bursting the girl's bubble ball.

"Hey!" she says as she almost falls after the bubble pops.

"Dutch! Alisha! Something tells me this year's game will be the best of our lives! I'm betting my own life on that." He begins to rise off the ground as larger rocks float and swirl around him. "HORSEMEEEN!" he shouts to rally them to attention with Dutch standing tall and Alisha smiling wildly at him. "Let the games," raising his finger to the sky. "Begin!"

The moment he points to the ground below, he flies off north, Dutch jumps off the stones and lands on a wave of fast moving rocks and dirt carrying him at an alarming speed up north. Alisha looks around with an annoyed expression as she taps her foot.

"CECIL!" she yells. Wind builds around her, lifting her off the ground. "Now that's better," immediately looking cheerful as she's zipped north behind the others.

All of these coming events are marching all three realms to what is known as the end. Each decision all of these major players make is counting the realms' Doomsday clock. Many don't realize it and others think they have more time. The truth is... the greatest threat to ever endanger man and demon has been...

"It's true to this day," Bonnie says, standing in a dark cave in Armagevion, lit by the torch she carries. "No matter how well prepared you are and no matter how powerful you become, no empire can last forever. Derexen puts on a good show, but with each passing day his power over the realms is weakening. We've never had so many open seats in the government circle like this. The threats, the dangers, the restless rebellion that dwells at his feet grows more hungry every minute. I don't think his world has another good year to give."

Bonnie turns, facing Agonda and Takahashi. The two of them sit on stones within the cave, seeming quite serious. "Then what will you do?" Takahashi asks. "You've been with him for a very long time. Doesn't it kind of bother you that your king's in trouble?" Bonnie just darkly smiles at him, clearly not going to answer him. "In any case, what is it you need from me?"

"A simple request. Be sure that you and the rest of the world leaders quit being so impatient. The more they push, the harder Derexen will push back. He's right where he needs to be and so are we. The situation with Ludwig was bad, but the recklessness of Chloe was downright foolish. Can I count on you to relay that to the others?"

"Seriously? You called me here for that? A phone call would have done the job."

"Yes, but you owe me something."

Takahashi becomes a little threatening with his hard expression. "I don't like the idea, but the Prime Minister was generous. He has agreed to let you enhance me further."

A devilish smile rises from Bonnie. "Believe me. If you wish to stand toe-to-toe with the likes of him, you'll need someone who knows him better than anyone. Derexen is a man who prepares for every eventuality. If he wasn't, he wouldn't be where he is today. So, I thank Prime Minister Minami." She holds her hand out. Annnd?"

Takahashi stands and moves toward her. He stares Bonnie in the eyes for a moment before tilting his head. "Can A.N.T.S. and the world leaders trust you?"

Bonnie tilts her head as well and smiles almost innocently, "Of course. Our mutually assured destruction is a bond stronger than any friendship. After all, self-preservation is a primal instinct that drives harder than anything else."

Takahashi smirks. "Then they'll be no hard feelings in the end." She nods, still holding her smile. He goes into his pocket and hands her a folded paper. "A deal's a deal. You can have her. We wanted another ace in the hole, but I think we're more than safe in our current standing."

Bonnie becomes a little giddy. "I can't believe she's intact."

"Not really. Most of her body is gone. Being frozen in ice really helped preserve what was left. What are you going to do with a dead girl?"

"Nothing you need to worry about."

"Right. Anyway, I'm going. Good luck to you both," walking out the cave.

She looks to Agonda, "That went better than I hoped."

Agonda stands, "This is an amusing outcome for the king."

"Is it?"

"So many factions and underuse in a collective attempt to stop one man. If I were him, I would feel flattered."

"Hmph, I bet you would."

Agonda turns to leave. "Anyone would. It simply means you've made an impact that will span far beyond your time. It's impressive." He looks back at her. "Shall we return?"

"You go on. Derexen believes we're hard at work. I think I'll continue making preparations."

"We should thank Jodi for finding 'The Old One' and pretending that the foreign leaders found the fallen Lightbringer first."

"No need to thank him. He always acted in his best interest before anything else."

"And you and I are so different?"

Bonnie stares at him for quite a while, seeming almost willing to revel an intimate fact about herself. "It is different though," speaking softer as she turns her gaze. "Because there's no one—" She glances at him, regaining her sideways smirk. "You can go, Agonda. I haven't forgotten our arrangement."

"Heh," walking away pleased. "To be honest, at this point I think I follow you around because I'm amused by the depths of your depravity."

Once he was too far to hear walking, Bonnie drops the false smiles and stares dangerously where he exited. "Depravity? Fucking idiot... What I do is too astronomically comprehensive for you. After all," teleporting from the cave.

She reappears in a massive underground cavern where rushing streams pass over and through rocks and crystals of various colors being lit beautifully by them. Rare white glowing plants bundled like bouquets grow from the numerous cracks in the cavern walls like a grapevine, spewing bright spores of pure energy that go up and fade away in seconds.

Bonnie wasn't alone. A dragon-like claw rests pass the largest rushing stream. Scales and bone, this creature's claw had its flesh neatly cut away bit by bit. Bonnie stares up at the crystallized horned head of this creature who's skull can easily fill a football stadium.

"Excellence is at reach for anyone who's willing to take it. For the universe is simply trying to rediscover itself—through us," proudly emphasized, talking up at the crystallized wall that runs miles thick. Bonnie walks up to the crystal wall that seals the beast. She taps it loudly with a laid about pickaxe. The creature vibrates the cavern a little before opening its empty eye sockets at her, trying to shred her with its pinned claw. "Good day, my love," speaking cutely. She pulls out a scalpel and smiles. "It's time for your daily contribution."

The Series so Far in Chronological Order

Book One: The Way To Dawn

Book Two: The Way To Dawn: Ascension Zero

Lost Story Volume 1: The Way To Dawn: Apocryphal

Lost Story Volume 2: The Way To Dawn: Remnants

Book Three: The Way To Dawn: Dominion of Eden

Book Four: The Way To Dawn: End of Days

Facebook: https://www.facebook.com/CharlesLeeBooks
Twitter: https://twitter.com/CharlesLeeBooks

Glossary

Дорогой, вода: Sweetheart, water. (Chap: A King's Role part 2)

Вы называетеето водка: You call it vodka? (Chap: A King's Role part 2)

Да ладнух!? Маленькая девочка, ты плохо говоришь о Боге. Я тебя убью, сука: Come on!? Little girl, you speak ill of God? I'll kill you, bitch. (Chap: A King's Role part 2)

Мы не закончили: We're not done. (Chap: A King's Role part 2)

Repellendum malum hoc, et in hoc vivat inaeternum scream de tenebris lucem: This evil must be repelled, and in this lives an eternal scream of light from the darkness. (Chap: The Martyr of Our Story)

Retro invocabunt in lucem. Exspellam eum in tenebras: They will call back into the light. I will cast him out into the darkness. (Chap: The Martyr of Our Story)

About the Author

Charles Lee has always been a fan of stories with greater meaning than what the surface portrays. His love for profound fantasy began at a young age. His growing interest in thought-provoking stories ranged from a gamut of different areas of literature. These are experiences he's cherished and evolved with for over a decade. It's his key drive for creating compelling, unique, philosophical stories.

When he decided to begin his own novel, The Way to Dawn, he originally had no intention of pursuing writing as a career. But when he fell in love with his own characters, he became inspired. He was so proud of his creations that he wanted to share this part of himself with others. In no time, writing soon became more than just his way of expression. It became his wings.